Constable Crime Omnibus 1

CONSTABLE CRIME OMNIBUS
1

Face value
Roger Ormerod

Here lies Nancy Frail
Jonathan Ross

A question of identity
June Thomson

Constable · London

Face value
First published 1983
Copyright © Roger Ormerod 1983
Here lies Nancy Frail
First published 1972
Copyright © Jonathan Ross 1972
A question of identity
First published 1978
Copyright © June Thomson 1978
All three books first published in Great Britain
by Constable & Company Limited
3 The Lanchesters, 162 Fulham Palace Road
London W6 9ER
Reprinted 1991
The right of Roger Ormerod, Jonathan Ross and
June Thomson to be identified as the authors
of this work has been asserted by them in
accordance with the Copyright, Designs and Patents
Act 1988
ISBN 0 09 471040 6
Set in Linotron Palatino by
Falcon Typographic Art Ltd., Edinburgh & London
Printed in Finland by WSOY

A CIP catalogue record for this book
is available from the British Library

Face value

Roger Ormerod

1

The snow over the moors had been mostly unbroken, and I'd managed to plug along at a steady thirty, but heading down into the valley I lost it once or twice, and felt the tyres beginning to bite again only when the road began to climb. There was a feeling I was getting close. The slope down on the left was much as he'd described.

I saw his official Allegro first, then the constable himself, standing in the lay-by and staring down towards the copse, slapping his hands together vigorously. I drew in behind the police car. He came across and opened the door for me, his breath steaming.

'You made good time, sir.'

I nodded. 'Brason, isn't it? I'm Detective Inspector Patton. What've you got for me?'

He was hesitant, slightly embarrassed. For a burnt-out car he'd probably expected to get a DC, or at the best a sergeant. On a Sunday, particularly. But the rest day was mine, and it was none of his business.

'Snow's bad over the moors,' he commented. He was eager, reaching for an explanation. I smiled, then went to stand by the gate, and let him work on it.

The air was clean and crisp, the view spectacular. Farm buildings were spread on the other side of the valley, almost beyond the far rise. The copse was snuggling low, immediately below us, and there was a dark flash of water between the bare trees. Up along the road, the farmer had cut back his layered thorn hedge for fifty yards and erected an angled pine fence, then stuck his five-barred gate in the middle. It made a lay-by that just held the two cars.

I got out the old, knobbly black pipe and ran my thumb over it. 'Was the gate open?'

'Not when I got here, sir. The kids would've shut it, any-way.'

'Kids?'

'The ones who found the car. They'd been tobogganing. See . . .' He pointed to the right. There were footprints, and lines of sled runners down the slope. 'That was this morning. The snow came last night.'

I was fumbling flake into the bowl, my fingers already aching. I looked down to check they were working, then up again. The slope had been skimmed by the wind, leaving ridges and tufts showing through.

'You've been down?' I asked hopefully.

'Yes, sir.'

'No sign of anyone who could've been in it when it went down?'

'No footprints. But it would've gone down yesterday, before the snow,' cause there're no tyre tracks.'

'Hmm!' I thought. 'Anybody touched it?'

'No, sir. The kids just looked, then came running to me.'

I glanced at him. He seemed complacent about that. 'They run to you, then? In town they run away.'

'I wouldn't know about the town.'

I raised my eyebrows at his touch of pride, then jerked down my cap brim in case he noticed. 'Why're you sure it went down yesterday? What's the matter with the day before – Friday? Thursday, even?'

'The schoolkids from Neaton Prior short-cut past the copse. They'd have spotted it, sir.'

I had to turn and lean back against the bitter wind, and tent the flap of my camel-hair coat to get the lighter going. The tobacco tasted sweet in the clear air, and blue smoke was tossed away over my shoulder. I stared down the slope. The car was a black, scarred wreck, nose-in to the trees. I hoped that Brason was as bright as he sounded, because I didn't fancy scrambling down there and back up again.

He was as big as me, and nearly as broad, but he was well over twenty years younger. The cold was beginning to get through

to my bones, and there was a strong urge to get back to the
warm car, but Brason seemed to be enlivened by it. He stuck
his chin out at the wind, and pulled off his peaked cap to let
it play around with his fair hair. Showing-off, when he could
guess I always had to wear a hat or cap to stop the cold eating
away at my balding patch.

'Did you get the registration number?' I asked.

He had. He passed me a bit of paper. I didn't glance at it,
but fumbled it into my pocket. Hell, there was just no point
in standing out there and freezing, staring down at a heap of
twisted metal.

'Any thoughts on it?' I asked hopefully. If not, I'd just have
to go down myself.

He hesitated. You could see the idea seeping into him. He
didn't want to make a fool of himself to a DI, but there was a
chance that he'd make a good impression.

'Assuming the gate was open,' he said, raising his face to the
wind, 'it's just possible somebody lost control and headed for
the gap as an escape road.'

'Possible.' I blew down the pipe and sparks flew back into
my face. 'If the gate was open.'

'It'd be unusual, sir.'

'And?' I prompted.

'The gear lever was in neutral, the ignition key still in, and
the engine turned off.'

'Ah!' The lad was bright.

'I did think, sir, that it could've been pushed off the road
and down the slope.'

'What made you think that?'

'You don't take a car down a slope in neutral, do you, sir? I
certainly wouldn't. No engine and no control. It'd get kind of
hectic. If you see what I mean.'

Oh, I did, I did. What had seemed to be simple and straightforward, suitable for a Sunday afternoon jaunt, was beginning
to sound too blasted interesting for my liking. Just at that time,
I wasn't keen on facing an interesting case, not facing it full
on, anyway. I shrugged, not meeting his eager eye.

'Somebody dumping an old wreck,' I tried hopefully.

'Hardly that, sir,' said Brason happily, raising himself to his toes and sniffing at the challenge. 'You'll see from its number . . . it's only three years old. A Cortina.'

I cursed to myself silently. I had to turn and tap out the pipe, not letting him see my expression. I'd slipped up. My memory wasn't what it used to be. In some report or other, recently, there'd been mention of a three-year-old Cortina, and nothing jumped to my mind. I stuffed the dead pipe into my pocket and got out the piece of paper, frowning it into focus as it fluttered – and still nothing. The number did not prod a single idea.

'Too much of it on the tely, sir,' Brason was saying.

'Sorry. I missed that.'

'Cars going over cliffs, plunging down slopes, turning over on fast bends – and every damned one of 'em goes up in flames. People get to think it's the thing they all do. But . . . I bet they don't. I never see statistics, though. But that car's still sitting on what's left of its tyres, and there's no reason for the tank to have split, and the ignition was off. I'd say the thing was fired deliberately, if only in imitation. Wouldn't you . . . sir?'

He said it anxiously, as though he thought I might not have been attending.

'Fired down there, you mean?'

'It'd be the easiest way of doing it.'

'But . . . no footprints?'

'The ground was hard. Frozen.'

I couldn't help laughing. You hold it in as long as you can, and then it bursts out. Like fury. I never could control either of them for too long. He stared at me, but I couldn't stop it. How the devil could he know I was laughing at myself? There I'd been, driving out in such lousy weather to find something totally unsuggestive of interest or involvement, and I'd run into it at the end of the journey! He stared, then grinned tentatively. I controlled myself.

'You've got an answer for everything, haven't you, Brason?'

'Sorry, sir. But it seemed logical.'

'No, no. Go ahead. The next step. Why fire it deliberately?'

'To hide it?' he tried.

I had to carry it on – no good backing out now. 'There'd be plenty of better places than here. Why leave the number plates on it, in that case?'

I was pushing him a little at that stage, but he rallied neatly. 'Fingerprints, sir? If it'd been used in a robbery, say. There'd be none left now, for sure.'

A robbery. Was that where I'd read about a Cortina? No, that wasn't it. I was furious with myself. 'But you could be right,' I said. 'Except that it wouldn't be done here. It's too open. You'd expect that sort of thing to be done secretly and quietly. Isn't there a quarry around here?'

'Yes, sir. Baggott's End. About four miles from here.'

'Well, then.'

I turned away. Suddenly I was feeling tired, and Brason's eagerness only made it worse. I reached the Stag and had the door open. 'You've been very helpful, Brason.'

He couldn't leave it alone. 'Perhaps it was intended to be found.' Nothing ever happened on his patch. His open, friendly face was brushed red by the wind.

'I'll send somebody to have a look at it,' I promised. One foot was in the car, one cheek sliding onto the seat. 'There's one other thing you can help me with. Rennie's farm. Do you know it?'

'On the edge of my district. I know Rennie.' And it didn't seem as though the knowing gave him any pleasure. 'What's he done, sir?'

'He's reported a stolen shotgun.'

'Not to me he hasn't.'

'Then perhaps you can lead the way, and you can ask him why he phoned Central and not you.'

That was another little mystery solved. I'd decided to take in the trip to Rennie simply because it seemed to have no overtones, apart from the single fact that he'd phoned direct to Central. Now Brason had explained that. The two men jarred on each other. I relaxed. It left nothing to worry me.

Brason to-and-fro'ed the Allegro and led the way. He took us along the flank of the hill and through the village, then turned left through a slough of muddy, patched lanes and eventually to the river, which he followed north for three miles before swinging away from the water. I got the impression he was pressing it a bit, trying to shake a car he considered a bit sporty for a man old enough to be his father. I hugged his tail.

11

He flicked his braking lights, testing my nerve, but I'd come across that one before. He drew up at the entrance of Rennie's farm, Borton Fall, got out, and walked back to me.

'This is it, sir.'

'You took it easy, lad. The snow worry you, did it?'

He grinned, and I turned back to look at the farmhouse. It was a new building, large and solid, and built close to the road.

'Where'll he be?' I asked.

'Sunday morning. He'll be in his office, round the back.'

There'd been a forced lack of expression in his voice. I reckoned it hid contempt. 'A gentleman farmer?' I suggested.

'It's how he'd put it, I'm sure,' he said, with prim precision. 'Never put a hand to a plough in his life, but he's been swallowing up one farm after the other around here. Swallow's End, Mere Borton, Andrew's Fall . . . opening out hedgerows and woodland . . .'

'It's called intensive farming,' I told him soothingly.

'All the same . . . the countryside's littered with empty and rotting farmhouses and cottages, where my friends – my father's friends – used to live.' He suddenly stopped and stiffened his shoulders. 'Perhaps you'd care to go ahead, sir. I'll wait here.'

I shrugged, looking away, suddenly ashamed of being there at all on a purely domestic incident. I was imposing myself on Brason's patch for a selfish reason – my wish to keep a low profile.

'It's your patch, Brason. Go ahead. I'll be right behind you.'

He'd got himself in hand by the time we got to the office. It was an outbuilding behind the house, with an exercise yard beside it and stables behind. No sign of manure, so he probably didn't ride, except in the Bentley I saw crouching in the garage at the end.

Rennie was at a bench desk, working on figures. They seemed to be giving him satisfaction. Brason had tapped on the door and walked right in, running his hand down the lintel to draw my attention to the line of splintered wood.

'Good morning, Mr Rennie,' he said, his voice neutral.

Rennie lifted his head and regarded him sourly. I might not have been there, the uniform taking precedence. Rennie was a slim man with a florid face, and a small, sandy moustache that partly disguised a loose mouth. There was a hint of jowls softening his aggressive chin.

'Oh, it's you,' he said. 'I phoned –'

'Yes, sir, so I've been told,' Brason cut in. 'Or I'd have been here sooner. It's a shotgun, I believe. Perhaps you'll just show me . . .'

Rennie waved an arm towards the rear wall. There was a whole row of racked guns along there. I saw two .22-bore rifles, and a dozen assorted shotguns. One rack was empty.

'Take a look,' he offered. 'If it helps.'

'Show me, sir.' Rennie was standing with his shoulders lax, the car keys swinging in his left hand.

There was a pause, then Rennie got to his feet, his chair rattling angrily on the bare wood floor.

'Can't you see? The empty rack.'

Brason drew close, with me nudging his shoulder. He was doing all right so far. He said: 'All twelve-bore, I see. Was the missing one the same?'

'Yes. Of course.'

Brason raised his eyebrows. 'Of course?'

'Then you've only got to buy one gauge of cartridges.'

'That'd save him a bit of trouble. I suppose he helped himself?'

'There's a box missing.'

'Anything special about it?' Brason was refusing to react to Rennie's terse tone.

'It's a Remington over/under model. Damn it, it *looked* good. They'd go for that at first glance.'

Apart from a couple of single-barrelled ones, the rest of the shotguns were the more standard type with the two barrels side-by-side.

Brason turned away. 'We'll do what we can, Mr Rennie. But really – with such poor security, you've been asking for it, you know.'

'I didn't ask for any lectures.' Rennie was tossing his chin. 'And when I phone your Central people I expect something a bit more positive. I shall certainly report your attitude.'

It was about time to introduce myself. I did. I told him his remark had been noted, added a bit on the aspect of security and his responsibilities regarding that, and turned to leave. 'Oh!' I remembered just in time. 'When exactly did it go?'

He waved a hand vaguely. 'We've been away, and only got back last night. In the last ten days, if that helps.'

I thanked him. We went out, and walked back to the cars. I shouldn't have done it, but I asked Brason what he made of it. Fatal, with Brason.

'Well . . .' he said, tapping his teeth with the ignition key. 'It's an over/under model, this Remington. If it'd been pinched with the idea of a hold-up, they'd want to saw it off, and an ordinary side-by-side would be a better bet for 'em. Look more dangerous, sir, you see. And a youngster . . . he'd surely go for one of the rifles. There's more challenge in a twenty-two rifle. One bullet instead of hundreds of pellets. But I'll sniff around, sir.'

I didn't like the idea of a shotgun on the loose. 'You do that,' I said encouragingly. 'But it could've been gone a week, and nothing's leaked back to you yet. Anyway, keep in touch, and I'll send a man to look at your car. It's been a pleasure to meet you, Brason.'

He stiffened. There was a faint tint to his cheeks. He couldn't know that I was silently cursing him.

I drove away. His lively brain had irritated me. There I was, wondering which way to turn, when Brason knew exactly where he stood and why.

I was three days from retirement. Two months before . . . even one month . . . there hadn't been a doubt in my mind regarding my attitude to it. My career hadn't been notable, and somehow I hadn't always been in line with official policy, so that I'd equally not been in line for promotion. I could look back to years of abrasive endeavour, always with my head down and forcing on against some sort of opposition. Oh yes, the thought of retirement and the freedom from pressure had been heartening. On the calendar on my office wall I'd started crossing off the remaining days.

But with each day deleted, I was simply one day closer to something I couldn't see clearly, and what had been brash confidence gradually slipped into a vague uneasiness. Even with a twinge of fear.

A fortnight before, I'd stopped crossing out the days. They mocked me. And yet I'd savoured the prospect of freedom from the routine and discipline for so long! I had, I had! There'd been a trumpet call to renewed action. Up and at 'em, Richard! I'd told myself there were hobbies and interests to be investigated, and that tour of Europe I'd always promised myself. All the world to play with . . . but suddenly a complete lack of interest for the game.

I suppose I'd pushed myself too hard. There'd been a time, three years before, when I'd needed to throw myself into the job, working myself to exhaustion. It gets to be a habit. The routine and concentration became part of my life, and I realised that by losing it I'd be faced by nothing but emptiness and uncertainty.

But . . . if I was going to lose the blasted routine anyway, there was still the method of abandoning it to be considered. Out with a triumphant bang, working flat out to the last moment, or ease out gently, gradually sliding away from under to ease the impact? I'd opted for the second alternative. The thought of walking away with an important and absorbing case pounding in my brain, and never to be resolved, was appalling. So I'd begun a paltry dabbling into minor matters, which I should have handed to a DC, not letting myself care too much, and not offering any imagination in case the unusual or the bizarre offered back.

Such as a strangely burnt-out car, a stolen shotgun – and that damned Brason mocking me by extracting interest from them and sticking it under my nose.

I was driving dangerously. Driving away from it. Damn it, I was afraid of interest now, when I'd equally been afraid of boredom. You're going paranoic, Richard, I told myself. You're on the way out.

Then I found myself crowding a tricky S-bend, and flicked the car through it, double declutching and catching the slide just right, and thought, what the hell! Suddenly I'd got my head back, laughing – God knows what at – and at least I was in control of the car.

There was no desire to drive home to the empty house. I thought round for a diversion, nothing too interesting, nothing too boring, and the obvious thing was to call in at Clive Kendall's place, to see whether there was any sign of the bastard. I was back into routine. I felt relaxed.

The information was that Kendall had been released from Long Lartin Prison three weeks before, so we'd been keeping a general eye open for him, just in case he came back to his home town. If he'd dare, that is. But he'd never shown any remorse or evidence of human feelings, and his bungalow had not been sold. The suggestion was that he might risk it, in which event there'd be trouble. So the bungalow was an obvious place to visit, because trouble just at that time I could do without.

The light was going early. The clouds were low and threatening, and I could hear the sound from the tyres taking on a new crispness. By the time I reached the outskirts of town the steering was becoming light. Here, the new motorway spur was slicing a scar through the stretches of waste land and the deserted shells of the old heavy industry complexes. I took a short cut through the new industrial estates that the council had thrown up. The aspect was depressing. So far it had not been a success, attracting very little in the way of new businesses. Orange streetlights were flashing on with an early dusk, but there was very little traffic, and no pedestrians. Then I was into the parallel streams of terraced dwellings that the ironworkers used to live in, mostly boarded up now, but with a few tatty curtains here and there and the odd blanket nailed up behind the glass. Beyond were the newer estates. Here, at least, the houses did not quite lean against each other.

There was a crumbling Victorian house at the junction of the by-pass and a minor road. The council had converted it into an old people's home, and sold off part of the land for residential development. Maybe they'd planned a whole squat group of bungalows, but only one had been built, and that in the most distant, private corner. The entrance to it was from the minor road, along a narrow lane flanked on one side by the wall surrounding the home, and on the other by a tall, sagging fence. I left the Stag parked out on the road, and walked up the lane.

The snow had partly melted, but was now freezing again. I took the torch from my car and fanned it over the surface. No foot or tyre prints. All right so far. I relaxed a little.

16

The sky was orange with reflected light, the fence at my elbow just visible. At the end it just gave up, leaving a gap. Kendall's bungalow sat facing me, low and threatening. No light showed. The traffic was a distant hum, emphasising the silence.

I moved in closer. Snow was hanging raggedly on tired shrubs and tufted grass. The garden, if it'd ever had any attention, was now far gone in rank growth. A few trees stood lank and bare to the right, against the wall, and two cypresses were towering one each side of the bungalow's front entrance, pleased at the unexpected freedom and throwing themselves at the sky.

I approached from the side. The slabs had lifted unevenly. The first thing I noticed was that the curtains were clean. That there were curtains at all was surprising, because Clive Kendall had been away for eight years. I went on round, fanning the torch through the windows, and in every room it seemed that the furniture was clean, even polished. I didn't like the look of it. In the living-room grate there was what looked like grey ashes and cinders. I'd have expected soot and mortar dust, after eight years. There was a recess for the side door, and in it I discovered a reinforced brown paper bag, nearly full of Coalite.

I was beginning to feel unhappy about it, and moved round faster. The double bed in the main bedroom was made, the covers drawn up neatly. In the empty second bedroom there was an untidy pile of what looked like sheets, and had probably been dustcovers.

He'd been back! Mind you, the suggestion was of a woman's touch, but I couldn't imagine that Rona, his wife, would have returned. She had hardly been the type to face out the situation, and hadn't been able to get away fast enough. The word was that she'd got herself a judicial separation with all the speed that the law, very sympathetic, had allowed.

It hadn't been my day. If he'd been there I could've backed him against a wall and told him all the dire things that could happen to him unless he disappeared smartly. Then I'd have put a guard round the place until he did, and set a watch on the Clayton brothers. If he was on the loose, then the possibilities were horrifying.

As I turned away from the kitchen window, a variation in

the reflection on the glass caught my eye, and I edged round until I got it clearly. Written in the dust with a stubby finger, backwards for reading from inside, but with the esses the wrong way, was printed:

THI2 FOR YOU – BA2TARD →

I turned quickly, stabbing the torch in the direction of the arrow.

One of the naked trees had a branch that sprang from the trunk horizontally. A child's doll, around two feet tall, had been strung from it by its neck with two feet of cord. I approached slowly. The doll was swinging gently, though I could feel no breeze. The noose was carefully made, just as a hangman would have fashioned it. There was a small tuft of black hair stuck to the doll's chin, and its neck was broken. The tuft had the appearance of having originally been the bristles of a half-inch paintbrush.

I fetched out a penknife and slashed it down. My hand was unsteady. I carried it by the string back to the car, and tossed it onto the rear seat.

When arrested, Clive Kendall had been wearing a small goatee beard, as black as his hair. He'd worn it through the months of preparation and trial, only shaving it off when he went into Long Lartin Prison. It'd begun to look strange, I guess, because his hair had gone completely white.

2

'It's bloody Sunday,' said Ted Clayton. 'Come back tomorrow.'

'It's Sunday for me, too,' I told him. 'Just a few minutes, Mr Clayton. A little chat.' I treated him to my best smile. I'm told it frightens people.

Of the two brothers still around town, Ted was the one to tackle first. He was the more aggressive, but he was apt to slip in the odd mistake when pressed. He looked a bit better off than when I'd seen him last, and there were touches of grey over his ears, and a bit more weight. But he still jerked his head in emphasis, and stuck out a prodding finger towards my chest, though never quite daring to reach. He was wearing old slacks in cavalry twill and a maroon roll-neck sweater.

'If it's about what I think it is . . .' he began, but I held up a patient palm and interrupted.

'It's about that. Can I come in?'

'We was watching a show on the tely.'

'Too bad. It won't take long.'

He looked doubtful, but backed away. 'Better get it said, I suppose.'

It was a neat semi-detached, a mile or so from Kendall's bungalow. From a door on the right of the hall there was the thud of throbbing rock, and a voice over it screaming: 'What is it, Ted?'

He stuck his head inside the door. Decibels floated hotly around my head. He withdrew quickly, grimacing.

'We'll use the kitchen.'

It was cold in the kitchen. The surfaces were clean and tidy, apart from the stacked washing-up in the sink. Ted glanced at it, and his head jerked. 'That young bitch Edna. Sneaked out again. I warned her . . . she does the washing up, or else.' Ted, being tough.

I sat at the table. There didn't seem to be much chance of a cup of tea. I remembered Edna, a bright, dark child with snapping eyes. She'd have been about seven when it all happened, just the age for Ted to lavish all his fond affection on her, and see in her a reflection of his niece, Coral. He'd used his own child to boost his anger and revulsion.

'Why don't you sit down?' I said quietly.

He glared at me. 'Get it said.'

'Clive Kendall's back in town.'

'You've come to give me the tip?'

'I rather guess you already know.'

He leaned forward, chin out. 'What the hell does that mean?'

'I think you've seen him, maybe spoken to him, and threatened him.'

'Heh, now . . .' His slightly bulging eyes popped with surprise. Then he wiped his hand over his mouth, just in time not to cover a smile of superiority. It seemed that my guess was wrong, somewhere.

'Sit down, Ted, I want to talk.'

'I don't wanta listen.'

'Sit down. You'll wear a groove in the floor.'

He looked at me doubtfully, but he'd got a wrong guess to play on. He sat down, hooked his elbows on the table surface, and laced his fingers in front of his chin. 'I ain't seen him, Mr Patton.'

I leaned back. He hadn't denied the threat. 'How's business these days, Ted? Still doing the painting and decorating?'

The eyes were suddenly wary. 'I still ain't seen him.'

'You know, that's probably the truth, or you would've known he's shaved off his beard.'

'Well, then . . .' He frowned, not sure it was the right answer.

'So it was a waste of time to stick one on the doll. What was it – a half-inch paintbrush?'

His voice rose. 'What the hell . . .'

20

'I've got the doll in the car,' I went on. 'Maybe there'll be fingerprints on it.' I paused. He'd allowed himself a grunt of derision. 'No fingerprints, then.' I laughed at his expression. 'All right, Ted, I'll cut out the fencing. I know you've been along to Kendall's bungalow. I know you left him a warning, but I'm not going to make a fuss. All the same, we ought to discuss it.'

I smiled again, but it didn't relax him. He was tense and twitching, and for a couple of seconds actually dangerous.

'Didn't I tell you what'd happen if he came back here?' he jerked out. 'Didn't I?'

'You did, Ted. I was in court – remember?'

'So nothin's changed.'

'You're eight years older, that's what's changed. Time to forget . . . well, not forget, perhaps, but cool it off a bit. You know.'

He slammed his fist on the table. 'Christ, you've got a nerve!' he shouted. 'Comin' here with your damn preachin'!' He took a breath. 'I ain't forgotten a bit of it, mate. It's as clear as yesterday. I said I'd get the bastard, and by God I'm going to.'

I was playing with the pipe on the table surface, keeping my eyes on it. I spoke down to it, quietly and easily.

'And then what, Ted? We've got a threat already, so where d'you think we'll look if Kendall turns up dead? You'd be inside like a shot, and what good'd that do, to you or your family? Talk sense. And don't tell me you'd plead justifiable homicide . . . it wouldn't work, not after eight years. You'd go down, Ted, as sure as I'm sitting here.'

I looked up. His eyes were dark with anger. The tented fingers were clenched into fists, the knuckles white.

'By God, but you make me sick,' he whispered. 'That . . . that bleeder raped and killed our Arthur's little girl. He took her and he raped her, and she was just one year older than our Edna. Don't you *know* – don't you feel anything, you cold bastard, sittin' there and comin' out with your cheap, snide warnings! If he comes back, I'll kill him. Put that down on paper. And don't give me any daft talk about juries. Show me one jury that'd convict me. They'd get up and cheer! Cheer, they would. They're not all like you . . .'

21

I'd known it was going to be difficult. He hadn't changed, nothing had changed. I watched him warily.

'I was there,' I reminded him. 'There on the job, from the beginning.'

'Oh sure. I remember you. All efficiency, and not one bloody second when you might've acted like a human being.'

'We do a job. We try . . .'

'You couldn't even protect her, damn you.'

It was true. I couldn't meet his eye. 'That's unfair.'

He jerked his head back, getting a better view. 'Oh dear me, and now I'm unfair. Oh, I'm sorry for you, I'm sure. It must be difficult, this job o' yours, going round and threatening ordinary law-abiding people.'

'It's how I want to keep it. Law-abiding.'

'Then ask somebody else. You know where you can stick your law.'

I began to fill my pipe, taking it slowly. There comes a time when you need to give out information instead of extracting it. 'Sometimes the job isn't pleasant, Ted,' I told him. 'Sometimes it's not easy. Talking to you isn't easy.' I risked a glance at him. I'd been trying to lighten the atmosphere, but he glared. 'Arresting people like Clive Kendall isn't easy, if you've been on the job from the beginning. Difficult to keep your hands off 'em. You can understand that. One bruise, though, one complaint about police brutality, and it could be built up at the trial. Admissions under duress, that's what they call it. But that one we did right, Ted. We got him sent down for life.'

'Life!' he croaked derisively. 'But you've bloody well gone and let him out!'

'Not us, Ted. We put him away. It's just that the Prisoners' Aid people got interested. One of their pets. They put on the pressure . . . and you know how it is.'

He was losing control. So much for my cooling technique. 'You're all the same,' he spluttered. 'Society . . . Authority . . .'

'The Establishment, Ted,' I offered. 'It's there to throw bricks at.'

'It stinks.'

'Then why make it smell worse by forcing it to put you away, when all you've done is put an end to a creature who doesn't

22

deserve to live?' He was staring, trying to take that in. I pressed
on with the advantage. 'But I'm not going to let you do it, Ted.
It's part of the job, so I've got to protect him.'

'A lot of protection you gave to little Coral!'

I gave it ten seconds. Then I went on: 'All right, Ted, I'll tell
you something, shall I? I admit it. We fell down on that. *I* did.
But it doesn't mean I've got to fall down on protecting Kendall.
From you, Ted, and from your brother, Foster . . .'

'You can always try.'

'And we'll succeed, you know. So why not leave it to us?
We'll run him out of town, and leave you in peace.'

'I ain't gonna rest till he's dead.'

'Oh, for God's sake! It's gone, Ted. It's in the past. You can't
do any good, so try to forget it.'

'Forget it! Jesus!'

I finally found time to light the pipe. I got to my feet and
refastened my coat. 'I'll get moving. There's more snow on
the way.'

I paused in the doorway and turned. By his expression, Ted
was indicating he knew I hadn't finished. But there was the
third brother to worry about, the most important – Coral's
father. He'd been the youngest, the least aggressive, but I had
to know about him, and place him.

'Whatever happened to your brother, Arthur?' I asked casually. 'I heard he and his wife moved out of the district.'

'Somethin' you don't know!' His face came alive with triumph. 'Oh, you don't have to worry about Arthur. They went
south. Gabby's people came from around there. They thought
they could forget.'

I didn't like the look in his eye. I was cautious. 'And couldn't
they?'

'He had a breakdown. Six months after the trial. He took
something.'

'Something?' My teeth were hard into the pipe stem. I had
to unclench them with an effort.

'One less for you to threaten,' he said. 'And then Gabby was
in hospital for another few months. Gabby! We called her that
because of the way she kept rattling on. Never get a word in
edgeways, you couldn't.' He spared a brief softness for the

23

memory. 'Last I saw of her – this was when me and Foster visited her in hospital – you could hardly get a word out of her.'

I wanted to say I was sorry, but I thought it would be received as an insult. 'But she's better now?'

He shrugged. 'We hear from her. A postcard now and then. You know. Reckon she's just about living.' Then he went wild again. 'You hearin' what I'm sayin', Mr Patton – Mr Bleedin' Patton – you hear? When he's dead, that . . . thing – when he's dead it won't just be for me an' Foster, it'll be for Arthur and for Gabby. I'll send *her* a postcard. I'll put on it: HE'S DEAD. In capitals. That'll cheer her up no end. You bet. So don't tell me about your duty and your protection, don't tell me nothin' . . .' He chopped it off with his hand.

His voice had been loud enough to cut through the rock next door. The voice behind me was frightened.

'What is it? What's going on, Ted?'

It was Clayton's wife, a poor waif of a woman, looking worn down by his angers and his bitterness. She peered anxiously from face to face.

'I'm just leaving,' I calmed her. 'It's nothing. Just a friendly visit.'

I went and let myself out. I could hear him shouting at her. 'Di'n't I tell her about the crocks? The lazy bitch, all she cares about is boys . . .'

I sat in the Stag, feeling moist and exhausted, and wiped my face with a tissue. It'd been bad, worse than I'd expected. Talking about it had brought it all back, all too close, when I'd thought there was no emotion left. I felt empty, and just a little sick.

Taken all round, it'd been a bit of a disastrous Sunday.

I drove myself home, taking it slowly because there was nothing drawing me, and slowly because the snow was falling again and the wind was buffeting the car.

The house was old and solid, a big Georgian semi. It'd been too big for Vera and me, and somehow the family we'd expected hadn't come along. On my own, I rattled around in it. I drove the car into the garage and fumbled the keys from the ignition. The porch was dark, and the hall smelt of damp. It always did that when I got home, never when I left. I went straight into the kitchen and slapped the kettle onto the gas stove, reached inside the fridge and put out a couple of chops to unfreeze, and decided on frozen chips because I hate peeling potatoes. Then I went to stand in the one room that still gave me any comfort. Vera had called it my library, but I thought of it as a study.

The gas fire gave enough light for standing and thinking. I didn't want to settle in my old leather easy chair, in case I couldn't get up again.

Ted Clayton had said about Gabby Clayton: 'Reckon she's just about living.' I tried to remember her, but there was no reason why we'd have met during the investigation. I'd been a sergeant then, on house-to-house work. No image of her came. Arthur Clayton – yes. I'd been at the station the day he came along, a short, thin husk of a man with horror in his eyes. I'd met Rona Kendall, too, just after the arrest. But of her, the only image was of a distraught face.

'Just about living.' I reckoned I was a fair way towards joining her.

That Sunday had been my last rest-day in harness, so I'd decided to treat it as a trial run for all my glorious days of freedom ahead. I'd rolled out of bed. A new day. Tra-la! But it hadn't lasted long. After breakfast, the grey day had seemed insupportable indoors, and all I had to fall back on was the same old routine. It had therefore occurred to me to drive out into the country and dicker around with a couple of minor issues. But Brason had to go and upset the equilibrium by offering interest, and Ted Clayton had presented a clear line of action I wasn't going to be in a position to carry through. It left me tense, my mind racing, and staring out at the wind-blown drifts of heavier flakes past my window. Like my life, I thought in disgust, colourless and insubstantial, and blowing past.

I went and put half a bottle of Barsac to cool in the fridge, and rescued the kettle. A pot of tea while I grilled the chops, then the meal itself, chops and chips and white wine, with a seed catalogue propped against the bottle, calling me to interest but failing.

I was digging a spoon into pineapple and cream when the front door bell rang.

At least it was a friendly face. Detective Sergeant Ken

Latchett stood in the porch, his dark hair blown and snow-flakes standing on his leather-inset cardigan. He was smiling, his wide face alive with it.

'Cath said to come and fetch you over,' he said. 'There's a chicken in the oven.'

I backed away. He was already walking past along the hall. He paused.

'Seems like I'm too late. You've already eaten?'

'Always the detective, Ken.'

'Lamb chop?'

'Nine out of ten. Plural. Come on through, and help me finish a bottle of wine.'

'Can't stay, really.' But he didn't seem to be in a hurry. He reached the kitchen, and took it all in with one glance. 'And seed catalogues, eh? Hardly your style, is it, Richard?'

'I'm looking for a new style.' I found him a clean wineglass. I waved it. 'Sit down a sec. I'm celebrating.'

'Oh . . . what?'

'My new life.'

'I envy you. Really I do?'

'Liar. You love the job. Lap it up like milk, you do.'

'Who trained me, Richard? But there's all the continent waiting for you, and the Stag raring to go. In the spring . . .'

'That was really Vera's idea, you know. I don't seem to be able to work up much enthusiasm.'

He looked at me sharply, and changed the subject with heavy diplomacy. He'd always been as transparent as hell.

'You've been out, I see.' He was settling into the chair lazily.

'Out into the wide open spaces,' I agreed. 'I went to see a burnt-out car.'

'Exciting.'

I gave him the bit of paper. 'That's it. I just can't recall . . .'

'A three-year-old Cortina? Yes, I remember that. A woman reported her husband missing. I saw her. Had a few words with her.'

'A husband? This is a car.'

'He took it with him. A Mrs Amelia Trowbridge. The car's hers.'

26

I thought about it. Nothing clicked. 'All right. Get along and have a look at it, Ken, first thing in the morning. Have a word with the local man. Brason. He's bright. You'll be interested.'

'Something special?'

'I don't know. Just unusual.'

We were silent for a couple of minutes. We'd worked together long enough to respect each other's silences. At last he spoke up.

'We're getting Inspector Donaldson. Had you heard?'

'A whisper.' He was a good man, as far as I'd heard. Hard, though. 'He's not likely to be pleased.'

'No promotion, you mean?' A man expected promotion with a new posting. 'Perhaps they'll give him Chief Inspector.'

I didn't follow that up, but drew on my pipe until the subject was dead. 'I saw Ted Clayton today, Ken. I think Clive Kendall's been back to his bungalow.'

'Sticking his neck out, then.'

'Yes. But he could've been scared off. Somebody had left a doll hanging in his garden, with a noose round its neck. It was a pretty strong hint.'

He nodded. 'So naturally you went to see Ted Clayton.'

'It seemed the obvious thing. But nothing's changed, you know. Eight years, and nothing's changed.'

The pipe was going well as I considered my own attitude. Nothing had changed there, either. I'd been the arresting officer. We'd pinned Kendall in his bungalow, and there'd been rumours of him being armed. As it turned out it was only a shotgun, and when I went in after him I put a lot of faith in the assumption that it wasn't loaded. One of my hunches. That one turned out all right, but in disarming him, alone in that place with him for a few minutes, I could've justified using some of the violence that was bubbling away inside me. But there wasn't a mark on him when we got him to the station. God knows why I was proud of that.

'Better get a general call out on him, Ken,' I said, as though I'd been working it out. 'Tip off the team for that area to keep an eye on the bungalow. If . . .' I said, cocking an eye at him '. . . if Donaldson'll go along with it.'

'Sure. I'll persuade him.'

'Oh, and Ken, when you're out that way, have a word with a farmer called Rennie. Brason'll show you where.'

'What's he been up to?'

'He's had a shotgun stolen. It's a rather expensive piece of equipment.'

'And?' He was eyeing me with a smile on his face.

'I was wondering whether Ted Clayton's done any painting or decorating for Rennie recently. He might have noticed the guns.'

Ken cocked his head at me. 'One of your fancy ideas, Richard?'

'The hanging doll could be a blind. Get us thinking in terms of hanging, then blast Kendall's head off.' Though that would be a bit too subtle for Ted and Foster Clayton.

He slapped his palms on the table, levering himself to his feet. 'Well ... better get home. You're talking as though you won't be coming into the office tomorrow.'

'Not first thing. I've got an appointment. Atlas Electronics. They want a Head of Security.'

The wind wafted in through the front door as he opened it. 'I'll do what you say, Richard. Best of luck at Atlas.' Then suddenly his eyes were shrewd. 'But you're not keen, are you?'

'I'll see, Ken, I'll see.'

Security. The happy hunting ground of all senior police officers who've been put out to graze. But maybe I wouldn't be sufficiently senior for them, and maybe I wouldn't be feeling quite ready for their pastures.

Atlas Electronics was the only business doing any good on the industrial estate. Starting with the largest complex, in five years it'd spread to absorb three others.

By the time I'd found the Visitors Only slot I'd already noted that the gate security was lax, and that the canal running through the site offered a clear security headache. But during the interview I found that none of that mattered. What needed guarding was not items you could grab hold of, but ideas too slippy for anybody less than a genius. It would all resolve itself into something close to spying, personal intrusion into the lives of people I'd come to know, and perhaps come to admire and like. Key scientists might require constant and individual surveillance, I was told.

Inside ten minutes I decided it was not for me. All the same, I was agreeable enough to a conducted tour, though when the Chief Personnel Officer said he'd find me somebody to show me around, I knew I wasn't for them, either.

Foster Clayton met me outside the offices, smirking at my surprise and delighted at the advantage it gave him.

'I'm a Production Controller here,' he told me. 'When I saw your name on the list I volunteered for this.'

'Good of you.'

'Where d'you want to go first?'

'Somewhere we can talk. There's no point in showing me around.'

He gave me a dry smile. 'Saved you coming to see me at home.' He offered it as a gift. 'There's no sense in upsetting the missus.'

'Nobody needs to get upset.'

'Let's slip into the canteen.'

The long, narrow building was empty, apart from the canteen staff, who were busy at the far end preparing for lunch. He sat me at a table by the window, and went to persuade a couple of cups of tea from the counter assistant.

'Their own pot,' he said, returning. 'Not the bulk rubbish.' He winked. 'Gladys owes me a favour.'

At fifty, Foster was thickening about the middle, beginning to lean back to balance the weight. His face was more puffy than his brother's, his hair thinner. There was a sly look to his eyes. He obviously fancied himself with the women, and clearly believed his attentions represented a favour.

'Ted phoned,' he said. 'He told me you'd been there, tossing your threats around.'

'Suggestions,' I said mildly. 'Ideas.'

Still smiling, Foster went into his prepared speech. 'But don't try pushing me, Mr Patton. Don't try it. That's all I want to say.'

I didn't reply. I tried the tea. How could the bulk rubbish possibly have been worse?

'Ain't you got anything to say?' he asked at last.

'You've come a long way,' I congratulated him. 'Production Controller. Well, now . . . that's a responsible job. I'm pleased for you. That's why I think I can ask you a favour, as a responsible man.'

'What're you up to now?' His smile was twisted, his head tilted.

'Ted's wild. He's not maturing at all. I'd like you to have a word with him. Point out that he's doing himself no good.'

'You're joking.'

'Do you own a shotgun, Foster?'

'Don't talk rubbish.'

'Or Ted?'

'What'd he want a shotgun for?'

'I don't know. Rats, perhaps?'

I was well aware that Foster could be a more dangerous man than his brother. Ted would charge right in, but Foster would wait his chance and sneak in from behind. I had to be more subtle with Foster.

'Clive Kendall's disappeared,' I said casually. 'We can't trace him. So you'd be wasting your time trying to.'

'Now . . . Inspector . . .' He was affable. 'You know that's not the point. Kendall disappears – that's fine with me. I'm not going to hunt him out. But if he comes near me . . . if I hear he's back in town . . . then I'm going to kill him.'

'That sort of talk's not going to help.'

'Oh, don't get me wrong,' Foster said amiably. 'I'm not like Ted. He ain't going to be happy till Kendall's dead. But me . . . well, now, I can rest if I don't set eyes on him. But if I do, well, then it's quite possible I'll get very angry, and there'd be no knowing. I'd like to get my hands round his throat. Yes, I think I'd like that. Then I could look into his eyes and watch him die. Now . . . doesn't that make it easy for you? Just keep him away from me. Well away.' He was twisting a cigarette in his fingers.

All hot air, I told myself. Kendall wouldn't be easy to take on with bare hands – he'd been a tall, strong man. And Foster wouldn't risk physical contact.

'Good,' I said. 'Then you won't be too disappointed if you never get the chance? I'm glad of that.' I smiled into his little, piggy eyes.

'What the hell does that mean?'

'It's just that I've got the idea he's dead already.' I had no reason to believe that, but there was no harm in putting out feelers. The threat might already have been finalised.

For a moment he was very still. Only his jaw muscles moved. I got to my feet. He flicked his lighter into flame.

'Thank you for the tea. Congratulate Gladys for me.'

'Heh – what d'you mean, already dead?'

'I mean I might be coming to see you again. If he's been strangled when we find him.'

I walked out into the crisp morning air. The snow of the night had added only two inches to the previous fall, but small drifts were lying against the canteen wall. I realised that Foster had smelt strangely of shellac. It had seemed to form a hard coating around him, like a pungent armour.

For a moment I paused and looked back. He was standing in the canteen entrance. As I watched he jutted his lower lip and blew a cloud of smoke in front of his face, managing a supercilious smile at the same time.

Now there was nothing left but to report in to the office, though the thought was a mild comfort. They still had us in a red Victorian monstrosity with a whole list of disabilities, but with the smooth-worn assurance of long acquaintance.

Ken hadn't returned from his trip into the country. I was glad of that. There was paperwork to be considered, and a small advantage in being able to cuss it in privacy.

I'd shared the same office with Ken for a long while. Nothing was convenient. Filing cabinets partly blocked the tall, narrow windows, and you could slide behind the desks from only one side. The floor beneath the door had worn into a deep dent, allowing a draught to cut into my ankles, and the slatted blinds had long since given up the task of preventing the window's cold air from falling across the desk surface. The single radiator bubbled and hissed, just to prove it was working, but didn't extend itself to throwing out any heat.

But it had the advantage of familiarity. You didn't have to waste any effort in hunting out a correct form, and no thought was disturbed in putting a hand on a stub of pencil. There was a dark patch on the wall behind one shoulder, where I'd made the habit of leaning back with one foot in the opened lower drawer of the desk. It's an ideal position for a quiet smoke. There had been talk of a move to new premises on the by-pass, but nothing had come of it. But who wants concrete and double-glazing, if it means open planning and impersonal efficiency? Not me. The present battered-wire trays did their job. Just as many flies perched in the IN tray, just as few in the OUT. It'd always been a minor mystery to me that it never arranged itself the other way round. Perhaps, I thought, settling in, that happy situation would have come about in new premises, with different trays. I pondered the possibility.

I lit my pipe. I stared at the calendar, then re-read the note Ken had left me.

> *Brason phoned. He's found somebody who saw smoke early on Saturday. His big case! I'll have a word with him. Ken.*

The car, I thought. I hunted for the file on Amelia Trowbridge, and found it in my IN tray.

Around two weeks before, she'd reported her husband as missing. No suggestion of a crime involved – no foul play hinted. It wasn't a police matter. The circumstances would simply have been noted, for future reference. But now the car had turned up, and the matter took on a new dimension.

I sat back. I relit the pipe, and was thus contemplating the passage of time when the door opened, and my boss, Chief Superintendent Merridew, stood in the doorway. His expression was poised between disapproval and jocularity.

We'd worked together for years, me in charge of the local CID, but somehow we'd never been close. I think he sensed a certain lack of respect in me, but he hadn't managed to work out whether it was for himself or for law and order in general. It still worried him. He was a tall, lean man with sloping shoulders, a long face, a long nose, and so little used to smiling that the present result was painful and embarrassing.

'Ah, there you are, Richard. I heard you were out and about, yesterday.'

'Shut the door, there's a good chap.'

He did. It gave him the opportunity to abandon the smile.

'No harm in getting out for a bit of fresh air, I suppose,' he said doubtfully. Then he reached over Ken's desk for his chair, and sat on it backwards, to indicate that this was all informal, friend to friend. The lines above his eyebrows were etched deep.

'Never find time to get out and about, myself,' he observed. 'I often envy you. Turn up anything?'

I grunted, and stared at my pipe. He hadn't expected any reply. I waited till he got going again.

'No . . . well . . . you'll be tapering off.' This time it was a question, but I didn't rise to it. 'I'll tell you what I'd like you to do, though. Donaldson's coming down . . . today . . . tomorrow . . . it's not certain.'

'Donaldson?'

'Your replacement. Hadn't you heard?'

'Not officially,' I said gently. 'Not from you, Paul.'

'Ah!' He touched his fingers to his upper lip. 'Sorry – must have slipped my mind. Well, it is Donaldson.'

'On promotion?'

He stared at the patch beyond my shoulder. 'They're offering him Chief Inspector.'

I leaned forward, indicating impersonal satisfaction. 'There now, I always complained that nobody listened to my suggestions. I flogged the point to death – this job rates the higher grade.'

He stuck out his lower lip and rubbed it against the arms across the chair back. It remained unsaid, that the upgraded post wouldn't have come my way. He could have explained, patiently and politely, that I'd never been too orthodox, but I can match him for politeness. I rescued him.

'You were saying?'

'Ah, yes. He's just calling to have a look round, and I'd like him to see things as I want them to continue. By the book, Richard. Every current file initialled, and every possible action initiated, and that . . .' He glanced at it in distaste. '. . . that IN tray empty, even if the OUT has to be overflowing. I want reports commented on, and statements countersigned, and every . . . every . . .' He paused, running out of inspiration.

'Criticism thwarted?' I suggested. 'I get the general idea.'

'Good. Fine. Then you'll do that?'

'It will make,' I observed, 'a fine exercise in tapering off. I wouldn't want to leave him any work.'

He stood up, leaving the chair where it was. His eyes were bleak, but he played it safe. 'Good man. I'll leave you to it.'

The door closed behind him. I got up and replaced Ken's chair carefully. He'd been very delicate about it – no direct order. My hands were shaking.

His idea of tapering off. But his life was paperwork. For me, to adopt his suggestion would be sudden death. Now. That very second. Already, it seemed, I was discounted. Richard Patton, who used to work here. That's his desk, when he was around. Left things neat, didn't he! What's he doing now? God knows! Who cares?

All my instincts rebelled against it. I had to walk away from the prospect, but training led my mind in search of a valid reason to justify it. My eyes fell on the file relating to Amelia Trowbridge. It would do, I decided, and I made a note of her address. I reached down my camel-hair coat and my soft tweed hat, and went out to tell the lady her car had been found. It was nothing too interesting, nothing that might get me involved.

I can't always be right, though, can I?

3

'Well,' she said, 'how nice! I reported it a fortnight ago, and no action. Two more visits, and still no action. And now – a whole Inspector to myself.' But there was no real sarcasm in her voice. The strain on her face told me she was forcing it.

What do you say to five feet four inches of nervous energy? Had she been hugging the window, waiting for signs of official life? She was looking up at me with dark, almond eyes slightly mocking, tossing her head to flick a lock of auburn hair from her left cheek.

'I'm sorry,' I said. She'd put me on the defensive.

Instantly her eyes were startled. 'There's something happened?'

'Could we perhaps sit down somewhere?'

'Oh, yes. Silly of me. Come through. Will you take off your coat?'

We were in the tiny hall, the white-painted staircase rising beyond her left shoulder, me towering over her and feeling that I cramped the narrow space. The hall-stand was digging into my thigh. I wriggled out of the coat, hung it up carefully, and placed my hat on the polished surface of the cupboard, next to the phone. The house was a new property. I'd noticed its matching twin, still unfinished, on the other side of the cul-de-sac.

As I followed her into the front room I could feel the anxiety pressing her. She'd given her age as thirty-nine, but I'd have guessed her as younger. When she turned to me she had a tentative smile on her face, and the lines from the corners of her eyes were deeply-etched, I thought from laughter, but I

35

didn't expect to get any confirmation. She had a wide forehead, widely-spaced eyes, and tiny vertical lines separated them like a small fence.

Her movements were energetic. She gestured to an easy chair, but I'm old-fashioned and stood until she found a seat for herself. Impatience drew a tiny sound from her tongue as she reached round for a padded stool and plumped herself down on it. She was wearing slim slacks, and made a small play of adjusting the hang of her matching cardigan. Then she was still, her eyes on me, waiting.

I cleared my throat.

'Tell me,' she said quickly. 'You've found him . . .'

'No.' I was gentle and casual. I sat down facing her. 'But we've found the car.'

'Oh.' She brushed her fingers across the material stretched tight on her knee. 'The car.'

'Burnt out, I'm afraid.'

'And he . . .' She said it on an indrawn breath.

'No sign of the driver. Nothing but the car.'

She looked away from me and out of the window. At that angle I got the impression from her jaw of strength and determination. There was nothing out there but the immature garden, with a few pitiful roses thrusting through the snow. And a distant burnt-out car.

I glanced round the room, waiting, noticing there were no ashtrays, when I was dying for a smoke. There was a vague feeling of unreality, as though I was watching myself sitting there and wondering what the devil I thought I was doing. Anybody could've told her about the car. But . . . and I brought my attention back to Mrs Trowbridge . . . there was no reason why anybody else should have the pleasure. She was trim and neat, in a setting that was close to repressing in its polished and pristine tidiness.

Her eyes came back to me. She was now completely in control. 'Where is it?'

'Where we found it, and I'm afraid it's going to take a bit of trouble dragging out. At the bottom of a sloping field, nose-in to a copse . . .' I was padding. Her eyes were intently on my face, and I sensed a small impatience. 'The other side of town from here. Eight or ten miles, I'd reckon. Do you want to see it?'

If she'd said yes, I'd have had to drive her there myself. I added quickly: 'Have you got transport?' There were buses, but they were infrequent.

She gave a small, immensely attractive grimace, partly a smile. 'The Cortina was mine. No, there's nothing else.'

I wanted to help her, though she seemed self-reliant. 'You'll have to let your insurers know. I'll let you have a note of the location, and they'll contact us.'

She nodded. 'I'm sure I can manage.'

'I was confident you would,' I said blandly. 'But if you want to see it . . .' I raised my eyebrows. The offer still held.

'I'm sure that's not necessary. Burnt out, you said?'

'Completely gutted. I've seen it myself.'

A small crack appeared in her composure. Delayed action. Suddenly she was shaking her head, now with distress in her eyes and with her lower lip caught between her teeth. 'Oh, I don't understand!' she cried, annoyed with herself. 'What could have happened?'

'We'll no doubt find out,' I assured her emptily.

The trouble was that I was finding I could no longer watch her closely. One thing I'd always had was an ability to switch off my own emotions and maintain an impersonal attitude of observation. But now it seemed to be an intrusion. I realised I was twisting my pipe in my fingers, embarrassed that I couldn't offer her a reasonable explanation.

She made a small gesture, attracting my attention. She was again in control of herself. And she, too, was embarrassed, smiling to cover it. 'Do smoke if you want to.'

I lifted my hand, indicating the room. 'I thought –'

'It's all right. You did say there was no sign of . . . him?'

'There was no indication that anybody was in the car when it was fired.'

She was quick. 'Was . . . fired? That's a strange way of putting it.' She cocked her head. The vertical lines were bitten deeply now.

'That seems to be how it was. The car was run down the slope, and then set on fire. That's what we believe.'

'And that interests you?'

'It's unusual.' I was cautious. It was not a crime.

'It's why they sent an inspector?' She was anxious to know that.

'Not really. I sent myself.'

'But all the same, it's out of the ordinary,' she insisted. 'I mean – why ever would anybody want to do that?' Her eyes were wide and intelligent.

'I can think of a number of reasons why anybody might, but certainly none why your husband would do it.'

That seemed to disconcert her. I held my eyes on her now, squinting through the smoke as I got my pipe going. The mention of her husband had reminded her that it wasn't an impersonal problem. She was abruptly so moved that she got up from the stool. There was a shelf of ornaments in an inset beside the fireplace, and she found an item she could adjust by an inch. If any prejudged image had entered my mind, she did not fit it. Most wives with missing husbands are either so quiet that they can barely offer an explanation, or so bitterly shrewish that they don't need to. Amelia Trowbridge was neither. The reason for her husband's sudden departure was clearly going to be complex and intriguing, and neither of these was I going to be able to handle. But, though she repressed it firmly, she was plainly crying out for help.

'Tell me about him,' I suggested softly.

'What? Oh . . .' She turned to face me and her eyes flickered. Then: 'Excuse me a moment, will you?'

She marched quickly from the room, her movements rapid and lithe, and returned in a minute carrying a glass ashtray and a packet of cigarettes, flashing me an apologetic smile.

'We don't usually smoke in this room.' Her expression was suddenly intimate and conspiratorial, and touchingly childlike.

'We could move elsewhere.'

'It doesn't matter.'

'Very well. Your husband . . .'

She placed the ashtray on the carpet between us, lit her cigarette, and tapped it in the air above it. She was nodding, believing she now understood the reason for my presence.

'It's why you had to come. An inspector – that means you
think it's serious.'

'Not necessarily. I'm just interested.'

'I do read books, you know.'

'You shouldn't make too much of it. There's no suggestion of
– shall we say – a crime, or even that your husband isn't alive
and well.' I didn't want her worrying unnecessarily. I smiled,
made a fantasy of it. 'Heavens, if we suspected anything, I'd
have a partner with me, taking notes.' Hell, I was saying all the
wrong things.

'Ah, yes.' Her eyes were on me, challenging. 'I understand
completely. Am I a suspect, Mr ...?' She was rushing ahead,
suddenly anxious. Her imagination was intuitive.

'Patton, ma'am.' I was taking it very steadily now, very
calmly. 'And nobody's suspecting you of anything.' I leaned
forward, taking her into my confidence, trying to give her
confidence. 'Between you and me, Mrs Trowbridge, I've drifted
away from official procedure a little. I'm here now because I'm
interested. Frankly, I don't *want* to be interested. But I am. So
... we try to decide what's happened to your husband. Tell
me about him. No – first of all – tell me something else. You
haven't lived here very long, have you?'

'Six months,' she said, and I was pleased to see I amused her.
'We came here in July. My husband was made redundant, you
see. We were living near Birmingham, and there seemed to be
no chance, no chance at all of anything in his line.'

'And what's that?'

'Electronics. He worked for a firm specialising in high quality amplifiers. You know, what they call hi-fi. He's a circuit
designer.'

The picture was coming together. 'I can see why you came
here. But Atlas didn't want him?'

'No.' Her lips were a bleak line.

'Then perhaps it was a mistake to move before the job was
confirmed,' I said casually.

'There were other reasons. I wanted to come here ...' She
glanced away, gestured with the cigarette, and gave me a weak
little smile. 'But never mind that.' It'd perhaps been a mistake
to mention it at all.

'But moving house is expensive.'

'I have some money of my own.'

Which explained why the Cortina had been hers. 'But it made him even more dependent on you, perhaps?'

Her eyes flashed. 'What do you mean by that?'

'Oh . . .' I shrugged. 'A man, out of work, his wife with a little money, and moving into a strange district where he'd feel unfamiliar and perhaps a bit lost . . .' I smiled engagingly, but it doesn't always come out right. It bounced off her. She was expressionless.

'Please explain what you mean.'

'I'm trying to understand why any man should suddenly leave a wife who is so . . .' How the hell could I go on with that? I knew next to nothing about her. I took a breath. 'Mrs Trowbridge, I've interviewed perhaps a hundred women whose husbands have disappeared suddenly, and believe me, it's been quite obvious why they've gone. The only inexplicable point was usually not that they'd gone, but that they'd stayed so long.'

I peered cautiously at her. Her frown of concentration was not encouraging, but I could swear I detected a hint of mischief in the line of her mouth. And yes, they were lines of amusement round her eyes, after all. I went on: 'And frankly . . . well, it does seem there's no reason in this case. No obvious reason,' I qualified, just to stop her laughing out loud at me.

She leaned back, slapping her palms on her knees. 'Another woman?' she asked briskly. 'Is that what you're nervous of saying?'

It hadn't crossed my mind. I nodded solemnly.

'He would have said,' she told me calmly. 'We always had that closeness, you see. We could tell the truth to each other, and trust . . . no, I'm putting this badly. Not trust blindly. Something like that – it suggests a kind of smug acceptance of each other. Don't you think? It was not like that.'

I wasn't prepared for such honesty. Her eyes were remote. She looked far beyond me, into an inner awareness. Then she continued softly, as though trying to understand it herself.

'It was a trust simply in the truth of each other. Yes, that's it. Does it sound silly? We made promises, but we did it warily, and only if we knew they could be kept. He didn't promise he wouldn't leave me, because the possibility never arose. It wouldn't have been possible, because he said: always. He said "always" the day before . . .' She swallowed. There was a catch in her voice. 'The day before he left me,' she whispered. 'The very night before, he said: "Always, Amelia, always."'

There was a moment when I thought she was going to break down. She stared at the palm of her left hand for several seconds, then brought it up briefly to cover her mouth. Then she gave a tiny shudder, and her shoulders straightened.

'I'm not usually so stupidly sentimental,' she apologised, trying a smile that didn't quite succeed.

I cleared my throat, realising rather desperately that I was becoming involved deeper than I'd intended. Just tell her about the car, I'd decided, then clear out.

'If he said: always,' I murmured encouragingly, 'he might not have meant being with you in a physical sense, but being with you . . . in his thoughts.'

She was considering me seriously, as though with a new and unveiled eye. Then she lowered her head and fumbled for another cigarette. I leaned forward quickly with my lighter, but the moment of intimacy was lost in the smoke.

'Describe him for me,' I said, leaning back, suddenly relaxed and confident.

'But I did. At your police station.'

'That was on paper. But now . . . in your own words.'

'Well – a tall man. As tall as you, but not so . . .' She hesitated.

'Bulky?' I grinned, and she glanced away.

'If you like. Slimmer, but very strong, and very gentle. He's a shy man, self-effacing. Perhaps that's a weakness. I'm not sure. Often I've wished he was firmer and more . . . well . . . dominating, I suppose. Quiet, restrained.' She stopped, her eyebrows raised.

It wasn't what I wanted, but I wasn't going to stop her. Was she hinting that she yearned for somebody more forceful? She'd seemed to want to impress that on me. I nodded gravely.

'But you wanted a physical description,' she declared. 'As I said, six feet or so, with wide shoulders. A kind of broad face, kind, crinkly. He was always laughing. And blond. His hair was so light I used to tease him that he bleached it when I wasn't looking, but . . .' She stopped abruptly again.

'But he'd have told you the truth?'

'It was a joke,' she told me severely. 'A private joke.'

'Of course.'

'He's got,' she said, 'small hands for a man. Long legs and large feet, but small hands. He could – can manage very delicate operations with his fingers. I . . . I . . .'

'And how was he dressed?' I asked quickly. 'When he went away.'

'Oh, his working jeans and a check shirt, with a blue cardigan. Sneakers – those blue and white running-shoe things, and . . . and . . . well, nothing else, really.'

'In this weather?'

'It wasn't in this weather. Three weeks ago it was fine and warm. And he had the car.'

'He hasn't got the car now. And it's this weather now.'

She looked at me as though I'd slapped her. 'Oh.'

'Nothing else?' I waited. She said nothing. She'd stopped thinking. 'Anything wearable in the car?'

'Oh, yes, yes. An old anorak.'

'But that still isn't much. Did he take any shaving equipment?'

'Nothing else. Nothing. And anyway, his shaver's electric.'

'There are shaving points in hotels.'

She gave a small, choked laugh. 'Hotels? I reckoned . . . I did work it out.' Her laugh had been edging near to hysteria, and now she was suppressing sobs. 'He couldn't have had more than twenty or thirty pounds with him. And it's been three weeks, and where could he have gone, with no car and no money left, and not a decent coat to his back . . .'

I stared at her miserably, but I had to dig for possibilities. 'And no cheque book, cheque card, credit cards?'

'Don't be ridiculous,' she said sharply.

I couldn't see why it was ridiculous, but if she said so . . . I twisted my pipe in my fingers, letting her take her time. I glanced up, and she was reaching forward tentatively.

'I'm sorry. It was just . . . I do apologise. But he had

42

nothing like that.' She paused. 'And you're only trying to help.'

I'm not sure that my smile always helps. In the shaving mirror there's just a craggy, square face, with a long scar on one cheek, but I don't usually smile at myself. I risked it, and she didn't flinch.

'I just want you to trust me.'

'You know I do.'

I didn't know that, but I nodded. 'It's the car that's upset you?'

'I did think that maybe he'd gone back home. You know what I mean – back to his own district. He was terribly depressed, and perhaps being with his old friends . . .'

I knew exactly what she meant.

'I tried phoning,' she told me. 'But I couldn't drop on anybody who'd seen him. And without the car I couldn't just go there myself, and I didn't dare to be away from here too long.'

She was lonely and frightened, and hanging on to everything by sheer force of personality. The interview was running out of enterprise, and in a minute we'd be chatting generally, but I had to get back to the office. Any minute now she'd realise she'd not offered me anything, and be dashing into her kitchen for the kettle. I heaved myself to my feet.

'But now – you can leave it to us.'

She smiled. Rising, for her, was one lithe movement. 'The full majesty of the law?'

'At least that,' I assured her gravely. I led the way into the hall and took up my hat and coat. 'I'll be in touch.'

She reached out and touched my arm briefly. 'And thank you. For what you've done.'

'We haven't done anything yet.'

'I think perhaps you have.'

Because I sensed her watching from the window, I couldn't sit relaxed in the car for a few minutes and gather my thoughts. I drove away, realising that Donaldson wasn't necessarily going to treat it as a police matter at all. Not the Donaldson I recalled. He'd probably say: 'Get out of it! He's gone off with some fancy piece. You can bet on it.' And I'd never be able to explain to him why I thought that was impossible.

I was feeling angry and disturbed. The anger was easy to tie down, because it was at myself. I'd made a botch of it. Going myself to see her had been a mistake to start with. It'd given the matter an importance I'd never be able to justify, and Donaldson, just to be contrary, would probably tear into it with disgust and his usual lack of restraint. Or just do nothing. More than likely, I'd done Amelia Trowbridge a disservice, simply because I'd forgotten how close I was to my last day. I should have treated her with official reserve and formality. That I hadn't been able to annoyed me.

But my uneasiness I couldn't isolate. It had something to do with the weather, I thought, and something to do with Clive Kendall.

I drove directly back to the office. The sky was clouding, the heavy grey layer pressing in from the west. It was a day when the office offered some attraction, and maybe Merridew would get a few files looked at, after all. As I drew into the car park behind the station the snow had begun to fall, swirling round the building. A sudden gust nearly took the car door from my hand.

I stood, holding down my hat and leaning forward against the wind, and recognised the reason for my uneasiness.

It had happened on just such a day, but three years before, and it'd been the same hat, if not the same coat. A similar snow swirl had caught me, walking down the steps out at the front, heading for home. The Stag had been in for its MOT, but Vera had promised to pick me up with the Mini. For a moment, paused on the steps and realising how bad the weather was, I'd wished she hadn't made that promise. There'd have been no point in going back to the phone – she'd have left home by that time.

But she was unused to snow, and a nervous driver in the best weather. Only . . . she'd promised. Somehow, she'd manage it, because she'd promised.

(. . . a trust simply in the truth of each other . . .)

So I'd walked, head down, towards home, hurrying against the slant of the snow on the side facing oncoming traffic. My eyes were searching for the first sign of the Mini. It was red, so should've been easy to spot in the white blanket, even though the orange streetlights seemed to be beaten down and blunted. When the ambulance howl came up behind me, my heart began to race. It swept past. I broke into a stumbling run, feet unsure and my mac flying. Yes, I remembered, it'd been my belted mac with the shoulder flaps ... God, it was so clear, every detail sharper than the snow-swirled reality.

The Mini was nose-in to a lamp post. Vera was dead. Her blood was grey in the wan light, her eyes open as though she was still searching for me.

It'd been on just such a night as this ...

But it wasn't night, not even lunchtime. I shook myself, and let myself in through the rear door next to the canteen. The smell was of curry. Not curried chicken again! I stumped up the back stairs, and there was Merridew in my office, just banging down my phone.

He turned. His mouth was a tight line. This was my Chief Super in one of his forced calm moods. He'd told me once that to lose your temper reduced your effectiveness. With him, it worked out that he restrained his impulses to such an extent that it all came out as a chill acidity.

I pretended not to notice. 'Chief?'

'How many times,' he wondered, 'have we discussed this, Richard? If you want to go around in your own car, then have the thing fitted with a radio.'

'A bit late for that, surely.'

He drew himself up. 'I am quite aware that you're not wildly interested in what's going on around here. That's natural, I suppose. I can understand it. But you leave me high and dry ...'

'Something's happened?' I moved round the desk. The IN tray had grown considerably.

'That was Latchett,' he said. 'They've found a man's body in a cottage.'

A man's body! 'They?'

'He and a local man.'

'That'd be Brason.'

'All right. Brason.'

'Where?'

'On a farm called Swallow's End. Wherever that is.'

45

Brason had mentioned Swallow's End. I snapped a mental finger. Yes, it was one of the farms Rennie had acquired.

'I'll arrange for a team to get out there.'

'A team? Something you know?' He was teetering on his heels, staring along his nose. It was a trick he used to gain in stature.

'Any description?' I asked.

'You seem convinced it's serious, but you haven't heard any details. It could be a tramp, for all you know, died of exposure.'

'But it isn't? All right. Let's have it.'

He gave a snort of disgust at my abruptness. No respect. 'There's not much to tell you. It's a man, in an isolated cottage. All they've got is what they can see through a window. But I'm told there's a shotgun involved, and Latchett said it's murder.'

'From a look through the window?'

'He says so. They hadn't got in when he called. Apparently, everything's sealed.'

'Sealed?'

He shrugged. 'Locked or fastened.'

It was the classic set-up for accidental death or suicide.

'But Ken says murder?'

'He said that.'

It was what I'd dreaded, something big breaking at the last minute. I wanted no part of it. 'Then I'd better get moving,' I said. Even to me my voice sounded harsh.

But he was standing between me and the door. 'Sit down a minute, Richard. I'd like a word.'

I had an idea what that word would be. I stared out of the window, at the snow slanting past it. Witnesses had said that Vera had braked hard to avoid a pedestrian, and really, she hadn't been moving fast enough . . . I slid into my chair and thrust the files aside.

'Come on, then, Paul. Out with it.'

He remained standing, and spoke to a point a few inches over my head. 'Donaldson's coming along today.'

'Looks like I'll miss him. Pity.'

'You know what I mean. Don't pretend to be slow, Richard,

when I know you're way ahead. I could phone through and *ask* for him . . . now. On the strength.'

'His posting's not due –'

'A formality. I could put him in charge of this case.'

'Oh, come on.'

'It makes sense. Assume it really is murder – well, it's common sense to maintain continuity, the man starting it off carrying it through.'

'It's my case.'

'And it's my station. Let's not have a ridiculous argument.'

'I'm the DI here. Therefore I take charge.'

'And for how long? Ask yourself.' His voice was cold. 'You know damn well . . . with a murder case HQ will have a Super along here in no time. But if I get Donaldson . . .'

'Who's also a DI.'

'But not for long. It could be covered. We simply put his transfer forward a couple of days, and his promotion comes with it. Then – maybe – I'd be able to keep the case to ourselves.'

'That'd be nice for you.' I stared at the middle button of his uniform jacket. 'You'd like that. Provided Donaldson pulls it off. But for now – it's my case, Paul.'

'I wish I could say I'll be sorry to see you go, Richard,' he said softly.

I smiled. 'Continuity, Paul. And I've got a feeling I'm already way ahead on this one.'

'I could simply make it an order.'

I levered myself to my feet. 'Certainly you could, but I'm heading out there right now. Have you thought of this? Brason and Latchett will've been out there all morning. It's snowing, and there's no dinky café to drop into for a cup of tea.' I glanced out of the window again. It hadn't stopped. 'So I'll get out there as tea-boy, take 'em some sandwiches and coffee. No harm in that, now is there! Hell, as far as the murder's concerned I might as well not be there. How'd that suit you? Just standing around, drinking coffee.'

He stared at me without expression for a full ten seconds. He was making a mistake, and he knew it. There'd have been no harm in sending me out for a preliminary look at it. *Then* he could have contacted HQ, and maybe they'd have let Donaldson handle it. Maybe not. But Merridew had his pride. He and I had struck sparks against each other, but something had always come from it. Now he had to tell himself he wouldn't miss the abrasion. Pride, that was his trouble.

'Let me have something in writing before you go home,' he said sharply, tossing his head.

He left the door wide open.

'Could be late,' I said softly, but already his door had slammed.

4

I found the place easily enough, from the open gate on the right
and the tyre tracks in the snow. The two cars were way up the
slope, the tracks heading in a straight line along what must have
been the farm approach road. Beyond them, on the brow of the
hill, was the old farmhouse. Even from the road you could tell
it was falling down.

I plugged up the slope. It had stopped snowing. Each side
of me, wheat stubble was sticking up through the latest fall. I
went through two more open gates, two more fields, but it was
still the same old stubble.

Latchett and Brason were standing by the cars, Brason stamp-
ing his feet, though the surface wouldn't be hard enough to
help. I stopped the car and got out. Ken approached and said I'd
taken my time, and I told him I'd been to see Mrs Trowbridge.

'Your burnt-out car, Brason,' I called, but he seemed unresponsive.

Ken helped me out with the carrier and the two thermos
flasks. Brason stood and watched.

'Lonely out here,' I said, pausing to look round, trying to be
friendly with Brason.

He stiffened, and became all formal. 'It is now, sir. A few
years back you'd have seen smoke from the farmhouse, and
from a couple of tied cottages just behind that line of pines
there. And from this one behind us. Now it's like a lost
kingdom.'

I couldn't see a cottage behind him. A straggly, layered thorn
hedge headed off up a rise, at right angles to the farm drive. The
building must have been over the brow.

Ken saw me raise my eyebrows at Brason's attitude. He said:
'Brason wants to bugger off home. The missus'll have his dinner
ready.'

'Really?' We were loaded up. I slammed the car door with my
knee. There'd be more to it than that. 'But how can we possibly
manage without his advice, Ken?'

'I was about to tell him that.'

'That's why I brought sandwiches and coffee,' I told Brason.
'A bribe. Or don't you chaps in the country take bribes? We
do, don't we Ken?'

'All the time,' Ken agreed. 'What've you got?'

'Tell you what.' I ignored Ken. 'You pop along to that phone
box I spotted just down the road, and call your missus. Tell
her where you are and why, and say you'll probably be late.
Huh?'

'Yes,' said Ken. 'And if you're not back, she can keep your
tea ready. Maybe supper, too.'

Brason saw he was being ribbed. For a second, colour rose
to his cheeks. Then he grinned, and turned away to his car,
with a sloppy kind of salute.

'We'll keep you something,' Ken called after him.

We watched him drive away.

'Trouble?' I asked.

'He's been grumpy. Helpful as hell, and looking forward to
meeting you again, till I told him you're on your last few
days.'

'Yes. Yes, I think I can understand that.'

'He said *he'd* work right up to the last second, and go out
with a bang.'

'I might do exactly that.'

So Brason had believed he'd been part of my tapering-off
process, and resented it. I couldn't say I blamed him. I shook
my head. Work to do.

'Well – tell me what happened. How'd you come to be out
here?'

We had turned away from the farm drive and were walking
up the line of hedgerow. What I could feel through the snow
didn't seem to be plough furrows, so perhaps there was still a
yard or two of approach-way left for the cottage.

As the path rose, the chimney and then the roof of a square dwelling came into sight. It was set back from the hedge, and trees had been planted in the space provided. Fruit trees of some sort, I reckoned, though they looked lifeless at that time.

There was a rustle under the hedge and a rabbit scrambled away. I watched it with interest, having thought they'd all died off. Ken was busy explaining.

'I was waiting outside Rennie's place, letting Brason work his own patch.'

'Oh yes, Rennie. Did Brason find out anything about Ted Clayton?'

'Nothing. Rennie swore he'd never heard of him. Come to that, he hasn't had decorators in for a couple of years.'

'Ah well, it was worth a try. You were saying?'

'Well, I was leaning against the bonnet, and these two young-sters . . . oh, seventeen or eighteen . . . came belting down the side lane in a Ford pick-up, heading for Rennie's place. When they saw it was a police car they had a word with me instead. They'd been up here, looking for somewhere quiet . . . you get the idea?'

'I can remember the basics.'

'And they looked in through the window, seeing if it was worth while getting in. Well, you'll see. They were a sensible couple, and dashed off to tell Rennie. It's his property.'

'I know.'

He'd stopped. The fruit trees on the left were backed by a line of evergreens I hadn't noticed, and no part of the road below was visible. Behind us there was nothing but sky, in front a continuation of the rise, and to the right the cottage. Beyond it was a long vista down the valley, chequered and scarred with snow and isolated copses. In the far distance there was the tiny movement of a toy wagon.

'Isolated,' I murmured.

There was a tatty wooden fence enclosing a yard or garden, it was impossible to tell which, and then the cottage. The footprints of Latchett and Brason drove a straight line to the front door, and two other sets went off at an angle towards the window. There was a small, collapsing porch over the door, and the remains of a rustic framework each side. The distance from the gap in the fence – there was no gate – to the front door was about thirty yards. It was large, I thought, to be considered as a cottage garden, and had probably been used as an open yard, with hens scratching, and perhaps a goat wandering round. Maybe somebody had once been very proud of their roses up the trellis each side of the door.

The cottage seemed small, but that was possibly because of the immensity of space around it. The front door was set to the right, as I looked at it. There was a small window a few feet to its left, with a matching window above it and an even smaller one above the door. The woodwork showed no remnants of paint, and a few slates had slipped free from the roof. Two of them were standing on end in the gutter, which was close to collapse. Apart from a single, fist-sized hole in the living-room window, the glass seemed to be intact. In town, there wouldn't have been one sliver left in the frames.

'Have you been in?' I asked.

'Yes. We went round the back. The front door's solid, and all the windows are shut, and in the end Brason put a tyre lever to the back door.'

'A tyre lever? You don't see many of those around, these days.'

Ken glanced at me, amusement in his eyes. 'Brason says a lot of people around here run old cars with old tyres. He carries tyre levers just in case. You get the point?'

'I guess they'll miss him.'

'Is he leaving?'

'Sure to. He'll be moving up.'

'Yes.' He rubbed his face. 'Keep to the path,' he added, as we moved on.

'Oh?'

'There're trip wires.'

'You can't mean . . .'

'We've had time to scout around a bit. It's wired everywhere except the gateway and this path. Nothing fancy, just string and old electric wire and the like, finishing up looped over the trees, with rusty cans tied to the ends. It'd make some sort of a warning system.'

We paused in front of the door. There was a leaking water butt to the right of it, and to the left the window. One or two toe-prints tripped towards it from the porch.

'You've been to look at the hole in the glass?' I asked.

'I had a peep inside. He's lying against the grate, with a shotgun leaning next to him against the wall. The hole looks new.'

'So we go round to the right.'

'It's the way we went.'

The side wall was blank brick that had been cement layered, but chunks of it had fallen off and made a rough surface beneath the snow. We walked round to the back.

There were two doors, and a small window beyond the second one. The first door was a plain coalhouse type, easily opened with a finger through the hole. The second door also had a finger hole, but beneath it there was a mortice lock. Brason's efforts had taken the plate from the jamb, but the lock's brass tongue was still protruding and intact.

We went into the kitchen. The floor was blue brick, damp and cold. There was an earthenware sink beneath the window, with no draining board and only one tap, which was dripping dismally. In the back left-hand corner was an ancient boiling copper, with a round lid on top. I lifted it. In the spherical boiler there were a dozen empty beer cans and several screwed-up packages, two of them for light bulbs. When I replaced it, Ken at once put the carrier on the top, and I added the two flasks.

'I just asked for sandwiches,' I told him. 'What've they given us?'

Ken reached inside. 'Cheese and pickle, and egg. By the look of it.'

'I'll try the egg. Straight through, is it?'

He nodded, his mouth full.

There was no door in the doorway between kitchen and living-room. The blue brick floor became red quarries. We were standing in a large room, maybe fifteen by twelve, which had a small, low door to our immediate left, I guessed to a between-wall staircase. Dominating the right-hand wall was an iron fireplace, now almost red-brown with rust, with an oven on each side.

We were getting a little light from the doorway behind us, and not much more from the window – the one with the hole – which was facing us. Four feet to its left was the front door.

Ken said: 'Take a look.' He waved his sandwich.

The man was sprawled on his back, head and shoulders against the cold grate, his legs tangled as though he'd tripped when he fell. Beside him, leaning against the wall, was the shotgun Ken had mentioned. In the squalor of the room, the gun seemed shining and clean. I could see it was an over/under model.

The floor around him was black with dried blood. It had flooded onto his clothes, so that the flannel shirt was almost unrecognisable, a check or two peeping out here and there. The anorak was caked with it. He was wearing jeans with a hole in the knee, and blue and white sports shoes, so filthy that I barely recognised them from Mrs Trowbridge's description. At a rough guess, I'd have said he'd been dead for two or three days.

I raised my head, and realised the light was diving. 'Isn't there any bloody light?' I demanded, ridiculously, because we wouldn't have been able to use it anyway.

'The electricity's on.'

'In a deserted cottage?'

'The meter's in the kitchen,' he said tonelessly, his reaction to my anger. 'The company's seal's been broken, so he probably shorted it out with a bit of wire.'

'We'll find out. Later.'

I finished the sandwich. I stood in front of the body. Not wanting to, I nevertheless tried to get an idea of his height. Six feet – perhaps five-eleven. And yes. Peer a bit closer, and I could see that what hair was still clinging to his skin was blond or white.

'Where the devil's Brason got to?' I demanded savagely.

Ken raised his eyebrows. He said nothing.

Where there had been a face there was now a mess of mangled flesh, with slivers of bone standing whitely against it. Very little of the skull was left, just enough for the bit of hair to hang on.

Ken's guess of murder had to be correct. How could it have

been more than a guess, from a glance through the window? That amount of massive damage couldn't have come from less than both barrels, and he'd had his hands up to his face when they were fired. The blast had shattered both hands on the way through, leaving little more of them than tatters of flesh clinging to the bones.

'Seems your guess was right, Ken,' I conceded.

'Guess?' he asked. He nodded towards the gun. 'If he'd shot himself, who leaned that against the wall?'

I should have realised it at once. My brain was slowing. I usually got there, but I had to have time.

'Try the cheese,' said Ken. 'They're quite good.'

'Not just now, thank you.'

In the right rear corner of the room there were several cardboard boxes. I glanced into them. Tinned food mainly, condensed milk, sugar, powdered coffee. A number of larger cardboard crates had been squashed into a shape vaguely resembling a bed. There were two army blankets on it, with a kit-bag as a pillow.

The only thing that could have been used as a table was a tea chest, the only seat a five-gallon oil drum, so rusty it could have been rescued from outside, with another army blanket folded on it as a cushion.

There was a saucepan on the hob of the grate, and a black kettle in front of it on the floor.

'How anybody could exist like this . . .' I shook my head.

'I don't think he's a tramp. A drop-out, perhaps?'

'When he almost fortified the place? No.' And who the hell was going to have to tell her? 'Where the devil's that forensic van?'

'Give 'em time,' said Ken soothingly. 'The weather's bad.'

'I made good time.'

'Not my impression.'

I glanced at him. 'Don't *you* start. I've had one session already, with Merridew.'

Ken poured coffee into plastic cups. 'Oh yes?' Casually.

'I think we might expect a visit from Donaldson.'

'Has it got to that?'

'It has.'

55

It seemed to satisfy his worry about my evil mood. I allowed him to absorb the assumption, watching his shoulders relax.

There was a cough behind us. Brason stood in the rear doorway.

'Come in,' said Ken. 'Don't bother to knock. Squared the missus, have you?'

We joined him in the kitchen, and he at once investigated the plastic bag. 'Nobody wanting the egg?' he asked.

I was worried about the forensic team. 'Did you see any sign of a large, black van?'

'No, sir.' Brason poured himself coffee. There was less than half a cup.

I picked a bit of hard-boiled egg from the corner of my mouth. 'Better finish that other flask, or that forensic lot'll clear us out.'

Ken and I walked back into the living-room.

'They'll have to give special attention to fingerprints,' I told him. 'It's about all we've got for identification. And I'll want a special check on that window latch, Ken.'

'Yeah. I had the same idea myself. Somebody could've reached in through that hole and opened the window.'

'We'll see. Opened it to get in, and closed it when they left. Perhaps. I don't like the look of that shotgun. I suppose it's been fired?'

I went over and had a sniff at the barrels.

'Been fired right enough,' I decided. 'Both barrels, I'd say.'

'And it would've taken both barrels,' Ken said, sticking out his lower lip in disgust.

'That's always assuming he was killed with this gun. Maybe *he* fired both barrels, at somebody coming, say.' I shook my head. 'Then why would he place it so carefully against the wall, probably not even reloading it, if that somebody was just about to stick another shotgun through that hole in the window and blast him? There's something that doesn't make sense. And another thing – that hole. Where's the glass splinters, if it was done recently? Can't see any on the floor, can you? So perhaps the hole wasn't bashed in – or even blasted in – from outside.'

We advanced to the window. Ken said softly: 'You're rushing it, Richard.'

By that time the light was poor. We bent together, and obligingly, standing in the doorway behind us, Brason put on the overhead light.

I turned on him angrily. 'Touch nothing!' I snapped.

Brason held up his ball-point pen meekly, indicating he'd used only the end of it. His smile was weak, and fading fast.

I relaxed. 'Oh Lord, lad, d'you want to give me a heart attack! Can't you find something to do?'

'I could go and wait for your van,' he suggested. 'They might miss the entrance.'

'Yes. Good idea.'

He was turning away. 'And anyway,' he added, 'Henry Rennie might be along.' It was a remark he obviously expected would make a favourable impression.

'Wait!' I caught him in half-turn. 'What the hell did that last remark mean?'

'It's just . . . while I was on the phone I thought I'd call Rennie and ask him to come and check it's his gun.' Brason was frowning. I could hear Ken humming quietly to himself. 'Sir . . .' Brason said questingly.

Ken turned away diplomatically, and began to examine the floor beneath the hole in the window pane. I took a breath.

'Something you'd better understand, Brason,' I told him evenly. 'I'm in charge of this investigation. So far, anyway. I'm the one who gives the orders around here. Is that clear? Right. Now . . . I do not intend to allow civilians in here, to look at guns or otherwise. Nobody's going to touch it until the forensic wizards have been over it, and it'll take 'em a day or two. Am I getting through?'

'Yes, sir.'

'Good. Now you've landed yourself with the job of heading off Rennie, and telling him he can't put a foot on his own property. If that embarrasses you, that's too bad.'

'I'll do that. Sir.'

'You will, indeed. And now you'll come over here and get a close look at this gun.' It brought him very close to the body. 'That's right, keep clear of the legs. Put your head down. Down, lad, and take a good look at the maker's name engraved on the plate.'

Brason straightened. He was pale. 'Seen it, sir. Remington.'

'We're progressing. How many over/under shotguns d'you reckon there are around here?'

'Well . . . Mr Rennie's . . .'

'And? Come on, an honest guess.'

'I'd say – none.'

'Good. Then can I assume – would you say – just as a working hypothesis, that this weapon could be the one he reported missing?'

Brason lifted his chin. 'I should say so, sir.'

'So you see, there was no point in getting him to have a look at it. Not yet. Slow down, Brason, and don't go jumping the gun.' I winced, not having intended that. 'So to speak.'

He turned to leave. 'I'll go and look for the van, sir. And Rennie.'

'And if you're not feeling too well, try to be sick outside the boundaries of this property.'

'Sir.'

We stood by the window, watching him stomp up the path. Ken stirred, and glanced at his feet.

'Can't see any signs of glass,' he said quietly. 'But I'll get 'em to run a vacuum over it. Have you noticed, Richard, how clean the floor is? No dust. No footprints.'

I grunted. Things were bad enough without Ken noticing that. I agreed to the vacuum. They'd find the smallest of traces. 'But have 'em look under the snow outside,' I said. 'But gently, Ken, gently.' I glanced sideways at him. His face was impassive. 'I was too rough with him, wasn't I?'

'Not really. He's too eager.'

But Ken was being quietly reproving. However disturbed I was, Ken knew that I'd never been in the habit of dispersing my anger around. Lucky it hadn't been Donaldson, though, who'd have torn Brason apart. Mind you, I had to admit that Brason wouldn't have put on the light for Donaldson.

'There's no room in the force for idealists and romantics,' said Ken. Was that how he saw Brason?

I merely nodded, recalling my own idealistic and romantic beginnings, and every detail of the painful compromises I'd had to make. The force had nearly broken me.

Not many minutes later the forensic team turned up, but there was no sign of Brason. The wind had eased, and the sky glowed in the west behind the scattering clouds. The MO formally pronounced death, and took the body away as soon as the photographers had finished with it. They were now all working with floodlights, hooked to the generator in the van.

I went outside to stand in the back garden snow for a quiet smoke. My feet were cold and my brain feverish. I knew Ken had it in hand, so I relaxed to the sunset spreading through the sky. The glorious death of one more of my days! Then Brason came up quietly to my elbow and cleared his throat for action.

'Took you a while,' I said. But I was calm now, and it came out placidly.

'I drove down to Rennie's place, sir, to cut him off before he set out. He was . . . difficult.'

'I can imagine.'

'Wants his gun back, of course.'

'He'll get it. When we can prove it's his.'

'Oh, I'm sure it's his. I noticed a notch in the stock, and he identified that. I told him he'd have it in due course, sir.'

'Good. Nice observation. So now we know where we are. Ever fired an over/under shotgun, Brason?'

'No, sir.'

I was getting a 'sir' with every sentence, now.

'Single trigger, you know, unlike most of the side-by-sides. There's a special selector, so that you can choose which barrel you want to use. But it does mean you can only fire one barrel at a time, not both with one good squeeze. It worries me. Can you see why? It's the separate firing I'm getting at.'

I was hoping that a fresh and younger mind might rescue me from a rather horrible thought I was stuck with. But he seemed uneasy and restless, no longer trusting himself. I waited quietly, wondering whether he could bounce back. At last he fished tentatively.

'Is this on the assumption it was the Remington that killed him?'

'It's been fired. It's a distinct possibility.'

'But the cottage was fastened up tight.'

'Not quite tight. There's a hole in the window pane, and it's right beneath the latch. You could stick a hand through from outside . . .' I tailed it off, letting him absorb the thought.

He took a breath. 'Or somebody could've stuck another shotgun, instead of a hand, through that same hole?'

When he became involved with an idea, he forgot the 'sirs'. His face was caught in an orange glow, jaw muscles deeply shadowed. A young man of mature purpose.

'Yes . . . I see,' he went on. 'I see. I don't know too much about shotgun wounds, but that . . . that mess in there – hands and face – it'd have to be both barrels, I'd guess.'

'The pathologist will no doubt tell us. It seemed so to me.'

'But if it is, and the over/under did it, then . . .' He hissed through his teeth. 'Then it would've taken two separate and deliberate shots. Yes, sir, I see what you mean. Nasty. Kind of vicious.'

'And yet . . . it does look as though that was what he was expecting, doesn't it? Something nasty. He made a fortress of the place, trip wires and all.'

Brason moved his head. He suspected a trap. 'If you think so . . .'

'But?'

'He could've hidden out here for months, and nobody know it. Not till the spring ploughing, anyway. No need to make a fortress of it. The whole farm's been deserted for five years.'

'Hidden, yes. But he was afraid, Brason. Terrified. Hence the trip wires and the shotgun. So he expected to be traced.'

He was doubtful. 'But all the same . . . Begging your pardon, sir, but there's another explanation for using both barrels. Something less vicious.'

'I'd be pleased to hear it.'

'Identification. It could've been meant to hide who he is.'

'With the place full of his fingerprints? With his clothes to work on? And with the rest of his body intact?'

'It was a thought.' He pondered. 'One shot for the face, one for the hands.'

I looked sideways at him. Was this the Brason whom Ken had described as a romantic idealist?

'Does that make it better?' I asked.

'More . . . well, practical, sir. Less vicious.'

I couldn't find an answer to that. Either way, I found it difficult to accept.

Then Ken came to tell me they'd found particles of glass beneath the front window, outside. I said absent-mindedly that I'd be round in a minute. Ken grunted and went away.

I was turning my mind to something else. 'Five years, did you say, it's been deserted? Did they chuck them all out together, farmer, labourers . . .'

'Not all together, sir. This one's been empty for six or more years. Since the old lady died. Mrs Kendall, that'd be.'

'Kendall! Did you say Kendall?' I swung to face him, and he looked startled.

'Well, yes.'

'Now, I need to get this straight. Did this Mrs Kendall have a son called Clive?' My heart was tripping.

'That raping bastard – that's him! Born and bred here, but fortunately he'd been gone from this district for . . . oh, three years, before he started his nasty habits. Fortunately for him.'

I guessed him as around twenty-five. 'But you weren't in the force then, surely.'

'My father, sir. He'd got the patch then. But I can tell you – if he'd had the arresting of Kendall . . . well, now, perhaps there'd have been an unfortunate accident.'

'Hmm! But as it happened, it was me. Arrested him.'

Then, while Brason was staring at me in indecision, a throat was cleared, and Donaldson was standing at my elbow.

5

'Well now . . .' Donaldson was holding himself stiffly, almost in defence. 'How're things going, then?' There might have been half a smile in the corner of his mouth, and he had his head cocked beneath the felt trilby he always wore. 'Perhaps you'd better bring me up to date, Inspector.'

There'd been a flash of white shirt cuff and gold cuff-links. Two comments, and he'd told me the lot. He'd got his rank of Chief Inspector, and he expected my full co-operation.

'Yes,' I said. 'Have you been inside, yet?'

'Not yet.' He waited. He'd got to know where he stood with me. He was a trim, slim figure, maybe forty-five, holding himself as though he thought he was in the army. I happened to know he'd come straight from University to the force. A pity about the moustache, I thought, and the sideboards were really a little long.

But there was something in his eyes I couldn't interpret. A pity the light was so poor. He'd been thrown into this – his new rank and a murder case – and he hadn't even located his desk. He was nervous, but afraid to show it.

I set the position straight. 'Sergeant Latchett's running things inside. He'll give you the background. This is Brason, the local man. I'll be at my office, if you want me.'

He nodded. His eyes caught the remnants of the light, glowing red and reflecting what could be anger, or simply satisfaction. Then he turned around smartly and went into the cottage.

Brason was uncomfortable, eyeing me sideways with raised eyebrows.

'Mr Donaldson's in charge now,' I told him. 'You'll be working for him, so you'd better trot along inside. Oh, and I wouldn't offer him any bright ideas, he might not appreciate them.'

Then I nodded, and ambled off round to the front of the building. No hurry now. It was strange, taking it slowly, with no pressure. Something else I'd need to get used to.

Ken wasn't waiting for me to inspect the glass splinters, but was now inside, talking to Donaldson. To hell with the glass, I thought, then I wandered over to have a look.

The man from forensic was still working on the snow beneath the window. He'd used a spatula to scrape it aside, meticulously, probably flake by flake. I stood and watched him for a moment, then crouched at his side.

The glass splinters were scattered in a patch about a foot square, and a cameraman was taking flash shots of it from various angles. I held up my hand, and he lowered the camera.

'What d'you make of it?' I asked the technician.

He was cheerful, waving the spatula, though his trousers were soaked to the knees. 'Oh, it's certainly window glass, sir, so I'd say it's from the hole in the window. See – that piece on its edge. It's dirtier on one side than the other.'

We stared together at the piece of glass, then at the hole in the pane.

The window was a simple wooden-framed design, four feet wide by three high, half of it – the right-hand half, from where I was squatting – consisting of an opening section. It was now firmly latched. I could see the latch inside, a simple downward swinging arm of curved, cast metal. The hole, six inches across on average, was in the pane immediately beneath the latch. Its edge was only an inch or so from the central, vertical bar.

'That hole,' I asked, 'would you say it could've been done by a shotgun blast?'

'It's the size you'd expect, if it was fired close to the glass.' He was dubious. 'But fired that close, you'd expect the glass to fly further, and it'd be in smaller fragments, I'd have thought. We could do some tests, if you want them.'

'No. But pass it on to Mr Donaldson.'

I eased my knees. There was no point in pursuing the

subject – it wasn't my case any more. 'But it wasn't blasted out, was it?'

'Sir?'

'Take a look at that hole, and then at this glass in the snow. One isn't beneath the other.'

The small patch of glass fragments was about two feet from the cottage wall, and a foot or more to the right of the hole. I edged round, not an easy thing to do when you're in a crouch. Looking straight on at the wall, the patch of glass was closer to the hinge than to the central vertical bar.

I told the photographer what to do about it. 'Get a shot from here. It could matter. Show exactly the relationship between the hole and the bits of glass.'

He'd have done that, anyway. But he nodded, looking solemn. The two men seemed impatient to get on with it. I creaked to my feet and headed for the Stag.

It was almost completely dark. I sat quietly for a while, my pipe going, drifting the smoke out of the half-open window. It was necessary to rearrange my emotions. I'd been a damn fool to stand on my paltry authority and come there. I'd seen it now. I'd become interested and involved, and the best I could hope for was second fiddle to Donaldson's confident leadership. To hell with that! It was like a marriage gone sour – better to break clean and walk away from the case with a blank mind.

I started the car, edged round, and drove away, leaving behind me an oasis of light in the middle of desolation. Heading into desolation.

Yet there were compensations, I told myself. From what Brason had said there was a direct link with Kendall, and the body could be his. Even thinking of him was disturbing. The life sentence had been a source of complete satisfaction to me, as a private individual and as a policeman, so that his early release had produced a choked feeling of outrage, as though something had been kicked away from under me. No . . . better out of it, if it turned out to be Kendall. I'd have been blocked by emotion, and torn apart.

And yet . . . the possibility of the body being Kendall's naturally turned my thoughts to the Clayton brothers. But how could they possibly have known about this remote refuge? The

Claytons were, at least, still mine. Them, I could approach unemotionally.

I drove on, pleased with this rationalisation, and for some minutes pleased with myself, too.

The road surface was worse than when I'd driven there. I hit the main road into town, fortunately facing the commuter stream, and there'd been some gritting done. But all the same, there were difficulties. From a long way away I could see that Turner's Gap was blocked, with a trailer-wagon slewed across the hill. I slipped into a minor road.

This took me in a loop that eventually ran along the outskirts of the building estate in which Amelia Trowbridge lived. There was an abrupt urge to drop in on her, and I found myself testing excuses to do that. But though the description fitted her husband, the location of the body suggested Kendall. I would not even dare to mention it, and what else was there? It would be completely unprofessional to visit her . . . and the case was Donaldson's. I turned away from it.

I entered town past the railway station. Every day, it seemed to me, they messed about with the diversions round the work on the new by-pass. At the bus stops there were long queues, with miserable feet shuffling in the slush. Suddenly I felt tired, picking it up from their strained faces, I suppose. I didn't think I could persuade myself to return to the office, to the IN tray, and to Merridew's satisfaction, however well he managed to control it. Tomorrow would do. There were a lot of tomorrows completely untouched.

I saw her, standing in a bus queue on the other side of the street. I was in the outside lane of a tail-back from the traffic lights at the pelican crossing ahead. There was no oncoming traffic. On impulse I swung out from the stream and across the street, winding down the window.

'Can I give you a lift?'

She bent to the opening, features peaked, with a little woolly hat tilted on her head. For a moment she was startled and defensive. 'But you're not going my way.'

'I could. Very easily.'

I tried to make my voice match the warmth that must have been wafting out at her. The very sight of her had flushed away all my weariness, and tomorrow had another name.

'If you really wouldn't mind,' said Amelia Trowbridge. There was relief in her voice.

'Hop in, then.'

She skipped round like a teenager. The lights had changed, and the oncoming traffic was pressing close, flicking indignant headlights at me. She had difficulty opening the door wide enough, but at last she fell into the seat beside me, throwing her head back with a breath of released tension. She was wearing a skirt, I saw. I preferred her in a skirt.

'And now you're in trouble,' she said, as one who knows, staring into the advancing headlights.

'I'll manage.'

Tempers on the whole were short. Nobody seemed pleased when I forced my way back through the stream. Horns were blasted. I grinned. A bit of opposition was like a blood transfusion. I achieved my original stream at last.

'I'll turn down from the square,' I told her. 'We can do a circle at the island at the bottom.'

She sighed. I glanced at her. She was jutting her lower lip. 'Shopping's been simply terrible,' she told me. 'You can't imagine . . .'

'Yes, I can. I do my own.'

'Your wife . . .'

'My wife's been dead for three years.'

'I'm sorry. You're quite alone?'

'Yes. But I manage. I can always send a constable out to the takeaway.' I wanted to get off the subject.

She hesitated, unsure whether it was a joke, but then she got the hint. 'I'm sure you can do no such thing,' she said gravely, reproving me.

'How d'you feel about a cup of tea?' I asked wildly. 'We could drop in to a café.' I risked a glance. 'If you're not in a hurry.' My own evening stretched away into emptiness.

'I'm in no hurry.' A pause. 'There's something you want to tell me, isn't there?'

Something I didn't. 'Nothing that comes to mind,' I said smoothly.

'Then you should not have stopped for me.'

'There you were, miserable and cold. I thought: just what she needs, a cup of tea.' Had I? I couldn't remember.

'You're a detective inspector,' she reminded me. 'Already you've taken some trouble over my missing husband and the car, and I'm sure they were very minor matters to you. And now you make a point . . .'

I interrupted. They never see past the uniform, even when you're in plain clothes. 'Funny, I had it different.' I'd stopped just beyond a meter space and was backing, my head twisted. I didn't dare switch my eyes to her. 'I simply thought it would be pleasant – a chat over a café table. Was I wrong?'

Perhaps my voice was slightly challenging. Her attitude had irritated me a little. She sat still for a moment, not opening the door.

'Yes,' she decided. 'I think it would be very pleasant.'

I got out and locked the car. There were forty minutes left on the meter. I went round and took her arm in my fist, and steered her into the covered shopping complex.

'We might find room at the Crystal Orb,' I said.

It wasn't quite as I remembered it. The café was a narrow slice inserted in the shop fronts, on one side a long counter and on the other a row of small tables, at which four people would have been cramped. There was a two-chair table in the far corner unoccupied.

I was sure she'd expected something better – crisp table linen and a silver pot of tea, tiny cakes and a soft background of gossip. But she'd been reluctant and I couldn't afford to march her all around the town. I thrust her ahead of me, and sat her with her back to the door, my habit from years of facing entrances. Then I went to the counter and returned with two cups of tea.

I caught her expression as I put them down. Nothing for it but to face it out, hoping I didn't look like an embarrassed boy on his first date. 'I got it wrong, didn't I! They must have altered this place. Never mind, we'll find something better next time.'

'Next time?'

Why was I saying the wrong things? I covered quickly, watching her play with the sugar dispenser.

'A figure of speech. I certainly shan't be seeing you officially.

Her eyes were dark above the rim of the cup. 'So that's what this is. Official.'

'Pleasure,' I persisted. 'An interlude.'

'A break, you mean? In your work, or out of your own time?'

I'd spent forty years interviewing people, one way or another, and always there'd been the same damned barrier. They wouldn't let you get inside. Maybe it was guilt, maybe suspicion, even pure ingrained opposition to what I represented. But I always tried to see behind their eyes. What were they like? How did they click? How could I gain their confidence? But always that veil in between. Always I was a copper. How long did I have to go before I became an ordinary human being?

I laughed, showing her I'd got a laugh in me. She was still grave, nowhere approaching my mood.

'The trouble with CID work is that nobody can tell when you're off duty,' I told her. 'Now, for example, I'm supposed to be on my way to the office to clear a few files.'

'This will make you late, then.'

'I'm not sure I'll trouble to go. So – you decide – am I on duty or off?' I tried to make it a little game.

'Give me a clue.'

'On duty I wear a dark tie, off duty a flashy one.'

'This one's dark.'

'Is it?' I fingered it. 'The other's in the car. Shall I dash back and change it?'

'Would that make this meeting unofficial?'

'It *is* unofficial. Me – Richard Patton – drinking tea and talking nonsense.'

She raised her chin. There was pain in her eyes, as though she felt I was being cruel by imposing suspense. 'Something's happened, hasn't it?'

'I have never,' I said, clattering the spoon in my saucer, 'met such a persistent woman. It's no wonder your husband ...' I stopped. She could know nothing of my outrageous sense of humour. 'I'm sorry. It was supposed to be funny.'

'You're trying to cheer me up,' she decided. 'But I'm not

really in the mood, Inspector. My feet are freezing and my head's aching.'

'Even reprimanding me, I think you ought to call me Richard,' I suggested. That, I saw, had touched some nerve of amusement in her. 'If there's to be a next time,' I ventured, taking advantage.

She flushed like a young girl, and for a moment her mouth softened to something close to a smile. 'Well . . . Richard,' she told me, 'my feet are still freezing, and . . .'

'And I should call you Amelia?' I cut in.

'I ought to know better than to talk to a detective without my solicitor present,' she told me. And now at last she'd tuned in to my mood.

'It's all right if I give you a warning first.'

'Warnings now! Warn away, then.'

'Anything you say will be noted, and used in your favour if I get half a chance.'

Then she laughed. It was the first time she had really treated me to her unrestrained laughter. Her face lit up. I grinned at her. She looked down, glanced up.

'This tea is quite undrinkable,' she said.

'It's not really for drinking, it's for talking over.'

Still smiling, she said: 'And is it likely you'll need to speak in my favour . . . Richard?'

I slapped my left palm down on the table. 'Oh hell.'

'What's the matter? What have I said?' When I did not meet her eyes she reached over and put a hand on the back of mine. 'Richard?'

'You never miss a word,' I whispered. 'Any slightest intonation, and you're on to it. I merely said . . .'

'I know what you said. It was your subconscious peeping through. Warnings, Richard. Something's happened, and you don't want to tell me. That's what it is,' she decided firmly, sitting back.

I sighed, pushed away my tea in case I picked it up again without thinking, and looked directly into her eyes. The smile was still there, but I could see she was not the sort of woman who'd let me go on skating around it.

'Something has happened,' I admitted. 'Several things, though it's not clear whether they involve you. One of them . . .' I paused. Did *that* involve her? 'One of them is that I've been out-ranked, and in effect been tossed aside to tidy up the paper rubbish. But that doesn't really matter, because I'm retiring in a day or two, anyway.'

'You should have said. Are you looking forward to it?'

'Not really.'

'A man like you, you'll soon find something to occupy your mind.'

'But it's not a matter of finding something to do – to fill a gap. Is it? It's a matter of finding something that you want to do. Then there aren't any gaps.'

She leaned forward, genuinely interested. 'And what do you want to do, Richard?'

'I don't know. I haven't planned. What I didn't want was to get involved in another case, this close to the end.'

'You should have said,' she repeated, 'that you're retiring.'

She couldn't know the extent of my involvement, nor what the case was. 'But when,' I asked, 'if not now? This gives me a chance to tell you, in case I never see you again.'

'That would be a pity.' Her eyes were soft.

'And in a mood of depression – I suppose – I saw you, and I wanted to talk. But really, you know, I shouldn't even speak to you, because it's too early, and too indefinite.'

For a moment she was uncertain what I meant. Then she nodded.' You see, I was right.'

'There was no point in causing you distress, when it could be unnecessary.'

I needn't have worried about that. She was a woman of strong character. A finger touched her lips. The nail was polished, but not varnished.

'We've found the body of a dead man,' I said, suddenly relieved that it was out.

She drew a long, shuddering breath. 'It's . . .'

'I don't know. It's going to be difficult, due to the nature . . . Amelia, it's a shotgun business. They do a lot of damage. The face . . . nobody could know him. He's the correct height, and the clothes fit your description. But thousands of people dress like that.'

'I must see him.' Her fingers to her mouth, still.

'No!' I produced my pipe.' No,' I said, more gently.' Not yet. There are other aspects to it. The body was found in a rather remote cottage . . . are you all right?'

Her eyes had flickered, and she'd gone very pale. She nodded, lower lip caught in her teeth.

'It's a good four miles from where your car was found,' I told her.' If it *is* your husband, it'd be strange for him to be there, and it doesn't link at all with your car being set on fire.'

'You're making a point.'

'I'm making the point that it's too soon to be making assumptions.'

'No. It's something else.'

'Let's get out of here.'

'Richard . . . please.'

I didn't want to go on with it, and continue to stare into her liquid, hurt eyes. I'd already gone too far. I half rose to my feet, but she put out a hand, and I sat down again. Wasn't there anything in which I could oppose her?

'There's another man,' I said miserably. 'He's recently returned to the district, and a number of people could mean harm to him. There've been threats, and he's disappeared. But . . . and this is the point . . . this cottage is where that man was born. He'd even have reason to know it would be empty. He'd shut himself away in such a manner that suggests he was scared to death, and heaven knows he'd got good reason to be. And on top of all that, there was a shotgun in the cottage which he, coming from the district, would know how to put his hands on. You can see, the set-up fits that man exactly, but the description could fit your husband. I didn't want to discuss it at this time. You can surely understand that.'

'Then why did you offer me a lift?'

'For heaven's sake . . . I explained.'

She gave a little grimace of apology. 'Sorry. You've been very frank with me, Richard, and I'm grateful for that. I truly am. But I've been prepared for something. He's been gone for so long, and the car . . . All you've got to do is take me to see him.' It was all so clear and uncomplicated to her.

'I'm afraid you couldn't see him now, anyway,' I told her.

'The medical officer's got the body. And anyway, it might not be necessary. The cottage is full of his fingerprints, and the other chap's well known to us. *His* prints are on file. You see, by tomorrow we'll know. Come along, now, I was going to run you home.'

This time I was going to accept no arguments. I bustled her to her feet, urging her ahead. 'But Richard . . .' I strode along, my usual heavy strides, she trotting at my side and clutching my arm. 'But why are his fingerprints in your files?' We got to the car, and I held the door open for her.

She slid in, her face raised. 'You haven't told me – why are that man's fingerprints in your files?'

'Because he's only just come out of prison.' I said it angrily, choking on the thought of Kendall's early release.

Then I walked round and got in behind the wheel. She was strangely still.

'Amelia?'

'You said – only just.' Her voice was weak. 'How long ago?'

'Two or three weeks. What . . .'

'Oh . . . h . . . h!' It was a shuddering gasp.

I'd slid in the ignition key, but now I didn't turn on the engine. 'What is it?'

'It's just . . .' She gave a nervous little rattle of forced laughter. 'In either case – if my guess is right – I could probably identify your man.'

'What *is* this? What're you saying?'

'I know a man who could have reason to be afraid, who's recently come out of prison. It's Clive Kendall you're talking about, isn't it?'

'You know him?' The surprise jolted my voice. Suddenly things began to fall apart.

'Yes.' She nodded. She was staring straight ahead, her profile in silhouette against a bright shop window. 'I know him very well. I've spoken with him many times, as a counsellor in the Prisoners' Aid Association.'

'Oh dear God!' I whispered.

'He's been my own special case. I managed to get him paroled.' She said it in pathetic pride.

I woke the engine into life, hitting the throttle wrong. It

howled for me as I crashed into a gear and forced the car out into the traffic stream.

'Richard . . . please!'

I'd run a red at the pedestrian crossing and forced the car forward. The rear wheels were skidding wildly, the roundabout coming up. I knew what I was doing, watched myself doing it, and couldn't control the impulse. I was running away. Everything had suddenly become insupportable, and I couldn't handle it. The roundabout was too close, and I had to do something. Brake hard. I scrambled it into some sort of control, but still rocking, and shot into the roundabout under the nose of a wagon. Sweat ran down my face and into my eyes, from the strain of running away. And yet . . . I was carrying it with me.

Then we were round the island and I was flicking the winker for the turn-off. The car, at least, was under control. I slowed, glanced sideways, almost afraid to look at her. She had her face in her hands. I was ashamed. I knew what I had to do. I had to get her out of the car and drive away, and think it out alone.

'What's the matter?' she whispered. I had to read her lips.

But I couldn't say anything. I was remembering what I'd said to Ken, when we'd heard of Kendall's release. 'By God, I wish I could meet the stupid, bumbling bastard who's done this! I'd tell him . . .' But it wasn't a him, it was a her, and a very special her. Amelia. She didn't fit the image. She couldn't . . . How could I trust my voice?

The obvious thing to do was to drop her at the bus stop. Where I'd picked her up. But even at that time I retained enough manners to realise it would be no more than a petty show of ill-humour. It would be an insult, and it was insult I was choking down.

She'd gathered her shopping bag onto her lap. Her voice was cold and distant. 'If you'll let me out along here . . .'

'No.'

'I'd best catch the bus.'

'I'll take you home.'

'I don't understand you. Richard, please stop the car.'

'I'll drive you home. I promised,' I replied, the words bouncing back at me from the windscreen.

I drove on, and past her bus stop. The length of the queue added point to the decision. But I was silent, driving with controlled tension.

'You're frightening me,' she said at last, reaching to me with her voice. 'Is that what you want?'

'I want to take you home.' My jaw muscles were painful.

'Such temper!' she commented, her voice gaining strength. 'And what when you get me home?'

'Then I'll ask you to get out of the car, and I'll drive away.'

'Well, at least you're speaking normally now. I just can't understand this . . . this exhibition. But you must do as you wish, I suppose.'

'Thank you.'

No more was said during the rest of the journey. I was aware of her there, sitting stiffly upright, but I sensed a relaxation in her. She had persuaded herself to go along with my decisions. I was ashamed, but still burning with rejection. Now I didn't want the situation to remain unresolved. There was just a chance I'd misunderstood, and that I'd misjudged her.

The cul-de-sac stood in front of us, the snow layer in the unmade street unbroken. I drew up in front of the house. It was very quiet. I switched off the engine and sat back. She made no move. I could not look at her.

'No explanations, Richard?' she asked softly. 'No apologies?'

She was putting me on the defensive. 'Apology, yes. I don't know what . . . I'm sorry.'

She left it at that. It was pure nervous reaction when I reached for my pipe and fumbled with it.

'You must come in,' she said, nodding decisively. 'We've got to talk. Surely you can see that. You terrified me, Richard. You owe me an explanation. We were . . . so . . . we were communicating. Do you know what I mean?'

I knew very well. 'I don't want to come in. Not now.'

'Then why have you switched off the engine?' I turned to her. She gave me a tiny, searching smile. 'Oh, come along. You mustn't be childish.'

Women's blackmail. You don't ever have to give in to it.

'For a minute, perhaps.'

It would have been better if she hadn't smiled with such

complete lack of restraint. I followed her into the house, feeling awkward and hesitant.

'You know where to hang your coat,' she said. 'I'll put on the kettle.' On her home ground, she was taking control. I was limping along on injury time. 'Do go into the back room,' she called, walking away, but I prowled after her into the kitchen. 'They called it the dining-room in the specification,' she told me more loudly. 'It's more comfortable than the front. Oh!'

I was at her shoulder. The warm smell awakened my hunger, but I could hardly ask her to feed me. 'Very pleasant,' I said, looking round.

It must have come as a fitted unit, long sink beneath the window, flanked by the cooker, fridge, cupboards and washing machine. She had slatted blinds at the windows, and everything matched, the surfaces to the Formica-covered table and the chair seats. Along beneath a side window there was a counter, with four stools, clearly a dining alcove. It wasn't suitable, I decided. I wouldn't be able to sit facing her.

I sat at the table, then I got up again to place two chairs against the wall. Might as well demonstrate my intentions, I thought. Seeing this, she grimaced ruefully, but said nothing.

She filled the pot, slid crockery onto the table, and sat opposite me. She poured. I tasted mine.

'Much better.'

'Now please explain,' she demanded. 'Why were you so upset?'

'Very well. But first of all, I'll need to get it clear. You said you know Clive Kendall. You said you're a worker for the Prisoners' Aid people. You said this was your own, special case.'

'Yes.' She sipped.

'Does that mean it was you – your actions – that brought about his release?'

'Oh yes. My first triumph.' She tossed her hair, her eyes glowing. 'I'm very proud of it.'

I tried again. 'I suppose you know he got life imprisonment?' A nod. 'And that the judge recommended it shouldn't be less than twenty years?' Another nod. Why was she so complacently unresponsive? 'And that your efforts . . .'

'I can't claim it all as mine, Richard. Our President – his lobbying and persistence . . .'

I talked her down, not being able to take her pride and false modesty.

'But – I assume – they were your recommendations?'

'Certainly. Oh, please relax. You can be so severe, you know.' She pouted. She was trying to keep it on a light level.

'So presumably you know what he did to earn a life sentence?'

'Of course I know. Is it relevant?'

'It's all that matters, damn it.'

'I could argue that with you.'

'Not now, for pity's sake. You know he raped and killed a child?'

'I know that.' A paltry defiance. 'I had all the documents.'

'Documents! I was on the case. Four months of it. Coral Clayton wasn't the only girl he raped, you know. We had a hundred men working on it. Five rapes, and three indecent assaults. I went through the lot. But we got him in the end. The whole town breathed a sigh of relief. Then six months to get him to trial, the Director of Public Prosecutions, solicitors, barristers, a court, a jury and a judge. All that to show the world that it'd been done right and proper. Then he was put away.'

'I do understand all this, Richard.' Her eyes pleaded. I'd touched something, perhaps.

'Then perhaps you can explain why you – you and your recommendations – should override it all. Why you'd *want* to! Just so that he can start another lot . . .'

'Now, that's ridiculous. There's no reason to suppose he'd do it again.'

'It's almost certain he would. Who in God's name gave you the right to interfere with law and justice, and . . .' I controlled myself, shaking my head.

'You were going to say: and the public's revenge,' she said in a flat voice. 'Don't you think that's archaic – a pagan emotion?'

'Do I hell! It's still there in everybody, and you can't deny it. The public wants to *see* that revenge. They saw him put away, but I bet that most people don't even know he's been let out again. God damn it, you should've been here at the time. The town was boiling. Revenge? They'd have torn him apart, if we hadn't got to him first.'

'We?' she demanded, attacking. 'You mean the police? Where's *their* instinct for revenge, then? Don't tell me they're the only civilised people around! But I see what you mean. When it came to it, when it came to making an arrest, they'd pick the subhuman types, who'd had all the human feelings and imagination knocked out of them.'

She was hot and angry. I sipped my tea. 'It only took a bit of self-control,' I said. 'No – it took a great deal. But no fancy principles. I was the arresting officer, Amelia.'

She bit her lip, shook her head, and said: 'Damn!' bitterly.

I felt empty, my spirits low. You only see the outsides. I'd probed and wormed around, trying to get to know her. I sensed that even now this was not the true woman. But I was light headed, my brain craving rest. I sighed.

'Can I get back to what I was saying? Tell me, please, why you wanted to undo all that effort, and get him released.'

'Not me alone. There were numerous examinations and reports by psychiatrists.'

'Psychiatrists now! My God.'

'Any objections . . .'

'They don't even come into it. Nobody said he was insane. He was put away because of what he'd done.'

'Because of what he *was*,' she corrected. 'He was a danger to the public at that time. But, after eight years, he was showing not one sign of any instinct for assaults on young girls.'

'There weren't any for him to get at. That's the whole idea.'

'That's a very cynical remark.'

'Realistic. He was a vile man, and you decided to let him have another go.'

'I was convinced he'd do no such thing.'

'Ah, then we're all right. You're the expert.'

'I didn't think you'd sink so low.'

'I feel low, right down at rock bottom.' I rubbed my face with both hands. I had to keep control. 'But tell me – have you thought what it might mean to you, personally, if another little girl dies? Have you given any thought to that at all?'

77

'What d'you think I am?' she demanded angrily. 'Of course I have. But I saw him, in Long Lartin, oh, maybe a hundred times. I've looked into his face, and he was a human being who was suffering. To you he was a finished case, discarded, and shut away like his file in a drawer, gathering dust. All I saw was that he needed help.'

'Perhaps a bit of that pity could've been spared for the parents of Coral Clayton. Perhaps *they* needed help,' I said in disgust.

'But you're so lacking in imagination! What help – what possible help – could've been given to those poor people? It'd be a personal distress. Who could've intruded? But something could be salvaged from it. You have to go forward. It was in the past, and nothing could be retrieved, except for him.'

I groaned. 'From you!' But hadn't I said much the same thing to Ted Clayton?

'Clive Kendall could be helped. I helped him.'

I stared into my cup. I couldn't believe I'd been completely wrong about her. Call it pride, if you like. She'd seemed normal, with no hint of the fanatic. I wondered whether her husband had been unable to live with it, wondered how much longer I could, myself. I spoke from an exhaustion I was unable to oppose. But I had to hang on to something.

'There're some things, Amelia, that people can't forget and forgive. And never excuse. Clive Kendall will never be normal, and never fit to be amongst ordinary people.'

'I can assure you, his reactions to me were normal enough.'

'Oh Lord! He was married. Rona was quite beautiful. Was. I mean, she must have been, before all that business started. I talked with her quite often, after the arrest. His sex life with her had always been normal.'

'You questioned her about that?'

'We talked.' I flicked a smile at her. '*She* needed a bit of help, around that time.'

'Then *she* couldn't have been normal, telling you that. How d'you know she was telling the truth?'

'Did he tell you anything that makes it a lie? I suppose you questioned him about his sexual appetites.'

'Richard . . .'

'Well, that was what it was all about.'

She became dignified. 'I found him to be a perfectly normal man. He was polite to me, a little domineering, very masculine. But easy to talk to.'

I was on my feet, unable to remain still any longer. 'Then perhaps you'd better tell that to Coral Clayton's mother. She'd be pleased to hear how normal he is. Or to her uncles. I can take you to the uncles. Would you like me to arrange that?' I asked bitterly.

Her eyes were angry. She bounced up, all tense fury. 'Now?'

'Not now,' I said wearily. 'I must go. We're getting nowhere. But . . . I forgot to ask you. Do you know just what this normal, masculine and charming man did?'

'I know he raped and killed . . .'

'Yes. Goes together, doesn't it? One single and ungovernable act of a man who ought to be pitied because he couldn't control what he was doing.' I shook my head, trying to clear my eyes of the streamers of anger. Or were they tears? She had seated herself again, white-faced, and I tried to go on in a flat, emotionless voice.

'Clive Kendall raped little Coral Clayton. She was nine years old. It was the only one in daylight, so there was a chance she'd know him and recognised him. We got her to the hospital. We thought it was enough – for the doctors to say she'd live, and maybe, in a day or two, be able to talk to us. But two nights later he walked into the ward. Nobody saw him. He walked into the side room where she was sleeping, and silently took what remained of her life with a pillow. I've always blamed myself not putting a guard on her. But I thought, like you, that he was just a sexually perverted man, acting from some obsessive drive he couldn't control. But I was wrong. Nobody conceived such a depth of evil. . . . There, you see, and I was feeling proud I could talk about it so calmly. But I can't, after all. And that was what he did. And the parents – who couldn't be helped? Six months after the trial, the child's father, who I suppose couldn't help the images that wouldn't leave him alone, took his own life, because that was the only defence he had. That's what Clive Kendall did, and you've got him out to do it again, and I can't . . . I can't talk to you any more about it.'

I turned away. I thought I was moving like a stricken old

man, but I was at the front door and outside before she could stop me. She ran after me, out through the snow, and was at the car window as I reached forward to start the engine.

'Richard . . . don't hate me so much,' she whispered.

'Hate?' I managed a twisted smile. 'It's not that.'

She had her hand on the sill of the open window. I reached over and clamped my fist on it.

'When I saw that dead man in the cottage,' I told her, 'I thought at first it was your husband. I knew it'd make you very unhappy, if it was, but . . . heaven help me . . . I was rather hoping that's how it'd turn out. But now . . .' I released my hand. 'Now d'you know what I'm doing? I'm praying it turns out to be Kendall.'

I switched on the engine, not turning to look at her again. I felt the wheels through the turning circle at the end, and drove back past her. She was standing in the snow, watching me leave. She did not wave.

6

Ken had left a report on my desk, when I got in the next morning. It was clearly a photostat of what he'd submitted to Donaldson. He must have been up half the night. There was a note stapled to it.

> *Richard. I've starred the points you probably don't know about.*
> *I don't like the smell of it. Ken.*

That was my friend, determined to keep me involved. I shoved it to one side. My head was still aching from a sleepless night, but I was stubbornly determined to do just what had been asked of me, no more and no less: tidy up the paperwork.

I reached for the IN tray and got the first file, and my mind was tracking two lines behind my eyes. I lit my pipe, and concentrated. Seven files later I'd scrawled seven signatures, but I couldn't have told you what I'd authorised. Angrily, defeated, I flung them aside and drew forward Ken's report.

There were bold pencil asterisks at several places, and here and there a scribbled note in the margin. It was long and detailed. I skipped most of it, and concentrated on what he'd marked. After a minute or two my mind creaked into gear, and I sat back, absorbed.

Many of the points possibly held no significance, but they added to the general background.

The upper floor had been completely stripped of floorboards, and the main staircase dismantled. Clearly used as firewood.

Evidence in ashes that a small amount of furniture also burned. Scarcely anything burnable left. No reports of smoke being seen, but Con. Brason states there have been either strong winds or mists.

About a week's food left. Cans and rubbish in rear garden indicate he had been in the cottage around two weeks. Water was available from underground well. (Location not discovered.) Pump and tank in outhouse. Pump is electric and automatic. Company's fuse box was shorted. Water very pure.

Keys were found in their appropriate locks. The rear door was locked when found, but the lock in the front door was unfastened. However, the front door was wedged in its frame and immovable.

The shotgun has been identified as belonging to Henry Rennie, comparison of numbers having been made. Both barrels had been discharged. There was an open box of cartridges found beside the wall in kitchen, only two having been taken out. The weapon had not been reloaded. Fingerprints were found on the weapon. (See para on fingerprints.)

Preliminary examination of fingerprints in cottage indicate as belonging to one person only. This has a theoretical confirmation in that entry from outside seems impossible. (Prints on window latch match those on the shotgun and in the cottage.)

Glass fragments on the ground surface outside front window are indicative of the discharge of a shotgun from inside, as is the size of the hole in the pane. Disposition of glass indicates that shotgun was fired at an angle through the window pane, in the direction of the porch outside the front door??? (The inference from this is that a second shotgun was afterwards discharged through the same hole from outside, killing the subject. See separate report – DCI Donaldson.)

I raised my eyes at that, and turned the page sideways to read Ken's pencilled note.

He told me to put this in. What d'you think of it? He's already convinced himself that we've found what's left of Kendall. Wish I was that certain. But we'll know when the prints have gone through the PNC. Going home now. I'm whacked. Ken.

I folded the report and slipped it into an inside pocket, then drew a fresh batch of files towards me. I started off with determination, but after a quarter of an hour it ran out. I put down my pen, then reached for the phone and asked for HQ – Computer Section.

'Harry . . . it's Richard. No – I'm at my desk. Anything yet on those prints? The Swallow's End murder, what d'you think?'

He commented that he'd heard I was not in charge of it. Damn it all, I'd bought him a pint last time we'd met! I talked him down cheerfully.

'I know Donaldson's got it, but that doesn't mean I'm not interested . . . yes . . . you fed them in when? Eight this morning. Well, you ought to have heard something by now, Harry. Thanks. One I owe you.'

I put down the phone and settled a shoulder against the patch on the wall. I'd been sent, grumbling, to a short course on the Police National Computer, but now it was useful to know how it clicked. They'd have fed it with a code covering all the recognised characteristics of the prints they'd found. Then it would make a search. If it found a positive match straightaway, it would throw it out. But failing that, it would search for all characteristics minus one, and throw out a dozen or so possibles, then minus two, and produce a hundred or more, and then minus three . . . and so on, until somebody punched a key to tell it to stop playing the fool, and lay off.

A positive ID of all characteristics, as you'd expect for prints already on file, might take the computer as long as four seconds to locate. Non-positive took longer. They had fed the computer at eight. It was now ten-thirty, and it hadn't disgorged. The body was therefore not that of Clive Kendall, always provided that nobody had botched it up.

I reached for my hat and coat, and Merridew walked into the office.

'Going out, Richard?'

'Something I'd like to check.'

He fingered his lower lip. 'I've put Donaldson in the room opposite mine.' He gazed along his nose. 'If you should want him.'

'It seems unlikely.'

'Latchett in yet?'

'He was here very late last night.'

'You've seen him, then?'

'No . . . o . . . He left me a note.'

He frowned. 'Did he, now! I'll have a word with him. He's to report direct to Donaldson.'

'Then I'm on my own,' I observed pleasantly.

'Your own pace, Richard. No sweat, huh?' He was addicted to Americanisms. 'But let me see the files you're shedding. Oh . . . and it looks like we can close down the watch for Kendall.' He smiled thinly.

'Perhaps a little early for that assumption.' I laughed. 'No, perhaps already too late.'

Then I went out, leaving him wondering.

The sky had cleared that morning. The weatherman had said there was a stationary high-pressure system right over my house, which brought a distinct drop in temperature, but clear air and a snap to my walk that hadn't been there the day before. Something I could get my teeth into. The low sun was in my eyes and I flicked down the visor, and headed for Kendall's bungalow, which was only half a mile from the station.

The snowfall in the narrow alleyway had been undisturbed, but had melted on the surface before freezing again, nicely preserving two sets of footprints, one in and one out. I walked carefully, left shoulder brushing the fence. They were cleated rubber soles. I compared the size with my own shoes, which were tens. About size eight, I decided, allowing for the fact that they make rubber boots on the large side.

There was no apparent change to the bungalow. Walking round it in daylight I was able to confirm my previous impression that some period of occupation had occurred. The Coalite in the bag had not gone down any more, though.

Then, standing close to the kitchen window, I noticed something different. The message of warning, which had accompanied the hanging doll, had been rubbed off.

I had a think about that. Had Kendall been back, and wiped it clean in anger? But why trouble? Why, even, wait to rub it off? He'd been a strange mixture of cowardice and arrogance, completely egotistic. This had seemed to fit in with his attacks on girls – they would arise from a necessity to assert. Perhaps his wife hadn't been too easily impressed. She had been a bitter, belligerent woman, and I'd always wondered whether the anonymous phone call that ended the investigation might not have come from her.

No, I decided. If Kendall had seen the warning, he wouldn't have stayed around long enough to clean it off. Although, I realised, the doll hadn't been there for him to see.

Still theorising uselessly, I went round the corner, and there, on the back window, was the answer. Something new had been substituted. In white emulsion paint applied with a paintbrush, as though Ted Clayton had used it in a gesture of personal defiance to me, there was a crude drawing of a man's face. The mouth was open in a perfect O, the eyes wide, smaller Os, and the hair standing on end as six spikes. Framing the face on each side, two hands were roughed in, palms extended in horror.

It was too expressive. To be the work of Ted Clayton, he'd have had to witness the killing – must have been there. Must have done it? And then he'd come back here to tell the world all about it? Oh, come off it Richard, I thought. This is Ted Clayton you're thinking about. Dear old thick, unimaginative Ted.

I turned very slowly. Pointing directly at the drawing – and therefore at me – was a double-barrelled shotgun, side-by-side model. It was wedged in the fork of a tree and tied roughly with rope.

I skirted it carefully. It wasn't going to fire itself, but I was remembering all those trip wires at the cottage. Then, as I got closer, it became obvious that it couldn't possibly fire. It was so rusted that it probably hadn't been fired for twenty years. Its stock was grey with rot, with deep clefts in the wood, and was riddled with worm holes.

There wasn't anywhere smooth enough to take fingerprints, but all the same I untied it carefully, and used the rope to bind round it and carry it away.

I sat in the Stag with the gun on the seat beside me, drew smoke into my mouth thoughtfully for a few minutes, then drove to Atlas Electronics.

As I was checking in at the gate the Chief Personnel Officer was just driving out. He saw me, and drew up.

'Ah . . . Mr Patton. Did you receive our communication?'

'Not yet.'

'I'm sorry. There were a large number of applicants.'

I hadn't wanted it, hadn't expected it. 'That's all right.' Yet all the same, there was a plunge in my self-esteem.

'If you were coming to ask about it . . .'

'No. I'm here on my own business.'

He looked worried. 'Police business?'

'Nothing serious. I just want a word with one of your staff.'

Then I walked over to the Production Control building and hunted out Foster Clayton in his office. He had a glassed cubicle at the far end of a long, narrow room, which was clattering with computer consoles and typing machines.

He was dozing over a cup of tea, a cigarette smouldering in the hand resting on his desk, the other hand supporting his forehead. He looked up with a start when I opened the door.

'Can't you knock?'

'Had a bad night?' I drew up a chair. The ashtray was full, papers scattered all over his desk, and at one end of it an open package of half-finished sandwiches.

Foster groaned. 'I've been here half the bloody night. A breakdown on M line, and all our damn schedules thrown to cock . . .'

'Are you trying to tell me something?' I asked pleasantly.

He glared at me. 'Such as?'

'Such as an alibi for last night.'

His head came up. Eagerness lit his eyes. 'Something's happened? Don't tell me somebody's done the bleeder in.'

I shook my head slowly. 'Didn't I warn you about issuing threats?'

'Threats! Is that all? You come here, worrying me about paltry threats . . .'

'Not paltry.'

'The word's around that you're on your last few days, Mr Patton. Of course, you wouldn't want to see much action.'

'Do you own a shotgun, Foster?'

'A shotgun! You've asked me that before.'

'And didn't get an answer then, either. Do you?'

'Find out. If I had a Firearm Certificate, you'd know.'

'I didn't ask about a certificate, I asked if you've got a shotgun.'

'No. And never had one.' His eyes slid away. 'Nor Ted, neither.' He looked suspicious. 'You been to Ted?'

'Not yet. Do I need to?'

But I'd got him uneasy. I waited patiently, realising what was worrying him. He was well aware that his brother was weak and unpredictable. That I'd gone first to Foster, who could be much more difficult to break down, meant that I probably had something definite, and was confident with it.

I waited while he worked it out.

'What's this about a shotgun, anyway?' he grumbled at last.

'What size shoes d'you wear, Foster?'

'What the hell!' Then he laughed hoarsely, slapping the desk with his right palm. 'By all that's holy – you've found some footprints! And what does Holmes make of 'em?'

'What size?'

'And where were they?'

'Down the little entrance drive to Kendall's bungalow. Let's have a look at one of your shoes, there's a good chap.'

He glared at me. 'You can just bog off outa here.'

'These were size eight or nine wellies.'

'Wellies don't mean anything. Anybody can flop along in big wellies . . .' He stopped. 'I take sevens.'

'Well now!'

I leaned back, took out my pipe and started filling it, relaxed and waiting. That pipe's a useful psychological weapon. He spoke grudgingly at last.

'Where's the shotgun come into it?'

'Don't you know?'

He thumped the table.

'Mind you,' I conceded, 'the drawing was done with a paintbrush, and Ted's the one for paintbrushes. Have you seen him lately?'

He got to his feet. 'All right, Mr Patton, you've had your bit of fun. Charge me with something, or get out.'

I grinned at him, stood up, and headed for the door. I paused. 'And there's no sense in phoning Ted, because I shan't be seeing him. No point, really.'

I walked the full length of that long office with every eye on me. They might not have heard, but they certainly could have seen.

But my show of confidence was empty. I was worried. There was still an outside chance that the man in the cottage was Clive Kendall, so the obvious suspects had to be the Claytons, even though the cottage was isolated, and they'd be unlikely to know about it. The two threats had all the marks of their work, but the second – and the first, for all I knew – had been rigged after the killing, which was a bit late for threats. It indicated an unawareness that Kendall was dead. All right, so it could have been a clever bluff, but I wouldn't have thought those two could put together one subtle thought between them.

When I got back to the office I discovered I'd been wasting my time on conjecture. Ken was in, looking red-eyed and jaded, and he had the computer print-out on the fingerprints.

There were seventeen possibles on the minus one sheet, one hundred and eighty-seven on the minus two sheet, and Clive Kendall's fingerprints failed to match on five similarity points.

'Has Donaldson seen this?'

'Yes.' Ken tried to smile.

'So now he knows it's not Kendall.'

'He doesn't want to believe it. Says all the evidence shows it's got to be Kendall. So he's furious. Quietly furious,'cause he thought he was going to wrap it all up in a couple of days.' His eyes met mine. He was worried. 'So now it's back to routine. Wading through all the missing persons lists. Got any ideas, Richard?'

'Wouldn't I tell you?'

He didn't return my smile. 'You know where we've got to go first.'

'Mrs Trowbridge.'

'No comments? Nothing to offer, Richard?'

'Why should I have?'

He shrugged, painfully uneasy. 'You liked her, didn't you?'

'I never said that.'

'I saw her when she made the report. I thought to myself: Richard would like this woman.'

I grinned at him, though it cost a lot. 'Liar.'

'You were getting along just fine with her, in the Crystal Orb.'

'Now how the hell d'you know that?'

'Young Peters was in there, having a coffee.'

'It's as well he didn't try the tea.' PC Peters. Nosey young bugger. He'd do fine in the CID.

I began to fiddle with a few files, wondering how far Ken would dare to take it. At last he ventured:

'She'll have to be seen. I thought – you've got another day – I thought you'd like me to put it to Donaldson for you to see her . . .'

'Put nothing to him,' I snapped.

He couldn't understand me. Shook his head. 'Then I'll go myself.'

'You do that.'

'Oh, for God's sake, Richard, can't you see what I'm trying to say? I don't want to go tramping in, not knowing . . .'

'Take it as it comes, Ken. As it comes.'

'So you're just backing out, is that it? You're going to sit there, just laughing, while we scrat around –'

'Am I bloody laughing?' I asked quietly.

He made a weary gesture. He'd been trying to goad me, and it hadn't worked. 'It's *her* toes I didn't want to tread on – and yours, Richard.'

89

'Yes. Of course.' I felt deflated. 'Sorry, Ken. But I just don't dare to get involved. Hell to it, I'm going out to lunch. Out of here, somewhere I don't have to look over my shoulder. Coming? It's on me.'

'Thanks, but I can't. He's called a conference for one o'clock.'

'Right. Then I'll see you . . .'

'Don't go.'

I stopped with my hand to the door. 'There's more?'

He spread his hands in exasperation. We'd been friends for years. 'Damn it, don't look at me like that. I'm not fighting you – and you'd bloody love it if I was.'

'What were you going to say?'

'You can see what it's going to come to. The man was guarding the place with a shotgun. He even fired off a couple of barrels at somebody.'

'And missed.'

'At full range, that's quite possible. Sideways through the glass – still possible. But Richard, it's most likely that he allowed the murderer to get close, because he knew that person. And the most likely suspect in a man's murder is his wife. A wife might have been able to get close enough.'

'You know too much, Ken. Or you guess too much.'

'Just making sounds,' he said soothingly. 'Try that new place in Cheshire Close. I hear it's good.'

'I'll do that.'

It might be worth looking at, I decided. The usual depressing dumps I used – almost absentmindedly, as a supply of calories – were clearly not suitable for what I had in mind.

I parked at the top of the multi-storey just behind the church, and made my way on foot to Cheshire Close. The new place certainly looked attractive, so I crossed to one of the phone boxes on the corner.

From habit I'd noted the number on her phone in the hall. After a few moments of recall, I dialled it.

'Amelia?'

'Yes. It's Richard.' A flat statement.

'I'd like to give you lunch. Can I come along and fetch you?'

I'd said it in a neutral tone, not sure what attitude to take, but I could hear that it couldn't have sounded enticing. There was a pause before she replied.

'Is there anything we could possibly discuss?'

'We could try.'

Another pause. 'But not there, please.'

'You don't know where I had in mind,' I protested.

'Wherever it is. I just couldn't take your dogmatic old fashioned philosophy in public again.'

'Then where?' Teeth barely separating.

'You'd have to come here, anyway. I could prepare you something for lunch. If you'll promise not to be too overbearing. Will you do that, Richard?'

I found I was very hot, sweat standing on my forehead. She was actually teasing me! Was it that I was taking the whole situation too seriously?

'I'll do that,' I croaked. 'Twenty minutes?'

'That will be quite splendid.'

I hung up. Blast her. Did she think I was a teenager? Yet I was quite relaxed when I drove the car down the spiral.

She smiled at the door, smiled as she took my hat, watched me hanging up my coat, as though it was a rare accomplishment I was demonstrating.

'If you'd care to sit in the back room . . . Ten minutes, and it'll all be ready.'

'The kitchen will do fine.'

Not only was there an appetising smell in there, but it also had the advantage of her presence. I liked to watch her, turn the pipe in my fingers – because she might not like me to smoke while she was cooking – and toss odd remarks of an innocuous nature to her back, just to enjoy the swirl of her hair as she turned her head to answer.

'I had a casserole on, anyway,' she told me.

'Well . . . really . . .'

'Enough for two. I'm sorry there's no beer. Do you drink beer? All policemen spend so much time in pubs.'

'I drink beer. But I don't get withdrawal symptoms if I can't.'

'There's some wine. Yes, I believe there's a little wine.' She ended on a question, eyebrows raised.

'Fine.' I laughed. How long since I'd laughed? 'What goes with casserole?'

'Whatever there is.'

We sat side by side, perched on stools at the counter at the side window. The view was of the undeveloped end of the cul-de-sac, earthwork thrown up and the foundations trenched, and a site hut desolate and cold. The wine was a surprisingly good hock.

'Coffee at the table,' she said, aware that we had to talk face to face, but teasing me, still.

I waited until she'd stirred in sugar and cream. I was sufficiently lulled to light my pipe now, and held my lighter to her cigarette, reaching across the table.

'You'll remember,' I said amiably, 'that there were indications the dead man might be Clive Kendall.'

'You said you were praying that it was.'

'Well . . . my prayers weren't answered. There were just one person's fingerprints – in fact, it would've been surprising to find more. I can tell you, there was no other person could have got in.'

'Just one person,' she echoed softly.

'And the same fingerprints were on the window latch.'

She watched me wide-eyed. 'Is that important?'

'A hand could've been reached in through a hole in the glass. But seemingly it wasn't. I was saying . . . the fingerprints were not Clive Kendall's. So we have an unknown man. The normal routines will have to be applied, now.'

She blew smoke upwards. She tried a tentative smile, then looked away, the fingers of her left hand tracing the pattern on the table surface. With anyone else, I'd have diagnosed nervousness. But her voice was quite steady when she spoke.

'I've been thinking about everything, Richard, and I realise you've been very rash, haven't you? You came to see me about the car, and then you told me about the dead man. And both times, I really did feel that what you were saying was more personal than official. No, let me finish what I want to say, please. I'm guessing that neither of those interviews has been reported – does it all have to go down on paper? I see it does. And it hasn't.' She nodded. 'But

... because I reported a missing husband, and you've got an unidentified body, then I can expect some very official enquiries before very long. You've come to tell me that. Is that it?'

She was making everything too easy for me. 'There's more to it than that.'

'It places you in a difficult position, though?'

'To hell with that.'

'Will you have to be very severe with me, when you come again, all official and formal?'

'It will not be me.'

'Richard! Relax. It's all right. There's nothing unpleasant going to happen.'

'There's something very unpleasant going to happen, and very soon. You're going to be asked to identify the body. It's at the path lab at St George's hospital at the moment, and nothing about that place is pleasant. Donaldson will take you there, and I don't think he's capable of handling anything delicately. Amelia, I want you to come along with me, and get it over and done with.'

She had lost colour. She stubbed out the cigarette with short, impatient movements.

'This is for you, Richard?'

'No. For you.'

'So that you can get in first, put it in your report, and turn an official reprimand into a commendation?'

I put that down to her uncertainty, to her necessity to eliminate the unpleasant possibilities first. 'It's not that.'

'Because, if it's to help you, I'll willingly do it.'

'It's because we must know.'

'We? You and the rest of your crew?'

'You and me. Us. Don't you want to be sure?'

She got up from the table with one quick movement, turned back to me, bit her lip, and said: 'How little you understand ...' Then she made an abrupt decision. 'I'll do what you say. Whatever you say.'

'Damn it.' I was on my feet, too. 'It's not what I say.'

'Oh, but it is.' She made a small gesture, and smiled ruefully. 'My husband never told me to do anything. How pleasant it is

not to make my own decisions for once. He always deferred
. . . but he was such a gentleman. Oh God, such a wonderful
and gentle man . . .' Her voice broke.

'Please, Amelia, what did I say?'

'I'm sorry. It's not you. I'm being silly and emotional. Why
do you always do that to me? Give me a quarter of an hour, and
I'll be ready.'

'But . . .' I raised a hand to detain her. 'I've got to phone and
arrange it. Preparations will have to be made.' She just couldn't
imagine!

'The phone's in the hall.' She'd made up her mind, and that
was that. She walked away from me.

'I know where the phone is.'

To my annoyance, I found that they were expecting me.
Sergeant Latchett had phoned to say that Inspector Patton
would probably be along. It was therefore in a morose mood
that I drove there, with scarcely a word for Amelia.

She was dressed for the cold, slacks and a cardigan, with a
dark green duffle coat over them. The very thought of a hospital
autopsy room must have been chilling, but in practice it was
warm inside. She opened up the coat and threw back the hood.
I put a hand to her arm, and she was shaking. She said nothing
as I led her forward.

The naked, sterile room had been prepared for us. There was
only a single white-enamelled trolley in evidence, and the smell
was of a sweet disinfectant. There was no death present, only
the shell of it.

They had covered his face with a white cloth, and had laid
another across his middle, extending sideways and spread to
mask the remnants of his hands. Apart from that he was naked.
The attendant gestured, then stood aside.

She drew back. My hand closed on her arm more firmly.

'But I can't . . .' she whispered, eyes down, shaking her
head.

'I told you,' I encouraged her softly, 'that you couldn't see
the face,' and she looked at me with entreaty.

I drew her close again. 'The body, my dear.'

She shuddered again. 'But I can't say.'

'Is that his body?' I insisted.

She put a hand over her mouth, her eyes horrified above it.
'But I tell you, I can't say.'

'You must surely know.'

'I . . . think it is.'

'Say. Please say. Yes or no.'

'Take me out. Let me go, Richard.'

I gave the attendant an apologetic smile. The man shrugged.
Amelia was already at the door. I lengthened my stride, and
when I reached her she was leaning back against the gloss
green of the wall in the corridor, taking deep gulping breaths,
the green reflected in her pallor.

I waited. She tried to smile. 'You must understand, Richard.
How can I be sure?'

'But . . . if he's your husband, you must know his body.'

She shook her head. 'He was . . . oh dear Lord, he is a
strange man. To you he'd seem unusual. I have never seen him
undressed, Richard. He was very modest, too shy altogether.
He would always undress in the bathroom. We . . . made love
invariably in the dark. Is it improper of me to say . . . to say
I always thought that was some sort of withdrawal?' She was
feeling her way through it with careful delicacy. 'I'm trying
to explain – get it right in my mind. We were always so frank
together, holding back nothing. But that was the emotional
aspect of it. In the physical . . . God help me, I felt he was
ashamed of his own body. Oh, we discussed it. Discussing
it, he was frank, yes, never too modest then. But physically it
was a mania. I have never seen him undressed.' She searched
my face for disbelief. 'That was why . . . if that in there is him,
that was the reason I felt suddenly faint and somehow indecent,
looking at him. As though I was taking advantage.'

'Then you're unsure?' I didn't dare to try any other comment.

'I think it must be him,' she said worriedly.

'Not think. Thinking's no good. You must be certain.'

'How can I be?'

'But if you felt as you did, then surely that means you
recognised him, if only subconsciously.'

She looked at me with pity. 'And did you want that so
much?'

'I'd hoped for a definite answer.'

'Or had you hoped for something neat and tidy that you could put on paper?'

'You're upset,' I whispered. 'I'll drive you home.'

We were both silent on the journey. I was struggling with implications, attitudes, impressions. The engine hummed. We were silent.

'You're very quiet,' she said after a while. She sounded apologetic, but no longer distressed.

'What you told me, about not recognising the body, that's what's worrying me.'

'Is this something else you can't fit into your conception of what life is?'

She could annoy me, sometimes. I said, steadily: 'It's not that.'

'It'd be strange, wouldn't it, being upset first of all by an idea too modern and advanced for your prejudices, and now just as upset about a point of view so old-fashioned.'

I refused to be drawn. 'It's not that. I *can* accept it. Not go along with it, perhaps, but understand. But you see, you're going to have to tell the same thing to Chief Inspector Donaldson, and I can't see *him* understanding. To him, it'll seem that you're just stalling. To him, it'll simply mean you're refusing to admit it's your husband.'

I had drawn to a halt in front of the house. She gave a little choking laugh of disbelief.

'But why should I deliberately refuse?'

'Because, in any case of sudden death by violence, the surviving spouse is the first suspect.'

She was silent for a few moments. Then: 'Aren't you coming in?'

'I've got to get back to the office.'

'Yes. Of course. Your report.' She tried to steady her voice. 'Will you use that splendid phrase in your report? Surviving spouse! It sounds as though you lifted it straight from a police manual.'

'It's not for my damned report!' I burst out. 'Can I please explain, without you interrupting . . .'

'Of course you can.' Calmly.

'In the circumstances – the gutted car, for instance – the link with you and the dead man is rather close. Closer than with the wives of the other dozens of missing men who're on the list. If you're uncertain about the identification, Donaldson will tear into it, because he'll believe you're actually quite positive, but you're refusing to admit it. So he'll be even more suspicious. If you admit it now, that might make things –'

'Admit? You keep saying admit.'

'If you say it, then, he'll be equally suspicious, but he could well go more easily with you. And Amelia . . . it would be now. I've got very little time left. From midnight tomorrow I shan't be involved at all. Give me as much time as you can. Please.'

She answered quietly. 'You're talking as though you're sure it's him. Do you think I'm deliberately lying to you?'

My knuckles were white on the wheel. 'I thought you might be afraid.'

'What's there to be afraid of?'

'A murder investigation.'

'I'm not afraid. There's nothing for me to fear.'

I looked at her. She could not meet my eye. She *was* afraid.

'Then I'm asking too much?'

She shook her head. Her mouth was a firm line, but her lips were twitching. She spoke softly, even warmly.

'Then for you, Richard, I'll make it positive. That man is my husband. There. Now you'll know what to do. Unleash the dogs of law.'

I bent my head, baffled. 'You're misunderstanding me.'

'I don't think so. Now just you run along and do your little report. You can state quite positively that I've identified the body as that of my husband. I'm sure you'll word it exactly like that. And I shan't deny it.'

'Now just you wait a minute!'

But she had opened the car door. I reached over for her arm, but she eluded me, and stood outside with the wind ruffling her hair. 'Richard, my dear . . .'

Then she was gone, up the dark path to her front door. And I was not certain what she had offered me.

7

The meeting was just breaking up when I got back to my office. I'd hoped to slip in quietly, unobserved, but Merridew's eyes have always been sharp.

'Richard. So there you are,' he called from along the corridor.

Chummy, I thought. Donaldson loomed at Merridew's shoulder, looking slightly cynical, perhaps a little repressed. Merridew advanced. They crowded me into my own office.

'Why weren't you at the meeting?' Merridew asked, but still keeping it friendly.

Ken edged round the door and to his own desk. Brason was hovering in the corridor. I wondered what Brason was doing there.

'Well,' I answered, 'I wasn't invited. And I was clearing up one or two details of my own.'

'But you've got an identification for us,' Merridew said. 'So I heard.'

Across the room I caught Ken's eye. He raised his eyebrows and gently shook his head.

'Nothing positive,' I said casually, taking my seat, spreading out the files on the desk as though anxious to plunge into them. 'I was looking into a missing husband case, and when this dead man cropped up, I thought it might be a good idea to take his wife along.'

'They phoned from the hospital,' Merridew told me.

'It looked,' put in Donaldson, 'as though you were sort of anticipating me.'

I hoped my expression was soothing. 'Not really. Wouldn't

98

think of such a thing. You know that. And it was no more than a chance.'

Ken turned his face away. Merridew glanced sharply at Donaldson. There was a warning in his eyes. I could read it. Let me handle Patton, I know him, and he can be an awkward cuss.

'Then we could have struck lucky?' Merridew asked casually.

I shrugged. 'It doesn't seem so. I can't be sure. *She* can't be sure.'

Donaldson wasn't prepared to leave it all to Merridew. He'd understood the warning, and he resented it. 'Oh, come on!' he cut in sharply. 'Of course she'd know.'

'There's no face.'

'His body, for Chrissake.'

'She was unsure,' I said very gently, not prepared to discuss Amelia's married intimacies. 'I'll put it all in a report for you.'

'How can she be uncertain?' Donaldson nodded around. 'She'd know her husband's bits and pieces.' He looked at Ken for his agreement in this proposition, but Ken looked blank.

'She told me,' I said, picking carefully through the words, 'that she could not be certain.'

'Oh, good Lord . . .' Then Donaldson restrained himself. He looked miserable. 'You're not telling me she's had so many men that she can't sort out their bodies!'

I said: 'No doubt you'll make up your own mind about that.' How I managed to smile at all I don't know. It couldn't have been very warm.

'That I will. They don't *look*, that's the trouble. You have to push 'em a bit.' Donaldson was crisp and decisive.

'All right,' Merridew cut in. 'We'll get your report, Richard . . .'

Donaldson interrupted abruptly. 'We could apply for a search warrant.'

His eyes, I saw, were soiled chips of ice. He felt himself to be isolated, and he was suspicious of what he saw as deliberate interference in his case. But his statement startled me, and I looked away. He was pushing too hard.

'A search warrant?' Merridew turned. 'What on earth are you talking about?'

Donaldson cocked his chin. It made little jerking movements, lending accents to his words. 'There's a simple way
to settle this. If it's her husband, then his fingerprints'll be all
over their house. We'll get a warrant and a team of men to go
through the place . . .'

Merridew clawed at his arm. 'Take it easy . . . easy . . .'

'A warrant, that's all we need.' Now Donaldson's impatience
was directed at his Super.

'There are no grounds,' said Merridew firmly.

The two men stared at each other, while I clutched my pen
and tried to control my dismay.

'In any event . . .' I began, and they turned to me as though
they'd forgotten I was there. 'In any event, she's a tidy woman.
Houseproud, even. And her husband's been away for around
three weeks. You can bet she's polished every inch since then.'
I was unable to prevent myself from smiling openly, though I
was thinking of Amelia, rather than expressing any feeling of
triumph.

But Donaldson saw it only as contempt. He bristled.

'And I'll bet she's polishing right now. This very minute. And
we stand here while she does it! I could get round there . . . she
wouldn't know about warrants. She'd let us in, and once over
the doorstep . . .' He smiled thinly.

Everybody in that room knew that there were no grounds,
legal or otherwise, for applying for a warrant. Not at that stage,
anyway. In any case, it would have to weave its way through the
usual channels. His suggestion, then, was at least unethical,
and he couldn't know Merridew's fetish for sticking close to
the book.

I felt a flush of anger, hot in my neck, and I knew that
it was me he was pressing. He was suggesting, even, that
it was I who should be elected to thrust my way into her
house.

Ken cleared his throat. 'It might not be necessary . . .'

I rescued him quickly, holding my voice level. 'No need to
use force. I'll phone her. I'll ask for her permission.' Donaldson
raised his eyebrows. 'Shall I do that, Paul?'

Merridew was stiff with disapproval. 'Do that,' he said, short,
clipped words. 'Do that . . . Richard.'

Calmly, I reached for the phone with the outside line and dialled her number. I lifted my eyes to Donaldson, challenging him to comment on the fact that I hadn't needed to look it up. He was smiling complacently.

'Amelia?' I lowered my eyes, drawing a pad forward, the pen in my hand.

'It's you, Richard?'

'I'm at the office. The opinion here – from my superior – is that the question of identity, as far as you're concerned, can be settled very easily.'

'Then you haven't told them I'm positive about it?'

'No. Because I'm not sure you are.'

She whispered my name, but I thought she sounded annoyed with me. Then: 'How easily can it be settled?'

'They want a team of men to come to your place and search it for fingerprints, and then see if they can find a match with the ones in the cottage.'

She had made light of what could be in store for her – had tried to – but I'd known she'd really been nervous and afraid. She'd now be imagining a troop of large men swarming all over her house, her peace and privacy invaded.

'No!' she gasped. 'They can't do that. Surely they can't march in here . . .'

'Not without your permission.'

'Then they haven't got it,' she said, so quickly that the words trod on each other.

'Or they could apply for a warrant.'

'A lot of good that would do them,' she said scornfully. 'There's not an inch I haven't polished.'

'I've told them that.' I smiled into the phone. She must have detected it in my voice.

'Well, what else have I got to do all day?' she demanded, confiding with me her boredom.

'I'm sure you've covered every inch. But an expert might discover something you've missed.'

'You're not alone, are you? They're standing over you, I can just feel it. Do you want this, Richard? You, yourself?'

'No.'

'If they're forcing it on you . . .'

101

'It was my idea to ask you. I want to know the truth. But not necessarily in this way.'

She sighed. 'I can't face it. Not tonight. Tell them that, will you.'

'I will.'

I hung up, and looked at their solemn faces. I offered up the top sheet of my note pad, on which I'd printed: NO!

'This is pure fantasy!' cried Donaldson angrily. 'We stand here while he asks. Asks, blast it. Amelia! We're on bloody Christian names!'

'That's enough,' said Merridew.

'What *is* this?' Donaldson exploded. 'Is this how you conduct murder investigations?'

'We'll discuss this in my office,' Merridew grated.

'Discussions!' Donaldson dismissed them with contempt.

'You know damn well you can't barge into people's homes,' I told him calmly. 'The proper way is a search warrant, if you can justify it. Which I doubt.'

'You're deliberately blocking this,' he said tensely, and Merridew rasped: 'My office!'

He turned and went out, white with anger. For one moment Donaldson glared at me, then he snapped round and followed his superior. He must have felt furious with frustration, trapped in a personal atmosphere that Merridew and I had built together over the years. Certainly, already, Merridew was uneasy.

Ken waited until the door was shut, but I got in first.

'What's Brason doing here?'

'Helping. Local colour. You know.'

'Then keep him away from Donaldson. The lad'll get corrupted.'

He was amused, but dismissed it with a nod. 'What're you trying to do, Richard?'

'Trying to sort something out.'

'Yourself?'

'You're too smart.' I'd miss working with him.

'You're going at it bull-headed, and you know it. What's got into you: This woman got under your skin, has she?'

'You don't know a thing about it, Ken.'

He shook his head, smiling but unhappy. 'Then take it easy.

Try coasting the last lap, and get out of it in one piece. The way you're going, they'll cut you in little pieces. Instead of letting you walk out of the front door, they'll toss you in the ash can out back.'

'Very poetic, Ken. Look, I'm grateful for the advice, but I'm still on duty. Throw me over an application form for a search warrant.'

'You're going to apply for it?'

'Not there, you idiot. I want to get into Clive Kendall's bungalow. That, at least, is still my case.'

'After what you said about Donaldson's chances, I can't say much for yours. Here. This do?'

The form, a four-sheet set in non-carbon reproduction, was crumpled. I smoothed it with a heavy palm.

'Ken,' I said, 'I'm beginning to smell a few unpleasant possibilities. I'm sure Kendall's involved in this somewhere. I'm applying for a warrant, but I can't possibly get it in time. So . . . if I have to lean heavily on the back door, I'll at least have some sort of a reason.'

'What d'you want me to do?'

'Just keep out of it. You're working for Donaldson now. Just don't be around if things go wrong.'

He considered me silently for a moment. Then he pressed his palms on the desk and levered himself up. 'I'm off home. Can't bear to stay and watch you sticking your chin out.'

I crouched over the desk. Said nothing.

'It's what you'll miss most, Richard, and you're not even seeing it.' He was being kind. His voice was relaxed. 'The aggro – the opposition. You always liked a good fight.'

It hit me between the eyes. I hadn't realised it, and he was so damned right. I looked down at the surface of my desk. 'But I'm getting slower coming out of the corners, that's it. D'you reckon it's time I retired to the dressing-room?'

'In your own time.' He wasn't even looking at me now, pretending to be searching for his coat. People ought to listen to Ken. He understands things. 'Not in theirs, that's the point. They retire you – that's their end of it. You're no longer on the books. But it's what you feel that matters. Nobody's got the right to tell you when you're finished.'

I waited until he looked round. 'But that's exactly what they do.'

'For God's sake,' he said, 'there's a whole world out there for you to take on.'

I grunted. The concept was too big to absorb in one thought. 'I'll bear it in mind. You say you're going?'

He relaxed. 'For your information, Donaldson's got several teams following up routine missing husband and son reports, and we've put out a general trace. See you.'

'Oh.' I remembered, pointing the ball-pen. 'One thing. If Brason's still around, ask him to meet me tomorrow – say at ten o'clock, at the cottage.'

He was curious. Suddenly worried again. 'It's sealed.'

'I guess it would be. Will you fix that up for me?'

He nodded, and by the time he'd closed the door behind him I was well into: Reason For Application. I could hardly put: because he's a tricky bastard. I tried to treat it with due solemnity. After I'd completed it, and was dictating my report on to tape, Ken put his head in, stuck up a thumb, and said: 'Ten o'clock it is.'

I sent down the tape and waited for the typescript. As this'd take some time – I'd put everything into it that I knew – I went down to the canteen for tea and a sandwich. I was wishing I knew for certain, then I could've circled my intentions around the single fact that Amelia's husband was dead.

It was late when I left, quite dark. I used the side door into the car-park. The Stag stood almost solitary on the stretch of tarmac, and Amelia was leaning against one of the wings.

I did not see her until I was nearly upon her. 'Amelia?'

She was bundled up in her duffle coat, sheepskin mittens on her hands, and that little woollen hat on her head again. On the car's bonnet was resting a white plastic bag.

'You've been waiting for me?'

She nodded, a small, embarrassed smile on her lips, which looked purple in the dim orange light, standing meekly like a schoolgirl about to admit to an indiscretion.

'But you should have come up. They'd have sent you up to my office from the front desk.' There was time we might have spent together, now lost. 'You look frozen.' I put fingers to her cheek. 'You *are* frozen. Why didn't you come up, Amelia?'

'I didn't want to embarrass you.'

I snorted. 'You're coming for a drink.'

'No.'

'Right now. There's a pub on the corner. Get some blood into your cheeks.'

I took her arm. She drew back, then reached across for the carrier bag. She offered it to me.

'What's this?'

'Lock it in your car,' she said. 'It's only an old shaving-soap bowl.' She stared past my elbow. 'After you phoned, I made a search. There could've been something I hadn't polished or cleaned. You know, I think I'm getting obsessive – yesterday I found myself wandering round the house with a duster in my hand . . .'

'You were saying?' Slowly I said it, but with my heart racing.

'I found it in a corner of the bathroom cupboard. How I came to miss it . . . But of course, it's a long time since he used it – since he bought the electric one.'

'You didn't touch it?'

She giggled. 'I lifted it out on the blade of a knife and tumbled it into here. I felt so silly.'

'Not silly. Not silly at all.' I was suddenly very serious. 'You understand what this'll mean?'

'I know.'

'Your life could become very uncomfortable.'

'But I thought you'd be pleased to have it.'

'Oh, but I am. Let's go and get that drink.'

I locked the carrier in the car and led her away, one hand on her arm, bending my head to hers. I took her into the Snug and sat her at a table in the corner, then went to get her a double brandy, and a pint of bitter for myself.

'I'm sorry,' I said, sitting down. 'I didn't ask if you like brandy.'

She found a weak smile for me, but there was strain in her eyes. 'I certainly need something.'

I watched her with concern as she took a sip, and then another, watched the tenseness ease from the line of her jaw.

'It wasn't that it was necessary to steal it,' I encouraged her softly. 'No reason you should feel ashamed.'

'No, no.' She shook her head, then fumbled in her bag for cigarettes, but I knew it was because she didn't want me to read what she was thinking. 'You don't understand.' But now there was a cigarette to play with, and movements she could hide behind. 'It was as though ... giving you that shaving-bowl ... as though I was handing over the last chance I have that he could be alive.'

'It's not really like that.'

'I know. I'm too fanciful.' She smiled bleakly.

'And you're making assumptions. The fingerprints might not match, anyway.'

'But they will. I feel that.' She drew deeply on the cigarette. 'You know, Richard, thinking back – and how could I help thinking about it? – thinking back to that terrible place at the hospital, I can be a lot less emotional about it now. I wouldn't need to go there again. Every detail's as clear as crystal in my mind. And I realise I was blinded by ... oh, confusion and distress and fear, I suppose. That sort of thing. But now – now I'm quite sure it's him. My husband. I know it is, so I'm sure the fingerprints will match.'

'I hope you're right.'

'You're not sorry it isn't Kendall?'

We'd buried something between us. 'Not sorry at all, my dear.'

She pushed her half-finished drink towards me. 'Can you finish this, Richard?'

I shook my head. 'I'll get you something else.'

'But I'm all right now. It was just me, being silly.'

I saw that she was speaking the truth. She was all right. In fact, she was more relaxed than I remembered seeing her at any time, smoking now with one elbow on the table and the cigarette poised beside her face. Her eyes were fond, almost provocative.

'What will you do with it?' she asked.

'When I've run you home, I'll drive over to Divisional HQ with it, and take it into their lab.'

'This late at night?'

'No time to lose. There'll be somebody on duty.'

'You *are* determined, aren't you?'

I couldn't match her relaxation. I felt stiff and exhausted, the tension clamping down on me. 'Yes, I'm determined. It's still my job.'

'Your job!' Her eyes were mocking. Feigning disinterest, she stared absently beyond my shoulder.

'I want it tied down. No holes anybody can climb through.'

'Pride, Richard? Determined to beat your Mr Donaldson, is that it?'

I shook my head, aware that I must be appearing simply stubborn, and angry with myself. 'Don't sneer, please. Never at Donaldson. I want to be able to convince him. Then maybe he'll take it easy when he comes to see you.'

'Oh, I see.' She pouted. 'Then it's not pride and determination. Just being gallant, asserting your masculine protection.'

'It's not that. I'd call it helping, while I'm still in a position to.'

'And it hasn't occurred to you,' she asked daintily, 'that I can look after myself? Perhaps I'd prefer to?'

'Oh, I'm sure you're quite capable. But you've no idea . . .'

'Now you're annoyed. But I don't want you to be. I just hoped to get you to see something a bit more clearly . . .' She hesitated, then plunged on. 'You do a job, to the best of your ability, and you're proud of it. Success boosts you – I'll bet it even makes you feel intoxicated.'

I was staring at her, not understanding. She reached forward and put a forefinger on my forehead. 'Oh, please don't frown at me. You look so frightening. Did you know you can frighten people? It's true. But now I want you to listen and try to understand. Will you do that?'

'Of course I'll listen.' I wasn't sure about the understanding bit. I produced my pipe and tobacco tin, just in case the listening became too painful and I found myself in need of comfort.

'You blamed me,' she said softly, 'so very severely for what I did for Clive Kendall. To you, I was just being a stupid, interfering woman, who ought to have known better. But can't

107

you understand that for me it was a job, a task, something I might take pride in completing? Allow me that, Richard. And if that task became difficult, then of course the pride in success was even stronger. I see you can appreciate that. There were difficulties, you see. Kendall himself was difficult. In some ways he was an impossible man to deal with, arrogant and self-opinionated, and resenting like hell that I was a woman. But I had to handle that. At any time at all I could've handed the case over to somebody else. But it was my first big, personal case, and I'd chosen it myself. Yes, I chose it. And d'you know why?'

'Let me guess.'

'Go on, then.'

'Nobody else would touch it.'

'You see, you're not even trying to understand. No. Our President himself wanted it, but I persuaded him to let me try, simply because it *was* so difficult. So how could I allow myself to fail? The more Kendall jeered at me, and the more he tried to assert his emotional aggression, the more I had to fight him, and fight for him. He made demands. He wanted this and that and the other concession. His cell didn't please him, the books he could get didn't interest him, his cell-mate was a homo and was importuning him. Oh, the demands streamed from him, and every one was a challenge to me, as a person and as a woman. It got to the point where I could have screamed for help. Screamed at him. Every demand ... I had to take it up, tackle the Governor about it, and fight for it. And win, Richard, not so much for Kendall as for myself. Me, as a person. And all the time I was wasting time and effort on minor details, when I should have been concentrating on trying to get his release considered, trying for a parole hearing ...'

'He knew what he was about,' I murmured. 'I told you, didn't I? I said he wasn't in any way insane. He could control every movement and demand he made. That's what he was doing with you.'

'He was trying to force me to quit. Because I'm a woman.'

'No.' At last I lit my pipe. This was my own ground, and I was sure I'd got it right. 'He really needed you, and he knew it. And he read you like a book. The more he threw at you, the more determined you became.'

'That was certainly how it worked out,' she conceded, but warily, warningly.

'Because he wanted his freedom, and he knew it'd take something special to pull it off. So he manipulated you. He picked you up and he manipulated the necessary hidden strings to get you to do what he wanted. And in the end you'd have done anything for him, just to prove to yourself that you *were* yourself. Anything!'

'I knew how well you'd understand,' she said bitterly. But of course she'd have to reject it.

'But you didn't prove it, did you?' I asked. 'Not to your own satisfaction.'

'I succeeded,' she claimed, her chin lifting.

'He didn't deserve you, my dear. You tried too hard. What he deserved was to rot in prison. But you failed, by getting him out. That didn't prove yourself. Not you as your own individual self. In the end, you were his.'

My palm came down hard on the table surface. For a moment I was having difficulty in controlling my temper. There was a vein throbbing in my temple, and my jaw ached.

'I don't think you understood one word I said,' she told me with miserable anger.

'I could kill him.'

'We talk,' she said, 'about *him*. Kendall! Kendall! I thought I was talking about me, hoping you'd understand.'

I gave a grimace, partly humour, partly distaste. 'It seems to me we can't think about you without Kendall sticking his nose in.'

'You're upset.'

'Not now. Shall we go?'

'We must speak about us.'

I rose to my feet and went round the table to draw back her chair. She was reluctant to leave. Nothing was settled. She thought it took only a few words, but my entanglement was too complex for me to explain. I got her outside, and still I wasn't sure how to smooth it over. Kendall had come back

into my life, but this time as a very vital and personal factor.
I resented it like hell.

I handed her into the Stag. 'How can we talk about us?' I
burst out. 'He's always there, in the middle.'

She pouted, and folded her hands in her lap. Women always
assume you can't understand what they're trying to tell you.

So I drove silently for a while. On the seat behind us there
was now a broken doll, a rusted shotgun, and a plastic carrier
containing a shaving-soap bowl.

I was not annoyed, merely disturbed. Now I was confident
that what I had detected between us was an affinity that went
beyond friendliness. But I felt it grew from what she'd indicated
she admired in Kendall, a forcefulness, a masculinity, a control.
I wasn't happy with the comparison; they were characteristics
I couldn't admire in myself. I even hoped she'd hint at a dislike
for him. Just for once.

I wondered grimly to what extent she had opposed Kendall.
Whether, in practice, she might have relaxed in the end, not
from confidence but from sheer exhaustion. In that event,
he wouldn't have hesitated to take advantage of her weakness.

At last I had to speak. She cocked her head. I could see it
was a nervous reaction, her responses taut.

'And what did your husband make of all this?' I asked,
keeping my voice casual. 'This Kendall business.'

She brightened. 'Dear man. He was so helpful.'

'To the extent of encouraging you to go on with it?'

'He knew it was what I wanted to do.'

'That wasn't quite what I asked.'

She moistened her lips. 'Well – at first – he took the same
old-fashioned view you have, Richard. No . . . really . . . you're
very patient with me . . .'

'He was patient?'

'Amused, rather.'

'But he wouldn't have been pleased, seeing you spend so
much time and emotional energy on a creature like Kendall.'

'You can't hide that hatred, can you?'

'Did your husband hate him, too?'

'No.' She bit her lip. 'You tangle me up. Is that what comes

110

of being a detective? My husband was very patient,' she reproved me.

'Unlike me?'

'Damn it, you're too blasted abrasive!'

She didn't often swear. I was silent. It was clear she wasn't going to compare me with her husband, whom she'd described as a gentle man. All the same, I was surprised at how she'd put it. Had I always seemed like that to other people? Too abrasive? Too aggressive, perhaps? It was not a pleasant thought, when I'd imagined my career had been undermined by my attempts to be sympathetic. Damn it, I'd always thought I was not sufficiently assertive.

I decided to discard the subject of character. 'Did your husband ever meet Kendall?'

'Oh, yes. Several times. He went with me to the prison. He said he ought to see for himself. He was making a real effort to show interest in what I was doing.'

'And Kendall, at those times?'

'The dear man, he made such an effort. He could be very charming, you know. He set himself out to praise me. He told my husband how much I was doing for him, and how much he appreciated it.'

'And you didn't see through that?'

'Of course I did, silly. Kendall even had the cheek to wink at me. It was between us, you see. To Kendall, it must have seemed that I was bringing in reinforcements – and that I needed them. He was teasing me, another of his challenges. But just between the two of us. Now do you understand?'

'Oh dear Lord,' I groaned to myself, leaning forward over the steering wheel.

'Pardon?'

'Nothing.' I leaned back. 'And your husband – so gentle and kind – he didn't object when you moved home to this district, just in order to be near Kendall when he came out of prison?'

It was a pure guess, but it seemed an obvious conclusion. We hadn't touched on this before, but I'd been waiting for the opportunity to bring it up.

She was silent a moment, but her voice was steady when she replied. 'You always put the worst construction on everything.

111

It wasn't really like that. Of course I wanted to carry it on through, and see how he coped. But at the same time, there was always Atlas Electronics to consider.'

'That was a poor chance, surely.'

'But it suited both of us, moving here.'

'Both you and your husband?'

'Of course,' she said shortly. 'And at the same time I could keep an eye on Kendall.'

'Just in case you'd made a mistake, I suppose,' I said grimly. 'In case a fresh batch of little girls caught his attention.'

'That's unworthy of you, Richard.'

I grunted. Unworthy!

'It was . . .' she began.

'Another of his challenges, I suppose?'

'If you like.' Then, with abrupt anger. 'If you *like*.'

'It's how you've explained things.'

'All right,' she snapped. 'It wasn't finished – with Kendall. He said . . . said he supposed I'd drop him like a hot cake, once he was free. I had to deny that, or his confidence would have been undermined. It's a difficult and frightening thing, coming out of prison.'

'I can understand that, with the reception he could expect. So you went as far as preparing his bungalow for him? That as well?' Another guess, but there'd been a woman's hand in that, his home, neatly welcoming him.

She glanced at me sharply. 'The least I could do,' she murmured defensively.

Though I'd been driving slower and slower, the cul-de-sac eventually appeared. I was not really sorry to see it, and drew up in front of the house, pointedly not switching off the engine. I needed time to think, and alone.

'I won't ask you in,' she said, 'because I know you've got things to do.'

I said nothing.

'And because,' she went on, 'you're in a very funny mood.'

She waited. Then she opened the door. But I couldn't restrain myself.

'And your husband,' I wondered, 'what did he think of this bungalow-warming business?'

112

'Oh.' She poised the door to shut it. 'He helped me. He was pleased to, if you must know. It seemed to intrigue him no end.'

'But this was all before Kendall was released. Have you seen him since then? Has he contacted you?' I desperately needed to know what had happened to him.

'No.' Her eyes briefly caught a reflection of light. 'Not a word. Not a sign from him.'

Then she slammed the door, and there was anger in it. When I'd managed the circle at the end, and drove past again, she was no longer visible.

She must have run into the house, I decided. She'd run from me. I wound up the window.

Kendall, I was beginning to realise, had come out of prison just about the time her husband had disappeared.

8

The new premises of Divisional HQ were spread over a couple of acres of pastureland, on which most of the trees had been preserved as landscaping. The forensic lab was separate, a low building projecting out from the three-storey main complex, and enclosing a covered tarmac expanse where vehicles involved in crime were retained. I ran the Stag in beside a crashed and battered Rover 3500. The building was flooded with light from inside, and with an outside light over the entrance in the corner, a door at the top of six stone steps.

The interior was one long room lined with benches, resembling a laboratory of an exotic and unorthodox nature. The light was artificial daylight and shadowless, the air dust-free, the heating controlled. I had to enter through two doors, the second of which refused to open until the first was shut.

The activity was subdued, as the time was then after eleven. I looked along between the benches, hoping to spot something that was clearly from the cottage, but the Swallow's End case was obviously one of a multitude. The lab was packed with assorted crime. A pistol barrel under a microscope, and two bullets lined up for comparison – not from the cottage. A bloodstain on a pyjama jacket – again not from the cottage.

'Can I help you?'

I turned. Somebody I didn't know. 'Is Charlie on duty? Charlie Finch.'

'No. I'm sorry.' He was unresponsive. They don't like to be pressured.

'I'm Inspector Patton. The Swallow's End case.' I produced my warrant card.

'Yes. That's over there, under the window. Have a word with Frank.'

I thanked him. Frank was a young man, dark, wearing large metal-framed glasses. His eyes peered with the unfocused look of a man at the other end of a microscope. I spotted the window latch from the cottage, lying on a sheet of white paper on the bench.

'The Swallow's End job?' I asked.

The eyes considered me. 'You're from there?'

'Inspector Patton. I've got something for you, son. I want a nice, quick check on fingerprints.'

I offered the plastic bag. He was immediately interested. His eyes flashed. 'This from the cottage?'

'You tell me.'

While he worked, I sucked at my cold pipe, careful not to light it. The young man was precise and quick, without seeming to hurry. He found time to make the odd remark while lifting a print delicately, or searching for a comparison.

'We got nearly four hundred prints from that place,' he told me proudly. 'Smears, partials, palms. Marvellous.'

'And there's no doubt they're all from the same person?'

'No doubt at all.'

He straightened from his comparison check. 'And we've got another here. Several.'

'They check?'

'Oh, absolutely. Nearly as good as the ones on the soap.'

'Tell me.' Because he was going to, anyway.

'There was a tablet of Pear's, on the quarry-tile windowsill behind the sink. You know how it is with Pear's, you get down to a thin oval, and this just fits the dent in the new cake. Well, that was what happened. You've got to press the old bit in the dent. This chap'd pressed, with both thumbs, fingers underneath. Perfect!' he said, with enthusiasm.

'A good job he didn't get round to using it,' I said.

'Eh?'

'If he'd washed with it after the pressing bit, he'd have washed away the prints.'

'Yes. Never thought of that.'

'Did you find any shaving tackle?'

115

'Well, no . . . heh, and now you've got a shaving-bowl. That's strange.'

'I didn't say it'd come from the cottage. Don't jump to conclusions. I see you brought the latch here.'

'We lifted it from the frame. Seemed it could be important . . . you know, with that hole in the window just below it.'

I was pleased. 'Just what I wanted to ask you. That hole seemed to be just too damned convenient. A hand could've been stuck through it, and reached up to the latch. Now . . . the prints on it? I hope it's not too rusty, but I heard you'd got some.'

'They weren't too good,' Frank admitted. 'But we got enough, partials here and there. Yes, it's the same hand.'

'There's another possibility, though. Suppose that you wanted to close that latch without blurring or overlaying the prints already on it. Now . . . a hook of wire . . . the latch moves down to fasten, and it'd take no more than a pull . . . a hand reaching in from outside.'

He'd been watching me solemnly, making no attempt to interrupt. It seemed, I thought, that his patience was extended only while I talked my way into absurdity. At last he smiled. There was pity in it.

'We thought of that. Mr Donaldson made a point of it. Hasn't he told you, sir?'

'I've been away from the office.'

'Yes. Well, there's no chance that was done. The handle was near vertical, the way we found it, pointing downwards. Any length of wire, bit of string, or what-have-you just couldn't help but to have slipped a bit. It would've left some sort of trace. We did three separate microscopic checks. Nothing at all. Nothing.'

I smiled at him again, because I was feeling a sick despair, and I didn't want it to show. It kept coming back to the same thing – a locked and fastened cottage, into which nobody could have entered, and nobody left. All there was to go on was that hole in the pane, through which a shotgun might have been discharged from outside. And that had to come back to the only answer – somebody who'd be able to bring a shotgun that close. The dead man's wife.

'Can I have a written report on the fingerprints?' I asked.

'It'll take a time.'

'I've got time. A little.'

Frank stared at me for a moment. 'Then I'll get on with it.' He grinned, his face suddenly transformed. The dedicated scientist became the naughty boy. 'Better fix yourself some coffee. Boiling water in that flask over the bunsen, coffee powder in that can marked DRIED BLOOD, and milk . . .'

'I'll find it, thanks.'

'Use a two-fifty millilitre pyrex beaker, sir. I do.'

I waited. The coffee, when I'd finally satisfied myself that STRYCHNINE – CRYSTALLISED was in fact sugar, was very good. Frank eventually returned with a report that included comparison photos, and a certificate that exhibit A was from the shaving-soap bowl delivered to the lab by Inspector Patton.

'Oh, one thing,' I remembered to ask, turning back. 'Now you've been over it, let's have a look inside.'

Frank removed the lid. It was a plastic container, which had started life filled with a cake of soap. The inside was empty, clean, nothing but a shiny brown plastic.

'Son,' I said, 'if you can think of any reason why a man should clean out a shaving bowl, and then hide it in the back of a bathroom cupboard, then tell me now. My mind is getting just a little tired.'

He shook his head. 'Not my line, sir, detecting. Can't think of anything logical.'

'That's what it has to be. Logical. And this logic I don't like.'

Wearily and discouraged, I drove back to the office. It was one-forty when I entered the side door from the car-park, and I'd started on my final day. That fact, alone, undermined me. Passing the canteen, I wondered when I'd last eaten. But now only a smell was available, and that not very encouraging.

This part of the building seemed deserted, though there would be limited activity in the front office. I climbed the back stairs ponderously, and was just reaching for the handle of my own door when I noticed a line of brighter light under a door farther along the corridor.

I hesitated, then walked along, opened the door, and broke in on Chief Inspector Donaldson.

Donaldson was alone. He sat behind his desk in a thick fug of cigarette smoke, with his forehead supported on the palm of his left hand, his right forefinger moving along the lines of a typed report as though it commanded his reluctant eyes. He was in shirt sleeves, one rolled up beyond the elbow, the other flapping loose. There was a thinning patch in the centre of his slicked hair, and a pair of horn-rimmed glasses sliding forward along his nose.

Hearing the door open he looked up. His eyes were red-rimmed, with heavy pouches beneath them. For one brief moment I couldn't help feeling pity. The man was trying, really trying.

'Patton?' he asked, blinking, his voice hoarse. 'What brings you here?'

'Brought you a report.'

'What time is it?'

'Getting on for two.'

He groaned. 'What've you got?' His tone was almost pleasant. Exhaustion had beaten the crisp aggression from him.

'I've been saving you the trouble of a search warrant, or the unpleasantness of persuading Mrs Trowbridge to let you take a team into her house, whichever you had in mind.'

He blinked. 'Not for my benefit, I'm sure.'

'Very true. For her sake. I'd impressed on her that you'd be around, anyway, so she did a search. She came up with one of her husband's old shaving-soap bowls. Plastic, so it took a good print. I ran it along to the lab, and they did a quick check for me. There's their report.'

I flicked it across the desk. He leered at me, as though I'd revealed a weakness. Then he put his head down and began to read. I took the spare chair, crossed an ankle over the other knee, and started my pipe. He coughed, and lit a cigarette in self-defence.

At last he raised his head, his eyes hooded, peering over the rim of his glasses. 'I suppose I ought to be grateful,' he conceded.

I inclined my head.

'But it doesn't alter anything, really.' He looked away, and then back. 'I was going to work on the assumption that it's her husband. So far, nothing else fits. The case seems straightforward, with only a few details to clear up. I'll go round there in the morning . . .' A thin smile. 'This morning. No need to bring her in, I think, not for a first interview. This report simply makes it easier for me – gives me a firm basis on which to build a case. I'm . . . grateful to you.'

He paused. I said nothing. He moved restlessly.

'You've got to realise,' he went on, 'that I'll have to treat her in exactly the same way as any other suspect.'

'Of course,' I said, my voice tight. That was what she was – a suspect.

His voice took on an edge. 'Then what did you expect to get out of it? Why go to all this trouble?'

'I'm finishing at midnight. I just fancied the idea of seeing an end to it before I go.'

He grunted. 'I think we'll have an end before then. There's nothing unusual about it, nothing complicated.' Then his eyes opened wide. His tongue flicked out to moisten his lips. There was pain in his voice. 'Are you asking to be present at the first interview?'

'No.' I shrugged.

'Then what?'

'Just a couple of points. I'd hoped to persuade you to think very carefully about the glass on the ground outside the window, but not beneath the hole it came from. And it'd be nice if you could find an explanation for the Remington shotgun – both barrels discharged but not reloaded, and leaning against the wall by the fireplace.'

I got to my feet. He failed to meet my eye, but managed to speak with confidence. 'That'll all become clear when I've had a few words with her.'

'Do you really think so? I'll be surprised if she'll tell you any more than we've got now.' I paused at the door, and tried to speak kindly. 'I'd get off home, if I were you. You'll be whacked in the morning.'

His head jerked. Advice from me he didn't need. 'Just do that yourself. I'll look after myself.'

119

I shrugged, and closed the door quietly behind me. I hesitated at my own door. There seemed no point in going in now, but all the same, instinct had the door open, the light on, and the four strides completed to my desk. Then I was glad it had. There was a note from Ken on my pad.

Damn you, Richard, you've got him working us to a frazzle. He wants to get it tidied into a neat bundle before you leave us. Just to show you won't be missed, I reckon. Here's one who'll miss you. Ken.

It was meant to be amusing, even encouraging, but I crumpled it angrily and tossed it into the wastebasket, then stood hesitant for a moment before deciding to go home. My mind was so tired that it wouldn't turn up a good reason for meeting Brason at Swallow's End at ten, as I'd arranged.

But all the same I wasn't late. Heavy-eyed and stiff, I still managed to climb from the Stag and confront Brason briskly. He was waiting beside his official Allegro.

'Didn't keep you waiting, I hope?' I asked.

A DI is entitled to keep a constable waiting. He blushed. 'It's a pleasant morning, sir.'

And so it was. The sun was mildly warm, with no wind to take the edge from it. Nearly all the snow had gone, with only scattered pockets lying in the shadow of the thorn hedge leading up to the cottage. I looked round. The air was crisp and clean. I felt alive again. Even eager. There was so much living still left unexplored. I glanced at Brason, who was poised and very official, and briefly envied him his youth. Then I noticed his inexperience, and pitied him. Why, I wondered, had I asked for Brason to be there? Then I remembered, and couldn't match his smile.

'The cottage is sealed, sir.'

'Yes, I know. But I don't want to go inside.'

We strolled towards the cottage unhurriedly. Blue smoke drifted from my pipe. Brason didn't speak, waiting for me to take the lead. He matched me, pace for pace.

We stood in front of the cottage. For the first time I noticed there was a number on the front door. 'Three?' I asked, looking round. The place was totally isolated. 'Where're the other two?'

'Two other tied cottages, over beyond those pines, sir. It's the postal number.' He seemed surprised at my interest.

I shook my head in wonder. A postman travelling half a mile between numbers two and three! 'The keys,' I said. 'I was going to ask you about the keys.'

'How d'you mean, sir?'

'They were both found in their locks inside the cottage, and there hadn't been any break-in. The place was unoccupied for years, but it's impossible to lock it up and leave the keys inside. So . . . how would anybody be able to get in?' I glanced at him. 'And don't tell me the keys were taken from Rennie's office when the shotgun was pinched, because . . .'

'Oh no, sir. Certainly not. It'd been lived in for at least a fortnight, and the gun was taken no more than ten days ago. But it's easily explained.'

'I'd like to hear.'

'The keys would be in the outhouse. It was the first place I looked.'

'That's a funny arrangement.'

He allowed himself a little quiet satisfaction. 'Not out here, not in the country. You've got to realise . . . two rather big keys, and a family living here, say. They wouldn't want to carry one around, and they couldn't afford half a dozen duplicates, anyway. And so – the last one out locked up, and left the keys in the outhouse. First home knew where to look.'

'I see.' I found it naively amusing. 'I wondered why that courting couple seemed confident they could get in. Generally known, is it?'

'Around here, yes.'

'Not much security, then.'

'We get trouble, but not that.'

'Hah! Show me where.'

Brason, uplifted by the interest and warmly smug with his low crime rate, led the way round the building. He put a finger through the hole in the outhouse door, lifted the latch, and swung it open. We stepped inside, wedged together.

It was the general size, with the same stifling atmosphere, of a coalhouse. The dust was thick on the floor, scuffed near the door by forensic feet. Just around the corner, and hard against the side wall, was a structure of brickwork, which raised a square, galvanised water tank so that its upper rim was above our heads. Crouched behind it in the far corner there was a solid ancient block of cast-iron machinery, still bearing traces of its original green paint, and smelling strongly of oil.

'There,' said Brason, pointing.

A nail, level with the tank top, protruded from the cement between the plain brickwork. It was festooned with cobwebs, recently broken and not yet repaired.

'They'd be hung there,' he said.

'So that even a stranger might find them. Looking round for a way in, without having to break anything.'

He protruded his lower lip. 'A stranger who'd lived in a place like this . . . yes, I suppose so.'

'This the pump?' I pointed my pipe stem at the machinery. 'It doesn't look too efficient to me.'

He calmly reached over the tank rim, felt for the ball, and pressed it down. At once the pump began its operation, a thump, thump, thump that shook the cement floor beneath our feet. Water splashed into the tank.

'They fit a micro-switch instead of a plunger valve,' Brason was pleased to explain.

I was relieved to back out of there. Too claustrophobic for my liking. As he was swinging the door closed, the thumping stopped. I reached out and caught the door.

'Hold on a sec. Something I wanted to check.'

Then, shaking my head at my forgetfulness, I plodded away and back to the Stag. When I returned, Brason was looking puzzled, no doubt because I was carrying the rusted old wreck of a shotgun that I'd found at Kendall's bungalow.

'Spotted something,' I said, and re-entered the outhouse.

In the back, left-hand corner the dust layer had not been disturbed by feet. It consisted of countless years of brick and cement dust shaken into the air by the intermittent throb of the pump. Six inches from the wall, way in the corner, there was an indentation in the dust. I tried the butt of the stock in it. The fit was absolute.

'Would you say this could have stood here?' I asked.

'It's possible.' He obviously thought it couldn't matter, as the gun clearly couldn't have fired.

'And would it rust away like this?'

'Oh, sure. In here it'd always be damp. Ten or twenty years in here, and the best of guns'd be like that.'

'Mmm!'

I carried the gun out into the daylight. It was strange that it should have been taken from the cottage all the way to Kendall's bungalow, just to take its place in a threat to Kendall. Both threats, the doll and the gun, looked very like the Clayton brothers in action. But if this was so, it indicated their innocence in anything beyond threats. And when I came to think about it, so did the fact that we were no longer considering the body as being that of Kendall. My heart beat a little faster. Somewhere along the line the murderer always makes a mistake. I felt I held that mistake in my hand. It would've been too easy for the murderer to assume that the rusted gun would never be traced back to the cottage.

Calmly, pretending I was not elated, I went along and peered through the kitchen window.

'What had we decided?' I asked. 'Ah yes, that a stranger might have found the keys.' I straightened, facing him squarely. 'I suppose you've heard we've got a positive identification?'

'I heard that, sir. Mr Trowbridge. It kind of links with the gutted car.'

'Doesn't it? But it's unlikely he'd know about this place . . . anyway, assume he came across it, and we've decided he might have located the keys easily enough . . .'

I'd hung it on a question. Brason frowned. 'If you're satisfied about that . . . sir.'

'I'm not. But assume it for now. Then, it's reasonable to suppose he'd let himself in by the back door, this one here, then leave the keys in their relevant locks.' I waited, but he disappointed me. So I went on: 'And if the necessity didn't arise, he might not even try to open the front door, and discover that it's wedged solid.'

'Yes.' He relaxed. He'd got the point. 'Not until the day he died, say, and unlocked the front door in order to . . .'

'Welcome a visitor?'

'Yes, sir.'

'Or am I stretching it a bit?'

He was thoughtful. 'Well . . . I suppose . . . it's no more than an argument about human behaviour.'

'Yes.' Then I suddenly laughed, and slapped him on the shoulder. 'You're thinking in terms of the evidence you'd need to make an arrest. But when you're thinking about having to present a case in court – and you have to keep that in mind all the time – then little details like that can suddenly become critical. A defence lawyer could well think up an explanation that's quite convincing, and at the same time makes it impossible for his client to be guilty. You have to allow for that, and get in ahead with your own reasonable explanation.'

He smiled in embarrassment. 'But surely, sir, that sort of thing, it's for officers a bit higher ranking than me.'

'And you're assuming you'll never be that? Don't be a defeatist, son. It's all good practice.'

'I understand that.' He was grave, already with the weight of responsibility on his shoulders.

'Good. Now, there was something else . . .' I wagged my head, trying to shake it free. 'Oh yes – the light switch. Do you remember, Ken Latchett and I were standing inside. The daylight was fading, and you came in and put on the switch.'

'I'm sorry about that, sir. I wasn't thinking.'

'I know you weren't. It was instinct. It was almost as though you knew there was electricity available. A kind of absent-minded confidence.' I said it casually.

I cocked my head, smiling slightly, but I could see I'd overdone it. He knew I'd been serious, and was instantly confused. The mood had changed.

'I know I shouldn't . . .' he began awkwardly.

'It's not that. I'm not blaming you. But you *knew* the light would come on.' I was pressing him on it.

Then Brason realised he'd been trapped. The idle chat about keys might have been intended to lull him, but this was in

124

earnest. 'Well ... I ... I,' he fumbled. 'Of course I knew, sir,' he recovered. 'The sergeant had already spotted the broken seal on the company's fuse box.'

'But that didn't prove anything at that stage. Think, man, think. When you and the sergeant first arrived, you broke open the back door with a tyre lever. Then you and Ken went in. He'd have been in the lead ...'

'Yes.' He was hot, hurt and baffled.

'But at that time,' I reminded him, 'it was daylight. And you, with your actions dictated by instinct rather than procedure ... Brason, when you walked with Ken into the living-room, was it perhaps that the light was *on*, and you put it off without considering, instinctively, as you'd have done at home? Because *then* you'd have known the electricity was connected. It'd register itself in your mind.'

There was immediate relief. 'Oh no, sir. I didn't do that. The light wasn't on.'

'A pity.' I shook my head. 'It could've explained a lot of things.'

He was staring at me. I laughed at his expression. 'You're thinking this could be another of my piffling details?'

'Oh no, I wasn't thinking that.'

'Then we've achieved something, at least. Come on, let's go and have a look at the front.'

By that time I'd got Brason's brain working flat out, and he'd relaxed into a new confidence. When we got there, he said:

'I've been thinking about the glass, Mr Patton.'

I was staring down at the small patch of glass shards beneath the opening window. I nodded approvingly. 'And what did you come up with?'

'Well, sir, Mr Donaldson said the hole might've been blasted at an angle from inside the room by the Remington, but somehow ... and I've seen a shotgun hole in glass ... it's not like that hole at all. A shotgun leaves a rounder hole, with the edges not so jagged. And anyway, I can't really see that the bits'd fall where they are, closer to the hinge than the hole itself. Not even with Mr Donaldson's idea of a slanted shot. It'd kind of spray out, anyway.'

He paused. I nodded encouragement. 'Go on, son. You're doing fine.'

'So I reckoned . . . it must've been knocked out, and at a time when the window was open, not when it was shut.'

'That's what I thought. Something was poked through the glass.'

'Say, if the window was flung open,' said Brason eagerly.

'In welcome?'

'By the person inside, having turned the key in the front door, and found it was wedged solid.' He was going well now, his imagination leaping at every little flick of my mental whip.

'And the hole in the glass was made by?'

'The muzzle of the other shotgun. The one he was killed with. And then . . .' But he faltered to a halt.

'And then?' I asked quietly.

He shook his head, but I persisted. 'Go on. Take it from there.'

But he was winding down. 'The man inside slammed the window shut, because he'd seen the shotgun coming through the glass.'

'And? You're not carrying it on through.'

'Hell, sir, it doesn't make sense.'

'What doesn't make sense?'

He was miserable that he'd allowed himself to be led on. Maybe he'd already seen this dead end. He shrugged.

'The man inside, waiting there for trouble – he'd fired both his barrels and hadn't reloaded. He'd probably had the window open when he fired . . .'

'Seems likely.'

'So he must have seen somebody coming, fired . . . and then realised it was a . . . well, a friend. But hell, sir, that person must've been carrying a shotgun. It isn't the sort of thing you can hide in a pocket. And that doesn't make it look friendly, does it? I mean – he fired the Remington, two separate barrels, and missed both times – must have done – when the range couldn't have been more than thirty yards. *Then* he sees it's a friend, and even so he doesn't see the carried shotgun. And shuts the window, sir! It's just too much to swallow.'

'But it's pretty good, son. Needs more thought, of course. I only wish I had time for it.'

He grinned weakly. 'I get plenty of time for thinking, out here.'

I said: 'Come on, let's go. I think I've seen all I want to now.'

We walked back to the cars. He seemed embarrassed. Cleared his throat. 'Perhaps I'll meet you again, sir.'

'I'll look forward to that,' I said, tossing the rusted shotgun onto the rear seat.

I drove back to the station. It was getting on towards midday. Everything was quiet. In the general sergeant's office they'd all got their heads down, the two officers Donaldson had borrowed from Division looking lost and bored. Nobody spoke to me. At the front desk I'd sensed an awkwardness. Of course, Donaldson had had the morning with Amelia, but nobody was anxious to tell me about it.

'Anybody seen Ken Latchett?' I asked the desk sergeant.

'He didn't come back with Mr Donaldson, sir.'

'Back from where?' I tried to make him say it, but he looked past my head at a wall poster about Colorado beetle.

'Where they'd been, sir.'

I hadn't wanted to tackle it that early. A pattern seemed to be coming together, but I wanted more time with it, and there was something missing from it somewhere. I didn't want to be pushed.

He said hopefully: 'I'm sure he'll be back, sir. Mr Donaldson's called a conference for three-thirty.'

I turned away, and went out to my car again.

Ken was parked at the lead-in to the cul-de-sac, and reached me before I'd climbed from the Stag. I took one look at his face, and knew why he'd waited for me.

'Donaldson's finished, I'm told.'

'We were there for two hours, Richard. Now listen . . .'

'What did she tell him?'

He put a hand on my arm. 'What did she tell you, Richard? That's the point.'

'It was all in my report.'

'Then Donaldson got further. Her relationship with Kendall . . .

'I know about that.'

He was silent.

'How did he treat her?' I asked quietly.

'You know Donaldson.'

'How, Ken?'

'There were just the two of us. He was gentle as you like at first, very careful, leading her on. She started all confidence, but Lord, he can really dig in. Kept at it, and at it, insinuating, not accepting anything. She just had to justify herself, and he didn't give her one second to take a breathing space. You handed it to him,' said Ken, with more than a hint of contempt. 'That shaving-soap bowl!'

'I had to know where I was,' I growled. 'We had to know.'

'It's like that, is it?'

'I'm not going to spell it out.'

'Oh hell!'

'This conference he's called . . .'

'Three-thirty. All sergeants, and Phillips and Kelly they lent us from Division, Merridew, and Brason. You're not thinking of busting in there!'

I jutted a lip at him and managed a light tone. 'I'm not thinking at all, Ken. Not one thought. Now . . . get out of my way, will you.'

'Anything I can do . . .'

'I know, Ken. Thanks.'

She opened the door before I'd reached it. She did not speak, simply stood back. Even that small movement was stiff and formalised, as though her brain could spare nothing for physical control. I took one look at her face, then slid an arm round her waist and led her through into the kitchen, sat her down at the table, and put on the kettle. It was impossible, until I'd taken a stronger grip on my emotions, to look again at her face.

She whispered: 'You did warn me.'

I found crockery, placed cups and saucers and milk and sugar in front of her. Her fingers clawed towards my hand, but I withdrew it gently. The kettle was singing. I asked: 'Where d'you keep the tea?' But she did not reply. I hunted it out, and every movement had to be carefully controlled to the task at hand.

128

Then at last I sat opposite her. Her eyes were huge, red with strain and weeping. 'What have you told Donaldson, Amelia?' I asked.

'Everything I said to you, Richard.' Her voice was weary, drawn from somewhere way back.

'What have you told him that you haven't told me?'

'He went on and on, repeating, going back, insisting . . .'

I'd caught the note of hysteria in her voice, and noticed the shaking of her fingers. I poured the tea myself, and pushed her cup towards her.

'Drink your tea.'

'He wouldn't give me time to think.'

'Your tea.'

She sugared and milked it. I'd forgotten: milk first, for her. The cup clattered against her teeth. It was too hot, and she gulped, gasping, but the shock seemed to steady her.

I spoke gently, drawing it from her. 'What did you tell him that you were afraid to have me hear?' She shook her head. 'I must know.' There had to be something, to justify this.

She gave me one startled, terrified glance, then she looked down at her cup, and answered into it.

'There was one thing he couldn't understand. All the rest . . . oh, the bitterness and the contempt he threw at me! I'd told him about Clive Kendall, how I'd wanted to help him, and he kept saying yes, yes, yes. Just wouldn't let it alone. Wouldn't *believe* I'd want to help him. Wouldn't *accept* that I'd get his bungalow ready for him. Sneered at everything I said. He made me, Richard . . . made me justify myself. As though I needed to! He made me feel like something cheap and dirty. There . . . there was this one thing he couldn't get round. My husband, a stranger to the district, and he'd been discovered in a cottage he just couldn't know about. And it was the place Kendall was born. Kendall's own early home, and my husband was there! He wouldn't believe it could be chance. Threw it at me. As though I'd got to prove something. How could a stranger find *that* cottage? He kept on and on . . .'

'He thought originally that it had to be Kendall's body. But go on – how *did* your husband know about it, my dear?'

'Kendall . . . in the end he was afraid. I had to encourage

him, and persuade him. I told him he'd got to face up to it, or it was all worthless. All my work.'

'He'd love that.'

'And so . . . so, I had to agree, finally, to take a look at the cottage, too. Well, not clean it up. Just go inside and look round it. You know.' She looked up into my face in desperation. 'You *know*, Richard. Don't stare at me like that. Please,' she whispered, and I tried to smile. 'I promised I'd go there, and tell him that at least the glass was still in the windows. I didn't approve of all this, Richard, but he wanted somewhere in case he had to hide. I went – and of course my husband went with me. That's all there is to it, Richard. All there is.' She looked bewildered and pathetic.

There seemed to be an inability to focus. Her face swam in front of me, and I felt lost. Suddenly I needed her, and she'd given Donaldson all there was, all he needed – the evidence that she, too, knew the location of the cottage.

Somewhere inside there should have been an angry grief, that she'd kept it from me, but there was nothing.

'All there is!' I said softly. 'Oh my God!'

Then my hand found hers.

9

The instinct was to remain with her until they came, but it would have meant inactivity, and I couldn't face that. Yet I told myself that I must not go to the conference. All they would be doing was polishing Donaldson's case, so that he could march in with a warrant for her arrest. And I had nothing to throw back at him. It would be all formal and unemotional. I tried to explain the process to her.

'You make it sound as though I'm lucky,' she said ruefully. But she was certainly more cheerful than she'd been. 'Lucky he didn't take me away straightaway, I mean.'

'He's not a man who acts on impulse, and you're not going to run away. He's got to give himself time to think.'

I looked round vaguely, feeling confined.

'Is that a hint?' she asked.

'Was I so obvious?'

'You're restless. Go if you must. But . . . be back here, will you? Be back when he comes again.'

'Of course, my dear.' But I looked at her blindly.

I drove to Clive Kendall's bungalow, for the very good reason that I could think of no other place to go. And because I had to feel, still, that Kendall was involved. She had given me lunch, on my insistence, to give her something to distract her. I felt heavy and uncomfortable with the food, my mouth harsh because I'd been smoking too much. My mind was in a turmoil.

Once again I left the car parked on the road. There was now no trace of the cleated-sole prints. Overhead, the clouds were gathering again. I could smell the snow in the air, and feel again

131

that subliminal uneasiness that didn't seem as though it would ever leave me.

The bungalow seemed unchanged. I walked carefully round it, but there were no more threatening gestures or messages. I peered through the windows. Nothing indicated a visit by Kendall since I'd been there before. I eased my bulk into the recess, in which the back door was set sideways, and suddenly it seemed that Kendall was to blame for more than the rapes and the killing of Coral Clayton. All this was a legacy of Kendall, all that was happening now being a proliferation of Kendall's personality.

I wedged my feet against the brickwork behind me, put my shoulder against the door, and burst it open with one savage thrust.

The kitchen, which had seemed bare from outside, had small indications of one visit, at least. An unwashed plate and tumbler were on the surface just out of sight from the window, and when I opened the refrigerator door the electricity was connected – had Amelia arranged that? – and the light came on. There were two frozen beefburgers in the freezer compartment, and half a packet of peas. The milk in a bottle in the door was curdled. There was a packet of unopened cheese, and a block of butter, merely scraped. I shut the door, and went on through to the hall.

There was nothing to find, I grumbled to myself, but every instinct told me that there ought to be. When I walked into the hall, there was a smell of stale violets, and on the hall stand was a note. *You must do your own shopping, but I've started you off. A. T.* The paper smelt of violets, too.

Started him off!

Beneath the letter-box slot there was an envelope on the floor. I picked it up by its edges, training warning me about fingerprints. The flap was not sealed, and I edged out a single sheet of paper. On it was printed:

CORAL DIED AND SO WILL YOU.
BUT SLOWER, YOU BASTARD. SLOWER.

I crumpled it up angrily and tossed it on to the hall-stand. Why the hell should I worry any more about the Claytons?

Then I went on through into the living-room, and all was neat and tidy. There was no indication that the place had ever been used for living in. The tidiness was impersonal, like the institutional perfection of a spare hospital bed. But then, standing there, I became aware that this was *her* doing. This, Amelia had done for Clive Kendall, and the thought revolted me. I flung a chair away from my path, and watched it almost with detachment as it fell on its side against the wall. There was a ringing in my head, and a dull, bellowing fury inside me, thrusting for release. My restraint was stretched to its limit. The chair was a gesture, a tiny valve, a micro-switch that needed only a touch to provoke the thump, thump, thump of the more powerful pump.

I stood, then, in the chaos of the room, blood in my eyes and my fury boiling. Whatever she had done for Kendall had to be destroyed. That I saw with clarity. I ran into the bedroom, toppled the wardrobe on to its face, tore curtains down and the sheets from the bed, smashed the mirror over the dressing table that had been Rona Kendall's, tore drawers from beneath it and shattered them in a blind, mad fury against the wall. And stopped, very still, staring down at my feet.

Amongst the debris there was lying a small revolver, black and shining. I reached for it, and hesitated, then moved quickly to the doorway and put on the light. Then I returned to it, down on one knee, examining the pistol without touching.

One connecting link I'd needed. Was this it?

It was a Smith & Wesson, and seemed to be of .32 calibre. The cylinder was fully loaded. I hooked a pencil into the trigger guard and brought it out beneath the light, and smelt the barrel. The only smell was of oil, as though it had been well preserved for an anticipated long wait. It was possible he'd had it, even before his arrest, but had been afraid to flaunt a loaded weapon.

Even with the naked eye I could see that the oil film was quite undisturbed. There were no traces of fingerprints. I risked, then, handling it, the butt slippy in my hand. I flipped out the cylinder, and peered along the barrel, against the light. I was looking for evidence of fouling. But even inside the barrel it was well oiled, with only a fleeting glint here and there. I tilted the barrel this way and that, trying to catch the light, and then realised that what I was looking at was the refracted light thrown by several tiny slivers of glass, caught in the film of oil.

For a moment my mind darted towards a conclusion, but then retreated. I couldn't force it to complete the equation. I thrust the gun into my pocket, and looked around at the damage I'd done. I couldn't remember doing it. Then, decisively, I tramped through the bungalow and out through the back door.

The light was failing. Heavy clouds were pressing low. I raised my head and saw that Foster Clayton was leaning against one of the stark trees. Smiling, he eased his shoulders upright and strolled towards me.

'What the hell're you doing here?' I demanded angrily.

'I could say the same for you.'

'Where's Ted? I bet he's around somewhere. Ted! Ted Clayton.'

Ted came from round the end of the building. He was walking with a bouncy gait, his head cocked, his voice, when he spoke, defiant.

'Somebody called? Did somebody call me, Foster? Well now, if it isn't the Inspector! Been breaking and entering, have we?'

'I warned you . . .'

'Warnings!' said Foster in disgust. 'Who the hell're you to chuck around your warnings?'

They were advancing on me from two directions. I set my shoulders against the wall. 'You damn fools,' I said. 'We've got a murder investigation going, and you haven't got the sense to keep your heads down.'

Neither of the brothers seemed impressed. With their shoulders relaxed, they pressed in close to me.

'What've you done with Kendall?' asked Foster, maintaining a pleasant tone.

But Ted was more aggressive. 'Where've you hidden the bleeder?'

I took a deep breath. 'I've got evidence of your activities. A doll hanging from a tree over there, and a shotgun tied to that one there. And now a threatening note through the door.'

'Not us,' said Foster, smiling.

'Coral died, and so will you,' I quoted. 'But slower, you bastard, slower. What does that sound like, if it's not you?'

Foster's face was immediately blank, but Ted crowed: 'That's what he's gonna get.'

'Shut up, you idiot,' Foster hissed.

'And that drawing on the window,' I shouted, feeling I was on the ascendant. 'Who's that but you, Ted?'

'Gerraway.'

'Look at it. On the back window.'

'Don't need to look.'

'Go and look at it, damn you!'

Ted leaned his face close, sneering, but then his eyes slid away and his face withdrew. He turned away to stare at the window.

Foster said: 'We ain't done anything around here, and you know it, Mr Patton.'

Ted whirled. 'He's done that his bloody self!' he claimed, gesturing towards the window.

I sighed. 'Talk sense for once.'

But Ted was furious, feeling that a trap had been laid for him. He came close to me and poked out a finger.

'Don't you put a finger on me,' I warned him. I could feel my anger rising again, and it scared me.

Ted thrust out his palm against my shoulder. More to avoid contact than anything else I stepped back, and was thrust forward at once by Foster, who had stepped sideways to get behind me. They'd played this game before. I twisted away from between them, reaching out my left hand to grab a portion of Ted's pullover, and brought my right hand from my pocket. It happened to be clasped around the revolver.

'Take your hands off me!' I roared, and the muzzle was under Ted's chin, with Ted staring back at me in surprise and horror. Foster stepped back. 'Heh, he's bloody insane.' And I was shouting: 'I warned you, Ted. I warned you!'

It was the first time I'd ever pointed a pistol at anybody, in all my career. And this one was loaded. What are you doing? I asked myself. Take a grip on yourself. Stop! Stop now!

'Now you're going to talk,' I was snarling. Ted's head was

135

going back, back under the impulse of the pistol, until I wondered if his neck would break. 'The doll! That was you. Wasn't it you?'

Ted croaked: 'Get him, Foster.'

'I'll blow your head off,' I snapped. 'Talk. The doll.'

'Oh no. It wasn't me.'

'It was Foster, then?'

'No. Neither of us.'

'And the shotgun?'

'Don't know what you're talking about,' Ted appealed weakly. 'Watch what you're doin' with that thing!'

I was so caught up in a blind fury of frustration that I was nearly choking him with the muzzle. There was a groaning, but it could have been me, and fingers were clawing at my elbow. Foster, finding his confidence failing him, was appealing: 'Now, Mr Patton. Mr Patton. Go easy.' His voice was a frightened whine.

'And the note, Ted? The note through the door?'

'No.'

'The truth, or I'll kill you.'

'All right. Lemme go. That was me. Just now. Before you come along. It's the truth. But only that.'

I thrust him away. My heart was beating wildly and I felt insecure on my feet. I stared blindly at the revolver in my hand, then put it away in my pocket. When I looked up I could see the brothers running away, Ted staggering. I shook my head, muttering to myself, and began to walk after them slowly, my eyes to the ground.

I sat a long while in the car before my heart settled and my mind focused. Slowly I lit my pipe. The clock on the dash said three-thirty. The conference should just about be starting.

10

Lord, the number of conferences I've been to! And they're all the same – a waste of time, to my mind. You get to a point where the officer in charge of a case knows what he's got and what he's going to do about it. So he calls a conference. It's just to be polite. He gets a lot of suggestions and opinions, and probably intends to ignore every one of them.

There was really no hurry, because I could have written the script. But in any event, I hadn't got a hurry left in me. I'd plodded past the desk, aware of the sudden silence when they saw what I was carrying, and I'd forced my weak legs up the four flights to the top floor. Here we had the only room big enough to take the two borrowed men and all the sergeants who'd been involved, but who really hadn't been given time to dig into it. And Brason, I hoped.

I could hear them before I reached the top landing. It was all partitions up there, empty side rooms, and the one big one at the end. By that time I was moving quietly, and made not a sound when I slipped into the cubicle next to the conference room. No chairs in there – they'd bagged them all. I leaned into the corner, and slowly, not taking any notice of my instructions, my legs gave way, and I slid down to a sitting position on the floor.

Merridew was into his preamble, trying to exert his authority, but I could tell, even through the partition, that he wasn't happy about things at all.

'. . . but if anybody thinks of any point, however trifling . . .'

I could hear him fading off with a sigh, but the throat clearance was Donaldson's.

'I don't think there's any doubt we've got a straightforward domestic murder here. A wife kills her husband. She seems to have shot him with a shotgun . . .'

'Seems to . . .' Merridew cutting in unhappily.

'. . . through a hole in the front window,' Donaldson pressed on, unshaken. 'We might have some discussion on how that hole was caused, and on other small details.'

Merridew raised his voice. 'We haven't even got a murder weapon.'

'A shotgun,' said Donaldson in a flat voice, 'which was then thrown away. Exactly where it was thrown should emerge during later interrogation. I propose to charge Mrs Trowbridge with murder, and bring her back here. I'm sure we can persuade her to clear the few remaining points.'

'But there're too many points,' Merridew grumbled. 'So very many we can't explain.'

'Details,' said Donaldson incisively, dismissing them.

'Then suppose we discuss one or two.'

'All right, sir, we'll discuss them.' The disgust in Donaldson's voice came through very clearly.

They did that. You get the same thing every time. Several of the men clearly didn't appreciate what was going on, but had to get themselves noticed. Two marks for trying. But as far as most of them were concerned the case was ended. A woman had shot her husband. It had happened before, and it would happen again. Simple and uncomplicated. You therefore had her in, and in due course she would sign a statement in which she admitted it.

What the hell did it matter that the victim's shotgun had been standing, fired and not reloaded, against the wall? Who cared where the glass from the pane had fallen? And what possible importance was it that the light switch might or might not have been on?

I nearly thumped the wall with exasperation, but my fist would've gone through. That would've been a laugh, a fist sticking through the other side! I heard myself chuckling, and it threatened to run out of control, so I stuck the fist in my mouth instead, and held on.

In the end, Merridew tapped it down, calling them to order.

'All right. I think you've all had your say. Now, let's take the difficult points in order, and perhaps Mr Donaldson will outline what he's got in mind. Now . . . motive?'

I could see the smile in Donaldson's voice. 'I think that's fairly obvious. She's given us a long rigmarole about her relationship with Kendall – all that guff about trying the best she could for him, and not refusing any of his demands in case it undermined his trust in her.' Contempt dripped from him. 'She tried to convince us it didn't spill over into her private life, but I don't know. We'd have to get the psychiatrists on it. But I'll remind you, gentlemen, that we don't have to produce a motive. Only show that she killed him. Oh, they'll put it up as a defence, no doubt. They'll plead diminished responsibility, on the grounds that she couldn't help herself. And that's not our worry, either. So let's forget all this psychology nonsense, and get on with the case.'

'Oh no,' I whispered.

'Now,' went on Donaldson, having disposed of motive, 'we come to the discharged shotgun inside, and the hole in the window pane. Assume Mrs Trowbidge reached the front door unobserved . . .'

'As simply as that?' Merridew that was, being acid.

'Assume she did, sir, for the moment. The victim heard her in the porch, rushed to the window, and discharged his shotgun sideways through the glass, though the angle must've been too fine for him to hit her.'

Merridew interrupted. 'You've got something to say, Brason? Come on. We've heard nothing from you yet.'

Brason came in, all hesitant. Good lad. 'The hole, sir, I don't think it was caused by gunshot. I've seen such a hole. It should be more regular than the one we've got.'

'You've got an alternative?'

'Yes, sir. If the window was flung open, and if somebody was standing by the porch holding a shotgun, then the muzzle could've gone through the glass and the splinters would've been just where they were found.'

A silence. Donaldson no doubt absorbing that. Then he came in crisply.

'Flung open? Why?'

139

'In welcome. After all, this was his wife.'

'Welcome, by God! But she'd have been carrying a shot-gun.'

'The idea of a welcome, sir, is borne out by the fact that *his* shotgun was put aside, as though he'd no longer got any fear from somebody he knew so well. Then he rushed to the window and flung it open.'

It was the same theory as we'd already discussed, but Brason seemed to have the confidence to carry it through. Donaldson tried sarcasm.

'He welcomed her! Carrying a shotgun, she came across that yard, and he welcomed her. But first of all, he took a couple of shots at her, then leaned his shotgun against the wall, and decided to welcome her, instead. Oh, come on, man.'

'Let's hear the rest of it,' said Merridew, interested. '*Can* you give us any more, Brason?'

But Brason had given some thought to the linking clue I'd offered him. I could've hugged him.

'I can go on, sir. I know that on the face of it it's self-contradictory. But we've got a man who'd kind of fortified himself in that cottage. So you'd think that only somebody very close to him would stand a chance of getting anywhere near. It's his wife we're considering, but even she wouldn't stand a chance if she was seen coming down that path with a shotgun. But we're only saying that, because we found him in daylight, and the light switch was off – so everybody assumed the murder was done in daylight. But if you imagine a different scene – a night-time scene – then it's all very different.'

He stopped. Thought he'd finished, perhaps. Donaldson was very gentle with him, considering.

'I hope this can be substantiated.'

Led on, Brason continued: 'He could've been sitting there, with the light on. But against a bright night sky he could've detected a movement.' Romantic imagery, now! 'He'd dive for the light switch and flick it off, then go to the window and open it . . . see a shadow out there . . . give it one barrel, then the other, and miss both times. Slam the window shut and run for his spare cartridges . . . and she'd shout out: "It's me, darling, Amelia." Or something like that. And then . . . well, what I've already said. He'd be in the dark by then. He'd lean the shotgun against the wall and rush to the window again, open it . . . and realise she'd got a shotgun of her own, because it went through the glass. In a panic he'd shut the window, but there was the hole. He saw the gun shoved through, put up his hands in front of his face . . . and I suppose that's all there is to say.' He ended on an exhausted downbeat.

I made a move. It took me ages to lever myself to my feet. I'd never felt so old. I nearly forgot the shotgun and the doll, but managed to move slowly into the corridor. I made it to the door into the conference room.

'Good,' Merridew was saying, while I did all that. I edged the door open a couple of inches, and his voice came in louder. I waited to pick the best moment. 'Very good. Thank you, Brason.'

'It's all very well,' said Donaldson. 'But it still leaves . . .'

'What?' snapped Merridew impatiently. He'd enjoyed Brason's little story.

'A few points.'

'Such as?'

'The pathological evidence is that the shots were fired from no greater range than three feet.'

'Brason's theory covers that.'

'But he was found nearly ten feet from the window.'

'The force of the charge. Two barrels, remember, together.'

'But there was no blood at all near the window.'

Merridew made a dismissive noise. His right hand was in view. I could just see it moving.

'And besides,' Donaldson persisted, not intending to surrender all the credit and plunging hectically into his imagination, 'if a shotgun barrel was pushed through glass, *some* bits of it'd get down the barrel. And the autopsy . . .' I could see him clearly now. He began to search for the autopsy report in his file, but Merridew put a hand to his arm.

'I don't think it would be likely.'

'There was no mention of glass particles in the flesh,' protested Donaldson.

It was time. I pushed the door open, and said: 'You started without me.'

141

They turned. Judging by all their expressions I must have looked a bit rough. My legs were spread, because I didn't feel too firm, and my voice had matched their weakness. There was a silence. In one hand I was dangling by its string the doll with the broken neck and a tuft of beard, and in the other the rusted shotgun.

I walked forward. There was a general shuffle as the men clambered to their feet, and a rattle as chairs were moved from my path. I made a straight line to the table, and banged down my two burdens on the surface under Merridew's nose.

'What's all this?' Merridew growled.

My gesture could have done with more authority. 'Two things,' I said, 'that've been used as threats to Clive Kendall.'

'We're not talking about Kendall,' said Merridew wearily, though with a hint of kindness.

'Aren't we?'

'Richard, we're discussing the murder of her husband by Mrs Trowbridge.'

I turned, one hand supporting me on the table surface. My eyes ran over the faces, surprised and shocked, with only Ken in any sympathy with me at all, and that perhaps only pity. I turned back. Took a breath.

'But the doll's got a beard,' I explained to Merridew, shaking it by its floppy neck.

'Richard . . . now please go away,' he said softly.

'And we all know Kendall hasn't got one now,' I said, not too loudly.

Donaldson had been remarkably patient. I could hardly have expected it to last any longer. 'We've got to get on with this.'

'And this shotgun's from the cottage,' I went on. 'It was used as another threat to Kendall.'

'We're not discussing Kendall,' hissed Donaldson, now becoming more angry. 'He's trying to break this up, sir.'

'I'll handle this.' Merridew was pale, control almost stifling him. I could see he wanted anything but this. 'Latchett, can't you take Mr Patton for a cup of tea in the canteen.'

Ken was on his feet, but I caught his eye warningly. I had to have time, judging by the way my mind was mangling it up. Ken sat down again.

I turned back to face Merridew. 'And there's this,' I said with an effort, producing the revolver. 'I found it in Kendall's bungalow.'

'Kendall! Kendall!' shouted Donaldson.

'You've broken into –' began Merridew.

'Yes. And found that. It's not been fired.'

'And you *handled* it?' Donaldson demanded in outrage.

I flicked him a glance. 'It was slicked with oil. No prints. It'd been cleaned. I brought it here. To show you.'

Merridew decided to be firm. 'Richard, I'm ordering you to leave this room at once.'

'Look down the barrel, sir.'

'He's trying to confuse the issue!' Donaldson appealed, I thought a bit frantically. 'This!' He swept the doll from the table with a furious gesture. 'And this!' He picked up the rusted shotgun and hefted it. 'Oh my God, a gun that hasn't been fired for a century!'

'Look down the barrel, sir.'

Merridew lifted the pistol, humouring me. He flicked out the cylinder and stared down the barrel.

'See it?' I asked, my voice rough. 'The light catches the sparkles. It's glass. Tiny splinters of glass.'

The rusted shotgun crashed against the wall as Donaldson hurled it away from him. 'That's it, then,' he growled. 'That's the bloody limit. He comes in here, determined to break up my conference . . . Sir, he's got that pistol – God knows from where – and he's shoved it through a pane of glass somewhere, and brings it here . . . Christ, it's just a fraud. You can't listen to this . . .'

'Be quiet,' said Merridew icily. He stared Donaldson in the eye, until the Chief Inspector slowly sat down again. 'Now . . . Richard . . .' He moved to come round the table, but hesitated when I faced him down. He leaned towards me and spoke softly.

'Richard, I know this has hurt you. You *like* the woman. I'm aware of that. And perhaps she's felt something for you. But she's killed her husband, and I don't think there can be any doubt about that. She did it because of the control Kendall had over her, and I can see how that'd hurt you, too. But you can't

143

affect things, now. These things you bring us . . .' He shook his head sadly. 'Oh, Richard, you're not helping her at all.'

I held his eyes for a moment. I was swaying. His face blurred.

'Go home, there's a good chap,' he said gently.

Then I turned away. I passed Brason blindly. He was on his feet, but I had to ignore him. He'd done as I wanted, and now I couldn't carry it on. Ken was at the door. I shook my head when he tried to follow me, and as I moved away down the corridor I heard the door close quietly behind me.

11

It had begun to rain by the time I reached Amelia's place. I was reluctant to get out of the car, but whether that was physical or mental I don't know. I sat there for a good five minutes. I could see that she was standing at the window in a darkened room, but I gave her no sign. In the end, she came out with a raincoat over her shoulders.

'Aren't you coming in?'

I lifted my head. Her face was stiff with tension. I made no answer, simply opened the door and got out beside her. I took her arm, and we went into the house together.

'Go into the back room,' she said. 'It's warmer there. You're shivering.' She watched me turn away, with worry in her eyes.

I stood with my back to the gas fire while she went into the kitchen. It was quite dark outside. I waited for her to return, as I'd expected, with a tray of tea things.

'I'll do some sandwiches,' she said enquiringly.

I realised I was hungry, and nodded. As she turned away I said: 'There might not be much time, Amelia. We've got to talk.'

'I'll only be a minute.'

I sighed, stared at the tea tray, my thoughts floating unfocused around it, and I still hadn't got hold of them when she returned.

'They'll be here soon,' I told her. 'Donaldson's going to charge you with the murder of your husband. Then he'll take you away.'

'Do sit down,' she urged me. 'Try a cheese sandwich.'

'They won't let me get near you, then. I'll be able to do absolutely nothing for you.'

'If you *must* stand, put your cup on the mantel shelf. But eat something, Richard.'

I picked up a sandwich and waved it at her. She wasn't comprehending. 'I've shown them the threats made against Clive Kendall. The hanged doll, the rusted old shotgun, and the note.'

'Note?' She frowned, shaking her head, confused.

'But they take no notice,' I complained. 'Even the pistol meant nothing to them.'

'Pistol? You're not making much sense.'

'I found Kendall's revolver. It hadn't been fired, but it'd got slivers of glass in the bore.'

She was watching me with concern. I felt restless, yet at the same time unable to move. I didn't want to watch her reactions.

'I'm sure you've done all you could,' she said soothingly.

'You're not taking this seriously, that's the trouble.'

'I'm frightened. Yes, I'm really very much afraid. But it seems kind of unreal, as though it's not happening to me. How can they say I've killed my husband, when I loved him so dearly? Tell me that, Richard.'

I gulped tea and spluttered, then reached for my pipe and stared at it in disgust.

'They're going to come at you with a substantial case, my dear. They don't have to explain to you what case they have, nor the motive they'll put to it. They will merely charge you and take you away. At this stage. So . . . I'll tell you now, so that you can be prepared.'

She nodded eagerly, agreeing simply to calm me, as though I wasn't acting rationally.

'Smoke if you want to,' she told me.

I shook my head, and put away the pipe.

'They're going to say you went to that cottage at night. They will say that your husband had gone there in fear of his life. He'd thought his danger was mainly from Kendall, and you'd already taken him to the cottage, so he knew he had a place to hide. It was a good place to be in fear. He'd had time to prowl the district in the dark, and he'd got himself a shotgun from Rennie's place. That's what they'll say.'

'But why? What would be the reason behind all this?'

'I'll come to that,' I said, my voice clipped. 'They'll say you went to him in darkness, and that he saw you only as a shadow, so he fired at you through the open window. But you called out to him that it was you. He believed there was nothing to fear from his wife, so he ran to open the front door, but it was wedged solid. So ... failing that, he flung open the window again, but by that time you'd reached the porch, and suddenly he realised he'd got a great deal to fear from you after all, because you too had a shotgun. The window opened against it, breaking a hole in the pane, so he slammed it quickly. But you thrust your shotgun through the hole and shot him with both barrels. Even though he held his hands in front of his face, palms out in entreaty. But it was dark. You might not have seen what he was doing,' I conceded. 'That's what they're going to say.'

'And you ... you believe this, Richard?'

'No. I've told you what *they'll* say.'

'It's ... Richard, it's quite absurd.'

'But how can I prove it is?' I asked, my voice sounding plaintive to me, not forceful enough.

But now she was worried. 'Don't tell me they can say that without putting a reason to it. It's not right. I'm not having it. Oh, it's so stupid! I can't even discuss it.'

'They know all the details of your relationship with Kendall,' I grated. 'To you it might seem that you were just doing a job, a difficult job, and had to do it in the only way you could. But from outside – to other people – it all looks different. Damn it all, hadn't you ever given one thought to Kendall's attitude in this? He was a forceful and self-confident man, a supreme egotist, and he was helpless, there in prison. He had to submit himself to the tender hands of a woman. Hell, he probably despised women. But you had the control, you were the one he had to depend on completely. He'd writhe at your condescension.' My face felt hot. My brain was working again.

'I never treated him like that!' she said indignantly.

'To Kendall it would seem that you were patronising him.

147

And, by God, he'd hate you. Why d'you think he sneered at your efforts, if not in pure self-defence? Why else did he throw challenges at you, if it wasn't to prove to himself that *he* was in control? He had you dancing to every damned demand he could make, and he hated you, and he lived off it. More than likely, he never had any faith in your ability to get him released, on *any* grounds. And believe me, a man like that'd even hate you all the more for succeeding.'

'What good is all this doing?' she asked, a little nervous that I was no longer capable of controlling my emotions.

I merely raised my voice. 'And when he did succeed, and he was due for release, by heaven he'd hate the thought of losing you. Rona, his wife . . . I don't think he ever managed to dominate *her*. Maybe that was what caused him to turn to little girls. God knows. But you'd proved to him that he could still dominate somebody.'

'You're accusing me!' she cried. 'I don't want your contempt. I've got as much as I can put up with.'

'Contempt?' I shouted. 'I'm talking about Kendall.'

'And aiming it at me,' she flashed back.

I gave a furious snort. 'I'm trying to get it clear in my mind. Kendall. That creature! Why d'you think he got you involved in cleaning his bungalow? Not because he couldn't do it himself, but to see if you'd go that far. And then got you to check out the cottage! Not because he was really afraid. He wouldn't need to stay in this district, if he didn't want to. Ask yourself. But he'd need to prove to himself that he'd got you – there in the palm of his hand. Only got to snap his fingers, and you'd go flying in any direction he chose. He'd got you jumping.'

'Why are you saying this to me?' she asked in bemused misery.

'It's Kendall . . .'

'No. It's me you're talking about.'

I tried to speak more softly, more persuasively. 'A thing like this, it grows. You can easily lose control of it.'

'I never lost control!' she snapped. 'I knew exactly what I was doing.'

'One concession, and it seems so small. Then a slightly larger one. You feel that to protest at that would be petty, and the whole

148

thing would be lost for a minor annoyance. It's so much easier to give way – and do it.' I was appealing to her. 'Then gradually it grows until you're taken over, though you might not realise it at the time . . .'

'Why don't you sit down, for pity's sake!'

'. . . until there comes a point when *anything* will be conceded, because you're too damned tired to say: no – go to hell.'

'Sit down,' she cried, controlling her temper with an effort. 'Sit down . . . please.'

'There can come a time when you find you're taking actions completely opposed to your nature,' I persisted.

'Have you got the utter nerve to stand there, and tell me that he sent me out to kill –'

'Not me!'

'That he put a shotgun in my hands and said to me: go and shoot your husband!'

'Listen to me, for heaven's sake.'

'And that I would!' she screamed.

'Be quiet!' I shouted at her. 'Listen – will you. They're going to say that. They, they, they! Not me. They'll say that Kendall could tell you to do even that . . . and you'd do it.'

'By God, just let them!'

'So you'd deny it to their faces?'

'I'd walk out of the room,' she declared hotly. 'If it wasn't you saying it now . . . I tell you, Richard . . . I'd be doing just that right now. And,' she said fiercely, 'you can just take that look off your face.'

'Look? Look? What look?'

'Like a thunderstorm, hovering.'

'You're trying to change the subject. This isn't something you can run away from, Amelia. You wouldn't be able to walk out on them. On me, perhaps. Not on them. They'll arrest you, and they needn't even put a motive to it. You'd be left with nothing to deny, only seeing the look on their bloody faces, and knowing what they were thinking.'

'I'd have my say . . .'

'At the trial, oh yes.'

'Trial? It'd come to that?'

149

'What else am I trying to say, for heaven's sake? After a few months in Holloway, you'd come to trial . . .'

'I could never stand that,' she said decisively.

'And then, perhaps, there'd be discussion in court about your motive. And *then*, in open court, you'd get your chance. They'd claim he dominated you, sent you out . . .'

'You're saying it again!' She was almost in tears with frustration and anger.

'And you'd deny it?'

'Of *course*. At the top of my lungs.'

'And fall right into their trap,' I told her wearily.

'Oh, I'm tired of this. You're talking such nonsense. What trap?'

I'd got round to it at last. I almost sighed myself to my knees. 'They'd have offered you that as the easy way out, and you'd have refused to take it. They'd then say that if you weren't claiming that you killed your husband because of Kendall's domination – because *he* wanted it – then you must have killed him because *you* wanted it yourself.' I waited. 'Amelia?'

She was shaking her head, hardly able to get a word out. 'From you, Richard? You can say such a thing!'

'The only answer would have to be that you were fascinated by Kendall. His arrogance and domination. Perhaps that's what you were looking for. Your husband deferred to you. You want a man who led and controlled.' Such as me, I thought. Standing there, shaking, pleading, and afraid.

'What're you saying?' she whispered.

'They will say you killed your husband for the simple and usual reason – that it was what you wanted. Because you were in love with Kendall.'

I let it hang in the air, mocking us.

She got to her feet abruptly and turned her back to me, staring out of the window. I approached her quietly and put a finger on her shoulder. She shrugged herself free angrily. She was shaking, I could feel in that second, and I hated myself for going on with it.

'Don't you think I've got a right to know?' I asked gently. 'If you saw something in Kendall that you couldn't resist, then maybe I could understand it. Sexual chemistry's a strange thing. If what you really feel for Kendall is what you'd call love, then say it. For me, my dear, just for me.'

She whirled on me so abruptly that I took a pace backwards. Her face was red, her eyes staring, her mouth distorted.

'Love him?' she choked. 'I hated him. With all my heart and soul I hated him! I could not possibly hate a person more . . .'

Then her face crumpled and tears streamed down her cheeks, and she fell into my arms, burying her distress in the breast of my jacket.

I was smiling past her head, my palm spread between her shoulder blades. 'Thank you, my dear,' I whispered. 'Thank you for that. And now, maybe, there's still something I can do.'

After a few moments I eased her away from me. 'They'll be here soon.'

She tossed a hand through her hair, and sniffed. 'What do you want me to do?'

'Can you say that to Merridew? Can you convince him that it's the truth?'

'I can repeat it a hundred times. Shout it from the roof-tops . . .'

'That won't be necessary.'

'It's boiled up inside me, all the time trying not to tell you, Richard.'

'I know.' I smiled at her, but the effort of extracting it had drained me. I swayed where I stood. 'Let me speak to them first. I'll take them into the front room. There's something I've got to try and get across. You'll stay in here?'

She dipped her head without reservation. 'If you say so.'

'That sounds like them now. I'll get out into the hall.'

I didn't look at her again, giving her no chance to retract a word. Perhaps, alone, she'd realise what she'd admitted. I went to meet the invasion.

As I stood in the porch I saw that they'd brought three cars, transport for Merridew and Donaldson, the two outside inspectors, Ken Latchett, and Brason. A policewoman hovered at their shoulders.

I was not pleased to see Brason. He made it more difficult. But I'd come so far now, and had wagered so very heavily. I managed not to meet Brason's eye, not to flinch from him.

'She's in the back room,' I said. 'But I want to talk first. There's something I've got to tell you.'

Donaldson had recognised the Stag, and was in no mood for obstruction. 'Now look here, Patton, I've had about as much as I can take from you.'

I looked past him, and said: 'We'll talk in the front room. I'd advise it.'

Something of the confidence I was now feeling seemed to get across.

'We'll hear what he's got to say,' Merridew decided.

'We know what he's after,' Donaldson claimed, easing his way to the front. 'He's blocking. We've got it all put together, and now he wants to confuse the issue.'

'We'll listen,'decided Merridew. 'There's no hurry. It does no harm to listen.' He nodded to the policewoman, who walked past me towards the back room. I heard her speak to Amelia as the door opened.

I smiled weakly, and flung open the door to the front room, switching on the light. They trooped past me, Ken with a conspiratorial wink, Brason with an uncertain grimace. Then they stood around, no one willing to look for a seat unless Merridew did, and he standing four-square, poised, ready to plunge in quickly if I said anything to upset Donaldson. Brason took up a position by the window, gloomily staring at the streaming night, miserable because he'd already seen me make a fool of myself once, and could see another coming.

'Say it,' said Donaldson. 'Let's get it over and done with.'

'So you've got it put together,' I said, trying for quiet control. I put a shoulder against the mantel, and now felt sufficiently relaxed to fill my pipe. 'A theory you couldn't even work out yourself – you had to rely on an inexperienced constable.' I was aware of a sudden movement by the window but kept my eyes on Donaldson. 'In too much of a hurry, that was your trouble, Chief Inspector.'

'All right, Richard, that's enough.' Merridew had allowed as much as he dared.

Donaldson growled, and tossed his head. I nodded to him, but he didn't take it up.

'But look what you've worked out,' I said. 'Just look, and

don't imagine I wasn't listening while Brason got it off his
chest. There were two absolutely contradictory themes: that
the dead man should've fired two barrels at an intruder, placing
the shotgun carefully against the wall and not even reloading
it . . . and that the intruder should have been able to get close
enough with his – or her – own shotgun, which would have
offered a threat. To cover both, Brason came up with the grand
idea that it would work if his wife'd come to the cottage in the
dark.'

I stopped. I lit my pipe. There was dead silence. I blew smoke
at the ceiling.

'What a load of nonsense,' I said amiably.

Donaldson moved. Merridew clamped a hand on his arm.

'But sir . . .' Donaldson appealed. Merridew said: 'In what
way nonsense, Richard?' And Brason turned sharply, his face
pale. He'd realised that I'd set him up.

'Just look at it. This man, in the cottage, he's sitting and
waiting for trouble. In the dark, with a loaded shotgun at
his side. He hears a sound. What would he do? Creep to
the window and open it, and stick the gun out, more than
likely. And blast away? No shout of: who's there? And *then* she
calls out! What the hell's she been doing out there? Surely she'd
have seen the shadow movement when the window opened –
and would have called out straightaway. But no – he fired two
shots, and then she called out, and he ran and leaned his gun
against the wall. No . . . my mistake. The theory has to have
him slam the window shut after he's fired. So she *still* hasn't
called out.' I considered the bowl of my pipe for a moment,
then looked up with a new idea. 'But perhaps she hadn't got
her wind back, having thrown herself flat on the ground after
the first shot.'

Brason was a rigid shadow by the window, his back to the
room. Merridew coughed. Ken hummed quietly to himself, his
eyes on the ceiling.

'All right,' I said, 'so she hasn't called out, and he'd shut
the window. He dives for his cartridges, but her voice halts
him. How do I know that? Because he didn't get there, to the
cartridges, but instead leaned his gun against the wall. But at
that time he'd have been near the light switch. This was now

a friend outside – his wife. The light worked, Brason showed us that, but it wasn't put on. It would've been very dark. No streetlights there, not even snow at that time to throw back a sky-glow. But he ran around in the dark. How do I know that? Well, I don't. But his wife must have had time to get all that way to the window. I wondered how he wasted all that time. Trying to open the front door, perhaps. But eventually it occurred to him to open the window again and say: "Hello, darling, fancy seeing you." And then her shotgun went through the glass! Lord, what a shock that'd be. But all the same, he must have taken time out to shut *and* latch the window again. We know that, because only his hands touched that latch. And what does he do then? He gives her time to push her gun through the hole and line it up on him. Still in the dark, remember. By that time he's only three feet away, but holding his hands up in front of his face. It hasn't occurred to him to dive sideways into the darkness, or run for his own gun. Oh good Lord, what a botch-up!'

'I'm not having this!' Donaldson roared.

I raised my eyebrows. 'It's your theory. And it includes the peculiar fact that he was shot three feet from the window, and didn't shed a drop of blood till he fell back against the fireplace, eight feet or so away.'

'I did mention that,' said Merridew sadly, forgetting that he hadn't.

I'd waited until then to look directly at Brason. He was quite firm, head up and chin out, and in his eyes a pain that hit me. I looked away quickly. Somebody laughed quietly.

'And all that,' I said, 'completely ignores the fact that there's been no other shotgun turned up, except a rusty old wreck, which couldn't possibly have fired.'

Donaldson was breathing with difficulty. 'And I suppose,' he said heavily, 'you know where to find the gun that killed him.'

'Certainly I do. It's in the forensic lab at HQ. It's the Remington over/under shotgun, which was found leaning against the wall in the cottage. There was only one gun. Why complicate matters by assuming a second one.'

'Come on, Richard,' said Merridew softly. 'What d'you know?'

'Well . . .' I straightened. 'The trouble's always been that we've assumed the fingerprints had to belong to the dead man – and that no intruder could have got in or out. But it doesn't mean anything of the sort. It simply means that the fingerprints belonged to the man who'd just spent a fortnight hiding away in there. Invert it, and assume that the murderer was the one who'd been hiding away there, and that the dead man was his visitor – and it all falls into place.'

There was a light in Merridew's eye. 'You'll have to substantiate that.'

I looked away. The next bit was difficult. 'It all depends on motives, on Amelia Trowbridge's attitude to Clive Kendall, and it's no good oversimplifying it and saying she was in love with him. It was more complex than that. Certainly she was dominated by Kendall. He was too strong a personality for her to handle. He could get her to do anything for him – but she's always insisted it was only related to her job. I couldn't see how it could reach out beyond that and grab hold of her private life. But . . . well, she and I seemed to get on well. I soon realised she saw something in me that reminded her of Kendall. I wasn't too keen on that, but you have to use what you've got. So I came on a bit stronger, trying to get her to reveal whatever emotional tangle she'd got herself into with Kendall. It worked, to some extent. I thought I'd gained her confidence, but I still couldn't get through to the basic truth, though I felt it was there, just out of reach.'

I gazed round cautiously, as though seeking their approval. Ken was no longer humming. Brason was staring at me with disgust.

'So where did you go from there?' asked Donaldson softly. His lip curled. 'We can only gain from your technique.'

I shrugged. 'I needed something that'd help me put on the pressure, and it couldn't simply come from me, as *my* idea. In the end, Brason came up with it. That wonderful theory I've just outlined . . . by heaven, it was just what I needed. I gave her the lot. At first, she just wouldn't accept that she could be arrested, and actually locked up. I had to paint a pretty vivid picture for her. You can see what I was digging for . . .' I looked from face to face, making the effort, though I nearly flinched. Beamed instead. 'Having realised that the dead man could, after all, be Kendall, there was still one great snag. Motive. Why would Trowbridge want to kill Kendall, when he'd seemed to go along with everything his wife had done for him, and quite happily? In the end, she broke down, and told me what I'd guessed – that she'd hated Kendall, and quite bitterly.'

I looked down at the pipe in my fingers. 'All the while she's avoided having to face that admission. How the hell could she admit that she'd worked so hard for the release of a man she'd come to hate? Damn it all, it'd be an admission of failure. But she admitted it to me, because that was the only thing that'd save her – or so I made her believe.'

'God,' whispered Brason.

'And you see how that's cleared the air,' I claimed. 'Certainly, Clive Kendall had brought about a great deal of domination, but that should have ended with his release. But her husband saw it carrying over. He agreed to move into this district, even though it didn't help his job prospects. He helped her to prepare the bungalow for Kendall. He was even with her when she went to look at the cottage. And *he* knew his wife hated Kendall. If she'd been in love with Kendall, he might simply have bowed out, thinking only of her happiness. But he could see this Kendall taking over her life, and nothing coming from it but misery for her. So . . . what was this quiet, ineffectual man to do? There was only one way out. The Kendall his wife had released to destroy them had to die.'

'You're saying . . . that body is Kendall's,' Merridew demanded, 'and that Trowbridge killed him?'

'Exactly that. Trowbridge knew that Kendall would eventually go to the cottage. He'd left a hanging doll at the bungalow to scare him away from there. Meanwhile, Trowbridge went to the cottage and waited. He searched the locality and found himself a shotgun. And waited. His wife, in the meantime, had reported him as missing, because he would not have dared to tell her what he intended. Probably he hadn't expected to have to wait as long as he did.'

Merridew grunted. He was worried about Donaldson.

'That pistol, now . . . it was Kendall's and he'd need that, frightened, and driven from his bungalow. He'd bring it with him to the cottage, where he expected he could hide. And there he'd find . . . well, Trowbridge had taken his wife's car, and it would be there. Kendall would think it meant the wife was there, but I'd suggest he'd be wary, and drew the pistol, and Trowbridge, seeing that, would run and take up the shotgun, and get himself into position. Kendall walked round to the back door. Not locked, you see, because Trowbridge was waiting for his victim. But in spite of the pistol, Trowbridge wouldn't have expected somebody to pop up suddenly with a shotgun. His head would be blown off in a second.'

'You're not tying it up,' Donaldson grunted, disappointed that I was.

'I'm trying to find logical action,' I retorted. 'I don't know what Trowbridge originally intended. Possibly a faked suicide. Why else would he rig the trip-wires? But suicide was way out of the question, the way the hands were destroyed. But then, maybe, he'd think it was just possible he could confuse the identity of the body. His own fingerprints were everywhere, and Kendall had touched nothing. Except the revolver, which Trowbridge would have to take, and return to Kendall's bungalow. For the rest, he simply had to leave the set-up as we found it, door locked at the back and the hole in the window. That hole, he did when he got out of the window, pushing the pistol through the glass. Then he reached through from outside and fastened it. No tricks with fingerprints there, they were *all* his. Then he'd simply drive away.'

'And that's it?' asked Merridew.

'A few minor details to be tied down.'

'Then we'll put out a general trace for Trowbridge.'

'If it's not too late. He'll be convinced we'll take the body as his own, and that we'd suspect Kendall, not his wife. But he'll be far gone by now. Or . . .' I looked from one face to the other, another bright idea bubbling to the surface. 'You could arrest her, and hope his conscience brings him back.'

They stared at me. Donaldson swallowed, but had nothing to say. Ken moved restlessly, and Brason was edging to the door.

'To play safe,' I put in, 'it'd perhaps be best to ask Mrs Trowbridge her opinion of Kendall. Just to make certain this isn't just another of my obstructions.'

157

They filed out into the hall. Merridew closed the door softly behind him. Then I heard their voices in the other room. I heard their voices! I hadn't expected that. Were the walls that thin? It went on too long for the single question I'd urged on them, but I sat very still in the chair by the window. After a few moments I put off the light, then sat in the same chair, waiting for them to leave. The third vehicle, I saw, was Brason's official Allegro.

Then at last there was movement in the hall, and the front door slamming. I stood, and watched them walk down the path, and Amelia wasn't with them. The WPC, I saw, was Marjie Crane. I knew her well, and tried to smile at her, but she met my gaze with white, tense dislike.

When Amelia entered the room I was sitting with my head in my hands. It was still buzzing.

'Richard?'

I lifted my face. 'You heard?'

She nodded. 'Every word.'

Her voice had been so empty and her face so stiff that I looked away quickly. Brason's car was still there, I noticed. As I watched, I saw the glow of an indrawn cigarette.

'I must have a word with Brason,' I told her, and was out of the room before she could say anything. I had to get away from what I'd seen in her eyes.

I slipped into the passenger's seat. Brason glanced at me, then away.

'Sorry about that,' I said.

'You tricked me,' Brason whispered, his eyes on the white knuckles clasping the steering wheel. 'You fed me that theory.'

'I had to have it, son. Who better from than you!'

'They drove away, and not one of them said goodnight.'

'I needed somebody to put forward a solid theory, something I could throw at her.'

'That much,' said Brason, 'was clear.'

'And it couldn't be Ken.'

'Of course not.' Cold, his voice was, toneless.

In his self-absorption, he failed to realise that I had another reason. Later, perhaps, it would occur to him that my own theory gained strength because it followed his very good one, which I'd been able to break down. Psychology, that was, and he'd need to learn how to use it.

'Don't take it to heart,' I said at last.

'I'll have to resign.'

Then I was angry with him. 'Don't be a damn fool. Give yourself time to cool down.'

He glared at me, slapped his palm on the wheel. 'I could tear your theory to pieces – the same way you did mine.'

'So why didn't you?' I smiled, and opened the door. I got out into the rain. 'I think you made a good impression, whatever you might see of it.'

'The revolver!' Brason said savagely. 'The car . . .'

'See what I mean?' Then I slammed the door.

I watched him drive away, then turned back to the house. It was going to be difficult to explain to Amelia, how my hands would have been tied, once they'd arrested her and had her tucked away. She had seemed stiff and hurt.

The front door was closed. I rang the bell, but there was no response. I hammered with the knocker and peered through the letter slot. Then, when I turned away in exasperation, I saw her face at the front window. I gestured, and called her name in appeal, but she was unmoving, simply a white face, drawn with rejection.

It had been necessary to force her into admitting that she'd hated Kendall. I'd not intended she should hate me.

After a while I went to the Stag and drove away. I never recalled the journey home.

12

In the morning I went to the office to clear out my desk, and collect together the accumulated debris of my life. Not early. There had, first, to be the luxury of lying late in bed, and persuading myself I was going to enjoy a life of leisure.

They had cleared all the paperwork from my desk, and taken the trays into Donaldson's room. Ken put his head in, but seemed to remember somewhere else he should be. Then there was the embarrassment of going round to remind everybody about the do at the Carpenter's Arms on Saturday night. I'd hired the upper room for a booze-up, and the invitations had already been accepted with pleasure. But there had not been time, the day before, for the routine round of handshaking. Nobody actually backed out of the party, but all the same there was a coolness. There was also a pain in my chest.

It seemed only manners to put my head into Donaldson's room and invite him, too. Ken was in there with him, and tried to smile, whilst Donaldson put on his expansive manner and said he'd be delighted, because after all a free pint or two was not to be refused lightly, especially when you haven't contributed to the traditional retirement clock.

'Er ... Richard,' he added, 'we can't quite find a logical reason why he'd burn the car, especially where it was done.'

That cost him a lot, I could see by the strain round his mouth.

I shrugged. 'Pity I'm retired. Have you tried asking Brason?'

'I'll do no such thing.'

'Then you've only got to give it a bit more thought. See you Saturday, Ken?'

'What? Oh . . . sure. See you.'

It had been a painful morning. I couldn't get away fast enough. I'd willingly have forgone the pleasure of acquiring another clock, but there was no possibility of withdrawing at that late hour.

For the rest of the week, mainly I stayed home, but never far from a phone. It hadn't rung by the time I left the house for the party, best suit on, and rehearsing in the taxi my Lord-am-I-glad-to-be-out-of-it speech.

At first the whole thing was terrible. The formal presentation was made, Merridew reciting his few sad words. The purchasing committee had been highly original – not a wooden-cased mantel clock, but something very quartzy, guaranteed not to lose a second in ten years. It even showed the year, and some joker had set it at year one. The first year of a glorious retirement.

But of course, after a few pints comfortably absorbed, the atmosphere lightened. Arms became strung across stalwart shoulders, and sentimental rugby songs were sung. Ken, sober still, came to me and said:

'When're you going to tell me, Richard?'

'Tell you what?'

'Why you did it.'

I grinned, and called for another pint. 'Going out with a bang, Ken.'

And he had the grace to smile.

Eventually, clutching my precious clock to my chest, I was escorted to my taxi and sent on my way with roars of alcoholic best wishes.

Sunday was hell. Monday and Tuesday, which should have improved with practice, were worse, and each successive day seemed to contain more hours. On the Wednesday evening Ken came visiting. I welcomed him with a friendly face, though he seemed nervous and repressed. I fetched cans of lager from the fridge and we sat in the untidy kitchen, small talk covering his intentions. But at last:

'It's not going well,' he said. 'Not a trace of him anywhere. It's weird.'

'What did you expect? He had a good start.'

161

'And there's the car.'

'What about it?'

'It just doesn't make sense, Richard, pushing it off the road and setting fire to it.'

'What's the betting Brason could explain it?'

'He's not talking. Probably expects to be slapped down.'

I grimaced. 'Somebody's asked him, then? Surely not Donaldson?'

'No, me. I'm not sure Donaldson's normal – but we'll live with him, somehow.'

I made no comment.

'He's asked for Brason, you know. On transfer to CID.'

I raised my glass, giving myself time to think. 'And he's accepted?'

'He's coming next month. But in the meantime . . .'

'The car?'

He nodded.

'Donaldson's sent you, hasn't he?'

'I wanted to see you. Me.' He looked uncomfortable. 'We've always been friends, and there's something you're keeping from me.'

'Am I? About the car?'

'About the way you treated that woman . . .'

'Drop it, Ken,' I growled. 'I'll talk about the car.'

'Richard . . .'

'The car. There's a reasonable explanation. Trowbridge knew nothing about fingerprints, and everything depended on fingerprints. For all he knew, they might well go stale. He'd have to get things moving. The car was a beacon, Ken.'

'I'll put it to Donaldson.'

'But you've got everything else in hand, I suppose? Description out – fingerprints – Interpol?' I glanced out of the window, wondering what she was doing at that moment. 'And a surveillance on her house?'

He spoke defensively. 'There's always a chance he'll try to contact her.'

'Discreet surveillance?'

'Of course. There's an empty site hut quite near.'

'I noticed it. Tell you what – let her see she's being watched.

Then I might be able to help. God knows I've got nothing better to do.'

'Christ, Richard!' Then he took a look at my face. 'All right. I'll do that . . . if you really want it.'

'I want it.'

He hesitated. 'You've changed.'

'Of course I have. Maybe I'm seeing things from the other side. Have you ever realised, Ken, how much we're told to think? We're shown the law – reams of it. We have to know what's legal and what isn't, and all the shades of it, and what we can expect to prosecute, and whether we can. Well . . . now I'm trying to use my own decisions. It's all very strange. You see things differently. Before – everything was legal or non-legal. Now there's only right and wrong. So much simpler, I find.'

He looked at me doubtfully. Had it sounded pretentious? 'I'll see if I can lay on what you want,' he said, and he reached for his coat.

When he'd left, the house was big and quiet. I waited, and six desolate days later she phoned. I'd been about to decide what might interest me as an evening meal. I dropped an egg on the floor and ran to the phone.

'Richard?'

'Yes. It's me.'

'I must see you. Please.'

'I'll be right round.'

I hung up before she could thank me, in case it should deflect me from my purpose.

13

She seemed to have every light on in the house, as though in welcome, and the door was open before I reached it.

'Come in. Let me have your coat.'

She took my short motoring coat. I was wearing no hat.

'No flashy tie?' she asked, her eyes on my roll-neck sweater.

'I'm retired. Ties are out.'

She looked very worn, I thought, her eyes dull, and not even attending to the tired banter. She moved with less grace and her energy seemed exhausted. I followed her into the kitchen, where she turned quickly and fixed on me a long and determined scrutiny, looking, I thought wryly, for any loss of flesh.

'Have you eaten?' she asked.

'I was about to scramble a couple of eggs when you phoned.'

'We could both do with a hot meal,' she decided.

I did not reply. As she peered, frowning, into her fridge, I prowled the floor, touching surfaces, turning the taps on and off, until she told me to sit down for heaven's sake and let her get on with it. I sat, extended my legs and spread my feet, and put my head back with my eyes closed.

'They're watching the house,' she said suddenly.

I opened one eye. 'That's only to be expected. They're waiting for your husband to contact you.'

She bit her lip. 'And the phone sounds . . . different.'

'That's possible, too. They'd apply for a legal order to tap it.'

'But when's it going to end?'

'It will gradually ease off,' I assured her. 'Better, perhaps, than being in custody. For you, I mean.'

'I'm not sure about that.'

I grunted. 'They'll assume you'll want to help him. As you probably have already.'

She made no reply, just stood watching me.

I went on: 'I've no doubt Donaldson will try to get a positive identification on the body. He'll try to trace Rona Kendall. Some wives can recognise their husband's body, you know. They're not all like you.'

Her eyes widened, searching for a hint of humour in this remark, but I hadn't intended any. 'You know very well that wasn't my husband.'

'Of course it wasn't. It was Kendall. But I can understand you'd want to do what you could for your husband.' I allowed a bit of reproach to creep into my voice. 'I suppose you'd promised?'

She pouted at me. 'Don't be so scornful about promises, Richard.'

'I'm not,' I said sincerely. 'I'm not, my dear.'

'But I suppose it's different for you,' she shot at me.

'I made promises?'

'Oh, not verbally, but all the time, by implication, by gesture, by your tone of voice.'

'Ah!' I stirred. 'Want any help there?'

She shrugged, and changed the subject quickly. She was putting out pork chops. 'Isn't there anything you can do . . . to get them to leave me alone?'

'I'm not a policeman any more.'

'You're so cold. Why did you come, if you don't want to talk to me?'

'I'm having to get used to people not wanting to talk to *me*. Maybe I've grown just a little wary,' I admitted.

'It was the way you went about it,' she declared. Her voice was toneless, but she was searching for reaction.

'I never got a chance to explain that. But it was for you.'

'Please don't explain,' she implored me. 'I don't think I could stand that. I've got frozen peas. How are you at peeling potatoes?'

'My speciality. Every eye carefully dealt with,' I assured her, heaving myself to my feet.

'I've got a potato knife if you want it.'

'No. I prefer an ordinary kitchen knife. Yes, that one'll do.' I picked up a potato and considered it carefully. 'Donaldson's already asked me about the gutted car, and I managed to put him off with a plausible explanation. But he hasn't even realised the significance of the other important details.'

'The last grain of truth?' she asked, peering into the grill.

'Well, yes. Now you come to put it like that.'

She was suspicious of me, I could tell that. 'What,' she asked softly, 'hasn't he realised?'

'The significance of the pistol with the slivers of glass in the bore, the hanging doll, and the rusted old shotgun.'

I flicked out an eye with a dexterous movement of the wrist. She asked me, slipping the pan under the grill: 'And can you really hope he'll come to you and ask?'

'Hardly.'

She was unable to control the tremor in her voice. 'But I thought that was what you wanted – for him to come crawling to you, so that you could explain the last little dribble of detail to him. Being careful not to be too condescending, of course. Then you could close it all up neatly.' She laughed, and there was a hideous note of hysteria in it. 'Your triumph! Patton's last case!'

I paused. The knife was stilled. I stared out of the window into the darkness. 'That's a very attractive idea, but I'm afraid it'll have to remain a dream.'

We were circling each other warily, the effort to maintain a casual tone putting sharp edges to it.

'But you've already succeeded, Richard. You've supplied Donaldson with the truth – the details can't really matter.'

What a statement! Details were the picture, frame and all. 'I've supplied him with a reasonably good case. Knowing him, it'll seem to him to be the absolute truth. But it isn't, you know. Not till every action makes sense. Will that be enough potatoes?'

'It depends how hungry you are.'

'Any afters?'

She smiled. 'No.'

'Then I'll do a couple more.'

'Why are you teasing me?' she burst out. 'You keep suggesting that there could be more, more, more . . .'

'Perhaps I've got a tidy mind. You, at least, ought to appreciate that.'

'Oh I do, I do,' she told me angrily, clattering the grill pan. She cursed softly at a splash of hot fat on her wrist.

'Run it under the cold water.' I advised solicitously, turning on the tap.

She stood close to me, her hair falling over her eyes. I could smell her hair, and yearned to touch the soft down beneath it at the nape of her neck.

'There,' I said. 'Is that better?'

She dabbed her wrist dry with a towel. 'And what is fidgeting around inside that mind of yours, Richard?' she asked, smiling now. But her eyes were on my hands, clasping the knife, nervously fingering it.

'Donaldson and Merridew seemed satisfied with the explanation I gave them. I just wish I was.'

'You're not satisfied with your own explanation?'

'I put it together in a hurry. I knew the body was Kendall's, and I thought up a theory that'd save you from arrest, however shaky the logic was. But I ask you! Your husband waiting there, in the cottage . . . and searching out a shotgun! Does it *sound* reasonable?'

She was staring at me in exasperation. 'But it was *your* theory. What's the matter with you, for heaven's sake?'

'It was a sloppy way for your husband to go about it, that's all. There was no guarantee that Kendall would go to the cottage, and surely no certainty of being able to find a weapon to confront him with.'

'But Kendall did go to the cottage. Why argue with fact?'

'Yes.' I pointed the knife at her. 'That fact can't be disputed. Kendall went there – his body was found there.'

She glanced at me, then slid it past my head. 'Reach me that saucepan, will you?'

I did so. She turned away from me to the cooker.

'If you'd care to put out the place mats, Richard . . . they're in the drawer with the cutlery.'

I did it. The mats had dog portraits on them. I'd never owned a dog. The reaches of the moors called out for walking boots and a dog, and Amelia at my side.

At last she spoke softly. 'Where is all this talk getting you?'

'Simplicity. Logic. And maybe the truth of something . . .' For a moment that thought clouded everything. Then I shook my head. 'Coral Clayton's father took his own life, you know, because of the thoughts he couldn't live with. I'm beginning to understand that.'

She looked at me with distress. 'Do you think I could help?'

'Perhaps. By listening, and telling me where I'm wrong.'

'Then say it, and I'll try.'

But then, not giving my words the attention they deserved, she returned her concentration to her two saucepans.

'It's all a matter of logical behaviour,' I explained. 'I can't see your husband relying on the threat of a hanging doll, and waiting nearly a fortnight for Kendall to put in an appearance. Long before then it would've looked as though it wasn't going to work.'

'Does everything have to be logical?' she asked, flicking hair out of her eyes. 'Life's not like that.'

'Acceptable, at least. And I can't accept that your husband would have been able to search out a shotgun, in a district he didn't know. Do you agree?'

'Oh, if you like. I don't see what you're trying to say.'

'Only that I worked up a theory that doesn't really work.'

'Theories!' she said scornfully.

I stared bleakly ahead. 'But it *is* logical for your husband to have taken the pistol to the cottage. After all, he went with you to Kendall's bungalow, to help you clean it, so he had a chance of getting his hands on the pistol, before Kendall even came out of prison.'

'You're sure the pistol did go to the cottage?'

'It's got glass fragments in the bore, and that links neatly with the hole in the window pane. You do get my point, though! It's more logical for Kendall to have gone to the cottage and waited that length of time. He'd be afraid, and hiding. It's more logical that Kendall should be the one to be able to hunt out a shotgun, because he was born in that district. And, because he found it necessary to obtain a shotgun, we can assume he didn't find his pistol where he'd hidden it in his bungalow. Which would be logical, if it'd already been taken away from there. I can't get round that logic.'

'So why try?' she asked, lifting out the chops with a fork. 'Why upset yourself about it?'

'Because it takes us right back to where we started, with Kendall waiting at the cottage, and your husband as the intruder. And that makes complete nonsense of the way I managed to explain the fingerprints.'

'Then there doesn't seem to be much point in talking about it,' she said in a reasonable tone.

'But perhaps there is. It was a nice twist, explaining how the body could be Kendall's, and the fingerprints somebody else's, but unfortunately it does require Kendall to have been the intruder. It's much more sensible the other way round, him waiting there and scared. I mean, it'd explain the trip wires and the cans. It'd explain the revolver with the glass bits in its bore. And it'd explain how somebody could've got close enough to kill Kendall, because a pistol will hide in a pocket, when a shotgun can't be hidden. In that way, a visit would appear to be friendly, so that Kendall would logically run to unlock the front door from inside, find it was wedged solid, and then fling open the window. And that explains the glass in the pistol bore, the hole in the window, and the glass fragments on the ground where we found them. Damn it, everything falls into place.'

But it didn't get past the big snag that the fingerprints in the cottage had not been Kendall's. I eyed her, wondering if she'd pounce on that.

'The hand could've been wearing a glove,' I suggested. 'It was cold, after all, though there hadn't been any snow. From that moment – window wide open, the shotgun already placed where he couldn't reach it, Kendall would've been helpless.'

She put the plate in front of me. 'I got some beer in for you, Richard. Lager. Would you like that?'

'Please.' Wondering when she'd got it.

I watched her moving about the kitchen, opening the can and carefully pouring it into the glass. Her hands were unsteady.

'Aren't you drinking?'

'No,' she said.

169

'I don't like to drink alone.'

'You're my guest, Richard. Do stop criticising.'

I raised my eyebrows, took the glass from her, and watched as she took her seat opposite me. For a couple of minutes we ate silently. I waited, wondering whether she would be able to let it alone. But no . . .

'This is just talk, isn't it?' she asked, the vertical fence lines again between her eyes.

'Not really.'

'But he wasn't shot with a pistol. And you know that the fingerprints weren't his.'

'I've already explained that you shouldn't assume that the fingerprints in the cottage had to belong to the man who was found dead there.'

She was silent. She glanced up once from her plate, but my eyes were on her, and hers were full of pain.

'Then what are you getting at?' she asked at last, a meekness in her voice.

'Something I hate to think about,' I admitted. 'Let me come at it from another direction. I'd found the hanging doll and the rusted shotgun at Kendall's bungalow, and I'd made my mind up what they had to mean. I didn't like the answer very much. But then, suddenly, I came across another shocking idea. *Kendall wasn't shot with the pistol.* You said that yourself. Then – why not? He was shot with a shotgun, when a pistol must have been available, purely and simply to hide his identity. Brason suggested it, but I couldn't see it at the time, because I was surrounded by a whole cottage full of fingerprints. Yet now . . . as I said, it's a fallacy to assume those fingerprints belonged to the dead man. *Now* d'you see what I'm getting at? If there's to be any reliance at all on logic, then I have to come down to one really shocking fact. Kendall must have been killed with the shotgun to hide his identity, and that was done by two separate and deliberate barrels being discharged into his face. One after the other! When the first must have had him down, the second shot couldn't have been more than cold and vicious destruction.'

She choked, and clattered from the table, rushed to the sink, and drew herself a glass of water. I got to my feet and went to her. Her face was red, her cheeks shining. I took her elbows and led her back to the table.

To apologise would have seemed insincere. 'Such revolting details when you're eating,' I murmured.

She gulped. Her voice was hoarse. 'You seem to be able to pick your moments.'

'Are you all right now?'

She nodded. I resumed my seat. 'We'll say no more about it,' I assured her.

Then suddenly she flared at me. 'To say that now! Go on with it, for God's sake!' Then she was more calm, controlling herself as abruptly as her anger had broken free. 'You came here, and you were determined to say it. You seem to have forgotten I might want something from you.'

I flinched at that, and took a sip of lager, merely to moisten my lips. I couldn't taste it. 'Perhaps I'm doing both at the same time,' I suggested. 'Let me say it?' I watched for her nod, which was minimal. 'All right, then. I'll tell you about the doll and the shotgun. That couldn't upset you.'

She smiled weakly.

'The doll, you see, had been hanged by a noose from one of Kendall's trees. The significant thing about it was that it had a little beard. When Kendall was arrested, he had a beard, and he kept it until he went into Long Lartin. Then he shaved it off. You know that, and I know that, but the Clayton brothers didn't know it.'

'The Clayton brothers . . . that would be the uncles . . .'

'Of little Coral Clayton, the girl Kendall assaulted.' I was being cautiously delicate. 'Yes, it was their brother who later took his own life, and Coral's mother, Gabby Clayton, who had a nervous breakdown. So you can see, they had a score to settle with Kendall, and I can assure you it gave us a bit of a headache. But if Kendall had shown himself in this town, and was killed, then the Claytons would've been the first we'd go to. If there were no alibis around, then they, or one of them, would've been in serious trouble.'

'I can see that.'

She was very subdued, I thought, very quiet. Surely I couldn't be wrong about her!

'And Ted Clayton's a painter and decorator, and the beard was the bristles of a paintbrush. I was round to see Ted Clayton like a shot.'

'Pouncing.'

'If you like. But the doll was only a warning, after all. Kendall was simply not around. No more than that. But later, after we had a body – which might or might not have been Kendall's – a rusty old shotgun turned up. It was tied to a tree, and pointing right at a drawing in white emulsion paint on the back window. You see the emphasis there? The drawing was done with a paintbrush – Ted Clayton again. Emulsion paint – Ted Clayton. But if this was simply a threat, then in practice it proved their innocence. It'd been rigged after the murder. Who'd threaten after the event? I didn't think either of them was clever enough to rig it as a blind. And yet . . .'

I paused, gathering my thoughts.

'Yes?' She was leaning forward tensely.

'Think what those two warnings said. No . . . shouted out. One, that they were set up by the Claytons. Two, that they proved their innocence. But there was something strange about the second warning. The rusted shotgun was from the cottage. I'd never be able to prove it, but I was certain. And the drawing on the window was too expressive – a psychological throwback to the actual murder. It was probably not even recognised by the artist as being a dead giveaway. But that was what it was. It meant that the two warnings were rigged by the murderer, and intended to prove the innocence of the Clayton brothers.'

'Who'd be in danger of arrest if Kendall died?' she asked innocently.

'Exactly. And everything that happened regarding the actual murder was also slanted in the direction of the Claytons' innocence. Why was Kendall scared away from the bungalow to a remote cottage? Because the Claytons knew the bungalow, but had no reason to know the cottage. And what happened regarding the identification of the body?

'Look at it. What we found was a body that could have been Kendall's, or could have been your husband's. If it *had* been Kendall's, then again the Claytons might have been in danger. But we accepted that the body was your husband's, and once again the danger to the Claytons drifted away.' I sighed. It was almost a groan. 'And the reason we accepted the body as your husband's was because of the shaving-soap bowl – and because there were no hands and no face.'

'Richard!'

I set my jaw. Merridew had always flinched when I did that. She smiled encouragingly. 'Don't you see what I'm getting at? It was planned ... planned ... planned.' I emphasised each repetition with a pound of my fist on the table. 'Everything was to keep the Claytons in the clear, which meant the mutilation was also planned. Even if it meant it had to be done with a bloody meat axe, if that was all there was.'

She gave a small whimper, fists tight against her teeth to control it. 'Oh please ... You don't have to ...'

'I have to,' I said savagely. 'It's nearly driven me insane. I couldn't help but conclude that the shotgun was used because it happened to be there, to kill him, and then deliberately – the second shot carefully aimed – to make sure those hands and the face were smashed to a pulp.'

'Stop it!' she screamed.

'And all to protect the bloody Claytons,' I said heavily. 'As with the car.'

She peered at me between her fingers. 'The car?'

'It had been planned,' I sighed, 'some time before. But the death took place in an isolated cottage. The body could have remained undiscovered for a couple of months, three, more. That wouldn't do. By that time the doll and gun threats – all the carefully worked out protection for the Claytons – would've gone stale. The police had to be alerted ... to something out of the ordinary. So the car was fired. It triggered something. It got me interested, and then I couldn't leave it alone. God help me, I couldn't drop it, and I've agonised over that shotgun ...'

She didn't understand what she could do to help me. Her lips moved, but no words came.

'The fact that the mutilation was planned!' I hammered the table with my fist.

She whispered: 'Can you be so sure of that?'

I shook my head, not so much to dispel the uncertainty as the vision. 'There was the shaving-soap bowl, you see,

the one thing that gave us the identity fitting the fingerprints.'

'I thought you were grateful for that.'

'Oh, I was. Until I looked inside.'

'Was there something inside that upset you?'

'Yes, it upset me. There was nothing inside.' Then I managed
a weak smile. My face creaked. 'You know, I doubt there're
many women who ever see the inside of a shaving-soap bowl.
The cake of soap wears down in the same way every time.
A dip in the middle, which gets deeper, like a crater, the
further down you use it. That would be a difficult thing to
match, if you wanted to fake it, without actually scrubbing
out the soap with a shaving brush. Maybe, to play safe, it'd
be better to leave no soap in at all, rather than a small amount
that might look wrong. But why should a man clear out the
last vestige of soap? It'd mean washing it out. Well, all right,
I know. I've done it myself. I keep cuff-links and oddments in
an old shaving bowl. But I don't wash one out, and then tuck it
away into the back corner of a bathroom cupboard. It was the
point that finally told me the truth. A woman had done that. It
had to be a woman who'd want to protect the Claytons from
trouble, and the only one I could think might fit was Gabby
Clayton, who was called that because she talked so much –
but whose proper name could well have been Amelia.'

I squinted at her. Her eyes were huge.

'You didn't dare to allow the fingerprint men into your house,
Amelia – this house. They wouldn't have had to search very
far for one odd print that matched the ones in the cottage. It
would've been filled with them. Or they might've found one
of mine! That was because the ones in the cottage were yours,
weren't they? It was the reason you had to produce *something*
for me, with a set of prints on, and you chose a shaving bowl.' I
reached over and touched her wrist. 'What was your husband's
name, Amelia?'

'It was Arthur,' she said softly, but quite steadily.

'Arthur Clayton.' I nodded. 'That was another thing. Try as I
might, I couldn't get you to use his name. It was always: my
husband. On the missing person report he was called Henry,
which I suppose was his second name. But you couldn't speak

of him as Jack or Fred, or even Henry. My wife was Vera. In my mind she *has* to be Vera. So you played safe, and called him nothing.'

She was silent. I inclined my head. 'Not so gabby, are we, now? But I suppose, things have happened . . .'

'Don't play with me, Richard. Like a cat with a mouse.'

I drew back. I'd meant it kindly. 'There's no missing husband. You are Gabby Clayton – I suppose Amelia Clayton – the mother of Coral. Maiden name, I wouldn't be surprised, Trowbridge.'

'How long have you known this?'

'I've lost count of time,' I admitted.

'Then there was really no point in working so hard to discover that I hated Kendall,' she said bitterly.

'I had to be sure.'

'For your wonderful theory? For *this* theory?'

'For me,' I protested.

'But you had to pretend, and lead me on.'

'No,' I said violently. 'I had to persuade them, Merridew and Donaldson. It didn't matter how. I just had to keep you free, and let them go rushing off on a false trail. Do you think I could help in the arrest of whoever killed Kendall – even if it hadn't been you? But it *was* you. I used every bloody dirty trick that I could, just on the chance that I'd hear the truth. I didn't really want to hear it, because it involved that ghastly planning to mutilate . . .'

My eyes pleaded. But she wasn't sufficiently prepared to offer me what I wanted. She had to deal with it in her own way.

'I'd promised, you see,' she said. Her voice was calm, now, resigned. 'My husband had a breakdown. He was in a mental hospital. I was trying to hold on to my reason, but he was very ill. He made me promise that Kendall wouldn't be allowed to go on living. Oh, I promised. I thought it would help him, but he'd handed it over to me. That night he got hold of something and swallowed it, and died. It about finished me. But I remembered what I'd promised, and it was for myself, too. And that helped me.'

'But to sustain it. To hate him so intensely for so long!'

She gave a flat, humourless laugh. 'It's ironical, when you

175

think about it. I joined the Prisoners' Aid people, just to see if it was possible to get him out. How could I kill him in there? But there seemed absolutely no hope of a release at all. His sort of criminal, you know, they're loathed even amongst the worst of the prisoners. But I had to try, and in trying I got to know him very well, and he himself managed to keep my hatred alive. Without that, of course, I couldn't have gone through with it.'

'You're a remarkable woman.'

'To a man it might seem so. I don't know. But any woman would understand.'

'But would they be able to plan it so completely? There he was, believing he'd completely dominated you with his personality, when all the time you were leading him on, offering to prepare his bungalow for him, moving into his own district, and pretending *that* was for him, discovering for him the details of his cottage . . .'

She smiled, softening a memory. 'He was really a most abject coward,' she said. 'All that forceful masculinity he threw around, and at the first threat – the doll – he ran for the cottage.'

'Would it take much courage to rape . . .' I stopped.

She grimaced. 'The pain has gone, Richard. It's all right. I can live with it, now. Now, I can.'

'So you'd got him running to the cottage. It was what you wanted, because that place couldn't have been known by the Claytons.'

'I'd found Kendall's pistol in the bungalow, when I was tidying it. I like to get into all the corners . . .'

'I'd realised that.'

'So I'd found it. I thought to myself that dear Ted and Foster – now don't you smile like that! – they'd been so kind to me. Anything at all I could do to keep them safe . . . well, I thought Kendall really ought to die by his own gun. Kind of poetic, you see. And that suggested a faked suicide. And he'd fortified himself away so well that it fitted. I visited him there twice, you know, the second time to do it . . . the first to check that it could be done.'

'That *what* could be done? That you could mutilate . . .'

She reached out quickly, and this time managed to capture my hand. She kept hold of it, the pressure telling me something.

'Now, now . . . Richard, let me explain. A substitution had been my original idea . . . but I didn't know anything about fingerprints and things like that. I'd rather thought I'd set fire to the cottage, but then that nice sergeant of yours . . .'

'Ken Latchett.'

'Yes. Well, I'd gone to report a missing husband, and sillylike, laughing because I was nervous, I asked him if he'd need my husband's fingerprints, and he smiled and said no, because they wouldn't be on file – is that the correct phrase? – unless he'd been in prison. And Kendall had. So then I knew I wasn't going to be able to fake the body, and I couldn't see that the cottage would burn, either. I didn't plan anything so nasty as . . . what you said. I simply changed the plan to pretending it was suicide.'

I blew out my breath in one long, continuing sigh. 'Go on.'

'I went there. The pistol was in my pocket, as you said. He saw me coming. He didn't shoot at me, or anything like that, just tried to open the front door, but it'd jammed.'

'I wasn't so far out, then.'

'And by the time he'd flung the window open I was beside it with the pistol in my hand – and that was when it went through the pane. He couldn't believe it. He backed away, and I climbed through, and then suddenly I knew I couldn't *do* it. I couldn't be sure of actually killing him – and I couldn't stand the thought of leaving a wounded man, not even him. So I made him back away, playing for time, to think.'

I nodded. 'And?'

'He'd leaned the shotgun against the wall. I didn't see what he intended to do before it was too late. He snatched the shotgun up, but his hand slipped or something. It half fell, and half twisted, and suddenly it fired – right up into his face.'

Her mouth was distorted. She whipped a handkerchief from her sleeve and dabbed at her lips. Her eyes seemed deep-set above it, and dark.

'He . . . went down, Richard. No sound . . . but he was writhing. I could *feel* his scream, feel it tingling right through me, but there was no sound. His hands . . . his fingers . . . were clutched into his face, and he didn't die. I was screaming all the time, and it went on and on. There was only the shotgun. The pistol – somehow I'd put it into my pocket – it seemed so useless and paltry, and he wasn't . . . still. There was only the shotgun. I picked it up, but I couldn't see how to make it work. I kept pointing it and pulling the trigger . . . but he threshed around, and I couldn't help him. Then suddenly it did fire. I didn't know what I'd done, but it worked.' She drew a deep, shuddering breath. 'And at the time it was pointed at his face. But – he stopped moving, and he was at last still, and I was on my knees, sobbing . . .'

I was round the table in rapid strides, took her shoulders in two rock-firm hands, and bent close to her head.

'It's all right,' I whispered. 'Don't say any more.'

She shook her head.

'Shall I guess for you?' I offered. 'You'd be there, and you couldn't say how long. And there was panic . . . but not for long, knowing you. And . . . you realised you'd got to go on with what you'd planned. But nothing was like you'd planned at all.'

She looked at me with swimming eyes. 'I wanted to run. The window was open, and it would've been so easy. But . . . there was that hole in the window pane, so I couldn't make it look like suicide, and there was Kendall, and he couldn't have done that to himself. And I'd really made it worse for Foster and Ted. So I sat on that seat and tried to steady myself, and think. And gradually I realised that I could use my original idea after all, because now I could really claim him as my missing husband, because he hadn't *got* any fingerprints.'

I smiled, trying to encourage her, because it was costing her a lot to say it. 'But he had. He'd got 'em all over the cottage. But that wouldn't stop you. The world champion cleaner-upper. All you'd got to do was a complete clean-up of anywhere his hands might have touched, and the substitution of your own.'

'It took me five hours, Richard. Five hours, in there with him.'

'You were very thorough. We never found any print but the one set – your own. And that . . .' I snapped my fingers in realisation. 'That was how you came to find the rusty old shotgun.'

'I was doing the soap –'

'The soap!' I cried. 'I knew there was something strange about that. The last time he'd touched it hadn't been to wash himself, but to open a new packet . . . what a coincidence!'

She smiled weakly at my enthusiasm, and went on as she'd started. 'I was doing the soap, my hands under the tap, squeezing one piece into a new one to leave a good impression, when that thumping started. It gave me quite a turn, so I went to see what it was . . . and there was the gun . . . and it gave me an idea . . .'

'Clever you. And all the time . . .' I stopped. Abruptly she'd buried her face in her hands. I spoke in anguish. 'Amelia! I didn't realise. You must have been so very upset. More than that – the drawing on Kendall's bungalow window! It took you . . . how long to recover? A day? Two days?'

She lifted her face, drawing her fingers down her lips. 'I thought I'd never stop shaking. But after two days I knew I'd got to get things moving. I was keyed up, with my story all prepared. It was all true, you know, everything relating to Kendall, and everything I told you about Arthur. There, you see, I can use his name now without thinking. Everything, of course, except that he hadn't left me recently. He left me seven years ago. So, I had to face it, and quickly. I could have simply left the car, anywhere, but I needed something more dramatic, something to attract police attention. So I set fire to it.'

'And got me.'

'I suppose it could've been worse.' A hint of a smile.

'But I wasn't really what you wanted, was I? You wanted somebody who'd start a nationwide search for Kendall, as the murderer of your husband. But I didn't get going on it, and you fumbled the identification.'

'It was so *silly*!' she said. 'There I was, and I'd gone through so much, and when it came to it – the one thing that I needed to make it all so reasonable – and I just couldn't do it. I couldn't claim that the . . . the creature on that trolley was my husband. It would've been a complete betrayal of Arthur's memory. Is that very stupid, Richard?'

'Not stupid at all.' Stupid, perhaps, to ask such a question.

She straightened her shoulders, and laid her knife and fork neatly on her empty plate, staring at it, not believing that it could be empty.

'I've got some tinned rice pudding, if you'd like me to warm it up,' she suggested dully.

I nearly broke into laughter. 'Not really.'

'Then what do you want?' she burst out. 'What now?'

I waited for her to look up. I tried to be very serious.

'What I really wanted was for you to marry me, Amelia, though of course that wouldn't have been possible if they'd put you away.' I held up my hand. She'd been half on her feet. 'No, let me say this. You've made things very difficult, you know. Legally, we can get married at any time. But Donaldson's busy hunting for a live husband, and how would it look . . .' I grinned. 'Imagine . . . Donaldson as best man!'

That broke her up. It was some time before I could edge another word in.

'No – seriously,' I said. 'They wouldn't even let you leave the district without somebody, somewhere, keeping an eye on you. And there're the Clayton brothers. Your lovely brothers-in-law. How long before *they* see the truth?' I had a thought, abruptly shocked. 'I suppose they know nothing about it all?'

She shook her head. 'And I've been terrified of meeting either of them by accident. But now . . . d'you think they'd say a word?'

'I'd kill 'em both first. All right . . . so it's a matter of time. In the end, the case'll be put in the pending run, and the watch for your husband will be closed down. But I can't wait for that.' I reached for her hand. 'Can you?'

Her eyes shining, she shook her head. 'But what can we do?'

'I've laid something on,' I said briskly. And after all, I'd used Ken! I got up from the table, spurred by the thought, standing and looking out of the window. 'Already I've suggested it to Ken Latchett. I'll appoint myself official watcher of Amelia Trowbridge. My sense of duty carries me on into retirement! I've at last found something I really want to do with it. I, personally, will make sure that Amelia Trowbridge, of this parish, is kept under close surveillance. They'll love that. It'll save three men on duty per day, and the cost of the phone tap and the letter interception.'

'And how d'you propose to manage that?' she asked to my back. I heard her chair scrape back.

'You'll pack up what you'll need, and you'll move in with me. How much closer could you be watched? The beauty of it is that nobody will be surprised. That bastard Patton's capable of anything, my dear, and it'll just be another of my underhanded tricks.' I turned quickly from the window. 'What d'you say to that?'

'We'd be living in sin,' she pointed out. As old-fashioned as me!

'So we would. For a while.'

'I've always wanted to live in sin. It's so romantic.'

I turned and glanced out at the site hut. 'The news will already be on its way, but I don't see why they should be in on everything.'

I twitched the blind cord, and watched the slats overlap, and felt her arms come round my waist from behind, her head against my shoulder.

'I'll help you pack,' I offered. Turned to her. Saw beyond her eyes at last. 'Later.'

Here lies Nancy Frail

Jonathan Ross

1

Nancy Frail had been a whore of a sort.

Whoredom is a business. It has a high level of profitability, the overheads being minimal. Its practice needs only a man with a lust and the money to gratify it. And the right kind of woman. Some of them are craftswomen at their trade: others have all the response and skill of a badly stuffed pillow.

There are independent whores who set a high price on their exclusiveness. There are whores organized by pimps and hired out like saddle-sore hacking ponies.

Whores range from the unbelievably beautiful to the horribly grotesque; from those pandering to the needs of a small exclusive circle of professional or industrial executives to the gutter trollops who consider a pull at a meths bottle on a building site sufficient reward.

Nancy Frail was beautiful and talented and sold herself on the smaller market. She was as far removed from the acned whore a drunken man used tepid and gruesome against the back wall of a pub urinal as the London Hilton is from a shoddy transport café off the Edgeware Road. Both provided a service at different levels of comfort and personal attention.

If she ever rationalized her whoredom she thought of herself as a courtesan. Less slavish than a mistress, more selective than a prostitute, she chose her lovers, requiring total discretion and gallantry in lovemaking.

There were historical precedents for considering herself superior to a tart but the difference was illusory, founded as it was only on her cultured selectivity and her chosen surroundings.

She had latterly been on intimate terms with Detective Inspector David Alistair Lingard, apparently forswearing the harlotry neither had discussed in other than euphemisms. He, like many another man who had loved a whore, believed he could cage and tame her compulsive concupiscence by marriage. Whether he would have succeeded would now never be known.

For Nancy Frail was dead.

She had been discovered at dawn in a weedy, web-strung lane near the railway tracks. Situated at the edge of town, it was only a few minutes' drive from the flat she occupied with her seven cats.

She lay stiff and livid, slumped in the driver's seat of her own white Mini Cooper. The railway linesman who found her had been too shaken by her horrible deadness to do more than stumble to a telephone kiosk and dial 999 with a trembling finger.

A constable despatched to the scene in his Panda car had opened the door and examined the body without touching it. Recognizing the dead woman, he had possessed sufficient service and nous to call Detective Chief Inspector Rogers. Rogers, not normally approachable on non-criminous deaths the dark side of his coffee and marmaladed toast, was Lingard's immediate superior and likely to want to do something about it. And Nancy Frail being found dead in a car was reason enough.

When he arrived, there remained a smoking mist in the air. The bushes, wet and cobwebbed, loomed dimly, their leaves hanging lack-lustre. Busybodying gnats jigged around Rogers' head and he trod wry-faced on liquefying toadstools in the mud. He was very much a cement-footpath man with no particular liking for the country. It was nice that it should be there but he didn't want to involve himself in it.

The car's white enamel was dulled and the shattered windscreen silvered with a fine mist. It had been there some considerable time. Rogers, standing away from it with his fists jammed in the pockets of his raincoat, regarded it sombrely, seeing the vehicle and body as a whole. He noted the freshly damaged wheel arch and the two football-sized holes in the windscreen.

While he observed and evaluated, Detective Sergeant Coltart arrived and joined him. Rogers nodded, not speaking, not removing his steady regard from the car. The sergeant stood slightly behind him and waited. They were following a well rehearsed drill.

To Rogers, the morning was of the *couleur de merde*. Fine strands of web, drifting across his swarthy unshaved face, were an irritation. His dark brown eyes were gritty and tired and pouched from too little sleep. His stomach rumbled its emptiness and he shivered at the early morning chill. He was often unreasonable enough to wonder why the hell people never died during his office hours. Not yet thirty-two, he felt a clapped-out debauchee with none of the pleasures of recollection. He had brooded on his non-ambience with his wife through the night just dead and buried. And had drunk too many undiluted whiskies to help the brooding along. At that moment she occupied a decidedly jaundiced corner of his mind. A small vein pulsed in his temple and the alcohol's hangover hammered rivets in the sutures of his skull. His hat sat square and uncompromising on his forehead. This alone warned Coltart not to walk inadvertently on the shadow of his senior's distemper.

Rogers held a pipe between his teeth, as much a part of himself as his vermiform appendix. Clouds of smoke drifted above the two men.

He had never seen Nancy Frail as a living, breathing, warm-blooded woman and had disapproved heavily of Lingard's infatuation, riding his displeasure lightly only because it had been essentially Lingard's business. Officially, she could not be classified as notorious and thus within the ambit of Police Regulations. Nor, in the absence of a conviction, could she be judged of ill-fame and unfitted to be a policeman's wife.

Lingard was a man with a promising future and, had she lived, had she married him, Nancy Frail might well have reached the *éminence bleue* and tortured respectability of a Chief Constable's wife.

Beneath the stiff mask of death she was still beautiful, her amber hair loose over her shoulders. A mole on one cheekbone was clear on the blanched flesh. The unpainted mouth, no longer sweet, was open. A dry tongue showed between lustreless teeth. Her eyes were secret behind closed lids, her face tilted upwards at the quilted PVC of the roof.

The fawn woollen dress she wore was creased. She carried no jewellery other than a watch clipped on one thin wrist. Rogers checked it against his own. It was showing the correct time. There were a few fragments of glass from the windscreen caught in the folds of her dress. He noted others on the floor to one side of her.

He cleared his throat. He thought of what had been until a short while ago the exciting mechanism of shared orgasms and which was now so much cooling muscle and tissue and blood. But he dismissed his contemplation of dead emotions. Their ashes were for others to warm themselves by. There remained only death; a solitary experience, rarely other than obscene. Rogers was easily irritated by people who romanticized it.

'I don't like it,' he said to the big sergeant with him. At that particular moment it was unlikely he would have approved of the Creator Himself.

Coltart waited. What Rogers didn't like would be made clear enough in his own time. To ask was to invite rasping sarcasm and to expose one's ignorance of the obvious.

Rogers' formidable eyebrows were scowling. 'So,' he grumbled, 'we've got trouble. The car's been involved in a collision and she's dead.' He was sardonic. 'A simple matter of finding out what she's doing here and what she died of.' He leaned into the car and poked about beneath the dead woman's legs and in the parcels shelf. 'No tablet container. No weapon.' He slid a flat hand between the body and the back of the seat and withdrew it, examining the unmarked palm and pulling a face. 'No evidence that one was used. No apparent injuries from the accident. Christ! You can't have a crack-up like this without *someone* being hurt.'

'And not in this lane,' Coltart rumbled. 'There isn't room.'

'No, there isn't. Anyway, most of the broken glass seems to be missing.' Rogers spread his fingers and placed them delicately over the top of the smooth hair, rotating the head back and forth. 'The neck doesn't appear to be broken.'

Coltart nodded his head in agreement. He was a meaty man

with small green eyes and tea-leaf freckles on an oatmeal skin. His fists were terrifyingly large; pale uncured hams covered with a sandy fuzz. A slow and ponderous thinker, his single-minded tenacity made him a better thief-catcher than most of his more brilliant colleagues. The trousers and jacket he wore fell in creases and folds like the skin of an elephant's hindquarters. His suits were loose-fitting, seemingly on the premise that he would grow even bigger and fill them before they became shiny and threadbare. He was a happy man in that his sexual appetites ran sluggishly and not very deep.

He peered intently at the upturned face. 'There's a distinct bluishness about her,' he said.

'Yes, there is. It could be asphyxiation of some kind.' Rogers put a finger under the chin and lifted the head up further. The throat was smooth and unmarked. 'Not by ligature. Nor, I'm sure, by manual strangulation.' He shook his head. 'The tongue would be out anyway.' He was speaking around the stem of his reeking pipe. 'Everything about this worries me and I'm struggling. There's nothing logical about it. For a start, she's sitting on the buckle of her safety belt. Assuming a suicide, she would at least do it in comfort. They always do. And why? Have we had a hit and run accident reported?'

Coltart looked dubious and pulled his bottom lip out between finger and thumb. 'I don't know. But it'd be a silly reason for suicide. Unless, perhaps, she killed someone.'

'Check on it, will you.' He scratched his bristles. He was always blue-chinned first thing in the morning. 'Her clothes don't look right . . . too untidy. As if they've been put on in a hurry.'

'All of which could mean nothing,' Coltart pointed out. He was a non-smoker and chewed on things. In this instance, a stalk of grass. One day, Rogers thought, this habit would result in his swallowing the worm of a parasite and his harbouring thereafter a fluke in his liver. 'You're not thinking it's murder?'

'Not particularly. Only trying to fit the picture into the fact of either suicide or accidental death.' He pushed back the cuff of his shirt sleeve and read the time on the stainless steel watch nestling in the black wool of his thick wrist. Its purchase had been a calculated extravagance at a time when he hadn't been able to afford it. That was Rogers. 'Go back to the van,' he said, 'and tell Control to call out Doctor Rees. I want him to examine her *in situ* before he starts his carving. After you've arranged for the coroner to be told, get some screens and the photographer up here. The nosy bastards with nothing better to do will soon be herding.' He tapped a fingernail on the door pillar of the car. 'I want this dried out and dusted for fingerprints. And don't forget to check with Traffic Branch for an accident.'

'Inspector Lingard?' Coltart's face was expressionless.

Rogers didn't hesitate. 'No. It wouldn't help. Later perhaps when we've tidied up.'

With Coltart at the van doing things, Rogers peered again into the car, not touching anything, his fists neutralized in his pockets. Idle hands touched things without knowing and an investigator's fingerprint found at the scene was an embarrassment. To an officer of junior rank it meant also a flea in his ear. Apart from underlining ineptness, thoughtless handling obliterated other marks and dislodged fibres and hairs. Opening the door on the passenger side, he took a closer, more sustained look, his jutting nose with its wide nostrils sniffing up information, his brain tabulating and filing the minutiae of the dead woman in her metal coffin. Layered beneath the fleshy smell of death he believed he could identify the elusiveness of perfumed soap. He noted the slim curved fingers with the unpolished nails, the long legs pressed primly together; the tan leather shoes resting on the rubber matting of the floor of the car. The skirt of the dress was rucked and folded between her buttocks and the seat.

In the ignition switch was a key with a St Christopher medallion fob. He stretched an arm over her lap and turned it. The needle of the fuel gauge flickered to show the tank was a quarter full.

On the parcels shelf was an RAC Continental Guide, a packet with six Gauloise cigarettes in it, a self-charging torch and a black plastic wallet. Opening the wallet, he checked its contents: a three-year driver's licence in the name of Nancy Elizabeth Dominis, the surname being crossed through and FRAIL printed in ballpoint ink above it; a cover note for the car, index number AGL 145B in the name of Frail and expiring the month following, a test certificate issued by a local garage and an RAC membership card. None of which was anything for Rogers to get excited about although the change of name on the driving licence interested him.

The ashtray beneath the fascia was stuffed with Gauloise cigarette stubs and grey ash. Most of the stubs were stained with a tangerine lipstick. There were no matchsticks.

A fleece-lined car coat and her handbag were on the rear seat. Rogers unsnapped the bag and examined its contents without touching them with more than a fingertip. They were a butane gas lighter with a lizard-skin binding, a fragrant handkerchief, a bunch of five keys, a wallet containing banknotes and postage stamps, letters with a local postmark, a tiny phial of *L'Air du Temps* perfume, a tangerine-coloured lipstick in a gilt case and an enamelled compact.

The seat which the dead woman occupied was a clear four inches behind the passenger seat. He checked the adjustment, finding it at full extension. He grasped one of the ankles and unflexed the leg. The shoe on it only just reached the clutch pedal.

Transferring his attention to the outside of the car, he examined the damaged wheel housing. The exposed metal was bright and shiny, not yet oxidized by exposure, although streaked in places with a stone-coloured powder. The glass remaining in the windscreen frame was striated and clouded. A few glass diamonds from it had been trodden into the mud beneath the driver's door. There was a confusion of unidentifiable footprints around the car.

Rogers searched the index of his memory for details of what Lingard had told him of the dead woman before his infatuation chopped short the confidences. Out came the card of total recall.

Nancy Frail. Aged twenty-five years and interviewed by Lingard only four months previously in connection with the movements of one of her lovers, Harry Quint. Rogers remembered her morals being defended by Lingard with more force-fulness than Rogers, at the time, thought warranted by the short acquaintance. She lived alone with seven cats and no dirt of public scandal had ever smeared her reputation. Rogers had been incredulous and nonunderstanding when Lingard explained that each time she took a new lover she had saved a stray cat from destruction at the local vet's compound. To him, it had seemed a convoluted expression of a guilt complex.

That Lingard proposed marrying her was a fact he had to accept. But Lingard was touchy with his senior about it, obviously regretting confiding in him prior to his infatuation. He had kept the two apart and Rogers was glad he had. No moral snob himself, he yet could not stomach the seeming coldbloodedness of her paid orgasms with the seven men, repeated he assumed at biologically necessary intervals. Her saving of the cats from a saucer of strychnine-dosed milk went some way to soften his inflexibility, but it was not enough to appease Lingard. He sensed Rogers' disapproval and a coolness kept the two colleagues apart outside their hours of duty.

When he had committed the external details of her death to his memory, Rogers removed a slim green notebook from a pocket, unclipped a pen, thumbed it and exposed the ball point and began writing. He filled three pages with his close-packed and large italic scrawl. Occasionally he grimaced at the burning harshness of his pipe. When it made a bubbling noise he held the hot bowl between finger and thumb and flicked the liquid from the mouthpiece. It was a filthy habit, he thought. He couldn't think of a vice that wasn't.

While he was sketching the position of the body on a page of the notebook, a pillar-box red MG bounced over the ruts of the lane towards him. It was an old car and blue smoke came from its tail end as if it were propelled by a badly mixed charge of gunpowder. It was also a very dirty car. Mud and dead flies masked the glass of its headlamps and fan-shaped segments of clarity showed on the dirty windscreen.

The driver was a woman. A special kind of woman with orange eyes, clear and precise, her straight brown hair swinging carelessly against the creamy flesh of her cheeks. She wore no mascara or eyeliner, only the pale ghost of an apricot lipstick. As she slid gracefully from the car, Rogers turned towards her.

She was dressed in a white military-style raincoat with a tobacco-brown silk neckscarf beneath her chin. She looked well-scrubbed and superlatively healthy. After pulling out a leather case from the rear of the MG, she slammed the door shut, shaking the car. She was Bridget Hunter, Doctor of Medicine and Graduate in Morbid Pathology: unmarried and assistant to Doctor Archibald Rees, MA, MB, B. Chir., FRC Path., DMJ, Senior Consultant Pathologist, whose eminence and distinction she would one day parallel should she remain unmarried.

Rogers raised his eyebrows and then smiled. Perhaps the morning might become of the *couleur de rose* after all.

'Archie still in bed, Bridget?' he asked.

She glanced at the body in the car and then returned her gaze to Rogers. 'He was guest speaker at the Medico-legal Society's old chums reunion last night. He left me on call. I think he'll probably want to die this morning.' She rarely smiled but her eyes creased with sober humour. 'You'll make do with me? I'd just arrived for an early post mortem when your call came.' She gave him a steady appraisal. 'When I heard you were in trouble I ran all the way.'

'It was sweet of you,' he said. 'I don't know anyone I'd rather have slice me up the middle.'

They knew each other well. Once they had clashed violently, bruisingly, on the issue of sex. Rogers had retreated, trammelled partly by his almost paranoical adherence to Police Discipline Regulations, equating such intercourse with discreditable conduct. He had always regretted it for Bridget burned with a rare fire. He later recognized himself as a pusillanimous fool and in his present discontent with his wife the arrogantly discarded opportunity rankled.

Time having unstarched his stuffed shirt attitude he had rationalised his approach to the regulations defining discreditable conduct, deciding that unadvertised, unboasted adultery need cause no heartburning to an authority that would rather not know that it was happening.

He was not unique in his problems. Few detectives were able to approach the investigation of a crime in a state of euphoric content; not complicated by intrusive worries about either women, their health, their wives, mortgages or income tax. Or all the lot lumped together into a black ball of disgruntlement.

Rogers'alter ego had been kept in check by the dictates of his profession and disarmed by his wife's needs. Now they were mutually bored with the sameness of their responses, needing a domestic and marital explosion to bring them together again. It was nothing that hadn't happened to a million other marriages. He and Joanne were at the beginning of a period of tight-lipped, unforgiving silence over a stupid disagreement. Her brother – in Rogers' opinion the most dreary bore outside the political scene – was occupying the guest room. And had been since the death of his mother with whom he had lived his cossetted bachelor selfishness. Now the house revolved round his overly prolonged grief and his sister was no person to douse its sickly flame or to suggest he should find other lodgings. His indolence and greed over food grated on Rogers' never very thick-skinned sensibilities and he found crime enquiries to occupy the time he would normally have spent at home.

So he was in a mood to ignore regulations and work off his black frustrations in the only way he knew. And that meant with the first bedworthy and willing woman that caught his eye. Anyway, he assured himself, he had had a triple gutful of the same routine of sex. There was never any significant variation he and Joanne could be bothered with and both were conscious of its staleness. So he regarded Bridget with something more than his usual neutered professionalism.

She placed her case on the ground and studied the body, a frown line between her eyebrows. Both were silent. She touched the pad of a forefinger on the flesh under the jawbone, then opened an eyelid. The sightless fixed iris was the colour of a bloomed sloe and the eye, remaining open, gave her features a satirical cast. Bridget closed it gently. When she opened the other she frowned and tapped the eyeball with her fingernail. 'A contact lens, George,' she said. Lifting the other eyelid again, she pursed her lips. 'But this one's missing.'

'Could she wear only one? You know, like a monocle?'

She was doubtful. 'Could be. But I've never heard of it. That's out of my field.'

'Can they be lost easily?'

'Not easily.' She removed a glove and slipped the lens out from beneath the lid. 'It's easy now only because the

194

flesh is relaxed. But I doubt if they'd fall out under normal conditions.'

Looking at the tiny plastic lens on the palm of her hand, he said, 'It isn't going to be a pushover to find, is it?' He waved a hand at the mud around the car, then took the lens from her, sealing it in a glassine envelope.

'You're not happy, George,' she observed. He was standing close behind her. Engrossed in her contemplation of sudden death, his body's nearness was nothing.

'Are you?' he countered. This near, she smelled of formalin and a hyacinth fragrance. It raised the hair on the back of his neck.

Leaning forward, she sniffed near the open lips. 'She's the right colour for asphyxiation, George.' She looked puzzled. 'In the absence of external signs I'd normally plump for a heart failure.'

'In the middle of nowhere and in a damaged car? The facts don't fit, Bridget.' But it was a factor and he worried at it.

She replaced her rubber glove and put a finger in the mouth, sniffing again. 'I thought so. There's a distinct smell of brandy.'

'Take a swab of it, will you. At least it indicates she was out drinking some time before she died.'

After she had wiped the inside of the mouth with a blob of cottonwool on a stick and sealed it in a glass tube, she put her hand inside the dress of the dead woman, feeling the now flaccid breasts, forlorn like punctured bladders. Then she lifted one of the arms a few inches. 'At a wild guess she's been dead six to eight hours. Rigor mortis is well established in the upper trunk.'

'Check on her neck, Bridget,' Rogers suggested. 'She might have broken it in the accident.'

She was as deft and tactile in what she did as an osteopath, her fingertips feeling beneath the stiff flesh of the neck, reading the bone joints and flexor muscles.

'No,' she said at last. 'Nothing like that.' She raised her eyebrows. 'You've no other information than what's here?'

'None. I'm even guessing about the accident she had. But I'm thinking on the same lines as you. That it's asphyxiation of some kind. And having thought that, I've to accept it might be a criminal act. And I do that because I cannot believe she came up here alone.'

'You don't think it might be suicide?'

'What with? There's nothing to indicate she's taken a poison.'

'And she certainly hasn't any of the symptoms,' she conceded. 'But I won't really know until I've examined her thoroughly.'

'You know now why I've a general niggle on me that it's not right.' He looked down at Bridget's adequate breasts pushing out the stuff of her raincoat and suddenly wanted to make love to her. The mere wanting did something to his sombre mood.

She lifted a camera from her case, adjusted the lens turret and took a series of colour photographs of the body. While Rogers watched she spoke her comments on the condition of the body into a small battery-operated tape recorder.

None of these refinements were for the police. Rogers would be required by the courts to produce black and white photographs; despite the undeniable fact that black and white was an anachronism in a multi-hued world. But black and white it had been since photographs were originally admitted as evidence and so it would continue. The photographs would need to be supported by solemn testimony that they had not been fiendishly altered in any way and by handwritten notes made at the time. Rogers had often wondered if it was all right using a ballpoint pen and not a goose quill. He had once, in his youthful inexperience, used a tape recorder when interviewing a suspect. At the trial the defending counsel had, because there was no other defence, accused him of doing things to the tape that would have baffled an engineer with a degree in electronics.

Rogers made a sudden decision. 'I'm going to treat this as murder, Bridget, until it's proved otherwise. Will you check her for wounds or bruising before she's removed? I'll have her out while you're here and when the screens arrive.' He looked irritably at the small knot of curious idlers who were gathering like vultures around a kill and held at the entrance to the lane by the guarding constable.

On Coltart's return with a newly arrived photographer and

two searchers, Rogers growled his criticism of their tardiness. It meant nothing. They would never arrive soon enough for his approval. The searchers were trained to find the evidential equivalent of needles in haystacks and to find them expeditiously and without fuss. They carried a stack of hessian-covered screens between them.

Coltart nodded briefly to Bridget. Not offhandedly. Not warmly either. He disapproved of women doctors, women anything; believing they should stay aproned in kitchens or knitting at home. On the other hand, career women didn't like him either, sensing his Victorian disapproval.

Coltart rarely wasted words. 'No accident reported,' he told Rogers.

'No hit and run?'

'No. Hospitals checked, garages being done now. I've put a couple of our men searching the roads for fresh glass.'

Rogers was neither surprised nor particularly disappointed at the lack of information. In his experience, useful evidence came only from the expenditure of time and sweat.

It was after nine now and the pale autumn sun had fired the dying leaves to yellow and dispersed much of the mist. With the screens in position, their metal legs pushed into the earth, one of the searchers laid a sheet of shiny black polythene on the ground. From a varnished wooden box, Coltart took out a bundle of transparent plastic gloves and handed a pair to each of his helpers.

At a nod from Rogers they lifted and manoeuvred the stiff-limbed body from the car. It folded in their grasp and sagged like a water-filled rubber dummy as they placed it face upwards on the polythene.

Bridget Hunter stooped over it, fingering the clothing. She lifted the dress above the thighs, examining them, depressing the skin gently, feeling for warmth. She stiffened, twisting her face up to speak to Rogers. 'The briefs, George,' she said, perplexity in her voice.

He hinged his knees and looked. They were white briefs and freshly laundered and appeared no different from those he had seen on other occasions. 'There's something special about them?'

'They're on back to front.'

'That would matter? I mean, it's not so necessary a requirement as it would be for a man.'

She was doubtful. 'I suppose a woman could if she dressed in the dark or if she was in a hurry. Understandable but unusual. Nevertheless, while some briefs do not, these do have a front and back.' She ran a finger down a leg. 'And the stockings. Laddered and twisted.'

'That too could happen if she dressed in a hurry?'

'The laddering? A cheap pair might.' She felt the material of them. 'These aren't. They've been roughly handled.' She pulled off a shoe. 'And the heel of this one hasn't been pulled up properly.'

'So I see,' he said, frowning. 'It adds to my unhappiness. There's something so damned wrong about all this and yet I can't put my finger on what it is. It confirms me in not going overboard for suicide. You're really telling me she was dressed after she died. And if she was, her being naked in a car on a cold night – and somehow I can't imagine it – doesn't make sense. And *if* it happened, why should someone go to the trouble of dressing her?' He scowled. 'Or was she dressed somewhere else and brought here?'

Bridget had been examining the surface of the body while he talked. 'No injuries, George, or bruising either. Until I've got her on the table I can't take it further.'

'Will you do the post mortem straight away? I'm fumbling in the dark until I know the cause of death.' He signalled to Coltart who covered the body with another sheet of polythene.

Bridget stripped her hands of the rubber gloves and replaced them in the bag. 'You'll be joining me at the mortuary?'

'Of course. I'll have her moved when she's been docketed and itemized.' He allowed his eyes to show his interest in her body and she was aware of it.

'I haven't breakfasted so allow me an hour.' She snapped shut the bag, not giving his interest any encouragement. She was serving notice on him that this time he was going to have to work hard at it and make all the running.

She left him with a cheerful wave of her hand, her scarlet

car belching out blue smoke, and he turned back to the contemplation of the job before him. The truth was, he admitted to himself, he wanted it to be suicide or an accidental death: an uncomplicated death with its issue as disposable as a paper handkerchief. Murder was an unwelcomed challenge. Each a showpiece demonstration of the investigating officer's competence or lack of it. A successful investigation never demonstrated more than the obvious. An unsolved murder, on the other hand, diminished a man's professional standing. For someone to clear it later, adventitiously or not, was a humiliation not easy to live with. And obtruding into the foreground of Rogers' consciousness was the pressing need to resolve his own personal problems.

While he waited impatiently for the photographer to complete his finicky adjustments and interminable readings of his exposure meter, he absent-mindedly stuffed tobacco into his pipe and used several matches to fire it properly. When he heard the deep rumble of a powerful vehicle entering the lane he recognized trouble like the sighting of an approaching storm cloud and he walked to meet it.

The open Bentley, a gleaming dark green with a polished brass radiator shell, had a long strapped-down bonnet with chromium tubes sprouting from it. Its driver, white and haggard-eyed, his blond hair disordered by the wind of his passage, braked the car to a halt. He alighted slowly as if unwilling to meet the inevitable. He was coatless and wore a modish dog-tooth check suit with a high-collared shirt and a maroon knitted tie.

Rogers lengthened his stride towards him, waving him to stop. When he reached him he put a restraining hand flat on the man's chest. 'No, David,' he said, his expression wooden. 'It's no good. She's dead.'

Lingard's mouth gaped and he collapsed with suddenly boneless legs on to the rubber mat of the car's running board. 'They ... they told me at the station,' he jerked out from his bloodless lips. 'They ... you ...' He stopped, shook his head as if to clear it and looked up at Rogers. His blue eyes were damp with what Rogers feared to be the prelude to weeping.

'I was going to tell you later.' Rogers felt an irrational guilt and not knowing why he should, was annoyed. He was having difficulty in drawing air through the hard-packed tobacco in his pipe. He opened a smoker's pocket knife, selected a cigar-piercer and stabbed it in the bowl. Then he lit the tobacco and puffed fiercely. The sight of another's grief was always an embarrassment to him. A man's particularly so. He talked quickly, hoping to stave off the brimming over of tears.

'Go home, David,' he said. 'Take some time off. There's nothing here for you.'

Lingard shuddered and wagged his head. 'How was it done?' He wasn't reciprocating Rogers' friendliness.

'I don't know that anything was done. She was found dead in her car. With no indication of how she died. Nothing to show how she got here; whether she drove herself or was driven.' He added carefully, 'It could be suicide, David . . .' He stopped as Lingard glared at him but held his regard until the younger man's eyes fell. '. . . it could be natural causes. So don't jump the gun. Bridget . . .' He halted. Mention of the pathologist would provoke a picture in Lingard's mind of the post mortem examination with its attendant cutting and disembowelling. He would have seen too many in the past to suffer any illusions that it wouldn't take place.

'I want to know what happened,' Lingard persisted. 'And find out who did it.'

'Apart from her dying I don't know that anything *has* happened.'

Lingard's voice rose. 'Then why are you here?'

'I'm here because nobody can be completely satisfied, David. You know that as well as I . . .'

'I don't know anything.' He stood and faced Rogers, his narrow cheeks bloodless, his eyes wild. He took a small ivory box from a waistcoat pocket and opened it with shaking fingers. He pinched snuff from it and inhaled deeply, brown grains falling on his lapels. His usual elegant aplomb couldn't live with grief. He looked boyish and vulnerable. Rogers' own troubles shrank

200

to nothing beside the enormity of the younger man's sorrow. 'I want to see her,' he insisted. 'To know for myself.'

'It won't do you any good.' Rogers' face was sharp-planed and stern. 'I know you've been hit hard, David,' he said in softer tones, 'but you're not to interfere. That's an order. You can't touch this job. If,' he added carefully, 'there *is* a job. You're emotionally involved for a start.'

Lingard yelled, 'Of course I'm emotionally involved! How did you think I'd be? Laughing my head off! I was going to marry her.' His features were distorted, his expression fierce. In the background the few spectators, their attention attracted by his raised voice, looked at him curiously.

He suddenly pushed past Rogers and strode to the concealing screens. Behind him, Rogers waved a hand at Coltart and the photographer, telling them to move away. He waited several minutes, relighting his pipe and puffing smoke thoughtfully. Then he followed Lingard into the screened area.

He found him crouched by the side of the body. He had uncovered the face and was staring numbly at it, his eyelids red-rimmed. He held one of her hands in his own. With the other he flapped away worrying gnats. Not from his face but from hers.

Rogers waited silently, his expression pitying.

Then Lingard, as if suddenly conscious of his presence, said, 'Her hair.'

'What about it, David? Is it something I should know?'

'She never wore it loose.' He was speaking to himself rather than to Rogers and there was an unutterable sadness in his voice. 'Only in bed.'

'How normally?'

Lingard had difficulty in getting the words out from between his stiff lips. 'Piled up, Grecian style. Sometimes in a chignon . . . with a ribbon thing. She never went out like this.' He turned his face towards Rogers, suddenly accusing. 'She was murdered!'

'Look at her again, David,' Rogers said tersely, 'and tell me how. Because I don't know. Nor Bridget either.'

'She's blue.' He smoothed a knuckle on the cold cheek.

'Which could mean anything. Or nothing.'

'But you're treating it as murder.'

Rogers hesitated. 'Only as a precautionary measure. You know that's a standard drill.' He asked gently, 'When did you last see her, David?'

Lingard was surprised, his eyes jerking. 'Yesterday. Yesterday afternoon.' The misery of recollection twisted his mouth.

'You know nothing of her movements last night?'

He shook his head dumbly. Then his mood changed again to anger. 'No. But I'll find out.'

Rogers was sharp. 'No you won't. That's my job.'

'Is it? Is it?' Lingard stood, his blond hair disordered, his tie pulled out from behind the waistcoat. 'Well, I'm making it mine as well! When I get the bastard I'll . . .' He checked the wild words, sucking back the saliva on his lips. 'Never mind,' he ended abruptly. He pushed his tie back into place and shouldered past the grim-visaged Rogers, rocking a canvas screen as he blundered through the narrow opening.

After a while, Rogers heard the Bentley's engine cough on a viciously applied accelerator pedal, then catch and thrash its pistons at full throttle. When he emerged from the screening he saw the tail of the big car bouncing and swivelling in the mud and the departing Lingard being saluted by the constable guarding the lane's entrance.

Where the Bentley had stood were deeply scored tyre marks and the torn halves of a square of laminated plastic. There was no need for Rogers to pick them up to recognize the remains of Lingard's warrant card.

He said, 'Stupid sod,' in a remote voice to nobody in particular. As an afterthought he went to the van and unhooked the radio handset, calling Control and ordering a guard to be put on the door of the dead woman's flat. He nearly added that Lingard in particular was to be denied access but thought better of it. He couldn't believe the elegant detective could be that kind of a bloody fool.

Then he dictated a message to be passed to the Chief Constable.

Woman, Nancy Elizabeth Frail, found dead in car in unnamed lane off Bourne End at 7.15 a.m. Cause of death unknown. Pathologist

examined at scene. Car appears involved in accident. Coroner
informed. Precautionary drill for possible murder. Post mortem
follows. Have authorized press release. Report first available
opportunity. Rogers.

He called Coltart over to him and showed him the contact
lens. 'Put the searchers on looking for the twin of this,' he
instructed, 'in the immediate area of the car. Call the laboratory
and ask them to run a complete check on the exterior and
interior of the car. I want every particle of dust from it, every
hair and fibre.'

Before he left, he sat in the driver's seat of the car and
operated the foot controls, finding the reach a comfortable
one for his long legs.

2

The constable waiting in the porch of Nancy Frail's flat was an incongruity in the quiet thoroughfare in which knobbed, arthritic trees discarded their yellow leaves gently, almost apologetically, on to deserted footpaths. To Rogers, braking his car outside the tall Edwardian building, it seemed that nobody living in Queen Anne's Road could possibly make much more noise than that needed to call in a cat from its airing. It was all so eminently dignified and withdrawn from contemporary vulgarity.

He joined the constable in the small jungle of potted geraniums almost filling the porch, their dying scent cloying in the October air. Four tiny brass frames containing white cards and flanked by bell pushes were attached to the door stile. One read *Miss N. E. Frail, No.1* in stylish steelplate script.

The constable saluted and said, 'All correct, sir. Mr Lingard's just left.'

'Left?' Rogers stared blankly at the constable. 'He's been here?'

'Yes, sir. He was here when I arrived a few minutes ago.'

Rogers, badly jolted, swallowed his bile. So Lingard had been that kind of a bloody fool. He cursed himself for his unthinking confidence in his deputy's obedience. Anger against him soured his stomach. He said, 'Did Mr Lingard take anything away with him?'

'No, sir. Not that I saw.' Rogers' anger was difficult to hide and the constable wondered what the hell.

'Not that it matters,' Rogers assured him with the best grace he could muster. 'I just wondered.' But it mattered a lot and he

204

hoped he hadn't made a serious error in not putting a guard on the flat earlier.

Inside he found a white door with the figure 1 painted on it. It was ajar and there was a fresh scar in the wood near the lock to show why. The lock was a flimsy one needing no more, Rogers judged, than a wet loofah to force it. He pushed the door further open with the toe of his shoe. Carpeted steps led to a short passage and into a spacious living-room. The curtains were drawn and he switched on the lights.

It was a sage-green and gold room with hopsack panelled walls and a vast expanse of fitted white carpeting. His first impression was of a superfluity of pulpy airskin-covered settees and chairs and green drum-shaded reading lamps On shelves, on occasional tables and in niches were figurines and statuettes of cats modelled in glass, ceramics, wood and enamel.

Hearing a soft bumping noise, he opened a door and found himself in a kitchen. In it were seven cats. Real flesh and blood cats, each wearing a blue collar with a silver disc hanging beneath its chin. On the floor were dishes and on a working top three empty cat food tins. There was a smell of meat in the air. That they had been fed went some way to mollifying Rogers' anger with Lingard. He hoped it had been his only purpose in visiting the flat.

He made a hurried survey of the bedroom. Its rank voluptuousness made him swallow. The headboard of the huge unslept-in bed was quilted in white satin and richly encrusted in gilt scrolls. There were heavy rugs making islands of fur on the carpeting. Gold fabrics hung against the white walls. A large mirror dominated one wall and was so angled that it provided an obvious *opéra charnel* for any couple using the bed.

It was a bedroom designed for making love in rather than for sleeping. He wondered if Lingard had used it, savouring his own fornication in the mirror. Then he rejected his own naïveté, knowing there could be no doubt he had.

The bathroom leading from it complemented the bedroom with its feminine luxury. The huge pink bath with its gold-plated mixer tap took up most of the floor space. But it left enough room for more rugs, glass shelves bearing soaps and jars of crystals and another full-length mirror.

Rogers looked in it, seeing himself in an odd, different way; infected had he known it by the sensuality of his surroundings. The flesh of his face was Spanish-swarthy and drawn tight over the cheekbones. His eyes were a warm brown that could darken with anger to a frozen black. The nose, wedge-shaped and thrusting out from the sharp-planed features, possessed an arrogance redeemed only partly by the humorous mouth beneath it. Neither sentimentality nor credulity had moulded its structure. Cynicism had. He was a hard man with little tolerance for another's weaknesses. Burly without being lumpy, he carried himself with the smoothness of a man owning to an unshakable confidence. He dressed soberly and well, rarely wearing any suit but a grey worsted: any shirt but a white one. His ties ranged through a muted spectrum from quiet red to modest green. He needed no colourful plumage to emphasize his basic attraction. It was all there in the man himself. Women liked him, usually for the wrong reasons; first being attracted to his even white teeth and the close-knit black hair growing thick on his neck and behind his ears.

To his credit he never thought much of his own looks, his only acknowledgement of them being his conscious use of the authority and power they carried as a tool of his profession.

He returned to the living-room, feeling the vacuum of quietness, the forlornness that invaded a room on the death of its occupant. Even the cats, he thought, looked orphaned. He promised himself he would do something about them.

A rosewood bureau stood in a recess and he opened it. The interior was a disorder of papers pulled out from the rear compartments of the desk. Someone – he knew it must be Lingard – had searched it and his expression grew flinty, his lips thinner. Sorting through the jumble of documents, he put aside a bank paying-in book, a plastic folder containing bank statements, bank receipts relating to the purchase and lodgement of $8\,3/8$ per cent income unit shares, a desk diary (he noted that the preceding day's space had not been completed) and a bundle of correspondence. He snapped open a leather spectacle case. On its inner lid was a label; *James Hacker, FBOA,*

FSMC with a local address and telephone number. It contained a pair of spectacles with bifocal lenses.

A cream and brown telephone handset stood on a table near the bureau. By its side was a mechanical index. Rogers put the tip of his forefinger on the tab marked L and pressed, springing open the gilt metal cover. He read the short list of names on the exposed card and found what he looked for: L(David) followed by his personal and office telephone numbers. He put the index with the other articles for later examination.

A thought striking him, he returned to the kitchen and picked up one of the cats, a fat-faced tabby with unblinking green eyes. The disc under its chin was engraved Rodney with a date. Under the throat of a ginger tom was the name Waldo, also with a date. Not all the cats were so amenable to handling and he suffered a number of scratches in finding them to be named Philip, Jimmy, Andrew and Harry. There was no cat named David. But the name Harry nudged a ready recollection.

He retrieved the mechanical index and dabbed his fingertip at Q. Harry Quint was there, discreetly but definitely recorded as Q (Harry) with his well remembered telephone number. Rogers knew Quint to be a compulsive lecher. He had, on a previous occasion, endeavoured to justify (Rogers never knew how seriously) his sexual activities on the grounds of his having been bitten in the scrotum by an Indonesian warble fly, *Chrysomyia macellaria*; acquiring his ineradicable goatishness as a result.

Rogers was going to enjoy meeting Quint again although he doubted the ex-colonial Resident Councillor would reciprocate the feeling. He thought of Quint's wife, Judith, with her treacle-brown eyes and mellifluous voice that had so nearly charmed him into her bed.

He looked at his watch. Bridget, rubbered and talced, would be waiting his arrival at the mortuary. As he left the flat, so he started to worry about Lingard. Unless he could find him and hammer some sense into him, there was the matter of his contemptuous discarding of his warrant card to report to the Chief Constable. For all his anger, this was a step Rogers wished to avoid taking.

3

'You can't mean it!' Rogers stared at Bridget, his eyebrows down, his face expressing an emotion between relief and incredulity, still unable to believe a murder case had just flown out through the mortuary window.

'I do,' she assured him. 'There's no room for doubt. It's just a plain ol' ornery coronary occlusion.' She was cool and competent in her green gown draped with a red plastic apron, her glossy hair confined in a surgeon's linen cap. She was mopping blood with a small sponge from the inside of the heart she had dissected out on the marble bench before her.

Rogers, doing his caged lion act of pacing to and fro, puffed furiously at his pipe. It was his only defence against the raw stench of the disembowelment and dismemberment of a human body.

'You mean a thrombosis?' he said.

'I mean just that, George. A thrombus blocking the coronary. Have a look at it.'

She put a rubbered finger on the pea-sized black blood clot in the exposed tube of the artery, moving aside and allowing him to peer at it. 'Such a tiny thing to bring someone's life to an end.'

'Not so small as a cancer cell,' he said. As much as looking at the blocked artery, he was regarding her bloodied fingers, thinking incongruously and perversely of their use in the act of love.

'But preferable. She wouldn't have known what hit her.'

'It doesn't make sense. It can't be as simple as that.'

Bridget frowned and tapped the blade of her scalpel on the

marble. There was a slight chill in her voice. 'Obviously you aren't satisfied, George. Would you be happier if Archie had a look?' Her orange eyes held his steadily.

He halted his renewed pacing and looked surprised. 'Of course I damned well wouldn't. If you say it's a thrombosis, then it's a thrombosis. I'm just not happy about its cause.' His frustration was obvious. Had he been able to believe it as a simple natural death he would have been happy. 'I mean, she's a young and apparently healthy woman. Not even a fatty. And dying of a coronary thrombosis doesn't explain away her being in a godforsaken lane with a damaged car; her having been dressed after she died.'

'She had to die somewhere, George.'

'Did she? Well, tell me what causes a thrombosis.'

'Offhand, the list runs pretty wild. Old age, over-eating and over-drinking, high blood pressure, advanced syphilis.' She was cutting along a large artery in the heart and mentally searching back on the mnemonics of her early medical studies. 'Chronic nephritis, gout, plain worry and bad luck.' She looked pointedly at his pipe. 'Also the excessive use of tobacco.'

'Leave my addiction alone,' he growled. 'It costs me £14,000 a ton.' They laughed together. 'Still, I doubt if any of those apply to her. Is there anything else?'

'You could find out whether she was taking an oral contraceptive. There have,' she said, 'been some disquieting reports of the pill's side effects. The formation of thrombi in the blood, for instance. Some of the pills have a much too high proportion of the hormone oestrogen in them.'

'Would it be traceable in the body?'

'I'm sure it would but it's a laboratory job. We haven't that sort of equipment.'

He nodded at the dead woman. 'Is there anything else that might support it in the meantime?'

'Nothing I've seen. Bloating from fluid retention?' She shook her head. 'Obviously not. Depression and headaches? You'll have to ask her doctor or look in her medicine cabinet. And even assuming she was on the pill, it doesn't have to be the answer.'

'Is there any other drug that might cause clotting?'

'If there is, I don't know of it.' She quirked her lips. 'Shall you and I spend the evening together with a copy of *The British Pharmacopoeia* and find out?'

He smiled. 'Leave the book in your office and I'd be interested.' When she made no reply, he said, 'I think I'll use the Home Office laboratory on this if you'll bottle up the viscera for me. I just can't accept this was an unassisted happening.'

Bridget had cut out a wedge of heart muscle complete with the artery and its fatal clot and was manoeuvring it into a glass jar. 'I'm inclined to be with you on this, George. She was physically what my veterinarian brother would call a good doer.' She stoppered the jar and put it in a rack. Then she elbowed a tap on and held her hands beneath the water, cleaning her gloves. 'I can see you're anxious to be done. Do you want the usual swabs?'

'Please,' he said. 'I'd be particularly interested in knowing whether she entertained a lover last night.'

'Call in my office later and I'll let you have a copy of my report. Also some facts about oral contraceptives you might find interesting.'

He was anxious to go. He still had Lingard on his mind. But he found the few seconds necessary to brush the back of Bridget's neck with his lips and feel pleased that she didn't shrug him off.

The Chief Constable's office was a dark panelled room with closed windows and a humming air conditioner dissipating tobacco smoke to form stratus clouds beneath the lofty ceiling. Anigoni's portrait of the Queen occupied a prominent place. Propped in one corner of the room was a cased shotgun and a bag of golf clubs.

James Huggett sat at an oak desk, hemmed in by filing trays, a *Who's Who* and a Kelly's *Handbook to the Titled, Landed and Official Classes*; green leather framed portraits of his wife in hunting gear and his son in a barrister's wig and gown, an unfolded copy of *The Times* and a rack of old pipes with saliva-bleached mouthpieces.

His hair was sandy, wiry and cut too short. The spare flesh

of his autocratic face was a newly scrubbed pink. His nose was bulbous and disfigured by a pitted floridness. He powdered it to camouflage its resemblance to a pale strawberry. It was an unearned blemish for he drank nothing stronger than dry sherry. He was known to the more irreverent junior ranks as Old Strawberry Nose, a scurrility undreamed of by him in his lofty isolation. A close-clipped military moustache gave his expression a bonus of a Sandhurst authority. The neat Donegal tweed suit he wore was completely appropriate for blasting at driven game birds.

A black and white spaniel lay on a rug and lifted a lip at Rogers, displaying yellow teeth in a token snarl before going back to sleep.

To Rogers, Huggett was more a politician than a policeman. As he needed to be to survive in his world of trimmed service estimates, a zealous Home Office Inspectorate and forced liaisons with pressure groups of vocal citizenry criticizing the increase in crime on the one hand and denaturing criminals to the level of naughty wayward children susceptible to persuasion and reproof on the other.

He motioned Rogers into an easy chair at the side of the desk. Although smoking his own, he ignored the fully charged pipe Rogers held in his hand. That meant his cordiality was surface and iced at the edges. But neither man much liked the other anyway.

'Ah, Mr Rogers,' he said, picking up a sheet of paper and flapping it. 'Before you start. Lingard has put in his resignation. You know?' He was already making it Rogers' fault, a mishandling of his staff. Man management was his latest obsession; he himself practising an embarrassingly flabby bonhomie with the rank and file, thwarting and blunting as a consequence the authority of his Divisional Commanders.

'I thought he might, sir,' Rogers said. 'You know he had an association with Miss Frail?'

'Vaguely, vaguely,' he admitted. Which meant something more definite.

'Naturally, her death upset him and he is not altogether satisfied that its investigation should exclude him. I considered it should.' Rogers produced the torn halves of the warrant card.

'He left this at the scene. I don't take it too seriously. He was shocked and emotional. I think he'll change his mind. He was very much taken with her.'

Huggett leaned back in his chair. 'I'll see him, of course, but I want you to speak to him first. He's too good a man to lose this way.' He dug into the bowl of his pipe with a straightened paper clip. 'But now, fill me in on this woman's death.'

4

Returning to his office, hardly aware of those he passed en route, Rogers chewed moodily over his interview with the Chief Constable. It hadn't pleased him. A vinegary Huggett had not been impressed with Rogers' theory that Nancy Frail had died elsewhere than in her car, that she had been dressed after her death or that there was much in it about which to be concerned. Huggett was a glutton for easily assimilable facts and he distrusted unsupported theories. In the process of pontificating on this he had irritated Rogers; never a very difficult thing to do. While conceding the peculiarity of the circumstances in which the body had been left in the car, Huggett stuck mulishly to the unarguable fact that Nancy Frail had died from a coronary thrombosis. Which, he argued, eliminated murder and, as a corollary, any expensive stirring up of unprofitable mud by the mounting of a large-scale investigation. He was so insistent on this that Rogers had, for a wild and joyous moment, wondered whether Huggett was the 'Jimmie' on Nancy Frail's call sheet. He had abandoned the notion regretfully. Huggett would as soon shoot a broody pheasant from its nest as sleep with a woman not his wife. He had, before picking up *The Times* and abruptly terminating the interview, told Rogers he was to ensure that Lingard retracted his resignation. He had been unable to order Rogers not to further his investigations but had underlined his opinion that it should be no more than a routine low-profile enquiry into the unlawful disposition of the corpse of – in his nose-wrinkling opinion – a distastefully loose woman.

On his way out, Rogers had left Huggett's door not quite

closed, a thing he knew would irritate the Chief Constable into getting up from his desk and slamming it. The sound of its slamming down the corridor had cheered him a little as he puffed at the tobacco long denied him.

There were two telephone message forms waiting on his desk.

The first was from Bridget and read:

Preliminary chemical test indicates presence of spermatozoa in vagina of NF. Thought you would want to know post haste. BH.

The second, from Coltart, was longer.

Possible stone dust on damaged wheel-housing. Blue woollen fibres area of windscreen damage. Contact lens not found. Glass fragments at scene insufficient to account for holes in windscreen. Witness found, says car not in lane at eleven p.m. Interior of car wiped clean. No fingerprints. Car now under cover pending examination of exterior. E. Coltart, D/Sergt.

He dropped the forms in his 'pending' tray, a glimmer of satisfaction in his expression. Reaching for the telephone, he dialled Lingard's flat number. When there was no reply he left and walked the corridor to Lingard's office.

Lingard was there, his blond hair still disordered, pulling open the drawers of his desk and sorting papers.

Rogers was surprised. 'I thought you'd left us,' he said. 'Are you back on the job?'

Lingard, grim-faced and not looking at Rogers, replied, 'I'm clearing out my things. I shall be gone in a few minutes.'

Rogers closed the door behind him and turned the key. 'The Chief Constable isn't very happy about accepting your resignation, David.'

'That's too bad. I'm going anyway.'

Lingard's office reflected exactly his personality. It contained a well-fleshed easy chair into which Rogers sank. On the walls were hung a series of coloured prints of *The Cries of London*, a steel engraving of The Royal Crescent at Bath and a wash drawing of Beau Brummell. On his desk, paraded in a cut glass tray, was a row of small aluminium tubes of snuff: Attar of Roses, Brown Rappee, High Dry Toast, Macouba and Golden Cardinal. Lingard admired – and emulated as far as the twentieth century would allow him – the customs and mores of the Regency. In his own way he was as dandified as the posturing fop whose picture hung on the wall.

'I think you're being hasty, David,' Rogers said. 'You know Miss Frail died of a coronary thrombosis?'

Lingard froze. 'Who says so?'

'Dr Hunter.'

'It can't be. How could she?'

'That's what I said. But she did.' He paused. 'I saw it myself.'

Lingard abruptly sat in his chair and Rogers knew he was hated for having seen the dead nakedness of Nancy Frail. The younger man peered at him with suspicion. 'What about her being in the car with her hair down; the car damaged?' His voice rose. '*That* needs as much explaining as the reason for her death.'

Rogers nodded. 'Yes, it does. It's what I intend finding out.'

Lingard groaned and buried his face in his cupped hands. 'I loved her,' he said in muffled tones through his fingers. 'I've got to know what happened.'

Rogers puffed his pipe alight, eyeing Lingard over the flame of the match. 'So you will but first we're going to talk about it. I'm the Investigating Officer and I need information. Will you co-operate?'

Lingard uncovered his face. 'I'm sorry about that.' His eyes were watery but steady. 'I'll help you all I'm able. It can't make any difference now.' He withdrew his tiny ivory box and inhaled snuff, flicking the dropped grains from his tie with a red Paisley handkerchief. Its perfume hung in the air around him.

'If I'm less than tactful in the choice of my questions, David,' Rogers said gently, 'bear with me. It's better I ask you than someone else.'

Lingard grimaced. 'You can't do more to me than has already been done.'

'I can,' Rogers promised gravely. He recognized that Lingard was going to be difficult. 'I know most of the background from what you told me before: the business with the cats; that Quint was one of the seven men. Now I want more detail. Who are the other six?'

'I don't know. I didn't want to know. All I was concerned about was that it had finished.'

'Miss Frail said this?'

Lingard bristled. 'That it was finished? I know it was. Nancy was a finer woman than you could possibly imagine.'

'All right, David. I'm not quarrelling over that. You knew her. I didn't.' *Judas*, he thought, *what infatuation will do to a man's judgement*. Aloud, he asked, 'She never discussed the men?'

He made an angry gesture. 'Of course she didn't. All that was forgotten, dead and buried.'

'The names on the cats' collars meant nothing to you?'

'Nothing. I never looked at them.'

Rogers considered him a classic example of a man ignoring what he didn't want to see. 'You were seeing Miss Frail regularly?'

'Yes. We were engaged.'

'The last time being yesterday afternoon?'

'Yes.'

'I have to ask you this, David.' Rogers hesitated, groping for the right words. What he was going to ask was brutal but, in the long term, probably cathartic. And, he hoped, a healing surgery. 'Did you have sexual intercourse with her that afternoon?'

Lingard gasped. His blue eyes blazed in his white face, his nails digging into the palms of his hands. 'No,' he ground out at last. 'We did not have sexual intercourse. There was no question . . .' He stopped and glared at Rogers. 'Why do you ask? You've a good reason, I hope.'

'I've a very good reason, David.' His eyes were pitying.

Anger drained from Lingard, leaving him limp and shaken. 'You mean somebody . . . somebody else did?' he said dully.

'I'm sorry, yes.'

There was a long silence in the room. Then Lingard said, 'She was raped.' It was an allegation, not a question.

That hadn't occurred to Rogers. 'It's a possibility, David.'

'It's more than a possibility. It's the only answer.' His face came alive again. 'That would explain a lot of things.' He pushed more snuff up his nostrils, this time not using the handkerchief and brown powder flecking them.

Having rapidly considered the possibility and dismissed it, Rogers was non-committal. 'But not everything. What time yesterday afternoon did you leave her?'

'At a quarter to six. I went from her flat straight to the office.' He took his notebook from an inside pocket and passed it to Rogers. 'It's all recorded. I was working until ten-thirty.' His lips twisted. 'Then I went back to my rooms. Is that what you wanted to know?'

Rogers didn't answer. He read the entries for the previous evening.

6.00 p.m. Office Cnfd D/Ps Hagbourne: preparing crime files.

7.30 p.m. Town Centre: enquiries re B & E (Woods, jewellers).

8.50 p.m. Telephone I/Room: check record Charles Wm. FOWLER.

9.00 p.m Observation on Tico-Tico Club for FOWLER (negative).

10.30 p.m. Booking off duty: D/Pc Vowden

'No luck with Fowler for the breaking and entering then?'

'No. It's all there.' He clearly wasn't interested in Fowler.

Neither was Rogers. 'Did Miss Frail tell you what she intended doing last evening?'

'No. And I didn't ask her. She knew I was on a split duty and not available.'

Rogers held out his hand, palm upwards. 'Her flat key, please.'

Lingard hesitated, then took it from his trousers pocket and dropped it on the desk. His eyes brooded on it. 'I didn't have to use it,' he said. 'The door had been forced.'

'Why did you go there this morning? You knew that was wrong.'

'To collect some personal property.'

'Such as?'

217

The blond detective bit his lip. 'Letters I'd written to her. Of no concern to anyone but myself. There's a copyright in letters, implying at least a part ownership. I considered myself within my rights in taking them. In any case, they've since been destroyed.' There was a clear defiance in his words.

'Don't push it, David. I could properly define your action as obstructing my enquiries.' When Lingard remained silent, he said, 'I'll accept they would throw no light on Miss Frail's death. Is that all you took?'

His chin went up and he flushed.

'Of course.'

'Did you examine any of the papers in the bureau?'

'Some. I make no apology for doing so.'

'I don't need one,' Rogers said shortly. 'All I need is your assurance that you aren't going to interfere.'

Lingard's eyes were as expressionless as glass marbles. 'You told me that Nancy died naturally. That leaves nothing in which I can interfere, as you put it.'

Rogers wasn't convinced. Lingard was dismissing both the damaged car and the entering of the flat far too lightly. He had seen them and they must have meant something to him. 'Well don't, David,' he said brusquely. 'If I suspect you are, I'll jump on you. Did you know Miss Frail wore contact lenses?'

'No.' His surprise was a complete answer. 'Does ... did she?'

'Yes. Do you know the name Dominis?'

'I do.' Bitterness was in his voice. 'That's the name of her former husband. Park Dominis. She divorced him two years ago.'

'Do you know the circumstances?'

The flap of Lingard's hand made it a question in bad taste. 'The usual, I imagine. Cruelty, adultery. He was a vicious, unscrupulous bastard.'

'Where does he live?'

'I neither know nor care. He's a pilot with some air charter firm.' He stirred restlessly. 'I don't even know where.'

'You mentioned Miss Frail's hair earlier on, David. How was it worn when you last saw her?'

'A Grecian style. At least, I call it Grecian. It was done with

218

curl things at the back.' He made circles with his forefinger;
vaguely, helplessly. 'Worn high at the back of her head.'

'How was she dressed?'

'As she was this morning.' The dark shadow of sad recollection crossed his face.

'Did she use the safety belt in her car?'

'Always. She had a thing about the possibility of scarring her
face in an accident.'

Rogers searched his memory for other matters and, finding
none, asked, 'Is there nothing else you can tell me, David?'

He stared at Rogers sombrely. 'No. You've asked me all these
questions. Now tell me why, if Nancy's death is the natural one
you say it is.'

Rogers looked in the bowl of his pipe as if seeking guidance.
He chose his words carefully. 'I'm satisfied about the cause
of her death. I'm not with the circumstances surrounding it.
Somebody drove her to the lane and left her there. The car, as
you noticed, had been involved in a collision. That, so far,
remains unexplained.' He gestured irritably. 'You know most
of this yourself.'

He waited for Lingard's reply. When he said nothing, Rogers
continued. 'About the matter of your resignation, David. Will
you now reconsider it? It doesn't help the enquiry or your future
for you to go charging off in a dudgeon.' His voice softened. 'I
know the worst possible thing is inaction in something with
which you are personally concerned but you've got to leave it
with me to sort out.'

Lingard's head was bowed, his chin flattening his tie, his
eyelids shuttering whatever was in his mind from Roger's
observation. Then his head jerked up, his eyes open and cold.
'Bollocks to my future and stuff the bloody service. Bollocks to
you too, Rogers. You've never bothered to hide your jealousy.
So far as you were concerned . . .'

'Jealousy?' Rogers' face darkened as he interrupted Lingard.
'Are you mad? Jealous over th . . .' He swallowed the contempt
he was about to unleash, breathing heavily through his nostrils. 'I'm telling you now,' he warned him harshly. 'Don't
interfere.'

Lingard stood. Despair had made him a dangerous and

unpredictable animal. 'My resignation stays where it is. On Huggett's desk. So don't tell me what I can or can't do.'

Rogers pushed himself out of his chair. He was pale with anger and near explosion point. 'All right, David. Man to man if that's the way you want it. The woman was a bloody whore and you know it. I believe she was knocking it off while you were supposed to be engaged to her. You're a fool if you think differently.' His knuckles were balled, ready for him.

Lingard was shaking but he rounded the desk in a sudden rush. Rogers knocked aside the wildly swung fist and hit him a paralysing blow on the bottom button of his silk-figured waistcoat, stopping him dead. Lingard's face was contorted agony, his mouth opening with the outrush of his breath.

Grabbing a handful of collar and tie, Rogers pushed him hard into the chair he had himself just vacated. He waited while the other man struggled to breathe. When the blue eyes opened in his cheese-coloured face and he groaned, Rogers said, 'That was just between you and me, David. Pack your things and get out. I'll tell the Chief Constable you're taking the leave you're entitled to and won't be back.'

When he closed the door behind him he realized he was trembling, his anger not yet gone from him. He returned to his own office and retrieved the two message forms from the 'pending' tray, locking them in one of the desk drawers. From another drawer he took a bottle and poured out a whisky. He drank this undiluted before going to see Huggett.

He didn't fool himself that the Chief Constable was going to be very pleased to hear the news about his blue-eyed boy.

Before calling on Bridget at the hospital, Rogers mowed his whiskers with a spare shaver operated from his car battery, not slowing the car appreciably to do it.

Bridget was typing her report when he arrived. She rolled it from the machine, signed a carbon copy and handed it to him.

'I'm glad you shaved,' she said. 'You were beginning to look like the late Che Guevara.'

'And feeling like him. Do you happen to have a bottle of skin conditioner in your filing cabinet?'

'It's sherry,' she said. 'I'll pour you one while you read my report.'

He perched on the corner of her desk and read it. Addressed to Her Majesty's Coroner, it was headed:

PRELIMINARY REPORT.

Name of Deceased: Nancy Elizabeth FRAIL.
Apparent Age: 25 years.   Height: 5' 4" (160cm 25mm).
Hair: Fair; long and straight. Pubic hair matching head hair.
Teeth: Dental chart attached.

'You've worked fast, Bridget,' he observed, taking the glass of sherry from her. He lifted it in salute. '*Gesundheit!* as we Deutschlanders have it.'

'Only for you, George.' She was wearing a blue linen dress, taut across her flat belly and outlining her thighs. To Rogers she looked eminently edible.

He read on:

EXTERNAL EXAMINATION. *The body of a young, lightly built adult female. It was clothed in a fawn woollen dress with a belt, a silk slip, white briefs, a suspender belt, stockings and tan shoes. The briefs were worn back to front: the stockings twisted, one not being fully on. The clothing was all better-than-average quality. A watch was worn on the left wrist and was showing the correct time. There were no finger rings or costume jewellery. The fingernails were long and unpolished, their condition suggesting a sedentary occupation.*

The body was lying in the driving seat of a Mini Cooper car. The arms were relaxed, the hands resting on the thighs. Both knees were flexed, the feet on the floor. The head was tilted back at an approximate angle of 45°. Rigor mortis was present in all limbs.

There was a blue discolouration of the lips and both ears. The eyes were closed. The right eye was fitted with a contact lens. None was evident in the left.

INTERNAL EXAMINATION.

Thorax: The trachea, bronchi, lungs and pleura were normal.

The Heart: All chambers were dilated. The muscles and valves appeared healthy. There was no evidence of atheromatous degeneration in the coronary arteries but the lumen of the left coronary was blocked one inch from its origin by a clot.

Abdomen: The liver, spleen, pancreas, kidneys, suprarenals and intestines were normal. The stomach contained about six ounces of well-digested food. There was no smell of alcohol. A vaginal swab subjected to Barberio's test (picric acid) produced typical yellow-tinted rhomboid needles indicative of the presence of male sperm.

Skull and contents: No damage was present to the cranium and there was no evidence of any intercranial abnormality. The vertebrae were intact, showing no damage.

Opinion: Death in my opinion was due to coronary thrombosis, the post-mortem appearances being compatible with death occurring between 10 p.m. and midnight prior to my examination.

(sgd) Bridget Jane Hunter, MD, MRC (Path).

Rogers folded the report and put it in his pocket. 'Were the spermatozoa alive and kicking, Bridget? Or does the picric acid stun them?'

She smiled. 'You'll have to wait for me to do a stained preparation to identify them at all. I believe them to be fresh only because I found the majority in the vestibule of the vagina.'

'Foreign territory to me, Bridget,' he said solemnly. 'I assume it means there was very little time for dispersion?'

'Yes, but don't let me mislead you. Although I'm fairly certain, I can be wrong. What I found could be trichomonads which aren't uncommon phenomena in a woman and mean nothing at all.' She was putting the sherry bottle back in the filing cabinet drawer. 'I did a Barberio's test only because it can be done in a few minutes.'

'I love you for it,' he said, sliding off the desk and standing behind her. When he saw she was waiting for him, he put his arms under her armpits and cupped her breasts. She twisted in his arms and faced him, her body pliant and responding, burning against his through the thin linen dress. His voice was unsteady. 'Under these flimsy bits of haberdashery you aren't so cool and clinical, are you?' He nuzzled aside her hair and kissed the warm throat. Beneath the perfume she wore he could detect the ghost of a ghost of a whiff of formalin.

She put her hands flat against the lapels of his jacket, her body arched into his, looking at him gravely. 'Is it the sherry, George? Or do I actually have a definite biological effect on you?'

'You do. Highly aphrodisiacal. My pulse keeps slipping a cog.'

'I was beginning to think you a neuter. After the last time . . .' Dark orange lights were in her eyes. The last time had been an embarrassing fiasco for both of them.

'Normally I'm as frigid as an Eskimo's back porch,' he lied. He touched her mouth gently with his own. Then he looked at the uncurtained windows and the unlocked door. 'Should we not fear discovery *flagrante delicto*? And with the sun still shining.' He unhitched himself from her and moved away. He was physically moved and showed it. 'Judas, Bridget. Keep at least a yard from me at your peril.'

'Would you be interested in another sherry, George?'

He pulled back his shirt sleeve and looked at his watch. 'Not now, Bridget. I'm due at the Frail flat. The laboratory people are doing a check on it for me.'

'I didn't mean now,' she said calmly. 'I meant later.'

He had a suffocating feeling in his chest but his face was impassive. He had reached his watershed and he splashed through it. 'You mean later like about ten o'clock? When I'm possibly finished?'

'Yes.' She held his regard without coquetry. 'You know the way up.'

As he opened the door to leave, she held out a folded pad of papers. 'You forgot these, George. Everything you'll ever need to know about oral contraceptives.'

Rogers' desk, normally of a regimented neatness, was now a disorder of papers and items taken from Nancy Frail's flat and from her car. Here were the significant statistics and artifacts of her life for Rogers to pore over and interpret as best he could. Among them were other artifacts; those of his hurried lunch: an empty coffee container, sandwich wrappings and coiled orange peel.

Of the more interesting items found in the bathroom medicine cabinet had been a small cardboard box. Rogers read its inscription: *PRŌESTOLIN* ♀ *: fifteen tablets. Progestogen 2 mgms. Oestrogen 100 microgrms. Mestranol. Norethynodrel.* It supported Bridget's hypothesis that the probable cause of Nancy Frail's thrombus was her use of an oral contraceptive.

Rogers smoked his pipe continuously, refuelling and lighting it without conscious thought as he checked through the exhibits.

A newspaper clipping dated eighteen months previously and pinned to a handwritten letter caught his attention. The clipping referred to a Sir Andrew Wallace JP of Spye Green Hall opening a philatelic exhibition in aid of The Commonwealth Cancer Research Fund and, among a plethora of platitudes, expressing a lifelong interest in nineteenth-century postage stamps with a self-confessed obsession with the French *Classiques*.

The letter, dated six days after the clipping, read:

Dear Miss Frail,
    Thank you. I would, indeed, appreciate viewing your collection.

*From the description you give they undoubtedly include the 1852
and 1853–1860 issues of President Louis Napoleon and these
would, of course, be of particular interest to me. Would you
prefer I call at your address?*

Yours sincerely,
Andrew Wallace

The mechanical telephone index yielded seven entries (excluding Lingard's) identified – and thereby made significant – only by an initial and a bracketed first name. He jotted them on his scratch pad as he found them:

G(Donald): 31881. G(Philip): 22430. H(Jimmy): 21206. J(Rodney): 24319. N(Waldo): 33764. Q(Harry): 21618. W(Andrew): 23222.

He opened the spectacle case and rechecked the inscription inside: *James Hacker, FBOA, FSMC* with the telephone number given as 21206. Although he felt a tiny spark of regret for the final elimination of the Chief Constable as 'Jimmy', he was pleased at identifying Hacker. He knew him slightly although only by repute. He had been described as a hard-living, hard-drinking handsome bachelor, very popular with women between fifteen and fifty with occasional forays into age groups outside that limit. Rogers had never considered him as needing to pay for their favours.

It required no mental gymnastics to equate the philatelic-minded Sir Andrew Wallace with the entry W(Andrew).

Without lifting the receiver of his internal telephone, he twice depressed the red switch labelled Coltart. When the huge sergeant entered the office, chewing the end of a wooden pencil, Rogers wrote the telephone numbers on a piece of paper and gave it to him. 'Go and see the Head Postmaster, sergeant, and screw the names of the subscribers owning these numbers out of him. He'll tell you it's against the rules and Holy Writ but that's only a vestigial twitch from his union days. He's very co-operative if you ignore his first two refusals. But before you see him, lay on two of the plain clothes aids to do a house-to-house enquiry in Queen Anne's Road. Don't advertise it. The Chief Constable thinks we're wasting our time.' He rubbed the ball of his thumb against the grain of his newly emerging chin stubble. 'Probably we are but I'm in the mood to be bloody-minded.'

225

Coltart spat a splinter of pencil on to Rogers' carpet. 'For what it's worth,' he said diffidently, 'I've a theory.'

'Thank God for that,' Rogers said without sarcasm. 'I'm glad some bugger has. *I* haven't.'

Coltart blinked. 'She's driving her car with her married boyfriend on board. They've done their thing and she's taking him home. Then she has her heart attack and piles the car into a wall. Chummy in the passenger seat puts his head through the windscreen but does no damage, except perhaps to his bowler hat. Which wouldn't be unusual, the glass being made that way. So now chummy's in a real fix. He can't leave her dead in the middle of the road. She'd be found straight away. So he panics, gets her out of her safety belt and into the passenger seat, knocks a hole in his side of the glass for visibility and drives to the nearest lane to his own place. Then he replaces her in the driving seat, forgetting to do up the safety belt, and walks home.'

'What about the windscreen glass all over the road,' Rogers pointed out. 'So far you've been unable to find it.'

'He could have spent a minute or two brushing it into a ditch. We'd never find it there. Or the wall could have been on a verge. We haven't checked the grass edges.'

There was a long silence in the office while Rogers brooded on it. Then he said, 'I warned you I was bloody-minded, sergeant. I'll take the likely arguments against its feasibility, not because I necessarily disagree with you but to give it a good airing. First, her clothing. According to Doctor Hunter – and she's the expert on how to wear them, not you or I – the briefs were on back to front. Also the stockings were disarranged.'

'She'd had sexual intercourse,' Coltart said, his oatmeal eyebrows heavily disapproving, 'and I'm told the removal of briefs facilitates it. Their being wrongly put back on doesn't seem unusual to me. The same goes for the stockings. They would have to be unhitched from the girdle thing she wore.'

Rogers eyed his sergeant with ironic amusement. 'Casanova Coltart,' he derided him. 'I suppose I'll have to defer to your detailed experience in such matters. All right, what about the missing contact lens? No, don't bother.' He stopped him answering. 'That's too simple. There can't be any significance in its loss, only in where it might be found.'

'It's such a small thing; so difficult to actually see,' Coltart said, 'that its not being found means nothing.'

'Her hair,' Rogers continued. 'I'm reliably informed she wore it loose only in bed.'

The sergeant's deep green eyes glittered. 'I understand sexual intercourse in a small car can involve a fair bit of thrashing about.' He was unsmiling, stating what was to him a disgusting fact. 'Would it be so unusual for her hair to have become undone?'

'I suppose not. But wouldn't there have been pins or one of those tortoiseshell comb things in the car?'

'There weren't, I'll admit. But the intercourse could have taken place behind a hedge, in a hay rick . . . anywhere.'

Rogers snorted. 'Not with a woman like Nancy Frail, sergeant. You're thinking of a thirty-bob transport café job. Knee-tremblers. I know your idea of a whore. She's someone with a tight skirt up around her buttocks, fishnet stockings and a shiny black handbag as big as a suitcase. She'd wear an ankle chain, two-inch nylon eyelashes and her face enamelled like a repainted second-hand jalopy.'

Coltart's expression remained unchanged. 'I've seen one or two. They've also snakes tattooed on their arms.'

'The universal phallic motif,' Rogers said. 'Well, there are others. My own assessment of Frail is a woman demanding silk sheets, a pre-performance shower in Chanel No. 5 and a fair amount of ritualistic gallantry to deodorize what she was doing.' He shook his head. 'If she ever did it in the back seat of a Mini Cooper or in a haystack, then I've learned nothing about women in all my thirty-one years.'

Coltart possessed a suety streak of stubbornness. 'I read last week of a well-known actress being caught knocking it off in a back row seat of a Hollywood cinema with her ex-husband's chauffeur. So it does happen.'

'I know of the lady,' Rogers said carelessly. 'She was a Grade A nymphomaniac when Errol Flynn was around to do something about it. If it hadn't been the chauffeur it would have been the cinema commissionaire. And she'd even pay if she couldn't get it any other way. She's just a woman who likes sweaty under-shirts. But,' he hastened to say with a placatory smile, 'there's a lot of merit in what you say and you could be so right. It's just I'm not in the mood to agree with anybody at the moment.' He looked puzzled. 'But why bring in the bowler hat?'

Coltart screwed his small eyes up in a spasm of humour. 'I put that in to give my theory some sort of respectability.'

Neither man had mentioned Lingard but he was very much in their minds.

With Coltart on his way to the Head Postmaster, Rogers dialled the number of the Blakehill Airport Police Authority. He spoke to Godson, the duty Chief Inspector, asking him to do an unpublicized check on the pilots' records for the details and background of Park Dominis.

'I know him, George,' Godson said, 'but having company with me I'll call back.'

The bank paying-in slips Rogers thumbed through were interesting. Checking back two years, he found that Quint had, until four months previously, paid twenty-two sums of £5 by cheque; 'DG', fifteen of £10; Hacker, twelve of £10 and 'AW' one of £850 eighteen months previously. Quint, Rogers thought, appeared to be getting it with a discount; being the only one paying amounts of £5.

There were no cheque payments in respect of 'RJ', 'PG' or 'WN' and Rogers assumed they had merely shown more discretion than the others, paying their way in unidentifiable bank notes. There were bankings of a number of sums of £10 and its multiples to support this.

The bank statements, addressed to Nancy Elizabeth Frail, 1(a) Bushey House, Queen Anne's Road, revealed she was receiving monthly payments of £100 from P. Dominis and a small regular income from unit shares in concerns indicated cryptically as INT. BRI. FD and AUST. C.N. CORP.

Rogers did a rapid casting of the figures and assessed her annual income to be only a little short of £2,500 which, he thought, a not inconsiderable amount to be garnered from an end biblically condemned as being bitter as wormwood and sharp as a two-edged sword. Furthermore, on this occasion it had proved as lethal.

The desk diary contained little that was comprehensible at first reading. The same sets of initials occurred at regular intervals, most coinciding closely with the payments of cheques or cash into her account. After each pair of initials appeared the notations (a) or (h). Quint's initials did not appear after June. Nor the initials 'RJ' after April. One entry for 'AW', a month previously, had the words *Rajput Cat* bracketed after it. There were a number of entries recording 'DL', all within the past four months. Some, Rogers noted cynically and without surprise, on the same dates she had entertained one or other of her paying guests. They justified his harsh words to Lingard and to that extent buttered his gritty conscience.

He tabulated his findings, hoping they would mean something:

Recordings since Jan 1	Number of visits	Cheques paid over period of two years	Notes
RJ (h)	6	None	No diary entries after 6th April
PG (h)	9	None	Last visit 1st October
JH (a) and (h)	7	£120	Identified James HACKER. Last visit 5th October
AW (a) and (h)	8	£850	Single cheque. Last visit 16th September
HQ (a) and (h)	12	£110	Identified Harry QUINT. No diary entries after 2nd June
DG (h)	5	£150	Last visit 4th September
WN (h)	9	None	Last visit 11th October, day before NF's death

Judas, Rogers marvelled under his breath, *but she must have been accomplished. Certainly hard-working. And no income tax to pay on it either.*

Most of the remaining entries referred to twice-weekly appointments with a Monsieur Paul (whom Rogers quickly disposed

of as her hairdresser) and three-monthly checks with her
dentist who, fortunately for him, possessed initials entirely
dissimilar from any recorded. There were reminders for renew-
als of licences and subscriptions and theatre and orchestral
engagements.

There were no diaries for the previous years nor, in her desk,
had there been any correspondence other than gossipy reams
of paralysing dullness and rectitude from other women.

In her wallet was a £10 note, several £1 notes, correspondence
and bills. The letters – from a woman friend Cynthia – were
chatty and uninformative.

Like a black cloud boiling up over an otherwise clear
horizon, Rogers' case-hardened cynicism was insisting that
the worst was yet to come.

His friend, Godson, from Blakehill went some way in justify-
ing his gloomy view. 'This chap Dominis,' he told Rogers over
the telephone, 'is a Flight Captain with the Concordant-Global
Airways, flying DC8s. I remember him because a few weeks
ago he took a boozy swing at his navigation officer in the
crews' bar here at the airport. He nearly tore his head off.
A nasty-tempered cove, so I understand. But popular with
the ladies. And proficient enough at flying to get away with
anything short of murder.'

'That sounds good, Bill. What's his form?'

'An ex-Squadron Leader with an AFC after his name. He
refused to bale out of an experimental tactical fighter that was
dropping him and a couple of million pounds worth of secret
ironmongery into the Irish Sea. He landed it more or less intact
on a strip of beach just long enough for a No. 2 iron shot. By
all accounts he's got guts enough for two. Let me see . . .'

Rogers heard him turning over paper at the other end. 'Ah,
yes. He's thirty-two and married to one Mrs Nancy Elizabeth
Dominis with the unlikely maiden name of Frail. *Frailty, thy
name is woman*,' he quoted and laughed.

Rogers laughed with him. It was a time for being polite. 'Go
on, Bill,' he said. 'This is very interesting.'

'No children and they live at 18 Broken Cross, High Moor.
He runs a black Sunbeam Stiletto, index number Q361 KAM.
His personal description: six feet two inches, heavy build,

black hair and moustache, brown eyes, prominent scar on left temple – that's the one he collected earning his AFC.' Godson neutralized his voice. 'Is he in trouble, George? Something I should know about?'

'I don't honestly know, Bill. I'm in the process of digging out backgrounds on a sudden death enquiry. When you're passing the office, drop in and I'll explain. In the meantime, don't fret. There's nothing you need report to your headquarters yet.'

When he put the telephone down he said aloud, 'Married! The bitch was still married!' It was Lingard he was most concerned about. The scars were going to last a long time.

When Coltart entered the office, it was with a broad grin on his freckled face. The shoulders of his gaberdine coat were waterlogged with rain. He never drove a car where he could walk. 'You didn't tell me the Postmaster was under report for driving through a red light, having an out-of-date licence and no MoT certificate,' he complained. 'It helped a lot. He said "No" three times and meant it.' He handed Rogers a square of paper. 'I had to butter up the Exchange Supervisor and she's an old dear with breath like a blow torch.'

'I'll recommend you for a Queen's Police Medal,' Rogers promised him. 'Many have got it for less.'

He read the notes made by Coltart and they jolted him.

22430. *Vosper, Vosper, Carradine & Galbraith, Solicitors, High Street.*
24319. *Lt. Col. Rodney Jagger, DSO, MBE, MC., Dormers, Castle Road.*
21206. *James Hacker, 21 Regent Crescent.*
23222. *Sir Andrew Adrian Wallace, JP., Spye Green Hall, High Moor.*
31881. *The Sun & Evening Echo, Commercial Street.*
33764. *Waldo Cecil Norton, Goshawk House, Spye Green.*
21618. *Harry Edmund Quint, The Old Rectory, Spaniards Rise.*

It wasn't difficult for Rogers to identify 'PG' as Philip Galbraith of the legal firm. He sucked in his breath. Not because he was particularly surprised but because he was a friend of the Chief Constable's. 'DG' he guessed to be Donald Garwood, assistant editor of the highly moralistic *Sun & Evening Echo*. He added the names in pencil. At first glance he thought there must be a rational explanation for the inclusion of Wallace's name. Then he wrinkled his forehead in vexation and told himself not to be so bloody simple.

To Coltart, he said, 'Good stuff, sergeant. You've made my day if not the Chief Constable's. God knows what he's going to say when he knows that Galbraith, plus one of our own magistrates and a DSO and MC colonel have all been hammering on Frail's door with £10 cheques in their sweaty hands.' He turned down the corners of his mouth. 'Probably blame me for not leaving well alone.'

Coltart, who had been standing patient and bulky and steaming, said, 'I haven't finished, sir.' His green eyes were glinting his satisfaction. 'Young Lashley turned up some information with his first knock. A chap called Midgley – he lives in a flat somewhere above Frail's – says he saw her leave with a man in a Rolls-Royce at about nine last night.'

Rogers said 'Agh!' with satisfaction. 'He did? What about her own car?'

'I don't know. That's all Lashley said. He thought it important enough to telephone in and leave a message for you. Do you want me to see this Midgley?'

Rogers regarded the array of papers on his desk with dislike. 'No. I've collected a migraine sorting this lot out. I never was an armchair detective. I want some fresh air, even if it is wet and laced with carbon monoxide.'

He shrugged himself into his raincoat. The afternoon was dying in a drizzle of grey rain. 'Leave Midgley to me, sergeant. I'd like you to go to the laboratory and see what, if anything, they've turned up on the Mini Cooper in particular.'

Before he left the office, he underlined in ink the name Sir Andrew Adrian Wallace and the amount of £850. It was beginning to bother him, not fitting the general pattern, irking his sense of orderliness.

There were too many 'AW' entries to equate with a common interest in French postage stamps, even if – and Rogers couldn't believe they did – the passions of stamp collectors ran that high.

His earthy mind rejected the improbability but decided to read up on the French *Classiques* before interviewing Wallace.

Getting into his car, he remembered Quint's wife Judith and the occasion she had driven him up on to the moors, intent on an open-air seduction. The nub of his recollection was that she had driven him there in an elderly Rolls-Royce.

6

For the third time that day, Rogers dismounted from his car in Queen Anne's Road and climbed the cement steps to the geranium-smelling porch. This time he thumbed the bell-push at the side of the typed card reading *Martin Midgley Esq., No. 3*, opening the door to the common entrance and stepping inside.

The door to Nancy Frail's flat was now securely locked; Rogers' signature, inked on a strip of tape stretching from door post to stile and fastened by thumb-impressed seals, forbidding admission.

The little man who limped down the stairs to greet Rogers was in the grey fifties with prominent thyroidic eyeballs. His scalp shone pink and hairless. His limp moustache was yellow-fringed with vaporized nicotine tars. The detective could smell the staleness of tobacco smoke on his clothing as they shook hands.

'Midgley,' the little man said in a soft limp voice. 'You are?'

'Rogers. Detective Chief Inspector Rogers.'

Midgley rubbed his palms together making a slithery sound. 'Come on up, chief inspector.'

Following him up the stairs, Rogers saw that he was club-footed.

His flat smelled of confined tobacco smoke and peppermint. His wife (a mountainous and pallid hybrid between a frog and a pekinese bitch, Rogers thought) sat on a blue satin settee, eating violet-sugared peppermint creams from a bulging paper bag. A cigarette smoked in an overflowing glass ashtray at her side. She was provisioned for an evening's hard reading with an

234

opened box of chocolates, a drum of Turkish Delight, a twenty-packet of Players No. 6 cigarettes and several paperback books. Her fingers, pale magenta-tipped slugs, pushed creams into her tiny cupid's-bow mouth. Her eyes were cold blue; more frog than pekinese. They pinned Rogers with an unwinking sexless stare, taking in his raincoated bulk and swarthy maleness, but not letting it divert her from masticating. She remained hulked on the settee, her dropsical legs tucked beneath her. Rogers tried to visualize her *in coitus* with her little bald husband and failed.

There was a table at one end of the room stacked with account books and invoice files. 'I'm an accountant, chief inspector,' Midgley said, noticing Rogers' glance at them, 'and unfortunately I find it necessary to bring work home.'

Refusing a sherry, Rogers sat and smiled encouragingly at them both. He wasted his time with the fat woman but Midgley responded, the eternal little man basking in his warming moment of importance.

Rogers said, 'I understand you saw Miss Frail last night, Mr Midgley.'

He clucked. 'A sad business, chief inspector.' He glanced sideways at his wife. She was reading, her jowls bulging, seemingly a world away. 'A very popular young lady with, er, lots of friends.'

'So I understand,' Rogers said blandly, accepting the euphemism. 'You saw one of them last night?'

'Yes. About nine o'clock,' he said eagerly. 'I was looking out the window to check the weather. I happened to see a big black car down below, further along the road. I recognized it as a Rolls-Royce. There aren't many of those about. Even around here.' He made Queen Anne's Road seem the equivalent of Park Lane, W1. 'Nobody got out immediately and that alone made me wonder.' He looked at his wife. 'Didn't it, dear?'

She nodded indifferently, the rolls of fat under her chin flopping.

He continued. 'Then a man got out from the driver's side of the car.' He waited.

'All right,' Rogers said. 'You knew him?'

'Not by name but he'd called on Miss Frail on a number

of previous occasions. He'd blond or white hair, a slim figure.'

'Age?'

'Oh, fiftyish, although I never saw him in daylight.'

The description fitted Quint sufficiently for Rogers. His use of a Rolls-Royce added weight to it.

Midgley's pouched eyes fixed on Rogers', making his next remark significant. 'I rarely saw her friends in the daytime, chief inspector. And they always left their cars at the end of the road.'

Rogers defused the innuendo with irony. 'They probably didn't want to cause an obstruction, Mr Midgley. You are on a slight curve here. What happened after the man got out?'

'He came up the steps and, I presume, went inside Miss Frail's flat. I left the window then, not expecting his departure until at least the . . . the, er, small hours.'

Rogers' face was impassive against the revelations of this nosy little sod. There was one in every road thank God, he thought. 'And then?' he asked.

'After about five minutes I heard the car door banged and I looked out again. I saw the Rolls being driven away. When it passed under the road lamp opposite I saw Miss Frail in the passenger seat.' He lit a fresh cigarette direct from the stub of the old one.

'Good,' Rogers said. 'What was she dressed in?'

Midgley lifted his eyebrows. 'Oh, it was too dark for me to see that, chief inspector.'

'But not too dark to recognize her?'

Midgley peered at him as if doubtful whether he was a friend or an enemy. 'Well, I didn't actually see her . . . I mean, it must have been her . . . his having just come . . .' His voice withered under the frost of his wife's regard.

'But you did see her features?' Rogers persisted.

He was crestfallen. 'I must be frank,' he said bravely. 'I only assumed it was Miss Frail. Wasn't it?'

'I don't know, Mr Midgley,' Rogers said. 'You may be right. But I have to know just how sure you believe you are.'

'Well, after what you've said, not very.'

'He should be,' the fat woman surprisingly interjected, her

voice glutinous around the bolus of chocolate cream in her mouth. She spoke as if Midgley wasn't there. 'He knows her well enough.' An unspoken *dirty little sod* hung in the air.

The accountant smiled like a kicked dog but for a microsecond there was murder in his eyes. Rogers didn't miss it and he thought that one day Midgley might find the courage to poison his vicious wife with a nasty caustic like oxalic acid that hurt both being swallowed and vomited back up.

'Oh?' he said politely.

'It's nothing, chief inspector,' Midgley said hastily. 'My wife is joking. A professional relationship only. I occasionally advise on buying and selling – particularly selling . . .' He cackled as if he'd said something clever. '. . . on the Exchange.'

'He spoke to her last night,' she said flatly over her open book, admitting of no argument.

Midgley swallowed. 'On the way in . . . coming back from a walk.' He had flushed a bright red on his naked scalp and was agonizingly embarrassed. 'We discussed the weather . . .'

The woman's 'h'm' was barely to be heard but it reached their ears like a small black malevolent moth.

'What time was this, Mr Midgley?' Rogers smiled at him, recognizing a sexually frustrated bitch when he saw one and happy to help the little man along.

'Just before six.' He hesitated, then bit at his bottom lip. 'She was . . . oh, it couldn't be important.'

'Let me be the judge.'

Midgley glanced sideways at his wife. She was coughing on a cigarette, her face dangerously crimson, her eyes bulging. 'I'm not sure you'd want to know,' he said. 'I mean, it could be completely innocent. I wouldn't want to blacken a man's character . . .'

Realization came to Rogers. 'I see. You're trying to say I know the man?'

'Yes. You do know?'

'You tell *me*, Mr Midgley.'

'He was on his way out.' His eyes shifted. 'When he'd gone I naturally stopped and passed the time of the day with her.'

Rogers searched his face. 'There's more to it than that,' he said.

Again Midgley glanced at his wife. 'He was angry. She wasn't but he was.'

'In what way?'

'White-faced angry . . . bitter. As if he'd lost a quarrel with her.' He spoke as a man with some experience of losing quarrels. 'Miss Frail was quite calm, I thought. Not particularly caring. She acted as if nothing had happened. But that, of course,' he said, 'may have been her good manners.'

'You know the man's name?'

'Mr Lingard. He left in his green Bentley. He was about the only man who ever parked outside the house.'

'You know the names of the others?'

Before he could answer, the woman slapped her book down. Rogers read its title, *Sweet Heartbreak*, upside down, not being surprised. 'No, he doesn't,' she snapped. 'He isn't interested enough.' She dared her husband to say differently.

Rogers ignored her. 'Do you, Mr Midgley?'

The eyes meeting his apologized briefly for his cowardice. 'I know of no others, chief inspector,' he said. He indicated the piles of ledgers. 'My evenings are usually so occupied.'

'Where did Miss Frail garage her car?'

'In the next road. Number twenty-five St Marks.'

'You have a car?'

He shook his head and his dentures clacked. 'No. I've never felt the need.'

He held out his hand when Rogers left and the detective shook it. It lay in his fingers like a lump of damp fungus.

'You might fool *him*,' the woman said when they heard the door downstairs shut, 'but not me, you dirty-minded lecherous pig. You can't keep your filthy paws off anyone.'

Her spiteful tirade flowed unregarded beneath the level of his awareness as he lit his fifty-sixth cigarette of the day and turned the pages of a Sales Ledger. When she finally stopped and opened the drum of Turkish Delight he was as indifferent to the glutinous chewing as he had been to her noisy malignancy.

Before calling on Quint, Rogers returned to his office. There was a message form from Coltart on the blotting pad.

Sir,   *13th October.*

Preliminary Lab. Report.

1 *Stone dust identified weathered fine-grain sandstone.*
2 *Lipstick on Gauloises cigs. similar lipsticks from flat and deceased's handbag.*
3 *Black head hair with living root bulb found in deceased's clothing. Report will say minus 0.4 medulla; 93mm long with nodule suggesting hair cut approx. eight days previously.*
4 *Result of oestrogen and other checks on blood/stomach contents unavailable for further three days.*
5 *Exterior of car definitely wiped clean of marks.*

(sgd) E. Coltart, D/Sergt. 7.50 p.m.

Rogers put it away in the drawer with the other case papers. Then he pulled the telephone handset towards him and dialled the Chief Constable's office code. He let it ring for a few seconds before shutting down. He hadn't expected him to be there but he had to know. Then he dialled the number of his home, hoping with his fingers crossed that he wouldn't be there either. When there was no answer he made a note of the time he had tried to contact him. He was pleased he wasn't to be deflected from his purpose either by any immediate considerations of the status of some of the names taken from Nancy Frail's diary or by Huggett's downgrading of the importance of the enquiry.

The Old Rectory at Spaniards Rise appeared as arrogantly shabby as he remembered it from his previous visits some four months previously. The iron gates, crooked on their stone columns, were, perhaps, rustier. The drive was certainly more lumpy with moss, the laurels a shade more unkempt.

Although the house was in total darkness, Rogers pulled hard at the cold iron ring of the bell-pull, hearing it clanking behind, it seemed, a dozen closed doors. When there was no answer he depressed the handle and pushed. The door remained solid and unmoving. He walked along the gravel to the rear of the house, shining the beam of his torch into the huge octagonal conservatory taking up the side of the house. Once it had been heated and lush with tropical plants; colourful with exotic birds and lizards and swarming insects; a miniature Borneo jungle for Quint's amusement and a nostalgic reminder of his service in the Fallic Islands.

It was now cold with broken panes of glass in the structure, the trees and plants no longer plump and glossy, their succulence wrinkled and blackened by an unheated English autumn. There were no birds in the drab foliage and nothing moved under the probing ray of the detective's torch. The small pond by which he and Judith Quint had so nearly copulated was dry and empty of its one time colony of frogs. There was desolation about its memories and Rogers shivered.

An old stable in a cobbled yard at the rear, obviously used as a garage, was empty.

Rogers looked at his watch. It was 8.40 and he had time to see Dominis before his appointment with Bridget. The thought of her was a warming ball of fire in his stomach.

Broken Cross was a rectangle of ferociously-shaved turf with a few silver birch trees clumped in its centre. Around the perimeter were clapboard, split-level chalet houses with too many windows and glass doors for civilized living.

He saw the window curtains of No. 18 being pulled aside as he slammed the door of his car.

She opened the glass and wrought-iron door a scant six inches before he could knock, peering at him through the crack. He saw a girl with long straight yellow hair, a disintegrating rope espadrille on the one foot visible to him and a floral smock that had surrendered any attempt at minimizing the huge paunch of her pregnancy. Very pregnant women made Rogers nervous. He always feared being required to cope with a messily premature birth.

She shivered in the cold night air. 'Are you the police?'

'Yes. Detective Chief Inspector Rogers,' he answered. 'Mrs Dominis?'

'Come in.' She was apparently satisfied he would not rape her. 'Have you found him?'

Inside, he studied her. She wore no lipstick; no anything on her formless face. She was pretty but not attractive; making, nevertheless, a pleasant change from the grotesquery of Midgley's wife. Her huge bloated belly made her unstockinged legs look spindly.

He didn't much like the house. There seemed square metres of uncarpeted, comfortless space only sparsely furnished with plastic chairs and metal tables. The walls were of natural pinewood, the spiral stairs of iron. There would be a Sauna bath somewhere up there. Rogers had felt more at home in his dentist's waiting-room.

He sat in a chair shaped like a surrealist motor tyre. It gripped his buttocks with a giant's warm hand. He looked around for ashtrays. There were none so he kept his pipe unlit in his fingers.

'Have we found who?' he asked, settling himself.

'My husband, of course. Isn't that why you're here?'

'I came to see Mr Dominis, if that's what you mean,' he said carefully. 'You say he's missing?'

She stared at him. 'Shouldn't you know?'

'Not necessarily,' he said testily. 'I am CID. Details of missing people come to me fortuitously or only when there appears some good reason why they should. May I use your telephone to check?'

She nodded. He extracted his buttocks from the almost human grip of the chair and went to the telephone in the hall.

'There's a completed form in your IN tray,' the Information Room Inspector told him incisively. 'I put it there myself this morning at three o'clock. When you were still in bed.'

Rogers swallowed his momentary ill-humour. Park Dominis wouldn't have meant anything to him either at that time. 'Tell me about it,' he said. 'I didn't get round to sorting through my trays today.'

'Park Dominis, Flight Captain with Concordant-Global Airways. Reported by his wife, Mrs Philippa Dominis of 18 Broken Cross at 2.05 a.m. today. Missing since he left his home in his car at 7.30 p.m. Said he was going out for a drink. Dress: dark blue lightweight coat, a buff pullover, light blue linen trousers and soft shoes.' He gave the missing pilot's personal description which tallied with that already known to Rogers. 'It says here,' the Inspector continued, 'there's no known reason for his absence: job secure, good health, financially stable, no domestic troubles other than his wife's expecting a child in three weeks time. We've made a check at Blakehill Airfield:

241

no help there. He's not flying again until tomorrow so they aren't concerned. Not yet. His description's circulated with the number of his car. We last checked with Mrs Dominis at six this evening when he hadn't returned home.'

'Good.' Rogers knew this had been well handled for what it appeared. Hundreds of persons went missing each year from the area; some for days, some for ever. Only a very few warranted special action. He lowered his voice. 'Recirculate it for special attention. On my authorization. Any results direct to me, please.'

'What about Mr Lingard?'

'What about him?'

'He's had his copy of the Missing Persons Form. Will he want to know of any progress?'

Rogers thought that one out. 'You don't know?'

'I'm sorry. What don't I know?'

'I can't imagine it's much of a secret. He's resigned.'

'That's a shaker . . .'

'Don't discuss it,' Rogers said brusquely. 'Nobody's very happy about it. Just leave the Dominis matter with me. And dig Sergeant Coltart out from wherever he is. I want to see him in my office in half-an-hour's time.'

He replaced the receiver and returned to the woman. She was standing, waiting.

'I've got the picture,' he said. 'I'm sorry.'

Her fingers twined together in her agitation. 'He's not been found?'

He shook his head. 'You've no idea why he should stay away so long?'

Her eyes dropped from his. 'No.' Then she said, puzzled, 'You said you wanted to speak to him. Can you tell me why?'

'I wanted some information from him.' His face was wooden, not revealing anything. 'You are his second wife?'

She clutched at the mound of her belly and sat abruptly. 'No,' she said. 'But you knew that already, didn't you?'

'Yes.'

'We live together because we can't get married. Not until Park can get a divorce from that poisonous bitch of a woman.'

'You mean Nancy Frail?'

242

'That's what she calls herself, thank God.' She looked sad. 'Will Park get into trouble, Mr Rogers? With his company, I mean.'

'I shouldn't think so. Not unless it affects his flying.' He grinned companionably at her.

'Did *she* send you?'

'I'm here because of her.'

Her forehead wrinkled. 'There's something wrong, isn't there? Because you're here looking for him. Not even knowing he's missing.' She hesitated. 'Is it about the stamps?'

Rogers' memory produced a mental picture of the newspaper clipping and Wallace's letter. 'The French Louis Napoleons?' he countered, fitting himself back into the embrace of the plastic chair.

'You *know!*' she cried despairingly. 'She told you.' She cracked her knuckles in her anguish. 'She had everything of his. Including the stamps. It was the first time he'd ever bought anything that turned out to have been stolen and she had to find out.'

He nodded as if he knew everything.

'He would have owned up when he found out because he hadn't known. But he'd brought them through Customs in his Flight Bag and that would have cost him his job.' She bit her bottom lip hard. 'Smuggling. It wasn't really. She said she'd report it to the police if he tried to get them back. Such stupid little bits of coloured paper,' she said sadly, 'to cause so much trouble.'

'So are bank notes,' Rogers said. 'Little bits of paper, I mean. Is that where he went last night? To her flat?'

'Yes,' she whispered, bowing her head, the hair falling about her face like yellow curtains. 'He was watching her. Trying to get evidence for a divorce. He wants it so desperately he was even willing to risk her saying something about the stamps. He's been watching her off and on for weeks. When he has the opportunity; which isn't very often with so many night charter flights.' She flicked her hair back with a shake of her head. 'She's a filthy little cow, you know. And clever with it. She's blackmailing Park, Mr Rogers.'

'She is?'

'Yes. She sucks a hundred pounds separation allowance from him every month. For bloody dam' all.' Her blue eyes sparkled with the first showing of real spirit. 'Park never deserved a bitch like her.'

'He definitely said he intended watching her last night?'

'Yes. He doesn't otherwise go out.'

'Always at her flat?'

'Mostly, but sometimes he's had to follow her to other places.' She clenched her hands into small fists. 'All this time and he's never *seen* anything. Nothing he can use . . .'

'Do you know the men she was meeting?'

She was wary, pulling a strand of hair across her face and holding it between her lips. 'No.'

'But he mentioned names?'

'Is any of this going to hurt Park?'

He stared at her. 'You should be the best judge of that.'

'Park isn't a criminal, Mr Rogers,' she said earnestly.

'All right, I'll accept that. Now tell me about the men.'

'He thought one was her optician. A man called Hacker. She stayed with him all one night. I remember that because he didn't come home until dawn. Then there's Gal . . . Galbraith I believe it is. A lawyer.' She laughed without humour. 'He handled the separation proceedings for her and got Park to agree to paying her all that money. He should have fought it but he didn't want it splashed in the newspapers. It doesn't seem right, does it? Her own lawyer . . .'

'Go on,' Rogers said patiently.

'There was a man living in a big house at Spye Green. She's been there a lot, Park says.' She searched her recollection. 'There's a man who flies hawks and a man with a very old green car. A veteran model, Park called it. Oh dear,' she said, 'I've such a wretched memory and it's all so beastly and squalid.'

'Life usually is,' he assured her. 'Was there a man with a Rolls-Royce?'

'Yes, there was. His name was Qu . . . Quill . . . ? Something beginning with a Q.'

'Quint?'

'That's it,' she said. The flesh tightened over her cheek-bones. 'You know all this, don't you? Like you knew about me.'

'I know a little.' He shrugged deprecatingly. 'I can never know too much. Is there anything else?'

'Park thought she knew he was watching her. It wasn't anything he was very good at. She was so horrible in her promiscuity I don't expect she cared.'

'I don't think you need worry about her any more,' he said casually, but watching her closely. 'She's dead.'

Her hand flew to her mouth. 'Oh, dear God! Not by Park! What have I done! What have I said!' Her eyes rolled from side to side.

'Don't distress yourself,' Rogers said calmly. 'She died of natural causes. Of a coronary thrombosis.'

She was silent for a long time, retrieving the fragments of her lost composure. Then she said, 'That wasn't fair of you. You could have told me before.'

'I could. But I didn't.'

She gave him an unhappy smile. 'I'm sorry. You have your job to do and you must do it as you think best. You know,' she said, tightening her mouth, 'I can't say I'm sorry because I'm not. I'm even glad. But where's Park if she's dead? That's what I have to know.' She held her belly again. 'I'm frightened, Mr Rogers. Things are happening . . .'

'Such as?'

'I had a telephone call earlier on. About two hours ago. A man asked for Park.'

'Just like that?'

'No "Mr Dominis", he said. I thought he was a policeman. When I told him he hadn't returned he shut down on me. When the inspector telephoned at six, I asked him. He said they hadn't called before. It worried me . . . here on my own . . .'

'Don't let it,' he reassured her. 'I'm sure there'll be a simple answer to all of it.' But the little comfort he gave her was illusory. When he found him, Rogers would require Dominis to answer some uncomfortable questions.

'Does he smoke?' he asked.

'No, never.' Her nose wrinkled her disgust and Rogers was glad he had kept his pipe unlit in his hand. Dominis could, of course, be a secret smoker in the toilet but he didn't think so.

'An odd question, Mrs Dominis, but it might prove useful. Do you know when your husband had his hair cut?'

Although perplexed, she was grateful to him for his courtesy in addressing her as Dominis's wife. And it kept her talking. 'It is an odd question, Mr Rogers.'

'Please answer it,' he said, smiling. 'It really could help.'

'About a week ago. I did it myself.'

'Have you a photograph I could use?'

She produced one from the drawer of a scarlet-painted sideboard.

It showed Dominis in his Airways uniform. He was a handsome, rakish man with a lecher's narrow moustache and eyes a woman would be a fool to trust. Rogers thought he must have been tamed considerably since the photograph was taken.

In the hall he saw the missing man's dark blue cap with its shiny braided peak and the gilt winged badge with a C-GA motif. 'May I?' he asked, taking it from its peg. There were a number of hairs inside adhering to the plastic lining. Unobserved, he slid one out. Later he would put it between two unused pages of his notebook.

He hesitated as he left the house. 'Get someone to stay with you,' he urged. He looked at her swollen figure. 'I'll let you know as soon as I get some news.'

7

Rogers made a hurried return to Spaniards Rise, flogging a hot engine up the steep hill leading to it. On the way he had been blinded by the undipped plate-sized headlights of an approaching car. As it passed him he had had a momentary glimpse of a brass radiator shell and glittering exhaust pipes sprouting from a long green bonnet. It could only have been Lingard's Bentley.

The house was still in darkness and Quint had not returned. The wheels of Rogers' car left furrows in the gravel and moss as he took off in a mood of frustrated irritation.

Coltart was in his office waiting his return, his jaws bulging on a wooden toothpick.

'Did I drag you away from television, sergeant?' Rogers asked, knowing he never watched it. He was in the mood to quarrel with someone.

'No,' Coltart replied mildly. 'You had me pulled out of The Saracen's Head.'

'They must miss you,' Rogers said ungraciously.

'Mr Lingard might. He was there earlier on.' Coltart's bull mastiff face was expressionless.

Rogers thinned his lips. 'I want to see him.'

'You should choose some other time.'

'Oh?'

Coltart didn't like Lingard: had liked him even less since he had learned of his resignation. But he was still reluctant. 'He was knocking back Pernods like milk shakes. And not being what I'd call gregarious.'

'Be explicit, sergeant.' Rogers was frowning.

'All right. He was nasty-drunk. Ready to hang one on the

247

barman's chin if he so much as coughed for the wrong reason.' Coltart bit hard on the toothpick, blinking his eyes. He might have wanted it to happen.

Rogers checked his watch. It was nine thirty-five. He had wasted time returning to Spaniards Rise. 'What time did he leave?'

'About nine.' His face was serious. 'In the mood he was, he's probably tearing some poor bastard's arm off at this very moment.'

'He's cutting his losses, sergeant, rationalizing his gullibility. We all do it in different ways.'

That was difficult for Coltart to understand and he shrugged Lingard and his problems away.

Rogers abruptly discarded the subject of his former second-in-command. 'I want some urgent background information. Tonight if possible. And I'm sure it is. Dig out the Area and Beat constables concerned. Check Vehicles and Firearms records, anything you can think of that will provide useful facts.' He ticked off names on a list with his pencil. 'A complete rundown on Jagger, Hacker, Wallace, Garwood and Norton. I know enough about Galbraith and Quint to be getting on with. See me at eight-thirty in the morning and brief me on their domestic set-ups, what they do to scratch a living, what cars they run, their general reputations. That sort of thing.' He gave the sergeant the photograph of Dominis. 'Get Sergeant Lucas to run off a dozen copies of this. Tonight. It's Exhibit A, Nancy Frail's missing husband. It's too bloody convenient she should die just when he so badly wanted a divorce. More than significant that he's coincidentally vanished.'

It was pure Coltart that he made no comment about Rogers' giving him a full night's work. 'Shall I telephone you if I get anything really useful?'

Rogers kept his expression straight. 'I hope to be off the air for an hour or two. Leave any message with the Information Room Inspector.'

When Coltart had lumbered from the office, he lifted the telephone receiver and dialled the number of St Jude's Hospital. The operator finally located Bridget in the pathological laboratory.

'Still working, Bridget?' he said lightly. 'I thought you'd be polishing sherry glasses.'

'At the moment I'm working overtime, finishing off the staining of some interesting little wrigglers for you.'

'That sounds fine. I rang to say your visitor is likely to be about twenty minutes overdue. Does it matter?'

Her voice was neutral. 'I shall be here in the lab.' Which left Rogers wondering and he chewed his lip uneasily.

He next dialled the Chief Constable's home number.

He was in, sounding distended with someone else's dinner. 'I telephoned earlier, sir,' Rogers said. 'You told me to keep in touch.' He gave him the lot, including his interviews with Midgley and the woman calling herself Mrs Dominis. Telling him thus made it seem as if he had been digging into a sewer. Which he knew would upset Huggett's rather prissy, unworldly views on the nature of humanity.

Huggett found his voice. 'You're certain of all this?'

'Most of it. Not all. It's the general picture I've got.'

'I can't believe it,' he said flatly. 'Not Sir Andrew . . . Mr Galbraith: this Lieutenant Colonel . . . you *must* be mistaken. People like that don't do those sort of things.'

Rogers was irritated that Huggett's snobbery equated professional and social position with a strict sexual morality. 'With respect,' he said bluntly, 'I fail to see why not. You don't have to be an unwashed illiterate to fornicate with a whore. I'll quote some national names if I have to,' he added helpfully, sailing very close to the wind of insolence.

'Thank you, Mr Rogers,' Huggett said frostily. 'I am well aware of the point you are trying to make. I meant these particular men. I am equally aware that it could be none of our business. I still believe you may be mistaken.'

Rogers said patiently, 'I concede that Sir Andrew's cheque may have been for the purchase of the French stamps. But those, being apparently stolen, certainly need investigation. Nor does their purchase explain Miss Frail's three visits to his house. Or his five to hers.'

'Visits to his house? To hers?'

'I'll admit they could have stayed at an hotel but that would be dangerous. I believe the bracketed "h"s and "a"s after each set

249

of initials indicate Home and Away visits.' He laughed briefly. 'She seemed to have had a sense of humour, whatever else.'

The noise Huggett made was indicative of a vast disbelief.

'I could be wrong,' Rogers admitted, 'but it fits. Anyway – leaving Wallace aside for a moment – the other payments need explaining. And, as an important corollary, the matter of who dumped her body in the lane. She may not even have been dead. Which would aggravate the offence considerably.'

'I don't like it, Mr Rogers.'

'Neither do I, sir,' Rogers answered, wilfully misunderstanding him. 'It smells like a privy to me. One of the old-fashioned kind.'

'When I say I don't like it, I mean I don't like our getting so involved in what appears to be a moral issue.'

Rogers scowled into the mouthpiece. 'You know already, sir,' he said patiently, 'I'm not concerned with any moral issue. I'm concerned with one fact only. Who had sexual intercourse with her before – or while – she died. Not why. Anyway, we're already involved. I've the Pathological Laboratory working on it. I've sent exhibits to the Forensic Science Laboratory and I've made the enquiries I've already mentioned.' Before Huggett could object again, he continued, 'There are also the other matters I've mentioned. Dominis hasn't gone missing for nothing. The woman he's living with is about nine-and-a-half months pregnant and he isn't going to default on a highly paid job with C-GA for a triviality. Stretching a point, Quint's missing from his home too. Why he called at Miss Frail's flat is something only he can answer.'

'I don't quarrel with any of that,' Huggett said stiffly. He was liking it less and less and it sounded in the tone of his voice. He was also having to concede points to Rogers' argument. 'But I insist we cannot afford a profitless scandal involving public figures.'

'We'll have one anyway,' Rogers promised him stubbornly, 'if I don't get to these people before Lingard does. He's got it into his head Frail was raped and he's in the mood to do something bloody-minded about it. I believe he's already looking for Dominis and Quint. He won't miss out on the others either.'

'You must stop him.'

Rogers allowed his exasperation to sound. 'If I may say so, that's easier said than done. Neither of us has any effective authority over him.'

'He is still a police officer and subject to my instructions.'

Oh God! Rogers groaned to himself. Aloud, he said, 'And he's liable to tell us . . . me, anyway . . . to get stuffed. He knows there's nothing to stop him from asking questions, making what enquiries he chooses as a private citizen. Unless he actually obstructs my own enquiries I can't touch him.'

'And that's that,' he growled as he replaced the receiver after several minutes more of querulous doubts from Huggett. He would be exposed and naked to disciplinary trouble if there was no more in the investigation than a simple coronary thrombosis and a reasonable explanation from somebody to account for her being where she had been found. It was a sobering thought but he wasn't going to allow it to give him an ulcer.

Before he left the office he swallowed a whisky, washing and scrubbing his teeth in the cloakroom at the end of the corridor. He scowled at his face in the mirror; shadowless and clear-etched under the unflattering strip lighting. 'You bloody lecher,' he mouthed at it. 'You should know better.'

In the car he shaved his whiskers as he drove, holding the steering-wheel rim in one fist. He afterwards smoothed his chin and jowls with the back of his hand, checking he'd made an acceptable job of it.

Bridget, trim in a grey woollen dress, was alone in the laboratory, writing notes.

She smiled at him on his entry. An easy, friendly smile that said nothing at all. 'A positive on the semen test,' she greeted him without preamble. 'All the spermatozoa you'll ever need. Your girl-friend was carnally known, possibly during or immediately prior to her coronary. An over-excited orgasm, I expect,' she murmured drily.

Rogers turned down the corners of his mouth. 'It's a sobering thought,' he said. 'To drop dead *in situ*, I mean. More particularly if either you or your partner isn't supposed to be where it happens.'

Bridget remarked calmly, 'If the need ever arises, I'll take my

251

partner's blood pressure first.' She said it as if the circumstance was highly improbable and Rogers had a depressing moment of doubt.

She stood and moved to a bench, removing a glass box cover from a binocular microscope. She peered into the eyepieces and adjusted the slide stage with the twist of a gear wheel. She flicked a light switch and moved back, saying, 'Have a look, George. I'm pleased with them.'

Three violet whip-tailed tadpoles wobbled into his field of vision. They were lifeless and unmoving. 'Why violet?' he asked. 'The last time I saw any, they were cobalt.'

'I used Biebrich scarlet and methylene-blue,' she said. 'It's the Van Gogh factor in me coming out. Next time they might be emerald.'

'How many are you going to need to allow you to stand in the witness box and prove intercourse?'

'One. Out of, perhaps, the five million in a single ejaculation.'

'Bless my soul. And you found only three?' He was sardonic.

'Idiot! These are in the thinnest film from a wrung-out swab. Anyway, three lovely little fellows like that will be sufficient to prove sexual intercourse for you. And each only about point o-five of a millimetre long.'

'But not identifiable to any particular man,' he said glumly.

'Not unless you'd like to wait a few years while I rear one in a test tube.' Much of what they were saying was nonsense, a camouflage for their need: Rogers', clear-cut and unambiguous; hers, shallow-rooted and very much at the mercy of chance emotional currents.

She replaced the glass box over the microscope. 'Are you happy now?'

'I'm thirsty.'

Her eyes were dark orange as she regarded him coolly, baiting him. 'Oh, yes. I asked you up for a sherry, didn't I.' She snapped off the lights. 'You'd better come on up.'

Her apartment was on the top floor of the annexe. In the lift they were unspeaking and preoccupied. Rogers felt his visit had developed into a cold-blooded assignation and he fretted to say something. There was nothing that wouldn't be banal and he remained silent.

She slipped the catch on the inside of the door. It was a warm, lived-in place with cushioned furniture and small thickets of potted plants climbing ceilingwards. Through an arch, its curtain undrawn, he could see her bed. There was no way of his knowing whether he was meant to. There were books everywhere and the wired-together bones of a spinal column occupied a place on a coffee table. He shed his overcoat and dropped it in an easy chair already containing Moritz's *Pathology of Trauma* and a fat textbook on bacteriology.

While she poured sherry at a trolley he went to her. She stopped, one glass filled, the bottle poised, her eyes questioning him over her shoulder. There was a shadow of mockery in them. 'No *hors-d'oeuvre* after all, George?' She put the bottle down and faced him.

He put his impatient hands on her waist and pulled her to him. His need for her was urgent, almost brutal, and she felt it.

Her hands were flat on his chest, pushing him back. 'The last time you were here, George, you had objections. You considered loving me inconsistent with your status as a police officer. Or something,' she added.

He kissed the tip of her nose. 'I must have been mad.' He was drunk with wanting her.

'You were,' she agreed coolly. 'Had you considered that it is *I* who might now have objections?'

He released her abruptly, his expression angry. 'I'm sorry,' he said slowly. He turned and picked the bottle from the trolley with a shaking hand, splashing sherry into the empty glass. 'So I've made a bloody idiot of myself. I'll drink your sherry and leave you to it.' He banged the bottle down.

She reached for her own sherry and drained the glass. Then she laughed in his face. 'You've taken a lot for granted, Detective Chief Inspector Rogers,' she taunted him. 'Did you expect me to unzip myself and fall flat on my back?'

There was only one thing he could say and he said it. Coldly and definitely. 'As a matter of fact, I did.'

They stared at each other for long seconds. Then she said

softly, 'How wrong can you be, George?' She moistened her lips with her tongue and turned her back to him. '*You* unzip me.'

He hesitated. His tongue was thick in his mouth. 'You aggravating bitch. Did that make you feel better?'

'Yes. Sadism becomes me.'

There was a spattering of tealeaf freckles on her glossy shoulders as he unpeeled the dress from her. She twisted in his arms and bit him hard on the throat, making him flinch. 'Watch it,' she said, her mouth hot on his flesh. 'I could also be a were-pathologist with a Dracula syndrome.' Her hands were pulling at his shirt front.

On the bed, her palms pressing on his shoulder-blades, she whispered, 'No. You needn't be *that* old-fashioned, poppet. You can't make me pregnant. It's one of the unadvertised emoluments of the medical profession.'

When they had each expended their stored-up lusts on the other, they lay side by side, their warm flanks touching. She ran a fingernail from the point of his chin, down the median line of his chest, along his flat belly to the genitals and kept it there.

'If I ever get you on the table, George,' she murmured, 'I'll bottle it in formalin and label it *Un Spécimen Formidable*. It would look lovely in the laboratory. In time,' she added drowsily, 'I could make a definitive collection of them . . .'

'You flatter me,' he grunted, 'and for God's sake don't say things like that. Not even in fun.'

When he left Bridget's apartment, Rogers was rubber-legged with fatigue and his neck ached. His conscience was an acid eating into his stomach. He felt that somehow he had been infected with the sexual aura of the death he was investigating and the dead woman's erotic shadow darkened his thinking. As he let himself in his front door he cursed himself for being old-maidish about it.

At four in the morning he awoke with a yell, than lay writhing and twisting with a black knot of worry in his gut. He suffered an enormity of guilt. Adultery was suddenly the ugliest word in the world. Stealing from the Force Imprest Account seemed by comparison a prosaic trifle. Although wishing futilely the night's happening could be undone he yet knew himself fallible enough for it to repeated. That women were attracted to his cynical masculinity didn't help. He grimaced in the dark. Bridget had called him a yummy dish. He was in the mood to be Calvinistic in his interpretation of sexual morality and it was dawn before he rationalized his guilt and stuck a less ugly label on it.

8

Waiting for Coltart in his office, Rogers thought he had made too much of the episode with Bridget. But the stump of his conscience was still there, nagging at him in a minor key. Even Joanne's stiff-necked obstinacy and a sullen breakfast hadn't seemed reason enough to excuse his lechery of the night before.

Coltart arrived freshly showered and shaved. His eyes were clear and unpouched. He would, anyway, refuse to yawn on principle.

'Sit down, sergeant,' Rogers said. 'You've had some sleep?'

'A couple of hours in the office chair.'

'Good.' Rogers absently stuffed tobacco into his pipe. It was the first few grammes of the ounce he would smoke during the day. He reached over and switched on the tape recorder. Then he leaned back and said, 'Right. Fill me in.'

Coltart had his notes spread on his knees. 'I'd better start with the late Lieutenant Colonel Rodney Jagger,' he said.

Rogers raised his eyebrows and sat up. 'Late?' he echoed.

'On the eleventh of April he was grubbing out some hedge roots when he had a cerebral haemorrhage. He died in hospital next day. I checked with the coroner's officer. He's dead all right.'

Rogers scratched his name from the list. 'Dying, no doubt, in an odour of sanctity,' he remarked. 'In one way that'll please the Chief Constable. Better dead than damned.'

'Number two. James Hacker. Thirty and unmarried. An optician: Fellow of the British Opticians Association, Fellow of the Spectacle Makers Company. And a hell of a feller with the women. One of those, I'm told, who looks down their bosoms while he's fitting them with glasses.'

'Who wouldn't be an optician,' Rogers murmured. 'What does he look like? I only know of him.'

'Black hair, slim build, Mexican-type moustache. Wears glasses.'

'Do you know an optician who doesn't?'

Coltart considered that. 'Now you mention it, no. This one wears octagonals. A natty dresser and drives an open Porsche. He has a record of minor traffic offences. A very nice chap apparently and good at his job. Lives in a flat over the shop and parks his car in a lock-up behind.'

'Like you, sergeant,' Rogers observed. 'A bachelor with nothing to lose but his freedom.'

That bounced off Coltart's imperturbability. 'Number three. Sir Andrew Wallace.' He shrugged meaty shoulders. 'Deputy Chairman of the Bench. Conservative big wheel. Birthday Honours list knighthood two years ago for political services. Runs a small dairy farm out of town. You already know what he looks like. He's a widower, his wife dying ten years ago. His sister, Constance, looks after the house. She's unmarried, about thirty-five . . .'

'I know of her too. I'm told she keeps it snapped shut like an Old Age Pensioner's purse and likes her gin. Not a bad-looking woman either but a bit on the hefty side.'

'That wasn't quite my information,' Coltart said. 'There's rumour of a boy-friend she sees on the quiet.'

'I asked for gossip. I'm getting it.'

'Sir Andrew runs an old silver-coloured Daimler, she has a blue Austin. They have a woman, Mrs Jacobs, who goes in daily to dust the Rembrandts or whatever. They've money but not enough to spare for a yacht after keeping the house together. His grandfather was Lieutenant General "Khyber Pass" Napier Wallace whose worthy statue blocks the view from the Law Courts.'

Rogers looked glum. 'And Wallace himself the most excruciatingly respectable bore of them all. They all are,' he muttered, 'until they're found out. Just the cosy sort of man to ask if he's been sleeping with a whore. His only known vice, French *Classiques*.'

'Yes?' Coltart said politely and uncomprehendingly.

'Postage stamps,' Rogers explained, 'issued in the eighteen-fifties. Some of them worth a small fortune. I only know because I took five minutes off yesterday and checked at a stamp shop. There's one – a ten-centime bistre – valued at over £650. So a collection of them isn't pimply schoolboy stuff.'

If the big sergeant was impressed he didn't show it. 'Number four. Donald Garwood. Assistant editor of *The Sun & Evening Echo*. You can cross him off your list too ... I think. He fractured his ankle three weeks ago.'

'Falling out of the Frail bed, I expect.'

'No. Stepping off a kerb or something similar. Anyway, he's immobilized in plaster. Has to hobble about with a couple of sticks. I did learn something useful though. Miss Frail was a copy-taster with the *Echo* before she married Dominis.'

'When Garwood probably got it for nothing. All right. He can't drive a car so I've crossed him off. Who's next?'

'A nasty little man. Waldo Norton. A bone-idle bugger who flies hawks and screws anything that stands still long enough. He's kept by his wife who has some money of her own.'

'She must be soft,' Rogers said disparagingly.

'I think he keeps her fairly happy as well. He's the type, I'm told, who can jump on a woman's face and make her come back for more.'

'Don't ever try it, sergeant. He's a smaller man than you.' All this was minimizing Rogers' own peccadillo and he felt happier. He smiled at Coltart.

'He runs a dark green Citroën Safari with a white roof. Carries his birds in it too. He's a quick-tempered man with a mean streak in him. Fortyish, five-feet nothing with an oversized ego. He wears ginger Elizabethan whiskers and a velvet jacket.' That seemed to finish him completely so far as Coltart was concerned. 'I quote the local constable, "All wind and piss".'

'I've seen him about. And his car. He always has a skinny liver-and-white pointer bitch with him. Frail wasn't as choosey as I imagined.'

'I think he bathes regularly and smells all right,' Coltart said solemnly. 'It's just he's such a bouncy, arrogant little sod.' He put his notes in his pocket and yawned behind closed teeth.

Rogers saw it make the sergeant's eyes water. 'You'd better get some sleep,' he said sympathetically. 'The first thing this afternoon I want you to arrange for Midgley to make up a Photo-fit picture of the man he saw visiting the Frail flat. It was dark and he was thirty feet up but I bet he saw every pore in his skin. 'He gave Coltart the hair he had taken from Dominis's flying cap. It lay coiled in a glassine envelope. 'Drop this in at the laboratory. Ask them to do a quick check of it against the hair they found in Frail's clothing.'

He read his watch. The Chief Constable normally arrived in his office at nine-thirty. If he wanted to avoid him – and he did – he would have to move fast. He made some brief telephone calls.

There was no answer from Quint's house and Dominis had not returned. Bridget was in the mortuary with a cirrhosis of the liver and unavailable.

He located Galbraith at his office. 'Yes, George?' he answered. 'What poor devil have you got inside this morning?'

Rogers cleared his throat. 'Nobody, Phil. They're all pleading guilty. An admirable attitude.' He waited a second. 'I'd like to speak to you myself.'

The solicitor sounded surprised. 'Of course, my dear chap. You're not in trouble?'

'No. I just want to speak to you, Phil.'

'This morning?'

'If I can.'

'It'll have to be soon. I'm due in court on a domestic in an hour.'

'Ten minutes, Phil.'

Constance Wallace answered his last call. 'Sir Andrew's on the farm,' she said. Although her words were formal, they sounded warm, her voice mellifluous. Rogers wondered how it had remained unsoured after thirty-five years of her being *virgo intacta*. 'He'll be back at eleven. Can I tell him what you want?'

There was an awkward pause. Rogers tapped his front teeth with the stem of his pipe. 'Strictly legal stuff,' he assured her cheerfully.

'Of course,' she said. 'You can't talk about it on the telephone.'

As he drove through the OUT gate, so Huggett entered through the IN. Rogers showed his teeth in the rear-view mirror. It had been a near thing. He had the day to himself now and things to do.

Galbraith rose from his overloaded desk and shook hands warmly, his round face ruddy with good living. He removed pink-taped bundles from a chair.

'Sit down, George. Nice to see you again.' His grey eyes told Rogers nothing. He was a short, barrel-chested man with a fruity voice. The smooth grey flannel suit he wore had been tailored to disguise an ambitious belly.

'Well,' he said comfortably, 'what can I do for you?' He lit a cigarette with an onyx desk lighter and smiled.

Rogers checked unsuccessfully for the microphone head concealed under a seemingly innocent newspaper or folder. He said, 'I came to see you about Nancy Frail, Phil,' leaving the words to hang in the air between them.

The cigarette jerked between Galbraith's fingers. A look of concern crossed his face. It didn't reach his eyes. 'I read about it in the *Echo* last night. How did she die?'

'Apparently quite naturally. Of a coronary thrombosis. She was found in her car.'

'Unbelievable.' He wagged his head sadly. 'She was a client of mine, George. I handled her separation.' He took a lungful of smoke. 'But why are *you* interested?' His eyes were veiled with wariness. 'I mean, if she died naturally . . .'

'She was taken to where she was found. Dumped there.'

'I see. That's not so good, is it.'

'No. I'm checking on her associates.' He didn't particularly like Galbraith but would get no pleasure from putting him through the wringer. There was a word for that sort of nastiness: *Schadenfreude*. It was absent from Rogers' make-up.

'You mean her professional and business contacts?'

'No. I mean her social contacts. You in particular.'

The thread of smoke from his cigarette zig-zagged like ribboned silk through a patch of bright sunlight above his head. 'I don't know what you're implying, George,' he said at last, a chill in his voice, 'but I think you should be careful. My connections with Miss Frail were entirely professional.'

'She kept a diary, Phil,' Rogers said casually.

The solicitor's ruddy face went pasty. Only the sound of the traffic outside could be heard in the quiet room. Then he forced out, 'A diary isn't evidence of anything or against anybody.' He didn't sound too confident.

'No, it might not be. But it could form the basis for some pretty searching enquiries.'

'I see. All right. Assuming Miss Frail made some notes, what do they amount to?'

Rogers produced his notebook and selected a page. 'They record your nine visits to her flat since the thirteenth of January, the last being on the first of this month.' He put the notebook back in his pocket and stood, moving away. 'If the answer's "no", Phil, I won't waste any more of your time.'

'But you wouldn't be leaving it at that?'

'No.'

'You're really going to dig for some dirt on this, aren't you.'

'I didn't put the dirt there. But the answer is yes, if I have to.'

'Sit down, George,' he said wearily. 'I don't suppose I'm the only married man to have had a mistress.'

'No. We all do what we can to spread it around.' It was as far as Rogers could go in acknowledging a common imperfection. In part, it was a confession. He returned to his chair.

Galbraith reached down and opened a drawer, taking out a brandy bottle. 'The good old therapeutic stand-by for uncovered sin,' he said with a chalky smile. He produced a small glass and poured a stiff dose into it. 'You can't, of course?'

'Not now, Phil. Are you going to tell me about it?'

Galbraith drank the brandy in one gulp. 'There isn't much to tell. I handled her legal affairs on her leaving her husband. We were attracted to each other and that was that. It happens all the time.'

'So it's nothing to get into a stew about.'

Galbraith measured Rogers with his wary eyes. 'How far does this go, George?'

261

'Not far if you aren't connected with her death. Or with the disposal of her body.'

'Well, I'm not. You know my wife, George.'

Rogers did. She was a sinewy, hacking-jacketed, hunting woman with a hardbitten face and a leather backside. She was older than her husband: the type to put him well down on the list of her affections. Certainly below her two horses and her dogs. As he remembered her, she wasn't likely to approve such a debilitating non-sport as sexual intercourse either with herself or anyone else.

'Yes,' he acknowledged, 'I do.'

'You know my partners.'

He knew them as well. Both active churchmen and as narrow with it as the horsehair hassocks they knelt on twice on Sundays. 'Yes,' he said again. He was content to let Galbraith tell it.

'It would mean domestic and professional ruin for me if this got out.'

'I think you exaggerate, Phil.' He was sympathetic. 'There aren't many who can boast a strict moral code. No doubt your partners had it off on the side when they were physically capable. There's no virtue in being moralistic when you're too old to be anything else. We're in the swinging, permissive decade now,' he added disapprovingly.

'The legal profession isn't,' Galbraith said. He looked deflated in his flannel suit. 'And you aren't being investigated,' he pointed out. 'I am.'

'Don't fret. I'm not going out of here and give an interview about it on television. But you haven't told me enough about your relationship with her. Was it a commercial one?'

'Oh, Christ, George,' the solicitor protested. 'You make it sound so damned sordid.'

'Well? Was it?'

'I gave her small gifts,' he defended himself. 'She allowed me to help her financially. She received only the hundred a month from her husband. It just wasn't enough . . .'

'What do you call a small gift?'

Galbraith shifted in his chair. 'Are you asking me to confirm what you already know?' He was getting prickly.

'Probably. But please answer my question.'

'Ten pounds now and then. Something of that order. It helped.'

'She could have got herself a job.'

'That, George,' he said sharply, 'was her decision. She was frightened, anyway.'

'Oh?'

'She was sure her husband was watching her.'

Rogers lifted his eyebrows. 'You were taking a chance if he was. Most unsolicitorlike.'

'No. She knew when he was on a night-flying schedule.'

'Why was she frightened of him?'

'He used to hit her during their marriage . . . he had a foul temper. He also wanted a divorce pretty badly.'

'Tell me about her, Phil. Unbutton your natural caution just a bit. Even the trivialities might help.' He cocked his head at him. 'And you do want to help me, don't you?'

'Bugger you, George,' he snorted. 'I'm more concerned about my own troubles.'

'Come on, Phil,' Rogers urged. 'Tell me what sort of a woman she was.'

'I'm relying on your friendship, George.'

Rogers, busy cramming tobacco into his pipe, grunted, 'Come off it, Phil. You've known me long enough. We needn't get sentimental about it.'

'Damn you.' Galbraith poured another brandy and lit a cigarette. 'It wasn't anything other than some extramarital entertainment.' He was trying hard to reduce his admissions to the level of clubroom chit-chat. 'I used to telephone her and make an appointment. Whatever the time of year I would arrive after dark, leaving the car in the next road. I'd carry a briefcase to give me some sort of cover.' His lips quirked. 'She treated each visit like an elaborate indoor picnic. We had everything but a bloody Fortnum and Mason's hamper and an aerosol of fly repellant. She'd keep me at arm's length until I was damn near puce in the face.' He laughed, seeking understanding from Rogers. The detective smiled with his teeth. 'Then she'd talk. Lord, how she loved talking.'

'What did she talk about?'

'Herself mainly. I remember she told me of her illustrious father – he was a brain surgeon. How he'd got the District Nurse with child and how her mother and the woman's family had all mucked in and covered things up.' He laughed mirthlessly. 'A commendable custom that seems to have died out. She spoke often of her husband, Dominis. How terrified she was of him. How he used to get drunk and chase her bollock-naked all over the furniture. Of course, she didn't quite put it like that but you get the general idea.'

'Yes, vividly. You handled her separation, Phil, on the grounds of cruelty. How much of it was true?'

Galbraith moved uneasily, pulling at his bottom lip. 'We have, more or less, to accept what we're told in domestic cases. She had no scar tissue, no bruises. But that doesn't signify, of course. Somehow I believed her.' He lost himself for a moment in recollection. Then he smiled ruefully. 'I oughtn't to tell you this. It doesn't show me in a very good light but it underlines my complete frankness. One evening there was a knock on the door. We lay quiet for a few moments hoping whoever it was would go away. Then it sounded as if the door was being battered down. Nancy put on her dressing robe and went to answer it. I heard a man's voice – I couldn't make out what he was saying – and Nancy was expostulating with him, saying it was late and she was in bed. At first I thought it was Dominis and that was enough for me. I put on my pants and socks, grabbed the rest of my stuff and was through the window into the garden. I dressed behind the bushes and got out quickly through the back way.'

'When was this?'

'Months ago. I can't remember exactly when except it was bloody cold with frost on the grass.' His brow furrowed. 'She told me later it was an old friend of her father's calling unexpectedly. But, you know, the voice had something familiar about it.' He shook his head, anticipating Rogers' question. 'It's no good. I've tried and I still can't place it.'

'Anything more, Phil?'

'Christ! I'm being more than obliging.' There was a tiny spark of resentment there.

'I know. It's so nice of you. Did she mention any other man?'

264

His forehead wrinkled. 'Yes. One man. She said she'd helped the police over the Clancy-Spiteli murders back in June. This man was concerned in the case, I believe. She didn't say anything other than he worried her.'

Nancy Frail had been Lingard's end of the enquiry and Quint had also been concerned in it. Rogers thought he could make his choice between the two of them. 'But no name?'

'No. It was an isolated casual remark. I didn't want to know about it anyway.'

'Did she ever visit you at your home?'

'My *home*!' Galbraith looked astonished. 'Are you mad?'

'Always at her flat?'

'Yes.'

'No Mr and Mrs Smith at small hotels?'

'Your humour is misplaced,' Galbraith said stiffly.

'I'm sorry. You had a key?'

'No.' He stared at the end of his cigarette. 'As I said, it was a casual affair. Nothing emotional. Certainly not permanent.'

'She had others?'

'Affairs? What makes you ask that?' He was annoyed. 'She was basically a nice, well-bred woman.'

'I wondered. Do you know she called one of her cats Philip?'

'Yes.'

'The other six had names.'

'I imagine they did. What are you getting at?'

'They all had men's names. And three of them are shecats.' He paused. 'You weren't the only one. Some of the others paid by cheque. So I know.'

Galbraith's face was expressionless. He expended his protest by viciously stubbing out the butt of his cigarette. 'You've a bloody cruel streak in you, George.'

'Yes, I have,' he acknowledged as if Galbraith had said he had black hair. 'It makes me ask awkward questions. Like, where were you on Sunday evening the twelfth of October?'

'That's the evening she died?'

'Yes.'

'What if I say I was home with my wife?'

'I'd check if necessary.'

'Damn you. Haven't you any humanity at all?'

'A bit. Where were you?'

'At home. As I said.' He looked anxious. 'But on my own. My wife went to her mother's place. What times do you need to clear me?'

'Say, up to eleven o'clock.'

His eyes were on the chaotic jumble of folded papers and books scattered on his desk. 'She didn't come home that night. It's not unusual. She sometimes stays. I was on my own. But she telephoned at about ten forty-five. I trust you'll take my word for that?'

'No more than I could before.'

'Are you suggesting I'm lying?' There was no friendliness in his eyes now.

'Don't come the court advocate stuff with me, Phil,' Rogers said sharply. 'You lied when you said your relationship with Frail was a professional one. Of course you'd lie. Particularly if you thought you'd get away with it.'

Galbraith swallowed his anger like a piece of jagged tin. 'I'm not lying now. I was at home all day and all night.'

'All right. Can I have one of your head hairs?'

'In God's name, why?'

'To check against one I already have.'

'One of mine?'

'I don't know. That's what I want to find out.'

'I see.' His lips tightened. 'Where was this other hair found?'

Rogers looked at him quizzically, not answering.

'You can't tell me?'

'No.'

'I'm sorry. There's no obligation on me to go that far. It wouldn't be unreasonable to suppose a few of my head hairs are in the flat. Hell, George,' he protested. 'You can see my point of view, surely.'

'Only if you've something to hide. Have you ever been in her car?'

'No.' He asked uneasily, 'Does Mr Huggett know about this?'

'Yes. If it's any consolation to you, he doesn't believe it.' Rogers smiled. 'He's your friend. Would you prefer to disabuse him yourself?'

'You're a bastard, George. You mean as an alternative to your telling him?'

'Somebody has to, Phil.'

'There's no chance . . .'

'No,' Rogers said warningly. 'Don't ask it.'

'Sorry. Can I ask you a question?'

'Of course.'

'Where did Nancy die?' There was a slight tremor in his voice.

'In someone's bed, I imagine. It left the particular owner of it with a pretty problem of disposal.'

'She didn't die in mine. You've got to believe that.'

'Then you needn't worry, need you.'

'I do. You'll respect my position . . . not see my wife unless you have to.'

'I won't see her unless I'm forced to.' He eyed the stocky Galbraith and grinned, not unsympathetically. 'Don't fret, Phil. So far you don't add up to being a very likely suspect. Not just at this moment.'

When Rogers left, the solicitor's handshake was tepid but he managed a pale smile. 'At the moment, I wish I'd never seen the bloody woman. Or you either, George, for that matter.'

The sun had burnt up the clouds and Rogers opened the car window. A warm breeze smelling of canal water and car exhaust fumes blew sparks and ash from his pipe into the back of the car.

Spye Green Hall, pink-bricked and Georgian, was set in a walled area of pruned greenery. Every tree and shrub stood symmetrical with its neighbour; the turf beneath shaved almost to the roots. Rogers approached it through two stone gate pillars decorated with armorial bearings, the car's tyres crunching on thick, freshly raked gravel.

The massive carved oak door was designed to make callers feel they should have slunk in by the tradesmen's entrance. Rogers lifted the heavy brass knocker on it with a forefinger and let it drop. Then he did it again.

The woman who opened the door was no dried-up, juiceless

spinster. She was soft-skinned and as well proportioned as an operatic Valkyrie. Her hair was yellow and cut short in small curls like the petals of a chrysanthemum. Her eyes were bright. If she was *virgo intacta* it was, Rogers admitted to himself, doing her the world of good. He could smell the faintest whiff of gin. That was all there was to support his earlier assessment of her to Coltart.

She smiled at him. She had dimples as well. And her teeth were surprisingly white. 'Chief Inspector Rogers,' she said. 'Do come in.' As she turned away the smile dropped and for a moment she looked worried.

He followed her along the corridor, admiring her well-fleshed body in the apricot jersey dress she wore. He could discern the outline of her briefs beneath it. They were very small briefs.

Her brother was in his study. He sat at a huge desk as if granting a vice-regal audience. He neither rose, offered to shake hands nor asked Rogers to sit.

When his sister had closed the door behind her, he said, 'And what can I do for you, chief inspector?' His manner was such that Rogers wanted to hit him.

He was a big man with smooth, buttery blond hair. His features were blobby and puffed out with his pomposity. He wore a hairy Harris tweed suit, a pheasant-shooter's check shirt and a purple and green college tie.

Rogers noted a current copy of Debrett's *Baronetage, Knightage and Companionage* on his desk. That didn't surprise him. Wallace would be in it. There were also copies of *The Farmer and Stock-Breeder* and *The British Friesian Journal*. An empty coffee cup and a plate of charcoal biscuits were on a silver tray. To the detective, he looked just the man to savour the flimflammery and fake feudalism of a political knighthood.

Rogers waited to be asked to sit. When he wasn't, he said, 'I'm making enquiries into the death of a woman called Nancy Frail. You know of her? And of her death?'

'Yes. It was in the newspapers. Why have you come to me?'

'Miss Frail was found dead in her own car. She appears to have died naturally from a coronary thrombosis. Later, however, she was left in a lane not far from here. The circumstances require my checking on her associates.'

'I still say, why have you come to me?'

'I thought you might like to tell me about your own association with her.' Rogers kept him pinned with his eyes, noting his reaction. There wasn't much of one.

'Just what do you mean by that, chief inspector?' He was trying to intimidate the detective; trying to make him feel like one of his herdsmen asking for an undeserved rise in pay. Apart from his natural contempt for titles, he was damned now if he was going to call him 'Sir Andrew'.

'I'm asking you if you had an association with Miss Frail.'

'If I did, I'm not so sure it would be any of your business.'

'If you did, I'm just as sure it would,' Rogers said calmly.

Wallace got up from the desk and stood with his back to the fire. It was burning sawn blocks of wood and smelt like autumn.

'I don't particularly like your attitude, chief inspector.'

'Oh? In what way?' Rogers asked politely. It was a deceptive politeness.

'I'd like you to remember who I am.'

Rogers almost smiled. Had Wallace two chins he would have led with them both. 'I know you are Sir Andrew Wallace and a Justice of the Peace. Is that what you mean?'

Wallace flushed with anger. 'As you choose to put it like that, yes.'

Rogers' manner was dangerously quiet. 'You mean I didn't knuckle my forehead? Call you Sir Andrew every other word?' Being left standing had put a cutting edge to his dislike. 'Are you complaining because I'm not crawling around you like a bloody lap dog?'

There was a quietness of shocked incredulity. Somewhere in another part of the house Rogers could hear the droning of a vacuum cleaner being used.

There were pink blotches on Wallace's cheeks when he spoke. 'How dare you, chief inspector.' He was shaking with anger. 'I meant nothing of the sort. Your attitude is insolent . . . outrageous.'

'And yours is arrogant,' Rogers said harshly. It hadn't taken long for the two men to start fighting and Rogers was taking a calculated risk in what he said. When Wallace started to say something, he interrupted, 'Wait a moment. Are you saying you're immune from being questioned by a police officer? That you expect special privileges? Is that it?' His fierce glare forced an answer from Wallace's pomposity.

'No, I do not. It depends on their form.'

In Rogers' opinion, Wallace had very little above his collar stud and it showed. He was uncertain of what he could do with the blackbrowed, challenging detective.

'Only, if you *do* consider yourself privileged,' Rogers pressed him, 'I'll be quite happy to make my enquiries about your association with Miss Frail elsewhere.'

Wallace puffed his cheeks. 'Is that a threat?'

'Yes.'

Wallace presented his back to Rogers and kicked at the logs in the fire. When he turned he had contained his anger although it still glowed in his eyes. In a choked voice he said, 'Ask your questions, chief inspector.' He didn't say, *and then get out* but Rogers knew that was what he meant. 'I warn you, however, I shall be complaining of your conduct to Huggett.'

'I expect you to,' Rogers said with indifference. 'While you are doing so, remember the terms of my office. They include the phrase, "without fear or favour". I don't recall their mentioning there were certain people they didn't apply to.'

'I repeat, ask your questions,' he ground out.

'Did you know Miss Frail?'

'I did.'

'In what connection?'

'I purchased something from her.'

'A collection of French Louis Napoleon stamps?'

Wallace's eyes jerked his surprise. 'Yes.'

'When?'

'In June of last year.'

'How much did you pay for it?'

'That's my business.'

'And mine. Was it £850? Paid by cheque?'

'You seem to know all about it.'

'Show me the stamps, please.'

He hesitated, then went behind the desk and crouched down before a small green safe. He turned a key in the lock and wrenched at its handle. From its interior he took a slim blue album. He placed it on the desk and opened it carefully. He seemed reluctant to expose it to Rogers' inspection.

The detective examined the stamps hinged to the black pages. They were interleaved with sheets of transparent paper. The fifty or so stamps were unused and in mint condition. The ten-centime bistre Rogers had checked on was there. He indicated it with his finger. 'That one's catalogued at £650. What is the value of the lot?'

There was all the cupidity of possession in the man's eyes. 'In *Thiaude's* catalogue, about £1700. But that,' he hastened to say, 'is a different thing from the market value. I paid Miss Frail the current valuation.'

Rogers was disbelieving. 'Half the catalogue value? Is that normal?'

'Perfectly normal. You obviously know nothing of stamps.'

Rogers closed the album. 'I know these were stolen abroad. Then smuggled through the customs.'

Wallace's jaw dropped. He looked from the stamps to Rogers and back again. 'What did you say?' he demanded in a strangled voice.

'I said they were stolen. Then smuggled into this country.'

'Rubbish!' His face reddened. 'They were willed to Miss Frail by her father some years ago. He was a well-known collector.'

'She said that?'

'Yes.'

'You don't know it as a fact?'

'No.'

'Why was she selling them?'

'She had very little income.'

'She lied to you,' Rogers said flatly. 'She had a good income and the stamps came from her husband.'

'I don't believe it. Can you prove your outrageous allegations?'

'Her income is a matter of fact. I propose checking through Interpol to find out about the stamps. I'll certainly know when we find Dominis.'

That produced a long silence. 'What do you mean, when

you've found Dominis?' Rogers noticed he hadn't asked who Dominis was.

'He's missing.'

'I see.' He turned and kicked at the logs again. 'Then I suggest you spend your time looking for him. Not asking me impertinent questions.' When Rogers remained silent, his face contemptuous, he said, 'What do you propose doing about the stamps?'

'I shall take them as an exhibit. Unless you wish to argue that you can justify the retention of stolen property.'

'Dammit you can't, man.' He was anguished.' They're unique . . . valuable. The wrong handling . . .'

'I won't hurt them,' Rogers said curtly. 'What do the words Rajput Cat mean?'

Wallace was furious. 'Have you been snooping around? Prying into my personal affairs before coming here?' His voice shook. 'By God, chief inspector, there'll be an accounting for this.'

'Miss Frail kept a record of such things,' Rogers said calmly. The man was a bladder of wind. 'When she died under the circumstances she did, her affairs naturally became ours.'

Although the voice retained a semblance of confidence, the eyes wobbled. 'She could record nothing about which I need be worried, chief inspector.'

'Good. So what did she mean by Rajput Cat?'

'It was something I gave her. A small painting in tempera colours. Of no great value but she loved cats. Does that satisfy you?'

'What was it like?'

He made rectangular motions in the air with a finger. 'About six inches square. In a black lacquered frame. It showed three female figures and a black cat.'

'Had she hung it?' Rogers couldn't remember seeing the picture.

'I don't know. She intended to.'

'Thank you. Now can I return to the question of your relationship with her. My information is that this year you visited her flat on five occasions and she visited you here on three. Is that correct?'

Wallace's complexion was mottled. 'I see,' he said quietly. He had lost a lot of his pomposity and arrogance. But not enough to make him likeable. 'Why is my social life being subjected to scrutiny by the police? Am I required to account to you for what I do? For what I have done?'

'Not really,' Rogers said mildly. 'But I am fully entitled to ask you questions. You, on the other hand, are entitled to refuse to answer.'

He cleared his throat. 'Miss Frail and I were friends, sharing a common interest in a number of things. There was nothing improper – as you appear to imply – in our relationship.'

'If you say so.' Rogers was non-committal.

'Dammit!' Wallace glared at him. 'I do say. You don't believe me, do you!'

Rogers remained silent on that. He didn't. He said, 'I don't want to waste a lot of time explaining that my only concern with your activities is in any bearing they may have on her death and the disposition of her body. To be blunt, your friendship with her only interests me in so far as that is concerned.' He paused, giving his words full weight. 'And then only if you were the last person to see her alive.'

Wallace said harshly and with emphasis, 'I repeat. I knew her only socially.'

'All right. Then give me some of her social background.'

He considered for a moment then said, 'She was definitely someone you would call a lady. Her interests were cultured and she lived a quiet life with very few friends. She never went out much. I think she wished to avoid her husband from whom she was separated.'

'Did she say why?'

'I believed her fears groundless but she thought he had a gun.'

'And the wish to use it?'

'So she told me.'

'But as a magistrate, you didn't advise her to complain to the police.'

He flushed, plainly resenting the reproof. 'I said I didn't believe the danger existed.'

'H'm.' Rogers showed he wasn't impressed. 'When did you last see her?'

'Last month some time.'

'When were you going to see her again?'

'I had made no arrangements.'

'Miss Frail died on Sunday evening. Would you like to tell me where you were?'

'No, I would not,' he snapped back. He had clearly made up his mind to say no more.

Rogers sighed. He picked up the stamp album. 'You'd like an official receipt for this?'

'Yes. And I know every stamp in it.' His voice trembled. 'God help you, chief inspector, if any harm comes to a single stamp. Or if I find that what you have told me is not true.'

'I'll see myself out,' Rogers said curtly. His spine ached from standing.

Wallace turned his back on him, his face thoughtful now as he stooped to throw a fresh block of wood on the fire.

Rogers didn't see the sister on his way out. He thought she might be busy emptying a gin bottle. Having experienced her brother crowing on his own dungheap, he didn't blame her.

9

The green and white Citroën Safari attracted Rogers' attention mainly because it was parked in a No Waiting area in the town centre. The very downward curve of its bonnet spoke of its arrogance.

Rogers pulled in behind it. There was a snuff-coloured hawk hunched inside on a log perch. It wore a leather hood with red-felt eye patches and a feather plume. A gaunt liver-and-white bitch lay near the bird and growled at Rogers through the window. A parking ticket was stuck to the windscreen.

Rogers lit his pipe and waited.

The little bantam of a man approaching twenty minutes later was easily recognizable. His pointed beard and thin moustache were coppery on a lean brown face that had damn-and-blast-you written all over it. The maroon velveteen jacket he wore with a polo-necked pullover was scruffy but of good cut. The trousers were shapeless and stained. He carried three dead unskinned rabbits under one arm. Two hundred years ago he would have been wearing a big sword and itching to slice somebody's gut with it.

Rogers smiled wryly. It wasn't his day for influencing people or winning friends and there was no reason to suppose it was going to change for the better.

Norton ripped the parking ticket from the windscreen. Without reading it he tore it into confetti and dropped the pieces into the gutter.

'That will still cost you,' Rogers said from behind him.

Norton swung around and glared at the detective. His eyes were slate-grey. 'Who the hell are you, cock?'

Rogers had his warrant card ready in his hand. He showed it to him. 'A few words,' he said, 'about Nancy Frail.'

Norton glanced at the card, unimpressed. 'I'm busy.'

Rogers smiled. 'So am I. But I'll make time to talk to you.' He said it as if doing him a favour. Deliberately.

'Oh, you will, will you?' Norton opened the door of the car. 'You've a bloody nerve, cock. What's it all about?'

Rogers felt happier. He could deal with outright, unconcealed hostility. 'It's about the death of Miss Frail.'

'So I imagined. What's it to do with me?'

'If you'll stop being so aggressive about it, I'll get around to telling you.'

'Tell me.'

'Not in the street. There are people listening and I'm not selling you a set of encyclopaedias.'

Norton showed his teeth between the whiskers. 'Funny bastard, aren't you.' It was a form of approval. He jerked his head. 'Sit in the car, cock. I'll give you five minutes, no more. I'm expecting my wife.' He closed the car door after him, throwing the rabbits in the back.

Rogers smiled again. Norton wasn't too happy about it. He opened the passenger door then paused, wrinkling his nose. The nylon plush seat was dusty and splashed with white.

'What's the matter?' Norton asked. 'You're not shy of a bit of hawkshit, are you?'

Rogers said, 'Yes, I am.'

The little man reached behind him and pulled out a grey blanket. It was covered with dog hairs. He draped it over the seat. 'Fussy bastard! I've had the Lord Lieutenant of the county sit there and he didn't complain.'

As Rogers climbed in the hawk gaped its beak and bated, its striped wings flapping wildly against the canvas screen attached to the perch.

'Also a clumsy bastard,' Norton grunted, reperching the bird. 'She can't stand coppers either.' He leaned back and lit a thin cheroot. 'All right, get cracking.' He was watching Rogers in the rear view mirror.

The detective slid the seat back on its ratchets and stretched his legs. It was comfortable in the big car. He opened a side

window. The bitch licked the back of his neck and one cheek.
She had bad breath.

'Make yourself at home,' Norton said sarcastically.

'Thank you. Nancy Frail was found dead . . .'

Norton interrupted him. 'Spare me the details, cock, and get
down to the nub. I do read the newspapers. I also listen to the
radio.'

Rogers continued as if he hadn't spoken. '. . . in her car in
a lane near the railway line off Bourne End. Not too far from
where you live. She apparently died of a coronary thrombosis.
You knew her?'

'You're telling the story.' Norton blew smoke against the glass
of the windscreen, thinking hard.

'I understand you saw her on Saturday night. The day before
she died.'

'So?'

'So I'd like to know something about it.' Rogers was bland
but in no mood to be ambiguous or tactful.

'Why? She wasn't murdered.'

'She was dumped in the lane after she was dead. It's something the Coroner doesn't wholly approve of.'

'Nor me, cock. If I saw her on Saturday as you say, I don't
suppose I'd be seeing her Sunday as well.'

'Why not?'

'Oh, Jesus! Don't play cat and mouse with me. You know the
score or you wouldn't be sitting so bloody smugly where you
are.' He scratched irritably at his small beard with a fingernail.
Then he glanced at Rogers cunningly. 'How many ten pounds
can a man afford to fling around?'

'Was it worth it?' Rogers was surprised at Norton's frankness
after the unpromising start. It was a pleasant change.

'Yes. Or I wouldn't have paid it.'

'Nine times this year?'

Norton shrugged his maroon shoulders. 'If you say so. I never
counted.'

'Where were you on Sunday evening?'

He thought for a moment or two. 'Out.'

'Which isn't good enough.'

'And which isn't worrying me, cock, if it isn't.'

'Where?' Rogers insisted.

Norton screwed his eyes against the smoke rising from the cheroot. 'Nosy bastard! First to The Saracen's Head, then The Ironmaster's Arms, then The Minster Hotel. In that order. Does that satisfy you?'

'Not yet. On your own?'

'Yes. I'm a solitary boozer.'

'Who can corroborate all this?'

Norton snorted. 'That's the sort of thing you get paid for. Don't ask me to do your dirty work.'

'All right. It's on your own head.' He held out his hand palm upwards and Norton stared at it. 'Let me have the key she gave you. You won't need it now.'

'Key?' he said blankly.

'The key to her flat.'

'Don't be daft. I never had any key.'

Rogers held the damn-and-blast-you glare for a long time. 'All right. Do you know any other friends of Miss Frail's?'

'God! How you coppers love a smarmy euphemism. You mean paying customers?'

'If you like.'

'She never told me and I didn't ask.'

Rogers took a chance. 'But you knew Harry Quint as one.'

'He told you?'

'He paints birds of prey. He'd know you. You'd know him.'

'For a copper you're a clever bastard.'

'I got it out of a training manual. Did you ever meet her husband?'

'I wouldn't know him if I did. Look,' he said impatiently, 'while I don't give a damn, my wife's due back any minute. She'll only . . .'

'I think she's here,' Rogers said.

Seeing the woman angling towards the Safari, he remembered her. She was slim with square shoulders and short cropped hair under a floppy hat. She wore an offwhite shower coat and buckled red shoes and carried a leather bag with small packages in it. Her features were neat and she looked too good for her husband. Rogers thought sourly that any woman would be too good for him.

He opened his door and got out, holding it open for her. She smiled at him and waited. He noticed her eyes were dark green and her teeth nicely white.

Norton leaned sideways and said, 'I've been clobbered for parking again. Meet the local law.'

'Rogers,' the detective said. 'Your husband's a born loser. It's going to cost him another two pounds.'

She shook his hand. 'It serves him right, Mr Rogers. I've told him so before.'

He shut the door after her. She didn't look the sort of woman to be fooled that easily. To her husband, he said, 'I'll see you around, Mr Norton.'

He beat an approaching traffic warden to his own car by a couple of yards.

After brushing dog hairs from his coat, Rogers entered a telephone kiosk and spoke to Detective Sergeant Hagbourne.

There were two messages left for him. Hagbourne read them out. The first, from Sir Andrew Wallace, asking him to return to Spye Green Hall as soon as possible. The second – from the laboratory – stated that the hair taken from Dominis' cap was identical in its colour, scale formation and in the measurement of its medulla to that found on the deceased woman's clothing.

Both messages pleased him. 'Has the Chief Constable been asking for me?' he asked Hagbourne.

'Yes. Round and about.'

'He left instructions?'

'Only to let him know when you'd returned. I told him you were booked out on general enquiries.'

'Good. You know Waldo Norton the falconer?'

Hagbourne laughed. 'I knocked his gin and vermouth over once. He wanted me to go outside and fight. I had a bit of a job to get out from under. I know him all right.'

Rogers knew Norton had been lucky that Hagbourne had refused his challenge. The sergeant could macerate an opponent into a bloody pulp with his small bony fists.

'Do a check on him. He's supposed to have visited The

279

Saracen's Head, The Ironmaster's Arms and The Minster on Sunday evening. If he did, someone saw him. I'm on the way to Spye Green Hall if you want me.'

Wallace answered the door to Rogers. He was in no better mood and motioned him curtly to enter. But he surprised him in the study by asking him to sit.

Wallace remained standing. 'Chief inspector,' he said, still the *grand seigneur*, 'distasteful as this matter has been, I have spoken to my sister about it. In order that you should make no unpleasant and possibly damaging enquiries about my movements, she would be prepared to corroborate that I spent the Sunday evening here at home.'

'Which is what you did?'

'Of course.' Wallace gestured his irritation. 'Dammit, I find it difficult to stomach your continued scepticism.'

Rogers was urbane. 'I don't disbelieve you. Why should I? If your sister will corroborate it, that's all I require. Your actual association with Miss Frail then ceases to interest me.'

Wallace frowned. 'You mean you want her to tell you herself?'

'It's the form,' Rogers said mildly. 'You can't expect otherwise.'

'I did. But if you insist, she will. Before you do, however, I require your assurance you will treat my affairs with discretion.'

'Naturally.'

Wallace hesitated. 'One thing more. Is it possible for me to obtain the return of my painting?'

'Not through me. You gave it to her and it forms part of her estate.'

'I see.' He looked uncomfortable. 'That is another matter in which I require your discretion. My sister may not understand the reason prompting my giving it . . .'

'I shan't mention it,' Rogers said curtly. 'I'm never very forthcoming. I just like other people to be.' He kept his face wooden. 'Did you have a key to Miss Frail's flat?'

A spasm of anger twisted Wallace's mouth. 'Damn you, *no*! You've a marked aptitude, chief inspector, for being too blunt.'

'It's only a question,' Rogers said with an irritatingly amiable smile, 'and you've answered it.'

Wallace moved to the door. 'I'll fetch my sister.'

Rogers said, 'Just a moment, please. I'd like to interview her alone.'

'Oh?' Wallace stopped dead. 'Why?'

'I never interview anybody in the presence of the person we are discussing.'

Wallace drew a deep breath. 'I still propose complaining to Huggett about your manner, chief inspector. I advise you not to make it worse.'

'On her own, please.'

He tried to stare the detective down and failed. He was savage with frustrated anger. Rogers followed him along the corridor. They stopped outside a white door and Wallace tapped on it with the knuckle of his finger.

Constance Wallace opened the door. She showed Rogers her dimples again. Her hair was slightly disordered and the perfume of gin was stronger.

'Mr Rogers wishes to speak to you on your own, Constance,' Wallace said disapprovingly. He was as magisterial with his sister as he had been with Rogers. He turned on his heel and left them.

She smiled at the detective again. 'Please come in, Mr Rogers. I was expecting you.' Her voice was beautifully modulated and meant for opening church bazaars.

The room and its contents appeared to have been handed down by a couple of generations of looters of *objets d'art* from Victorian India. There were lacquered tables in black and scarlet and ebony elephants; brass vases and oriental paintings and sepia-coloured photographs of topeed and heavily moustached polo players; Indian Army officers in self-conscious groups with speared hogs and turbaned retainers holding horses. The room was a monument to a long-dead British Raj. Only the bowls of white flowers in it gave the room femininity. The air was sweet with their scent.

The chairs – probably taken from an officers' mess, Rogers thought – were comfortable and he sat in one.

She went straight to a sideboard and clinked glassware. 'A drink, Mr Rogers?' she asked over her shoulder.

'A gin and tonic, please, if you don't tell anyone,' he replied with a friendly solemnity. Although she had the demeanour of a memsahib in the making about her, he liked what he saw.

They sat companionably, facing each other. She combed her hair back with her fingers. Where the dusty sunshine touched it, it glinted gold. She either had water in her gin or was drinking it straight. He couldn't tell. But she had had more than was usual by midday.

'I have had no experience of being interrogated by a policeman,' she smiled. 'Do you ask me questions?' She took a sip of her gin and put the glass down carefully.

'Yes,' he said. He had placed his own drink untasted on a coffee table. He would wait to see how the interview progressed. 'Your brother knew a Miss Frail through buying stamps from her. She died on Sunday evening of a coronary thrombosis in circumstances which require I check on everybody knowing her.'

'The thrombosis was a natural one?'

'So far as a post-mortem examination can tell us, yes.'

She nodded. 'I see. I understand there is something wrong with the stamps, that they are stolen property.'

'Yes.' He smiled amiably. It was an expression that sat uneasily on his hawkish face. 'Something your brother need not have known, of course. But I'm more interested in your confirming his whereabouts on Sunday evening, Miss Wallace.' Looking at her, he thought she had the smoothest flesh he had seen on a woman.

'We don't live in each other's pockets, Mr Rogers. He has his study.' She glanced around her. 'I have my room. But if he went out I would know. I would hear his car. Which I didn't.'

'You were here all evening?'

The point of her tongue licked her lips. 'I lead a very quiet life. I don't very often go out.' She occasionally slurred a consonant but it could have been the remains of a lisp.

'But you know he was here?'

'I know he was here.'

'Had you met Miss Frail?'

'No, never,' she said crisply, 'although I knew of her. And knew her by sight. I understand she wasn't quite ... you understand?'

282

'I understand.' He considered it safe to drink his gin and tonic.

She regarded him levelly. Her eyes were the amber of warm syrup. 'Just what is the background to a coronary thrombosis that sends a detective chief inspector out investigating it, Mr Rogers? I thought you were reserved for serious crimes.'

'She was dressed and taken to a lane and left there. It isn't something you can do and not invite investigation.'

'What do you mean by being dressed?'

'I believe she was undressed when she died.'

'I see,' she said thoughtfully. 'But nothing nasty . . . seriously criminal?'

'Not that I know of.' Which was less than the truth. But necessary.

She shivered. 'A sordid happening and I don't want to know anything more of it.' She stood and went to the sideboard. 'Another drink?'

'Thank you, no.' He held his glass up. 'You've left me behind.'

While she poured another gin, he studied her. He was in a state of relaxed euphoria. He didn't get it very often. When he did he felt free of physical imperfections and mental grittiness; floating a foot above the ground. So he imagined the state of nirvana to be. He liked her as much as he disliked her brother. She was a big woman and moved easily. She wasn't built for the frustrations and boredoms of a spinster's life. He wished he could do something about it. He judged her a strong woman, probably stronger in character than her self-important, strutting brother. Despite the gin. When she sat again her thighs were carelessly exposed. Rogers found it an effort not to look at them. He said, 'I see you're very interested in India.'

'I was.' She seemed in the mood for a talk. Rogers knew what it was to be used as a surrogate priest. She nodded at an open desk, directing his attention to it. He saw a flat portable typewriter and a pile of quarto typescript. 'I've been nearly ten years researching and writing the biography of my grandfather.'

'General Wallace?'

'Yes.' Something in his expression must have prompted her to ask, 'Don't you approve of ancestor worship, Mr Rogers?'

'No. Perhaps because I have none that deserve worshipping.'

'None of mine has done me any good.' She looked wryly in the gin glass. 'I don't suppose you give a damn for the British Raj either?'

'Not really,' he admitted cautiously.

'I can't think many people do. It was a different world. People now . . . they have different standards . . . are less inclined to be moral.' She was introspective.

'Are they?' Rogers twitched his mouth. *She knows*, he told himself. *The pompous sod hasn't got away with a thing.* He said, 'I think the Victorians and Edwardians were just as immoral. Only they didn't make a song and dance about it. They hid the dirt under antimacassars and behind lace curtains.' He nearly said under their bustles but thought better of it. 'Immorality's only condemned by social convention anyway. It depends what you mean by morality.'

'Being a policeman, I suppose you must possess all the virtues?' If there was any irony in her voice, he couldn't detect it.

'Good God, no,' he said, astonished. 'Did I sound all that bluenosed? I suppose we have our smutty little secrets like everyone else. Even the Queen's Police Medal is no guarantee of morality.' His swarthy face was discomposed. 'You embarrass me.'

She laughed delightedly. 'I can talk to you. Do you mind? You don't want to dash off somewhere?'

'I'm flattered. Perhaps I can have that second gin you offered me.'

While she got it for him, he said, 'You are proud of your grandfather, Miss Wallace?'

There was a large photographic portrait of him on the wall. He sported mutton-chop whiskers and a bushy beard. The left side of his tunic was running out of space for medal ribbons. He looked the sort of man who had flogged punkah-wallahs for exercise and the glory of the British Empire.

She had refilled her own glass as well. 'I've written about

three hundred thousand words extolling his undoubted virtues,' she said owlishly. She giggled, not happily. 'Then I
discovered my hero was an old lecher. That he made regular
contributions to the population of Anglo-Indian hybrids.'

'You were surprised?' Rogers knew she wasn't talking only
of her grandfather. She was drawing a not very subtle parallel
with her brother. 'It was probably the in thing in India at that
time.'

'I was shaken.'

'You shouldn't be. You were putting him on an impossibly
high pedestal.'

'But he was the best kind of Englishman, Mr Rogers.'

'You could say Julius Caesar was the best kind of Roman.
But the fact remains his sexual habits don't bear too much
scrutiny.'

'Julius Caesar wasn't my grandfather, Mr Rogers.'

They both laughed.

'You make too much of it,' he said positively. He waved a
hand around the room. 'Your grandfather collected all this?'

'Most of it.'

'And the paintings?'

The gin in the glass she held in her hand didn't slop over.
Not quite. 'Those too,' she said slowly, her expression noncommittal, shutting him out. 'You are interested in them?'

'They're unusual. What are they?'

'What is generally called Rajput art. Rajputa paintings are
usually religious in theme although those are not. They aren't
particularly valuable but I think a lot of them.'

'I like them,' he lied. They were too garish for his taste. If
there had ever been one showing a cat with three women it
wasn't there now.

He squinted at his empty gin glass. 'You make these strong.'
He felt he had known her always.

She took it and refilled it. She was friendly again now they
weren't discussing Rajput paintings. 'I suppose you think I
drink too much?' she said calmly. For the second time she
had succeeded in astonishing him.

'It's *your* medicine,' he observed. 'As it is sometimes mine.'

'Not a medicine. A panacea for a wasted ten years of research on the British Army in Rawalpindi and Peshawar. And three hundred thousand words of uncritical gush.'

'But you aren't disillusioned enough to chuck it all up?'

'Oh, yes I am. I only hope I can adjust.' She looked at him oddly. 'And I do want to adjust, Mr Rogers. To a lot of things.'

There was a knock at the door and it opened. Wallace put his head round it. 'Have you finished, Constance?' he asked reprovingly. 'It's nearly time for luncheon.'

She was short with him. 'I won't keep you waiting, Andrew.'

When he had gone she stood, not swaying but definitely holding herself steady. She said, 'Will you come again? I enjoyed our conversation.'

'I'd like to. But I think, somehow, your brother doesn't approve of me.'

'*I* am asking you, Mr Rogers,' she said, her hand warm and soft in his.

He felt an immense friendliness for her and it showed, he supposed. 'I will,' he promised her and meant it. He hoped the sun wasn't going to be bright outside. It wouldn't do his pre-lunch gins any good.

It didn't and he screwed his eyes against it. As he passed Wallace's Daimler in the drive, he stopped and looked at it. It had a rack fitted to the interior to hold two shotguns. It also had two cigar lighters and a pull-out picnic tray with a compartment for bottles of champagne. There were nine enamelled club badges – most of them French – on a bar over the front bumper telling the world what an important man the owner knew he was.

It was then that the thought hit him that Constance Wallace, despite her use of gin as a crutch, was a very clever woman.

10

The Henri et Camille bistro sold the only coffee in town that Rogers didn't consider tepid slop, tasting of old dish cloths. The menu outside said *Spécialités Particulières Couscous et Coq au Vin*. Rogers never ordered anything there more exotic than a sandwich.

With a Gallic sense of the fitness of things, the kitchen was clinically clean, the toilets uncared for; on the basis, Rogers assumed, that one didn't eat or drink in the latter.

Fat Henri was proud of his butter-cooked food and his wife. He told everybody unable to avoid listening that in his forty-odd years of marriage, he had never looked at another woman. Which seemed an absurd improbability. Particularly as Madame possessed, apart from a surly disposition, a pronounced squint in one dark snapping eye and a silky black moustache under a hooked nose.

'*Ah, Monsieur le Flic,*' he greeted Rogers amiably. 'The *Préfecture* is searching for you. Sergeant 'Agbourne wishes to speak to you in 'aste.'

'Coffee and sandwiches first,' Rogers said. 'Whatever it is will keep until I've finished.' What he wasn't cognizant of couldn't interfere with his eating. He suspected Huggett was on his tail and chasing him to earth.

While he watched Henri making his sandwiches with soft French bread and slices of glistening pink ham, he thought of Bridget. They were, in retrospect, pleasant thoughts. His conscience was on the mend.

He ate leisurely from a small formica-covered table, writing up notes of his interviews. He thought wryly that it would help if he could recognize what or who he was looking for. He was a blind man poking his stick ahead of his toes into impenetrable darkness.

When he had finished, he went to the counter and used the telephone. He dialled the Headquarters number and asked for Sergeant Hagbourne.

Hagbourne said, 'I've called every bar and coffee house in town for you. I was about to start on the churches. We've found the car.'

'Agh!' Rogers was happy again. 'Dominis's?'

'What's left of it. It's been dumped at the back of The Glue Pot and looks as if somebody's had his throat cut in it.'

The lane at the rear of The Glue Pot café was squalid and rubbish strewn. The base of its whitewashed wall was stained coffee-coloured with the urine of a thousand customers from the café. To leave a car like a Sunbeam Stiletto there was the act of a madman, providing an irresistible carcass for thieves to pick at. And those living near or frequenting The Glue Pot were nearly all thieves.

The car stood against the wall like a shattered black beetle, its wheels missing, its axles propped on four piles of housebricks. Children with depraved adult minds had chalked and scratched lavatorial indecencies on its shiny flanks. The number plates had been levered off; the lamp reflectors and bulbs, the wing mirrors, had all been stolen. The window glass had been smashed and the radio and instrument gauges ripped out, leaving nothing but coloured wires behind. Had it been left undiscovered for another night, the engine would have been unbolted and taken and the inside completely gutted. Then the useless shell would have rotted and rusted in the uncaring grey lane until an official of the Corporation Salvage Department tripped over it and caused it to be hauled away.

'They left the ashtray,' Rogers observed to Hagbourne as he regarded the dismembered Sunbeam. 'Which was goddam considerate of them.'

But he wasn't concerned with the cannibalistic dismantling of the car. His interest was canalized in the black gouts of blood he saw on the rubber floor matting and on the smeared foulness on the leather covering of the passenger seat; in the scraping of crushed stone on the control pedals and matting of the driver's side. In the stone powder he saw tiny flakes of yellow and ash-grey. Magnified under his pocket lens they appeared to be fragments of moss or lichen.

Covering the controls with a sheet of polythene and being careful not to touch the steering wheel, he fitted himself comfortably and easily into the driving seat.

When he and Hagbourne had finished their examination, he had the car's remains hoisted into a flat-bed lorry and taken to the police garage.

The two scientific officers he had summoned from the laboratory were already there. 'I want you,' Rogers said, 'to first of all confirm the blood. Then to identify the stone dust for me. You might also look particularly for a contact lens somewhere in the car.' He looked at his watch. It was nearly three. 'How long?' he asked.

Dagg, the biologist, said, 'Don't you ever want anything tomorrow?' He was an old friend of Rogers and could be allowed some sarcasm.

'No.'

'You want us to ignore the demands of the other seven forces in the region? To give you preferential treatment?'

Rogers smiled. 'Of course.'

'Somehow we thought you would,' Dagg observed drily. 'Is an hour or two's working like one-armed paperhangers and ignoring scientifically accepted testing procedures any good?'

'Thanks, John. I need the information today.'

Dagg snorted. 'You surprise me.'

When Rogers knocked at Huggett's office door the effects of the gin had worn off, taking his euphoria with them. He felt stale and stiff-jointed. He thought it would be nice to sit in a hot bath and read a book without worrying. To be able to smoke his pipe in the tranquillity of an overstuffed armchair. The trouble with a murder enquiry was that it wouldn't stand still waiting for the investigating officer to catch up with it. It meant eating sandwiches and wearing dirty shirts and living with the grinning monkey of possible failure on one's back.

Huggett was peppery and pacing his green Wilton with short irritable steps. Each time he reached his sleeping spaniel he would step over or around her as if she were a natural immovable obstacle.

'A most embarrassing day,' he trumpeted at Rogers as he entered the office. 'I've had Galbraith telling me about his liaison with that dreadful woman. I don't know who was the more distressed.' He wagged his head disbelievingly, incredulously. 'How can I ever ask the man to my home again,' he challenged Rogers as if it were his fault.

The detective waited, his expression saturnine, allowing the wash of words to flow over him.

'Then Sir Andrew.' Huggett's eyes blinked. 'I expected, I demanded, some discretion and tact from you. Not this witch-hunting, this stripping a man of the decencies . . .' He put on his colonel-of-the-regiment look. 'He complains you were insolent, that you used the word "bloody" in most offensive terms.'

'Sir Andrew Wallace – with respect – could do with a lesson or two in courtesy himself.' Rogers was coldly annoyed. 'To support that political handout of a title he's got. Nothing short of my kissing his ass would have suited him.'

'There is no need for vulgarity, Mr Rogers,' Huggett said frostily.

'He makes me want to be vulgar,' Rogers snapped. 'And he needs reminding at frequent intervals that we aren't his servants. He's a pompous bore and too full of his own imagined importance.'

'He *is* a magistrate and not lightly to be offended. Certainly not on a minor matter such as this. I warned you . . .'

'So you did.' Roger stuck his underjaw out aggressively. 'And I asked if you were prepared to instruct me to discontinue the enquiry. Which you weren't.' His anger was frothing up. He had always been intolerant of rebuke. 'Despite Wallace's complaint – which I think is a bluff anyway – I'm satisfied I dealt with him properly. He's a liar and in exactly the same league as Galbraith. But without his guts.'

Huggett slapped his flat hand on the desk in an excess of spleen, sliding a filing tray of papers across its shiny surface to fall on the floor. 'If you were investigating a serious crime I could understand it!' he yelled, his complexion mottled crimson. The spaniel flinched and growled at Rogers. It seemed to have more than its natural share of sycophancy.

'It so happens I am,' Rogers said brusquely.

'No you are not. You're investigating trivialities best buried and forgotten. A tuppeny-ha'penny death from natural causes and the unproved theft of some postage stamps. It's not a sufficient justification for you to go barging in with both feet . . . causing God-knows-what trouble in doing it.'

'I'm investigating a murder now,' Rogers said flatly. 'So that takes care of the trivialities.'

Huggett stopped pacing and stared at the flinty face of his subordinate. 'You're *sure*?'

Rogers bristled. 'Of course I'm sure.'

'Good God!' He went to his desk and dropped back into his swivel chair. 'Why the devil didn't you say?'

'Because you never gave me the chance. We've been discussing Wallace and Galbraith.'

'Shut up, blast you!' Huggett snarled at the bitch who was still growling at Rogers. He would have liked to have said it to the detective. 'Tell me now.'

Rogers detailed the finding of Dominis's car and what he had seen in it. 'The blood didn't come from a nose-bleed,' he said. 'It's thick, dead man's blood from the belly. The only conclusion possible is that somebody got himself killed. Either Quint or Dominis. As an outside chance, some X component we know nothing about.'

Huggett threw in his hand. He reached for the telephone. 'I'd better let Sir Andrew know. Cool him off a bit.'

Rogers reacted sharply. 'No, sir. That won't do any good at all. Let him sweat blood for a bit. I may get some more information from him.'

Huggett hesitated, then shrugged. 'As you wish. But you'll have to justify what you've told me.'

'So I will.'

'What are you going to do now?'

'Look for a body. It shouldn't be too difficult,' he said rashly. He had recovered some of his good humour. 'Something about six feet long, eighteen inches wide and beginning to smell a bit. It couldn't have been all that easy to dispose of.'

Hagbourne was waiting for him outside Huggett's office. A thin man with a pessimistic moustache and pouched brown eyes, he possessed a brash sense of humour.

'I couldn't help overhearing the uproar,' he said. 'Have you been reduced to the ranks?'

'Damn near,' Rogers growled. 'But don't go buying champagne on the strength of it. What's the trouble now?'

'Coltart. He's at Midgley's and asking for you to go there urgently. He wouldn't say why on the telephone.'

'I'm on the way. You go to Spaniards Rise and check on Quint's return. If he's there, grab him and hang on.'

Hagbourne said, 'Don't you want to know about Waldo Norton?'

'Not too anxiously.'

'Well, you're going to now I've done the checking. He was seen in The Saracen's Head and The Ironmaster's Arms but not in The Minster. The last sighting of him was at about nine o'clock in the Ironmaster's. He was then three parts cut.'

Rogers considered for a second or so. 'I'm not very interested in him now,' he said. 'Don't take it any further for the time being.'

Coltart answered the door to his ringing, coming out and closing it behind him. 'Before you go in,' he rumbled, jerking a banana-sized thumb over his shoulder. 'Lingard's been here pumping Midgley.'

'What!' Rogers stared at him, his jaw muscles bunched. 'When was this?'

'Last night.'

'The bloody fool!' he rasped. 'Now he has done it.'

Coltart held a blue plastic frame in one big fist.

'You've done the Photo-fit?' His mind was still on Lingard.

The sergeant offered it to him. 'The best Midgley could do with that bitch of a woman nagging in his ear.' He laughed deep in his belly. 'It's Salvador Dali in a blond wig although I can't imagine him being involved.'

Rogers examined it critically, holding it at arm's length. 'Quint wouldn't be flattered but it could certainly be a worm's-eye view of him.' He gave it back to Coltart. 'I'll speak to Midgley,' he said sombrely, 'and God help Lingard if he's interfering.'

'Then God help him,' Coltart muttered under his breath, 'because the sod is.'

The fat woman was still a flaccid hulk of pink flesh on the blue satin settee. She looked at Rogers as if he were a court bailiff repossessing unpaid-for furniture from a crippled widow. By her side was a loaded three-tier cake stand. She was pouring tea into her robin's-bum of a mouth from a tiny gilt and scarlet cup.

Midgley sat unhappily in a chair, a fuming cigarette held between the fingers of a limp hand. 'I should be back in my office, Mr Rogers,' he began querulously, eyeing his wife, indicating who had initiated his complaint.

'Ten minutes only,' Rogers promised briskly. 'So tell me about Mr Lingard's visit.'

Midgley flapped a hand in the direction of Coltart. 'As I told the sergeant, he called here last night. At eight-fifty exactly.' His Adam's apple bobbed. 'He said he wanted to recheck the statement I had made. In case I'd forgotten something vital.'

'So you went all through it again? Told him everything?'

'Yes. I'm sorry . . .'

The woman's expression was a fat belittling contempt. She said, 'H'm' through a mouthful of meringue.

Rogers scowled at her on behalf of her unwilling husband. 'You weren't to know,' he assured him, although he cursed him silently. 'Sergeant Coltart has now told you Mr Lingard isn't on the case?'

'Yes. But last night, I naturally thought . . . his being a detective, you understand?'

'Don't worry about it. What was his attitude?'

'Attitude? Oh, yes. Correct enough, I suppose, in what he actually said. But not very polite. I mean, he didn't say thank you or please.' He hesitated. 'He was very angry about something. He wouldn't sit down.' He glanced at his wife and moistened his lips with a yellow-furred tongue.

'Tell them,' she hissed at him.

'Er . . . yes. He smelled of alcohol. And his manner was most odd. He kept taking snuff and mumbling to himself. I thought . . .' He trailed off apologetically.

'You thought what?' Rogers pushed him.

'I thought he was a little unbalanced . . . you know?'

'But you told him just the same.'

'I knew he was a policeman. I could hardly not.'

'Tell them about his car,' the woman's spiteful voice ordered.

Midgley shuttered his eyes, looking down at his hands clasped on his lap. 'I'm sorry. I remembered after you'd gone that I'd seen Mr Lingard's Bentley go past on Sunday evening. No more than that.'

Rogers lowered his eyebrows. 'That seems an odd thing to forget, Mr Midgley,' he said forbiddingly. 'We were discussing him then. And his car.'

Midgley wrung his hands. 'You know . . . another policeman. It never struck me . . .'

The detective made a noise in his throat.

'. . . I'm a peace-loving man. I don't really want to be involved.'

'Well, you are,' Rogers assured him. For a brief moment he was on the woman's side. 'What time did you see his car?'

'About twenty minutes after the Rolls-Royce left.'

'You saw the driver?' Rogers thought, *The little sod spends all his spare time poking his nose out of the window.*

'Only momentarily but it was Mr Lingard. And he was on his own. He didn't stop, just slowed down and looked at Miss Frail's windows. I suppose he saw there were no lights showing and went on.'

Rogers cocked his head. 'And weren't there?'

Midgley's bald head flushed red. 'I . . . I assumed not,' he faltered. 'Having seen her leave in the Rolls.'

'I thought we'd agreed that was not proven?'

The little man shrugged helplessly. 'I don't know.' His wife visibly sneered at what she had married.

'But you're sure it was Mr Lingard's Bentley?'

'Yes, I'm sure.'

The woman spoke. 'She was a whore.' She said it as if stating a fact nobody else had the wit to recognize.

Rogers regarded her impassively, giving nothing away. 'What makes you say that?'

'You're fools if you think otherwise.' She bit the words out, nodding in the direction of her wilting husband. 'She'd have had him too if I hadn't been around.'

Midgley's head again flushed red and he opened his mouth, gobbling soundlessly like a fish.

'She was rotten. Filthy rotten and diseased.' The tiny mouth spat crumbs of cake on to the carpet.

'Thelma,' Midgley managed to get out. 'You mustn't slander ... she's dead ...'

She ignored him. 'I used to hear them at it.' Her currant eyes were prurient. 'Disgusting animals.'

'I'm sure they were if you say so,' Rogers said, tongue in cheek. 'Do you know any of them?' The woman's malevolence fascinated him.

'No, I don't,' she snapped, looking hard at her husband. 'And if I did I wouldn't tell you.'

Midgley was half-way through his third tortured and crumpled cigarette when Rogers and Coltart left. The fat woman was watching her husband with baleful eyes creased by the eating of a jam sponge slice. It made the little man's wish to be back at his office very understandable.

Before leaving the building, Rogers unlocked the door to Nancy Frail's flat and the two men searched it again. Nowhere was there a painting of a cat with three female figures. Nothing but an unoccupied brass hook in a wall that might once have supported it.

11

On his desk, Rogers found a bundle of message forms waiting his attention. Before he read them, he put out two departmental instructions marked Category A Urgency. One required a special search of unoccupied buildings and sheds, parks and gardens, streams and ponds and waste plots for a body. Whose body Rogers couldn't particularize. The other, ordering enquiries to be made to locate Lingard.

He read the message forms. Chief Inspector Godson from Blakehill had called. Dominis had not reported for his pre-flight briefing. Reading between the lines, Rogers got the impression that the C-GA hierarchy were putting pressure on an uncomfortable Chief Inspector Godson to find out why.

Mrs Jane Norton wanted Rogers to telephone her urgently and Dr Dagg of the laboratory had information for him if he could spare some of his valuable time in calling. A note from Hagbourne said that Quint had either not returned or had and gone out again.

There was nothing from Bridget. He lifted the telephone receiver and put a tentative finger on the dial. Then he changed his mind and dialled the Norton number instead. He experienced a tiny warm glow at his act of self-denial. Jane Norton answered as if she had been waiting by the telephone for his call.

'Could you see me, Mr Rogers? I'd like to speak to you.' She hesitated. 'On a confidential matter.'

'Of course. In my office?'

'Here if you wouldn't mind. My husband has the car.'

'I have a call to make first. In half-an-hour?'

Again she hesitated. 'Not any later,' she said. 'I wish to speak to you alone.'

That meant specifically without her husband being around to listen.

Before he left the office, a call came in from the Traffic Department. Lingard's Bentley had been located outside his flat, the engine cold. There was no sign of Lingard and no answer to the repeated ringing of his flat bell.

Rogers found a white-overalled Dagg in the dust-proof, sound-proof examination room of the laboratory.

'Bill's just finished your blood test,' he said. 'He did an old-fashioned microscopical on it. It's either blood from a human being or from an orang-outang. *Homo sapiens* or *Simia satyrus*, take your choice. If you're happy you haven't got an orang-outang mixed up in it, he'll plump for its being human. The precipitin test and grouping will have to wait until tomorrow.' He grinned at Rogers. 'He's guessing madly but says it's probably from the stomach.'

'Did he say why?'

'It's slightly turbid for a start and there's so much of it. Then there's marked clotting. But it *is* only inspired guessing. You can't have it all ways.'

'Can he put a date to it?'

'Fairly fresh. But anything less than three days is fresh to Bill.'

'And the dust?'

'Ah, my province. Although I used the petrographic microscope, I'm guessing too. But provisionally, common or garden carboniferous limestone with a *soupçon* of volcanic rock in it.'

'And what does that tell us?'

'That it's come from the moors. It's there in the form of outcrops. I think on the last count by the Ordnance Survey people there was about two thousand acres of it. All good rough going.'

'Clever stuff. I don't know what I'd do without you,' Rogers growled ungraciously.

'Fail lamentably, my friend.' Dagg handed him a glass microscope slide. In its hollow centre was a fragment of dark grey material. 'That's *Cladonia coccifera*. A lichen which grows on exposed limestone. I put them both together and came up with what I consider to be a scientifically inspired conclusion.'

'That the driver of the car has been hiking around on the moors?' Rogers took a gloomy view of that. There was so much of it and all in the open air. Most of the time in very water-logged air. 'I don't suppose you can say he walked with a limp and had a seafaring uncle, Sherlock?'

'No. But give me time,' Dagg said cheerfully. 'I might be able to tell you whether the lichen grows on the north side or the south of the outcrop.'

Rogers thought about that all the way to Goshawk House. He hadn't been there before. It was a timbered, thatched-roofed cottage with an unkempt yew tree covering too many of its small windows.

A row of wire-netting compounds filled one wall of the large enclosed garden. In one was an eagle with a disgruntled expression, tethered to a stump of wood. In the others were perched falcons, hawks and owls. The sun was throwing long shadows and the birds were fluffing their feathers against the growing chill. Shreds of rabbit fur and clean-picked bones littered the compounds. In several there were the broken bodies of tiny yellow chicks. Rogers disliked Norton for that alone.

Jane Norton answered his knocking, neat in a blue velvet dress.

'Waldo's flying a falcon at High Moor,' she said. 'He won't be back for some time.'

The room into which she led him was low-ceilinged and oak-beamed, suitable for an old lady and the sewing together of interminable patchwork bedspreads. Jane Norton was anything but.

Rogers saw her as an attractive woman with a ballet dancer's lithe, small-breasted body. Looking at her he experienced a nagging familiarity. Her face was finely drawn and taut with a sad mouth. In five years she could be gaunt, her face lined. But now she was very attractive and desirable. Despite the dark shadow of worry in her eyes.

She sat him on a settee and took a chair opposite. She tucked her dress primly under her thighs.

'I appreciate your work is confidential,' she began, 'but when it concerns interviewing my husband I think I should know.' She was a very direct woman. 'That nonsense about the parking this morning . . .'

Rogers measured her cautiously. 'It was nonsense, of course. But not of my making. On the other hand, the truth is nothing very important.'

'What was it about?' she asked. There was an obstinate resolve in her manner that put him on his guard.

'I was asking his help in a small enquiry,' he said evasively.

'Please be honest with me. Was it about Nancy Frail?'

'You know her?'

'You dodge the issue like a politician, Mr Rogers. Was it?'

He shifted uneasily on the settee. 'I could tell you it's none of your business, Mrs Norton. That you should ask your husband.'

'I have,' she said calmly. 'That's why I asked you to come here.'

'He told you?'

'Of course he didn't.'

He cursed Norton in his mind. Then he temporized with ambiguities. 'It's true I'm enquiring into the death of Miss Frail. And when I'm investigating a case, I ask all sorts of questions of all sorts of people.' He smiled reassuringly. 'Bishops, solicitors, jockeys, window cleaners, falconers . . . the lot. It means nothing.'

'Tell me why you think Waldo should know anything about her death.'

'He could know *of* her.'

'He could be one of her lovers, you mean.'

When he looked at her politely, not answering, she said, 'Please, Mr Rogers. Is he in trouble?'

'You shouldn't jump to conclusions.' *Christ*, he said to himself, *save me from determined women*. 'I repeat. It's a formal enquiry and there's no suggestion he's involved in anything. Miss Frail died a natural death. She died, in fact, from a heart condition. But she was taken to a lane and left there. Which makes it my business.'

'So I understand.'

'Good. Then there's no problem,' Rogers said lightly.

'Your diplomacy isn't very accomplished.' She was not unfriendly. 'I know about Waldo and Miss Frail, Mr Rogers, so you needn't beat so wildly about that particular bush. I just want your assurance he isn't in any trouble.'

'You're worried about him?'

Her sad mouth tightened. 'I don't wish to become the subject of public gossip. Would you like to be cuckolded and the town know of it?'

'That's different,' Rogers said weakly, caught off balance. She was very direct. 'In any case nobody's talking about that.'

'Nonsense,' she said crisply. 'You haven't given me one straight answer.'

Rogers felt a surge of baffled resentment and stood. His face was dark with irritation. 'I'm not a public information bureau, Mrs Norton,' he growled. 'You're not going to use me to flog a confession or something out of your husband.'

'Please sit down, Mr Rogers,' she asked him. 'I'm sorry to have been so blunt. You've told me most of what I wanted to know anyway.' She paused, eyeing him. 'I used to know Nancy Frail.'

He regarded her steadily for several moments, then sat. 'What do you know about her?'

'Are you going to be so tight-lipped about what I tell you as you are about Waldo?' A faint smile lightened her mouth.

'I wouldn't be surprised.' He was attracted to this woman. There was a quite tangible *rapport* between them even in their minor skirmishing. He could like her and not equate her with a bed. Which was unusual for Rogers.

'She is actually married. To a man called Park Dominis. You know?'

'Yes.'

'You know she divorced her first husband?' Seeing the look in his eyes, she said, 'I see you don't. He was an American, an assistant military attaché or similar at the Embassy. I was never quite sure but he carried a CD plate on his car. He returned to America about five years ago. Immediately after the divorce.'

'She told you his name?'

'I met him a few times. Swerdloff. Eugene Swerdloff. With two "f"s.'

'How long were they married?'

'A year. No more.'

'A woman of many parts,' Rogers murmured. 'He divorced her?'

'No, she him.' She looked at a point over his shoulder, unwilling to meet his gaze. 'I believe the reason was their disagreement over his unpleasant sex habits.'

'You have a good memory, Mrs Norton.'

'Women have for those sort of things. But don't ever ask me who the Foreign Secretary is. I wouldn't know.'

'So your husband would have met Miss Frail through you?'

A shadow crossed her face. 'How perceptive you are. To my regret, she did. My particular regret in this instance.' She met his sympathetic eyes and bit at her bottom lip. 'He can't help it, Mr Rogers. No more than he can help being besotted with his falconry.' She said wryly, 'If I and one of his birds were in collision, he'd call the vet first and the doctor second.'

'That only means he's a typical Englishman.'

She laughed for the first time. Quietly and for her own consumption. 'I used to spend my life running round after the blasted things with a shovel and a wet mop. Like an attendant votary round the Sacred Flame,' she said ruminatively. 'No more, though.'

'I noticed you hadn't done the car seats lately.'

She laughed again, sharing it this time. 'So you know what I mean.'

He said carefully, 'I would have thought it understandable had you spread your own wings and flown the coop.'

'I'm a Roman Catholic.' She said it as though it were answer enough.

'It must be pretty wearing on the nerve-ends,' he commented.

'It is. So can you help me?'

He inspected the fingernails of one hand. 'On the evidence I have,' he said at last, his voice neutral, 'I don't believe your husband can be connected with Miss Frail's death. But that's subject to my being wrong. Which I so often am.'

301

'Thank you,' she said softly.

'Your husband was friendly with Mr Quint?'

She stared at him surprised. 'Yes. Why do you want to know?'

'He also might have known Miss Frail.'

'I believe he used to.' She wasn't intending being very informative about Quint. 'I'm sure you'll be asking him.'

'Don't misunderstand me,' he said, 'but do *you* know him?'

She was cool. 'Slightly. Very slightly. But please don't ask me to talk about him.'

'He has visited here?'

'To draw the birds, yes.'

He said, 'Forgive my saying so but there's a quite surprising resemblance between you and Miss Frail.'

She returned his regard calmly. 'It's not so very surprising, Mr Rogers. She was my cousin.'

Dickersen, president of the High Moor Speleological Society, was a raw-boned man with thick pebble-lensed spectacles and muscular wrists and hands. There were rope burns on the palm he gave to Rogers to shake. He smoked shag tobacco in a cobby pipe. He had offered his rubber pouch to Rogers who, smoking the harsh black mixture with assumed satisfaction, wished he hadn't accepted.

Dickersen's bed-sitting room was cluttered with the impedimenta of his obsession with caving. There were collapsible aluminium ladders, coils of nylon rope, cordthreaded pitons and a scarred yellow-painted plastic helmet. The walls were decorated with sectionalized scale drawings of caves and fissures.

'It's a hefty-sounding job,' he observed through a cloud of villainous smoke. 'We've only a dozen or so teams. Even when they're all available.'

'I can limit it for you,' Rogers said. He coughed raspingly and laid his pipe aside. Courtesy for him had clearly defined limits. Charring his tongue and epiglottis was outside them. 'The hole I'm looking for should be near to a road. Or if a track, then one capable of being used by a car. And within reasonable distance of the town. Does that help?'

Dickersen went to a table and unrolled a large-scale map. 'It helps,' he said. He studied the map with Rogers at his side. 'If you want them with vertical drops, there's this one, this ...' He dabbed the stem of his pipe on several red-crayoned rings. 'None of them deeper than a hundred and fifty to the first elbow.'

'Those are the nine possibles?'

'Nine we can start with. None of them much good. Some are virtual craters, some just crevices. Some of them've got water running into them. Cattle and sheep fall down one or two, poor beasties. And that makes for unpleasant climbing. A couple of them have very crumbly pitches. Anyway, it'll take an hour or so in each. How sure are you about this?'

'Not very. But I'd guess more than a fifty-fifty chance.'

'You're assuming the body would have been dropped? Not hauled in?'

'Definitely dropped.'

'Um. A bit sick-making for someone to find.' He flexed his powerful fingers. 'You'll be there, of course?'

'What time do you think you can get started?'

Dickersen blew smoke over the map, then glanced at a clock on the mantelpiece. It was six-thirty. 'By the time I get the lads organized, not much before eight-thirty to nine.'

'I'll be there. Make our Operations Centre here at Blackbeg Rock.' He poked a finger on the map. 'I'll have a couple of communications cars and plenty of lights. And a personal radiophone for each team.'

'If we find something, you'll be going down?'

Rogers grimaced. 'If I have to. But I'm a Grade One claustrophobic. You people must be mad to do it for fun.'

Dickersen looked at him as if he were some grotesque insect. 'You'll love it,' he said with the utter conviction of fanaticism. 'It's a different world underground.'

'I,' Rogers said firmly, 'would prefer to delay the experience until I'm dead.'

Coltart was pacing back and forth outside the main entrance to the headquarters building when Rogers wrestled his car into one of the parking squares marked 'Staff'. The sergeant's usual low-key phlegm seemed to have taken a severe beating.

'I've been looking for you all over,' he rumbled disapprovingly at Rogers through the window of the car. 'We've located Lingard.'

Rogers pushed open the passenger door. 'Get in,' he snapped. 'Where?'

'The junction of Rooks Hill and Spaniards Rise.' The massive sergeant's entry into the car made it sag and squeak. 'There's a patrol constable keeping tabs on him until we arrive.'

They found Lingard standing in the protection of a high brick wall, making no attempt at concealment. A nearby street lamp threw its loop of dingy yellow light over him, fumid in the encroaching mist. He was in a position where no car could enter or leave Spaniards Rise without his seeing it. Quint's house was about five hundred yards from where Lingard stood and not in view. Spye Green Hall was not a lot further and, had it been daylight, would have been easily visible.

Although Rogers braked the car to a halt almost at his toes, Lingard neither moved nor acknowledged its presence. With Coltart a lumbering shadow behind him, Rogers flicked off the headlights and left the car, facing his former deputy.

This near, he could see the flatness, the emptiness, of the blue eyes. There was none of the amiable, elegant Lingard he had known. In his place was a haggard, grief-eroded stranger with an obsessional hatred burning acid holes in his stomach. His yellow hair was unkempt and he needed a shave. He was without an overcoat, his lightweight suit creased as if he'd made violent love in it. He was unsuccessfully trying not to shiver in the cold night air.

'I'd like you to come to the station for a talk, David,' Rogers began gently. He was warm enough in his fleecelined car coat and he felt pity for the frozen, delusional Lingard.

The empty eyes turned to his for as long as it took to say, 'Go away. Leave me alone.' His breath smelled of too many Pernods.

'No. There are questions I have to ask. Questions needing answers from you.' Rogers tried to force the eyes to meet his, to establish contact. 'We can't talk in the road.'

When there was no response, he asked, 'What are you waiting here for, David?'

'Justice,' he answered quietly, almost to himself. 'Now leave me alone.'

'You think you'll get it from Quint? That you'll find it here?'

Lingard did not trouble to reply.

'People taking the law into their own hands are seldom right, David. Police officers, never.'

'No?' There was indifference in the reply.

'What makes you so sure Quint will be returning?'

There was a flicker of uncertainty in Lingard's eyes. 'If I wanted to talk to Quint – or anyone else – I've a right to. I've all the privileges of a normal citizen. One of them being to stand on a pavement and wait. All night if I wish to. *You* say I want to see Quint. You've a right to think what you like. I've a right to refuse to say who I want to see or what I want to do.'

Rogers removed the friendly padding from his manner. 'Why did you quarrel with Miss Frail on Sunday afternoon?'

Lingard's lips thinned. They were livid under the yellow light.

'Was it because you found out she was still married?'

The dead eyes came alive, glowing with a burning anger. His voice shook. 'I warn you, Rogers . . .' He twitched his head and abruptly turned, walking away.

Rogers strode after him, catching him up and clamping his fingers on the narrow shoulders. He swung him around and slammed him hard against the wall. Lingard's breath exploded from his opened mouth and he clenched his hands into fists, holding them against his chest.

Rogers' face was sharp-planed with anger. 'You'll listen to me, David, if I have to knock you unconscious to make you do it.'

Lingard was docile in Rogers' grasp, making no effort to free himself. With his eyes not six inches from Rogers', he said dully, 'You know I could break both your arms if I wanted to.' Which was possibly true. He practised a lethal variant of karate which Rogers had never tested in angry opposition. 'You want me to resist you. So you can arrest me . . .'

Rogers removed his grip from the submissive shoulders. 'Yes, I do,' he growled. 'You should be locked up for your own good.'

Coltart had moved with Rogers and was stolidly waiting on events, his green eyes glittering his interest. He would welcome a personal showdown with the former detective inspector whom he had never liked. Nor did he want Rogers to be selfish about it.

'Tell me why you quarrelled,' Rogers repeated.

'We didn't quarrel,' Lingard said tonelessly. 'I don't know what you're talking about.'

'Why did you drive past her flat at nine-thirty when you were supposed to be keeping observation on the Tico-Tico?'

'I didn't.'

'You're lying, David,' Rogers said sadly.

'If you say I am.'

'You called on Midgley . . .'

'I made no secret of it.'

'You telephoned Mrs Dominis.'

'Did I? *You're* saying all these things.' He took his small ivory snuff box from his waistcoat pocket and with a touch of his former elegance inhaled the tobacco powder. The silk Paisley handkerchief he used was crumpled and dirty and left brown smears on his nostrils.

Rogers cocked his head on one side, measuring Lingard with squeezed-together eyes. 'You've stopped being a copper,' he said sombrely. 'All you've got left is a damn great bellyful of self-pity.' To Rogers, it was like discovering suppurating putrefaction in an apparently healthy leg. He did everything but actually spit. 'All over a bloody woman who wasn't worth it. Who wasn't even faithful to you . . .'

Lingard's cheek twitched in his grey face. The taut sinews in his neck showed with how much difficulty he was holding back from throwing himself in a screaming rage at Rogers. Somebody was breathing harshly. It was difficult to decide which of the two men it was.

Coltart's chest rumbled a warning in the background.

Rogers shouted at the blond man. 'Did she take your guts as well!' He prodded at his chest with a rough finger. 'You bloody spineless ninny! A little trouble and you cry your eyes out.'

Whatever it was he expected from Lingard, he didn't get it. Lingard blanked his eyes from his tormentor, scrubbing any expression from his face. His self-control was iron-hard and Rogers bled for him.

When he spoke it was in a tired voice. 'I know why you're saying these things. You want to arrest me. Well, I'm not giving you the excuse.' He added ambiguously, almost as an afterthought, 'I shan't always be so unobliging with you.' For a moment, he was Beau Brummell being aristocratically arrogant with a dunning creditor.

Rogers put away his aggressiveness. 'All right, David. I shall arrange for Sergeant Hagbourne to be here. He'll be instructed to arrest you if you so much as approach Quint. Is that clear?'

Lingard regarded him steadily. Then he said politely, 'May I go?'

When he received no reply from Rogers, he turned and walked away down the hill, not looking back, losing himself in the thickening mist.

'What do you make of that?' Rogers asked Coltart.

The sergeant grunted. 'Did you really believe he'd have a go at you?'

'I was as nasty a bastard as I dared be. Too nasty and his arrest wouldn't have stuck for five minutes. Undue provocation or some such.'

'He's got a thing about Quint.'

'If Quint's still about, I think Lingard could be mad enough to kill him. Given the right stimulus. And knowing how bloody-minded Quint can be, he'd give it to him.'

'But you don't know if Quint *is* about.'

Rogers bared his wrist watch of two inches of soiled shirt cuff. 'Ask me in a couple of hours' time,' he said.

12

Hacker hadn't been difficult for Rogers to locate. He was knocking golf balls with a No 2 wood at the Sporting Club's indoor driving range.

Rogers waited at one side while he drove at the canvas bull's-eye wired to the netting at the far end of the floodlit shed.

'I've been expecting you,' the optician said with a cheerful grin over his shoulder.

He was a handsome slim man with crinkly black hair. He wore a red crewneck pullover with white linen trousers and rubber spiked shoes. He gripped a thick unlit havana between his teeth and spoke around it. 'I hear in the bazaars you're getting all hot and bothered about Nancy.' The amiability that reached his spectacled eyes was strictly the small change of social intercourse.

'I'm not putting you off your stroke?' Rogers asked sardonically as Hacker teed a ball and waggled the club head behind it.

'No. I always practise my shots with coppers asking me questions.' The club swung up, paused and slashed down, sending the ball whistling towards the left of the target. 'I'm bloody useless with a two wood,' he muttered. 'I hook like hell with it.'

He put an arm around Rogers' shoulders and squeezed, showing his gleaming porcelain smile. 'Don't take any notice of what I say. I *like* coppers. You're all that stands between us lambs and anarchy and our being up shit creek.'

'I'm glad to hear it,' the unresponsive Rogers said, disengaging from the embrace. He didn't like being handled by another man.

'Some of my best friends are coppers.'

'And you'd let your sister marry one?'

Hacker looked blank. 'My sister . . . ?'

'A joke,' Rogers said dourly. 'It's supposed to be the acid test of sincerity.' Beneath the spurious bonhomie, both men were willing to dish out punishment.

'Ha! Ha! I see it now. Very funny.' Hacker squinted along the length of the club. 'You want to know about me and Nancy?'

'More or less.'

He reached down, teeing the ball carefully and precisely. Straightening himself, he said, 'It was a simple pay-as-you-enter relationship. Which you probably know already or you wouldn't be here. I won't give you any guff about lonely hearts and similar crap. A man can't help the dynamo of his testicles and he's got to do something about it. And to put it crudely, my dear chap, what Nancy had between her legs was a fur-lined cash register.' He lifted the club and whipped it down with a slashing motion, topping the ball and sending it scuttling crablike over the peat-strewn floor. Hacker swore.

'You dipped your left shoulder on the back swing,' Rogers commented, giving his unwanted opinion. 'Miss Frail. She was worth it?'

'Nancy? God, yes. The ultimate experience. With nothing barred, although she could spit and claw like a wild cat when the mood took her.' He wagged his head. Even with the odd-looking spectacles he wore, Rogers considered him too pretty for his approval. 'She liked her pleasures on the crude side. But money mad . . .'

'When did you last see her?'

'Sunday week. The fifth, I think it was.'

'At her flat?'

'Yes.'

'Had you ever noticed a painting there? A cat and three female figures?'

Hacker looked cautious. 'Has it been stolen?'

'You did see it then?'

He nodded. 'I remember the cat vaguely, the females distinctly. They all had little purple flowers painted over the interesting parts of their titties. And palm leaves over their whatsisnames.'

'You seem to have had a good look.' Rogers smiled inside at the man.

'Of course I did. I'm a post-graduate student of exotic porn. It makes a change from optometry.' He teed another ball, straightened and snapped a butane gas lighter at his cigar. 'I always relax after making a balls-up of a shot,' he said. 'Oh, yes. I nearly forgot. He raped her once.'

'Jolly good,' Rogers grunted. 'Who raped whom?'

'Her husband. Dominis. He raped Nancy.'

'You were looking through the keyhole?'

Hacker regarded him with faint mockery. 'She told me. And she had a gorgeous shiner under one eye to prove it.'

'How long ago was all this?'

Hacker removed the cigar and pursed his lips. 'Seven or eight weeks. About. I can't be certain.'

'You believed her?'

He held the cigar out to Rogers. 'Would you mind awfully, old chap?'

Rogers took the cigar. The rich leaf was smooth as satin between his finger and thumb, the perfume of the smoke reminiscent of a cooking cabbage.

Hacker drove the ball hard and straight and he smiled. In his mind the ball had represented Rogers. 'Believe her?' He retrieved the cigar from the detective. 'Not altogether. But then I don't believe much of anything women tell me.'

'She didn't report it to the police. I'd have known.'

'Of course she didn't.' Hacker looked amused. 'I expect she enjoyed it. She was that sort of a bitch. It's a compliment to a woman to want her so badly you are prepared to rape her to get it. The law should be amended to allow for this fundamental truth.'

'I'll mention it to the Home Secretary the next time I see him,' Rogers said drily. He added, 'I think she was a liar.'

'So? I was interested in her sex. Not her semantics.'

'You knew Dominis?'

'No. But I damn nearly did.' He threw back his head and laughed, showing his beautiful teeth. 'Some time last December

I think it was. Nancy was at my place over the shop. She looked out the window and saw him skulking on the other side of the street. He looked a right mean bastard. Likely to take a dim view of the whole thing. So she didn't leave and we had a ball of a night while we waited for him to go. Which was when it started to get light.' He sucked ruefully at his back teeth. 'That's the night that cost me the contact lenses. It's funny. Although she was badly myopic she could still recognize a ten-pound note at a hundred paces.' He raised his eyes to the polystyrene ceiling. 'Christ! I must have been mad!'

'Yes,' Rogers agreed. 'Did she trust you with a key to her flat?'

He shook his head. 'I didn't need one. All I had to do was to knock twice and make a noise like a well-filled wallet.'

'Do you know anything about her other playmates?'

Hacker glanced at him slyly. 'She mentioned an item or two about her detective boy-friend. None of it very flattering. She told me he had developed into the most monumental bore imaginable. That he amused her in the beginning but took her much too seriously.' He smirked. 'A brighter-than-white knight and incredibly naive . . .'

Rogers cleared his throat, his face stiffening.

Hacker grinned maliciously. 'You asked me.'

'Go on.'

'She said she wasn't used to being treated like someone's grandmother. He was too respectful, too deferential. It made her feel as old as the hills. She used to call him her "cucumber-sandwich-and-tea-on-the-vicarage-lawn man". Behind his back, naturally.' He guffawed. 'He should've taken a lesson from me and treated her like something escaped from the Casbah. She loved it.'

'I can imagine it,' Rogers said coldly. 'The pair of you must have been a rare giggle.'

Hacker wrinkled his nose at the cigar. 'Jealousy'll get you nowhere.' That was the second time it had been said to Rogers and it scratched at his *amour-propre*. Hacker continued, 'Are we going to talk about Lingard or me?'

'Stick to Lingard,' Rogers growled. 'Without the extraneous

311

comments. He wouldn't appreciate your advice on sex matters.'

'Charming man,' Hacker murmured. 'Anyway, when she realized he was serious ... on a copper's salary ...' He laughed, his eyes creased and wicked when he saw Rogers glower. 'She said it wouldn't keep her cats in sardines and milk. So she tried to lose him. But marrying him ... ?' He sniggered this time.

The detective was sour. 'She'd have raised her status considerably. Lingard was streets ahead of the deprived rubbish she pandered to.' His face was expressionless. 'Present company excepted, of course.' He didn't mean the exception and it showed.

Hacker, smiling with stiff lips, rammed the club back in his bag and selected a murderous No. 3 iron. He made a few preliminary swings with it. 'Kind of you, my dear chap. Have you finished? I'm busy.'

'Whose bosoms were you inspecting last Sunday evening?'

Hacker laughed in the detective's face. 'A married woman's. Seventeen miles away in a north-easterly direction. At the Acey-Deucey Club in point of fact. I returned at two in the morning. If you ask her nice and discreetly she'll no doubt confirm it.'

'She'll need to. Who is she?'

Hacker gave him her name and address. Rogers said, 'I'll know her by the free spectacles, I suppose?'

The optician ignored the jibe. 'Her old man's on a permanent night-shift at the steel pressing works. So see her when he's not about to cause trouble.' He regarded Rogers with distrust plain in his eyes. 'And no dipping your spoon in my private jar of honey,' he warned him, not wholly humorously.

Rogers sneered. 'Not even using a disinfected fencing post.' It wasn't brilliant – not even passable – repartee but the best he could do against a man already engrossed in the contemplation of his next shot and who had plainly lost interest in him.

The road glistened like moist liquorice in the headlights of Rogers' car as it climbed into the smoking grey fog of the moors.

Below him, resembling burning sulphur gases in a pit, was the vague yellow glow of the town he had just left.

He pulled into the lay-by where Dickersen, standing near the police communications car, was adding the acrid fumes of his pipe tobacco to the fog. The smoke hung around his head like small dabs of cottonwool with nowhere to go. He held his plastic helmet in one hand. Despite the cold he wore only a denim boilersuit over his trousers and shirt. He carried a folder of papers under one arm.

Coltart was with him, bulking large against his stocky companion. A radio transmitter and receiver stood on the bonnet of the car near them. An occasional disembodied voice floated out from it giving the location of the speaker in his descent into the moor's catacombs.

'All the lads are climbing,' Dickersen said to Rogers. He looked at his watch. 'We cleared the first – Lugs Bottom – about five minutes ago.' His words dropped like pieces of wet felt in the waterlogging mist.

Coltart rumbled, 'I've posted a CID man on top of each of the holes for liaison.' To Dickersen, he said, 'Excuse me a moment,' and led Rogers to one side, taking the radio set with him.

'Hagbourne's sitting on Quint's doorstep. Do you want a situation report?'

'I'll talk to him.'

Coltart's banana thumb depressed a button on the transmitter and he spoke, his bass voice vibrating the grille in its side. 'Foxtrot One calling Foxtrot Ten. Are you there?'

Rogers heard a glum-sounding Hagbourne answering and took the set from Coltart. 'Is there any sign of L?' he asked.

'No. But the fog's so thick he'd have to be sitting on my lap before I could see him.'

'And Q?'

'No sign either. And I'm out of cigarettes.'

'That's terrible. Where are you?'

'Inside the gates. On wet turf and beginning to take root.'

'Keep in touch, sergeant.' He added unsympathetically, 'And try chewing grass.'

He handed the set back to Coltart and shivered. The fog swirled around the two men, silvering their hair and the fibres of their clothing. Rogers filled his pipe before returning to Dickersen and the possibility of being offered his pouch of poisonous shag.

The news he waited for came at nine-fifty from the hole known as The Gawp Gut. The climber calling in sounded sick, telling Dickersen he was coming up to the untainted air of topside before he actually was.

The Gawp Gut was less than half-a-mile away. Rogers made it in just over fifty seconds in a blind-eyed drive through the dark muffling fog that had Coltart and Dickersen pressing their feet unhappily on imaginary brake pedals.

A pallid-faced youth wearing a red helmet was sitting on the pit edge with his head cupped in his hands. His companion was massaging the back of his neck.

Rogers walked to him across the soaking clumps of moor grass. 'Are you all right?' he asked.

'No. Anything but.' He grimaced and blinked. 'If I think about it, I shall chuck up.'

'Think just a little bit. What was he like?'

The pallid youth swallowed. 'I didn't stay to look. All I could see was a pair of legs sticking up from inside a dead sheep . . .' He twisted his head to one side and quietly vomited.

When he had finished and was wiping his bloodless lips with a handkerchief, Dickersen asked, 'Where was he, Mike?'

Mike gulped. 'At the bottom of the trough on the second stage.'

Dickersen nodded. He snapped on his helmet light, unfastened the folder he was carrying and selected a plan, holding it open for Rogers to see. It showed The Gawp Gut in section, shaped like a short two-angled fall pipe. After a vertical drop to an elbow, the cave sloped steeply to a level watercourse.

Dickersen indicated the first angle with his forefinger. 'The body would have hit the ledge here on the second stage, bounced off and slithered down the trough to where it's now resting.'

'How deep?' Rogers asked.

'Thirty-eight feet straight down to the first stage. We'll use Mike's ladder. That's kid's stuff. Then a rope-down through the trough for about sixty.' He smiled encouragingly. 'Old ladies have done it blindfolded.'

'Will I need an umbrella?' Rogers asked sarcastically.

'Not in this one. It's a dry run except when it rains. And if it does while we're down there, we'll be washed away like matchsticks in a drain.' He fastened a rope around the detective's waist. 'Keep that on while you're using the ladder.' He indicated Rogers' gloved hands. 'You won't want those. Not with wet nylon.'

'It's only a bloody ladder,' Rogers said impatiently. 'I've climbed them before. Up *and* down.' This particular ladder hung down into a yawning, unattractive blackness but Rogers refused to be intimidated by its apparent flimsiness.

'Maybe you'll find it a queerer ladder than you bargain for.' Dickersen lowered himself over the edge feet first, feeling with his toes for the aluminium rungs. Then he vanished, the ladder jerking with each step he took, only the reflection of his helmet lamp showing his progress.

His voice came up diminished by distance and thinned by enclosing rock. Rogers, his head squeezed into the sick youth's helmet, clambered on to the ladder and stepped downwards into the blackness, his pipe clenched between his teeth. Coltart held the safety rope, playing it out as Rogers descended.

The ladder was, indeed, as queer as Dickersen had warned although he was holding it as taut as Rogers' weight would allow him from below. It swivelled and lurched sideways under the detective's feet with unpredictable malice, skinning the knuckles of his fists wrapped round the white nylon side ropes and scraping the toes of his black oxfords. His stomach felt wobbly and he remembered he hadn't eaten anything since his sandwiches at Henri et Camille's. As he dropped down, so the wet grey stone slid upwards six inches from his nose in the disc of light from the lamp on his helmet. When he tilted his head he could see the vanishing perspective of his safety rope, metal rungs and distorted shadows. He didn't care to look down between his feet.

When he thought he must be getting short of ladder, he felt Dickersen tap his heels and heard him say, 'Six more rungs,' and after that finding himself balancing on a ledge big enough for two small chickens. A passage about four feet in diameter fell away below.

Dickersen's eyes glinted behind the pebble lenses. 'You OK?'

Rogers grunted. 'Apart from running out of skin on my fingers, yes.'

Dickersen untied Rogers' safety rope and knotted it to a steel piton already hammered into the rock face. 'Watch me carefully,' he said. He manoeuvred the rope between his thighs, around his buttocks and over a shoulder, allowing the tail of it to drop into the hole behind him. 'Let it slide between your hands,' he instructed. 'Like this.' He walked backwards down the steep trough of the passage, crouching to avoid the roof.

When the rope slackened, Rogers heard his faint words echoing up from the depths. 'Hurry up. There's not much room for the three of us.'

'Three?' Rogers called the word into the passage.

'Don't forget the sheep. It takes up a lot of room.'

Rogers, fitting the rope around his body, backed down the slope, the nylon burning his hands, his wrists aching from the strain. Warm-blooded humanity on topside seemed a long hour away from him. He was entombed in a hostile, suffocating and silent world. He swallowed his spit, wanting nothing more than the moral courage to scramble back up the ladder like a sensibly scared rabbit. His claustrophobic imagination made the walls tumble in on him in slow motion. He thought deliberately of a fleshy Bridget in his arms in an effort to take the sick foreboding from his fears.

Once he slipped, swivelling on his back, his heels scrabbling frantically on the rock for purchase and he had a horrifying picture of tumbling into the decaying flesh below. He pulled himself upright again and sweated. He imagined he could already smell its putrefaction.

Dickersen held his ankles and guided his feet as he reached the debris of small stones at the bottom. There was a gurgling of running water and the small sounds of their movement echoed. 'A born caver,' Dickersen said laconically. 'I'll get you enrolled as a member when we get back.'

'*If* we get back,' Rogers growled. 'This is my first and last time.' His nostrils twitched as the smell of corruption reached them with its evil miasma. 'For God's sake,' he said, 'smoke some of that tobacco of yours. Anything's preferable.'

He filled his own pipe as he studied the body at his feet. Dominis was not instantly recognizable. His head was buried in the distended belly of a dead sheep, his legs unnaturally and grotesquely twisted. One hand, held out appealingly, was frozen with bent fingers in their last grasp at the something they had never reached. The dark blue coat was rucked up over the hips, showing a bloodsoaked pullover. The pale blue trousers were concertinaed to expose livid shins.

Rogers disliked handling dead flesh and he used a handkerchief over his fingers to twist the torn face out from its fleece pillow; to recognize the lady-killing moustache and the AFC scar on the left temple; to see the dreadful fixed stare of violent death and the dried blood fouling the chin and necktie.

'He's the one you were looking for?' Dickersen asked.

'Yes, poor bastard. The prototype Do-It-Yourself private detective. He should have left it to the professionals.'

13

It took nearly an hour of grunting, straining effort at the ropes to haul up the stretcher to which the body of Dominis had been lashed.

Rogers stood with Bridget on the rim of the dark hole of The Gawp Gut. A semi-circle of hissing butane lamps poured hot beams of diffused light on to the stretcher being manoeuvred over the outcrop lip on to level ground.

Bridget, pulling on rubber gloves, said lightly, 'I hope you'll come as quickly when I whistle for *you*, George. I thought you'd lost my number.'

He stared into the orange of her eyes. 'A temporary amnesia. Events have been scything my legs from beneath me.'

'Along with David's?'

'Yes,' he said gloomily. 'You know?'

She nodded. 'He's in trouble?'

'He could be.'

'I'm sorry. He's a nice boy.'

'He's also a fool.'

She turned towards the body, now isolated on a square of polythene, and said casually, 'Talking of fools, don't forget you didn't finish your sherry.'

The pressure was on and Rogers realized with sudden clarity that there was rarely a single watershed. They came in pluralities. He thought he'd cross this particular one when he walked into it.

He stood behind her with Coltart and Dickersen and a small group of emerged potholers forming a silent semicircle, watching her deft fingers examining Dominis's face, hooking a finger inside the mouth, lifting up the eyelids. She paused in her scrutiny of the lacerated forehead, picking out a granule of crystal from the bloodied flesh with a pair of tweezers.

She held it out to Rogers. 'Windscreen glass?'

He looked closely at it and nodded. 'It fits the wobbly sort of theory I have.'

She unbuttoned and unzipped the dead man's clothing, exclaiming a soft 'Agh'of satisfaction when she pulled the shirt up and bared the dreadfully mangled stomach. She pressed it with the pads of her fingers.

The men watching moved uneasily for Dominis's mouth had opened in what looked like a soundless yell. Rogers smiled grimly when he saw Dickersen edge backwards out of the group, his face tallow-coloured.

'Gross crushing injuries to the abdomen,' Bridget said without looking up. 'Consistent with having been run over by a car. He must have died almost immediately.'

'Does the time of death fit in with our other problem?'

She flexed an arm and then a leg. 'Yes. Very roughly forty-eight hours. But don't hold it against me. It needs some higher mathematics in the mortuary.' She lowered her voice. 'He was with her?'

'Yes. But not necessarily inside the car. And the little I know is more about the How than the Why. I'm being lied to, of course.'

'Of course,' she agreed, standing and stripping her hands of the gloves. 'Isn't that the cross a policeman is always nailed to?'

'Yes. But more understandable when lied to by the guilty than by the presumably innocent.'

He crouched at the side of the corpse. 'No tyre marks on the clothing,' he commented to Coltart. 'That should mean something to me but doesn't. And no more bits of windscreen glass that I can see.' He straightened his legs and beat his hands together. The fog was freezing all his previous sweating out of him. 'Get Dr Dagg up here, sergeant. I'd like him to run his vacuum cleaner over the clothing before it's moved.'

To Bridget, he said, 'Can you do your examination first thing in the morning?'

She nodded. 'Tonight if you like. But the answer's going to be death due to crushing injuries.'

'No,' he said. 'Do it tomorrow morning. I'm walking on my chin strap already.'

She stared at him hard, her eyes bright. 'Telephone me about it later,' she said softly. 'I keep a stock of spare chin straps.'

A faint voice, querulous and demanding, came from Coltart's coat pocket. He dragged the radio out, bringing most of the lining with it. Hagbourne's voice became clear, asking for Rogers. 'Quint,' he said when Rogers answered him. 'He pulled into the drive in his Rolls a few minutes ago. He's now in the house.'

'No sign of L?'

'I wouldn't guarantee it,' Hagbourne replied pessimistically. 'This bloody fog! I haven't seen the ends of my legs since I came up here.'

'Do you know what Quint's up to?'

'Yes. I peeked through the window. He's been talking on the telephone since he arrived.'

'How does he look?'

'Worried.'

'Go and sit with him,' Rogers said. 'I'll be over in a few minutes. Talk to him, tell him jokes, do anything. But keep the . . .'

'Just a minute, sir . . .' Rogers heard the click of Hagbourne's thumb pressure being released.

He waited, hearing only the crackle and hiss of static. 'What is it, sergeant?' he asked sharply. 'Sergeant! Sergeant Hagbourne!' He stared at the mute set, his face grim. Then he tossed it at Coltart. 'Stay here and look after things,' he said, already running.

His car shuddered as he slammed the door and took off, accelerating downhill with the tyres rasping rubber on the chipping-surfaced road.

With his nose to the windscreen and the wipers clacking, he blundered into the blank wall of fog at a dangerous speed, alternately accelerating and braking. Twice, blinded by the headlights of approaching vehicles, he swerved, gouging lumps of earth and grass from the verge. When he finally reached the street lamps of Rooks Hill he was livid with frustration.

Turning into Spaniards Rise, he killed his engine and coasted silently on side lights to the gates of the Old Rectory, jumping out almost before the car came to a halt.

Hagbourne, his eyes protuberant with effort, had his shoulder-blades against the angle of one of the gate pillars, rubbing at the necktie binding his arms behind him. His radio lay on the gravel at his feet.

Rogers cut the tie with his pocketknife and the sergeant spat out a gobbet of blood. 'He's mad,' he gasped, rubbing the side of his throat. 'He came from around the wall and clobbered me.' He held his head lopsided, looking at Rogers' angry face. 'I'm sorry. I didn't expect him to hit me like that . . . no warning . . .'

'It's done,' Rogers said shortly. 'We'll argue about it later. I only hope I'm in time to stop him.'

Hagbourne spat blood again. 'This time I'll be ready.'

'No you won't. This time you stay here and make sure he doesn't get out. If he's still in there, that is. Use that radio of yours and get some assistance here.'

He saw there were lights in the lower rooms of the house as he ran up the stone steps. He opened the door and stepped into the dark hall. It was as cold in there as it was outside.

He recognized Lingard's voice behind a closed door. Although muffled by the heavy wood, it was sharp and vicious and what he said was answered by a groan. Rogers pressed down on the handle of the door and pushed. It remained solid and immovable. The groan came again and, on the heels of it, the sound of the smacking of flesh on flesh.

Rogers depressed the handle again and heaved his bulk against the door. The impact shook him to the marrow and rattled his teeth but the door remained solid. There were sounds of hasty movement behind it and a thud as he drew back and slammed the flat of his foot jarringly on the lock. With a splintering crash the door exploded inwards.

Quint, his face blotched and swollen, lay on his back. The door behind him was open. Rogers reached him in a few quick strides. The cream-haired man was staring vacantly at the ceiling and bubbling saliva, his breathing stertorous. One arm was twisted beneath his body. He groaned. To Rogers, it was a reassuring sound. A slim green-leafed cigar burned on the carpet at Quint's side and Rogers put his foot on it.

The open door led to the arboretum. Rogers knew its interior well. There was a short windowless passage and then a further safety door to the mini-jungle of tropical greenery. Four months ago it had been a steam-heated Mato Grosso, alive with exotic birds, lizards and frogs: swarming with the mosquitoes and fruit flies bred in their myriads to feed them.

He walked quietly along the passage. The door at its far end was ajar. He paused, pushing it wide open. It led to the enormous metal-ribbed structure towering dimly to the black sky. The reflected glow from the lamp outside in the road gave the interior an ochre luminosity. A giant tree fern stood in dark silhouette with its topmost fronds thirty feet above the ground. It was surrounded by palms and tall bamboos hung with creepers and hairy mosses. The shrubbery had grown rank and wild. There was a lifelessness and dankness in there with the pervasive smell of decaying vegetation. Fog billowed in through the broken panes of glass and torn lining of polythene.

For the second time that evening, Rogers felt himself in alien territory, away from his ordered and familiar world of stone and brick and tarmac. Here he sensed very strongly the menace of shadowed foliage and the feeling of being watched by a hunting animal.

He groped silently with his fingers for the switches on the wall and snapped them on. Nothing happened and he swore inside his mind.

'David?' He spoke conversationally. 'I know you're in there.'

There was a remote rustle of sound, so soft it might have been the pulsing of his own blood through his arteries. He suddenly felt old and tired and useless; his body aching from his climb into The Gawp Gut. His knuckles were raw and smarting and he thought that fighting even an ailing pygmy shrew might be beyond him. 'You can't get out,' he continued. 'Only this way. And I'm here.'

The quiet cold voice from the other side of the trees said, 'I'm going out. Please don't try and stop me.'

'I'm arresting you, David.' Rogers shifted his position, stepping forward into the arboretum. He turned his coat collar up, covering the whiteness of his shirt. 'You've forgotten everything a police officer should remember.'

'I'm not a police officer.' He wasn't making a point, just saying it. 'I resigned.'

'Does that stop your being fair? You were acting on the level of a street-corner lout.' There was cutting contempt in the words. 'You were trying to beat an admission out of him.'

'Pussyfoot Rogers,' the voice said tightly.

'Not so pussyfoot I can't take you, David.'

'You'll have to. You took me by surprise last time.'

Rogers moved forward two silent paces on the flagstoned path. 'Like you did with Hagbourne?'

There was a faint stirring of disturbed leaves and Lingard's words came from a different angle. 'Did I hurt him?' There was no anxiety, no curiosity, in the question.

'Enough.'

In the still, unbreathing silence, Rogers' hearing seemed unnaturally acute. He could hear tiny scratching noises he thought to be mice or insects. Somewhere above him water bubbled in one of the metal pipes used to provide the storms the miniature rain-forest needed.

There were pots of dried-up shrubs at his feet. He manipulated one pot between his shoes and slowly, not breathing, grasped its stem and pulled the plant out with its ball of soil intact. Against Lingard's undoubted adequacy at karate and his theoretical ability to kill by it, Rogers needed something more devastating than muscle, something less obvious than his own elementary knowledge of judo. He judged a lump of solid earth, swung accurately at the end of the shrub, might be it. That and jolting Lingard from his inhuman iciness: making him lose his temper.

Lingard spoke out of the darkness. He was appreciably nearer. 'Let me go out of the door. I don't want to fight you.'

Rogers answered that by ignoring it. 'Why did you pick on Quint?'

Lingard was a long time silent. Then he said, 'You know why. Because he killed Nancy.'

'There was no murder and you know it.'

'There are other ways. Not in the book. Things ... just as bad. He was with her that night.'

There was a soft contempt in Rogers' voice. 'So Midgley said. But that doesn't make it so. It could have been one of six others.' He remembered the late Lieutenant Colonel Jagger and the crippled Garwood. 'Well four. anyway.'

There was a ghost of movement from near the trunk of the giant fern. Rogers strained his eyes but could see only a confusion of dark shapes. He stepped sideways on to the peat soil, his shoes sinking deep into it.

'You heard me, David?' He was like a bat: sending words winging into the darkness that had their echoes in movement or sound.

'I heard you.' The articulation had the precision of polished steel balls. 'She was far above your grimy understanding.'

'You're deceiving yourself, David. Deliberately and against all the evidence. You know she was married twice?'

'*Liar.*' It wasn't much above a whisper.

'All right. I'm a liar. But hear me out. The first was to an American, Eugene Swerdloff. Does that mean anything to you?' His scalp tingled and his leg muscles ached with holding himself motionless. There were small, fragmentary sounds of movement around him. Water dripped on leaves somewhere, distracting his attention from keeping Lingard located. 'We've found Dominis. He was murdered.'

'The filthy pawing bastard. He deserved it.'

That came from behind him and Rogers turned slightly. Now he daren't stir. His only remaining move was out into the open and there he would be exposed. He had to draw Lingard to him. 'You're a paranoic, David. You need help ... treatment.'

There was a noise outside of tyres crunching over gravel and the glaring beams of a car's headlights swept across the arboretum, elongating shadows and sending them racing, piercing the gloom with sudden shafts of blinding light. Then there was darkness again, followed by the clunking of metal doors and approaching footsteps.

Rogers guessed he had been seen. 'I'll repeat what I said before,' he rasped cruelly, bracing himself to swing his soil

324

bludgeon. 'She was the Great Whore of Babylon. Opening her legs to anybody with a fistful of pound notes.'

He heard a sharp intake of breath at one side of him. Very much nearer now.

'Why don't you face up to facts . . .'

There came a soft whisper of the scraping of papery leaves, a displacement of air and Lingard was suddenly in front of him, his shadowed face murderous. A hissing noise came from between his teeth as he moved fluidly with the grace and rhythm of a striking snake, ducking his head and twisting his body, flashing an upward-curving kick at Rogers' jaw. Rogers flung himself sideways as the sole of the shoe slammed into his shoulder, spinning him backwards into the bush. At the same time, he swung desperately with the clod of earth, feeling it disintegrate against Lingard's cheekbone as he followed up his attack. It was a staggering blow but no more than enough to check him momentarily.

Rogers experienced a blighting spasm of paralysing fear. This was a Lingard he had never known or suspected. Completely berserk, his blows were being delivered with savage ferocity. Rogers, helpless in the tangling branches, covered up as Lingard chopped at him. He grasped a fistful of Lingard's jacket and pulled him down, his free arm taking the numbing blows. He jolted an elbow into Lingard's stomach and heard him gasp, smelling the Pernod and snuff on his breath. He was making growling noises, worrying at him like a mad dog.

Rogers, his arm aching from the punishment it was receiving, realized clearly that if the younger man succeeded in hitting him in the right place on his throat he would choke and die. That was when desperation gave him a viciousness of his own. With his arms tangling Lingard's efforts to get in a finishing blow, he drove his knee piston hard into the squashiness of his genitals. Although Lingard screamed hoarsely like a tortured animal, he continued his chopping, his ferocity diamond-hard. The cutting edge of his palm struck fire into the side of Rogers' neck, bringing tears to his eyes. He grunted and wrapped his arms bear-like around Lingard, pulling him down and snapping his own skull violently into the nose of his opponent. Feeling the abrupt relaxation of muscles, he balled a fist and drove it with a solid smack against the jaw exposed above him; a blow that flung Lingard across his legs in a sudden boneless collapse.

Panting harshly, Rogers pulled free from beneath him, grasping and twisting his arms behind his back. He knelt one knee on them, wrenching his handcuffs from a pocket and clipping them on the unresisting wrists.

Lingard's eyes were agonized in his soil-covered face, his nose pumping blood over his mouth and chin. When Rogers hoisted him upright he bowed his head and stood abject with shaking legs.

'I'm sorry, David,' Rogers said gently. 'I would have liked to have left you with your illusions. I can't see you've got anything else.'

14

Quint, slumped on a yellow plush chaise-longue, was being nursemaided by a uniformed constable. Still dazed and with one boiled-egg eye he had seen the handcuffed Lingard escorted from the arboretum by Hagbourne and the driver of the patrol car. Rogers stood waiting while the constable practised a rudimentary first-aid on Quint's arm, slinging it in two handkerchiefs knotted together. Occasionally Quint groaned and closed his eyes. He wasn't very anxious to talk to Rogers.

When he had been suitably prepared for later treatment by a doctor, Rogers jerked his head at the constable, telling him to leave. It was cold in the room and he kicked down the switch of an electric fire, moving it closer to Quint. The house had an unlived-in air about it. He opened a lacquered box on a table and took out a spinach-green cigar. 'A smoke?' he asked.

Quint nodded and Rogers pushed it between the swollen lips, holding a match to it. Then he lit his pipe, tamping down the burning shreds of tobacco with a fingertip long inured to incineration. While he did so he studied Quint.

Four months hadn't changed him. His creamy-blond hair still possessed the contrived shagginess of a middle-aged male interested in women; his skin still golden from regular exposure to a sun-tan lamp. He was lean and sinewy in his carefully tailored tweed suit. His apricot shirt, torn at the throat and with a button missing, was hand sewn with a high collar and four-inch cuffs. The knitted brown tie had been torn loose.

Beneath its lumpiness, his face was raffish and handsome with lids hooding secretive pale eyes. The thin arrogant nose was nostrilled with the miniature cheeks of a belly-dancer's buttocks, each possessing an astonishing mobility of its own. He was the sort of man whom other men, owning to bored wives, eyed warily and wished impotent or somewhere else.

'Don't tell me this sudden concern for my comfort is altruistic,' he said with sour mockery.

Rogers smiled with his lips together. 'I'm cold too. I'd rather ask my questions in comfort.' He pulled a chair nearer to Quint and sat facing him. 'A doctor'll be here soon. In the meantime, you're fit enough?'

Quint released smoke from his mouth as if he hadn't the strength to blow it. 'There's nothing wrong with me that a month in hospital and a bonesetter won't cure,' he said nastily. 'To be honest, I'd hoped to have seen the last of you.' He winced and touched the side of his jaw with a fingertip. 'The bastard! He was as unstable as an elephant in *must*.'

'And for much the same reason.' Rogers stared at him with the unwinking regard of a policeman. 'He didn't approve of your association with Nancy Frail.'

'So he said.'

Rogers was earnest. 'I want you to know he wasn't acting as a police officer. He'd resigned.'

'He told me that too. Before he started knocking me about. Which was bloody considerate of him. It made a difference.'

'You knew why he was like it?'

'He didn't go into details. A mere matter of accusing me of being responsible for her death ... of raping her.' His lips twisted in a humourless grin. 'Raping *her*! My God. He had to be joking.'

'No, he wasn't. To the deluded, all things are delusional. And they insist on ramming their delusions down other people's throats. Perhaps his knowing you were at her flat on Sunday evening had something to do with it.'

Quint examined the lengthening ash of his cigar and adjusted his arm in its sling.

When he didn't answer, Rogers said patiently, 'That was a sort of question, Mr Quint. What were you doing there at nine o'clock that evening?'

'I don't remember saying I was there, chief inspector.'

He knew this form of patronising address would irritate Rogers and it did. 'You're saying you weren't?' His shoulders and neck throbbed painfully, not improving a disposition that was never very merry at the best of times.

Quint held the cigar to his mouth and spoke around it. 'That's something you'll have to prove.' He blew smoke. 'If you can.' It was an act. Despite his nonchalance he was beginning to look worried.

'All right. Would the sighting of an old black Rolls-Royce car with a woman passenger and a Photo-fit picture by an eye-witness of a middle-aged six-footer with fair hair be enough?'

Although his fingers had jerked ash from the cigar on to his shirt front, he answered calmly enough. 'If you ask the Rolls-Royce people I expect you'll find they've built more than one black Phantom Five in their time.' He pursed his pulpy lips. 'And I vaguely recollect there exist a few other tall men with fair hair.'

Rogers smiled tightly. 'The self-delusory confidence of the layman. It's sustained some of them even on the gallows' trap. So don't lean too heavily on it. What were you doing there?'

Quint shook his head stubbornly. His tan had turned blotchy.

'There's another fallacy,' Rogers commented mildly, 'that if you say "no" enough times, a policeman will believe you and go away. You're dodging the issue,' he said sternly. 'And because you're dodging it, I know you've something to hide. And knowing that ...' He showed his teeth. '... your movements and statements deserve close scrutiny. Who was the woman with you?'

Quint grimaced. 'If I knew a socially acceptable way of telling you to get stuffed, I'd say it.'

Rogers smiled. It was the sort of smile more fraught with danger than another man's scowl. 'Lingard thought it was Nancy Frail.'

'Assuming – just assuming, mind you – I was with a woman, I can assure you it wouldn't have been Nancy.'

'And if it had, you wouldn't admit it anyway?'

'You're clairvoyant.'

'When did you see her last?'

Quint hesitated. 'Back in June. Not since.'

329

'You're sure about that?' He stared hard at him. Quint was held by his continued scrutiny. Rogers knew it to be an unnerving experience to be the object of another's unblinking regard. Quint was standing up to it well.

'I'm sure.'

'I don't understand why.'

'Why I'm sure?'

'No. Why you stopped being a paying customer.'

Patches of pink showed on Quint's cheeks. 'You've a singularly nasty way of putting things, Rogers.'

'So I've been told. At five pounds a coupling why should you complain of a little indelicacy in my describing it? Why did you stop?'

'I got bored.' He brushed cigar ash from his trousers on to the carpet. 'Much as I am now.'

'Or you met someone else.' Rogers noted the flicker in his eyes.

Quint's nostrils did their little belly dance of agitation but he only shook his head.

'Where have you been since Sunday?'

'I don't see that's any of your business.'

Rogers sighed. 'You don't know how many people have said that to me and how many times I've had to insist it is. Tell me, please. Where?'

'I don't suppose it matters. London. Room forty-two at The Tudor Court Hotel in Cromwell Road. It's within staggering distance of The British Museum of Natural History.'

'You drove there?'

'I caught the ten twenty-seven train Monday morning.'

'And your car?'

'I parked it on the station approach.'

'You went with your wife?' He could guess the answer to that.

'My wife,' he replied stiffly, 'left me after that last effort of yours about her brother.'

'You aren't blaming me?' Rogers bristled. He had so very nearly bedded with Judith that he was touchy about it.

'No. But then, I'm not thanking you either.'

'You were on your own?'

'Yes.'

'Doing what?' With Quint being so unusually forthcoming, he knew the London visit to be a blind alley. But he plunged into it nevertheless.

'Doing my thing. When I wasn't at the museum sketching a group of Harriers – Montague's and Pallid, if you want the details – I was being bored to the eyeballs with the weather.'

'You found yourself some female company? Forgive me, I remember a similar occasion . . .'

'You would. You coppers thrive on muckraking. You file it away and bring it up to confound the innocent.'

'Hardly the innocent,' Rogers said cheerfully, 'but otherwise yes. It all goes into a computer these days. And we don't make the muck. It rubs off from people like you.' He rasped the bristles pushing through the skin of his jowls with the back of his hand. 'If you didn't get yourself a woman, what were you doing about being bored?'

'I drank. I can give you the name of the bar if you want it.'

'I'll ask you later if I think it important.' He smiled again. 'I understand you did some bird painting at the Nortons' place.'

There was a quite marked searching for words. 'Yes. The Bonelli's Eagle and a Cooper's Hawk. An accommodating couple, the Nortons.'

'Particularly Mrs Norton,' Rogers said without expression.

Quint narrowed his good eye. 'Just what does that mean?'

Rogers was bland. 'Norton – as I believe you know perfectly well – was also a client of Nancy's. Mrs Norton knows this. *Ipso facto*, being still his wife, she must be accommodating.' Rogers eyed him closely. 'You look peaked,' he said. 'Can I get you something?'

Quint leaned back on the chaise-longue, brushing invisible cobwebs from his face. It looked scrubbed of its tan. His cigar stub lay unheeded and cold, having burned a scar on the table at his side. 'Brandy . . . in the sideboard. I took a fair beating from that mad assistant of yours.'

Rogers, rising, reacted sharply. 'I told you once before. He'd resigned. He's no assistant of mine.' He slid back the doors of the sideboard and found a bottle of four-star cognac. He poured an alcoholic's idea of a stiff drink into a balloon glass and handed it to Quint, holding it carefully by the stem.

'Take one for yourself,' Quint said.

Rogers didn't bother to answer. When Quint had drained the glass he took it from him by the stem, putting it unobtrusively out of Quint's reach.

'Better?' he asked, reseating himself.

Quint nodded.

'Tell me about Lingard.'

A spasm of distaste crossed the lean face. 'All right. I returned by the last train tonight, picking up my car and getting back about . . .' he looked at his wrist watch '. . . three-quarters of an hour ago. I hadn't been here five minutes when Lingard opened the door and just walked in.' Quint's features assumed the expression he had used against the intruder. It wasn't a welcoming one. 'I asked him what the hell he wanted.'

'You recognized him, of course.'

'I recognized him all right. I demanded to see his warrant. That's when he said he wasn't here as a police officer. He said "I am justice." It sounded silly and I thought he was being funny.'

'I don't think he was. He'd started up in business on his own account in the administration of justice.'

Quint made a noise in his throat. 'Whatever his reason, he asked me what I'd done to Nancy. His eyes were odd, staring, you know, not focused. I said, "What the devil! Get out! I haven't done anything to the bloody woman." He yelled at me then. "You raped her, you filthy bastard! Then dumped her like a sack of offal!" He came closer to me and before I caught on had hit me in the face with the flat of his hand. It knocked me backwards, ass over tit. I looked at him from down on the floor. He had *tears* in his eyes.' Quint shuddered. 'That frightened me more than anything else. I knew he was round the twist and – like I told you – as crazy as an elephant in *must*. It's a horrible thing to be up against somebody who's insane. I tried to wriggle away but he jammed his foot on my trouser leg, pinning me down.' He stirred on the plush of the chaise-longue. 'Give me another cigar, will you?' When he was drawing deeply at it, he continued, 'I didn't need to have much of an IQ to know the man was an expert at whatever he was doing. He grabbed me and pulled me upright with one hand, hitting me again with the other. As easily as if I'd been a baby. He shouted, "You were with her on Sunday! She was in your car!"' Quint's mouth turned down at the corners. 'On the same theme as you are now. I told him not to be so bloody stupid.' His nostrils rotated in the anguish of his recollection. 'So he hit me again. Somehow I managed to knee him in the gut and run for the telephone. I never made it. Not by yards. I felt this dreadful pain in the side of my neck and I tumbled over a chair on to the floor, twisting my arm and feeling something crack. I was paralysed down one side. He kept shouting, "You raped her, you bastard, you must have done. Tell me you did or I'll kill you." He pulled me upright again and did this.' Quint touched his swollen eye. 'I was getting to the point where I was going to say I had and chance what he did. That was when I heard a banging – I believe at the door – and must have flaked out. I can't even remember whether he hit me again. Then one of your chaps was lifting me on to this settee . . .' His mouth was ugly. 'I want him charged.'

'He will be. Whether you want it or not. Who told you about Nancy's death?'

'Lingard.'

Rogers shook his head. 'You're not curious enough about the details. Somebody else filled you in.'

'It was in the newspapers.'

'Not in the national press, it wasn't. And not in the local papers until after you'd left. You,' he said positively, 'have been in touch with someone knowing a lot about it, haven't you?'

'Believe me, chief inspector, you're on the wrong track.'

'All right. So put me on the right one.'

'I can't if I don't know.'

'That's a pity,' Rogers said, 'because I'm going to arrest you on suspicion of having committed an arrestable offence.'

Quint flinched and his head jerked. 'An arrestable offence?' he echoed feebly.

'Breaking and entering Nancy Frail's flat will do for a start. I can think of another,' he added grimly.

'Jesus wept! You *can't*.'

333

'Famous last words, Quint. I can and I am. There's a finger impression on the door-post that might just put you there.' He did not miss the shadow of unease crossing Quint's face.

'It could have been there since God knows when.'

'That isn't the opinion of the chap finding it. He says it's fresh. I assume you're not going to object to our taking your fingerprints for a comparison?'

Quint raised a small flicker of protest. 'I am indeed going to object.'

'All right. I can always get a magistrate's order to take them by force,' Rogers pointed out equably. 'It takes time, that's all. Your time.' He glanced at the brandy glass. 'But don't worry. I'll probably find all I want on that.'

'That's a dirty underhanded trick.'

'I know a thousand of them,' Rogers said unruffled. 'I use them against the dirty underhanded people I have to deal with.'

The telephone bell rang. Rogers went to it before Quint could object and lifted the receiver to his ear. 'Yes,' he said. There was a moment of light-breathing silence and then the purring sound of a disconnection. 'Guess who,' he said sardonically to Quint.

Quint stretched out his good arm. 'Let me make a call.'

'Of course.' Rogers trailed the handset to him.

Quint placed it on the chaise-longue beside him, carefully turning the dialling face away from the detective. Then, with the receiver pressed hard against his ear, he dialled a five-figure number, using the thumb of his injured arm and keeping his eyes on Rogers, grimacing the discomfort of it. After listening for a few moments, he asked, 'Did you call?' Receiving an answer, he said, 'I am being interviewed by Chief Inspector Rogers so do not call me again. I have said nothing. Neither have I mentioned your name. So do not allow yourself to be told I have.' He replaced the receiver quickly and stared defiantly at Rogers.

If he expected an angry reaction from the detective he was disappointed. Rogers' expression was amused. 'Not particularly clever,' he said. 'And you'll never know how helpful you've been. Had you a key to the flat?'

334

Quint snorted. 'You flatter me.'

'Is that why you had to break open the door?'

'It's your theory. It isn't a very good one.'

'We'll soon know. This other woman who isn't Nancy Frail and who telephones you with all the latest news. Who is she?'

Quint tightened his lips.

Rogers was deadly serious. 'It might be in your own best interests to tell me.'

'No.' Quint had chewed the end of the cigar soggy and brown nicotine tar stained his teeth. He pulled a face and rubbed his handkerchief over them.

'You're protecting her,' Rogers said. 'Because she's a married woman?' He watched closely Quint's expression. 'Ah! Because she's one of your . . .'

'Shut up! Don't say it,' Quint interrupted forcefully. 'Don't even think it.'

Rogers was unimpressed. 'I *am* thinking it,' he said flatly. 'What in the hell else would I think? If I'm anything, I'm surprised.'

Quint was bitter. 'Like I said before, you policemen never forget, do you? Never put anything but the worst construction on things.'

'We're logical. The background's the man so far as we're concerned. And it fits. All I'm getting from you are evasions. Innocent men don't evade issues. Tell me about this woman,' he persisted. 'Is she the one you chucked Nancy for?'

Quint was weary. 'Where's that bloody doctor? I could be dying for all he cares.'

'He's on the way,' Rogers assured him. 'I don't suppose he stands in his drive in running shorts and spiked shoes just on the offchance he gets a message you've broken a fetlock. It's foggy and the poor bugger might have been in bed.'

'Funny man,' Quint said sourly.

'You know Park Dominis, of course?'

'In detail. Nancy talked about the conniving bastard *ad nauseam*.'

'He's dead.' Rogers watched his eyes.

Quint's head jerked and more ash dropped on his tie. 'Dead!'

he repeated feebly, bewilderment on his face. His jaw muscles knotted in small bunches.

'I should have said murdered,' Rogers corrected himself. 'Although, at a pinch and with a smart alec barrister, it could be bulldozed into manslaughter.'

'Oh, Christ!' His one open pale eye hunted the room as if seeking the answer on the walls. He was paper-white and seemed shrunken, his suit made for a bigger man.

'Your Intelligence Section didn't tell you that? Not even that he was missing?'

Quint merely looked stunned.

'Didn't you see him outside the flat on Sunday evening? He was there.'

Quint groaned. 'What a mess . . .'

'Yes.' Rogers applied a match to his dead pipe and puffed smoke. 'Let's see if we can guess at what happened. I want you to know, to appreciate, exactly what you've let yourself in for. Go back to Sunday evening. Nancy and the man we'll call X were having their usual little romp in bed. It wasn't her own bed, of course. Had it been, none of X's troubles would have happened. She, at least, was starkers. When you pay for it, I suppose you can insist on the full treatment *au naturel*. In all this scrabbling around, Nancy suffered a fatal thrombosis, leaving X in an excruciatingly embarrassing position. A naked dead woman in one's bed takes some explaining away and X didn't propose to do any explaining. He's that sort of a man. After unsuccessfully trying to revive her with brandy, he dressed her as best he could in the clothing she had taken off. And that's a quite different proposition from undressing a live, co-operative woman. It shows.'

Quint, leaning forward, had covered his forehead with his hand, concealing his eyes. His cigar, wedged between his fingers, had gone out.

Rogers continued, 'I assume now that X, with a fair amount of reckless desperation, carried poor dead Nancy outside and into the passenger seat of the car in which she arrived. Which means,' he said pointedly, 'the man was on his own in the house. He could hardly do what he did with a woman wandering about on the premises. And that's an important point. What X didn't know was that Dominis was prowling around playing detective, trying to catch him and Nancy at it. Whether he saw X carrying the body or driving her in the car remains for X to say. I'm going to assume the latter because there's little doubt that X – in a moment of horrible panic at being caught red-handed or later, from sheer bloody-minded viciousness – ran the car at Dominis and did him in. So X found himself with two bodies to dispose of. Each connected to the other by an obvious association, hating each other in life, brought together in death. You're with me so far, Quint?' he asked politely.

Quint uncovered his eyes for a brief moment. They looked sick. 'You're a sadistic bastard,' he mumbled.

'Just an informative one,' Rogers said. 'Where was I? Yes, with two bodies. We'll assume X hid Dominis temporarily and got on with his plan to dispose of Nancy. The lane isn't too far away from his home. It hasn't to be because it is necessary for him to walk back. Once there, he put Nancy in the driver's seat of her car, hoping that the police with their well-known ability at jumping to conclusions might assume she had driven to the lane and died at the wheel. What we were supposed to make of the holes in the windscreen, God only knows. Woodworm or termite infestation, possibly. But X is a reasonably cool customer. He wasn't going to cart a blood-soaked Dominis around in his own car and provide the police with lots of scientific evidence to use against him. He looked for and found Dominis's car, put his body into it and drove to the moor. He probably thought it a good idea to dump the whole caboodle down a hole until he realized he had to get back to town. So it was Dominis only who was put down and his car driven back and abandoned. Again, within reasonable walking distance of X's home.' Rogers' expression was unsmiling. 'A nasty little story, eh? And somewhere you fit into it. So why shouldn't I assume X has a need to visit Nancy's flat. Perhaps to recover some incriminating papers.' He cocked his head. 'Or something else?'

Quint shook his head blindly. 'No,' he whispered.

Rogers shrugged. He had all the indifference of a man knowing his own mind. 'It's a tenable theory. And it'll do until I get something different. The irony of it all is that Dominis wasn't her legal husband. The records at Somerset House say she was still married to an American called Swerdloff . . .'

There was the sound of a car on the gravel outside, crawling along in bottom gear. Rogers went to the window and peered through the curtains. 'Here comes your doctor,' he said coldly. 'You'd better do some serious thinking between now and when he discharges you into our custody.'

Although he received no reply, Rogers was content. He knew precisely where he was going and what he had to do.

15

Seated at his desk, Rogers stared at the telephone handset in front of him for a long time. Without removing the receiver he dialled the number 23222, listening carefully to the clicking of the spring return mechanism, reproducing the delays he had heard in Quint's own dialling of his call.

Satisfied, he uncradled the receiver and dialled the number again. When a woman's voice answered, he said, 'Rogers here, Miss Wallace. Are you on your own?'

There was an indrawing of breath at the other end. 'Yes.'

'I thought you would want me to let you know Mr Quint has been interviewed concerning the death of Miss Frail.'

'I . . . I'm surprised . . .'

'I'm sure aren't, Miss Wallace,' he said matter-of-factly. 'He telephoned you less than thirty minutes ago.' When she made no objection to that, he added, 'He's in custody.'

'Oh . . .' It was a punctured sound. 'Can . . . can I ask on what charge?'

'There are two. The first is in connection with the breaking into her flat.' He heard the sound again. 'The second is a much more serious charge.'

'I don't understand . . .'

'It relates to my enquiries into the murder of Park Dominis. Miss Frail's husband.'

She made the sort of noise that comes from trembling lips. Then she whispered, 'Please say it isn't true, Mr Rogers.'

'He's dead, Miss Wallace.' He was gentle with her now. 'Killed by the same man who drove Miss Frail to the lane and left her there. And you know who that was.'

'Oh, God!' she moaned. 'What are you *saying*?' He imagined her holding herself from collapsing only by her courage and a need to know.

'It's true.'

There was a long, unhappy silence. Finally she said, 'Mr Rogers, I honestly didn't know. He didn't tell me . . .'

'It should make a difference, shouldn't it? About protecting him, I mean.'

'Yes.' Her whisper was muffled by the grey dust of defeat. 'How was he killed?'

'He was run down by Miss Frail's car. Then thrown into a hole on the moors.'

'It . . . it could have been accidental?'

'If it was, the distinction didn't help Dominis very much.'

'He wouldn't do it.' Her protest wasn't strong enough.

'Yes, he would. He did.'

There was a long silence. 'You wouldn't lie to me, Mr Rogers? Harry said . . .'

He interrupted her, a cutting edge to his stern voice. 'I know exactly what he said. I was there. What I'm telling you is that I've spent an hour or so pulling Dominis out of a pothole. I'm unlikely to be anything but very serious about it.'

'Forgive me, Mr Rogers,' she said quietly. 'I accept that.'

'And I accept you won't want to stick to the fiction of your being in on Sunday evening. Not knowing what I've now told you.'

'What can I say?' She was spiritless, beaten; her words dead flowers on a grave.

'The truth might be a good idea.'

'I thought . . . only her. She was dead . . . the scandal . . . it didn't seem that serious . . .'

'I knew you'd lied to me. But not why.'

'I didn't lie, Mr Rogers. Not directly.'

'Perhaps not,' he said ironically, 'but very much the next best thing. You were ambiguous.'

'I'm sorry . . .'

'You'll tell me now?'

'I have no choice.'

'No, you haven't.'

Her forlornness came through clearly. 'Oh, God. Andrew . . .'

'I'll come straight away.'

'Please . . . no. I'll come to you. I can't stay here.'

'Where is your brother?'

'He's attending a Farmers' Union dinner.'

'I'll be waiting.' He dropped the receiver on its cradle thoughtfully.

He spoke to the Chief Constable at his home. Huggett sounded like a man who wanted nothing more than to stay in bed and put his head under the pillow in the hope that the nastiness would all be gone by the morning.

While he waited for Constance Wallace, Rogers coordinated the eating of cardboard-thin cheese sandwiches from the canteen with a quick wash and a brushing of his stained clothing. He also found the time to mow his darkening chin and jowls and stick pink tape over his grazed knuckles. When he moved, pain twinged in the shoulder joint where Lingard had kicked him. There wasn't much he could do about the depression of his spirits.

He visited the chargeroom to sign the sheet authorizing Lingard's detention, glancing at his late colleague with a face of stone but feeling, beneath it, a deep pity for his hunched and silent wretchedness.

Quint, being splinted and bandaged in the Casualty Department of the hospital, was not injured seriously enough to be hospitalized – as he had no doubt hoped – and would shortly be joining Lingard in the cells.

A quick brushing of Quint's brandy glass with mercuric-oxide powder had produced the twin of the finger impression found on the door-post of Nancy Frail's flat.

When Constance Wallace arrived, the perfume of gin hung around her like a cloud of invisible smoke. She was sheep-skinned and tweeded; accoutred as if she had freshly come from the hunting and killing of an otter. The fog had left diamond points of moisture in her hair. Her expression was fixed and unsmiling; her eyes raw-rimmed from crying. Her voice had lost the pink wholesomeness it possessed on their first meeting. Rogers had noticed suitcases on the back seat of the car in which she arrived.

Before she accepted his invitation to sit in the chair at the side of his desk, she handed him an envelope.

He opened it and took out a blob of cottonwool. In it was a tiny curved lens. It looked as fragile as paper ash. He held it shining and dry in the hollow of his palm. 'Where, Miss Wallace?'

'Mrs Jacobs found it on the stair carpet and handed it to me.' She was seated with her legs tight together, her hands folded in an attitude of apparent submission.

'You knew it to be Miss Frail's?'

'Not at first. But I guessed, of course.' She was brooding on her fingernails, not meeting his regard.

'You told your brother?'

'No. There was no point. Not after he asked me to tell you I had been at home all evening.'

'It also suited your own purpose.' Rogers' cheeks were hard-planed and purposeful.

'Yes. But I don't think I would have gone that far for myself.'

He remained silent until she was forced to look at him. 'You were in the car when Quint stole the Rajput painting from Miss Frail's flat,' he said.

'What Harry did, he did for me,' she protested, as if that whitewashed the act. For her it obviously did. She was, Rogers concluded, in love with the man.

He showed his teeth. 'The law doesn't recognize that sort of altruism.'

'We didn't regard it as stealing, Mr Rogers. My brother had no right to give it away.'

'Legally he did.'

'But not morally.'

'No,' he agreed, wagging his head. 'Probably not. Anyway, a claim of right made in good faith is always a good defence. You knew she would be with your brother that evening?'

She gave an exhalation of contempt. 'Yes. He always made it clear when I should be out. I suppose because I didn't like her and made no secret of it.'

'This happened monthly?'

'Yes. You knew?'

'She kept a record of their meetings. There was a visit due for October.'

'I see. So that's how you knew about Andrew?'

'Partly. Do you like your brother?' His chin pressed on the knot of his tie.

'That's an odd question . . . not a very nice one.' Hauteur was not far away.

'Do you?'

She considered a second or two and submissiveness came back. 'Not enough to lie for him any more. Not if Harry has to suffer.'

'I didn't think you would. Did he know about you and Quint?'

'No.'

'And if he had?'

'He would have objected.' Her lip curled. It was a soft, pink, attractive lip. 'It might have interfered with my housekeeping for him.'

Rogers understood, although in his experience it was usually a selfish mother who kept her daughter chained to her needs. 'Wasn't he curious where you went?'

She laughed mirthlessly. 'Not in the slightest. Just so long as I came back.' She snapped open her handbag and withdrew a flat green leather case. 'May I smoke?'

He stood and reached across, holding the flame of his lighter to the cigarette between her lips. That near he could feel the heat of her body and smell both the odour of her femininity and the gin with which she had fortified herself against him.

Seated again, he filled and lit his pipe, tasting gratefully the narcotic woodiness of the smoke. 'You knew of Miss Frail's actual relationship with your brother?'

'I suspected, naturally. But it wasn't anything he was likely to discuss with me.' She licked her lips shiny as if needing more gin. 'And I wasn't interested enough to care. I knew he would never marry her.'

'Tell me, Miss Wallace, what happened Sunday evening.'

She looked at her fingernails again. 'We knew Andrew was expecting her because he'd asked me was I going to be out. So we waited outside until she arrived and . . . and was obviously

343

going to remain. Then we went to Queen Anne's Road and waited again, making sure there was nobody about. Then Harry stopped the car just short of her flat and I waited in it. He was gone for only a few minutes and returned with my Rajput. We both felt dreadfully guilty about what we'd done. Then we went to Harry's house. When I returned home at midnight, Miss Frail had left and my brother was in his room.'

'What if you had returned earlier?'

'I never did.' Her big breasts pushed against the stuff of her tweed dress. 'It was expected I would remain out until then.'

'And assuming Miss Frail had returned to her flat and discovered the painting missing?'

'My brother had never told me he'd given it to her. He could hardly tax me with its taking.'

'How did you know she had it?'

She shrugged. 'He wouldn't have given it to anyone else.'

'And where is it now?'

'In my bedroom.'

'When did you first suspect all was not well?'

'Not until Andrew spoke to me. After your visit.'

'Not when Mrs Jacobs gave you the contact lens?'

She made a moue, her brown eyes scornful. 'That meant only what I already knew.'

'You looked concerned when I first called.'

'I was. I thought you'd called about the painting.'

'After I'd spoken to your brother, what happened?'

'He told me Miss Frail had died of a heart attack while they were talking. That in order to avoid a misunderstanding, a terrible scandal, he had taken her in her car to a quiet lane and left her there. He assured me he had done nothing criminal. That his position as a magistrate, even his knighthood, would be in jeopardy. That she was dead and nothing could alter that.' Her mouth twisted. 'He pleaded the good name of grandfather ... our own position in the community.' There was a self-deprecation in the down-turning of her mouth. Rogers could visualize the whining cowardice of the man. 'And, as you have pointed out, my own motives weren't entirely selfless. If taking the painting was serious enough before, it became infinitely more so when I knew she was dead. Not wholly for myself. Harry would have been in a worse position. As he now appears to be. You yourself confirmed she had died naturally so I allowed you to believe I had been at home all evening.' She looked lost. 'I didn't think for one moment that anything else was involved – certainly not the death of Mr Dominis – or that Harry would be suspected.'

'Isn't that why he went to London?'

She was surprised. 'No. He'd arranged that long before. He left before either of us knew anything of her death.'

'But you told him later? By telephone.'

'Yes. I couldn't contact him until late this afternoon. When I did he returned by the first available train. He isn't the sort of man to avoid trouble at the expense of another.'

'No, he probably isn't,' Rogers agreed. 'And to his credit he hasn't involved you in any way. But he knows now what you and he have let yourselves in for and is busy thinking of an out for you both. He'll have put two and two together and come up with the name Sir Andrew Wallace.'

She sucked smoke into her lungs. 'It's a terrible thing to contemplate, Mr Rogers. That one's brother murd . . . killed someone.'

'People who do these things are always another's brother; another's father, mother or sister.' *Which*, thought Rogers in retrospect, *wasn't very consoling*.

'Dominis was watching Miss Frail,' he said. 'Trying to get evidence for a divorce.' He saw her wince. 'You didn't see him when you were waiting outside your own place?'

She shook her head. 'No. Please tell me. Did Andrew . . . was what he did deliberate?'

'I don't honestly know. Who knows what's in a man's mind?'

'Why did you think Harry had killed him?'

'I never said I did. I said his detention related to it. It is, in fact, a charge of impeding the arrest or prosecution of your brother. Not,' he admitted, 'a charge now likely to be pursued but one you may face yourself.'

That wasn't worrying her and she stared at him with her grandfather's empire-building eyes. 'You *knew* Harry didn't kill him.'

'I was fairly certain he hadn't.'

'You trapped me, misled me, in a way.' She screwed her cigarette to extinction in an ashtray.

'You misled yourself, Miss Wallace,' he said with coldness in his words. 'It would be ludicrous to suggest anyone could improperly trap a person into telling the truth. Blame your brother if you must blame someone. He used you and, in using you, must have realized you would become involved in more than the concealment of Miss Frail's death.'

'Whatever I feel about him,' she said dully, 'he's my brother . . .'

He spoke gently. 'I shan't use as evidence what you have told me. Nor need he know you have spoken to me. Mrs Jacobs' evidence of her finding of the contact lens will be enough to put Miss Frail in the house. The rest follows inevitably.'

'I've already told him.' She was looking at a point a million light-years outside the walls of his office.

Rogers was startled and raised his black eyebrows. 'You have?'

'I left a note on his desk. I can't go back now.'

He frowned. 'What did you say?'

'Just that I was coming to you. That I was telling the truth.'

'When is he due back?'

She lifted the cuff of the sheepskin coat and looked at her watch. It was a tiny thing on a gold strap. 'He should be there now.'

Rogers pulled the telephone handset to him and dialled 23222. He waited, listening to the call signal repeating itself unheard in an empty room. Then he replaced it. 'Not yet,' he told her.

'It won't make any difference,' she said. 'I'd still tell him. I'd have told him personally had he been there. I'm going away with Harry.'

'But not yet.'

'What do you mean?'

'You'll stay here until I've seen your brother.' He said it with the calm assurance of unarguable authority. 'If, after that, things are as you say, I'll release Quint on bail. I don't think either of you need worry too much about the charges.'

'No?' She was subdued and introspective. 'But that's not all of

346

it. Isn't there a name for a female counterpart of Judas Iscariot, Mr Rogers?'

'That's ridiculous,' he said harshly. 'And maudlin. You flatter your brother. I don't see anything Christ-like in dumping a dead girl – if she *was* dead – and running down her poor devil of a husband when he's caught doing it. And I don't think the grand-daughter of General Napier Wallace does either.'

That kind of gooey morality against informing on criminals always irritated Rogers to blasphemy.

16

'How did we do it?' Coltart asked, sitting at Rogers' side. In his stolid way he was being heavily sarcastic. They were in Rogers' car, driving cautiously through the thickening fog to Spye Green Hall. 'You played this one pretty close to your chest.'

'That's because I was doing a lot of guessing. If I was proved wrong I wanted to be wrong on my own.'

Coltart's eyes glittered his humour. 'And to be able to say how good you are when you turned out to be right.'

'Do I look that smug?'

'Yes.'

Rogers laughed. 'I don't mean to. It's probably a nervous tic. But I had nothing really. Only some scientific bric-à-brac that added up to very little. Not things that put a label on the man who did it but rather one that eliminated the others. And,' he added sourly, 'I'd had a gutful of gossip and defensive ambiguities from nearly everybody I interviewed. Even in a dirty country like we're living in now, men still don't like to admit they pay for it.'

Coltart chewed his toothpick, nodding his head in agreement at Rogers' opinion of the intransigence of witnesses.

'First of all, we knew it was a big man who drove Frail to the lane.' The windscreen wipers were sweeping triangles of transparency on the glass and Rogers occasionally pushed his head forward, sometimes tapping the bowl of his pipe against it.

'We did?' The car was filling with smoke and Coltart kept his face as near the crack of open window as he could without giving offence.

'The driver's seat was ratcheted back to its limit. I tried it for size and it suited me. *She* wouldn't have been able to drive it like that. Her feet wouldn't reach the pedals. Then there was Dominis's car. He's a big man and the seat was already adjusted to suit him. A smaller man driving it would have needed to pull it forward. So, in a negative way, I could eliminate Norton and Galbraith. Both men with their bottoms nearer the ground than average.'

'Leaving Wallace, Quint and Hacker.'

'And Lingard. I never forgot him.' Rogers braked sharply and swerved, nearly colliding with the rear of an unlit parked van.

'Bastard!' he swore absentmindedly. Glowing flakes of tobacco dropped unheeded on to his lap. 'He was in love with the woman and, I'll bet, the only one who hadn't done his thing with her. Even had he, he's a bachelor and there'd have been no overwhelming reason for him to dump her if she'd died on him. No,' he said reflectively, 'although I never overlooked the possibility, it was his flailing around like the Arm of the Lord that worried me. Hacker didn't fit in, either. If she'd had a coronary in his bed he'd have most likely written to *The News of the World* about it. And he was much too forthcoming about a similar instance of Dominis keeping tag on him. That would have been a far too sensitive point to bring up had he been involved. Whatever else he said, he'd have skated past that. And a town flat. I just couldn't see him carting bodies about in the Regent Crescent. Even on a Sunday evening. Asking his girl-friend to confirm he was at the Acey-Deucey Club was very much a formality.'

'Quint?' Coltart prompted.

'H'm. Quint could have cleared himself in five minutes. At the expense of Constance Wallace. Which gives him a decency I never suspected. He hadn't seen Frail for over four months. So why suddenly last Sunday? I would have accepted he'd got her out of his system by then. What is certain is that he'd called at her flat. And, as we now know, left his dab on the door-post. The by-product of all this is that the man who very carefully wiped Frail's car clean of prints isn't likely to leave one on a door he'd just forced open. As a corollary, Quint's breaking into the flat meant that the woman with him couldn't have been Frail. Wallace had given her a Rajput painting and it was missing. To me that signified Constance Wallace. And if it was Constance Wallace, then she had lied about being at home.' He yawned with his teeth clenched on the pipe stem. 'And lying about it meant her brother had something to hide. Of course, she could have lied to avoid being suspected of stealing the Rajput. But it left her brother very much on his own, having produced a lie for an alibi at the second time of asking. He panicked badly there. Unnecessarily too. You don't have to produce an alibi just because you're asked. All I had to do was to allow his sister to believe Quint was in serious trouble, to let her know there was more to it than just the dumping of a dead girl. She had a choice then and being the woman she is, she made the proper one. The one she thought her grandfather would have made.'

He changed gear to take the gradient of Rooks Hill. It was one o'clock and the streets were dead and cold. Even the cats seemed to be staying indoors.

'Quint thought he was being clever in telephoning her, warning her to keep quiet. But dialling a number with three twos on the end of it was almost as obvious as if I'd been looking over his shoulder. It was too much of a coincidence. He had to be speaking to her.'

'What evidence have we against Wallace?'

Rogers frowned. 'Nothing much. I'm not likely to get the Detective of the Year Award over it. I'm guessing that Dominis was killed in the drive of Spye Green Hall. If so, we should find something there. He probably saw Wallace carrying Frail's body out. He'd be baffled, not knowing what was happening. She could have been drunk for all he knew. But Dominis was, by all accounts, a man short on temper and long on action. It's not difficult to imagine him wondering what the hell and then, when he saw Wallace bundle her in the car and start to drive it, to charge out to try and stop his evidence for a divorce getting away from him. I can see Wallace panicking – I can't believe he'd do it coldbloodedly – and driving the car at him, crushing him against the gate pillar. Dominis's upper half would shoot forward over the bonnet, his head going smack through the windscreen, leaving one of his hairs on Frail's lap. To use the car, Wallace would have to punch himself another hole in the driver's side. I noticed the gravel had been freshly raked at the entrance and I've no doubt we'll find bits of glass there.' Rogers shook his head. 'But dear God! What bad luck he had. First she died in his house. Naked and probably in his bed. That would be enough to stun most men. On top of that Dominis had to be watching outside and is killed in the ensuing panic. Talk about troubles compounding themselves into disaster. Anyway, apart from the contact lens that's about the lot.' He pulled a face in the darkness. 'And you know how far that'd take us against the sort of barrister Wallace can afford. All he'd need to say is that she left him – after a cosy little chat about French stamps – alive and happy: that she died elsewhere under circumstances which only God and somebody else knows about.'

'It doesn't sound very convincing,' Coltart said dubiously.

Rogers looked sideways with a crooked smile. 'Since when did any defence have to? It needs only throw doubt on the facts and some mud at the prosecution's witnesses and acquittal's a certainty.'

'What about the contact lens?'

'On a stair carpet? So she went upstairs to use the toilet, to wash her hands. Any reason but that of going to bed will do.'

'And she drives her car away one-eyed?'

'If she lost a lens, she lost it. It needn't immobilize her.'

'So what are you going to do?'

'Question him. And tell him at the same time he needn't answer unless it pleases him to do so.' He snorted disgust.

'And if he decides to remain mute?'

'I shall probably get stuffy and point out that innocence claims the right of speaking, as guilt invokes the privilege of silence. Jeremy Bentham said that first,' he added, 'not me.'

'That'll shake him,' Coltart said ironically.

'He'll go white with fear,' Rogers said with equal irony.

'Anyway, it won't be the first murder case undetected because the murderer won't confide in us.' He made it sound as if frustration and failure were an acceptable part of the job. But for him they weren't. There was a deep need in him to ensure that justice was done. Anything else made what he did pointless.

With Coltart holding his torch and shielding its light with a flap of his overcoat, Rogers stooped over the gravel and sifted it through his fingers with the care of a miner prospecting for diamonds. He felt no more than a deserved satisfaction when he found the few tiny cubes of glass with which the laboratory would place Nancy Frail's car and the smashing of its windscreen firmly in Wallace's driveway.

Pulling aside a freshly planted cotoneaster bush, he exposed a fresh unweathered scar, made at the height of a car's bumper, in the sandstone of the gate pillar.

'We seem to be on the winning side, sergeant,' Rogers whispered, wiping dampness from his hands with his handkerchief. 'Let's take our fortunes on the flood.'

The house was silent except for a low, hardly perceptible murmur that sounded as if it were purring like a gigantic squatting cat. A thin light shone from between the edges of the curtains of Wallace's study, diffusing itself into the fog as soft yellow motes of luminescence.

Rogers rapped the big door knocker and waited, shoulder to shoulder with Coltart The insistent mutter of sound was louder now and all around them, the blanketing fog muffling the location of its source although they felt the tremors of it pulsing up through the soles of their shoes.

When the house remained silent, unanswering, Rogers untwisted the handle and opened the door, the two men stepping inside. The warm parched breath of central heating hit them as they closed the door. The hall was illuminated by the light from the study reflecting through its open door. Apart from the low murmur that had followed them inside the house, there was the absolute unbreathing quietness of an unoccupied building.

The study was empty. A screwed-up ball of grey lay on the carpet. Rogers went in and retrieved it, unfolding the stiff parchment paper. He read aloud the message written on it for Coltart's information:

'Andrew: I'm sorry. I cannot go on with it. I am going to see Mr Rogers and tell him the truth. I shall not be coming back. Constance.'

Rogers stepped to the door of the study and called into the emptiness of the house. 'Sir Andrew! Sir Andrew!'

He waited, listening; a dark premonition creeping up on him. Then recognition of the vibration and understanding came into his eyes. He cried sharply, 'The garage!', plunging along the hall and out into the fog, his shoes skidding as he raced along the wet cement walk to the rear of the house. Coltart was close behind, panting down the back of his neck.

The garage door was closed, the silver disc of a yale key glinting from its lock. From behind the aluminium panels came the throbbing they had heard before. Rogers grasped the handle, jerked it and swung the door up and over. The garage contained a blue fog of its own. Wallace's Daimler stood in it with the interior courtesy lights shining; its engine trembling the metallic lustre of its silver flanks and shivering the loose flesh of its owner's dead jowls.

He lay limp in the driver's seat with the window down, one hand hooked by its wrist on the steering wheel. The silk lapels of his dinner jacket and the rumpled white shirt front were stained with the brown liquid still dribbling from his open mouth. He was peering forward as if checking the petrol gauge and worrying that there wouldn't be enough. On the inside of the windscreen, still ghostly visible in the drying condensation, he had written with the pad of his finger, *An accident* . . .

Holding his breath against the harshness of the exhaust fumes, his eyes stinging with acid tears, Rogers leaned into the car and cut the engine. He coughed and spat on the oilstained floor. Wallace's skin was cherry pink and the detective, having seen too many dead men, knew any first-aid to be a waste of time. Nor had he ever considered mouth-to-mouth resuscitation a viable proposition with anyone not female and under fifty.

'He's chickened out,' Coltart rumbled disparagingly over his shoulder. He despised suicides.

Rogers walked out into the open air. The fog tasted clean and uncomplicated. He fumbled in his coat pockets for his pipe and oiled-silk pouch. 'He panicked for the third and last time,' he said, a sliver of compassion in his voice. He stuffed tobacco in the pipe bowl, not looking to do it. It was something he could do in his sleep and, were the paraphernalia of his addiction normally handy to his bed, probably would. 'I think his image was a front that held the rest of him together. Take it away and he was morally short-arsed with pomposity instead of guts.' Thinking he might be overly uncharitable to a dead man, he added, 'Of course, he might have liked Frail more than we imagined.' He didn't sound as if he believed it himself. He nodded in the direction of Wallace. 'Does this sort of ending depress you?'

'No,' the uncomplicated Coltart said, not really understanding why it should. 'It's cowardly but it tidies things up. Saves a lot of argument.'

Rogers sighed. Soon Nancy Frail, stored waiting in the bank of refrigerated green-enamelled drawers in the anteroom to the mortuary, would be joined by Dominis and Wallace. Rogers thought that if there was anything in the theory of survival after death, they could fight out their differences somewhere other than where he would be required to worry about them.

His own worries were earthy and more pressing. His biggest problem was, he knew, that he lived too much with those posed by other people and too little with his own. His wife and brother-in-law hovered exasperatingly at the periphery of his concern, waiting to demand their share of his attention. Before he would find time to get round to them he knew, with the certainty of experience, that someone would have his skull cracked with a pickaxe handle or his safe rifled, his troubles becoming Rogers'.

He looked at his watch. It was one-twenty and it had been a long day. A bit too long for anything more exacting than a final word with Huggett and sleep. He was drained of any further impetus. He felt as if newly come from having had a woman: physically deflated and mentally spent with hardly steam enough left to talk. Paradoxically, he needed Bridget to refill his emptiness.

But Bridget was tomorrow. When he had sloughed off the cloying miasma of Nancy Frail's sex and the troubles she had left behind her like a deadly slime.

With Bridget it was going to be different. It always was different when you did it yourself. . . .

A question of identity

June Thomson

1

As George Stebbing climbed over the gate into the lower meadow, he could see the members of the archaeological society still hard at work, despite the heat of that August afternoon. The trench they were digging now stretched almost half the width of the field, approaching close to the boundary hedge where his land ended and his neighbour's, Geoff Lovell's, began, while in the centre a large rectangle had been marked out from which the turf and top-soil were being removed. Girls as well as men were shovelling and digging, wheeling the excavated soil away in barrows or painstakingly sifting it through sieves.

He had to admit everything looked all right. There was no litter, not even near the tents where some of the younger ones were camping during the dig. And they were taking care to keep the top-soil, as he'd told them.

Not that this was the real reason for his visit, although it wouldn't do them any harm to think he was checking up on them every so often. He was really looking out for the girl, the one with the brief shorts and the long, brown legs. She had smiled and waved to him the first morning.

'There's life in the old dog yet,' he told himself, with a shamefaced yet half approving grin. 'And there's no harm in looking, although if I was twenty years younger, it'd be a damn sight more than a look I'd be after.'

He was glad now that he'd agreed to let them come. It made a bit of a change from the normal daily routine on the farm, although at first he hadn't been too keen. It was his son's idea. He was the one who had noticed the broken pieces of pottery,

359

turned up when the ditches were being re-dug, and who had taken them along to the local museum to have them dated. They were early Saxon, he had been told, and could indicate the site of a settlement or homestead. Would he allow some test diggings to be done?

George Stebbing had finally agreed. The field was a scrubby bit of pasture, too small for cultivation, although he was planning to have the hedges grubbed out and turn it into part of the adjoining field, ready for putting under the plough the following autumn. There seemed little harm in letting them make their dig before this was done, especially when it was pointed out to him that ploughing could destroy forever any archaeological remains.

Besides, as a relative newcomer to the district, it might do him a bit of good socially to be on friendly terms with the society, particularly as it included a few local dignitaries on its committee.

'All right. Let them come,' he had said at last.

He wasn't quite sure himself what he had expected. Long-haired students, most likely, making a damn nuisance of themselves by playing guitars and trampling down his corn; certainly not these hard-working men and women, some of them quite elderly, who had given up their summer holidays and were prepared to slog away hour after hour in the sun.

He started off down the slope, his blue eyes moving restlessly as he looked out for the girl. But it was Mr Rose, an earnest, middle-aged history master from the grammar school, normally a fussy man about his appearance but dressed now in a filthy khaki shirt and shorts and an old, floppy linen hat, who scrambled out of the trench to meet him, his face glistening with sweat. It was the first time he had been in charge of a dig and, knowing Stebbing's initial reluctance to let them on his land, he was desperately anxious that nothing should go wrong.

Stebbing watched him approach with dismay. He had been hoping to avoid Rose but, under the circumstances, there was nothing much he could do except stay and talk to him for a time, before finding an excuse to wander off on his own.

'Found anything yet?' he asked.

Secretly he had set his heart on their discovering something really valuable, like a hoard of buried treasure or, at least, some gold coins. But so far they had turned up nothing more exciting than a lot more broken pottery and some fire-blackened bones.

Rose's face lit up.

'Yes, indeed we have, Mr Stebbing! This very morning, as a matter of fact. Some post-holes! It's all very thrilling!'

'Oh, really?' Stebbing asked, trying to sound interested, although the discovery of post-holes didn't strike him as being particularly exciting. 'Is that important?'

'Dear me, yes. It could be very important. Judging by the size of them, they could indicate a building of some significance. A barn, for instance. Or even the house itself. And then, goodness knows what we might find. Grain storage pits! Perhaps even the original hearth-stone!'

Stebbing gazed about him uncomfortably, embarrassed by Rose's enthusiasm and pedantic style of speech. The farmer always felt at a loss as to what to say in reply.

Suddenly his attention was caught by the figure of a man, standing a little distance off in the adjoining field and watching them with apparent interest. He was a short, powerfully-built man, with heavy shoulders and, with his back to the sun, he gave the impression of a strong, dark, hostile shape against the light.

'There's Lovell,' Stebbing remarked.

Rose looked in the same direction and seemed uneasy.

'Who is he?' he asked. 'I've noticed him watching us on several occasions over the past few days.'

Stebbing laughed.

'It's the farmer who owns the land next to mine. A funny devil. Probably thinks you're going to start digging up his field next. I'll call him over and explain.'

Cupping his hands round his mouth, he shouted, 'Hi, Lovell! Come over and take a look if you want to.'

Geoff Lovell heard him but he made no reply and, after a few seconds, he turned and began walking away, trying to appear nonchalant and unhurried but inwardly cursing himself for having been such a bloody fool to come in the first place.

He should have waited until later in the evening when most of them had packed up and gone home, although even then it wasn't entirely safe. A few of them were camping in the field; he had seen lamps alight in the tents until quite late. But, at least, there'd be less chance of running into Stebbing. Seeing him standing there, he hadn't dared go too close to the hedge and get a good look and all he had been able to make out was that the trench was being extended, although he couldn't see its exact line.

Should he go back and complain to Stebbing, get him to call a halt to the digging, making as an excuse that, if they came too close to his land, they might mess up the drainage?

Then he decided against it. Stebbing was looking for an excuse to strike up an acquaintance and by going and talking to the man, he'd be playing straight into his hands. He'd be round at the house wanting to discuss it, and that would be even worse. Better to risk them digging in the field, for the chances of them turning up anything must be a thousand to one, although he didn't count on it. There had been too much bad luck over the past few years for him to believe that things would ever go his way again.

He came to the last meadow behind the farmhouse and stopped at the gate, reluctant to go any further. The land here sloped gently down on all sides so that the house and out-buildings were clustered in a hollow and he remembered, as a child, stopping at this same place, particularly in the evening when dusk was falling and the lights were shining out from the windows, and thinking how safe, how protected it seemed, held between the folds of earth as between a pair of hands. Then homecoming had been a special and secret delight. There had been a deep sense of belonging. Now, he saw the same scene with different eyes. It seemed to suck at the very roots of his strength.

Christ, if only I could get out of it! he thought. Stebbing would buy it for that son of his. That's what was at the back of his seeming friendliness. And if I'd sold out to him three years ago, none of this would have happened. I'd get rid of it like a shot now, only it's too bloody late.

As he stood there, he saw the figure of a woman in a blue

dress emerge from the house and turn to look in his direction, putting her hands over her eyes as a shield against the sun. It was Betty. She must have seen him, silhouetted against the sky at the top of the slope, for she waved tentatively. He made no answering gesture. From that distance, he saw her hesitate, look back towards the house and then, after a few moments of uncertainty in which she stood irresolute in the yard, she started towards him, disappearing for a time behind the trees that surrounded the farm. Still he didn't move. Presently she came into sight again and began climbing the slope towards him, stopping a little short so that the gate formed a barrier between them.

Always this space between us now, he thought bitterly. This holding back from any contact.

She was smiling at him nervously as she faced him; not a proper smile, more like a wincing of the mouth. In the bright sunlight, she looked ill. The shadows under her eyes were dark, like bruises, and he saw how thin and transparent her skin was, stretched across the delicate bones that seemed to shine through it.

She reminded him of a bird, fearful, fragile, light in the hands, and she roused in him the same instinct for protection and the same despairing sense of his own clumsiness.

He looked down at his hands as they lay on the top bar of the gate: a farmer's hands; strong and muscular; short-fingered; the nails broken and dirty; fit for work and that was about all, and he felt a sudden contempt and revulsion for his own body.

'You've been up there?' she asked, putting up a hand to hold back a piece of hair that had fallen across her forehead.

Despite the estrangement, he knew what she meant. There had never been the need for many words for them to understand each other.

'I had a look,' he admitted reluctantly.

'And it's all right?'

'I reckon so.'

Feeling her eyes on his face, he dropped his own glance, knowing that he had never been any good at lying to her.

'What are they doing now?' she asked.

'Still digging,' he replied, trying to sound off-hand. 'It's all right, I tell you. They're working in the middle of the field. They won't come anywhere near the hedge.'

Better not tell her about the trench, he decided. There was no point in frightening her needlessly.

'You're sure?'

No! he wanted to shout. I'm not bloody sure! Not about anything anymore. Instead, he tried to smile at her reassuringly.

'You worry too much,' he told her, but he had struck the wrong note: too light; too intimate. He saw her draw away.

'Don't go up there, though,' he went on. 'Stebbing's hanging about. He might see you.'

'He saw you?' she countered quickly.

'No,' he said, lying again. 'I made sure he didn't. The man's a damned fool.'

He meant it as a bit of a joke between them, a shared amusement at Stebbing's thick-skinned stupidity, but the remark came out with all the bitter anger and contempt that he really felt towards the man. And having once started to release his anger, he found it difficult to control, although he realised that Stebbing was only a scapegoat.

'Where's Charlie?' he asked, opening the gate.

He saw her back away at his approach, although he pretended not to notice.

'I don't know. Behind the barn, I think, seeing to the pigs.'

'Well, keep him away from the house. I don't want him talking to anybody.'

'You think someone might come?' she asked, sounding frightened.

His anger finally broke.

'I don't bloody think anything!' he burst out. 'Just keep Charlie away. And make sure the dog's off the chain.'

'It's my fault,' she said in a tone of flat assertion that was not expecting any answering denial.

His anger drained away, leaving him ashamed and awkward. Despite her frailty, there was this steely quality in her that he had never known how to deal with, that baffled him and made him helpless.

'It's no one's fault,' he muttered, turning away to fumble with the gate fastening.

She didn't answer but began walking away from him down the slope towards the farm. He let her go, following only when she was half the field's length from him and then walking slowly so that there was no chance that he should catch her up.

Stebbing, who had watched Lovell leave, turned back to Rose, his face flushed and his blue eyes hot with anger.

'Surly bugger,' he said, half to himself. Lovell had deliberately ignored him, an insult he found hard to take in front of other people.

Well, that's the last bloody time I'll speak to him, he decided. He can go to hell as far as I care.

Rose, aware of a certain tension and anxious that no disagreeableness should attach itself to him and his party, put in brightly, 'I don't know if you'd like to have a look at the post-holes, Mr Stebbing? As I was saying, they could be an important find. The proportions . . .'

'Ah, yes, proportions,' said Stebbing, walking away from him. He had caught sight of the girl, the one he was looking out for, a little distance away, kneeling down by a small pile of pottery fragments that she was washing in a bucket of water, and he felt his good humour return as he stood over her, looking down into the cleft between her breasts, revealed by the scanty sun-top she was wearing.

'Warm work?' he asked, grinning appreciatively.

Behind him, Rose, who had trotted after him, was saying with maddening persistence, 'The post-holes are over in this direction.'

Stebbing winked at her, indicating that he would much prefer to stay talking with her, and turned to follow Rose.

As it happened, he was not to see the post-holes that afternoon.

A sudden shout away to their left made them both turn. A young man was standing up in the trench on the far side of the field, waving his arms to attract their attention.

'Mr Rose!' he was shouting. 'Over here!'

'My word!' said Rose, pushing up his glasses excitedly on his nose. 'I believe young David's discovered something.'

He set off at a brisk lope, Stebbing following him and wondering if perhaps, at last, the excavations had turned up the treasure he had been hoping for; speculating how much of it, if any, he could claim for it having been found on his land.

The young man had climbed out of the trench to meet them. One look at his face was enough to tell Stebbing that whatever it was he had discovered it wasn't something pleasant. He was a deathly, greenish-white colour and he pointed wordlessly down into the trench where he had been digging before turning aside with a muttered apology to be sick in the grass.

Stebbing and Rose stood on the mound of earth at the edge of the trench and looked down into the newly-dug section where the young man's spade lay abandoned at the bottom. At first, neither of them could see anything unusual. The excavated sides were studded with stones, some of them quite large, and threaded with the fibrous roots that had spread out through the sub-soil from the trees that grew along the edge of the field.

Then Stebbing saw it and, taking Rose by the arm, pointed. At the far end, protruding from the loose clods of earth that had not yet been cleared away, was a foot. Or what remained of a foot, clad in the mouldering fragments of a boot, the leather rotting and falling away to reveal . . .

Stebbing averted his eyes.

'I think we'd better get the police,' he said gruffly. 'That's no bloody Saxon corpse down there. And,' he added, looking at the young man who was still retching miserably into the grass, 'I'll get him fixed up with a drop of brandy at the same time. Do you want to come for a swig yourself? You look as if you could do with it.'

'No I'll stay here,' Rose replied, with surprising firmness. 'I'm in charge of the site and it's my responsibility to see no one touches anything. Evidence, you know. Besides, I wouldn't like any of the women to see it. It's not a pleasant sight.'

'You're bloody right there,' agreed Stebbing and, thankful for the excuse to get away, he set off across the field, accompanied by the young man, while Rose, his back to the trench, stood on the mound of earth, shooing away with flapping gestures of his arms those members of the society who, realising something unusual was happening, had begun drifting down from the main excavation site.

2

He was still there three-quarters of an hour later when Detective Inspector Finch arrived, accompanied by his detective sergeant, Boyce, and a contingent of uniformed and plain-clothes men.

Finch saw him as he walked down the field towards the site, taking in with a few, quick, interested glances not only the small, dejected figure of the history master, now sitting cross-legged on the grass, a handkerchief draped over the back of his neck to keep off the sun, but the whole view.

The field was small and roughly triangular in shape, bounded on one long side by a ditch and a hedge, on the shorter side by a coppice of trees near which some tents had been erected, and on the third side by another hedge with a gate in it. This gave access to the large wheatfield round which they had walked on the way from Stebbing's yard, where they had parked their cars.

Across the field a line trench and a partly-excavated area in the centre, marked by mounds of excavated earth, showed where the archaeological society had been working. Wheelbarrows and tools lay abandoned here and there, for the digging had been called off and the members had retired to the tents to drink tea and wait for the arrival of the police. Only Mr Rose remained on duty, hot and miserable and feeling obscurely guilty, as if the discovery of the body were, in some inexplicable way, his fault.

He scrambled to his feet as he saw the group of men approaching, a little cheered by the appearance of the man who seemed to be in charge of them. He looked less like a policeman than a farmer, with a frank, open face and the slow, easy walk of a countryman.

'Mr Rose, isn't it?' Finch asked. 'I gather from Mr Stebbing you're in charge here.'

'That's right,' Rose replied. 'And I assure you I had no idea . . .'

Finch looked him over with a friendly eye. The man looked ready to drop.

'I think they're brewing up tea over by the tents,' he told him. 'Why don't you get yourself a cup? I'll have a chat with you later.'

'Thank you,' Rose said gratefully, and Finch watched sympathetically as he stumbled away.

'Poor devil,' he commented to Boyce, his burly, deep-voiced sergeant. 'He's dug up more than he bargained for here. Well, let's have a look at what's been found. Pardoe, you'd better come in on this.'

Pardoe, the police surgeon, a brisk man with heavy horn-rimmed glasses and a no-nonsense air about him, detached himself from the group of men and came forward.

Together with Pardoe and Boyce, Finch approached the edge of the trench and peered down into it. They contemplated the foot in silence for a few moments and then Finch and Pardoe clambered down for a closer look.

'About four feet down,' Finch commented, 'so it's a relatively shallow grave. The ground's dry, too. We shouldn't have too much trouble getting him out.'

'How long's he been down there?' asked Boyce. The trench was too narrow for the three of them and he remained on the top.

Finch squatted down to examine the foot in close-up.

'Hard to say,' he admitted. 'What do you think, Pardoe?'

Pardoe touched the boot with a fastidious finger.

'A fair time. The leather's well rotted. But I can give you a better idea when we've uncovered the rest of him.'

'Right!' said Finch. 'We'll get started on it straightaway.'

He climbed out of the trench, slapping his trouser legs to rid them of the clinging crumbs of earth, and began giving orders for the erection of a canvas screen round the site.

'Then I want a thorough search made of the field,' he added. 'Stapleton, you're in charge of that. Take the uniformed men and collect up anything you find.'

Stapleton moved off and Finch turned to McCullum, a tall, laconic Scot who, while awaiting orders, had seated himself on the grass and was slowly rolling a home-made cigarette.

'I'd like some photographs taken of the trench as it is now and then a series at successive stages as he's dug out. Get a few general shots, too, of the field.'

McCullum nodded and moved off, carrying his equipment, towards the screen that was being erected.

'And when McCullum's finished taking the first shots, I want you, Moody, to get your coat off and start digging him out,' he told a large, powerfully-built young constable. Turning to Boyce, he added, 'See that every scrap of soil's saved, so get those plastic sheets spread out and make sure everything that's dug out goes onto them. Denny had better take over from Moody when he's about three feet down. Barker and Frome can sift the soil as it comes out. I don't want anything missed, not even a shirt button. I'll leave you in charge, Tom, while I have a word with Stebbing.'

'Right,' said Boyce and, beckoning to Moody, disappeared inside the screens. As he walked away, Finch heard with some amusement Boyce shouting, 'For God's sake, man! It's not a pick and shovel job! You're not digging up the High Street. Get those turves off clean!'

Stebbing, who was waiting a little way off, had been craning his neck, torn between an anxiety to see what was going on and yet not wanting to observe too closely anything that might be unpleasant. Finch had already summed him up in the walk from the farmhouse where Stebbing had met them. He was a large, paunchy man, with a florid complexion and a bustling, self-assertive manner that, the Inspector guessed, covered up a much less confident personality beneath it.

'Nasty business,' he said as Finch approached.

'Yes,' Finch replied and added, 'the land's yours?'

'Up to the hedge.'

'And beyond that?'

'Belongs to a man called Lovell. He farms it with his brother.'

Finch turned to contemplate the further field. About half a mile away the roof of a house and its surrounding buildings was just visible below a gentle slope of grassland.

'That his place?' he asked.

'Yes,' Stebbing replied and added quickly, 'about that dead man they found. I swear to God I know nothing about it, Inspector. It came as a complete shock them finding it.'

'An archaeological society, isn't it?' Finch asked, ignoring the man's remark.

'That's right,' Stebbing said. He seemed eager to explain. 'We'd found these bits of pottery and we thought – that is, my son suggested – they might like to have a look at the field this summer. It's due to go under the plough in the autumn . . .'

'So they had your permission?'

'Oh yes,' Stebbing said and laughed a little too loudly. 'So it's hardly likely, is it, that I'd give them the go-ahead to dig, if I'd put the body there myself?'

Finch, who was well used to the over-anxiety of the completely innocent to establish their guiltlessness, said blandly, 'It never crossed my mind, Mr Stebbing. Have you noticed at any time that the earth in the field had been disturbed?'

'No, I haven't. Mind you, it's the tail end of my land and, as you can see for yourself, it's not much use at the moment, so I haven't bothered with it. It could be months before I'd walk down this far.'

Long enough, Finch thought, for the grass to grow again, especially if the turf had been replaced over the grave and well pressed down.

'Is there any nearer access to the field, apart from the road that runs past your place?'

Stebbing shook his head.

'No path or cart-track?'

'No.'

Finch looked across the fields to where a distant line of telegraph posts marked the road, along which he had driven a little while earlier.

'It's a fair way off,' he mused.

'Nearly a mile,' Stebbing replied.

'Have you noticed anything unusual over the past, say,

couple of years? A car parked in the road, for instance, or strangers about?'

'I can't say I have. As you saw for yourself, the road's pretty quiet. There's only my farm and Lovell's along it. But that's not to say someone couldn't have parked there and come across my land without me seeing him, especially at night.'

'I'll check with Mr Lovell,' Finch replied. 'He may have noticed something.'

Stebbing hesitated, as if about to say something and Finch cocked his head inquiringly, inviting the man to speak.

'Yes?' he asked.

Stebbing wetted his lips.

'It may mean nothing, Inspector, but Lovell's been hanging about since they started digging. I saw him myself this afternoon. In fact, I shouted to him to come across and have a look but he ignored me and walked off. Then Mr Rose remarked he'd seen him, too, on a couple of occasions. I'm not saying there's anything to it . . .'

'Just curiosity?' Finch suggested easily.

'That's right,' Stebbing agreed. He seemed relieved that Finch had put forward this explanation. 'Or he might have thought they'd move on to his land without asking his permission. He's a funny bloke, Inspector. Since I bought the farm three years ago, I've tried being neighbourly but he doesn't welcome visitors. I thought his wife and mine might get together, too, for a bit of a chat, but he made it clear he wants to keep himself to himself. Quite rude he was when I called. Mind you, that brother of his must be a bit of an embarrassment.'

'Oh?' said Finch. 'In what way?'

His face had relaxed into the friendly, listening expression that his colleagues would have recognised as part of his interviewing technique. It fooled Stebbing as it had fooled many others. Encouraged to go on, the farmer tapped his forehead significantly.

'A bit short up here. Simple. I'm not saying he ought to be put away or anything like that. The chap seems harmless enough. But I can see, with a brother like that, Lovell may not want many people calling.'

'Difficult for him,' agreed Finch. 'But I'm afraid I'll have to drop in on him and ask a few questions – about cars seen in the vicinity, that sort of thing. I suppose I could walk across the fields to his house?'

'I'd go round by the road, if I were you,' Stebbing advised him. 'He's got a dog that's kept loose in the yard so you'd be safer going in by the front way. It's pretty fierce; went for me when I called. I wouldn't like it to take a lump out of you.'

'Thanks for the warning,' Finch said and, nodding pleasantly, turned back to the trench. The canvas screen had been erected and, inside it, Moody was carefully removing the earth, throwing it to one side on to the large plastic sheets that were spread out on the grass and over which two constables were squatting, sorting it over with trowels.

The heat, trapped inside the screen, was stifling.

The makeshift grave, which lay roughly at right-angles to the trench dug by the archaeological society, had now been partly uncovered. The turf that had covered it had been cut into squares and was lying separate from the mound of loose earth. Finch contemplated them with his hands in his pockets.

'See those turves are parcelled up,' he told Boyce. 'The forensic boys may want to have a look at them. One thing's certain, he's been down there long enough for the grass to take root over him again.'

They watched in silence for a few more minutes until the soil had been dug out to a depth of three feet and then Finch moved forward.

'All right,' he said to Moody. 'You can take a rest. It's a trowel job from now on. Denny, you take over. You're the expert. I want him brought out as whole as possible.'

Moody retired gratefully, mopping his streaming face, and Denny, a thin, bright-eyed man, squatted down at the edge of the grave and began carefully removing the earth with a small trowel. Finch had seen him at work before and admired his patience. He would pick away, if necessary for hours, with the same delicate precision as an expert restoring an old master.

Finch drew Boyce outside.

'There's not much I can do here until he's properly uncovered and Denny's going to take at least an hour. Besides, I want to go over to the neighbouring farm.'

'Something interesting?' Boyce asked inquisitively.

'Possibly,' Finch replied. 'According to Stebbing the man who owns it, a chap called Lovell, has been hanging about watching them digging on the site. It could be nothing more than curiosity but he's an obvious person to call on anyway. It's his land on the other side of the hedge. Stebbing has noticed nothing unusual but Lovell may have done. Whoever put the body there must have carried it either across Lovell's land or Stebbing's.'

'Seems an odd place to choose,' Boyce remarked. 'Why take the trouble to bring it this far? If I'd killed somebody, I wouldn't want to go humping it across the fields, looking for a place to bury it.'

'That's assuming it was murder,' Finch pointed out.

'I think it's a fair enough assumption,' Boyce replied. He was feeling hot and tired and argumentative. 'If it was a suicide or a natural death, why bother to try and get rid of the body? The man didn't bury himself, that's for sure, but whoever did wanted him well hidden. If this archaeological society, or whatever it is, hadn't started digging, he might never have been found. Even then, it was just chance they uncovered him. If the trench had been dug a few feet to the left, he might still be down there and no one the wiser.'

'He might have died or been killed near here,' Finch replied, 'which would explain why he was buried in this particular field.'

'Then either the man who buried him happened to have a spade handy to dig the grave, in which case it suggests, if it was murder, it was planned beforehand; or he was able to get hold of one fairly quickly, unless he was willing to run the risk of leaving a corpse lying about until he could come back later and get it under the ground.'

'It's a point worth following up,' agreed Finch. 'I'll check with Stebbing and Lovell if they've noticed any tools missing from their farms. They're the two nearest places likely to have spades. He's been down there too long for someone to borrow the equipment the archaeological society brought with them.'

He glanced across at the tents where there were signs that the society was already striking camp.

'I'd better have a word with Rose before he leaves,' he added. 'Not that I expect he can tell me much.'

As he strolled over in that direction, Rose came forward to meet him, his face anxious.

'We're moving out, Inspector, I hope only temporarily. You see, we've found these post-holes . . .'

'You'll be allowed back,' Finch interrupted to assure him. 'I'll let you know when, Mr Rose. It should be within a couple of days.'

'Most distressing. Most distressing. And just when we were making such excellent progress. It's an early Saxon site, you see, which could be very important archaeologically, and some of my members have only a limited time to work on the dig.'

'You haven't noticed anything unusual yourself while you've been working here?' Finch asked.

'In what way?'

'Well, for example, an old spade left lying about?'

'No, I can't say we have. Everything that's found is most carefully preserved. All the earth is sifted and the pieces of pottery are washed, numbered and put to one side. You can examine those if you wish.'

It was clear Rose had no interest in anything on the site that wasn't of archaeological significance and Finch decided to leave it there. His own men, under Stapleton, were systematically searching the field. If anything of relevance to the dead man had been left behind, they would find it.

He put the next question with careful casualness.

'Fascinating, these archaeological digs. I gather Mr Lovell's been to have a look?'

'Not exactly to look at the site,' Rose corrected him. 'He's been watching us from the next field. I've noticed him myself several times.'

'Perhaps a bit worried you might start digging on his land?' Finch suggested lightly.

But Rose took it as a personal affront.

'I can assure him we would do no such thing,' he replied

375

stiffly. 'We are a responsible society. At no time would we excavate a site without first getting the owner's permission.'

Finch smiled and, thanking him, walked away. The interview hadn't been very productive, except to confirm that Lovell had been watching the excavation from his own land on the other side of the boundary hedge.

Had it just been curiosity, he wondered, as he skirted the wheatfield. It was certainly worth following up, and he found himself looking forward to the interview with Lovell, Stebbing's unfriendly neighbour, who kept himself to himself.

Meanwhile it was a glorious day, one to be enjoyed. Beside him, the wheatfield stretched away, the pale gold ears stiffly erect on their short stems, rustling as they rubbed together, under a sky of indeterminate hazy brightness that seemed to have had the colour bleached out of it by days of continual heat. A scent of warm grain filled the air, Mediterranean in its intensity, while, far off, a combine harvester droned lazily as it worked some unseen field.

3

Reaching Stebbing's yard, Finch collected his car and turned out of the farm entrance, heading for Lovell's place, about three-quarters of a mile down the road. He drove slowly, noting as he went the features of the area.

The road was narrow and tree-lined, little more than a hard-surfaced lane, with barely room for two cars to pass abreast. On either side were grass verges, heavy with cows' parsley and meadow sweet, and behind them hedges, broken here and there by gates, through which he caught glimpses of fields, growing wheat and potatoes mostly. Beside one, a narrow neck of trees ran down to the edge of the road. At no place, he noticed, was the field where the body had been found visible from the road.

As he drove, he had a growing conviction that his sergeant had voiced what he himself had felt from the beginning, that the location of the grave was in itself significant. Why had the body been carried so far off the road? He could understand why the nearby fields had not been chosen as a burial site. They were cultivated and therefore likely to be disturbed at some future date when they were ploughed. But the wood was easily accessible and a body buried there could remain for ever without being discovered.

On a sudden impulse, he stopped and, drawing the car on to the verge, walked a little way between the trees. In places they grew closely together and after only a few minutes' walk he saw, on glancing back, that his car was no longer visible between the dense foliage. Stooping down, he picked up a handful of the leaf mould that lay inches thick under the trees and let it trickle out between his fingers. It was soft and light. And yet, whoever had buried the body, had chosen a field at least half a mile away from the road where the earth was tighter packed and covered with turf that would first have to be removed before the grave could be dug.

Why? Because of its inaccessibility? Or was there some other more positive reason?

Thoughtfully, he walked back to the car and drove on down the lane.

A little distance further on, a gravelled opening on his left indicated the entrance to Lovell's farm and, parking the car at the side of the road, he got out and walked back towards the five-barred gate, fastened with a padlock and chain, that shut off the end of the drive.

As he put his hand on the gate, a dog came tearing up the slope from the farmyard and flung itself against the bars, snarling and barking savagely, its lips drawn back to expose sharp, white teeth.

Finch kept his distance as he contemplated it. It was a large black dog, a mongrel but with a lot of labrador in it, and quite clearly it was not going to be appeased with a few kind words and a pat on the head.

Beyond the gate, a rough, wheel-rutted drive led down an incline to a yard and outbuildings at the bottom. The house itself stood at right angles to the road, presenting a blank gable end, its windows looking out across the yard to the huddle of sheds and barns that faced it. It was an old building, with plastered walls and a roof of uneven, weathered tiles that was curiously shaped, the back of it sweeping down lower than the front to cover the first storey. Beyond the house, the ground sloped upwards again towards a meadow that would lead, Finch guessed, in the direction of the field where the body had been found.

There was no one about. The yard was deserted. Meanwhile, on the other side of the gate, the black labrador kept up its hysterical onslaught against the bars and it was clear to Finch that, unless he was prepared to be savaged, there was no way of approaching the house. It seemed to be stalemate.

Behind the barn, Geoff Lovell heard the dog barking and

guessed the reason. In a way, he had been half-expecting it. His luck had run out years before and he realised, with a morose fatalism, that he almost welcomed this final down-turn of events as a kind of relief. The waiting was over. The worst had come.

All the same, he stood irresolute, wondering what to do. It was Charlie who decided it for him. He had grown increasingly uneasy as the dog's outcry continued, glancing alternatively in the direction of the road and then towards Lovell, his round face anxious.

'There's someone a' the gate,' he said at last.

Geoff Lovell ignored him, thrusting the fork into the straw and carrying it over to the heifer pen where he stood at the fence to watch the soft-eyed animals trample it underfoot. A fine, sweet-smelling, golden dust rose in the sunlit air.

Behind him, Charlie touched his arm.

'Geoff, there's someone at the gate,' he repeated. 'The dog's barking.'

'I know,' Lovell replied impatiently. 'Leave it be, Charlie.'

'Shall I go, Geoff? Shall I see what they want?'

Lovell stifled his rising anger. It was no good, he realised. Charlie would go on and on about it until he went to silence the dog. Besides, whoever had called was evidently going to stand his ground until someone came.

Thrusting the pitchfork into the straw-pile, he turned to his brother.

'Listen, Charlie,' he told him. 'You stay here. Understand? I don't want you coming out. Whoever it is, I'll get rid of him as quick as I can. You finish seeing to the heifers.'

He saw the familiar, stubborn look pass over Charlie's face, his mouth drooping sulkily.

'Why can't I talk to him, too, Geoff? Nobody comes to see us these days.'

'Stay here,' Lovell said shortly. 'I'll be back in a few minutes.'

'It ain't fair,' Charlie replied, turning his face away. 'I don't ever get to talk to anybody.'

Lovell looked at him with a mixture of baffled anger and pity. It was hard on Charlie. He had few pleasures and, like a child, he welcomed any diversion. But he could not be trusted. God knows what he might say if allowed to talk.

'Listen,' Lovell said to him, trying to keep the impatience out of his voice. 'You stay here, like I told you, and I'll give you a game of cards later this evening. All right?'

'All right, then,' Charlie agreed reluctantly. 'But I still think it ain't fair,' he added, raising his voice as Geoff walked away round the end of the barn.

Finch, who had stayed where he was at the gate, letting the dog bark itself hoarse, watched Lovell approach up the drive. He was stockily built, broad-shouldered and, Finch estimated, in his forties. Although not bad-looking, there was a dark, surly air about him, accentuated by his sun-burnt skin and thick, black hair, turning grey over the ears, that hung low on his forehead. He gave the impression of strength and masculinity and smouldering energy that was kept banked down, apparent in his heavy, deliberate walk and the deep crease between his eyebrows.

'Mr Lovell?' Finch asked pleasantly, over the gate.

The man didn't acknowledge the greeting but shouted at the dog, which cringed immediately and came to heel.

'What do you want?' he asked belligerently. 'This is private land.'

'I'm a police inspector,' Finch replied. 'I'd like to ask you a few questions.'

He saw the expression on Lovell's face close over.

'What about?' he asked.

Finch regarded him with a cool eye. He had no intention of conducting the interview across a five-barred gate. It was time, he decided, that Lovell, too, should be brought to heel.

'If you'll tie that dog of yours up, we'll talk in the house,' he said. 'Otherwise we can go into headquarters for a proper interview. It's up to you.'

Lovell stared at him for a few seconds and then his gaze dropped.

Not so tough after all, decided Finch, once his bluff's been called.

'All right. Wait here,' Lovell said in a surly voice.

He dragged the dog off by its collar down the slope into the yard, where he fastened it up to a piece of chain attached to the wall of the barn. Like its master, the fight had gone out of it. Or so it seemed. But as Finch climbed over the gate and strolled down the track towards the farm, the hair round its scruff and along its spine rose and its lips drew back in a threatening snarl. The Inspector gave it a wide berth as he walked past it.

Lovell was standing at the door of the house, his hand on the latch, wondering whether to open it or not. The Inspector was alone and it was evidently an informal visit. Lovell could see that, if he kept his head, it might be possible to get rid of the man fairly quickly. To ask him inside would show some willingness to cooperate and, besides, Charlie was less likely to see them and come out to join them than if they were standing outside in the yard.

'You'd better come in,' he said shortly, pushing open the door, and Finch followed him into the house.

The door led directly into the room beyond that was long, low-ceilinged and shadowy after the dazzle of the sunlight outside. Finch, pausing in the doorway, took in its features in a few rapid glances as his eyes got used to the dimmer light. On his right, an oval, gate-legged table stood under one of the small casement windows, with four round-backed, Victorian chairs drawn up to it; while against the nearby wall an old-fashioned oak dresser stood beside a door that led presumably into an adjoining room. A sofa and a pair of armchairs, covered in worn cretonne, faced a coke-burning stove of mottled enamel, the only modern looking object in the room. The stove was placed in the deep alcove of what was probably the original fireplace opening, for the smoke-blackened beam was still in position above it and the high mantelshelf. A door next to the fireplace stood ajar, giving a glimpse of the two bottom treads of a narrow, boxed-in staircase that extended upwards, Finch guessed, alongside the chimney breast.

But what struck him most about the room was its neatness and cleanliness. There was none of the comfortable clutter that most farmhouses collect. The furniture, though old and well-used, was highly-polished; the ornaments and pieces of china on display over the fireplace and on the dresser shelves were neatly arranged and, apart from some bills tucked in behind a vase and a pair of wellington boots standing tidily on a sheet of newspaper in the hearth, there were few signs of family occupation. A shotgun propped up in the corner near them seemed out of place.

'Well?' asked Lovell.

He had taken up a position in the centre of the room with his back to the circle of chairs, blocking the Inspector's approach. It was obvious he had no intention of asking Finch to sit down.

'Just a few questions, Mr Lovell,' Finch said casually. The man seemed more at ease although it was, he guessed, largely a pose. He was standing with his hands in his trouser pockets but the powerful forearms, bare below rolled-up shirt sleeves, were still tense. Finch could see the bunched muscles under the dark skin.

'I believe you own the land next to Mr Stebbing's?' Finch continued.

'That's right.'

'And yours and Mr Stebbing's are the only farms along this road?'

'Yes. What of it?'

'You haven't seen or heard anything suspicious in the past couple of years, have you?'

Lovell's reply came a little too quickly.

'No, I haven't.'

'No cars parked late at night? No strangers about on your land?'

'No.'

'You seem very sure, Mr Lovell.'

'I've a right to be,' Lovell replied. 'That dog of mine's loose day and night in the yard. No one could set foot on my land without him letting me know about it. That's why I keep it.'

It was a reasonable answer, as Finch had to admit to himself. The dog had been quick enough to notice him and give warning as soon as he approached the gate. Under the circumstances, it seemed futile to put the next question, but Finch asked it all the same.

'No tools missing from the farm?'

The query seemed to disturb Lovell for some reason. He had

become more relaxed and confident as the interview continued. Now the old bristling, suspicious manner returned.

'Tools? What tools?' he asked sharply.

'Any tools. But I was thinking specifically of something like a spade or a garden fork.'

Lovell was about to speak when the sound of the door opening distracted the attention of both of them. Turning, Finch saw a man standing in the doorway, blinking as his eyes got accustomed to the subdued light. It was difficult to tell his age. He had the round moon-face and soft, unformed features of a child but, judging by his height and build, was probably in his thirties. As he stood there, peering at them from the threshold, his hands dangling loosely in front of him, Finch guessed he was Lovell's simple-minded brother of whom Stebbing had spoken.

Lovell's face had darkened and his voice when he spoke to him was angry and yet, underneath his impatience, Finch thought he heard a certain gruff affection.

'What do you want, Charlie?'

Charlie looked from his brother to the Inspector with a shy smile, as if hoping to be introduced, but Lovell quickly recalled his attention.

'I said, what do you want?'

'Cup o' tea,' Charlie replied.

'Go through to the kitchen, then,' Lovell said, jerking his head in the direction of the door at the far end of the room.

Charlie crossed the room slowly, his boots scraping on the floor. As he passed Finch, he ducked his head to give him a bashful, sideways look and grinned up at him.

'Hurry up,' Lovell told him.

He still seemed reluctant to go.

'There's men up there diggin',' he told them, indicating vaguely with his thumb somewhere outside.

Lovell made an impatient sound and, opening the door, bundled him into the further room that Finch only caught a glimpse of. It seemed to be a kitchen, for he noticed saucepans on a shelf before Lovell shut the door on the pair of them.

'I thought I told you to stay away,' Lovell said furiously to Charlie, as soon as the door closed behind them.

383

Betty Lovell, who was mixing pastry at the table, looked up, her eyes troubled.

'What's the matter?' she asked. 'I heard the dog barking and then you talking in there with someone. Who's come?'

'The police,' Lovell replied briefly, pushing Charlie in front of him, 'and *he* has to come nosing round.'

'I only wanted a cup o' tea,' Charlie protested. 'It's hot work, Geoff, humpin' that straw about. The dust'd got down my throat.'

He coughed unconvincingly.

'Make him one, will you, and see he keeps in the kitchen?' Lovell asked Betty. She had remained standing at the table, motionless, her hands still in the bowl. Her face had a rigid expression that he knew meant she was fighting against panic.

'What have they come for, Geoff?' she asked. 'What have they found?'

He shook his head in warning and glanced significantly in Charlie's direction. She understood and, for a brief moment, in that silent interchange, there was greater intimacy between them than there had been for a long time. She had even called him by his name.

Christ, he thought bitterly. It takes something like this to bring us together.

'It's nothing,' he said, making it sound unimportant. 'And there's only one of them, a Detective Inspector. All he's done is ask questions about who owns the land round here.'

The moment of intimacy had passed. She turned away, wiping her hands, and with lowered eyes brushed past him to put the kettle on to boil.

'I suppose I'd better get back to him,' Lovell said awkwardly. To Charlie he added with more anger than he intended, 'Stay here. You understand? Don't you move a foot out of here until I tell you to.'

'Can we still have that game o' cards?' Charlie asked appealingly. He had pulled a chair out from the table and was sitting obediently, like a good child, his hands grasping his knees.

Lovell looked down into his round, anxious face.

'Yes, Charlie,' he said in a softer voice. 'We'll have that game of cards.'

On the other side of the closed door, Finch could hear Lovell's deep voice, although he couldn't distinguish the words, and then a woman's lighter tones answering him. For the first time since his arrival, he remembered Stebbing had referred to Lovell's wife and assumed she was keeping deliberately out of the way. Stebbing had said they didn't welcome visitors and it could have been this natural dislike of strangers that had prevented her from coming out to speak to him. All the same, he was intrigued and he began walking casually towards the door in the hope that, when Lovell came out, he might catch a glimpse of her. But the farmer re-entered the room unexpectedly, shutting the door so quickly behind him, that Finch saw nothing more than the same shelf of saucepans and the end of a wooden table on which a blue and white mixing bowl was standing.

'I was asking if you'd noticed any tools missing from the farm,' Finch reminded Lovell, picking up the conversation where it had been broken off.

'I've missed none,' Lovell replied shortly. He remained standing with his back to the door, as if to prevent Finch from entering the kitchen or someone from leaving it.

'You're quite sure?'

'I'd've noticed.'

The interview seemed to be over. And yet Finch lingered. It struck him as strange that Lovell hadn't asked why these inquiries were being made although, given Lovell's natural taciturnity, it might not be in his character to do so.

'The men your brother was referring to are probably mine,' he continued, dropping into his easy, gossipy style, although he doubted if it would have any softening effect on Lovell. 'There's been a body of a man discovered in that field of Mr Stebbing's. You know, the one where the archaeological society has been digging. I believe you've been along to have a look a few times.'

He was hoping the remark might provoke some reaction in Lovell but he merely shrugged and said, 'What of it? I was checking up they didn't come trespassing on my land.'

Finch waited, giving Lovell the opportunity to question him about the dead man, as most people would have done. But, as

Lovell said nothing, Finch felt compelled to ask, 'It doesn't interest you that a body's been found there?'

'Why should it? It's none of my business. It's on Stebbing's land, not mine.'

It was said with an air of triumph, as if Lovell knew he had scored a point, and Finch had to agree that, in a strange way, he had. After all, why should Lovell concern himself about a dead body that wasn't even on his property? The man was perfectly entitled to shrug his shoulders and dismiss it as nothing to do with him.

'Has Mrs Lovell been to have a look at the dig?' he asked pleasantly, unwilling to let the subject drop.

'No,' Lovell replied.

'Not interested either?'

The slight emphasis that Finch put on the last word wasn't lost on Lovell. He scowled.

'She's got better things to do with her time,' he said abruptly. 'And so have I. So if you've finished . . .'

As he spoke, he had begun walking towards the front door which he opened pointedly. He clearly considered the interview at an end. All the same, out of some irrational perversity, Finch was determined to have the last word. On the doorstep, he paused to say in his official voice, 'There are no more questions for the moment, Mr Lovell, but I may have to come back to make further inquiries.'

A strange expression passed over Lovell's face as he confronted the Inspector across the threshold. It was a look of unutterable weariness and defeat and, seeing him in the strong sunlight that flooded the yard, Finch was aware that the strain was not of a recent origin. It had settled in his eyes and round his mouth; the look of a man who has been carrying an intolerable burden for too long.

He's close to breaking point but he's covering up well, he thought.

The next instant, the expression had vanished and Lovell was looking at him jeeringly.

'Look out for the dog, then,' he said. 'Don't blame me if it's off the chain and sets on you.'

With that, he went back into the house, slamming the door

shut behind him. As if on a signal, the dog, that had been lying quietly in the yard, began barking again, leaping forward the length of its chain and falling back, choking and snarling.

Finch walked away slowly. If Lovell thought he was going to be frightened off, then he had picked the wrong man. In the centre of the yard, he paused deliberately, ignoring the dog that strained and snarled a few feet behind him, and, turning to face the farmhouse, looked it over with a calm and interested scrutiny.

It was a long, low building, probably only one room deep, with plastered walls, once painted cream, that showed discoloured patches where they had been amateurishly repaired. The paintwork on the door and windows was shabby, too, and the outbuildings across the yard also showed signs of poor repair. A tractor, standing by the barn, looked old.

Was this the burden that Lovell was carrying? A run-down farm that was a constant struggle to keep going?

It might account for his lack of neighbourliness that Stebbing had commented on. Pride, combined with a lack of money, might make Lovell wary of mixing with his more prosperous and successful neighbours. Or was there some other reason that had forced Lovell to retreat from the world, shutting himself and his family away from any contact with outsiders?

With these thoughts in his mind, he strolled up to the gate and, as he climbed over it, he looked back. Lovell, without so much as a glance in his direction, had emerged from the house and was crossing the yard. Stooping down, he unfastened the chain and the dog, set free, came racing up the track towards the Inspector, barking furiously as it came.

The inference was obvious. Lovell had had the last word after all and was seeing him off.

Damn the man! Finch thought with exasperation, as he got into the car and started the engine. Any further inquiries he might have to make at the farm were not going to be easy. There would be no dropping in for a casual gossip. At the same time, as he admitted to himself with a rueful grin, there was something he had to admire, however reluctantly, about Lovell. The man possessed a certain strength and hard-ness, as well as sheer bloody-mindedness, that the Inspector found himself responding to. He was no fool, either. Unlike Stebbing, it wouldn't be easy to trick him into giving anything away.

4

Stebbing himself came out of the house as Finch drove into his yard, and he strolled over, eager for a chat.

'Any luck?'

'Not much,' admitted Finch.

'You saw Lovell?'

Finch hesitated, half-inclined to make some pleasant but noncommittal remark that would discourage Stebbing's curiosity. But Lovell intrigued him and he was curious himself to find out more about the man. There might be some piece of gossip that Stebbing had picked up about his neighbour and would be willing to pass on, even though he admitted knowing little about him.

'Yes, I saw him,' he said, 'although I didn't find him very forthcoming.'

'I did warn you,' Stebbing said with a grin. He seemed to be enjoying the idea of Finch's possible discomfiture. 'The dog go for you?'

'Lovell chained it up eventually.'

'It'll have somebody one of these days,' Stebbing commented. 'No wonder no one goes near the place. The postman won't deliver at the house any more; leaves the letters, when there are any, in a box by the gate, or so I've been told.'

'Has Lovell always been like this?' Finch asked.

Stebbing shrugged.

'I can't really say. I've only been in the district myself for the past three years, when I bought this place and, like I told you, I had a couple of tries at being friendly. I don't bother now.'

A man crossed the yard at this moment and Stebbing broke off to shout at him.

'Hi, Len! Come over here a minute, will you?'

To Finch, he added, 'That's Len Wheeler. He'll know a bit more. He used to work on Lovell's farm a while back.'

Wheeler came reluctantly towards them. He was a man in his fifties, with a small, brown face and wary eyes. Years of hard, outdoor labour had pared him down to essential muscle and sinew, so that he gave the impression of the tough, well-weathered strength of leather or whipcord.

'The Inspector would like a word with you,' Stebbing told him.

Finch silently cursed Stebbing's bluff and unsubtle introduction. Wheeler was clearly put on his guard.

'Oh ah?' he said carefully. He came no nearer, remaining a few feet away from them.

Keeping his distance, Finch thought disgustedly. In his own way, he's as bad as Lovell.

Stebbing stood by, smiling, pleased at having effected the meeting and quite unaware that a silent confrontation was taking place.

'I've just called at Mr Lovell's farm,' Finch began. Wheeler made no reply and Finch, rarely at a loss, felt uncertain how to continue in the face of his obvious reluctance to talk.

'Mr Stebbing tells me you used to work for him.'

Wheeler's eyes flickered momentarily in Stebbing's direction. Then after a long pause, he said slowly, 'That's right.'

'How long ago was this?'

Again the pause, before Wheeler replied, 'About twelve, thirteen years.'

It's like getting blood out of a stone, Finch thought angrily, but he kept his expression bland as he put the next question.

'You left?'

'I got given me cards.'

It seemed a promising opening and Finch pursued it.

'Oh, really? Why was that?'

'Not enough work.'

There was an odd undertone of sarcasm in Wheeler's voice as

he said it and Finch looked interested. Wheeler was unbending but it was a slow process.

'Or so he said,' Wheeler added, without any prompting this time. The sarcastic note was stronger, too, or perhaps Finch's ear was better tuned to picking it up. He felt Wheeler was hinting at something more than the mere words implied and he cocked his head inquiringly.

'Who works the farm now?'

'Lovell and that brother of his, seemingly. They've not taken on anyone else as I know of.'

'Seemed a run-down sort of place when I saw it,' Stebbing interrupted. 'Not enough capital put into it if you ask me.'

Wheeler immediately looked blank, withdrawing from the conversation and Finch, sensing this, turned a shoulder deliberately against the farmer, excluding him. He doubted if Stebbing would notice. He was too thick-skinned. But the gesture wasn't lost on Wheeler. For a moment, something like amusement showed in his eyes.

There's a streak of malice there, thought Finch, if only I can get at it.

'I shouldn't think Charlie could do much,' he commented, fishing for an opening. But it wasn't the right one. Wheeler merely shrugged indifferently.

'Charlie's all right. He's strong and he's willing and that's something these days.'

So it evidently wasn't Charlie who had aroused Wheeler's spite. Finch tried another tack.

'Does Mrs Lovell help much on the farm?' he asked off-handedly.

The gleam was back.

'She looks after the poultry and the garden. Leastways, she did when I was there,' Wheeler replied with a half-grin that implied some hidden animosity. But whether directed at Mrs Lovell herself or women in general Finch couldn't tell. But quite clearly the mention of her name brought back some old bitterness.

'I didn't see her this afternoon,' Finch went on, with seeming casualness.

He had the feeling that he and Wheeler were playing some

verbal game, the rules of which he wasn't yet sure about, although he was beginning to understand them a little better. But he realised there would be no short cuts. Wheeler would play it out under his own terms.

Beside him, Stebbing opened his mouth as if he were about to interrupt again and Finch plunged on, over-riding him.

'How long have they been married?'

He asked the question more for the sake of something to say to keep Stebbing out of the conversation than in expectation of any significant answer, but Wheeler's reply was surprising.

'Who?' he asked.

'Why, Lovell and his wife, of course.'

'She ain't his wife,' Wheeler announced with a look of triumph.

Finch was silent for a moment, nonplussed by the unexpectedness of the remark, and Stebbing took the opportunity to come in himself at this point. During the conversation, he had been fidgeting at Finch's side, feeling excluded and anxious to play his part. Now he said sharply, 'Not his wife? But you never said.'

'You never asked,' Wheeler retorted. He seemed to get a perverse pleasure out of scoring this point off his employer.

'But when I spoke of her as "Mrs Lovell" you didn't put me right,' Stebbing said angrily. 'Damn it all, when I went to call on the man, I referred to her as "Mrs Lovell" to his face and *he* didn't say anything either.'

He was clearly annoyed that no one had taken the trouble to acquaint him with this particular piece of local knowledge and Finch guessed that, under it, lay a deeper resentment that, although he had bought land in the district and invested money, he was still treated as an outsider.

Wheeler looked amused.

'Maybe that's because she is Mrs Lovell.'

'You mean she's Charlie's wife?' Stebbing asked incredulously.

Wheeler laughed out loud at this.

'Is it likely?' he asked. He was ready to go on playing Stebbing for some time yet, teasing the man into guessing his way into the truth but Finch, who had had enough, had no intention of letting him do so.

'Whose then, Mr Wheeler?' he asked with quiet authority.

Wheeler turned a cool glance on him.

'Ronnie's,' he said.

Stebbing, on whom the subtlety of the game was lost, opened his mouth to ask another question but Finch silenced him with a warning gesture of one hand.

'Go on,' he told Wheeler.

Their eyes met and Wheeler, with an almost imperceptible flicker of his eyelids, acknowledged that the time for fooling was over.

'Ron Lovell,' he explained sullenly. 'Geoff Lovell's younger brother. Cleared off and left her about fifteen years ago.'

Was that the reason for Wheeler's malice? Finch wondered. Did the man resent, or perhaps disapprove of the Lovell household? It was an interesting line of inquiry that might be worth following up, provided he could talk to Wheeler on his own, without Stebbing's presence.

'Local girl?' he asked. He put the question because it was possible Wheeler had known her before her marriage to Ron Lovell and perhaps resented the fact that, by marrying into a local farming family, Wheeler's employers, she had risen above what the man considered to be her station.

'No,' Wheeler replied. 'From Dorset. Ronnie met her when he was doing his National Service in the fifties. Geoff Lovell got exempted. Old man Lovell was alive then but ailing and Geoff was needed on the farm. But Ron got called up and came back after doing his two years with *her*.'

Finch was doing some rapid mental calculations.

'So they were married how long before he left? A couple of years?'

'Nearer three.'

'And then he left her. Do you know why?'

'No, Lovell took me on after he left; said he needed someone else to help him on the farm. Old Lovell had died by then, so there was only him and Charlie left to run the place. But Ronnie was always a bit wild and seemingly he couldn't settle down to the life after the army.'

'What's she like?' Finch asked.

Wheeler lifted his shoulders indifferently. The game being over, he seemed to have lost interest in the subject.

'Quiet,' he said. 'One of them women who don't say much. Maybe too quiet for Ronnie.'

Turning to Stebbing, he added, 'If that's all, I've got work to get on with.'

Finch nodded, letting Stebbing dismiss him. There would be other opportunities to talk to him later. Meanwhile, Stebbing was saying as Wheeler walked away, 'I don't understand it. Nobody told me. I thought they were married. I could have put my foot right in it when I was talking to Lovell.'

'You saw her when you called?' Finch asked.

'Yes, but not for long. She was in the yard and went into the house almost as soon as I arrived. Fair-haired woman. Thin. Not my type. Looked nervous.'

A brooding look came into his face as he recalled the encounter.

'Do you know, Lovell didn't even ask me inside the house? Kept me out in the yard. I don't call that friendly.'

Lovell's lack of neighbourliness evidently rankled with him still. Finch, his thoughts elsewhere, grunted a reply. An idea was beginning to take shape in his mind but he needed time and a little peace in which to think it out more fully.

'I'd've been willing to help the man out, if he'd've met me half way,' Stebbing continued, still pursuing his own particular obsession. 'Lent him equipment or one of my men for half a day, if he was short-handed. But I'm not putting myself out now.'

It was with relief that Finch saw Boyce approaching and, making this his excuse, he walked away, leaving Stebbing standing alone in the yard.

'Denny's nearly uncovered him,' Boyce announced as Finch came up. 'Are you coming to have a look at him or shall I tell them to hang on?'

'No, I'm coming,' Finch replied abstractedly.

Boyce looked at him inquiringly.

'Found out something at Lovell's farm?' he asked.

'Not from Lovell himself,' Finch replied. 'He claims he noticed nothing unusual.'

394

'Claims?'echoed Boyce. 'You mean he may not be telling the truth?'

'I don't know,' confessed Finch, moving his shoulders uncomfortably. 'Lovell's an odd bloke. According to Stebbing, he's frightened off any visitors to the farm, including the postman, and I certainly wasn't welcomed with open arms. I got the impression, too, that Lovell was deliberately keeping Charlie, that's his subnormal brother, and his wife from meeting me. At least, I thought she was his wife and so evidently did Stebbing. But I've been having a chat with a man called Wheeler who used to work on Lovell's farm and, according to him, there was a third brother, called Ronnie, who was married to Betty and who cleared off and left her about fifteen years ago. So that means she's Lovell's sister-in-law. But why all the secrecy? And why, if Lovell left her all those years before, has she stayed on at the farm? Most women would have gone home to their own family long ago. It can't be easy for her, running a house for her husband's two brothers.'

He paused for a moment, wondering how to put into words the other impressions he had picked up at the farm: Lovell's expression of strain; his anxiety to hustle Charlie out of the way; even the excessive tidiness of the living-room. They were all significant, he felt, of something more than their surface appearance, in much the same way as Wheeler's remarks had hinted at more than the mere meanings of the words.

'Sounds a funny set-up,' Boyce was saying, without a lot of interest, and Finch decided to leave it there.

'There's another thing,' he went on. 'I'm more than ever convinced that whoever buried that body was a local man who knew the field. It can't be seen from the road and, anyway, there's a wood on the way to Lovell's farm that would make a much better place to dump a body, supposing the man who did it was a casual visitor, looking for somewhere to get rid of an unwanted corpse. So, assuming he's a local man, it's more than likely that the dead man was in some way connected to this area, too: somebody known to him; somebody whose body he had to get rid of because it could be recognised as having links with him. And it crossed my mind, after Wheeler had told me about the other brother, that the body we've dug up might be Ronnie Lovell's.'

'What's the theory?' Boyce asked, looking interested. 'He returns after fifteen years? There's a family quarrel? Lovell kills him and . . . ?'

'Buries him on Stebbing's land,' Finch concluded for him. 'That bit doesn't make sense, does it? In fact, Lovell more or less said the same thing himself. Of course, I hadn't heard then from Wheeler about the third brother, Ron. But when I told Geoff Lovell about the dead body being found, he said he wasn't interested as it was none of his business. It was on Stebbing's land, not his; as if that proved something.'

'Well, it could,' Boyce pointed out, not unreasonably. 'It could mean the body had nothing to do with him.'

'I'm not sure,' Finch replied. 'He showed very little reaction; too little, if you get my meaning, as if he was prepared for the news. And yet he's under some enormous strain. I could see it in his face, although, to be fair to him, it could simply be money worries. That farm of his looks on its last legs. But if he *did* kill his brother, and we've got no proof that he did, I know what I'd do in Lovell's place – put him under my own ground, where I'd know he'd not be disturbed.'

Boyce was silent for a few seconds.

'I don't know,' he said, at last. 'It might still hold up as a theory. That field doesn't look as if it's ever been cultivated. It was pure chance that Stebbing got that society in to start digging.'

'According to Stebbing, it's due to go under the plough in the autumn.'

'Lovell may not have known that,'

'True enough,' agreed Finch. 'All the same, it'd be taking a risk. He's got fields of his own. Assuming it is his brother's body, why not bury it where he knew it'd be safe?'

Boyce lifted his broad shoulders in an indifferent gesture. He wasn't much interested in human motivation which, according to his way of thinking, didn't come into the category of factual evidence and was therefore merely speculative.

'People do funny things,' he remarked casually. 'Maybe he just didn't like the idea of it being on his land.'

'Superstition?' Finch asked quickly.

He thought of Lovell's dark, brooding face. He had struck the Inspector as a man of close and secretive temperament, not easily roused but nevertheless possessing deep passions. Supposing Lovell, having killed his brother, felt that to bury him on his own land was to sully it in some way? Perhaps bring bad luck? Or had it been a motive more twisted even than that? It was on Stebbing's land, after all. Supposing Stebbing had aroused in Lovell not just antipathy but such a deep-rooted hatred that Lovell had scored off him by burying the body on his property? But that suggested madness and Finch wasn't sure that Lovell would act in such a crazy way. He was a man under strain, certainly. But was he insane? Finch wasn't sure.

'Do you know what Ronnie Lovell looks like?' Boyce was asking.

Finch roused himself to answer.

'No, but I could ask Wheeler. He evidently knew him and I expect he could give us a description. All he said was Ronnie got called up into the army in the fifties, met a girl from Dorset, married her and left a couple of years later. But we'll have to be damned careful. We've got no proof yet who the dead man is and I don't want to start any rumours going round the village.'

He paused, thinking of the other things Wheeler had said or hinted at; for instance, that Betty Lovell was perhaps too quiet for Ronnie. Had he been suggesting there was another woman?

'Well, whoever he was, there's not much left of him now,' Boyce remarked. 'I doubt if his own mother would recognise him.'

They had skirted the large wheatfield while they had been talking and were approaching the gate that led into the smaller meadow that lay beyond, across which a line of men was moving as they carried out the search. More men were coming and going around the canvas screen that had been erected round the grave. On the opposite side of the field, the tents belonging to the archaeological society had already gone.

Finch, who had begun to climb over the gate, paused on the top of it to glance in the direction of Lovell's farm. From that elevated position, he could see the roofs of the house and its surrounding buildings that seemed, at that distance, to be huddled closer together. No smoke emerged from the chimneys, but he caught a glimpse of sunlight striking off glass on the tiled slope of the back of the farmhouse roof; a skylight, no doubt, to an attic under the steep pitch.

He tried to imagine the life that went on under that roof; Lovell left to run the farm with only a subnormal brother to help him and a woman who had been deserted by her husband years before; a funny set-up, as Boyce had remarked.

Boyce, who had dropped down into the field, asked, 'You stuck up there?'

'No,' Finch replied, climbing down. 'Just thinking.'

'The light'll be going soon, if we don't get a move on,' the sergeant pointed out.

Finch noticed, then, that the sun was setting behind the trees, casting long shadows across the grass.

'I'm coming,' he replied and, joining Boyce, they set off together for the far side of the field where a cluster of men were waiting outside the screen.

Inside, the heat was intense in that enclosed space and the air smelt strongly of hot canvas and crushed grass. Mingled with it was another odour, more subtle and less easy to define; the smell of earth and decay coming up from the oblong hole in the ground, six feet long and four feet deep, by the side of which Pardoe and Denny were kneeling. Finch joined them, squatting down on his haunches to look into the open grave.

5

There was, as Boyce had said, not much left of the man. The skeleton appeared to be intact, and scraps of decayed flesh and tattered, dirt-soiled cloth were clinging to it. Only the boots had survived relatively whole, but even these were falling apart. What remained of the head grinned up at them in the dreadful, fixed and mirthless grimace of death.

But it was the position of the corpse that interested Finch most of all. It was lying on its back, its arms neatly folded across its chest, the hands resting near the shoulders. Someone, it seemed, had taken the trouble to lay the body out before burial. It hadn't been roughly tumbled into its makeshift grave.

'Is this how you found it?' he asked Denny.

'Exactly,' Denny replied. 'Nothing's been shifted, except the soil round him. And I know what you're thinking. The same thought struck me as I uncovered him. Look at this as well.'

He pointed to an object that was caught against the chest. Finch bent down to examine it more closely. It was a large safety-pin, rusted and almost unrecognisable.

'I came across four more of them,' Denny went on. 'They'd dropped to one side, the length of the body, the first being up near the head, the last by the feet. McCullum's taken photographs so you'll be able to see the exact positions for yourself.'

Something else caught Finch's attention as he was bending forward. The body was covered with the rotted remains of fabric, the exact colour of which was indistinguishable from the surrounding earth, although its closely-woven texture and relative thickness were still discernible. It was, he guessed, probably wool; which might suggest the man had been wearing an overcoat. But an overcoat, however long, does not extend as far up as the head or down to the feet, as this clearly did, for pieces of the same fabric were clinging to the skull and some lay close to the boots.

He touched one of the scraps with a finger-tip and then turned to Pardoe.

'A blanket?' he asked. 'It could be. And five safety-pins. Do you know what that suggests to me? A shroud. Whoever buried him, laid him out and then wrapped him up, fastening the covering together with pins to stop it from falling off.'

Pardoe nodded.

'I noticed that myself. The cloth's too far gone for me to say exactly what it was but I agree, it could be a blanket. Forensic will be able to come up with more details on it and, once we've got him out, I'll be able to tell you if there's any more of the same material under him.'

'Anything else about him?' Finch asked.

'Not much at this stage,' admitted Pardoe. 'He's been down there at least a year, possibly two, but that's only a guess. One thing I can tell you though – you won't get any finger-prints off him. He's too far gone for that. And you'll be disappointed if you're counting on identifying him from his dental records.'

He pointed with the stem of his pipe at the head.

'I'd say he'd had most of his teeth removed to have dentures fitted . . .'

'None were found?' Finch asked quickly, turning to Boyce who shook his head.

'Not so far.'

'Height?' Finch went on, turning back to Pardoe.

'I'm not committing myself on that either,' the doctor replied. 'Not until I've got him back in the lab and can re-assemble the bits and pieces more accurately. Even then, I can't guarantee an exact measurement.'

'Hair colour? Age?' Finch suggested hopefully. But Pardoe refused to be drawn.

'I'll need to do some tests on him first. And I can't give you any idea how he died either, so it's no use asking. There's no obvious signs of violence that I can see, such as a fractured skull; and, with so little left of him, it's not going to be easy. If he was shot, we might find the bullet still in the body or at least marks of it on a bone. Stabbing's a bit trickier unless, again, the knife marked a bone. If it was suicide or a natural death, it may be even more difficult to prove. But I'll do the tests and see what they produce.'

'And nothing personal found on him?' Finch asked, turning back to Boyce. 'A signet ring, for instance, or a watch?'

Boyce looked a little uncomfortable.

'There was this,' he replied and, bending down, picked up a small, blackened lump that was lying on one side of the plastic sheeting that had been spread out to receive the excavated soil. Finch took it and, holding it in the palm of his hand, examined it carefully. It was a cross and chain, so corroded together that it formed an almost solid mass of metal.

'Barker found it in one of the spadesful of earth that Moody dug out, so we don't know exactly where it was in relation to the body,' Boyce explained. 'It was covered with dirt and looked like a piece of stone. But it wasn't all that far down. About six to eight inches, Moody reckons, so it may have nothing to do with the dead man.'

Finch rubbed it between his fingers, loosening the soil that clung to it. As far as he could see, the links in the chain were small and fine.

'It looks like something a woman might wear,' he remarked.

'Could be,' Boyce agreed. 'In which case, it might have been dropped accidentally.'

Finch contemplated it thoughtfully. It was a damned nuisance that Moody hadn't noticed it at the time and pinpointed its exact location in relation to the body.

'But what's it doing under the earth?' he asked. 'This field's never been cultivated. If someone had dropped it accidentally, it would still be lying on the top or, at most, trodden down into the grass.'

'Fell down a crack?' suggested Boyce. 'We've had two hot summers now. Last year in particular was very dry. Do you remember the farmers were complaining about lack of rain? If the ground dried out and opened up, it's possible it slipped down a hole and got covered over.'

'I suppose so,' Finch agreed, but without much enthusiasm. 'I'll check with Stebbing to see if he's noticed this field drying hard out at any time and we'll make inquiries locally in case anyone's lost a cross and chain – plated, by the way it's corroded. Solid gold or silver wouldn't have gone like that. In the meantime,' he added, addressing Pardoe, 'we'd better get him out. I'll leave you and Denny to deal with that.'

Pardoe nodded agreement and Finch, beckoning to Boyce to follow him, walked outside the screen where he took deep breaths of fresh air.

'When Pardoe and Denny have moved him,' he said, 'I want you to make a thorough search of the grave itself. Collect up anything that's left and keep your eyes open for a pair of false teeth. They may be essential in proving identity. Otherwise . . .'

He raised his shoulders in a gesture that Boyce had come to recognise as expressing a complex mood, partly exasperation, partly perplexity. The sergeant said nothing but tried to look encouraging.

'There's something odd about this case,' Finch went on, after a few minutes' silence in which he stared down moodily at the grass. 'Apart from the choice of the site itself, which I still think is strange, there's this question of the body being prepared for burial – the arms folded across the chest; the shroud, if that's what it is; even the missing false teeth could be significant . . .'

'Of what?' Boyce asked, looking perplexed himself.

'Of the body being laid out.'

'It could be, I suppose,' Boyce said, sounding unconvinced. 'Or it could be they just dropped out.'

'And then there's the cross and chain,' Finch went on, ignoring him and pursuing his own train of thought. 'I know it may have nothing to do with the dead man but I can't help feeling . . .'

Again he hesitated to put into words the vague impression he had in his mind. It was not so much a definite idea as a series of words that had begun to collect together. Superstition. Sacrement. Concern for the dead. Burial rites.

And for some reason that he could not explain, he kept

coming back to Wheeler's story of Ron Lovell's wife, deserted after a few years of marriage; the farm, isolated from the outside world with the dog on constant guard; the shotgun propped up in a corner of the living-room; and Lovell's dark, brooding, hopeless look as he stood on the threshold of the house.

He saw Boyce looking at him and he made an effort to rouse himself, switching his mind back to the immediate present.

'Proof,' he said briskly. 'We need proof. It's too late to do much today but we'll check on that cross and chain in the village tomorrow. I want a house-to-house done on it, but leave out Wheeler and Lovell. I'll question them myself. At the same time, find out if any strangers have been seen about the village in the past couple of years – a tramp, or someone looking for casual farmwork. Judging by the boots, the man was used to doing outdoor manual work. And ask if anyone's disappeared from the village – left home for any reason. I don't want Ron Lovell's name mentioned at this stage but if anyone brings it up, then get them chatting about him. He's a possible lead but we've got to tread damned carefully over that one. The question of identity, though, is going to be crucial to this case. Until we know who the dead man is, we've got nothing much to go on.'

Behind them, Pardoe and Denny were emerging from the screen, carrying a coffin shell between them.

'It looks as if they've finished,' Finch remarked. 'Take a couple of men with you, Tom, and get the grave searched. I want to have a last look round before we leave.'

Boyce nodded and moved off, collecting up Moody and Kyle as he went, while Finch walked away across the field, following in the wake of the line of uniformed men who had almost reached the far side.

What was he hoping they would find? Nothing of much significance, he imagined; only the assorted rubbish that fields and hedgerows always seem to yield in such astonishing quantities: old shoes, tin cans, bits of paper and plastic; all of which would have to be examined and none of which would be likely to have any bearing on the case.

At the corner he turned, walking round the perimeter of the field, looking for any gap leading to a path or bridleway along which the body might have been carried. But, apart from the gate leading into the wheatfield, there was none. The field was enclosed on two sides by thick, well-maintained hedges. On the third side, along which ran the boundary between Stebbing's land and Lovell's, the hedge looked older and could have been planted, Finch guessed, a long time ago, possibly at the time of the initial enclosure of the land, for it contained some large, well-grown trees. Here and there the bushes were sparse, with gaps between them; but on Stebbing's side there was a wide ditch that looked as if it had been recently re-dug, surmounted by a three-strand barbed wire fence, supported on posts that also looked comparatively new. Finch paused and thoughtfully pulled away a piece of loose bark from one of the posts, revealing the wood beneath that was still clean and unweathered. He could check with Stebbing when the fence had been erected, but Finch reckoned it had been up only a year, if that. So, before the fence had been built, it would have been relatively easy to carry a body to the field, over Lovell's land and through one of the gaps in the hedge, before burying it a few yards inside the boundary on Stebbing's land.

Stebbing's land. Always he came back to this crucial question. Why this particular field? And there appeared to be no rational answer; not yet, anyway.

He turned away, his shoulders humped, and started back across the field. The light was going fast now. The sun had disappeared completely, leaving behind a nimbus of brightness, streaked with rose-coloured clouds. Red sky at night. It was going to be another hot day tomorrow. In the coppice, a colony of rooks was settling down for the night, cawing hoarsely and flopping down with heavy wings into their untidy nests in the topmost branches of the trees. The men who had been searching the field were moving off towards the gate, their task finished. There was a feeling of completion; of the day ending.

Boyce, emerging from the screen, came across the field to meet him.

'Any luck?' Finch asked.

The sergeant shook his head.

'Apart from some more of that fabric, which we've collected up, there's nothing except a hole in the ground.'

404

'Damn!' Finch said softly. Without the man's false teeth, identification was going to be more difficult.

'I've covered it over with a tarpaulin,' Boyce went on. 'Do you want the screen left up?'

'No, it's not necessary. The site's been cleared. We shouldn't need to make another search.'

He turned to Stapleton, who had been in charge of the uniformed men.

'You've finished, too?'

Stapleton nodded.

'Then we'll pack up,' Finch said. 'It'll be dark soon. I'll get a Panda car to patrol the lane but I doubt if anyone from the village will bother to come sightseeing.'

'There's nothing to see, anyway,' Boyce replied gloomily, glancing round at the gathering dusk. He hated the country-side after dark, with its silence and atmosphere of indefinable menace, and was longing to get back to the lights and the cheerful bustle of headquarters.

'You coming back now, sir?'

'Later,' Finch replied.

He had an inexplicable desire to linger, now that the light was going and, as the others tramped away, he remained behind in the field alone, feeling the silence and the dusk settle round him.

The great rounded heads of the trees, massed with leaves, were merging into the sky and the contours of the land were fading, too, although he could still just discern the long mounds of excavated earth left behind by the archaeological society. They reminded him of photographs he had seen of mass war graves, dug to accommodate the countless, anonymous dead. The image stirred his imagination but he could make no connection between it and the oblong pit, the length of a man, that lay at his feet, except for the obvious metaphor of death and burial. But he felt instinctively that there was something more that linked them; something to do with the darkening trees, the falling twilight; the very air that still held the heat of the day and was breathing back a gentle exhalation of warm grass and earth from the ground beneath his feet.

Away to his right, a faint light showed where Lovell's

farmhouse stood among its surrounding trees and he gazed speculatively towards it.

Did another link exist there? He wasn't sure and yet he felt, with a strong sense of intuition, that somehow it all made sense and that the broken pieces could be brought together to form a pattern, if only he could find the beginning of it.

6

It wasn't until late the following afternoon that Boyce returned from the house-to-house inquiries in the village, looking tired and hot. Lowering himself gratefully into a chair, he bent down to loosen the laces in his shoes, commenting, 'Thank God that's over.'

'Any luck?' Finch asked eagerly.

He had remained behind in the office, working on the preliminary reports on the case, leaving Boyce in charge of the men who were carrying out the inquiry.

'Not much,' Boyce replied. 'Nothing on the cross and chain. No one in the village has lost one. I still think it could have been dropped accidentally by someone from outside – picnickers, say.'

'That's not very likely,' Finch objected. 'From what I've seen of people picnicking, they stay fairly near the road, where they've parked the car, or make for an obvious beauty spot. No one's going to hump packets of sandwiches and flasks of tea that far across the fields.'

Boyce lifted his shoulders wearily.

'What's the theory, then? That it's got something to do with the body? But it wasn't found on him. In fact, it wasn't even found near him. My guess is it's a waste of time as far as this case is concerned.'

'You may be right, but it'll have to be followed up, all the same, as soon as forensic have come up with a few more details on it. Then we can start making inquiries at jewellers' . . .'

'You mean, *I'll* make the inquiries,' Boyce corrected him. 'It'll be me who'll be hoofing it round the shops, I know that.

And a fat lot of good it'll do, if you ask me. That cross and chain's cheap, mass-produced stuff. You'll probably find any Woolworth's stock them and sell hundreds of them every year. Still, I suppose it could be evidence.'

He didn't sound very convinced.

'Anybody reported missing from the village?' Finch went on to ask. 'Any husband or son left home?'

'Not much on that either, although at one stage I thought we'd struck lucky – a husband who'd left his wife for somebody else's. It was the right timing, too; about two years ago. But as someone saw them together in the local Odeon the other Saturday night, he's presumably still alive and well and living in sin over at Little Fenny. So that was a washout. No one else has gone missing and there was no report of any strangers seen about the place, except for one old tramp who's well-known in the village; turns up at regular intervals, it seems. But as he's been seen in the past couple of months, it can't be him either.'

'That needn't rule out some outsider turning up,' Finch replied. 'I've been having a look at a large-scale map of the area . . .'

Walking over to the desk, he spread it out again for Boyce's benefit and the sergeant, with a martyred look, heaved himself up from the chair to cross the room and look at it.

'The village is here,' Finch said, pointing with a finger, 'and this is the main road that leads to Harlsdon, the nearest market town. It's also the bus route, so anyone arriving in the village from the Harlsdon direction would come along that road.'

His finger traced along it, turning off to follow the secondary road that led, by a circuitous route, past the fields, the boundaries of which were marked in, and the two farms belonging to Stebbing and Lovell.

'I see what you mean,' said Boyce. 'Anyone coming by bus from Harlsdon and making for Lovell's place would get off before the village and walk down the lane to the farm.'

'Exactly,' Finch replied. 'He needn't show himself in the village at all.'

'Any good checking with the bus conductors on that route?'

'We can try it but I doubt if we'll come up with anything

definite. It's at least two years ago, too long for anyone to remember one individual passenger.'

'This the place where the body was found?' Boyce asked suddenly, noticing a small pencilled cross in one of the fields.

'Yes. I marked it in,' Finch replied. 'And I checked the distances on the scale while I was at it. It's roughly equidistant from both farms; a little over half a mile.'

'Half a mile?' mused Boyce. 'It doesn't sound far but it's still a hell of a long way to carry a body. Whoever did it must have been a pretty powerful man.'

'Yes,' agreed Finch. He thought of Geoff Lovell's broad shoulders and muscular arms. Could he have managed such a burden? There was Charlie, of course, who could have helped him to carry it; but Lovell would have been taking a great risk in involving his brother, knowing his tendency to talk. But perhaps that explained why Lovell had been so anxious to keep Charlie at a distance when the Inspector called at the house, to prevent him from blurting out anything incriminating.

'The name of the field's been marked in,' Boyce was saying, bending low over the desk to read the tiny writing. 'Hollowfield, is it?'

'Yes. I rang up Stebbing to ask him if the field had a name. They often do and it seemed better to have something to refer to in our reports. It's probably called that because the land slopes down there from the meadow higher up.'

'You can see how far it is from the village,' Boyce continued, still studying the map. 'It must be all of four miles. I can't imagine anyone lugging a dead body that far.'

'Which would support the theory that it was carried there from this direction,' Finch added, jabbing a finger at the road with its two farms.

Boyce straightened up.

'That reminds me, Ron Lovell's name was mentioned twice during the door-to-door this afternoon.'

Finch, who had been folding the map, looked up with quick interest.

'Yes?'

'One old girl who Johnson interviewed brought his name up. Hang on a sec, I've got some notes on it.'

Getting out his notebook, he ruffled over the pages, looking for the right place.

'Here we are. It's not much but it might be useful. According to Johnson, when he asked about people missing from the village, she said, "There's only Ron Lovell, and he's been gone a long time. Used to live with his brothers on one of the farms down Hallbrook lane. Married a girl he met when he was in the army and then left her. Leastways, that's what I've heard. But then, he never was much good, not even as a youngster. Roaring round the village on that motorbike of his and spending half his time over at Harlsdon; in the public houses, I shouldn't wonder." After that, she veered off into a moan about young people generally; no respect for their elders; that sort of thing. Johnson heard her out. It lasted a good twenty minutes, he told me,' Boyce added with a grin. 'Any good, is it?'

'It adds a bit more detail,' Finch replied. 'The stuff about him marrying a girl he'd met when he was in the army I'd already got from Wheeler. But the bit about the motorbike and the possible drinking in Harlsdon could be quite useful. It gives us a better picture of him: the local tearaway, by the sound of it. It might also be worth checking on the pubs. Did she come up with a description?'

'No. You said not to ask too many questions about him and I'd warned the men to play it down, so Johnson didn't like to press it too far. The other time his name cropped up was when I was talking to the man who runs the local garage, name of Tidyman. His place also specialises in repairs to farm machinery and it seems Ron Lovell used to work there as a lad out of school hours and at weekends. He was quite good, too, with machinery, according to Tidyman; good enough for Tidyman to offer him a job there after he'd left school, which Ron Lovell wanted to take up. But his father wouldn't let him; insisted he joined his brother working on the farm. Old man Lovell was a bit of a tyrant, as far as I could make out; ruled those boys with a rod of iron. Tidyman went into a lot of detail about old Lovell which probably isn't of much use . . .'

'Let's hear it all the same,' Finch interrupted him. 'It could add to the picture.'

'Well, evidently he was something of a local Scrooge; wouldn't spend a ha'penny if he could get away with a farthing, and thought twice about parting with that – I'm giving you Tidyman's words, by the way – and it's one of the reasons for Geoff Lovell's present difficulties. Old Lovell let the farm go downhill and when Geoff came to take it over, it needed a hell of a lot doing to it and there just wasn't the money to put it right. He worked those sons of his hard, too. Towards the end, he had a bad heart and was supposed to take things easy but he dropped dead in the fields one day, checking up that Geoff was doing his work properly. None of them ever mixed much, except Ronnie, who tried to make a life for himself away from the farm; and, according to Tidyman, there was a bit of feeling in the village against Charlie. Tidyman agreed that he's quite harmless but some of the locals didn't like seeing him about and there was talk that he should have been put away in a home. So the Lovells have never been good mixers, or exactly popular.'

'Did he say anything else about Ronnie Lovell?'

'Not a lot. I got the impression that Tidyman felt sorry for him because he'd never had a proper chance. He did say something about him being a bit wild and wearing his hair in what he called "them sideboards". I've got a note here, by the way, of one comment he made that's worth quoting.'

Referring to his notebook, he read out in a deadpan voice, '"I know he was a bit of a telly boy, but that ain't to say there was no good in him."'

'"Telly boy?"' Finch asked, mystified.

Boyce grinned.

'I think he meant "Teddy boy".'

'It would fit, I suppose,' Finch said, 'assuming he's talking about the time he knew Ron Lovell before he went into the army. It'd be the fifties, the Teddy boy era.'

'That's the nearest he got to a description of him, I'm afraid,' Boyce added, a little apologetically.

'It all helps,' Finch assured him. 'We've got a much clearer picture now of what Ron Lovell was like: a bit wild; a natural mechanic who's forced to work on the family farm; escapes once into the army but comes back; escapes for a second time,

411

leaving behind a young wife. If we carry that a bit further, I think we can make a guess as to where he went. My bet is he made for a town. He sounds the type who'd be drawn by the bright lights of a city and I'll bet, too, that he got himself a job in a factory or garage. It's what he was good at. I know it's not much to go on but it narrows the field a little if we have to go looking for him.'

'Assuming we haven't already found him,' Boyce pointed out, 'four feet down.'

'That's still to be proved,' Finch replied, 'and for that we need a description.'

'Tidyman?' suggested Boyce. 'He obviously knew him quite well.'

'If we have to, but I'd prefer somebody who was in touch with him more recently, since his army days. Wheeler's the obvious choice. He knew the Lovell family well and worked on the farm for a time after Ron left, so he may have picked up a few interesting bits and pieces of information.'

He glanced at his watch.

'It's gone six o'clock so he should have knocked off work for the day. I want to see him at home, not at the farm. He's more likely to talk freely without Stebbing hanging about, sticking his oar in.'

'You know his address?' Boyce asked.

'Yes. I looked it up on the electoral register at the library and checked it on the map. If I see him this evening, we should have some details to compare with what Pardoe can tell us about the body.'

At the door he added, 'Get today's house-to-house down in a report, will you, Tom? We'll need it for the file.'

He left, ignoring Boyce's gusty sigh that followed him out into the corridor.

Wheeler's cottage was one of a brick-built pair, with a heavy, slated roof and narrow, sash windows, standing on the main road into the village, not far from the turning that led to the farms. There was a depressed, mean look about them, oddly out of keeping with the rural setting, as if they had been transported bodily there from the Victorian terrace of some inner city suburb.

Finch pushed open Wheeler's gate and, disregarding the front door with its forbidding, dark green paint and heavy, iron knocker, tramped round to the back of the house where a long kitchen garden, given over mainly to the growing of potatoes, stretched down to a ramshackle chicken house and wired-in run at the bottom.

The back door was set open with a half-brick and, as he knocked, Finch saw beyond into a dimly-lit and not very clean kitchen, with a deep, old-fashioned sink and wooden draining-board, and a table covered with worn American cloth that was stacked with dirty dishes.

Wheeler came out of an adjoining room in answer to his knock, chewing, his braces hanging loose, his shirt unbuttoned, showing a thin chest, knobbed with small bones and surprisingly white below his sun-burnt face and neck.

'Oh, it's you again,' he said in greeting. There was a small, self-satisfied grin on his face as if he had been expecting the visit.

'Just a few more inquiries, Mr Wheeler,' Finch replied in his official voice, wondering how he was going to introduce the subject of Ron Lovell into the conversation without it appearing to be the main reason for his call.

Wheeler jerked his head, inviting Finch to enter, and the Inspector followed him into a further room where Wheeler had evidently been eating his evening meal, for the round table in the centre was roughly set with a cloth laid across part of it on which were standing a plate of cold meat, a jar of pickles and an opened packet of sliced bread.

'Cup of tea?' Wheeler suggested and when Finch accepted, he went back into the kitchen to get another cup. While he was gone, Finch took the opportunity to look about.

It was a small room, crowded with heavy, dark, ugly furniture of the period that belonged, Finch guessed, to Wheeler's parents; an impression borne out by the framed photographs that stood on the sideboard: one of a wedding group in which the bride wore a huge hat that looked like a platter full of flowers and veiling; the other a stiff, studio portrait of a young man in

413

the army uniform of the First World War, standing to attention in front of a painted backdrop of rocks and a waterfall.

The thick, cotton lace curtains muffling the window, the array of vases and ornaments on every available horizontal surface, the patterned wallpaper of large leaves and flowers that age and dirt had darkened to an all-over sepia tone, gave the room an oppressive, claustrophobic atmosphere.

There was no sign that a younger woman had influenced it and, as Wheeler's occupation of it seemed to be of the makeshift quality of a solitary male making temporary camp, apparent in the hurried preparations of the meal and the clothes scattered about the room, Finch guessed his situation: that of a middle-aged bachelor who had gone on living in his parents' home after their death.

Wheeler came in, carrying a cup and saucer, still wet from being quickly washed under the tap, and poured Finch a cup of tea. It came out the same colour as the teapot, a thick, dark brown, that tasted strongly of tannin. Finch kept the grimace off his face as he drank it down, although it left a wry taste in his mouth.

'Well?' Wheeler asked abruptly. He had seated himself at the table, opposite Finch, and had started to eat again, cramming the food into his mouth.

Finch began with his official questions. Had Wheeler noticed any strangers about? Had there been any tools missing from the farm? To both, Wheeler answered 'no'.

There was a forced, unnatural quality about the opening of the interview as if both men knew that this was a mere preliminary formality that was to lead up to something much more crucial. Above his energetically chewing mouth, Wheeler's eyes were watchful and, Finch thought, amused.

Damn the man, he thought. He knows perfectly well why I'm here. There seemed to be no solution to it except to plunge in.

'We've been making inquiries in the village,' Finch began, 'about any local men who have left home for any reason, and Ron Lovell's name was mentioned.'

He paused, inviting Wheeler to speak, but he merely nodded and shovelled more meat into his mouth.

'It places me in rather a difficult position,' Finch confessed, with pretended naïvety. 'In any inquiry like this, we're obliged to follow up every possible lead, however unlikely. So I've come to you, Mr Wheeler. You knew Ron Lovell and I'm sure I could rely on your discretion not to gossip if I asked you a few questions about him.'

Wheeler watched him speculatively for a few seconds. He wasn't entirely taken in by the flattery and he realised Finch was setting up his own rules for the interview. In return for the Inspector's confidence, Wheeler would be expected to answer the questions in a straightforward and factual manner and not to talk about it afterwards.

'All right,' he conceded reluctantly at last, pushing his empty plate away. 'What do you want to know?'

'When Geoff Lovell took you on at the farm, did he give any reason why his brother had left home?'

'No. He just said, "Ronnie's gone so I'm left short-handed."'

'No mention of a quarrel?'

'Not that I heard of.'

'Did Charlie ever say anything about it?'

'Charlie!' Wheeler looked scornful. 'You've seen him, have you? Well then, you know what he's like. Given half a chance, he'd talk your ear off. Most of it's rubbish anyhow. I didn't bother listening to him.'

It was clear that Wheeler regarded Charlie and what he had to say as beneath contempt. But Finch wasn't entirely convinced. Even if Wheeler hadn't paid much attention to Charlie, he must have picked up some of his remarks. After all, Wheeler wouldn't have been human if he hadn't been interested in his employer's private life and Finch guessed that, although Wheeler might consider himself above passing on gossip, he had a malicious enough interest in other people's business to listen to it.

'How did Mrs Lovell seem to be taking it?' Finch asked, deciding to drop the subject of Charlie for the time being and circle back to it again later when Wheeler was less on his guard.

The spiteful glitter that Finch had seen before in Wheeler's eyes returned.

'Her? She didn't say much, but then she never does. She

kept to the house a lot of the time so I didn't see her all that often.'

'Shy?' suggested Finch. He had finished the bitter tea and sat back relaxed in his chair.

'Shy?' Wheeler repeated, tasting the flavour of the word with a small, ruminative movement of his mouth.

'Maybe,' he admitted, without much conviction.

'Stuck up?' Finch offered as an alternative. Wheeler tasted that, too, and seemed to find it more to his liking.

'Didn't mix and didn't want to mix,' he said with more warmth and then added, without any prompting, 'she were a bloody good cook, though. I'll give her that.'

It was said with an odd mixture of genuine admiration and personal animosity that revealed more than Wheeler intended and Finch thought he could guess what it was. Had Wheeler, a bachelor living alone, taken a fancy to Betty Lovell? It was worth testing out.

'She's never thought of remarrying?' he asked casually.

Wheeler's face closed over.

'Not that I know of,' he said shortly. 'She's still there, ain't she?'

'Funny she didn't go back to her own family after the marriage broke up,' Finch continued in a gossipy voice.

'Maybe she didn't want to. Maybe she reckoned she was better off as she was,' Wheeler replied. The half grin was back and with it the jeering undertone of innuendo.

Finch looked interested. The interview had reverted to Wheeler's rules, but the Inspector was prepared to tolerate this provided he learned something useful as a consequence. His difficulty was in finding the right question to ask that would provoke the response he was looking for. He decided to open tentatively.

'Can't be easy for her, though,' he suggested.

'Easier, maybe, than it was,' Wheeler replied.

Without Ronnie? Finch thought. Is that what he's driving at? Or does he mean something more than that?

'Happier on her own?' he hinted.

A complex expression passed over Wheeler's face, secretive and yet knowing. It was accompanied by one of his small, derisive smiles that had a twist of bitterness in it this time.

'You'd need to ask *her* that, wouldn't you?' was his reply.

It was an evasive answer, committing Wheeler to no opinion of his own and yet the wry emphasis he put on the word 'her' convinced the Inspector that Wheeler meant something by it.

'Perhaps I'll do just that,' he countered, hoping by this bolder, frontal attack to draw Wheeler out into the open.

His remark had some effect. Wheeler looked triumphant.

'Take my word, you'll get nothing out of her,' he told Finch. 'Nor out of him neither.'

The last comment was made after a pause so tiny that if Finch hadn't been straining to pick up every nuance of Wheeler's conversation he might have missed it altogether or passed it over as being of no significance.

You'll get nothing out of her – nor out of him neither.

And then suddenly Finch understood, although he kept his expression bland.

'You're probably right,' he agreed equably. 'I'd be wasting my time. Now, Mr Wheeler,' he went on, more briskly, 'there's a couple more questions I'd like to ask you, just for the record. You've no idea where Ron Lovell went to after he left the farm?'

'No,' Wheeler said sulkily. He knew that the game had passed out of his hands and he was aware, also, that he might have said too much. The Inspector's face gave nothing away but, all the same, the man was no fool.

'Or if he's been in touch with his wife or his brother since he left? Written to them for example?'

'Not that I know of.'

'Or visited them?' Finch asked cheerfully, dropping in the suggestion as a perfectly natural thing Ron Lovell might do.

Wheeler shook his head.

'I shouldn't think so.'

'But you have no proof?'

Wheeler took it as a rebuke.

'No, I ain't got no proof. But it ain't likely, though, is it?' he replied, looking angry.

Finch ignored his anger, although he understood the cause

417

of it. Wheeler had lost out, not only in the question and answer game but also in the situation at the farm which he had hoped to exploit. The roots of his malice and bitterness went a long way back, he decided.

'I'd like a description of Ron Lovell,' he went on.

'Just for the record?' Wheeler asked, with a flash of his former sarcasm.

'Exactly,' Finch replied, ignoring that too.

'It's been a long time since I saw him,' Wheeler said reluctantly. It was clear that, as a last throw, he was going to try blocking any of the official questions. However, Finch had no intention of letting him do so.

'Height and build don't alter all that much,' he replied promptly.

'I ain't much good at judging height.'

Finch countered that one.

'Well, was he taller or shorter than his brother Geoff? Or about the same height?'

'A bit taller,' Wheeler admitted.

'The same build?'

'No. Ron was thinner. Not so broad in the shoulders.'

Finch gave him an encouraging smile that Wheeler resented. He was sitting hunched up at the table, among the debris of his supper, in an attitude of angry defeat.

'Hair colouring?'

'Not so dark.'

'Brown rather than black hair?' Finch suggested.

'Maybe. Yes, all right, it was. Dark brown.'

'Eyes?'

But Wheeler had been driven too far.

'I never looked,' he said, jeering. 'And if that's all you want . . .'

'One more question,' Finch said. 'When you were working on the farm, did Geoff Lovell keep a dog?'

'Yes. A collie.'

'Was it allowed to run loose?'

'No. It were kept chained up except at night.'

'So he's got the labrador since you left?'

'Yes.'

'Any idea when?'

'No, I ain't.'

'That's all,' said Finch jauntily, rising from the table. 'Thank-you, Mr Wheeler, for being so patient.'

Wheeler looked up at him, his narrow face tight with dislike and resentment.

'You can see yourself out,' he said.

It wasn't so much a question as a statement.

Finch saw himself out, allowing his face to relax into a smile only when he reached the safety of the back door.

He was in the same jaunty mood when he got back to the office, where Boyce was still at work, laboriously typing out, letter by letter, the report on the house-to-house inquiry.

'You look pleased with yourself,' he commented, as Finch entered. 'Did Wheeler tell you anything useful?'

'Not *tell*,' Finch replied. 'Wheeler doesn't work that way. He throws out a few hints and leaves you to draw your own conclusions, if you can. I did manage, though, to squeeze something more direct out of him – a description of Ron Lovell. Not a very detailed one but it'll do to be getting on with. But Wheeler did come up with something interesting which, if I interpret it right, could suggest a possible motive, assuming it's Ron Lovell's body we've found. He hinted that Geoff Lovell and Ron's wife, Betty, might be lovers. It could be pure spite, of course. He's obviously got it in for the Lovells and I think I know why. He fancied Betty Lovell himself, at least, he fancied her cooking and my guess is she showed him he wasn't welcome. It could have been the reason why Geoff Lovell dismissed him; he was making a nuisance of himself hanging round Betty. But supposing there is something in what he hinted? After all, it isn't all that far-fetched. They're still comparatively young. Betty's alone and available now that her husband's cleared off and I can't imagine Geoff Lovell finding it easy to get a woman. He's too . . .'

He paused, searching for a word that would convey to Boyce the air of brooding unhappiness that Lovell conveyed. Not finding one, he left the sentence unfinished and went on.

'The farm's isolated. Even if they welcomed visitors, which they don't, they can't meet many people, so they'd be thrown together. It'd follow naturally that they'd develop some kind of close relationship. It could be another reason why Geoff Lovell got rid of Wheeler; he was afraid he'd notice that he and Betty were a bit more to each other than brother and sister-in-law. And it could be the reason, too, why they've cut themselves off from the outside world, with that dog virtually on guard. According to Wheeler, when he worked on the farm, Lovell had a collie but it was kept tied up during the day. He's acquired the labrador since. Now Stebbing mentioned that, when he called at the farm soon after he arrived in the district three years ago, the dog was loose then. So Lovell was actively discouraging visitors at least a year before Ron Lovell could have come back.'

'In case they'd see something they shouldn't?' Boyce suggested.

'Yes, and in case Charlie talked. Wheeler spoke of him wanting to chat and I noticed, when I called there, that Charlie seemed eager to start up a conversation with me, only before he could say much, Lovell hustled him out into the kitchen.'

'So the theory now is,' said Boyce, 'that Ron Lovell comes back, finds his wife and his brother are sharing a bed, there's a quarrel over it and . . .'

'Ron Lovell gets killed,' Finch put in. 'Not necessarily murdered. It could have been an accident. Supposing Geoff Lovell hit him and he fell and broke his neck? But, whatever way it happened, he's left with the dead body of his brother on his hands. He can't admit to it. There'd be an inquiry and awkward questions would be asked, such as, "What was the quarrel about?". So he says nothing, largely to protect Betty Lovell.'

'But it's not a crime, sleeping with your sister-in-law, is it?' Boyce objected.

'It's not incest, if that's what you mean,' Finch agreed. 'But I can understand someone like Lovell not wanting it known. Country morals are still quite a bit different to a city's. If the truth came out, you can imagine the gossip. Besides, he must have felt an enormous amount of guilt about it. So must she.'

'Come to that, if we go along with your theory, why couldn't Betty Lovell have shoved him down the stairs?' Boyce asked. 'She'd have as much motive as Geoff for seeing he kept his mouth shut.'

Finch was silent. The idea hadn't occurred to him.

'It's possible, I suppose,' he agreed at last, with a reluctance he couldn't have explained.

'You didn't meet her when you went to the farm?'

'No. She was in the kitchen; keeping out of the way, I suspect. But Wheeler hinted that her marriage to Ron might have been a failure and she was happier without him.'

'That would give her an even stronger motive,' Boyce pointed out. 'She's glad to see the back of him and then he turns up again, upsetting the apple-cart.'

'It's all theory,' Finch put in. 'We mustn't forget that. What we've got against the Lovells is pretty thin so far. A body's discovered near his land; not on it; we mustn't lose sight of that. Lovell is seen watching the archaeological society digging in the same field. His brother left home fifteen years ago and hasn't been seen since, as far as we know. It's nothing more than straws in the wind.'

'But at least they show which way the wind's blowing,' Boyce said. 'What'll you do now? Go back to see Lovell again?'

'Sometime,' Fiinch agreed. 'But not yet. I'm inclined to leave him alone for the time being. Let him stew for a bit. Besides, I haven't really got a good enough reason for going back to call on him. I'll wait until Pardoe comes up with something more positive on the corpse and see how far it tallies with Wheeler's description of Ron Lovell. If it fits, I'll have a little more to go on. And I'll make damn sure I see Betty Lovell the next time I call there. Meanwhile, we'd better get stuck into the routine stuff; check through the missing persons' files for a start and draw up a list of possible names. Get our liaison officer at the Yard to go through those outside the area. We can tackle the more local ones here.'

'Oh, God!' Boyce said mournfully. 'There'll be ruddy hundreds of them.'

'Not that many,' Finch told him. 'We'll begin with those reported missing two years ago and work forward from there. We know from the boots that it's not likely he was a professional man; an accountant, for example. Nor a teenager run away from home. He'd lost most of his teeth, so he must have been an older man. That'll shorten the list a bit. I'll chase up Pardoe, too. He may be able to give us something of a description of the body which will help.'

'It's still going to mean hours of bloomin' work,' Boyce said, only partly mollified.

'It'll keep you busy,' Finch replied cheerfully. 'And at least you'll be sitting down.'

7

But it was two days later before Pardoe was able to supply the evidence that Finch was waiting for. He was in the office, going over the reports of the case with Boyce, when the door opened and the brisk, upright figure of the police surgeon entered. The Inspector broke off what he was saying and looked up eagerly.

'You've got something?' he asked.

'Not a lot,' Pardoe admitted. 'You'll have to wait until the experts at the Yard come up with the more detailed stuff, such as the clothing. It's too far gone for me to be able to tell you much about it except this: the boots he was wearing were a size eight. And we were right about the body being wrapped up. There was quite a lot more of the same material under the corpse, including the head. It looks like a woollen blanket but, again, I'm not committing myself on that either.'

'A shroud,' Finch remarked, half to himself.

Pardoe looked at him quizzically under bushy eyebrows in a manner that put the Inspector in mind of a fox-terrier; alert, intelligent, but with a sharp edge to him that he didn't bother to conceal.

'What conclusion you draw from it is your business,' he replied. 'All I can do is give you the facts as I find them. The cross and chain I can't be much help on either. It's silver-plated and there's some kind of pattern etched into the crucifix, but I can't raise it in detail. The Yard may have better luck. As to the body itself, he seems to be a man between forty and fifty. I can't get nearer than that. Medium build. Height about five feet ten inches. Dark brown hair, going thin on

423

top. There were a few grey hairs mixed in with it but not a lot.'

Finch looked quickly at Boyce, who nodded in agreement at his unspoken question. The details that Pardoe had described agreed broadly with the description that Wheeler had given of Ronnie Lovell. But only in very general terms and, although it was sufficient to keep Ron Lovell in the running as a possible victim, it wasn't enough to prove positive identity.

'Any distinguishing features that might help us prove who he was?' he asked hopefully. Pardoe shook his head.

'Fingerprints are out. I did warn you of that. So is the possibility of finding any scar tissue that could be checked on. He's been under the ground too long for that. You've not found his dentures?'

'No,' Finch replied.

'Well, without them, you're not going to get much joy out of dental records,' Pardoe said brusquely. 'As I pointed out to you when the body was first uncovered, he'd had most of his teeth removed. There were a few back ones left but they're in such poor condition, I doubt if he ever made regular visits to a dentist. If you want some idea of what he looked like, the best I can do is take measurements of the skull and get a police artist to draw up a sketch from them, but all you'll get is an outline of the general structure of the face. It can't provide details such as the exact shape of the nose or mouth.'

He paused and looked questioningly at Finch.

'There is another way, assuming you've got a candidate for the dead man. Have you?'

'Perhaps,' Finch replied guardedly.

'Could you get a photograph of him?'

'I might. But that's not going to be much help, is it, if he's that far gone?'

'Not for normal identification, I agree. But there's another method. Ever heard of the Ruxton case?'

'Wasn't that the doctor who was hanged in the thirties for the double murder of his wife and her maid?'

'That's right. I've taken a special interest in it because of the medical evidence brought forward at the trial. If you remember, the dismembered bodies of two women were found in a ravine in Scotland and the prosecution had to prove that the bits and pieces belonged to Mrs Ruxton and her maid, Mary Rogerson, who were missing from their home in Lancaster. It wasn't easy because whoever killed them had done a pretty thorough job of getting rid of any physical characteristics that could have proved identity: fingertips; facial features; even down to a piece of skin that might have shown a birthmark on Mary Rogerson's right arm. But when the case came to trial, the prosecution were able to prove who the bodies were with some very clever forensic evidence; the final, crowning proof being a positive identification they made between one of the skulls and that of the doctor's missing wife. They got hold of a photograph of Mrs Ruxton in which she was wearing some kind of tiara, measured the actual piece of jewellery which they found, blew up the photograph until the measurements were exactly the same and then compared the facial details in the photograph, which was now life-size, with the head of the dead woman. That way they were able to prove by the jaw-line, the position of the nasal root and so on that it was Mrs Ruxton's skull. Fascinating case!'

His eyes were bright with the same kind of lively interest that Finch had seen in Rose's face when he talked about the Saxon site he was excavating.

'But I needn't go on about it,' Pardoe added. 'The point I'm making is this: if you could get a photograph of your candidate for the dead body and have it blown up to life-size, I could do a similar comparison between the two heads and tell you straight away whether you'd got the right man. It'd have to be exactly life-size, of course. McCullum will be able to advise you on that. He's the photographic expert. Well, I'll leave you with it.'

After he had gone, Finch turned to Boyce.

'What do you think?' he asked.

Boyce looked doubtful.

'It's a hell of a long shot but I suppose it's worth a try. Where are you going to get hold of a photograph of Ronnie Lovell?'

'Betty Lovell?' Finch suggested. 'She's almost certain to have a picture of him somewhere about the house. Failing that, there's Army records, or someone he knew after he left the farm, if we can find out where he went. He must have been living and working somewhere. Any luck with the missing persons' lists?'

'Not yet,' Boyce replied. 'I'm still working through the Home Counties ones with Kyle. The Yard haven't come up with anything either. Something may come of it, I suppose, providing he was reported missing. You'll be going back to see Lovell?'

'Yes, this afternoon probably, after I've had a word with McCullum about this photographic evidence. But what Pardoe was able to give me on the dead man is close enough to Wheeler's description of Ronnie Lovell for me to ask a few more questions. Besides, I've been looking for an excuse to meet Betty Lovell. If we're right in thinking Ron came home and that's his body we've found, she could be a possible witness.'

'What about the other brother – Charlie, isn't it? He might know something, too, and from what you've told me about him, he seems more likely to talk.'

'Too likely,' Finch replied. 'I don't want to make use of him unless I have to. He's got the mind of a child. You can imagine what a defence counsel would make of his testimony if we based a case on his evidence alone. It'd be thrown out of court. No, we've got to find something more reliable than that. And the first step is to prove that it *is* Ronnie Lovell we've dug up. Until we've done that, we're running about in circles. Pardoe's suggestion about the photograph is one way we may be able to do it. I think I'll go and have a chat with McCullum about it now.'

He found McCullum downstairs in the dark-room, developing the last of the photographs that he had taken at the site of the grave.

'Aye, it could be done,' he agreed, after Finch had explained Pardoe's theory to him. 'But I'd need one of two things in any photograph you came up with; either some detail in the clothing that could be measured, similar to the piece of jewellery in the case you were talking about. With a man, it's not going to be so easy. They don't dress themselves up with gewgaws as a woman does, but something like a tie-pin or a

426

watch might do. Or, failing that, I'd need a specific detail in the background that I could re-photograph and measure.'

'What sort of thing?' Finch asked.

'Almost anything could do. I'll give you an example. Supposing it was a snapshot taken of the person standing against a gate. If you could identify the gate, then it could be measured, photographed and I could use it as a scale to make a life-size enlargement from the original snapshot.'

'I see,' said Finch thoughtfully and, thanking McCullum, he went back to the office where he sent for Boyce.

'McCullum sounded hopeful,' he announced, 'so I'll be off to Lovell's farm later this afternoon to see if I can lay my hands on a photograph of Ronnie Lovell. By the way, I'd like to meet you afterwards at Stebbing's place; say about six o'clock. we ought to get that grave filled in and there's one more measurement I want to take; the distance from the grave to the main excavation site where Rose said he found the post-holes. Somebody forgot to take it and I'll need it for the large-scale plan of the field. I meant to mention it to you earlier when we were going over the reports but Pardoe came in and it slipped my mind. So bring spades and the tapes with you and a couple of men, then we can get the job finished today and Rose and his merry band of diggers can move back into the field as soon as they like.'

'Right you are,' Boyce replied. 'I'll round up Kyle and one or two others.'

He left the office and Finch settled down at his desk to complete the reports on the case.

Later he set off for Lovell's farm, parking the car near the opening. As he approached the gate, the dog came racing up as it had done on the first occasion and stood menacing him through the bars. But this time he didn't have to wait so long before it was called off. A woman appeared in the doorway of the house almost at once, looked briefly in his direction and then hurried out of sight round the corner of the barn. Shortly afterwards she returned, accompanied by Charlie, and stood watching from the doorstep as her brother-in-law hastened up the drive with an ungainly stride.

427

So Lovell must be out, Finch thought.

He had the feeling, too, that both of them were carrying out instructions, for the woman remained standing at the door, as if on guard, while Charlie slipped a leather strap that he had ready in his pocket through the dog's collar and dragged it off, without speaking to Finch or waiting for him to climb over the gate.

By the time he had done so, they were ready waiting for him in the yard below, Charlie by the dog that he had now chained to the barn wall and the woman on the doorstep.

Finch, who had come to a halt a little way off, stood looking at the pair of them with an amused interest that he didn't allow to appear on his face. Charlie was obviously ill-at-ease and Finch got the impression that he wasn't supposed to remain there, for he avoided their eyes and looked down at his boots that he was scuffling about in the dust.

'Charlie!' the woman called and he looked at her under his eyebrows and then walked away with a sulky air.

He wants to stay and see what happens, Finch thought, but he's under orders not to. What's he been told to do? Fetch Lovell as soon as I appear? It seemed a possibility.

It struck him then that Charlie might be suffering more than the other two from the self-imposed isolation. He seemed childishly eager to welcome anyone who called and perhaps he did not understand or share the sense of guilt or shame that kept Geoff and Betty Lovell apart from their neighbours.

Finch watched his retreating figure thoughtfully and then turned to Betty Lovell.

She was a slightly-built woman in her thirties, who probably had been pretty when young but whose fragile looks had been worn away by years of anxiety and work. Her hair, once fair, now faded to an indeterminate light brown still streaked with blonde, was tied back at the nape of her neck, although shorter pieces had escaped and clung round her forehead, softening the shape of her face. It was a drawn, harassed face, wide in the forehead, narrow at the chin, that still possessed a little of the childlike, elfin charm that in her teens would have been her best feature.

Had that been what had attracted Ron Lovell to her? Finch

wondered as he walked towards her, smiling and holding out
his hand.

He felt as if he were approaching a nervous animal that had
to be soothed and quieted. Absurdly, he wanted to stroke her
hair and thin hands. Her face was laid so dreadfully bare, with
all the years of worry and exhaustion stamped too vividly in
its drawn lines and hollows. He felt an immediate compassion
and tenderness, not just for her, but for someone she put him
in mind of but couldn't at that moment recall.

'Mrs Lovell?' he asked pleasantly.

She backed towards the door, putting her hands against its
surface as if for reassurance.

'You wanted to see Geoff?' she asked in a breathless voice.
'He's up the fields. Charlie's gone for him.'

'I see,' said Finch. 'You don't mind if I wait for him?'

'No,' she replied. 'But I've got work to do inside.'

'I'll come in, too, if it doesn't bother you,' Finch said
quickly, seizing the opportunity. 'It's hot standing out here
in the yard.'

She hesitated, but hadn't the courage to refuse him, and
he followed her through the cool, dark living-room into the
kitchen beyond, of which he had only caught a glimpse on
his previous visit.

It was better lit than the living-room for, being at the end
of the house, it had two windows, one overlooking the yard,
the other in the end wall opening out at the side of the
building.

Like the living-room, it was spotlessly clean; simply equipped
with a deep, white-glazed sink, a few cupboards and shelves,
and a two-burner oil stove that suggested that, although the
house had electric light, it wasn't wired up for power. A large
deal table occupied the centre of the room, on which lay some
shirts that she had evidently been mending, for a raffia sewing
basket stood beside them and one of the shirts was spread out
with a needle threaded through the collar, close to a frayed
patch that she had been darning with tiny, neat stitches in
white cotton.

She drew a chair out at the table and sat down but made no
attempt to pick up the sewing and Finch had the impression

429

that she was waiting anxiously for something, possibly for Lovell's arrival.

He stood watching her, for one of the rare occasions in his life uncertain how to proceed.

It would be so easy to question her before Lovell arrived. Too easy. Perhaps that was why he shied away from it. Her vulnerability gave her a powerful shield. Besides, he had remembered who her face reminded him of. Years before he had tried to dissuade a man from jumping from the fifth floor of a building. He, too, had worn the same exposed expression, as if all the nerve ends were too close to the surface of the skin, and his upper lip had lifted in the same ghastly parody of a smile, a rictus of pure fear.

Perhaps, she, too, was close to that extremity and he did not want to be the one who drove her beyond the edge.

Drawing out a chair next to her and sitting down, he began talking in an easy, chatty way, trying to get her to relax.

'How very quiet it is here, Mrs Lovell. No noise. No traffic. It must be nice and peaceful.'

She didn't reply but he went on nonetheless.

'Not many neighbours, have you? I suppose Stebbing's is the nearest farm?'

He forced her to answer this time, by cocking his head on one side and looking at her with a bright, interested expression.

'Yes,' was all she said, but it was a beginning.

'Seemed a friendly sort of man when I met him,' Finch continued. 'A good sort to have as a neighbour, I should imagine.'

'We don't . . .' she began and then broke off. Geoff Lovell could be seen coming across the yard, almost at a run, struggling to put his shirt on as he came, with Charlie, looking breathless and excited, stumbling after him.

There was a brief altercation between them, visible through the window. Charlie seemed to be protesting. Finch could see his long arms swinging, his slack mouth opening and closing. Then Lovell took him by the shoulders and, turning him about, pushed him towards the outbuildings.

'I told you, get them pigs seen to!' he shouted after him.

Then he came striding towards the house. They heard the front door slam shut and a few seconds later he burst into the kitchen.

Finch got to his feet and said equably, 'Good afternoon, Mr Lovell. I'm sorry to come bothering you again.'

The man was clearly in a temper, but whether with Charlie or on account of his own visit, Finch could not tell. His face was flushed and he was breathing heavily, the thick barrel of his chest rising and falling deeply under his unbuttoned shirt. But he had powerful self-control. Tucking his shirt into the top of his trousers, he said with a gruff attempt at politeness, 'I'm sorry if I've kept you waiting. I was up the top field.'

'No matter,' Finch replied. 'There's no hurry. I was chatting to Mrs Lovell.'

He watched for Lovell's reaction. It came in the swift glance he gave her, that she answered with a small, deprecatory movement of one hand. They knew each other well enough for words not to matter, which was only to be expected. They had shared the same house, the same closed-in life, possibly the same bed for long enough for them to know each other as well as any married couple. But, at the same time, he was aware of a tension between them, although Lovell seemed more relaxed after their wordless exchange. Betty hadn't said much and this pleased him. He was prepared to be more open and friendly himself in consequence.

'Fancy a cup of tea?' he asked Finch. 'I know I could do with one. Put the kettle on, Betty. You can take a cup across to Charlie. He's seeing to the pigs.'

Finch looked at Lovell with renewed respect. The ploy was not lost on the Inspector. The suggestion of tea was a device to get Betty out of the house and to keep Charlie away from it as well. The man, for all his apparent heaviness, had got that move worked out neatly enough.

Finch sat back, prepared to watch and wait. An opportunity would come. If need be, he could make one himself. But, for the time being, he was content just to sit there, absorbing the atmosphere of the place and feeling his way into the relationship between the two of them.

431

Betty Lovell moved quietly about the kitchen, filling the kettle, removing the mending from the table and setting out cups and saucers in its place. There was something self-effacing about her, as if she were perfectly happy to remain in the background. Lovell rolled himself a cigarette while Finch made a few remarks about the weather and the state of the harvest.

The tea was made and poured and Betty Lovell carried one of the cups out of the kitchen. Lovell waited until he saw her crossing the yard before he spoke.

'You've come about that man they found on Stebbing's land?'

It seemed a curious way of framing the question, as if Lovell were reminding the Inspector that the body had nothing to do with him, although Finch was prepared to admit he might be reading more significance into it than was justified.

'Found out who he is yet?'

Finch shook his head.

'The man's been dead for over a year. It's not going to be easy but we're making inquiries.'

'In the village?' Lovell asked, his eyes very bright. 'They'll tell you anything there.'

'They told me no one has been reported missing recently,' Finch replied. 'No one who's left home, at least not for a long time.'

Lovell was silent and Finch let the silence continue for a few moments before he added quietly, 'Someone did mention your brother Ronnie.'

There was no outburst of anger or bitterness as he had expected. Instead, Lovell went on stirring his tea before he finally looked up, a strange, crooked, half-smile on his face, and said, 'So they're still on about that, are they, after all these years?'

'You must understand my position, Mr Lovell,' Finch replied, in his negative, official voice. 'I have to follow up every possible line of inquiry.'

'Even one that's fifteen years out of date?' Lovell interrupted him to ask. 'What's on your mind? That Ron turned up here after all these years? That I killed him, I suppose, and buried him on Stebbing's land? I ask you, does it make sense?'

432

It was so near to the theory that Finch had indeed worked out, including the main objection to it, that he was nonplussed for a moment by Lovell's directness. There was, too, a new boldness about the man that he hadn't seen before. The sullen air was gone. He was almost triumphant.

'I have to follow it up, even though it may seem unlikely,' Finch replied, a little on the defensive. 'I'd prefer to question you, rather than your sister-in-law. However . . .'

He left the threat unspoken. Lovell looked at him, weighing him up. The heavy look had returned to his face and Finch realised he was close to losing his temper. Then he lifted his shoulders in a gesture that expressed contempt.

'You enjoy stirring things up, don't you?' he asked.

'I'm trying to avoid it,' Finch replied stiffly.

'All right.' Lovell had come to a decision. 'Ask what questions you want.'

'I'd like a description of your brother. Better still a photograph.'

'I can tell you what he looks like. We haven't kept any photos.'

It came a little too pat.

'None?' Finch asked.

'None. When he cleared off, I told Betty to burn everything, his letters, the photos, the lot.'

'Why?'

'Why d'you think?' Lovell countered with a sneer. 'He was no good. She was better off forgetting all about him.'

'Why did he leave?'

'I told you. He was no good. Never had been. The army made him worse. He'd never liked farmwork much anyway and he couldn't settle. He wanted to move on, so he left.'

'And that was the only reason?'

'It's the one he gave me himself.'

Finch crossed his legs. The interview had settled down to the quick give and take of question and answer that he was used to. But he remained on the alert. Lovell was no fool. He was more quickwitted than Finch had first given him credit for. Or he had his story well worked out.

'Do you know where he went?'

433

'No idea,' Lovell replied indifferently. 'He didn't say. He just packed a few things and went.'

'On his motor-bike?'

'Oh, so you've heard about that?' Lovell said with an amused grin. 'You have been busy asking questions, haven't you? Yes, he left on his bike.'

'Have you ever heard from him since he left?' Finch asked, ignoring the contempt in the man's voice.

The question was unexpected. Lovell hesitated, at a loss as to how to reply.

'How do you mean?' he asked.

'Has he ever written? Sent money?'

'No.'

'So how do you know if he's still alive or not?'

'I'd've heard if he was dead,' Lovell said quickly. 'Somebody would have let us know.'

It was acceptable as an answer, although Finch had the impression that Lovell had grasped it on the spur of the moment. He was certain of this when Lovell added, 'They'd've put it on the radio; an S.O.S. message, wouldn't they?'

Is he trying to convince himself as well as me? Finch wondered. But he decided to leave it there. It was a possible weak spot in Lovell's story that he might be able to exploit on another occasion. Meanwhile, he preferred to give Lovell the impression that he had been taken in by it.

'I suppose so,' he replied. 'Could you give me a description of your brother?'

'The man you've found isn't Ron,' Lovell said with conviction. 'You're barking up the wrong tree there.'

'Then you won't object if I go ahead and prove that it isn't?'

'All right,' Lovell said sulkily. 'What do you want to know?'

'Height. Colouring. Details like that.'

'Well, he was a bit taller than me; round about five feet ten, I'd say, and not so dark. More Charlie's colouring.'

'Any distinguishing marks?'

'If you mean moles or scars, no, he hadn't none.'

'Shoe size?' Finch asked.

'How the hell should I know?' Lovell replied angrily. 'I don't know the size he took in shirts, either, so it's no good asking.'

'Any of his clothes still about the house?'

'After fifteen years?'

'What happened to them?'

'He took his best stuff with him. What was left, Charlie wore. They fitted him; good enough for working in, leastways.'

'Including his boots?'

Lovell laughed as if he were beginning to find the interview amusing.

'No, not his boots,' he replied with a derisive look. 'They didn't fit. I think Betty chucked them out.'

'Who was his dentist?' Finch went on to ask.

The question threw Lovell. The smile, Finch noticed, quickly disappeared from his face.

'Dentist?' he repeated blankly.

'Yes, dentist,' Finch said, watching his face closely.

He took his time before replying.

'I don't think he went to one, not after he came out of the army. He may have seen a dentist then. I wouldn't know.'

'So his army records should have the details?'

The remark seemed to take Lovell by surprise.

'Do they keep them that far back?' he asked.

'I imagine so,' Finch said briskly. 'His dental records could be extremely useful, you see, Mr Lovell, in proving identity.'

He made the remark deliberately, to test out Lovell's reaction. The man didn't reply but looked away quickly, frowning, as if he were suddenly aware of unknown and dangerous areas of investigation, or so it seemed to Finch.

'What regiment was your brother in?' Finch asked.

'What did you say?' Lovell replied abstractedly.

Finch repeated the question.

'The Royal Engineers.'

'And I believe it was while he was in the army that he met and married Mrs Lovell?' Finch went on.

Lovell nodded. The sarcastic, jeering air had gone, leaving him subdued.

'Can you tell me where and when they were married?'

Lovell roused himself to ask sharply, 'Why? What need is there to know that?'

Finch had no intention of explaining that, with this information, there was a possibility that he might be able to get hold of a photograph of Ronnie and Betty Lovell taken on their wedding day, if the photographer were still in business and kept a back file of pictures he had taken. It was a slim chance but one worth trying.

'Just a line of inquiry we might need to check on,' he replied vaguely.

'I don't know the details,' Lovell mumbled.

'He didn't write to tell you?'

'Only that he was married and would be bringing Betty home after his demob.'

'I'll have to ask Mrs Lovell then,' Finch said, getting to his feet.

Lovell was on his feet, too, standing in front of the Inspector as if to bar his way.

'Do you have to?' he asked. His manner was almost supplicatory and there was a grave and touching dignity about it that made Finch realise the depth of affection he must hold for his brother's wife. Lovell was not a man who would find it easy to ask a favour of another.

'I need to know the date and the place of the wedding,' Finch insisted.

'Then can I ask her myself? I'd rather it came from me. She's been upset enough . . .'

He left the sentence unfinished and, when Finch nodded, went out of the room abruptly and Finch saw him striding across the yard.

8

As soon as he had disappeared round the corner of the barn, Finch moved swiftly into the living-room. He had at most, he reckoned, a few minutes. Lovell would have to ask Betty for the information and would probably spend a little while longer explaining why it was needed. All the same, knowing him, he wouldn't be gone for long. A man as suspicious by nature as Lovell wouldn't leave Finch much time to be alone in the house.

In a few quick strides, he was at the door beside the fireplace, had opened it and was going up the steep staircase, so narrow that his shoulders brushed the walls.

At the top, it ascended on to a tiny, square landing with a dormer window that overlooked the back of the house. A brief glimpse through it showed him the steep fall of the tiled roof and beyond it a kitchen garden.

Two doors opened off the landing. The one on his right gave on to a bedroom, simply furnished with a deal chest-of-drawers and a single iron bedstead, beside which stood a rush-bottomed chair with a man's jacket hanging over the back rail and some comic books with brightly coloured covers lying on the seat.

Charlie's room, thought Finch, shutting the door quickly, but not before he had noticed another door at the opposite side of the room that led, presumably, to a third bedroom, situated over the kitchen. There was no time, however, to examine it.

The door on his left opened into another bedroom, larger than Charlie's and better furnished although, like his, the back wall sloped sharply, following the angle of the roof. He took in the details swiftly. The floor-boards, on which lay some rugs, were polished to a high gloss. A vase of garden pinks stood on the deep window-sill. Against the far wall was a heavy, old-fashioned oak wardrobe, also highly polished. A chest-of-drawers of the same period stood across the corner near the window and held a small, oval mirror on a wooden stand, a brush and comb and a plastic bottle that looked as if it might contain handcream. There was no sign of any photographs and Finch knew he didn't have time to search through the drawers.

Immediately inside the door was a double bed with a cover of flowered chintz that matched the curtains, faded but still pretty.

The room had the same neat, spotless look of the other rooms in the house, oddly untouched and impersonal, and yet softened by the gentler touches of femininity in the flowers and the patterned fabric.

From the doorway, Finch could just reach the double bed. With one hand he pulled down the coverlet far enough to expose the pillows. On one lay a nightdress of pale pink cotton, on the other a pair of striped pyjama trousers, both neatly folded.

He had seen enough. Twitching back the cover, he closed the door and scrambled down the stairs in time to appear at the front door just as Lovell approached it from the yard, as if he had anticipated his arrival and had come to meet him.

His presence at the door didn't strike Lovell as suspicious. Finch wore a bland expression and, with his hands in his pockets, he looked unhurried and relaxed. Besides, Lovell had other things on his mind. The hasty, snatched conversation with Betty had left him disturbed and anxious. They had spoken in undertones so that Charlie could not overhear them. But, although Lovell had sent him sharply about his work, he had hovered nearby, clearly curious to know what they were talking about.

His presence about the place was a continual threat but there was nothing that could be done about it, except to try to keep him away from the house whenever the Inspector called, although Lovell could see it wasn't going to be easy. It no longer looked likely that Finch was going to restrict it to a few, infrequent visits.

Suppose he insisted on talking to Charlie?

Lovell wasn't sure what his rights would be in such a situation. Could he refuse to let him be questioned? After all, Charlie wasn't normal. Even Finch must realise that. He could, of course, deny anything that Charlie might say, pleading that he'd got confused over what had really happened.

Betty, too, was another source of anxiety. He knew he could count on her silence. There was no problem there. *She* would give nothing away. But the longer the investigation went on, the more strain she would suffer and God knows she had already been through enough. He could see it in her face when he asked the questions about her marriage that Finch wanted the answers to.

She told him and then asked quickly, 'What does he want to know for?'

'I don't know,' Lovell replied. 'He's just nosing about, that's all. It doesn't mean anything.'

It was better, he decided, to say nothing about the other inquiries that Finch had spoken of making; into Ron's army records, for instance. That was another source of worry that was best kept to himself.

How far back would the police be prepared to go? Not that they'd found out much, he told himself. Nothing that would be of any use to them in proving who the dead man was. Unless they got hold of a photograph.

Christ! He had forgotten the Inspector had asked about photos of Ron. He turned away, eager to get back to the house before Finch had time to start looking about. Downstairs was all right. There were no photos in the living-room, not even in the dresser drawers. But he could get a search warrant, Lovell supposed, and turn the place over.

And, God, if that happened . . .

Charlie delayed him, tugging at his sleeve to hold him back.

'Can I come to the house with you, Geoff?'

'No, stay here,' Lovell told him.

'But I fancied another cup o'tea. I always have a second cup.'

'Then you'll bloody well have to wait for it!' Lovell shouted.

439

Betty came forward, her lips set and disapproving at his outburst, to lead Charlie off, coaxing him as a mother might do to distract the attention of a difficult child.

'Not yet, Charlie. I'll make a fresh pot later. Come on, now. I want you to help me collect up the eggs.'

They walked off together, Charlie looking back over his shoulder at his brother with a sullen expression.

Lovell watched them both with a sense of angry and yet defeated despair before turning abruptly and walking rapidly back to the house where Finch met him at the door.

'You've not been gone long, Mr Lovell,' he remarked cheerfully. 'Were you able to find out what I wanted?'

'They were married at Bidderton registry office,' Lovell said shortly.

'And the date?'

Lovell told him.

'Bidderton,' Finch remarked chattily, as he made a note of the details. 'That's in Dorset, isn't it?'

'Yes.'

'Nice part of the country, Dorset,' Finch added.

'Is that all?' Lovell demanded.

'For the moment,' Finch replied. But he seemed in no hurry and remained standing on the doorstep, looking about him with a frankly interested gaze.

'If you've finished . . .' Lovell reminded him.

'Yes, of course,' Finch replied. 'I mustn't keep you talking, Mr Lovell. I'm sure you've got work to do. And so have I.'

It was said pleasantly enough and he was smiling in a friendly manner, but his eyes were cool and watchful and Lovell thought he could detect a warning note in the final remark. Finch was telling him that the inquiries were not yet over. And behind it, Lovell sensed something else. It was almost as if the Inspector were trying to provoke a response and, if that was what he was after, it was a game that two could play at.

'If you're leaving, then I'll let the dog off the chain,' he replied in an amused, drawling voice.

Finch's smile widened.

'As long as you let me get to the gate first,' he countered easily.

He didn't hurry, however, and went strolling off up the drive, his hands still in his pockets, as if he had all the time in the world. There was something exasperatingly confident about his back and the set of his shoulders that tempted Lovell to release the dog before he had climbed to safety over the gate. But he didn't and it was with a feeling of defeat and anti-climax that he finally freed the dog, after he heard Finch start up his car.

What was the point in it, after all? He couldn't hope to win. All he could do was postpone the final reckoning. Or trust to a miracle. And that wasn't likely to happen.

But, at least, there was something positive he could do, right now, while Betty and Charlie were safely out of the way and, with sudden decision, he entered the house and went up the stairs to the room with the double bed in it, where he began jerking open the drawers in the chest. The top one contained Betty's clothes, folded with the neatness that he had come to realise was almost obsessive, although he understood it, even sympathised with it in a strange way. A white blouse lay on the top. Next to it was a petticoat patterned with tiny blue flowers. At the sight of them, his resolution drained away. Their pristine, bridal freshness intimidated him and his hands hovered over them incapable of pillage.

'What are you looking for?'

It was Betty's voice behind him. He turned to find her standing in the doorway, her face taut, but whether with anger or anxiety he couldn't, in his own confused and guilty state of mind, decide.

'Nothing,' he muttered.

She crossed the room and he stood aside to let her pass. For a moment, she stood without speaking, looking down into the open drawer. Then she closed it quietly.

'You were looking for something,' she said.

'There was a coldness in her voice, as if he were a stranger, an interloper who had no right to be there and he felt his anger return.

All right! Let her know the truth, he thought. I've done with lying to protect her.

'Photos of Ron,' he told her.

'Why?'

441

'Because *he's* been asking for them.'

He jerked his head towards the window, to indicate the world outside, Finch's world.

She kept her eyes on his face as she asked the next question.

'What does he want them for?'

He made a helpless gesture with one hand.

'I don't know. He's heard gossip, that's all. He's checking up on anyone from the village that's gone missing.'

'Missing!'

There was an hysterical note in her voice and he looked at her with quick anxiety, frightened that he had said too much.

'Don't, Betty,' he pleaded.

He saw her stiffen at his concern.

'Oh, don't worry,' she told him coldly. 'I shan't break down, if that's what's bothering you.'

Averting her face, she went over to the wardrobe and, taking down a cardboard shoe-box that was hidden behind a suitcase on the top shelf, she handed it to him.

'If it's photos of Ron you want, you've been looking in the wrong place,' she said.

He opened it awkwardly and found it full of letters and photographs, held together in neat bundles with elastic bands.

'Is that the lot?' he asked. 'There's no more?'

'No. You've got them all.' Her voice was contemptuous. 'What are you going to do with them?'

'Burn them,' he said and added quickly, 'it's safest.'

She didn't reply, merely lifted her shoulders in a gesture that expressed weary acceptance before leaving the room.

He waited until he heard the staircase door close behind her and then, putting the box down on the bed, he began taking out the bundles and, removing the elastic bands, shuffled quickly through their contents, telling himself he ought to check to make sure they contained nothing that need not be destroyed. All the same, he was aware of a certain voyeurism, a jealous need to pry into the life she had shared with his brother.

The letters, few in number, were written on blue, lined paper in Ron's pointed scrawl. He caught sight of the words 'Darling

Bet' on the first one before, overcome with shame and anger, he thrust the letter back.

The photographs were mostly of Ron; snapshots of him taken in army uniform; several of a trip to some unknown beach: Ron in swimming trunks with his arms round the shoulders of two friends; Ron sitting propped up against a rock with a cigarette in his mouth. In all of them, he had assumed the characteristic pose that Lovell remembered with an odd mixture of bitterness and affection; the head flung back in that cocky, challenging manner; the swaggering look of self-confidence.

He could not bring himself to look at the wedding photographs, easily distinguishable from the others by their size and their white covers stamped with silver bells. He merely laid them on one side with the rest.

The box was now empty, apart from a few snapshots of Betty on her own, taken long ago, it seemed, before her marriage. He looked at them sadly. Betty at fifteen. Or thereabouts. Long before he had known her, anyway. Smiling, with her hair loose. Virginal.

Thrusting the lid on, he carried the box back to the wardrobe where he replaced it on the shelf, before gathering up the scattered letters and photographs into a bundle and making for the door.

At the bottom of the staircase he paused, listening. From the kitchen he could hear the rattle of crockery. Nearly half-past six. Betty would be preparing the evening meal. He heard the rush of water as she turned on the tap and then the knock of metal, as if she were placing a saucepan on the stove.

He crossed the room silently and, opening the front door, ducked round the far side of the house, so that she should not see him passing the kitchen windows.

The rubbish tip was at the end of the garden, behind a row of currant bushes and, as he squatted down and spread the letters and photos out in a loose pile, he could smell the hot, pungent odour of their leaves. Still crouching, he lit a match and, sheltering it in the palm of his hand, carried it down to the papers. The flame, almost invisible in the bright light of the late afternoon sun that flooded the garden with a level, golden radiance, touched the corner of a snapshot and ran quickly across the glazed paper. As he watched the smiling face char and buckle, he felt a sense of pleasurable satisfaction that at the same time shocked him. His decision to burn them wasn't, he realised, merely to prevent them falling into the hands of the police. Much stronger were his own motives of personal revenge, as if by burning the pictures and letters he could finally rid himself of the man. And that was as pointless as trying to beat Finch at his own game.

He got to his feet, staring moodily down at the burning fragments. The flames had almost finished their working, flickering across the last scraps of paper in little, licking spurts, smokeless in the still, warm air. The cover of one of the wedding photographs began opening slowly in the heat, as if turned by an unseen hand, but he didn't wait to see it. Instead, he began walking back along the path towards the house, remembering the contempt in Betty's voice when she had asked him what he was going to do with them.

Perhaps she was right. Perhaps he was contemptible. But whatever she thought, they were bloody well gone now. Too late to get them back. Too late to salvage anything from the God-awful mess.

He pushed open the door into the kitchen with a feeling of angry resentment. Charlie was already there, washing noisily at the sink, throwing drops of water over the floor as he swilled his face and arms.

'What you been doin', Geoff?' he asked, looking up, his hair wet and spiky.

'Nothing,' Lovell replied roughly. 'Move over.'

He washed his own face and hands quickly, taking the towel from Charlie before he had finished with it.

'Here! I ain't done drying myself,' Charlie protested.

'You take too bloody long,' Lovell told him.

Going over to the table, he jerked out a chair and sat down. Betty was placing a dish of potatoes in the centre of the table and he looked deliberately into her face.

'It's done,' he told her, watching for her reaction. Her face remained inscrutable. The lowered eyes, veiled by her lashes, gave nothing away. Perversely, he wanted to provoke a response, as Finch had tried to do with him.

'I said it's done,' he repeated in a louder voice.

'I heard you the first time,' she replied flatly and, moving away from the table, began getting out plates from the rack over the sink. He watched her covertly out of the corner of his eyes.

From the back, she still looked young, with her thin body. He saw the bony elbows jutting out from the rolled-up sleeves of her dress and the childlike upper arms, so small that he could span them with his finger and thumb. Her hair, which was tied back anyhow, had begun to spring back into waves in the steam from the boiling saucepans and he suddenly remembered the photographs of her as a girl, with her hair loose.

Christ! And she had to go and marry *him*!

Weren't there plenty of other women he could have taken and left her alone? That girl in Harlsdon, for instance. Nancy. He'd been knocking about with her before he went into the army and even after he'd come back, married to Betty, it hadn't taken him long to pick up with her again. And he knew Ron had been writing to her after he'd been called up.

God! Photos! Could he have given her a photograph of himself? Perhaps one of the snapshots he'd had taken. It hadn't occurred to him before but it was possible. It was the sort of thing Ron would do.

Supposing the police found out he'd known her? From what Finch had said, they'd evidently made inquiries in the village about Ron. It only took one person to mention that he'd been going out with a girl from Harlsdon to put the Inspector on her trail. Bob Deal and Frankie Cotter knew about her, for a start. They were two of that group who had been youngsters then, roaring off on their motor-bikes evening after evening into the town . . .

He had a sudden, vivid memory of Ron standing in front of the sink, ducking slightly at the knees in order to see himself in the little, square mirror that hung on the wall above, combing back his hair with long sweeps of the comb and then turning round, settling the collar of his jacket and asking with that bloody, pleased grin of his, 'Well, d'you reckon they'll fancy me tonight?'

Lovell thrust his chair back and got up from the table, aware of the startled expressions on the faces of Betty and Charlie at his abrupt movement.

'I'm going out,' he announced.

This time he did get a reaction from her.

'But I'm just going to serve up the supper,' she protested.

'Then stick it back in the oven,' he replied over his shoulder, as he made for the door.

It was how Ron would have spoken to her, confident, uncaring, selfishly absorbed in his own needs, and it gave Lovell a certain shameful and guilty satisfaction that, for once in his life, he could find the courage to behave to her in exactly the same way.

9

When Finch arrived at Stebbing's farm, he found Boyce already waiting with Kyle and two other constables, equipped with spades and measuring tapes. Boyce raised his eyebrows to indicate interest in how the interview with Lovell had gone, but Finch shook his head. It wasn't something he wanted to discuss in front of the other men.

They walked to the field, where Finch set the two constables to the job of filling in the grave. It had been measured, photographed, thoroughly examined. There was no more evidence that it could possibly yield and yet he watched them throw in the first few spadesful of earth with regret. A man's body had lain there. Soon it would be nothing more than an oblong patch of raw earth and that, too, wouldn't remain for long. The grass would take over again and by next summer there would be no sign that it had ever existed. It seemed to him the dead man should have had a more permanent memorial, although there was a rightness about it, too, that he recognised.

He turned away, leaving the men to their task, and began walking across the field to where Boyce and Kyle were measuring the distance from the grave to the excavation, the tarpaulin cover of which had been rolled back.

'Sixty feet five inches,' Kyle called out and Boyce, having made a note of it, began winding in the tape.

Finch strolled over and stood looking down at the site, his hands in his pockets. There wasn't much to see. For a few square yards, the turf and top-soil had been removed, revealing a yellowish layer of more densely-packed earth in which several darker patches, roughly circular in shape, were clearly visible.

Squatting down, he gently poked at the soil in one of them with a finger. It was finer in texture and more granular than the surrounding clay.

'Know what these are?' he asked, looking up. Boyce shrugged indifferently. Kyle, more anxious to create a good impression on a superior officer, frowned heavily as if trying to recollect some temporarily forgotten knowledge.

'Post-holes,' Finch told them. 'According to Rose, this could be the site of some Saxon building, a farmhouse, say. Interesting to think people were living here all that time ago.'

Expressing the thought out loud only partly exorcised the impression the field gave him. Besides, it was something more than a mere sense of history. If he had to define it, he would have explained it as a feeling of brooding presence, a weight in the atmosphere that wasn't, strangely enough, an unpleasant sensation, although there was a solemnity in it and an air of waiting. It reminded him of an occasion when, as a child, he had explored the empty rooms of a large, derelict house on the outskirts of the village where he lived. Like the field, they were full of sunlight so there was nothing sinister about them and he had felt no fear as he walked through them, only a sense of loss, even though he had never lived there, and the same feeling of sad withdrawal as if those who had once occupied those rooms had vacated them only temporarily and were waiting somewhere, he didn't know exactly where, to reoccupy them. It had been the first occasion that he had been aware of the concept of time; an endless chain of years, it seemed, stretching in front and behind him, which was probably why the memory and its attendant emotion had remained so vividly with him to be stirred into life again by the evocation of a similar response that, for some inexplicable reason, this area of rough grass with its surrounding trees and mounds of earth had roused in him.

'Saxons?' Boyce was asking. 'Aren't they the lot with the horns on their helmets?'

'You're thinking of Vikings,' Finch corrected him.

'Oh, well,' Boyce replied, lapsing once again into indifference.

'Angles, Saxons and Jutes,' Kyle announced unexpectedly.

Boyce and Finch turned to look at him in surprise. 'Came from the continent. First started raiding along the east coast before the Romans left. Stayed on to settle and farm. Took over from the Celts. Big, blonde people. Good warriors. Pagan.'

He tailed off, looking embarrassed.

'Well done, laddy,' Boyce remarked with heavy humour. 'Come and sit in the front.'

Kyle coloured up.

'We did the Saxons once at school,' he explained defensively. 'I don't remember much more about them except they used to build timbered halls where they met to drink mead.'

'"The flight of a sparrow,"' Finch said half to himself. He was struggling with a school memory of his own but it was too vague to put into words. Something to do with life being like a bird flying from the darkness into a lighted hall and out again at the far end, into darkness again. Who had said it? He couldn't remember but he felt sure it had some Saxon connection. Perhaps Rose would know.

'What . . . ?' Boyce began, but Finch was spared the embarrassment of trying to explain by the arrival of the two constables who had finished filling in the grave and were coming towards them, wiping their faces.

'We'll push off then,' said Finch. 'We've done all we can here. Better get the site covered over before we go.'

When Boyce and Kyle had rolled the tarpaulin over the excavated area, they set off to walk back to Stebbing's farm, skirting the cornfield, rich gold now in the dying sun, and then striking across the pasture beyond to the yard where Stebbing was waiting for them, exuding curiosity.

'Any news?' he asked.

'Inquiries are proceeding,' Finch replied in his best official voice and saw Boyce cough and cover his mouth to hide a smile. 'You can tell Mr Rose, by the way, that we've finished with the field so he and his society can move back into it any time they like.'

'Right. I'll tell him,' Stebbing replied. He was obviously on edge, fidgeting from foot to foot as he stood in front of them, his eyes roving across their faces, searching for any give-away

449

expression, and Finch wondered if Wheeler hadn't been stirring things up by dropping a few of his sly little hints in order to whet Stebbing's inquisitiveness.

'Mrs Stebbing would be only too glad to offer you a cup of tea,' the farmer went on. He seemed anxious to keep them there, no doubt in the hope of pumping them further. 'There's beer, but I suppose as you're on duty . . .'

Finch thought longingly of beer, cool and bitter, but even tea would be better than nothing. He saw the men's faces light up at the thought of something to drink and he was about to accept reluctantly for their sake when Stebbing glanced quickly over his shoulder towards the gate, where a battered grey van was just passing the farm entrance.

'Funny,' he remarked. 'That's Lovell. I wonder where he's off to at this time of the evening.'

Finch made a rapid decision. Looking at his watch, he said hurriedly, 'I'm sorry, Mr Stebbing. I've just remembered a conference at headquarters. Boyce, you'd better come with me. Kyle as well. You other two can make your own way back.'

As they walked towards the car, Boyce asked, 'What conference? First I've heard of it. I was dying for a cup of tea, too.'

He sounded aggrieved.

'Get in the back and don't argue. I don't want Lovell to see either of us,' Finch told him. 'Kyle, you take the keys and drive. You're to follow the van that's just passed. Don't get too close but, if you value your head, don't lose him.'

As he climbed into the back with Boyce, the sergeant asked, 'What's the idea?'

'Lovell's up to something. I don't know what but I think it's to do with my visit this afternoon. I must have got him rattled enough to leave the farm and I reckon he wouldn't do that without good reason.'

They had driven up the lane and were turning left on to the main road, in the direction of Harlsdon. Lovell's van, hidden from them round the bends of the lane, was now visible ahead of them on a straight stretch of road.

'Drop further back,' Finch told Kyle. 'I don't want him to see us.'

They slowed down to a sedate thirty miles an hour. There was very little other traffic about. A couple of cars passed them going in the opposite direction and that was all. In the gentle evening light, the countryside seemed empty and peaceful, resting quietly after the heat of the day.

'How did the interview go?' Boyce was asking.

'Quite well. Lovell didn't give much away but, then, he never does. I found out one thing, though. Two people are sharing the double bed in the best room.'

'Geoff Lovell and Betty?'

'It looks like it.'

'So if Ron Lovell came back and found . . .'

'Let's leave out the speculation for the moment,' Finch replied, with a warning look at Kyle's back. 'We'll need a lot more evidence before that charge can be made to stick.' He glanced out of the window at the passing fields. 'I wonder where he's making for and why?'

'It looks like Harlsdon,' Boyce replied.

He was right. Soon afterwards they were entering the town which began abruptly, with no intervening suburbs, the countryside that surrounded it giving way to a scattering of houses and then they were driving through the deserted main street, the shops closed, the pavements empty of people. It was a town that had escaped the worst of modern development, although there had been changes over the years. But, at heart, it remained unaltered: a country market town that served the surrounding villages and hamlets and where the slow, local dialect could still be heard in the streets.

Ahead of them, Lovell's van was turning into the car-park of the Blue Boar that faced the old market hall.

'Draw in at the side of the road,' Finch instructed Kyle.

With the engine turned off, the Inspector was aware of the silence of the town. The pealing of church bells being rung for an evening practice sounded unnaturally loud and insistent on the quiet air and added to the feeling of Sabbath calm. To it was suddenly added the sharp slam of a car door and Lovell came into sight, walking quickly, his dark head bent forward, and clearly unaware of their presence for he didn't so much

451

as glance in their direction as he went in at the front entrance of the Blue Boar.

'Give him five minutes,' Finch told Kyle, 'and then I want you to follow him inside.'

Lovell entered the saloon bar where he knew Nancy Fowler was most likely to be found at that time of the evening and noticed her straightaway, sitting at a table by herself against the far wall, an empty glass in front of her. As he walked towards her, she looked up, her face expressing astonishment and, to his embarrassment, pleasure as well.

'My God!' she exclaimed. 'Geoff Lovell! After all this time. You're a bloody bad penny, aren't you?'

'Hello Nancy,' he said awkwardly. 'Let me buy you a drink. What'll you have?'

'The usual.'

He couldn't remember what it was and, seeing the look on his face, she guessed this and laughed.

'Gin and orange, ducky. And a packet of cheese and onion crisps as well,' she called after him as he turned back to the bar.

As he ordered the drinks, Lovell noticed the landlord's expression, tight-lipped and disapproving. He banged the change down on the counter, ignoring Lovell's outstretched hand and Lovell could guess the cause of it. Nancy was on the loose again.

Well, it doesn't matter, he told himself. I'll be out of the place in half-an-hour at most.

Carrying the drinks over to the table, he sat down opposite her, taking in the details of her appearance for the first time. She had changed a lot since the last time he had seen her; coarsened and put on weight. The thin summer dress she was wearing revealed plump arms and too much of her breasts, pushed up high and close together so that the cleft between them showed as a dark crack. Her hair was a different colour, too, from what he remembered; reddish and unnaturally stiff so that when she moved her head it remained curiously static; more like a hat than real hair. She was sweating underneath her heavy make-up and tiny beads of perspiration had gathered across her forehead and in the folds of her nose.

'Well and how's the world treating you?' she was asking.

'All right,' he replied.

'Still got the farm?'

'Yes.'

He had forgotten how to talk to her and, besides, there was nothing much now that he wanted to say to her, despite her easy assumption that they could pick up the old topics as if they were back on their familiar footing.

'How are you keeping, Nance?' he asked, switching the subject away from himself.

She shrugged, her mouth suddenly going sulky.

'All right, I suppose.'

'Still working at the same place?'

'No. I chucked that. I'm at the egg-packing plant now. Bloody awful hours and on your feet all day long, too.'

'You're looking well, though. Your hair's nice.'

He offered the compliment clumsily but she was pleased and put up a hand to touch it.

'Noticed it, did you? I've had it tinted. It's called "Auburn Dawn".'

'It suits you,' he told her gravely.

'Well, you have to do something to cheer yourself up. You could rot in this hole and nobody'd notice.'

There was a complaining note in her voice and he turned the conversation again, shifting uncomfortably in his chair.

'The boys all right?'

'Oh, Christ,' she said. 'Don't talk to me about those little buggers.'

'I'm sorry, Nance,' he said and meant it.

'What for?' she asked sharply.

He made a movement with one hand, indicating everything and, understanding him, her face softened.

'It's not your fault,' she said. 'And don't take no notice of me. I'm a bit fed up, that's all. But I'll get over it. Bloody well have to, won't I?'

'I could lend you a bit of cash if it's money that's worrying you,' he said humbly and she leaned forward to pat his hand.

'You're a good old sod but hang on to your money,' she told him. 'You need it as much as me. Betty all right?' she added unexpectedly.

The question caught him off guard and he looked quickly into her face, wondering how much she knew. But she couldn't suspect anything, he decided. Besides, her expression was the same as it always was when she spoke of Betty, politely interested and a little pitying, as if she were asking after some sick relative. All the same, it was a subject that he wanted to avoid and it was time, anyway, he thought, that he got to the point.

'She's keeping well,' he said and added hurriedly, 'look, Nance, there's something I wanted to ask you.'

'About Betty?'

'No. About Ron.'

'Ron?' she asked quickly. 'You haven't heard from him?'

'No.'

He was finding it harder than he had imagined and wished now that he had taken more time to think out what he was going to say to her. He didn't want to give too much away and yet he would have to make it sound urgent enough to convince her.

'I've had the police round to see me,' he explained. 'They didn't say much but it's something to do with Ron. They were asking for a photo of him and, as I didn't want to get him into any trouble, I said we'd got rid of all ours . . .'

'He's in trouble with the police?' she interrupted.

'No. I don't know,' he said impatiently. 'They didn't go into details. But, look, Nance, suppose he is, I thought it best to come over and see you, just in case you'd got a photo of him and they came asking . . .'

'How would they find out about me?'

'I don't know. But they might. You know what they're like, snooping round, asking questions.'

'I wouldn't bloody tell them anything if they did.'

'But have you got any photos of Ron?' he asked, close to desperation.

He saw her face close over with the stubborn look he'd seen before.

'I might have. I don't remember. I might have chucked them out.'

'Will you have a look?'

'I might.'

'Will you, *please*?'

She became suddenly and unexpectedly angry.

'You and your brother make a right bloody pair!' she said, her voice rising. 'Both of you drop me like a hot brick when it suits you and then come whining back when you want some bloody favour doing.'

The landlord looked up and began lifting the counter flap as if to come across to them.

'Keep your voice down, Nancy,' Lovell urged her. 'People are looking.'

'Let them bloody look,' she replied, but he noticed she spoke more quietly. 'Let them have an eyeful. Him and all,' she added, nodding towards the landlord, who had retreated behind the bar again but was still watching them suspiciously. 'Rotten, sodding old git he is. Just looking for a chance to throw me out. Well, I don't bloody care. I'll drink where I like. My money's as good as anyone else's.'

'I'll make it right by you,' he said quickly, seizing on the mention of money and, getting out his wallet, took out a five pound note and slid it across the table towards her. 'For your trouble,' he explained.

For a few seconds, she looked at it without speaking, her face inexpressibly sad. Then she shrugged and picked it up.

'Why not?' she said. 'Ron's borrowed enough off of me in his time.'

'He owes you money?' Lovell asked.

'He owes me, but not money,' she replied bitterly and he was silent, not knowing what to reply.

'It's all right,' she said in a gentler voice. 'I don't blame you for what he did. And I'll have a look for them photos. I've got some somewhere. For, when all's said and done, I don't want to drop him into any trouble, more fool me.'

'I'll come back the same time next week to pick them up, shall I?' he asked, getting to his feet. 'You'll be here?'

'I'm always bloody here. Part of the fixtures, that's me.'

'I'll be seeing you then, Nance,' he said awkwardly and walked away, resisting the temptation to look back at her from the doorway.

10

Finch and Boyce watched him leave from the parked car.

'Are we going to follow him?' Boyce asked.

'No. My guess is he's only going home. We'll wait for Kyle.'

Five minutes after Lovell had driven away, Kyle too emerged from the Blue Boar and got into the front seat, bringing with him the warm, yeasty smell of beer which Boyce sniffed at jealously.

'I had a pint,' Kyle explained defensively. 'I had to. I couldn't stand at the bar and drink nothing. It'd've looked suspicious.'

'Never mind that,' Finch told him. 'Did he meet anyone?'

'Yes. A woman. He seemed to know her quite well. They talked normally for a few minutes and then she seemed to get angry and started raising her voice. The landlord didn't like it much. At one point, I thought he was going over to ask her to leave. He was watching her all the time after that.'

'Interesting,' murmured Finch. 'Why was that?'

Kyle flushed.

'I don't think he likes her being in there. By the look of her, she's on the game.'

'Go on!' Finch teased him gently. 'What did she say when she got angry?'

'I didn't catch it all. Something about him, Mr Lovell that is, and his brother making a right b. pair.'

In deference to Finch's rank, he thought he ought to censor the swear word.

'Then Mr Lovell calmed her down and I didn't hear any more. A bit later, though, he got out his wallet and passed something across the table to her.'

'Money?' Finch asked.

'I think so, but I'm not sure. It could have been a piece of paper. Soon after that, Mr Lovell left.'

Finch thought quickly. It seemed likely that the woman's remark about Lovell's brother almost certainly referred to Ron and this piece of information, added to the gossip that Boyce had picked up in the village about Ron Lovell spending his evenings in Harlsdon, suggested to the Inspector that she was someone he had known in the past. He got out of the car, announcing, 'I'm going to have a chat with her.'

'You can't miss her,' Kyle assured him. 'She's a big red-head sitting at one of the tables in the saloon bar.'

Boyce's face looked up longingly from the open passenger window.

'Bring us out a drink afterwards,' he begged. 'My tongue's sticking to the roof of my mouth.'

'If you can hang on, we might all be able to go inside later for a pint of the best,' Finch told him and, strolling over to the door of the Blue Boar, went into the saloon bar.

There was no mistaking her. She was sitting, as Kyle had said, at a table, although he doubted Kyle's assumption that she was on the game for, as he bought himself a pint and carried it over towards her table, she looked up at him with a startled and slightly hostile expression. A professional tart would have given a potential customer more of a welcome. He could understand, however, Kyle's mistake. Her low-cut dress and heavy make-up certainly gave that impression, although there was something naïve about her as well. Finch guessed she wasn't averse to picking up men but it would be on an amateur basis and probably only when she was a bit tight. He doubted if she ever did it for money. A few gins and the fleeting illusion of love would be enough.

'Do you mind?' he asked pleasantly, putting his hand on the back of an empty chair opposite her.

'Please yourself,' she said indifferently, although he noticed she shot a look across at the landlord who, pausing in the act of wiping down the counter, was watching them closely.

'Warm this evening,' Finch went on.

She ignored him and, swallowing down what was left in her

glass, began gathering up her handbag as if preparing to leave. There wasn't going to be time for any preamble. Finch would have to plunge straight in.

'Mr Lovell didn't stay very long,' he remarked.

She sat down again suddenly with a bump.

'How the hell do you know?' she demanded.

'I followed him,' Finch replied promptly and, flipping open his identification, he held it briefly towards her.

'Oh, Christ,' she said in a weary voice. 'The bloody police.'

'What did Mr Lovell want?'

She hesitated and then seemed to recover some of her assurance.

'Nothing. Just a chat.'

'About Ronnie Lovell?'

Her eyes didn't leave his face.

'We might have mentioned him in passing.'

Finch returned her gaze and, after a few seconds, her glance wavered.

'What's your name?' he asked in his official voice, kindly but impersonal.

'Mrs Fowler. Nancy Fowler,' she replied sulkily.

'Well, it won't do, Mrs Fowler. You'll have to think up something better than that. I happen to know Geoff Lovell and I'm quite sure he didn't drive all the way over here at this time of the evening just for a chat. So what did he want?'

She ran her tongue over her lips.

'He – he wanted to know if Ron owed me any money.'

'After fifteen years?'

'Well, not just Ron. He'd borrowed a bit of cash off me himself and he wanted to pay me back.'

So it was money that Kyle had seen Lovell pass across the table, Finch thought. That bit, at least, was true. All the same, she wasn't a very good liar. Lovell was, in his estimation, too proud to borrow money from a woman and besides, even if he had, Finch didn't believe he had come rushing over to Harlsdon on a sudden impulse to pay it back.

He leaned forward, speaking in a low and confidential voice.

'Look, Mrs Fowler, I don't want to make life awkward for you by taking you into headquarters in a squad car to make an official statement but unless you're prepared to help us . . .'

He left the threat unfinished and it had its effect. She looked alarmed.

'I don't want no trouble,' she told him. 'I've got my job to think of and the house. It's council, you see . . .'

'They're being difficult?' Finch asked. He switched roles quickly, assuming the sympathetic, listening air of an older relative, prepared to give good advice.

'I've got behind with the rent,' she explained. Her plump, heavily-powdered face had collapsed into creases like a child's on the verge of tears. 'And there's been complaints about the garden being left to go wild and the telly being on too loud. Bloody neighbours.'

She sniffed noisily.

And men friends calling late at night, too, I shouldn't wonder, Finch thought.

'But I don't want to drop Ron in it,' she went on.

'Who said anything about Ron Lovell being in trouble?'

Her eyes widened.

'But Geoff said . . .'

'Look, I don't know what Mr Lovell's told you . . .' Finch began, deliberately leaving the sentence unfinished.

'He said the police had been round asking questions about Ron and that he must be in some kind of mess.'

'Then he's got hold of the wrong end of the stick,' Finch assured her cheerfully. It was clear Geoff Lovell had told her nothing about the body of the dead man being found near his farm. 'Yes, it's true we'd like to find Ron Lovell and ask him a few questions, but it's only about a line of inquiry we think he can help us with. As far as I'm concerned, he may be useful but only as a possible witness.'

It was near enough to the truth, he thought.

'So you don't want no photos of him?' Nancy Fowler asked.

'Photos?' Finch asked too sharply and saw that he had put her on her guard. But it was too late to retrieve the situation and he went on, 'You've got some photos of Ron?'

'I might have,' she said warily. 'I'm not sure. I told Geoff I'd have a look.'

'He wants them?'

'Yes. He said he'd come back next week to pick them up.'

'I'd like to see them first,' Finch told her. 'They might be a great help in our inquiry.'

She still hesitated.

'If you're sure Ron isn't in no trouble?'

'No. I've already told you. We'd like to interview him as a possible witness, that's all. A photograph of him would make our job of finding him a lot easier.'

'You really think you can find him?'

The eagerness in her voice and face made the situation quite clear to Finch. Nancy Fowler was in love with Ron Lovell and, in order to have him found and possibly brought back to her, she was prepared to risk anything, even handing over evidence to the police.

'I'm certainly going to try,' Finch assured her.

She came to a sudden decision.

'All right!' she said, getting to her feet. 'I'll go and look for them. Do you want to wait here and I'll bring them back?'

'I'll come with you, if you don't mind,' Finch replied. He didn't think she'd give him the slip but, all the same, it would be useful to know where she lived.

She seemed reluctant at first and then agreed, shrugging.

'Please yourself. It's not far. You'll have to take the place as you find it, though. I haven't had time to clean it up.'

They left together, going out into the street where the long shadows were already falling across the pavements, Finch matching his pace to hers, that was slow and a little uncertain, a combination of high heels, a tight skirt and a few gins.

'Turn left here,' she told him, a little further down the road. At the corner, Finch glanced back and smiled to himself. Boyce was already getting out of the car with surprising alacrity for a man of his size and was making for the entrance of the Blue Boar.

Nancy Fowler's house was one of a small and new-looking Council development, tucked away behind the shops at the end of a narrow side street that suddenly opened out into a semi-circle of raw concrete and paving-stones, the houses fanning out round it, each with its own tiny front garden enclosed in galvanised wire netting.

As Nancy pushed open the gate and he followed her up the dead straight path to the front door, he could see what she meant by complaints about the garden. Knee high grass and weeds, heavy with pollen and seeds, grew on both sides of the path, in contrast to the minute lawns and rose beds, edged with lobelia, of the neighbouring gardens. The sound of the television was also apparent, blaring out of the open window where grubby net curtains stirred listlessly in the warm air.

They entered a tiny hall, with a staircase rising steeply, and then went into the living-room that opened from it.

It was quite a large room, but so crowded with furniture and so untidy that it appeared much smaller. A dining-table and chairs were pushed together under the window, while a three piece suite, covered with worn, rust-coloured fabric, was drawn up round a fireplace of mottled tiles, the empty grate of which was littered with spent matches and cigarette ends. Two boys, one about fourteen, Finch guessed, the other a year or so younger, were sprawled in the armchairs watching the television set that stood on a shelf beside the fireplace. Both had cigarettes in their hands and the air was blue with smoke.

Nancy, her lips compressed angrily, stalked over to the set and switched it off.

'I've told you before, don't have that bloody thing on so loud. And put those ciggies away. I'm not going out to work to keep you in bloody fags.'

'You're back early, ain't you?' the eldest boy asked, lounging to his feet. 'Got chucked out?'

'You mind your lip,' she told him, 'else you'll get a clump round the ear-hole. I've brought a friend back for a talk.'

'Oh, yeah?' the boy asked, his eyes moving insolently across to Finch. *Talk?*

'So the pair of you can clear off to the kitchen,' she went on, ignoring him.

'I ain't had nothin' to eat yet,' the younger boy complained.

'I told you, there's a pork pie and some cold potatoes in the fridge. You can have those.'

'Phil's eaten all the spuds.'

'Oh, Christ! Trust him! Come on then, I'll have to cut you some bread.'

She hustled them out into the kitchen, where Finch could hear her banging about and talking in a loud, angry voice. While he waited for her to return, he lowered himself gingerly into one of the sagging armchairs and looked about him. Signs of Nancy's housekeeping, or lack of it, were everywhere about the room. Dirty cups, plates and overflowing ashtrays stood on the floor, the sideboard and along the top of the mantlepiece while the furniture, although comparatively new, was already battered and scarred. The arms of the chair in which he was sitting were dark and tacky with dirt.

She came back into the room, red in the face and flustered.

'Bloody kids!' she said. 'Look at the mess they've made of this room.'

Finch made sympathetic noises, although the disorder was not a mere evening's untidiness. It had taken time to build up that rich patina of squalor. She began futilely to pick up some of the scattered comics and clothes that lay on the stained carpet and then plumped down on to the sofa, saying in an aggrieved voice, 'I don't see why the hell I should bother.'

'The photographs,' Finch reminded her gently.

'Oh, God, yes. I'll go and look for them.'

She evidently didn't have to look very far for she was back in the room within a few minutes and Finch suspected that she had known all along where they were.

'Ron had them taken soon after he went into the army,' she explained as she handed them over. 'I said I wanted one of him in his uniform.'

They were three small photographs on a strip, cut from one of those sheets of poly-photos that Finch remembered had been popular at the time. Despite their smallness, they were clear and showed in good detail the features of the man's face.

It was the first time he had seen a likeness of Ron Lovell and Finch studied them with interest. There was very little family resemblance, he decided. Ron was smaller-featured and more finely-boned, the jaw lighter and the hair-line further back from the forehead, although like Geoff he had dark hair and eyes and well defined eyebrows. But the face lacked the heavy, brooding quality of his older brother. In all three photographs he was smiling with a cocky, self-assured expression and a bold, almost flirtatious look straight into the camera, as if he were chatting it up.

It was a mistake, Finch knew, to read too much of a man's character in a photograph and yet he felt these three small portraits told him something about Lovell as a person. The Inspector had met his type before: self-confident; breezy; relaxed in his relationships with women; good-humoured; even generous when things went his way; but basically the sort who thinks that life owes him a living, a permanent adolescent, and therefore quick to take advantage of anyone who was fool enough to let him get away with it. It was often a woman, and Finch thought of Betty Lovell. Nancy Fowler, too, he guessed.

He examined them for a second time, wondering if McCullum would be able to find anything in them to use in the making of a life-size enlargement. There was nothing in the way of a background and all three were only head and shoulder studies, two full-face, one slightly turned towards a three-quarter profile. In all of them he was wearing a uniform battledress top and was bareheaded, except for the last one in which he had on an army beret, worn at a more rakish angle than regulations permitted.

Well, McCullum will have to do his best, Finch decided. He's the expert.

Nancy Fowler had come to stand behind his chair and was also looking at the photographs over his shoulder.

'They're a good likeness?' he asked, turning round to her. He saw her expression had softened and there was a sadness in her face.

'Oh, yes. They're the spitting image of Ron.'

She pointed to the centre photograph.

'I like that one the best. I wanted him to have an enlargement done and he promised he would but he never did.'

He noticed she was holding a piece of paper folded up small in one hand and he nodded towards it.

'Another photograph?' he asked. 'May I see it?'

She hesitated before handing it over.

'You can look if you like. It's not such a good picture of Ron, though.'

As he opened it out, he saw it was a newspaper cutting, old and well-handled, the paper already turning yellow, that contained a photograph of Ron and Betty Lovell on their wedding day. It was three-quarters length and showed them standing in what appeared to be a doorway, Ron wearing army uniform, Betty in a short-sleeved dress and a little hat, carrying a bunch of flowers in one hand while with the other she was clinging to his arm and leaning towards him, perhaps in order for both of them to be in the picture, her hair, shoulder-length and softly curled, touching his sleeve.

He could understand why Nancy Fowler had not thought it a good picture of Ron. He was unsmiling this time, staring out of the photograph with a surly look, more like his brother Geoff. Betty Lovell's face, younger, prettier, wore a nervous half-smile.

The caption below it read: 'Local Girl Weds Soldier'. It was followed by a short account of the wedding that Finch read through quickly.

'Miss Elizabeth Mary Walsh was married on Saturday to Sapper Ronald Lovell, stationed locally with the Royal Engineers.

'The bride, who wore a dress of blue flowered nylon voile, with a matching hat and carried a bunch of pink carnations, was given away by Mr Terence Bright, manager of the White Hart hotel where Miss Walsh worked as a waitress.

'After a reception at the White Hart, where the bridal pair were presented with a canteen of cutlery by the staff, the couple left for a short honeymoon in Devon.'

It was evidently a cutting from a Dorsetshire newspaper and Finch asked curiously, 'How did you get hold of it?'

'It just arrived by post one day,' she replied, her mouth twisting wryly. 'No letter with it, but the envelope had a Dorset postmark so you can guess who sent it.'

'Ron?' Finch asked quietly.

'Hadn't the bloody nerve to write and say he'd got married

465

so he sent the cutting instead. Do you think she's pretty?' she added unexpectedly.

Finch studied the photograph with apparent seriousness, aware he was on dangerous ground.

'In a way, yes, I suppose she is,' he admitted, but with the right show of reluctance.

'A bit washed-out looking, if you ask me,' Nancy said in a hard, positive voice. 'One of them pale blondes, but he always was a sucker for fair hair. She hooked him, mind.'

'Did she? How?'

Finch looked interested.

'How do you think?' Nancy asked scornfully. 'The usual way. Got pregnant so he had to marry her. I could have caught him the same way, if I'd wanted to, but I was only seventeen at the time and my dad would have beaten hell out of me. A right sod, my old man was. It's different today, though, isn't it? Bits of kids sleeping around, having babies. It's all wrong.'

There was a moralising tone in her voice that was genuine enough.

'She hasn't got a child, has she?' Finch asked sharply, wondering if this was another secret of the Lovell household that he hadn't yet uncovered.

'Miscarried,' Nancy told him. 'Had a couple more misses, too, after that one. They took her into hospital with the last and did something so that she couldn't have any more.' She made a vague, embarrassed gesture in the region of her own stomach, indicating an operation. 'Said it'd kill her if she did. Ron told me. Mind you, I felt sorry for her in a way. She was only a kid herself and Ron wasn't much help. He'd started drinking again. "You ought to be home looking after her," I told him. But he wouldn't listen. It wasn't long after she'd had the operation that he cleared out. "I've had about bloody enough," he said, "what with her sick half the time and Geoff ordering me about. I'll write," he said. But he never did.'

'So you don't know where he went?'

'If I did, I'd've gone after him,' she said promptly. 'It was me he should have married, anyway, not her. I'd've seen he kept out of trouble.'

'Trouble?' Finch asked. 'Was there some sort of trouble?'

'Oh, nothing much. He got drunk a few times, that's all. Being young, he didn't know how to hold his drink. And he got put on a couple of charges when he was in the army, once for having a punch-up with another soldier. He was quick-tempered, see. But he'd've been all right with me. I understood him.'

It was said with the absolute assurance of a woman who believes in the reforming power of love.

''Stead of which,' she went on, 'he marries *her* and I marry someone who clears off and leaves me with a couple of kids to bring up on my own and no money. Still, that's life, I suppose.'

'You've never met her?' Finch asked.

'No and I don't want to.'

Finch said nothing, although he understood her feelings. In Nancy Fowler's eyes, Betty Lovell had done the inexcusable thing of taking away her man. He thought of Betty, exhausted, her face drawn down to the bone, and saw the irony of it all.

'Still,' Nancy Fowler was saying with a triumphant air, 'he left her, too, in the end, didn't he?'

'Yes,' Finch agreed. 'He did.'

He had suddenly had enough and he got to his feet. There were other questions he wanted to ask but they could wait until another occasion.

'If I may keep the photographs for a few days, Mrs Fowler?' he asked, deliberately using formal, official language.

'If you like. But what do I say to Geoff when he comes for them?'

'I'll see that they're returned to you before then.'

'Well, you know where to find me; either here or round at the Blue Boar.'

'I'd be grateful if you didn't say anything to Mr Lovell,' he went on. 'There's no need for him to know at this stage.'

She shrugged.

'Please yourself. I'll just hand them over, then, and keep my mouth shut.'

She saw him to the door.

'You'll let me know when you find Ron?' she asked, with the same eagerness that she had shown before.

467

'Of course,' he assured her blandly.

'He might . . .'

She laughed suddenly, looking young and happy, but she didn't finish the sentence.

Come back to her, Finch supposed she meant.

As he thanked her politely for her trouble, he saw her colour up with pleasure. It was probably the first time for years that anyone had shown her that kind of courtesy and, as he walked away, he felt something of the same compassion towards her that he felt for Betty Lovell, the other woman in Ron's life.

11

All the same, the interview with Nancy Fowler had left a
sour taste in his mouth and later, when he joined the other
two in the saloon bar of the Blue Boar, he was relieved that
Kyle's presence made it impossible to discuss the interview at
length with Boyce, except for a brief and hurried explanation
in the few moments while they were alone at the table when
the constable lingered at the counter buying cigarettes.

Finch was still feeling angry and obscurely guilty. Angry
with her for the mess she had managed to make of her life;
the dirt and confusion that surrounded her; the futility of it
all. Angry with Ron Lovell who had walked into her life and
out again with no thought of the damage he was doing. Angry
with himself for reacting in so personal a way.

He found the guilt less easy to rationalise, except he felt he
had used her and, quite unwittingly, raised her hopes that
Ron Lovell might one day come back to her. But even that
exasperated him. It had all the ingredients of cheap, romantic
fiction and he knew that the reality would be very different
from the dream.

Kyle joined them at the table and the talk shifted to other
matters. Finch began slowly to recover his good humour
and, by the time they returned to headquarters, most of the
oppressive effect of Nancy Fowler's personality had lifted.

'There you are!' he said with a triumphant air, spreading
the photographs out on the desk for Boyce's inspection. 'Ron
Lovell!'

'And you got them off that woman Geoff Lovell met in the
pub?' Boyce asked, picking them up to look at them.

'Yes. Nancy Fowler. Evidently an old flame of Ronnie's. In fact, she was hoping he would marry her, but he married Betty instead.'

He pointed to the newspaper cutting.

'There's a picture of them on their wedding day. Read the bit underneath and see if you can find anything odd about it.'

Boyce read it through, muttering every third word aloud to himself. When he had finished, Finch asked, 'Well?'

'Nothing much that I can see,' Boyce replied, 'except it strikes me it was a bit rushed. "Short honeymoon spent in Devon." It doesn't sound exactly lavish. *He* doesn't look too pleased, either,' he added, indicating Lovell's sullen face.

'Shotgun wedding,' Finch explained briefly. 'Betty Lovell was pregnant. She lost the baby later and couldn't have any more.'

Some of the angry pity he had felt earlier in the evening returned to him and he broke off suddenly. Boyce, unaware of this, was saying, 'In that case, it's safe for her and Geoff to have an affair, if that's what they're doing. There'd be no risk of her having a child.'

'That's true,' agreed Finch. 'But to get back to the cutting – there's nothing about it that seems odd?'

Boyce shook his head.

'No mention of her parents,' Finch explained, 'even though it says "Local Girl Weds Soldier" under the photograph. And she was given away by the manager of the hotel where she worked.'

'Perhaps her people didn't approve, especially if she was pregnant,' Boyce said, without much interest. 'I've known it happen – to a girl I went to school with. Her parents washed their hands, as they say. Didn't turn up at the church and her mother used to pass her in the street and not speak. Daft.'

'It could be like that, I suppose,' Finch replied. 'I'll ask Nancy Fowler when I take the photos back. She may know something. From what she said, I gather she knew Ron before he went into the army and started seeing him again after he came out, although by that time he was married to Betty. According to her, he was fed up with the way things were going on the farm; fed up with his marriage, too, and told her he was clearing out, although she denied knowing where he went. And I've got good reason to believe her. She'd've gone with him if she'd known. She did let drop one interesting piece of information, though, and I'd like you to check on it tomorrow. In fact, if I'd had my wits about me, I might have tumbled to it before, from the gossip we've already picked up about Ron Lovell. It's possible he'd been in trouble with the police. Nancy said he'd been drunk a few times. So get hold of the records, will you, and see if he's ever been booked? She also mentioned he'd been put on a couple of charges while he was in the army.'

'I've sent for his army records,' Boyce put in. 'They're not through yet.'

'Right. There's something else, too, that's worth following up. When I see McCullum tomorrow, I'll get him to make an extra copy of one of the photographs to send up to the Yard for the Police Gazette, together with a description. Some other Force may have him on their books and recognise him. If he was in trouble with the law down here, the chances are he may have been picked up since. It could be a way of finding out where he went after he left the farm. Besides, it might explain why he came back, if that's what he did; a point we haven't considered yet. We've got a pretty good idea why he left. He was tired of the farm, his marriage, the life he was leading. Given those reasons, why did he come back? He couldn't have expected anything would be drastically changed. But supposing the police somewhere were looking for him? That could have been enough to force him home. It was the excuse, too, that Geoff Lovell gave to Nancy Fowler when he asked for the photographs: that Ron was in trouble with the police and he didn't want them falling into our hands. There might be some truth in it.'

'It shows one thing,' Boyce pointed out. 'Geoff Lovell has something to hide. He was damned quick off the mark in trying to get his hands on the photographs before we did.'

'Oh, yes,' Finch agreed. 'The man's no fool. I think I'll pay him another visit tomorrow. We've obviously got him worried and I think the time's ripe to stir things up a bit more. I'd like you to come with me this time: it'll make it look more official. But leave the talking to me. I want you to keep your eyes open, though. We'll tell him we want to measure the distance from his farm to the field where the body was found. How does that strike you as a reason for calling on him?'

'Feeble. It's something a couple of constables could do on their own.'

'Good. That's just what I hope Lovell will think, too, so we may get him even more rattled. By the way, I don't want the photos mentioned. He's not to know I've seen Nancy Fowler and borrowed them from her.'

He gave them a final glance before putting them away in the drawer.

'Let's shut up shop, Tom. We've done all we can for today. Tomorrow, I'll get McCullum to look them over and, with a bit of luck, we might be a step nearer proving who it is we've dug up.'

The next morning, as he spread the photographs out again for McCullum to examine, Finch tried to conceal his impatience as the man bent his long body over them, studying them intently through a powerful magnifying glass that he had taken from the bulging pockets of his jacket.

'Any good?' Finch was forced to ask at last.

McCullum merely grunted and went on looking. Presently he put the glass down and said grudgingly. 'The newspaper photograph is out; the definition's too poor. But the smaller ones are not too bad. I should be able to make a decent enlargement from one of those.'

'A life-size one?' Finch asked, trying not to sound too eager.

McCullum pursed his lips doubtfully.

'Well, now, that depends. There's not a lot of detail in any of them that I could use to make exact measurements.'

'What about the clothing?' Finch persisted, determined not to be put off by McCullum's lack of enthusiasm. 'The battledress would be standard issue. Couldn't you measure something on that? The collar, for instance, or the shoulder tabs?'

'Not one that would stand up as exact evidence, and I take it that's what you're looking for? We're dealing here with two different dimensions, you understand; the flat, two-dimensional

photograph and the living, three-dimensional man. Look at
your own jacket,' he added, taking Finch by the lapels. 'I
could take, say, the width of the collar and then measure it
again with you wearing it, but I very much doubt if the two
measurements would be exactly the same. You get me?'

'Yes,' Finch replied, sounding subdued, 'I get you. So there's
nothing in any of the photographs that you could use?'

'I didn't say that,' McCullum snapped, with the obstinate
expression of a man who doesn't like to have his decisions
made for him. Picking up the magnifying glass, he resumed
his study and Finch, realising he would take his time, waited
in silence.

'What regiment was he in?' McCullum asked suddenly.

The question was so unexpected that, for a moment, Finch
couldn't remember what Geoff Lovell had told him. Then he
recalled it.

'The Royal Engineers.'

'Then I could have good news for you,' McCullum went on,
permitting his face to break into a slow smile. 'See the last
photograph? The one in which he's wearing the army beret?
You get me a Royal Engineer's cap badge and I might be able
to make you that blow-up. The detail in the photograph is quite
good and if I used a lay head to get the exact angle, it might
work. Lighting it will be tricky though,' he added, lapsing into
his usual melancholy at the thought of it.

'That is good news,' Finch replied, subduing his jubilation.
'Mind if I have a look?'

McCullum handed him the glass and Finch held it over the
photograph. The badge leapt forward in amazing detail. He
could make out the wreath of leaves that surrounded it and
the crown that surmounted the central motto. Fascinated by
this new, enlarged dimension, he moved the glass across the
rest of the face, seeing the eyes and then the mouth in single,
disembodied close up. He turned it next on the newspaper
cutting and saw at once what McCullum meant by poor
definition. The individual grey and black dots with which
the picture was composed became, under the powerful lens,
too enlarged and broke up the outlines of the features. Betty's
face became a mere chiaroscuro of shaded circles in which

473

the details were lost. Holding the lens further away, he tried to adjust the magnification so that the nervous half-smile, diffident and shy, was in better focus.

Suddenly he stopped.

'McCullum,' he said quickly, 'take a look here.'

McCullum took the glass from him and bent over the cutting.

'The girl's neck,' Finch explained. 'What's she wearing round it?'

'Looks like a chain of some sort,' McCullum replied, after a maddening pause.

'Can you see what's on the end of it?'

McCullum moved the lens down a fraction of an inch.

'No. Whatever it is, it's hidden below the neck of her dress.'

'Damn!' Finch said softly.

McCullum looked up.

'Something important?'

'It could be. Remember that crucifix that was found in the grave? Could it be the chain to that?'

McCullum shrugged.

'It could be. I wouldn't like to commit myself, though.'

'It's gone up to forensic in London for a detailed examination. They'll send photographs of it once it's been cleaned up. Any chance you could make an enlargement of the chain the girl's wearing for comparison?'

'I could certainly enlarge it, but if you're hoping to prove they're the same by comparing the links, you're out of luck. The definition's too poor for me to raise that sort of detail.'

It was exactly what Finch had been hoping for, although he kept the disappointment out of his face. It was expecting too much. But at least it proved that Betty Lovell had possessed a chain. Whether or not a cross had hung on the end of it was another matter.

McCullum had put away the magnifying glass and was gathering up the photographs.

'If that's all I'll get started on the enlargement as soon as I get the badge. Anything else you want done with them?'

'I'd like several copies made of all of them – I've got to return the originals – and an extra one to send up to the Yard for the Police Gazette. It had better be one of the full-face photos. I'll leave the choice to you. How soon can you let me have them?'

'On your desk by lunch time?' McCullum replied. 'The life-size blow-up will take longer, say a couple of days.'

At the door he added, 'I'll do my best with the chain but I'm not promising anything.'

He went out, almost colliding with Boyce who came bustling in, looking pleased with himself and announcing, 'I've checked with the Harlsdon police. Lovell *was* picked up by them, three times altogether: twice for being drunk and disorderly; once for riding that motor-bike of his without due care and attention. He was fined on all three occasions. So you could be right about him being picked up by the police since.'

'It's worth a try,' agreed Finch.

'What did McCullum have to say?'

'There's a good chance he can make a life-size enlargement for us, using the cap badge in one of the small photos. So get hold of Kyle and send him out to borrow a Royal Engineers' badge from somewhere. The local army recruiting office ought to have one. After that, when McCullum's finished making them, I want him to take a copy of one of the photos up to the Yard for the Gazette. I'll draft out a description to go with it. That's one line of inquiry we can put into operation straightaway. The life-size enlargement won't be ready for a couple of days. But, as soon as it is, we can start work on the crucial issue in this case – proving whether or not it is Ronnie Lovell's body.'

Boyce looked at Finch covertly, aware of a peevish air about the Inspector that he couldn't account for. After all, with the investigation at last showing signs of getting off the ground, he ought to be more pleased.

'Something bugging you?' he asked tentatively.

'Yes, blast it, there is!' Finch replied with more warmth. 'The question of the crucifix has cropped up again.' He explained briefly how he had noticed a chain round Betty Lovell's neck in the newspaper photograph. 'Not that McCullum holds out

475

much hope of enlarging it so that we can compare it with the chain found in the grave,' he added.

'Well?' Boyce asked, puzzled why this small detail should cause the Inspector so much uneasiness.

'I still don't see where it fits in,' Finch explained.

It was only part of the truth, the rest of which he was reluctant to admit even to himself. Now that the case had begun to move out of the area of mere speculation and theory into the possibility of proof, he found himself in the unusual position of wishing to hold back. It was quite irrational, he told himself. He had no business to feel this way. And yet, their faces kept rising up in his mind to disconcert him: Betty's peeled down to the bone; Lovell's dark with a weight of brooding unhappiness that Finch could only guess at.

'Did you ask Betty Lovell if she's owned a cross and chain?' Boyce was asking.

'No, I didn't,' Finch replied snappily. At times he found Boyce's literal-mindedness a source of exasperation. 'I only saw her alone for a few minutes. I'll make a point, though, of asking her this afternoon.'

'I still don't think it's got any bearing on the case,' Boyce went on, hoping mistakenly that by playing down its importance he might put the Inspector in a more cheerful frame of mind.

'Why not?' Finch asked.

'Well, look at it logically. In the first place, there's no proof that it is a cross and chain she's wearing in that photograph, let alone the same one. Women wear all sorts of things round their necks – those pendant doo-dahs, for instance. Secondly, it wasn't found on the body, only near it. And what the hell was a cross and chain doing there anyway? Had he pinched it, hoping to flog it? But, according to Pardoe, it's only silver-plated, so he couldn't have hoped to get much for it. Or had he torn it off her neck, in a struggle, say? Got it tangled up in his clothing? That doesn't sound very likely to me and, even if he had, it'd still be on him.'

'It could have been placed there,' Finch said slowly. The impression that he had received when he stood alone in the field at dusk returned to him, only dimly, and all he was left with was a fleeting feeling of something significant that was vaguely connected with death and darkness, ritual and sacrifice, that was gone as soon as he tried to analyse it.

'By her?' Boyce asked.

'I don't know. By one of them.'

Boyce sniffed disbelievingly.

'Why?'

'As a token.'

'Of what?'

Finch felt exasperation rising.

'I don't know. Love. Family feeling. People bury their dead with all sorts of keepsakes: rings, love letters, locks of hair.'

'From what I've heard of him, I can't see Ronnie Lovell inspiring that kind of devotion,' Boyce objected.

'But we don't know,' Finch pointed out. 'He was, after all, Betty's husband and Geoff's brother. They must have felt something towards him. Or it could be meant for what it is, a Christian symbol. We've got good reason to believe that somebody went to the trouble of laying the body out.'

He offered the explanation reluctantly, knowing Boyce would have little sympathy with it.

'But they're not religious, are they?' Boyce demanded. 'They certainly don't seem to be churchgoers, or we'd've heard about it from someone. Instead, all we *have* heard is that they keep themselves to themselves and don't mix in the village.'

'That doesn't mean the crucifix had no significance,' Finch replied. He began to feel he was arguing intangibles. 'Look, I'll tell you what we'll do. We'll drop in at Stebbing's farm first and ask Wheeler. He might know if Betty ever wore a crucifix.'

But later that afternoon, when they called at the farm, Wheeler wasn't much help. He had been sent for from the fields and obviously resented this and Finch's renewed inquiries into what he considered a trivial matter.

'No, I ain't seen her wearing one,' he said. 'Is that all you've got me back here to ask?'

'You're sure?' Finch pressed him.

'I've told you, ain't I? She never wore nothing in the way of jewellery, except for her wedding ring.'

It was said with an air of angry certainty and yet Finch wasn't convinced. Wheeler didn't strike him as the type of man who would notice that kind of detail about a woman's appearance. Something of this doubt must have showed in his face for Wheeler went on, 'I made a point of looking, see? My mother left some bits and pieces, a couple of rings and stuff like that. I was going to ask her . . .'

He broke off and shot Finch a furious glance, aware that he had said too much in his eagerness to prove himself right. Finch kept his face bland as he asked the next question.

'Did any of the Lovell family ever go to church?'

'How the hell should I know?' Wheeler retorted and began stumping away across the yard, shouting back over his shoulder, 'Ask Stebbing. He'll be able to tell you.'

Finch went to look for Stebbing and found him hanging about in one of the barns, having been politely but firmly excluded from the interview with Wheeler. He came forward eagerly as Finch approached, putting the Inspector in mind of a large dog bounding up, tail wagging, for a little attention.

'You wanted me?' he asked.

'It's only a small point,' Finch replied. 'Wheeler said you might be able to help. It's this: do any of the Lovells attend church?'

'I can see why Wheeler suggested you ask me,' Stebbing replied, looking serious and important. 'I go regularly to church myself. Never miss a Sunday if I can help it. After all, when you come to live in a small community, like a village, it's as well to join in, make yourself known. Not that I believe it all, mind. Funnily enough, I was discussing that very point with the vicar only the other day . . .'

'But have you ever seen any of the Lovells at church?' Finch interrupted him.

'No,' Stebbing admitted, reluctant to come to the point. 'No. I can't say I have.'

'Thank you, Mr Stebbing,' Finch replied in his formal voice, walking away. Even then the man couldn't resist following him across the yard and, planting himself in front of Finch, announced with anxious officiousness, 'I've been in touch with Mr Rose. He's back in my field, with that society of his, digging. That's all right, isn't it? You did say I could tell him.'

'Yes, that's quite all right,' Finch assured him and was about to sidestep round him when he heard distinctly on the hot, still air the far-off sound of a dog barking savagely. He stopped and cocked his head inquiringly.

'That's Lovell's dog, isn't it?' he asked Stebbing.

'Sounds like it,' Stebbing agreed. 'I've got used to it so I don't take much notice when it starts up. It carries on like that two or three times a day sometimes. It's a good job there's a fair distance between the two farms or it could be a damned nuisance.'

'Two or three times a day?' Finch asked. 'But the Lovells can't have that number of people calling at the farm?'

Stebbing shrugged.

'I shouldn't think so. Maybe it just likes barking its head off from time to time. Some dogs are like that. Anything'll set them off. A bit of paper blowing past. A bird. A door slamming. Mind you, they're not much good as guard dogs in my opinion.'

Finch made no reply, except to wish Stebbing goodbye, and walked on to meet Boyce who was waiting in the car.

'Any luck?' he asked, as Finch got into the seat beside him.

'Not on the cross and chain. Wheeler was quite adamant he'd never seen Betty Lovell wearing one and I've got good reason to believe him. He was thinking of offering her some of his mother's pieces of jewellery and, cautious man that he is, he had a good look first to see what she owned herself before thinking of parting with them. And Stebbing, who evidently likes to think of himself as a pillar of the community, hasn't seen any of them in church, so that's a dead end.'

Boyce, leaning forward to start the engine, tried unsuccessfully to keep a smug, I-told-you-so expression off his face.

'There was one odd little incident, though,' Finch went on. 'Did you notice it?'

'Only the look on Wheeler's face when you were talking to him,' Boyce replied with happy malice. 'That man hates your guts.'

'I know,' Finch replied equably. 'I've rumbled his secret and he knows it. No, I was referring to something else. Did you hear Lovell's dog barking?'

'Can't say I did,' Boyce replied indifferently, turning the car into the narrow lane. 'What of it?'

'You'll see in a minute. I'm going to try a little experiment. When we pull up at Lovell's farm, I want both of us to stay in the car for a couple of minutes.'

'All right,' Boyce agreed. 'I don't see the point but . . .'

'You will,' Finch promised him.

They were approaching the entrance to the farm and, at Finch's directions, Boyce drew the car off the road, bumping it up on to the grass verge and then, switching off the engine, remained seated behind the wheel.

'Hear anything?' Finch asked.

Boyce listened. There was no sound except for the faint soughing of a light wind in the topmost branches of the trees and the piercing song of a lark somewhere out of sight in the dazzle of the sky.

'Not a thing,' Boyce replied.

'Come on,' Finch told him and, getting out of the car, slammed the door hard shut behind him. Again he stopped to listen but there was still no sound. Smiling, he beckoned to Boyce and began walking towards the gate. The sergeant followed, feeling a bit of a fool and wondering what all the pantomime was about.

At the gate, they paused, looking down into the yard. The concrete was blindingly white and almost shadowless in the sun; empty, too, apart from the black labrador that, with ears erect and scruff already rising, was beginning to stalk, stiff-legged, up the driveway towards them, its lips drawn back in a silent snarl.

Finch watched it carefully and then, putting his hand on the gate, shook it so that the chain and padlock rattled. The next instant, the dog broke into a frenzy of barking and came racing towards them to fling itself against the bars.

'Christ!' exclaimed Boyce, stepping back in alarm.

'See what I mean?' Finch shouted above the din. 'The dog didn't bark until I touched the gate and it looked as if I were coming in. But, according to Stebbing, it sometimes barks two or three times a day. So I ask myself, why?'

Boyce was about to shout back an answer when the figure of Geoff Lovell emerged from behind the barn, walked into the centre of the yard and, having surveyed them deliberately for a few seconds, his hands on his hips, began walking slowly towards them.

'Awkward devil,' Finch said happily and Boyce looked at him in surprise at the note of admiration in his voice. Now that the inquiry was under way, the Inspector had lost any sense of a special sympathy for Lovell, although he watched him with lively interest as he approached them.

'Take your cue from me,' Finch added quickly but Boyce had no time to reply, except to give a brief nod of agreement, before Geoff Lovell was at the gate, looking at them over it with a surly expression.

12

'What do you want this time?' he asked.

'If you'll call the dog off, I'll explain,' Finch replied.

At first, Lovell seemed reluctant to agree, glancing back at the house as if to assure himself of something and then, seizing the dog by the collar, he began dragging it down the slope towards the barn, where he fastened it to its chain. He seemed as if he were about to walk back towards them to speak to them over the gate but Finch had already forestalled him by climbing nimbly over it and, dropping down on the other side, walked forwards to meet him, leaving Boyce to follow more cautiously.

'Had visitors already this afternoon?' Finch asked Lovell pleasantly as they met in the yard.

'What do you mean?' Lovell replied belligerently.

'I heard the dog barking a little earlier.'

'My dog?'

'It must have been. There's no other dog along this lane, is there?'

Lovell didn't reply and Finch cocked his head expectantly. At last, Lovell said slowly, 'Oh yes, I remember. It started up barking when Charlie took the tractor out. Something fell off the back of the trailer.'

That's a lie for a start, Finch thought. If I heard the dog barking, I'm damned sure I'd've heard the tractor as well. Besides, it's not likely that something would fall off the back of it two or three times a day.

But, at least, it told him where Charlie was and Finch suspected that Lovell had deliberately sent him out to the fields in order to get him out of the way in case he returned to ask more questions. Lovell, then, had glanced back at the house to make sure that Betty Lovell was also safely out of sight.

By this time, Boyce had joined them and Finch introduced him.

'Two of you this time,' Lovell remarked with a sneer. 'Well, what do you want?'

'To measure the distance from your yard to Stebbing's field,' Finch explained.

'Is that all?' Lovell demanded angrily. 'Couldn't you have got it off an Ordnance Survey map without bothering me?'

It was a shrewd question and Finch silently applauded the man's quick-wittedness.

'It's the time it would take to walk it rather than the actual length I'm interested in,' he replied, improvising quickly. 'So, if you don't mind, Mr Lovell . . .'

As he was speaking, he began walking towards the end of the yard where a gate separated it from the adjoining field, giving Lovell no option but to follow. At the gate, Finch paused and ostentatiously looked at his watch, jotting down the time in a small notebook that he took from his inside pocket. Lovell watched these official-seeming proceedings with a sardonic smile but Finch thought he saw a look of alarm in his eyes.

The gate was not padlocked and Finch unfastened it and walked on, up the gradient of the field that led away from the farm, Boyce at his heels and Lovell, after a final backward look, following after them, although halfway up the slope he caught up with Finch.

'It must have been quite a job, carrying a dead body up here, if this is the route it came,' Finch remarked to Boyce over Lovell's head.

The sergeant, already out of breath, grunted a reply. Lovell, too, made no comment, although his face took on a heavy, obstinate look.

'Quite a view, too,' Finch went on, pausing at the top, as if casually, to glance back.

The farm lay below them, cradled in its surrounding trees, the old tiles on the house and the barns a warm red in the full sunlight. Through a gap in the trees, Finch caught sight of a woman moving in the kitchen garden behind the house. She stooped, picked something up at her feet and then held her arms above her head. A white oblong appeared above her. She stooped again and lifted her arms and another white oblong appeared alongside the first. Betty Lovell was pegging out sheets on a washing-line.

Finch made no comment but, turning away, went on into the second field where the slope gradually flattened out so that, although they were still walking uphill, the going was easier. It was pasture land in which a few cows were grazing over to their right. Ahead of them ran the boundary hedge that separated Lovell's land from Stebbing's and, as they drew nearer, figures could be seen working in the adjoining meadow, Hollowfield. It was Rose and his archaeological society back on the job, as Stebbing had already informed Finch.

It hadn't taken them long to resume their dig, he thought, although he could understand Rose's anxiety to finish excavating the site in the limited time he had available.

The field, busy now with people and activity, presented a different scene to the one when Finch had stood alone in the centre of it, with the light fading. A couple of brightly-coloured tents, one orange, one blue, had been re-erected at the far side, near the copse, while in the middle distance men and women were at work again in the area where the post-holes had been discovered, shovelling soil and wheeling it away in barrows. Closer to the hedge, the oblong of exposed earth showed the site of the grave. Finch noticed that no one was working on the test trench that ran along the bottom of it.

'Hard work,' Finch commented to Boyce.

'Must be,' the sergeant replied.

Lovell still said nothing but stood awkwardly, a little to one side of them, like an outsider who has been excluded from a conversation.

'It'd need a pick to get started on ground like that. Wouldn't you agree, Mr Lovell?' Finch went on, turning suddenly to address him. 'A spade wouldn't touch it. The earth's as hard and as dry as a bone.'

He stamped with one foot and they heard the parched soil ring with a dull, hollow sound under his heel.

Lovell's face had gone dark, the angry flush extending down his throat into the open neck of his shirt. But when he spoke, his voice was cool enough, almost drawling.

'I wouldn't know. I've never had any call to dig in this field. Nor in Stebbing's either,' he replied.

Top marks for nerve, Finch thought. He certainly doesn't rattle very easily.

'Somebody did,' he pointed out. 'Somebody dug a grave there. You know, ever since the body was found, it's puzzled me why that particular field was chosen. Have you any idea why it was?'

Lovell scowled.

'Why should I? If you ask me, it's a bit of rough, old pasture, not worth bothering with.'

'But I understand Mr Stebbing thinks it's worth bothering with. He's going to plough it up in the autumn.'

He watched Lovell's face closely for his reaction to this particular piece of information, but Lovell only shrugged.

'More fool him, then. It's not worth it. He'll have trouble getting the water off it for a start. Still, if he's willing to spend money putting in land drains, that's his business.'

'He's obviously spent money on fencing it off,' Finch said, pointing to the new-looking posts and barbed wire.

'Probably thought my cattle might stray,' Lovell replied. His voice held a note of amused contempt and he was more relaxed now that the conversation had shifted on to farming matters.

I'll get him to loosen up a bit more before I have another go at him, Finch decided.

'The fence been up long?' he asked casually.

'A year. Eighteen months.'

'And before that there was just the hedge and the trees?'

'And a bit of a ditch,' Lovell added.

'Not very deep, I gather, for Mr Stebbing had it dug out on his side.'

'Could be,' Lovell conceded grudgingly.

'You hadn't bothered much with it?'

Lovell scowled, as if angered by this apparent slur on his farming efficiency.

'It isn't so much a question of bothering,' he replied, 'it's time. I've got more important things to do about the place than clear out ditches.'

'Of course,' Finch agreed. 'There's only you and Charlie while Stebbing's got quite a lot of farm help.'

Lovell didn't reply and, after a pause, Finch picked the subject up again himself.

'So, until a year or eighteen months ago, the two fields were separated by a ditch, not very deep, and a hedge that had quite a few gaps in it?'

If Lovell saw the point in the question, it didn't show in his face. He merely lifted his shoulders indifferently.

'Yes. I reckon it was.'

'Rough pasture,' Finch went on musingly, looking again at the adjoining field. 'Good land for growing crops would you say?'

'No. Like I said, I wouldn't bother with it. He'll have to spend a packet on fertiliser to get it back in good heart. But then, he's got the cash, hasn't he?'

By 'he', Finch took it Lovell meant Stebbing.

'Poor soil?' he asked.

'Clay under a spit of top-soil.'

'So I noticed,' Finch said promptly, feeling it was time he closed in. Lovell was now sufficiently off guard. 'It couldn't have been easy, could it, digging that grave? Perhaps that's why it was relatively shallow. Only four feet deep instead of the usual six, although there were signs that someone had gone to a lot of trouble to lay the body out decently. Strange that.'

He assumed his listening stance, head on one side, a bright, interested look on his face, but Lovell wasn't to be drawn. Instead, he countered with a question of his own.

'I thought you wanted to find out the time it took to walk here?' he asked in a jeering voice. 'I haven't seen you look at your bloody watch since we started out.'

It was quick thinking on his part and even quicker on Boyce's who interrupted to remark, 'I've kept a note of the time, Mr Lovell. It took us exactly twenty-eight and a half minutes.'

Finch smiled broadly as he took out his notebook and wrote it down. He was thoroughly enjoying himself. The quick thrust and parry of the encounter was something he met only too rarely. It was more often a matter of plodding through an interview, question by question, trying to elicit facts.

'Longer, of course,' he couldn't resist adding, as he stowed the notebook away, 'if you're carrying a dead weight.'

Lovell looked from one to the other of them. For a moment, Finch thought he was going to lose his temper. The broad barrel of his chest rose against the thin cotton shirt as he drew in huge lungsful of air. The Inspector watched him warily. The fire that he suspected burnt under that heavy, brooding exterior seemed about to break through. But the expected outburst didn't come. Lovell subsided slowly.

'If you've finished,' he said in his usual surly voice, 'I've got better things to do than stand about yattering with you two.'

They walked back across the fields in silence, Lovell a little ahead of them moving with a deliberate and yet not clumsy gait. Finch watched his back with interest. The broad, muscular shoulders rose and fell with a steady rhythm, his feet were planted with a heavy and yet easy assurance on the ground, as if he were familiar with every inch of the earth he trod on. There was a fine physical balance in his whole body and the kind of economy of movement that a man, used to hard, outdoor work and heavy lifting, learns to assume.

Yes, Finch thought, he'd manage a dead body all right. He'd sling it over his shoulder like a sack of grain.

He pondered, too, the relevance of the information he had picked up that afternoon in conversation with Lovell.

First of all, as he had suspected, the fence had been put up and the ditch dug out fairly recently, probably since the body was buried, which meant that carrying it from Lovell's land into the field on Stebbing's side of the boundary would have been comparatively easy, if that was the way it had come. That much seemed fairly conclusive.

Whether or not Lovell had known that the field was due to go under the plough he was not so certain about, although it seemed unlikely, in view of the strained relationship between the two men, that Stebbing had told Lovell of his intentions. It followed, then, that Lovell could have believed that the field would remain as it was: rough pasture. He certainly didn't himself think it was worth cultivating.

The third point he had to consider was Lovell's knowledge that the field consisted of clay covered by a spit of top-soil, although he had denied ever digging in it. But wasn't it possible that he'd know that anyway? After all, he was a farmer. It would be his business to know what lay under his fields and the land that ran adjacent to his wouldn't be all that different to his own. As far as evidence went, that point was inconclusive.

The relationship between Lovell and Stebbing also intrigued him. The deepest animosity seemed to be on Lovell's side and Finch wondered whether there was more to it than mere exasperation towards an over-friendly neighbour. It could be jealousy, of course. Lovell wouldn't be human if he didn't feel some envy for Stebbing who, although a relative newcomer to the district, had capital to invest in his land while Lovell was struggling to keep his rundown farm going.

And yet Finch wasn't convinced that this was the main reason. Envy is a mean emotion and Finch was certain that, whatever else Lovell might be as a man, he wasn't a mean one. No, Stebbing had touched something deeper and stronger in Lovell than mere jealousy and Finch thought he knew what it was: his pride. Had Stebbing suggested, as Finch had done, only in stronger terms, that Lovell wasn't much good as a farmer? Or had he antagonised Lovell in some other way? Knowing Stebbing, with his officiousness, his know-all air and his superb lack of tact, and Lovell with his moody touchiness, it wouldn't take much for Stebbing to catch him on a raw spot, without possibly even being aware of it.

But one thing Finch was sure of, if Lovell had killed his brother, it had been under extreme provocation. Finch had deliberately driven him pretty far that afternoon, almost to the edge of losing his temper, and yet Lovell had held himself in check.

He was sure, too, that if murder had taken place and Lovell had carried the body to that field to bury it, it was for some perfectly sane reason. Lovell wasn't mad, not in any sense of the word, and the choice of the grave site would have been a rational one. But what it was Finch was no nearer to finding out.

By now they had crossed the pasture and, as they approached

the slope above the farm, Finch could see Betty Lovell still busy in the garden behind the house. The line of washing had extended, now taking up more than half its length but, as they jogged down the last field, the angle of view changed slightly and she disappeared from sight behind the massed foliage.

In the yard the dog, that had been lying asleep in a small patch of shadow against the wall, rose to its feet suspiciously, the chain clinking behind it. But it didn't bark. Presumably now they were on the premises and in Lovell's company, it accepted their presence.

Lovell stopped in the centre of the yard.

'You're off now?' he asked.' You've seen all you want?'

He seemed eager to see them go.

'Not quite,' Finch replied. 'There's one small question I'd like to ask Mrs Lovell.'

Lovell shot a backward look at the house.

'I don't know that she's in,' he muttered.

'She's in the garden behind the house and I want a word with her,' Finch said in his official voice.

Lovell turned back slowly to face him. The anger had burnt away, leaving him resigned and subdued.

'I've told you before, I don't want her bothered,' he said quietly.

'I shan't bother her,' Finch assured him. Without wanting to, he found himself responding to Lovell's mood. His own exultation had died down and he felt his compassion for the man return. 'You can be present when I speak to her, if you want to.'

Lovell looked at him, searching his face with troubled eyes.

'All right,' he conceded reluctantly and they tramped round the side of the house to the garden at the rear.

It was a long, narrow garden, surrounded on three sides by trees and hedges that formed a close, leafy background, the back wall of the house enclosing it on the fourth and presenting a curiously blank façade, the steep slope of the roof sweeping down to only a few feet above ground level, and windowless except for the small dormer casement of the landing and a skylight, set in the roof and propped open, presumably to let air into the attic.

Looking about him, Finch remembered Wheeler saying that Betty Lovell took care of the garden, as well as the poultry. He could see her influence on it. A path divided the garden into two plots, both of which were carefully tended. There was not a weed to be seen between the neat rows of vegetables. Soft fruit trees at the far end had been swathed in old net curtains to keep off the birds and the edges of the path were planted with herbs, among which Finch recognised chives and parsley.

A washing-line ran the length of the garden, slung between poles, on which pairs of pillowcases, sheets and shirts were hanging, hardly stirring in the hot, still air.

Betty Lovell, unaware of their approach, was in the act of pegging up another shirt that she had taken from a bright red, plastic laundry basket at her feet, shaking out the sleeves as she hung it up and smoothing out the cuffs with the palm of her hand. Finch remembered his mother doing the same, in order to remove as many creases as possible before the shirt dried to make the task of ironing it a little easier.

'Betty!' Lovell called when they were still some distance from her and she turned swiftly towards them. She was startled. Every line of her body expressed tension and alarm. Finch studied her face as they walked towards her. She looked more haggard and exhausted than the last time he had seen her, the shadows under her eyes more pronounced. The blue dress she was wearing accentuated her pallor and her hair, tied back for coolness, gave her face a scraped, bony look. A few loose tendrils hung damply on her forehead.

Finch remembered the young, pretty, tentative girl, clinging closely to the arm of her husband in the wedding photograph and knew that, as a man, he wasn't going to find the interview easy. As a policeman, though, every nerve in him was alert to observe the smallest nuance of voice and expression.

He noticed her eyes went immediately to Lovell's face as they halted in front of her on the path. There was an unspoken question in them. He wasn't quick enough to catch Lovell's answering look but whatever it was there must have been something reassuring in it for her own became more composed.

They make a pair, Finch thought. They don't need words to speak to one another.

And yet he was aware, too, of an undercurrent of something else between them. At first he thought it was hostility, until he realised it was more complex than this. It was more a clash of wills and he wasn't sure that, despite her fragility and seeming docility, Betty Lovell hadn't got the upper hand. Lovell's stance had subtly changed as he stood in front of her. His shoulders were a little rounder, his head held a little further forward as if, by his mere bodily presence, he was trying to placate her. He was, however, quick enough to get in the first word, as if warning her.

'The Inspector'd like a word with you, Betty.'

'Yes?' she asked quickly, turning towards Finch. There was a blind expression in her face, rigid with taut nerves.

'It's a very small point,' Finch said soothingly, trying to calm her down so that the question, when it came, should have the maximum impact. 'Have you ever owned a cross and chain, Mrs Lovell?'

For a second, the blank expression remained and then every muscle in her face jumped. It was an alarming experience, even for Finch who had seen many people on the verge of breaking down. It was as if the whole structure of her face was falling apart, every plane of it twitching into disintegration.

Then Lovell spoke.

'No. She's never owned one.'

Damn him to hell! Finch thought furiously.

'Let her answer for herself,' he told him. But the damage had been done. Betty Lovell had been given the time to recover. Her face tightened up again.

'No, I've never owned one,' she said in a voice that was barely audible. It was almost an exact repetition of Lovell's words.

'What's all this about a cross and chain anyway?' Lovell was asking. He was angry, but he seemed genuinely nonplussed by the question and Finch was sure he knew nothing about it, just as he was equally sure that Betty Lovell did.

'Just a line of inquiry we're following up,' Finch replied.

'Sorry we can't help you,' Lovell said with heavy irony. 'Is that the lot? Or have you any more damn fool questions you want to ask?'

491

There was an elated, confident air about him as if he knew he had got the better of Finch.

'For the moment, yes,' Finch replied.

He looked round for Boyce, who had wandered off to the end of the garden, where he was sauntering about, his hands behind his back, looking at a row of currant bushes with a bored expression. Catching his attention, Finch beckoned and the sergeant strolled back in their direction.

'We'll be off then,' Finch announced. 'I'm sorry we've taken up so much of your time, Mr Lovell.'

Lovell didn't bother to answer and there was nothing Finch could do except walk away, followed by Boyce.

As they reached the yard, the dog stirred again, rising at their approach. It seemed to know Lovell wasn't with them, for it began to growl, only tentatively, as if it wasn't sure how it was expected to react under the circumstances. All the same, they gave it a wide berth as they passed and walked up the rutted drive towards the gate.

'Funny bloke,' Boyce commented as they got into the car.

'Funny lot altogether,' Finch replied. 'And damned close. Lovell's not going to give anything away in a hurry, not even the time of day, if he can help it. And Betty Lovell may be a bundle of nerves, but there's a will of iron under it. Were you there when I asked about the cross and chain?'

'No, I'd wandered off,' Boyce replied negligently but there was a suppressed air of excitement about him that didn't register with Finch at first.

'She denied owning one, but I'm convinced she knows something about it. If Lovell hadn't shoved his oar in . . .'

He broke off, aware of the look on Boyce's face.

'What's up with you?' he asked. 'You look like the cat that's got the cream.'

'Just this,' Boyce replied, grinning broadly and, getting out his wallet, opened it to reveal five fragments of paper, the largest no bigger than a postage stamp and all of them charred along at least one edge.

'Where did you find these?' Finch asked.

'At the bottom of the garden, behind some bushes. There's a kind of rubbish dump there; mostly kitchen waste, old potato peelings and the like, but someone had lit a fire on top of it recently. Most of it was too charred to be recognisable but it had burnt into oblongs, if you get my meaning, like letters or postcards. A few bits near the edge hadn't burnt through and while you lot were talking I picked up what I could reach.'

Finch touched the fragments gingerly. Two were blue in colour with faint lines on them and one still retained part of a shape written in ink.

'These could be bits of letters,' he said. 'It looks like lined writing paper.'

He bent to examine the other pieces. The paper was different in quality and texture, thicker and with a glossy surface that he could feel when he rubbed his finger across them.

'Photographs?' he suggested.

'That's what I reckon,' Boyce agreed. 'And quite a collection of them, too, judging by what was left. Some snapshots, I'd say, and some bigger in size than that, more like studio portraits. One at least had been properly mounted. I saw a bit of deckle edging like the backing card a professional photographer would use but it was too far over for me to reach it.'

'You know what this means?' Finch asked.

'Geoff or Betty Lovell deliberately got rid of them.'

'Yes, and my guess is quite recently, since the last time I called and asked for photographs of Ron. Then Lovell must have realised Nancy Fowler might have some so he rushed over there to get his hands on those as well. And I've no doubt he would have burnt those too, if I hadn't got there first.'

'Destroying evidence,' Boyce pointed out. 'You must admit it looks suspicious.'

'Of course it does!' Finch snapped. 'The whole damned business looks suspicious. And yet . . .'

He bit furiously at his thumbnail.

'Something's not right about it, Tom. It doesn't quite add up, although I can't put my finger on it.'

'What doesn't add up?' Boyce asked. 'It all looks straight-forward enough to me. In fact, what we've found out this afternoon about the burnt photographs would support the theory: Ron Lovell comes home, finds his wife and brother are having an affair, there's a quarrel . . .'

'I'm not sure they *are* having an affair,' Finch broke in.

'But I thought you said the two of them are sharing a bed,' Boyce protested.

'They may be sharing a bed but that doesn't necessarily mean they're lovers.'

It was too subtle for Boyce, who looked both puzzled and outraged.

'I don't get your meaning,' he replied heavily. 'In my book, if two people are sleeping together, it only means one thing. But maybe I'm old-fashioned.'

'It's more complex than that,' Finch tried to explain. He thought back to the scene in the garden, the three of them standing on the path, under the hanging sheets and pillow-cases, drooping like flags, and tried to recapture the interplay of reaction that had passed between Geoff and Betty Lovell. There was something else, too, about the setting and he frowned with the effort of trying to recall it in all its detail.

Betty Lovell. He could focus in on her quite easily, standing against a background of runner beans, growing rich and luxuriant on their supporting poles. Her blue dress. The red laundry basket at her feet. Nearby something low and dark green growing along the edge of the path, only he couldn't quite see what it was. Then his memory sharpened. Of course! Parsley. The clump of dense, serrated, curled-back leaves came vividly to his mind.

He switched back to her face, changing swiftly in expression from alarm to rigidity and through the white terror of jumping nerves back to the taut mask of immobility again; her eyes flickering across to look at Geoff Lovell, a more shadowy figure in Finch's mind and one that he couldn't recall in anything like the same detail, only as a heavy, dark presence, oddly humble, oddly shy, quite unlike the man who had walked with such easy, physical assurance down the slope of the field. And yet a spark had jumped across the gap. There had been understanding and intimacy that was oddly mixed with something else.

No, Finch decided. He had been wrong to think of it as hostility, but he was hard put to it to describe exactly what it had been. It was as if she had drawn a circle round herself, a space, which Lovell was not allowed to enter and from the centre of which she spoke to him.

But before he could frame the idea properly, his mind had darted off again, ridiculously, to the line of washing above her head and he found himself counting along it. Shirts, sheets, tea-towels, pillow-cases . . .

'Well?' Boyce was asking.

The scene vanished and Finch struggled to return to the present moment.

'Well what?'

'You were saying something about their relationship, Geoff and Betty's, being more complex, and then you went off into one of your trances.'

'Oh, yes. What I meant was, whatever they may have been to each other in the past, there's a feeling of tension between them now.'

It was only a very rough approximation of what he really meant, but he couldn't explain it more exactly.

'Guilt,' Boyce said promptly. 'If they killed Ronnie Lovell, it'd be bound to come between them.'

'Yes,' said Finch, appearing to agree and Boyce, satisfied, started up the car and drove away.

Lovell heard the car and guessed they had been sitting in it, talking. He guessed, too, what about. The business with the cross and chain. The whole interview troubled him, but this particular part of it he could make no sense of at all.

What the hell was all this about a cross and chain? That damned Inspector seemed to think it was important and Lovell hadn't liked the look on Betty's face when Finch asked about it. For a moment, she seemed as if she were going to pieces.

As soon as Finch and the sergeant left the garden, he had turned to question her himself, but she had pushed past him and ran back to the house, shouting at him, 'Leave me alone, for God's sake!'

Baffled and hurt, he remained behind, brooding on it, going over and over in his mind what had been said. Finch had seemed very sure of himself. There had been an alert, watchful air about him all afternoon; at times, almost jubilant. He knew something, of course, and suspected a great deal more, but how much evidence did he have? Not much, Lovell suspected, or he would have been more open in his accusations. The reason he had given for calling, to time the walk to the boundary hedge, was only an excuse. And why had the sergeant come as well? Apart from a few remarks, he had said very little. In fact, when Finch had been questioning Betty about the cross and chain, Lovell couldn't remember where he had been. He certainly hadn't been present.

He had a sudden recollection of seeing him strolling up from the bottom of the garden when Finch was about to leave.

Oh, God! The bonfire! He hadn't thought of that. Could the sergeant have been nosing about round there?

He set off at a run down the path and, squatting down in front of the remains of the fire, examined it carefully. It looked all right. There were no obvious signs that anybody had been poking about in it and yet he couldn't be sure. The fragments of charred letters and photographs seemed to be as he had left them, although he was aware, for the first time, of unburnt scraps that remained, untouched by the fire. But they were too small surely to be recognisable?

All the same, to be on the safe side, he brought his foot down in the centre of them, crushing the brittle flakes of paper, churning them to dust under the heel of his boot.

Christ! he thought, as he felt them powder into oblivion, if only the whole, bloody, terrifying, crazy situation could be got rid of in the same easy way.

13

For two days after the visit to Lovell's farm, the case seemed to
come to a standstill. There was nothing Finch could do except
wait: for the Yard to send a report on the forensic evidence, for
McCullum to produce the life-size enlargement: for someone to
see the photograph and description in the Police Gazette and
come forward with more information, if there was any.

The only positive action he could take was to return the
original photographs and newspaper cutting to Nancy Fowler,
now that McCullum had finished making copies of them. He
had been hoping for a chat with her in which he might learn
more about the Lovell family background but, as he walked into
the lounge bar of the Blue Boar the following evening, it was
clear Nancy was embarrassed by his presence and unwilling
to talk as freely as she had done on their first meeting.

Had she regretted her outspokenness? Finch wondered. She
certainly seemed relieved to get the photographs back and
stuffed them quickly into her handbag, snapping the catch
shut with a quick, decisive movement, as if that were the end
of the incident.

'Ta,' she said briefly.

He had bought her a gin and orange which she drank
furtively, keeping an eye on the landlord.

'I can't stay chatting tonight,' she went on. 'I'm meeting a
gentleman friend later.'

It was said defiantly, but Finch was inclined to take it as an
excuse to get rid of him as quickly as possible. He had noticed
her as soon as he entered the bar and before she had seen him,
sitting by herself, a closed, sulky look on her face; the look of

a woman drinking alone and not expecting company. All the same, she couldn't pass up the opportunity to ask, 'No news of Ron yet?'

There was the same desperate eagerness in her voice that he had noticed the first time.

'Sorry, no. Not yet,' he replied. 'We're still making inquiries.'

'What do you want him for?'

'I told you, as a possible witness.'

'Witness to what?'

So she still hadn't heard about the body being found near Lovell's farm, Finch decided with relief. There had been a short paragraph in the local paper that morning, giving very little information, except for the fact of the discovery and its whereabouts. Either she hadn't read it or hadn't made the connection between the village, which was named, and Finch's interest in the Lovell family.

'Just a line of investigation,' he said vaguely and added quickly, to draw her away from any further questions about the case, 'how did you come to meet Ron in the first place?'

She seemed more inclined to talk, now that the subject had switched back to her relationship with Ronnie Lovell and she said, with a little laugh, 'He used to come here of an evening, drinking with his mates.'

'Here? You mean the Blue Boar?'

'Yes, only they met in the public bar in them days; played darts; had a few rounds and a few laughs, that sort of thing. I don't use the public myself anymore, being on my own. It's nicer in here.'

It struck him as an extraordinary example of her loyalty that she should go on drinking in the same pub, in spite of the obvious hostility of the landlord. Did it make her feel nearer to him? Or nearer, perhaps, to the green days of her youth when the future had seemed full of bright promise?

'And Geoff?' he asked. 'How did you come to meet him?'

It was mere curiosity that prompted the question.

'Oh, him. Well, Ron had a few too many one evening and couldn't get himself home on his bike. One of his mates went over to the farm and Geoff came out in the van to pick him up.

Talk about laugh! We had Ronnie out in the car-park, trying to sober him up but he kept falling about, singing and trying to take his shirt off.'

Her face brightened at this recollection of high revelry.

'On good terms were they?' Finch asked.

'Who, Geoff and Ron?' She looked surprised at the question. 'Yes, all right, I suppose. They're brothers, aren't they?'

As if blood relationship explained all and excused all.

'And Geoff came back to see you after Ron left to ask if you knew where he'd gone?'

'That's right. Like I said, I couldn't tell him 'cos I didn't know.'

She paused and gave Finch a sly, almost coquettish look.

'As a matter of fact, he hung about for a few months. I'm not saying he really fancied me, but I got the feeling if I'd taken a bit more trouble . . .'

She left the sentence unfinished, shrugged and laughed.

'Not that he was my type. Too bloody gloomy, for one thing. No chance of a laugh with him; not like Ron. And always on about that farm of his. I got fed up listening to it. Anyway, he stopped coming after a bit.'

Finch was silent, thinking over the implications of what she had told him. Without realising it, Nancy Fowler might have given him a clue to another possible motive for murder, and a powerful one at that, if he was right. Sexual jealousy. It seemed likely that Geoff Lovell had harboured a grudge for years against his younger and more attractive brother who, unlike himself, had no difficulty in picking up women. His own fumbling attempts at trying to establish some kind of relationship with Nancy might indicate this. Now that his brother had gone, she was free and Ronnie had already shown him that she was sexually available. Then he had stopped seeing her. Why? Because he realised his attempts were futile? That Nancy Fowler didn't fancy him? Or had he already turned to the other woman whom Ronnie had loved and abandoned: Betty Lovell? Not that Geoff's relationship with her could be compared in any way with the hankerings he might have had for Nancy. Finch had seen them together and had realised that, whatever Betty's feelings for him were now, his affection for her was genuine enough. It struck him that there was something deeply tragic about a man who could only approach the women his brother had discarded, as if he doubted his own powers of attraction.

And then, if Ronnie came home . . .

Nancy Fowler's voice broke into his thoughts.

'If that's all,' she was saying, looking pointedly at the clock over the bar.

'Just one more question,' Finch said, rousing himself. 'I was a bit curious about the newspaper cutting of the wedding.'

Her face went sulky again at the mention of Ron's marriage. 'Well, what of it?'

'Betty was given away by the manager of the hotel, not by her father, and there's no mention of her parents being there.'

'No they wouldn't be 'cos she didn't have none. She was brought up in a children's home. Ron told me. It was one of the reasons he felt he had to marry her. She had no one else and nowhere to go. It was a living-in job, see, at the hotel and she'd've been chucked out if they knew she was pregnant. "She got me in a corner," he said. Those were his very words.'

'I see,' Finch said thoughtfully.

It explained why Betty had stayed on at the farm after Ron had left her; a small point but one loose end, at least, that had been satisfactorily tied up.

He finished his beer and got ready to leave.

'Thank you, Mrs Fowler.'

'That the lot?'

'Yes. I don't think I need trouble you again.'

It was the wrong thing to say. Her expression hardened.

'You said you'd let me know . . .'

'Of course,' he put in quickly. 'I haven't forgotten. I'll be in touch the minute I know anything.'

'He'll turn up,' she said with an air of quiet conviction that had an odd quality of bitterness in it. 'He always does, like a bad bloody penny, borrowing a few quid when he's short, pissing off again when it suits him.'

I've underestimated her, Finch thought. There's no false sentimentality in her attitude to Ron Lovell. She knows him for what he is and yet she's still prepared to have him back.

As he rose to go, he looked at her with renewed respect. The heat had caked her powder and her eye make-up had been amateurishly put on, too heavy on one side, giving her face an uneven, lop-sided look, as if one side of it was in sharper focus than the other. Ridiculous. Comic. Pathetic, even. But Finch saw none of these qualities. He recognised, instead, a kind of courage and gallantry and a tough instinct for survival.

Apart from this one encounter, there was no other activity. Finch finished the paperwork, read over the reports already written, fidgeted about the office. He hated these periods of waiting in the middle of a case. They made him fretful and bad-tempered. Boyce, knowing this, kept well clear of him, to the cowardly extent of sending Kyle along to the office with the completed list of missing persons, aware that none of them were relevant.

Finch read it over with disgust. Only five were manual workers who approximately fitted the description and had been reported missing during the past two years, and all of them were vouched for by next-of-kin. Therefore none could possibly be Ron Lovell who, whatever life he had made for himself after he left the farm, certainly couldn't be traced back more than fifteen years.

Kyle scuttled out of the office as soon as he decently could, leaving Finch to bung the report into a file with the morose thought that the gods seemed to be conspiring against him.

The following morning, however, things began to move at last. The forensic report arrived from the Yard and, seeing the envelope lying on his desk as he entered the office, Finch felt his spirits rise. Peeling off his jacket and throwing open the window, he sent for Boyce before settling down at the desk to read it.

The report was detailed: pages of it, in fact; a lot of it medical evidence, which he skimmed over quickly with a practised eye, lifting out the guts of the information before Boyce's arrival.

The first few paragraphs largely tallied with the facts that Pardoe had already given him. The man had been dead for approximately two years. He was five feet ten inches in height.

Medium build. In his early forties. Hair dark brown beginning to turn grey.

There was more detail on the dental evidence, but in substance it amounted to Pardoe's comment: the man had had most of his teeth removed and those that were left were badly neglected.

The new information concerned the clothing that Pardoe hadn't been able to examine in detail. The man had been wearing cheap quality underwear of a cotton and nylon mixture; grey nylon socks; a blue and white checked cotton shirt, collar size fifteen; dark brown terylene trousers; a wool jacket of dark brown and green mixture, with leather patches on the elbows; leather boots, size eight, with metal studs on the soles, showing signs of wear.

The scraps of fabric that had covered the body were pieces of a grey woollen blanket.

He turned the page. More forensic information in greater detail under separate headings: the bones; the stomach; the tissue. Nothing much here to interest him, although it was all good medical stuff. One detail, however, caught his eye. The man had evidently suffered from early symptoms of rheumatism, discernible in the knee joints, suggesting he might have worked out-of-doors or in damp conditions. Otherwise there were no distinguishing features; no signs of old fractures or scars; no warts or moles. No chance of fingerprints either, as Pardoe had warned him. 'The tissue on the fingertips is in too advanced a state of decomposition,' the report stated laconically.

Boyce entered at this moment, a little cautiously, wondering what the Inspector's mood would be, just as Finch, running his eye further down the page, caught sight of the phrase, 'possible cause of death'. Raising a hand in warning that he didn't want to be interrupted, he bent over the type-written sheet, reading with concentrated attention, while Boyce creaked his way across the room to a vacant chair.

It came in a paragraph with the general heading 'The Heart', which went on to state:

'Although the heart was also decomposed, it was in a better state of preservation than the other internal organs and there was sufficient muscle tissue left intact for the following facts to be established:–

(1)The heart had been punctured by a wound in the left ventricle of sufficient depth to cause heavy if not massive bleeding and, although in the absence of other evidence it cannot be categorically stated, it was of a serious enough nature to be a possible cause of death.

(2)The wound was caused by an implement, weapon or blade at least four inches in length and varying in width, being broadest at the point of entry into the muscle tissue, viz, approximately $3/16$ of an inch in width, tapering to a point approximately $1/8$ of an inch. The implement, weapon or blade also had a downward curvature. It is, however, important to note that, because of the decayed condition of the heart, precise measurements could not be taken.

(3)There were signs that a second penetration had been made into the chest wall approximately six inches to the right of the wound in the heart and possibly of the same nature and depth, although no measurements were possible in this wound because of the advanced state of decomposition of the surrounding tissue.'

But Finch needed no careful hedging of the facts to convince him of the evidence.

'Stabbed!' he said out loud.

'Who's been stabbed?' Boyce asked, getting out of his chair and coming over to the desk.

'Our *corpus delicti*,' Finch told him, handing him the report. 'Read it for yourself. Last paragraph but one.'

'It certainly looks like it,' the sergeant agreed, when he had finished. 'Once you've picked your way through the three syllable jungle. Wordy lot, aren't they, these experts? Why can't they say it straight out – the bloke was stabbed in the heart, because that's what it amounts to?'

'Stabbed, certainly; and twice by the look of it, although whether stabbed to death is another matter. I can understand them being cagey about that one. He might have been dead or dying from other causes.'

'Odd weapon, though,' mused Boyce. 'At least four inches long and tapering off to a point. *And* curving downwards. I can't think off-hand of any knife that's shaped like that. A stilleto's got a long, narrow blade, but its straight, not bent down.'

'That would depend on which way this particular weapon was used,' Finch pointed out.

'I don't get you.'

'Then I'll show you,' Finch replied and, taking a sheet of typing paper from the drawer, he folded it over several times into a narrow strip about half an inch wide. 'There's the blade. I know it's not tapering but that doesn't matter for this experiment. Now look.'

He bent the last two inches of the paper strip so that it was pointing downwards.

'And now I shall proceed to stab you with it,' he went on and lunged at Boyce's chest, bringing his arm down from the shoulder. 'Result – one wound with a downward penetration. Get it?'

'I get it,' Boyce replied with a so-what-anyway expression on his face.

'I now turn the blade over so that the curve is pointing upwards and stab you again. A different action this time, you'll notice. I have to drive it in from below, leaving a wound with an upward penetration. Two different wounds but the same blade, depending which way round you hold it.'

'Yes, I see that,' Boyce replied in a slightly disparaging tone, 'but I still don't see how it helps us to identify what sort of weapon it was. It's not any kind of knife you'd find, say, in a kitchen. But could it be a farm implement? Assuming it's Ronnie Lovell we've dug up, then it's likely he was killed on the farm and more than likely with something that was lying about to hand. It's no good asking me what exactly. The sum total of what I know about farming could be written down in large capital letters on the back of an envelope . . .'

He broke off to add, 'You look as if that rings a bell.'

'Not for the weapon itself,' Finch admitted. 'I'm as much in the dark about that as you are. But it could tie in with something I noticed the first time I visited the farm. I asked Geoff Lovell about any tools that had gone missing. I meant something like a spade that could have been used to dig the grave. He reacted oddly to the question, I thought; denied it very positively as if it had upset him in some way . . .'

'Guilty conscience?' suggested Boyce. 'He could have used a farm tool to kill his brother and then got rid of it afterwards.'

'Possibly, but I don't want to read too much into it, not at this stage. I wish to God McCullum would come up with that life-size enlargement! Until he does and we've got positive proof it's Ronnie Lovell's body, we're working with our hands tied.' He paused and added, 'Let's have another look at the description of the wound. We may get an idea.'

He took the report from Boyce and began re-reading it. Suddenly he stopped and, turning back to the first page, started to scan it eagerly. Boyce, aware that he had found something important, leaned forward to ask, 'What's up?'

'Something I should have noticed the first time I read it. It says here "heavy if not massive bleeding" and yet there's no mention of blood found on the clothing.'

'Could he have been naked when he was killed?' Boyce put in.

'It's possible but I think there's a more likely explanation. There were signs that the body was laid out. Somebody had taken the trouble to fold the arms and wrap the body in a blanket. I think the same person also stripped it of its blood-stained clothing and dressed it in clean clothes before it was buried.'

'Crazy,' said Boyce.

'No, not crazy. Anything but that. Whoever did it had a perfectly sane and logical reason; the same sort of motive that was behind the choice of that field for the grave site . . .'

The telephone rang at this point and Finch stretched across the desk to pick up the receiver. A man's voice, deep and with a Midlands accent, asked, 'Detective Inspector Finch? I'm Detective Chief Inspector Mullen, stationed at Mill Edge. I saw the photograph and description in the Police Gazette this morning and I'm fairly certain that I recognise the man.'

'You mean Ronnie Lovell?' Finch broke in.

'That's not the name we know him by. The man we're looking for is James, or Jimmy, Neal who went missing three years ago.'

'Three years!'

That didn't fit in with the facts, but there was no time to discuss the point for Mullen was continuing, 'Over three years, as a matter of fact. We put out a wanted on him at the time.'

'And the charge?' Finch asked, signalling urgently to Boyce.

'Attempted murder.'

Cupping his hand over the mouth piece, Finch said hurriedly to Boyce, 'James Neal. Wanted for attempted murder. Over three years ago.'

Boyce raised his eyebrows and then, picking up the internal telephone, began giving instructions to someone at the other end.

Finch, meanwhile, was asking Mullen, 'Are you sure it's the same man?'

'Fairly certain,' Mullen replied. 'But I'd like to discuss it with you. Any chance of your coming up here? I'm anxious to get this case closed.'

And so am I, Finch said to himself.

'If you left now,' Mullen went on, 'you could be up here soon after midday. It doesn't take all that long on the motorway.'

'Mill Edge, you said?'

'That's right. It's about twelve miles south of Manchester. If you take the M1 and then the M6 and turn off at intersection 19, you'll find Mill Edge well signposted from then on. The police station's in the centre, in a turning beside the town hall.' He paused and then added, 'You haven't any more recent photographs of this man – what's-his-name – Lovell, have you?'

'Sorry, no. I'll bring what I have.'

'Right. We'll compare notes when we meet,' Mullen replied and rang off.

'A constable's bringing the "wanted" file,' Boyce said as Finch replaced the receiver.

'No time now,' Finch replied, grabbing up his jacket. 'You check it out for me. I'm off to Mill Edge. The Inspector there thinks he recognises Ronnie Lovell.'

'On an attempted murder charge?' Boyce asked, as Finch made for the door, but the Inspector waved a dismissive hand.

506

'Can't stop now. I'll see you later. I should be back by late afternoon, early evening. Stir McCullum up meanwhile,' he added, over his shoulder. 'Tell him things are moving and I'll want that blow-up.'

He went, slamming the door behind him and creating a small draught that stirred the pile of papers on his desk.

Once he got on to the motorway, Finch found the drive rapid but boring. The three-lane highway sliced its way north, busy with fast-moving traffic that gave the impression it was fleeing from some major catastrophe. Or feeling towards it, perhaps, for the cars and lorries on the south-bound carriageways were travelling at the same manic speed. Sunlight splintered off windscreens and chrome and glared back from the surface of the road. Alongside it, the countryside flickered past, anonymous fields for the most part, that looked as if they had come complete with the motorway, bought up as a job lot by the Ministry of Transport ready for rolling out beside the miles of sterile concrete.

Finch was glad to get off it, into the comparative sanity of the ordinary roads in the built-up area, where traffic moved at a more reasonable speed and where there were shops and houses and people, going about their everyday lives.

Mill Edge merged with it, part of the great, sprawling conurbation of Manchester, joined to it by miles of industrial suburb and yet managing to preserve something of its own separate identity. Finch drove into it slowly, noticing the grimy rows of terrace cottages, two up and two down, run up cheaply in the last century to house the mill-workers; and the mills themselves, grim, flat-faced, many-windowed buildings which, with their massive gates and sunless yards, put him in mind of Victorian prisons.

The town centre was a little gayer, tricked out with concrete tubs of flowers and coloured awnings. There was even a floral coat-of-arms with a grass border outside the town hall.

He took the turning beside it and drew up outside the police station, where he was shown upstairs to Mullen's office. Mullen, a large, grey-haired, baggy man, came forward to

507

shake hands, adding with a smile, 'Fancy a beer and cheese sandwich? Or have you eaten?'

'Yes to the first. No to the second,' Finch replied.

'Come on then. There's a pub round the corner that's got a snug where we can talk.'

It was a genuine snug, with a brown lincrusta dado, an ornate plaster ceiling and mahogany benches upholstered in worn, buttoned, red plush. Mullen ordered beer and sandwiches at the tiny section of the counter that served it, from the other side of which they could hear the roar and clatter of the public bar.

'Always peaceful here,' Mullen commented, as they carried the plates and glasses over to a round, marble-topped table. He drank deeply and then said, without any preamble, 'Jimmy Neal. Well, as I said on the phone, we're looking for him on an attempted murder charge. I'll give you his story, what I know of it, and you can see how well it fits in with the man you're looking for. Neal turned up in this area about eight years ago, as far as we can make out, and worked for a time at a factory assembling washing-machines on the outskirts of Manchester but left after a row with the foreman. We don't know where he was for about eighteen months after that. The next we heard of him, he'd been taken on as a mechanic at a garage and repair shop not far from here, out at Westbridge, run by a man called Maguire, Pat Maguire. Neal was there for just over a year and then there was a quarrel between the two men over Maguire's wife, Babs, who worked on the cash-desk for the petrol pumps. Evidently Maguire thought Neal was being a bit too friendly with her, and not without good reason as it turned out. Anyway, Neal got the sack. A few weeks later, Maguire's garage was raided and he was arrested on a receiving charge. I had a chat with the Inspector in charge of the case out at Westbridge. He told me the place was stuffed full of stolen spare parts and he'd been tipped off, although by whom he wouldn't say. "Acting on information received. Blah. Blah." But we can guess who grassed.'

'Neal?'

'I reckon so. It was his way of paying out Maguire for giving him the push. Anyway, Maguire got sent down, although that's neither here nor there, and Neal meanwhile turned up here, in Mill Edge, with Babs Maguire in tow, calling herself Mrs Neal by this time, and they installed themselves in a flat over a launderette just off the High Street, Babs working downstairs in the shop. Neal was in and out of jobs, mostly out, but when he did work it was usually in some small engineering firm or workshop. I gather he was quite a good mechanic when he wasn't quarrelling with someone and either getting the sack or asking for his cards.'

He paused and looked quizzically at Finch.

'It fits so far?'

'It fits,' Finch agreed.

As Mullen had been talking, he had been mentally ticking off the points that related to what he knew of Ronnie Lovell; the fact that the man had turned up in the area, without anything previously known about him; his mechanical skill; his tendency to stick at nothing for very long; the quarrelsome, belligerent character; the use he made of women: all coincided.

'Did he drink?' he added.

Mullen nodded.

'Yes, heavily at times. It was his drinking that first got him noticed by my lot. Nothing much to start with; mostly shouting matches with Babs Maguire late on a Saturday night when he'd had a skinful. The neighbours called the police out a couple of times but there's not much we can do in a domestic. There was one brawl in a pub for which Neal and the other man involved got fined. And then we come to the night in question: four years ago come next New Year, as a matter of fact. They'd been to a New Year's Eve booze-up and got back to the flat in the early hours. Soon afterwards, there was a violent row over another man, I gather, and Neal clobbered her with a chair. The police were sent for but by the time the patrol car arrived, Neal had skipped out, leaving Babs Maguire lying in the kitchen with serious head injuries. He was damned lucky he didn't kill her. We've been looking for him ever since.'

He took a photograph out of his pocket and laid it on the table.

'That's the only picture we have of him.'

Finch picked it up and studied it. By the look of it, it had

509

been taken by flashlight at a party in somebody's house. Three men and two women, all of them looking a little drunk and dishevelled, were standing in front of a sideboard, holding up their glasses in boozy salutation. But, despite the poor quality of the photograph and the intervening years, Finch had no difficulty in picking out Ron Lovell. He was the man in the centre of the group, tie loosened, hair flopping on his forehead; older and thinner-faced than in the photographs of him that Finch had got from Nancy Fowler, but unmistakably the same, still eyeing the camera with that bold, swaggering, come-on look and the same confident smile.

He laid the three copies of the photographs that McCullum had made beside it.

'Royal flush, I think,' he said.

Mullen examined the four photographs for a moment before commenting wryly, 'A handful of knaves, if you ask me.'

He pointed to one of the women in the group picture.

'That's Babs Maguire, if you want to know what she looks like. The man on her right is her husband.'

It was the woman who interested Finch the most. Blonde, plump, already showing signs of coarsening, with an incipient double chin and small belly showing beneath a too-tight, shiny silk dress, she put him in mind of Nancy Fowler; the same type, busty and well-fleshed, but with a harder, city gloss to her. He gave only a cursory glance at the husband who, wearing a paper hat, his mouth foolishly open, seemed to be propped up against Ron Lovell who was standing next to him.

'No doubt in your mind?' Mullen was asking.

'None,' Finch replied with conviction. 'It's the same man all right.'

'And you're looking for him too?'

'I think we may have found him,' Finch said, and went on to explain briefly the discovery of the body and what he knew of Ron Lovell's life before he left home.

'So your theory is he was on the run, with an attempted murder charge hanging over him, returned home and was killed in a quarrel with his brother?' Mullen asked, as Finch finished. 'It fits. He was a violent man; the type who was likely to end violently. I can't say I'm surprised. You'll probably find he started the fight himself.'

'The only snag is the time factor,' Finch pointed out. 'The man we've found has been dead for about two years. But your man, Jimmy Neal, skipped out over three years ago. That leaves about eighteen months unaccounted for.'

'Could be he spent the time somewhere else,' Mullen replied, 'under another name. It's obvious he was using false papers – a National Insurance card, for instance – when we knew him. He could have pushed off, assumed another false identity, perhaps even got into more trouble with the law before finally deciding to go home.'

'It's possible,' agreed Finch, although he didn't sound too happy with the idea. It was another loose end to be tied; another unsatisfactory part of the case that would need resolving.

He glanced at his watch.

'I'd better be pushing off myself. McCullum may have come up with that life-size enlargement which will clinch once and for all the question of identity. I'll let you know as soon as he does.'

'Thanks,' Mullen said. 'But I don't think you need to worry on that score. The description, everything, fits too neatly. I bet you a pound to a penny it's Ronnie Lovell, alias Jimmy Neal, you've got there and I for one won't be sorry. I shall close the file on him with a happy heart.'

But his confidence was to prove misplaced. Later, when Finch, hot, tired and suffering from the slightly disorientated feeling of a man who has driven too far and too fast, walked into the office to find Boyce and McCullum waiting for him, he knew by the looks on their faces that the news wasn't good.

McCullum put it into words.

'I'm sorry but there's no question of doubt, according to the photographic evidence. That body you've got is definitely not Ronnie Lovell's.'

He had spread the photographs out on the desk ready for the Inspector's examination, and in silence Finch crossed the room and bent down over them. The life-size enlargement of

Ronnie Lovell's face, under its jaunty beret, smiled up at him in what now seemed to be triumph. Beside it lay a transparent sheet, on which the outlines of a face had been drawn in black ink. McCullum, in a subdued voice, like a man present at a sickbed, began explaining.

'I had the features of the dead man sketched out from the measurements Pardoe took when he first examined him; length and width of skull, the position of the eyes and ears . . .'

He broke off, seeing the expression on Finch's face.

'But I won't go into the details now. The point is, it's accurate. Now see what happens.'

Lifting the transparent sheet, he laid it over the photograph, without speaking. No words, in fact, were needed. The evidence spoke for itself. At no point did the features of the dead man correspond to those of Ronnie Lovell. Eyes, nose, mouth, were all differently spaced. Even the jaw-line ran at a sharper angle.

Finch rested his hands on the surface of the desk and leaned his weight on them. He felt tired down to the marrow of his bones. Behind him, he heard Boyce stir and clear his throat.

'I'll send out for tea,' he announced. He, too, spoke in the hushed tones of someone addressing a patient who needed gentle handling.

Suddenly Finch was angry; not with Boyce, but with himself. It had been so damned easy to accept the obvious, to drift along with the comfortable and facile theory that had so conveniently seemed to fit the facts. Well, let that be a lesson to him!

He stumped over to the door and, flinging it open, said loudly, 'I'm going out!'

Boyce and McCullum exchanged startled glances.

'What for?' Boyce asked tentatively.

'What the hell do you mean – what for?' Finch snapped back. 'To start again, of course.'

Banging the door shut behind him, he felt a certain furious satisfaction at the rightness of the decision that he had made in anger on the spur of the moment.

To start again was the only answer. And where better than

the place where it had all begun: that scrappy bit of rough pasture that someone had chosen as a grave site for an unknown man; where he had stood alone and felt the first stirring of understanding; and where he knew he must now return – Hollowfield.

14

He had expected the field to be empty as it had been when he stood alone in the centre of it and felt close to the heart of the place. Instead, as he climbed over the gate, he saw Rose and a few of the younger members of the society still at work on the rectangular site where the post-holes had been discovered.

Damn! Finch thought. He had forgotten they would be there.

He stood irresolute, wondering whether to turn back and yet reluctant to retreat. There was nothing else he could do towards the case except return to the office and go over the files once again, and he was tired of reports and all the formal routine of investigation.

Besides, it was a beautiful evening. The sun was low on the horizon and the day's heat was dying with it, leaving only a gentle warmth and a promise of later coolness. After a day spent largely driving along motorways, it would be pleasant to wander about, with his hands in his pockets, while he tried to recapture the mood of that first day of the inquiry, before his mind had been cluttered up with all the useless theorising and the irrelevant detail that still lingered in his thoughts.

In the event, his mind was made up for him. Rose, glancing up, saw him and came forward to meet him, his face expressing both welcome and concern.

'Good evening, Inspector,' he said. 'I do hope you're not going to ask us to leave again just when we're so near to finishing our dig. Two or three more days should see it completed.'

There was nothing Finch could do except put a pleasant face on it.

'No. I just happened to be passing and I thought I'd look in and see how you're getting on,' he replied, lying agreeably.

'How very kind!' Rose said in his precise voice, his face flushing with pleasure. 'I shall be delighted to show you round.'

As they began walking towards the main excavation site, Finch remarked, 'You're doing overtime, I see.'

Rose gave his high, pinched laugh.

'Unpaid, I'm afraid, Inspector! But we try to keep going while the light lasts. As you can see, we're making very good progress.'

They had reached the edge of the site, which was now almost completely cleared, showing lines of circular post-holes in the clay, forming a rough box shape; the size, Finch reckoned, of an average room.

Rose was looking at him with a proud and slightly roguish expression.

'Now that you see it uncovered, can you make a guess as to what sort of building it was?' he asked in the teasing manner of a schoolmaster who, while knowing the answer himself, is determined to obtain the maximum scholastic amusement out of the situation by getting his pupils to make their own fatuous suggestions first.

Although exasperated not only by Rose's manner but by his presence there at all, Finch decided to go along with the game for a little while before making an excuse to escape. Besides, despite his impatience, he was genuinely interested in the findings of the excavation.

He studied the post-holes in silence for a few moments and then said thoughtfully, 'It's not big enough for a farmhouse. It could, I suppose, be a cottage or a small barn.'

'Wrong!' Rose announced triumphantly. 'Quite wrong! It's something much more interesting than either of those.'

'Then I'm afraid I have no idea,' Finch said firmly. 'You'll have to tell me.'

Although disappointed that the Inspector had given up so quickly, Rose was nevertheless determined to get the best effect out of his final revelation. Walking to the centre of the rectangle, with the absolute assurance of a man who has no idea that he might be running the risk of making a fool of himself, he lifted up his arms in a gesture that had a touch of theatricality about it. Behind his glasses, his eyes were shining with enthusiasm. Finch watched him with amused admiration, wondering how this style of instruction went down in the classroom. It was certainly more riveting than the average school history book.

'Imagine it as it was!' Rose was exhorting. 'The spaces between the posts filled in with wattle and daub to form the walls and rising up to support a thatched roof; sunlight filtering in through the cracks in the walls and through the open doorway to fall across the floor of beaten clay; outside a crowd of people, murmuring together in soft voices, some of whom had possibly come for miles to bring their offerings . . .'

'Offerings?' Finch asked quickly. Something more than just mere interest began to stir in his mind. He thought of the body, laid out with its arms crossed, the signs of ritual . . .

Ignoring his question, Rose turned to call in his normal school-masterish voice to one of the young men who was pushing a barrow-load of earth past the end of the site.

'Neil, be a good lad, will you pop over to my tent and bring me my little box?'

Neil, a strapping six-footer who looked mildly amused at being called a good lad, nodded and began walking towards the camp site.

'Offerings?' Finch repeated.

'You'll see, all in good time,' Rose replied, with an air of maddening secrecy. 'As a matter of fact, we only fully realised the significance of the place this morning when we found . . . But you'll see. I shan't spoil it by telling you.'

The young man had returned carrying a box which he handed over to Rose. Rose opened it, took out three small objects from its cottonwool-lined interior and gave them to Finch. He examined them carefully as they lay in the palm of his hand. They were tiny metal figurines, crudely fashioned into naked female shapes, with well-developed breasts and protuberant bellies.

'Bronze votive offerings,' Rose was explaining. 'We found them scattered about the site. Of course, there were doubtlessly other objects that haven't survived; offerings of food, for example; possibly wooden figures, too. We've found some clay pieces that may be parts of similar shapes but we'll have to re-assemble them before we can be sure. But what we are certain about is that this place was once a place of pagan worship, almost certainly to a local goddess. The name of the field bears that out: Hollowfield; a corruption, of course, of the Saxon word, "halig", meaning "holy". Isn't it fascinating how far place names go back into history? Never ignore them,' he added, wagging an admonishing finger at Finch as if he had been found guilty of such an omission. 'They can be vital clues to the origin of a site. Take the name of the lane that runs past the farms: Hallbrook Lane, another word that has Saxon origins, from "hael", which meant "health", suggesting a stream or brook that had healing powers, which may give us the reason why this place was considered sacred. Pilgrims would come to drink or bathe in the magic water and offer up gifts to the goddess of the place, here, on this very spot where we're standing now, where possibly the spring bubbled out of the ground. Interesting, isn't it?'

Before Finch had time to reply, Rose had plunged on.

'Then came Christianity; for the second time, as a matter of fact, although that's neither here nor there in our present study of the place. But the people didn't give up their old gods willingly. Do you know the story of the Saxon warriors, forced by their king to accept baptism and driven en masse through a river while a Christian bishop blessed the water up-stream, holding their sword arms high above their heads so they wouldn't be weakened by what they considered an effeminate religion that told them to forgive their enemies and turn the other cheek? The same attitude was found in many others. They clung to their old beliefs which, in fact, haven't entirely died out even today. There are still people about who worship the horned god of their ancestors. Indeed, Essex is supposed to be one of the counties where his worshippers are particularly flourishing.' He giggled deprecatingly. 'Not, of course, that I have first-hand knowledge. The Eucharist is the nearest I've ever been to ancient ritual and that's a long way from a Sabbat. But I'm digressing. The point is, faced with a pagan people who wouldn't readily accept a monotheistic religion, the Christian missionaries, rather cleverly I think, adopted some of the old gods and goddesses as their own saints and converted their shrines to churches, which is clearly what happened here.'

He took another object from the box and passed it to Finch, adding, 'Evidence, Inspector. You'll appreciate the importance of that, I'm sure. Indeed, you might say that you and I are in the same line of country, piecing together facts in order to arrive at the truth. *That* was found only this morning, but it's enough to prove that the site continued to be used as a place of worship into the Christian era.'

He had handed the Inspector a piece of bone, jaggedly broken and dirt-stained, that had been carved with what appeared to be the letters X and R, enclosed in an intricate, circular border. As he ran his fingers over it, Finch had the sensation that he was holding part of the key to the mystery in this broken fragment. It hadn't been a sense of death that the field conveyed to him, in spite of the anonymous grave and the heaps of excavated earth; nor a mere feeling of the past. He realised that now. But could he have been instinctively aware of the sacred and magic powers that had inspired all that past veneration and worship?

Another idea, too, began to take form at the back of his mind, but Rose's voice overrode his thoughts.

'The Chi-Rho monogram, an early Christian symbol,' he was saying, coming close to point at the carved letters. 'It's been broken off but that's undoubtedly what it was; the first two letters of the Greek word for Christ, set in a circle. Notice the border; a typical Saxon design with an interlaced ribbon pattern. It's a pity it's so damaged because we may never know what it was part of, unless we're lucky enough to find the other pieces; a crucifix, perhaps, or the decorative top to a staff or some other ritual object.'

'A crucifix, did you say?' Finch asked.

He was thinking of the other crucifix that had been found in the field; the cheap, silver-plated cross and chain that had been lying in the man's grave.

Sacred ground, of course. Holyfield. At last, that part of it made sense.

Rose had started to reply but Finch didn't wait to listen. He was eager to pursue his own particular, overriding interest.

'Could it still be known locally that this field had once been a place of worship?' he broke in.

'Strange that you should ask that,' Rose answered. 'The site must have been abandoned a long time ago, certainly before the wooden building was replaced by something more permanent in stone. Why, we don't know. Possibly the spring dried up. But some folk memory of the place must have lingered on. I was talking to one of Stebbing's men only yesterday and he told me that he remembered, as a boy, people saying that herbs picked in this field had particular healing power and that carrying an acorn in your pocket from one of the oak trees growing over there along the hedge was supposed to ward off rheumatism.'

'Was the man called Wheeler?' Finch asked with rising excitement.

Rose pursed his lips doubtfully.

'I'm afraid I can't recall his name.'

'What did he look like?'

'A small man, in his fifties, I'd say. Rather – well – sly, if you know what I mean, and not very eager to give away much.'

'Wheeler!' said Finch.

Handing back the piece of carved bone, he added hurriedly, 'Thank you very much, Mr Rose. You've been more help than you can possibly imagine.'

'Have I?' asked Rose, sounding bewildered but gratified, as Finch turned away and began walking rapidly across the field towards Stebbing's farm.

It fitted. It had to fit. There was no other possible explanation. And now that the question of the choice of the field for a grave site was explained, other details made sense as well: the tidiness of Lovell's house; the gun propped up in the corner by the fireplace; the dog turned loose in the yard. He remembered, too, the scene in the kitchen garden when he had questioned Betty Lovell under the washing-line. The significance of what he had seen then, that had eluded him at the time, now sprang into sharp focus and, with that realisation, the last piece of the puzzle dropped into place.

He found himself in Stebbing's yard without being aware

of making the journey there and, banging loudly on the door, brought the farmer out on to the step.

'I want to use your phone,' Finch told him, cutting short any possibility of time-wasting social preliminaries. 'And I'd like to talk to Wheeler.'

'He's knocked off work for the day,' Stebbing replied.

'Could he be sent for?'

Even Stebbing seemed aware of a sense of urgency.

'I'll get the car out and fetch him myself,' he offered with surprising decision. 'The phone's through here,' he added, showing Finch into a small room opening off the hall, and evidently used as an office, for it contained a desk and filing cabinets. As he ushered Finch inside, he couldn't resist asking, 'Something turned up?'

'Possibly,' Finch said shortly and waited until Stebbing had left the room before reaching for the telephone.

He made three calls altogether. The first was to Detective Chief Inspector Mullen at Mill Edge, whom he was lucky to find still at the office. It was a short conversation, consisting of two questions and Mullen's replies to them and, when he replaced the receiver, Finch had a look of quiet satisfaction.

Next, he rang Harlsdon police station and spoke to the sergeant on duty.

'Yes, I know Nancy Fowler, sir,' the man said, sounding amused. 'What's she been up to now to interest headquarters?'

'Nothing. I want to talk to her, that's all. Can you get her to ring me here as soon as possible?' Finch replied, giving Stebbing's telephone number. 'You know where to find her?'

'Yes. She'll be round at the Blue Boar at this time of the evening. I'll send a constable to bring her in.'

'Plain-clothes,' Finch said quickly. remembering the landlord's hostile interest. 'I don't want her harassed. You understand?'

There was a tiny pause in which Finch imagined the sergeant raising his eyebrows. But when he spoke, his voice was deferential. 'Very good, sir.'

While he waited for Nancy Fowler to telephone, Finch made his last call, to Boyce.

'I was just about to go home,' Boyce said. 'What's up?'

'A whole lot,' Finch replied. As he spoke, he saw Stebbing's car turn into the yard and Wheeler get out of the front passenger seat. He began to walk reluctantly towards the house, his whole body expressing hostility, while Stebbing fussed round him, attempting to hustle him along.

'I can't explain now,' Finch continued hurriedly, 'but I want you to meet me at Lovell's farm as soon as you can get there. It could be important.'

'Christ!' exclaimed Boyce. 'You don't mean you've got something definite on Lovell? But, surely, now we know the body isn't his brother's . . . ?'

'I'll explain it when I see you,' Finch replied and hung up just as the door opened and Stebbing ushered Wheeler officiously into the room. He refused to come too far and stood just inside the threshold, regarding Finch with open dislike.

'I'd just started my bloody supper . . .' he began.

'I'm sorry, Mr Wheeler,' Finch replied briskly, 'but there's a few questions I must ask you straightaway. I believe you talked to Mr Rose yesterday about the field where they're making the dig?'

'What of it?' Wheeler asked belligerently. 'There ain't no law. He'd come to fetch drinking water from the house and it was him who kept me chatting in the yard.'

'And you told him,' Finch went on, ignoring his reply, 'that there's a local story about herbs picked in that field having special healing powers. Am I right?'

Wheeler gave a slow, contemptuous smile.

'Yes and he believed it and all.'

'It's not true?'

Wheeler shrugged.

'Maybe,' he said cautiously.

'Do other people know of these stories about the field? Mr Lovell, for instance?'

Wheeler watched the Inspector carefully. He was unsure of the purpose behind the questions and didn't want to commit himself.

'Does he?' Finch persisted.

'How the hell should I know? I never talked to him about it.'

'Or Mrs Lovell?'

A bright, knowing look passed across Wheeler's face and was gone in an instant, but not before Finch had glimpsed it. He pounced quickly.

'You discussed it with her?'

'Maybe.'

'Not maybe, Mr Wheeler. I want a straight answer for once. What did you say to her about that field?'

Wheeler hesitated before saying in an offhand manner, 'Nothing much.'

Finch felt his temper rising and it was with difficulty that he kept his voice level as he replied, 'I haven't got the time for games, Mr Wheeler. I want to know exactly what you told her.'

It was Wheeler who became angry.

'All right, I'll tell you, since you're so bloody bent on finding out, but what good it'll do you, don't ask me,' he said, his voice rising and two ugly, red patches appearing on his bony cheeks. 'She had a headache one day, see, and I told her to pick a dock leaf from up that field and hold it to her forehead and that'd cure it. I was having her on, like,' he added, tailing off and sounding embarrassed and Finch guessed that, like a lot of country people, Wheeler had an ambivalent attitude to folk lore; part-belief, part-scepticism.

'Did you explain why?' he asked.

But Wheeler set his mouth stubbornly.

'I don't remember,' he said flatly and turned away.

Stebbing, who had been hanging about near the open doorway during the interview, bustled forward.

'If you'll go through to the kitchen, Len,' he said, 'and ask Mrs Stebbing to pour you a glass of beer, I'll drive you home in a few minutes.'

As Wheeler walked away down the hall, he added to Finch, 'A glass for you as well, Inspector, or are you on duty?'

His face was alive with curiosity and Finch parried the inquisitiveness behind the innocent-seeming question by saying vaguely, 'I've got a few calls to make later.'

To forestall any further questions from Stebbing while he waited for Nancy Fowler's call, he turned to a chart that was pinned up over the desk, detailing the fields belonging to the farm, with their acreage and crops marked in, and commented, 'That shows good organisation. Your idea, is it?'

'My son's,' Stebbing replied with pride. 'He's the expert round here; went to agricultural college and picked up all sorts of modern, farming know-how. Me, I'm just an ordinary working farmer.' He laughed deprecatingly. 'As a matter of fact,' he went on in a confiding tone, 'I'd got my eye on Lovell's place for him. It's been neglected, mind, and it'll need money spending on it, but I reckon we could run the two farms jointly and make it a going concern. No chance of Lovell moving out, I suppose?'

The remark seemed harmless enough, but Finch guessed the implied meaning behind it. Like Boyce, Stebbing had jumped to the conclusion that the case against Geoff Lovell was building up and was hoping that, whatever move Finch seemed about to make, it might benefit him. Finch now understood, too, why Lovell had so disliked the man, in spite of his professed neighbourliness. Behind it lay the same self-seeking motive that must have angered Lovell more than it angered Finch.

'I have no idea, Mr Stebbing,' he replied shortly and was spared further conversation with him by the ringing of the telephone.

'If you don't mind going outside,' he added and, showing Stebbing out into the hall, shut the door on him before picking up the receiver.

Nancy Fowler's voice, loud and breathy, vibrated in his ear.

'The police said you wanted to talk to me. What's it about?'

'There's a query you might be able to help me with,' Finch said quickly, before she could get on to the inevitable question. 'You remember you told me that Betty Lovell had been brought up in a children's home? Do you by any chance know whether it was Catholic?'

'Yes, it was. I know 'cos Ron said that's why she'd never divorce him. She'd been brought up by nuns and she didn't hold with it. But how did you guess?'

'I just wondered,' Finch replied, but added to himself that it was a fact he should have realised, if not on the first occasion when he visited the farm and the neatness of the living-room had struck him, then at least on the second when he had spoken to Betty Lovell in the kitchen where she was mending shirts. Only Catholic sisters could have taught her that exquisitely fine needlework.

It explained, too, a lot more about the case that had puzzled him at the time; not only the reason why, as Nancy Fowler had said, Betty Lovell had never divorced her husband, but the other details concerning the burial of the dead man.

'Is that all?' Nancy Fowler was asking, sounding surprised.

'Just one more question,' Finch added. 'Has Geoff Lovell been to collect the photographs yet?'

'No, but he should be calling round soon. He said a week. Have you found . . . ?'

'Thank you, Mrs Fowler,' Finch broke in. 'I'm sorry you've been troubled.'

He rang off guiltily. There was nothing he could do to shield her from finding out the truth eventually, but not now, he decided. Not at the end of a telephone with a policeman standing at her elbow. Later, he would break it to her himself.

He could do little to protect Betty Lovell but she, at least, knew the truth and had known it all along. The burden of it had worn her down. Her pale face with the bones showing through the thin skin rose in his mind but he thrust it quickly to one side. There was no room for sentiment. Not even for her. The process of justice that he would soon have to put into motion took no notice of the tragic circumstances of the individual and it was right not to do so. He would have to make the arrest.

Besides, he comforted himself, as he made for the door, there was that steely centre to her that he had recognised. She would bend but she would not break.

15

As he bumped the car up on to the grass verge by Lovell's farm and switched off the engine, Finch was aware of the silence. There was no wind. The trees were quite motionless. Even the long grasses that grew along the bottom of the hedge held themselves erect and still.

Getting out of the car, he was acutely conscious of the sharp snap of the door, even though he closed it quietly, and the sound of his feet crunching on the surface of the road as he walked towards the gate.

As usual, it was padlocked. Below, the yard lay in the last rays of sunlight that fell in sections between the long, peaked shadows cast by the roofs of the outbuildings. The dog lay in one of them, motionless on its side, its head stretched out in an attitude of exhausted sleep.

Finch laid his hand on the top bar of the gate, expecting it to spring immediately to its feet and come racing up the track towards him. It didn't move.

Surprised, he shook the bar, making the chain and padlock rattle. Still the dog didn't stir. At the same time, some fleeting impression of movement made him glance towards the house. But whatever he had seen – a curtain momentarily lifted, a face appearing briefly at a window – was gone in an instant. The house presented the blank façade, its door closed, its chimneys smokeless, of an empty building.

Cautiously, he began to climb over the gate, keeping his eyes on the dog that still lay in its patch of shadow and finding its silence more menacing than its normal ferocity. Dropping almost without sound on to the dusty ruts of the drive, he reached the grass edge in one long stride and stopped again.

He now had the house and the dog in plain view. It was possible to watch both without turning his head. The house presented the same lifeless appearance although he noticed, for the first time, that the windows of the upper storey were set open, so someone must be at home.

The dog remained where it lay and something about its stretched attitude struck the Inspector as strange. The legs were stiffly extended, the head bent back at an uncomfortable angle, as if the creature had been arrested in mid-howl.

He began to walk rapidly forward, his footsteps softened by the grass, keeping his eyes fixed on the dog.

It was dead. He realised that before he reached the end of the drive and, stopping at the entrance to the yard, saw the darker blotch of blood spread out in the shadow of the barn. He could make out the huge wound in its head, round which the flies were greedily clustering.

At exactly the same moment, a shot rang out to his left, from the direction of the house, its report so loud that he felt as much as heard it, like a physical blow, even though the bullet passed a few feet in front of him and thudded into the barn wall, blasting a hole in its wooden cladding.

For a terrible instant that seemed endless, he remained standing, confused and deafened, while, at the same time, another quite clear and logical part of his mind told him that if he stayed where he was he presented a perfect target and the second shot might not miss.

The next second, he found himself falling face downwards on the grass and then scrambling on all fours, with an alacrity he didn't know he possessed, back along the verge towards the gate.

Above him, rooks, startled from the trees, circled in a wide sweep, cawing loudly, and through their frightened cries came Lovell's voice.

'Get back, you bloody fool, unless you want your head blown off!'

The shout and the birds' clamour followed him as he made for the gate, still keeping low, out of the line of fire. Reaching it, he hesitated, not daring to climb over it, knowing that, once astride the top bar, he would be in full view of the house.

The hedge beside it was thick and well-grown but, with his arms shielding his face, he broke through it, his hair and clothes full of pieces of broken leaf and twig, just as Boyce's car drew up alongside. The sergeant's face appeared at the driver's window, which he was furiously winding down, at the same time shouting through it, 'What the hell's going on? Wasn't that a shot I heard?'

'Get back to Stebbing's farm,' Finch ordered him between gasps for breath. 'Use his phone. I want some men here as soon as possible. As many as can be spared. A couple of marksmen, too. While you're there, see if you can borrow a hacksaw, anything, to cut through the chain on that gate. We'll have to get it open for a clear view of the house. And keep Stebbing away at all costs!' he added, raising his voice as Boyce reversed and turned the car, its engine racing.

'I'll arrest him if he so much as pokes his nose near here,' he added aloud to himself as the car tore away up the road.

Meanwhile, there was nothing he could do except wait. Squatting down on the grass verge in front of the gap he had torn in the hedge, Finch contemplated what he could see of the house. It was silent again now. The windows, catching the last light of the sun as it slanted over the roofs of the outbuildings, glittered golden, allowing him not even the smallest glimpse of any movement inside. The body of the dog was no longer visible either, lying hidden from sight below a dip in the ground.

It occurred to him then to wonder exactly when it had been killed. Not during the last hour certainly, when he had been talking with Rose in Hollowfield. The farm was less than a mile away and the sound of a shot would have been easily audible at that distance. So it must have been fired sometime earlier, before he arrived, and he wondered what had happened at the farmhouse to precipitate this sudden violence.

He wondered, too, who was inside the house. Lovell, of course, and presumably the others as well, although there had been no sign of any of them at the windows. But if one of them had managed to get away, the alarm would have been raised and that hadn't happened.

Were they dead?

The thought struck him like a blow and he leaned forward to peer anxiously through the gap, focusing his attention on the blank, golden windows that gave nothing away.

Should he shout down to them? Or would that only make matters worse? Better, perhaps, to wait until the others arrived and he could have the place surrounded. That, at least, would give him a psychological advantage. Alone, there was little he could do.

He cursed himself for not having tumbled to the truth earlier and yet he knew he was being less than just to himself. There was no way he could have guessed at what had happened until this evening, when the full significance of the site chosen for the grave had been revealed to him, unwittingly, by Rose and, with difficulty removed, the other details had begun to make sense.

Boyce's car slid almost silently to a halt beside him and the sergeant got out and came to squat beside him.

'I've spoken to the Chief,' he said quietly. 'The men are on their way. Fifteen of them. And Rogers and Wylie who'll be armed. Davies will send on more later, as you need them, and any special equipment you want, like listening-in devices, in case it looks like being a long drawn-out siege.'

'I hope to God it doesn't come to that,' Finch said with feeling.

'And I borrowed these from Stebbing,' the sergeant continued, flourishing a pair of huge, long-handled wire clippers. 'They should cut through that chain. Shall I get started on it?'

'Keep your head down,' Finch warned him. 'I'll put you in the picture while you do it.'

Boyce crawled across to the other side of the gate where the padlock and chain hung and, as he worked to cut through it, Finch explained briefly.

'And that's what I reckon happened,' he concluded, 'although the proof of it's down there, in that house, and there's no chance of getting anywhere near it at the moment.'

'Do you think he'll give himself up quietly?' Boyce asked.

'I don't know,' Finch admitted. 'He may do once he realises

it's useless to hold out, but I'm not too happy about that dog being killed. It shows he's pretty near the edge.'

'Stebbing mentioned hearing a shot earlier this afternoon,' Boyce broke in. 'About five o'clock, he reckoned.'

'Then why the hell didn't he say something about it to me?' Finch asked bitterly. 'I nearly walked into his line of fire. A few more feet and I'd've got it in the head, too.'

'Said he thought it was Lovell out after rooks,' Boyce grunted. He was kneeling upright in the soft dust at the gate opening, trying to get a purchase on the wire cutters, the sweat standing out on his forehead.

Suddenly the link gave, the chain and padlock fell away and the gate began to swing slowly open, Boyce giving it a final push with his foot before scrambling back to the cover of the hedge.

They now had an uninterrupted view of the house at the bottom of the slope. It still presented its blank, silent face but, as they watched, a slight movement on the back slope of the roof caught Finch's attention At first, it was no more than a flash of brightness as glass reflected the light of the sun.

'The skylight!' Finch said urgently, pointing.

A few seconds later, the head of a man appeared, dwarfed by the distance, a mere dark blob against the steep incline.

Boyce opened his mouth as if to shout but Finch silenced him by grasping his arm.

'God, it's Lovell!' he said softly. 'He's going to try to make it down the roof. Don't move, Tom. Don't even breathe. If he loses his grip . . .'

He fell silent, watching absorbed as the figure struggled like a fly on the precipice of tiles that glowed a warm, deep red in the last rays of the sun.

Lovell was unaware of their attention. Having pushed the skylight open with his shoulders, he rested for a moment, breathing heavily, his whole weight carried on his forearms that were braced across the wooden frame. He could feel the muscles in them jumping convulsively and he knew that he had, at most, a few seconds in which to force his body upwards, over the edge of the skylight, before their strength gave out. Below him, the steep slope of the tiled roof seemed to avalanche downwards to a distant view of the garden, strangely and dizzily diminished at that unaccustomed height. But he daren't think of that. Kicking with his legs, he slowly drew himself upwards until he could feel the frame biting into his chest. He leaned forward gratefully, taking the strain from his arms, and then painfully drew first one leg and then the other through the narrow opening, until he was lying bunched up on his side, his knees touching his chin.

He waited, trying to listen for sounds below him in the house but the heavy rasping of his own breath and the pulsing roar of blood in his head and ears covered all other noises.

Clutching the frame with both hands, until his knuckles cracked and whitened, he let his legs swing over and down with their own weight, at the same time altering his grip on the edge of the skylight, so that he was now lying face downwards and fully extended, only his grasp on the frame preventing him from sliding down.

He could feel the tiles, warm and hard, pressing into his chest and could see, in close-up, those that lay immediately under his face, in one of those dazzling moments of complete perception in which every detail of their colour and texture was absorbed in an instant. He saw, too, the round blobs of grey-green moss with which they were patched and their coarse, porous, animal surface, like skin seen under a microscope.

The next second, almost without making a conscious decision, he had loosened his grip on the frame and was slithering rapidly down the pitch of the roof. He felt the edges of the tiles catch and tear first at his clothes, then at the bare skin on his chest as the thin fabric of his shirt was ripped away but, although he was aware of warm blood trickling down and a burning sensation in his fingertips as his hands scrabbled for any hold, however small, to slow up the falling rush of his body, he was not conscious of any pain, only of the sense of speed and the rough, bumping motion as he glissaded downwards.

Strangely, there was no fear either, until he felt his feet drop away into space and knew he was within inches of the edge of the roof.

It was not far to the ground, but a concrete path ran along the back of the house and Lovell knew that, if he dropped on to it at the speed he was falling, he would be lucky to escape with just broken legs.

Bracing his knees and hands against the tiles, he thrust himself away from the roof, at the same time tensing his muscles to turn and spring for the softer earth beyond the path.

All the same, he fell awkwardly and heavily, one shoulder striking the concrete before he was able to roll to safety. For a moment, he lay stunned and winded. The next, he was on his feet and, bent double, one hand clutching his shoulder, was making for the far side of the garden where a belt of trees and bushes separated it from the road.

He broke through it, in the same way as Finch had done higher up the lane, shielding his face with one arm, before collapsing on to the grass verge.

Finch and Boyce, who had lost sight of him behind the trees when he was halfway down the roof, ran forward to where he lay on his side. At first sight, his condition looked serious. His shirt and the knees of his trousers were torn to ribbons and through the rents Finch could see long lacerations and grazes from which blood was trickling.

'Get an ambulance,' he said to Boyce, but Lovell struggled to sit up, shaking his head.

'Not hospital,' he gasped. 'I'll be all right. Just let me get my breath.'

'Those cuts must be cleaned up,' Finch told him briskly and added to Boyce, 'there's a first aid kit in my car. Fetch it, will you? And then get back to the gate. Keep a watch on the house and report to me the second anything happens.'

As Boyce ran back to the car, Lovell made an effort to speak again.

'Betty and Charlie . . .' he began, his mouth shaking.

'We'll get them out,' Finch assured him. 'I don't think he'll do anything to harm them.'

'You know about him?'

'I guessed. Only this evening, unfortunately, otherwise I might have done something sooner.'

Boyce had returned with the first aid kit which he handed to the Inspector before moving away to take up his watch on the house, while Finch, ripping open Lovell's shirt, began dabbing his chest with antiseptic lotion, covering the worst of the cuts with gauze and plaster. His shoulder, Finch noticed, was badly bruised but not, he thought, broken, as Lovell seemed to be able to move it without too much pain.

'I fell on it when I came off the roof,' he explained and added urgently, 'Ron . . .'

'Don't talk,' Finch told him. 'Get your breath back. I'll tell you what I think happened and you put me right if I get any of it wrong. Ronnie came back nearly four years ago and expected you to take him in.'

He didn't add, as he could have done, that Ronnie had, at the same time, resumed his rights as Betty's husband. Had he known of the relationship that existed between his wife and his brother? Possibly not. But if he had, Finch couldn't see that he would have cared. Ronnie's attitude to women was one of sexual exploitation. Even after fifteen years' desertion, he would have expected Betty to share his bed again. As for her, Finch could understand her feelings. A Catholic upbringing that denied her the possibility of divorce must have also instilled into her a deeply-held sense of her obligations as a wife. Besides, Finch had recognised in her a rigid and unbending quality, perhaps an overdeveloped sense of shame, that was apparent in the excessive, almost obsessive, tidiness of the house. Whatever love she had felt for Geoff Lovell had been denied out of guilt. Finch remembered the occasion when he had seen them together in the garden and had been aware of the space she was deliberately creating between them that held him back from any real contact.

How Lovell had taken it, Finch could only guess, but the weariness and defeat that the Inspector had seen stamped deeply into his face on that first visit when Lovell had stood on the doorstep of the house in the sunlight had been eloquent enough. He had been forced to accept the situation because there was nothing else to do; because legally he had no rights; because she was stronger-willed than he was; because, like her, he felt a deep sense of guilt and shame; but, ultimately and tragically, because he loved her too much, with that humble and self-effacing devotion that accepts all and forgives all.

Lovell raised his head that he had been resting against his knees. His face was ravaged.

'How did you guess?' he asked.

'Something I noticed,' Finch replied. 'Only at the time I didn't realise its significance.'

It had been that same afternoon when he had seen her hanging out the washing in the garden. Afterwards, his mind had kept reverting to the scene when he was talking to Boyce in the car, only he hadn't then been able to make the connection. Four pillowcases, hanging in pairs on the line, when there should have been only three. A small, domestic detail but one he ought to have taken account of. It was a vital clue to the number of people who were sleeping in the house. And the gun, too, of course. That also should have registered more positively on him as a symbol of violence; Ronnie's signature on a room that otherwise contained only the signs of Betty's well-ordered routine.

'Yes,' Lovell said bitterly. 'He came back, after fifteen years when we hadn't heard a word from him, expecting to be looked after and sheltered, as if none of it mattered.'

'Did you know what the charge was against him?'

'No, not then. He said he was broke and in trouble with a gang for informing against them and he was afraid they'd come looking for him. I believed him. He was frightened of being seen. But there was something else about him, too, that was different. He was harder, almost vicious. He'd always been wild and quick-tempered but there'd always been part of him you couldn't help liking, even though he was out for himself most of the time.'

'Yes, I can imagine that,' Finch replied, thinking of Nancy Fowler who had gone on loving him. Even Tidyman, who ran the local garage, had had a good word for Ronnie Lovell as he had been in those days. 'Of course,' he went on, 'he'd been drinking heavily for years.'

'Yes,' Lovell agreed, with a wry twist of his mouth, and then fell silent.

'And so you got the dog?' Finch asked.

'What?' Lovell asked blankly. His thoughts seemed to be far away.

'You got the dog and let it run loose in the yard so that no one could come near the house without you knowing it?'

'It wasn't meant to be like that,' Lovell answered. 'I'd kept a dog before, a collie, only she'd died. The idea was to get another and keep it chained up in the yard during the day, like we'd done with Bess. Ron wanted it, as you said, to give him warning of anyone coming to the gate and, anyway, we'd been used to having a dog about the place. Only . . .'

He broke off and Finch took up the sentence for him.

'Ronnie turned it into a guard dog.'

I should have guessed that, too, Finch thought. It wasn't in Geoff Lovell's nature to allow a dog to become so fierce. He understood animals and, as a farmer, he'd know the value of having a well-trained dog, not a savage animal that would attack anything or anybody.

'He said he'd train it. Like a fool, I said yes. I thought it'd give him something to do. He'd been giving me a hand with the farm machinery but that's about all. He'd never cared for farming.

Anyway, I got the dog to please Ronnie but he didn't know how to treat it. It was young and needed proper handling. If it didn't do what he wanted, he used to hit it. In the end, of course, it turned on him. He couldn't go outside the door without it starting to bark at him.'

Which accounted, Finch said to himself, for the fact that Stebbing had heard it two or three times a day on occasions.

'Ron had let it run loose,' Lovell was continuing. 'I tried keeping it on the chain for at least part of the day but it only made Ron more tensed up, knowing someone could come through the gate without him being warned. This frightened him and, when he's frightened, he takes it out on other people. It was Betty and Charlie who used to feel it most, so I gave in and let the dog run loose and padlocked the gate. It made for a bit of peace, at least where Ron was concerned.'

'Until Maguire turned up,' Finch pointed out.

'You found out about him?' Lovell asked quickly.

'Only today,' Finch admitted, 'and even then the story didn't register with me. It wasn't until this evening when I knew without doubt that it wasn't Ronnie's body that had been found in the field that I realised it must be someone connected with him and Maguire seemed the most likely person. How did he find out where Ronnie was hiding? After all, he'd changed his name. There was nothing to trace him to this place.'

'He knew Ronnie had been carrying on with his wife while he was still working for him at the garage, somewhere up in the Midlands. I got the stoooooory out of Ron after it all happened. It seems Maguire guessed, from one or two things that Ron let slip when he'd been drinking, that there was something about his past that he was covering up. Then one day Ron left his jacket hanging up in the office and Maguire went through his wallet. Like a fool, Ron had kept his old driver's licence, with his name and this address on it, so Maguire knew where to come looking for him when he came out of prison.'

'He knew Ronnie had shopped him?'

Lovell gave a short, hard laugh.

'What do you think? He guessed as soon as the police raided the garage. In fact, I've often wondered since if that story Ron told about a gang being after him didn't have some truth in it; only it was just the one man who'd be out for his blood – Maguire; not only because Ron had tipped off the police but for what he'd done to Maguire's wife.'

'So after Maguire came out of prison, he came here looking for him?'

'Yes. It was two years ago, next October, about late afternoon. I was out ploughing when Betty came up the field to fetch me. She told me a man had come to the gate and Charlie had taken him down to the house. He was asking for Ron and didn't believe her when she told him that we hadn't seen Ron for years. When I got back to the house, Maguire was in the kitchen. I could see he was spoiling for a fight. I tried to get rid of him by repeating what Betty had already told him: that we hadn't seen Ron since he'd left home fifteen years ago, but he didn't believe me either. He said he knew he was somewhere in the house and he wasn't leaving until he'd searched every room to find him and then given him back what he'd given to his wife.'

Lovell shuddered.

'I could see he meant it, too. He'd picked up the poker from the fireplace and was waving it about, shouting obscenities about Ronnie and what he'd do to him. God! It was terrifying! Charlie was crying like a child and saying over and over, "I didn't mean it! I didn't mean it!" He knew he shouldn't have let anyone in without asking one of us first.'

'Was that the first time you knew about the attempted murder charge against your brother?' Finch asked.

'Yes,' Lovell replied in a quiet voice. 'Until Maguire turned up, I swear I didn't know Ron was wanted by the police.'

'Go on,' Finch told him. 'What happened then?'

'Ron was upstairs. He'd heard Maguire's voice in the yard, when Charlie brought him to the house, and he'd managed to get away without being seen. He was in my bedroom, the one at the end, over the kitchen, listening to what was being said. The ceilings aren't all that thick and, anyway, Maguire was shouting so loudly he could hear every word. When he heard Maguire threaten to search the house, he decided to try to make a run for it. He came down the stairs and across the yard towards the barn, only Maguire saw him through the window and went charging off through the house after him. I followed. I knew there was going to be a fight and I thought there was something I could do to stop it but, by the time I got there, it was too late.

'Ron had gone up into the hayloft. God knows what was in his mind, because once up there he was trapped. As I ran into the barn after Maguire, I saw Ron standing on the edge of the loft with a pitchfork in his hand.'

He rubbed his own hand over his eyes as if to erase the memory.

'I can't describe the look on his face. I knew then he was mad; crazy not just with fear but with the rage you see in a savage animal when it's been cornered. I'll never forget that look. He yelled something; what I don't know. All I can remember is standing there, thinking Christ! he doesn't look human. The next moment, he'd flung the pitchfork like a javelin and Maguire fell backwards with it sticking out of his chest, the handle of it still vibrating.'

Finch was silent. He understood now why his inquiries about tools missing from the farm had provoked such a sharp response in Lovell at the time. He also realised the significance of the nature of the wounds described in the forensic report. It hadn't been a double stabbing as he and Boyce had thought, but a single blow from a pitchfork with a sharp, curved, two-pronged head.

'He must have died almost at once,' Lovell was saying in a flat, exhausted voice. 'One of the tines had got him through the heart. He didn't have a chance. I got Ron back to the house and locked up the barn. I was in a daze and couldn't think what the hell to do. Charlie kept asking where the man had gone and Ronnie told him he'd sent him away. But Betty knew it wasn't the truth. She kept looking at me and I could see it in her eyes. Later, I sent Charlie out to shut up the animals for the night and got her on her own in the living room and told her what had happened. Ron was in the kitchen, drinking. He was on whisky. I used to go out in the evenings round the pubs and off-licences where I wasn't known to buy it for him. He couldn't give it up and that way he wasn't too much of a nuisance.'

Did he mean to Betty? Finch wondered. Drunk, Ronnie could be put to bed, his sexual demands diminished. It was probably the lesser of two evils.

'I had to tell her the truth,' Lovell continued. 'She'd guessed it anyway, when we came back to the house without Maguire. And, besides, I had to get her to agree to what I was going to do – turn Ronnie over to the police. I couldn't see any other way out of it. He'd murdered Maguire and nearly killed his wife. We couldn't go on harbouring him, knowing that.

'In the middle of it, Ron came out of the kitchen. He was drunk all right, but there was more to it than that. There was a sort of glitter to him; I can't describe it in any other way. He stood leaning in the doorway, with my shotgun over his arm and he said, "If you think I'm bloody well going to stand by while you hand me over, you'd better get one thing straight. I won't give myself up without making a fight of it and I don't bloody care who gets it; you, her, or Charlie, or one of the bleeding fuzz who comes to arrest me. But I can promise you this – one of you'll cop it with me. So what's it to be? Make up your mind." What could I do? I had to agree not to send for the police. I knew by then he was mad enough to do anything he threatened if he got pushed far enough and he knew it, too. It was like a game of dare that kids play, only in Ronnie's case we both realised it could be for real. It wasn't a risk I was going to take, not with other people's lives.

'After that he made damned sure there was either Betty or Charlie in the house or nearby to act as a sort of hostage. That's why I didn't dare risk warning you when you came to the house. Ron was upstairs, listening in to everything that was said and he always had one of my guns handy, either the shotgun or the rifle, and I knew that, even if you brought more men with you, by the time you got inside the yard, he'd've turned the gun on someone.'

The risk was real enough, as Finch had to admit to himself. With the dog loose in the yard, there was no chance of anyone approaching the house without Ron being aware of it. He realised, also, how close he might have been to death when he searched the upstairs rooms in the farmhouse. Ronnie must have been only a few yards away, in the one bedroom he didn't have time to examine.

Guilt, too, must have played a part in Lovell's decision to keep silent, Finch decided. How could he commit the final act of betrayal by turning his brother over to the police, knowing that he had slept with his wife? To go on protecting Ronnie was a kind of punishment and expiation. Besides, he had Betty's own sense of sin to take into account. Ronnie was also her penance and, as such, she needed him. In removing him, Geoff was in danger of destroying for ever the last fragile remnants of their relationship.

'Whose idea was it to bury the body?' he asked. 'Ronnie's?'
Lovell nodded.

'That was later, after we'd sent Charlie to bed. I said, "We can't leave it in the barn. What are we going to do?" "Get rid of it," he said. "Dig a hole. No one'll miss him."'

He had been right, Finch thought. No one had reported Maguire missing. It was one of the questions he had asked Mullen when he had telephoned him earlier; that, and the date of Maguire's release from prison; a date that coincided too closely with the length of time the body had been buried for Finch to be any longer in doubt as to its identity. Maguire had few friends. His business had gone bankrupt. His wife had moved away from the area after her discharge from hospital. Those who knew him had assumed he had moved on himself in search of her. Even Mullen had come to that conclusion when Maguire had dropped out of sight in the district.

'And then,' Lovell was continuing, 'Ronnie said something that started the whole bloody, stupid business off. "While you're at it," he said to Betty, "say a few prayers over him. He was a bloody R.C. the same as you." He meant it to be sarcastic. He'd always made fun of her religion. She'd stopped going to church years before but, deep down, she'd never really given up believing.'

'So she laid the body out and asked you to bury it in Stebbing's field because she'd heard from Wheeler it was sacred ground?'

'You know about that?' Lovell asked.

'There had to be some logical reason why that field was chosen. I only tumbled to the truth myself this evening, after I'd spoken to Rose and Wheeler. It was then it began to make sense.'

'She stuck out on that. Even Ron couldn't make her change her mind. "All right," he said. "Bury him where you bloody well like. There's no chance anyone's going to dig him up again." He knew the field and there didn't seem any likelihood anyone'd bother to cultivate it. It had never been anything else except rough pasture.' He laughed shortly. 'But he didn't reckon with Stebbing.'

'Go on,' Finch said quietly.

Lovell eased his shoulder, which was evidently giving him some pain, by cupping his hand under his elbow to take the weight. He was visibly tiring and there was a hoarse note in his voice as he took up the account again.

'I'll never forget the next couple of hours. We took a lantern out to the barn and I helped her wash and lay out the body. He was about the same height and build as Ron and we put some of his clothes on him. Then she asked to be left alone with him. I could guess why. As I went out, I turned and looked back. She was kneeling on the edge of the blanket I'd spread out on the floor. Later, when I went back, she'd wrapped the body up

in the blanket and fastened it together. I carried the body up
to Stebbing's field . . .'

'Was it your idea you should bury the body?' Finch broke in
to ask.

Lovell looked at him with a flash of his former belligerency.

'What the hell do you think? No, it bloody wasn't, but with
Betty and Charlie in the house and Ron sitting in the kitchen,
with the gun across his knees and half-drunk, I wasn't going to
argue with him. It was getting light by then and I didn't dare
stop too long, so I didn't have time to dig the grave very deep.
I laid him in it and put the earth back.'

'And the cross and chain?' Finch asked.

'I only found out about it later, after you'd been that day and
questioned Betty about it. I could tell by the look on her face
that she knew something about it and, afterwards, she told me.
It'd been given to her by the nuns for her first communion and
she'd always worn it until she married Ronnie. He'd never
liked her wearing it because, like I said, he hadn't any time
for religion. Besides, I think she felt she'd lost all right to wear
it. She'd sinned by marrying him in the first place; he wasn't
a Catholic. I don't understand it all. We talked about it a few
times and she told me her priest had tried to explain that the
church wouldn't reject her but she felt, because she'd sinned,
she didn't have any right to forgiveness. I can't put it clearer
than that.'

He didn't have to, Finch thought. He could perfectly well
understand how Betty Lovell, with her strong sense of guilt,
coupled with a masochistic streak in her personality, could
persuade herself that she was unworthy of forgiveness, not just
for marrying Ronnie but for committing what in her eyes would
be the sin of fornication, a fact that Lovell, with an innate sense
of discretion, had omitted to mention.

'Anyway, it seemed she'd kept the cross and chain and,
before she wrapped the body up, she put it between his hands.
It must have slipped out when I laid the body down to dig the
grave and got mixed up with the earth when I threw it back,'
Lovell concluded.

So that was the explanation, Finch thought. Simple enough,
although at the time it had puzzled him.

'And this evening?' he asked. 'What happened to bring things to a head?'

'It was the dog. I told you it had taken against him for the way he treated it. It went for him again this afternoon when he was crossing the yard. He'd got to the stage, anyway, where the smallest thing got him angry. Not being able to leave the farm was bad enough. That'd been going on for over three years. Then you started coming to the house, making inquiries about the body. I used to dread your visits. He always drank more heavily after you'd been and it was Betty who suffered most . . .'

No wonder Lovell had been so anxious to get rid of him, Finch realised.

'Then, this afternoon when the dog went for him, something seemed to snap inside him. He came raging into the house for the gun and shot it before anyone could stop him. I was up the top field so I didn't see what happened but the minute I heard the shot, I came down to the house. As soon as I got inside, he bolted the door after me. He'd got them in the living room. Charlie was terrified. He'd always been afraid of Ron. Betty was trying to calm him down. Ron was sitting by the fireplace with the gun across his knees and the same look on his face that I'd seen when he killed Maguire. After a bit, though, he seemed to go quieter. Betty started talking to him, trying to persuade him to let Charlie go out and see to the cows. I knew what she was thinking of – if she could get Charlie out of the way, it might be easier for us to get Ron to put the gun down. There were times when she could talk him round, if he wasn't in too much of a rage, because, in a funny way, I think deep down he trusted her. He seemed ready to listen and then we heard your car arrive.'

'And that finished it?' Finch asked.

Lovell nodded.

'He made us go upstairs to the bedroom he shared with Betty. I know why. From there, he had a clear view up the yard. He told us to sit on the bed while he stood at the window watching. He must have seen you coming because he put the gun to his shoulder . . .'

'He missed,' Finch pointed out. 'What happened?'

541

'I managed to get across the room and knock the gun to one side. Then I shouted to you. You heard me?'

'Yes, thank God. I was within feet of getting my head blown off.'

'There was a bit of a scuffle,' Lovell went on. 'Ron lost his balance and while he was on the floor, I ran for the door and through to the far bedroom where there's a ladder leading up to the attic. I didn't know what the hell else to do. He still had the gun and at the time I had no idea you knew about Ronnie. I wanted to come and warn you. I was scared you'd come back with more police and try to rush the place and I knew what that might lead to, Ronnie turning the gun on Betty or Charlie or on one of your men.'

He passed a hand over his mouth to hide its trembling.

'Maybe I should have stayed. I might have been able to get the gun off him in time, or, at least, talked him into letting Betty and Charlie go. They're alone with him now and God alone knows what he'll do.'

'Nothing for the moment,' Finch replied with more conviction than he felt. 'The men should be arriving any minute now and . . .'

'For God's sake, don't let him see them!' Lovell broke in hoarsely. 'He'll really go berserk if he thinks he's surrounded. I know him. He'll feel trapped.'

'All right,' Finch assured him. 'I'll make sure they're not seen.'

He walked back to the gate, where Boyce was still squatting under cover of the hedge, keeping watch on the house.

'Nothing's happened so far,' the sergeant began.

'Never mind that now. Something more important's come up. Lovell thinks Ron may blow his top if he knows we've sent for more men and we've got to go along with what he says. He knows his brother and the state of mind he's in. So what I want you to do is to walk along the lane and stop any cars or vans from coming too near. If the sound of my car set Ronnie off, God knows what the arrival of fifteen coppers will do to him.'

'Right,' Boyce said, getting to his feet. 'And what then?'

'I don't know,' Finch confessed. He looked back at the figure of Geoff Lovell, sitting on the verge, his knees drawn up and his head resting on them, in an attitude of total exhaustion. 'Maybe he'll come up with a bright idea. At the moment, though, I'm inclined to leave things as they are. Given time, we may be able to wear Ron down into giving himself up or, at least, letting the other two go. You'd better be on your way, Tom. Tell the men to approach on foot and they're not so much as to open their mouths.'

As Boyce walked away down the lane, Finch took up his position at the gate, peering down the drive towards the house. As Boyce had reported, all seemed quiet. The house still presented its silent façade, although the sun had moved round so that the windows no longer glittered golden. He was relieved to see they were still open.

Would it be possible to make use of them? he wondered. Get into the house through the front while Ronnie's attention was diverted to the back? Using the front door was out. Geoff Lovell had said Ron had bolted it, but he might be able to smuggle one of the police marksmen through the window at the far end.

Meanwhile, if he could persuade Ron to come to the landing window that overlooked the back garden, he could have already placed some of the men there out of sight. There was plenty of cover. The rest of the men could be positioned near the front of the house, hidden in the sheds and barns that faced it.

He looked towards them. Plenty of room there to hide as many men as he wanted. But could he get them inside without Ronnie seeing them? They'd have to be brought in through the back, out of sight of the house. He'd have to consult Geoff Lovell on that point. He'd know if there were any doors or windows facing away from the house that they could get in by.

The subdued tread of feet distracted his attention. Turning his head, he saw Boyce approaching up the lane, along the grass verge, followed by a long line of men in single file.

Finch got to his feet and began walking towards them, lifting his arm in a signal for them to stop.

What happened next occurred so quickly that there was no time, after all, to plan out any moves.

As the men drew to a halt and Boyce stepped forward to

speak to Finch, the sound of a car coming up fast behind them made the sergeant pause and then step rapidly into the road, waving his arms at it. It swerved, hooted violently and screamed to a stop.

Finch had only a second in which to glimpse the driver's face but it was enough.

Stebbing!

16

He had hardly time to register this fact when two shots rang out in quick succession from the direction of the house. As if jerked into action by the double report, Geoff Lovell was on his feet and was running past Finch, shouting something incoherent as he ran. Cursing Stebbing out loud, Finch turned and pounded after him towards the gate. At the entrance, he paused momentarily to look down again at the farm.

In the short time since he had last seen it, the scene had changed completely from its former blank, empty stillness. In the middle distance, Lovell was sprinting down the drive, running awkwardly, holding his injured arm against his body with his other hand to prevent it from swinging, the tattered remnants of his shirt flying out behind him.

Beyond him, from the upper window of the bedroom that Ron and Betty had shared and where he now held her and Charlie hostage, thick smoke was pouring, behind which Finch could see the bright flicker of flames.

Pausing only long enough to shout over his shoulder for someone to send for an ambulance and the fire brigade, Finch set off down the drive in pursuit of Lovell, who had now reached the front door and was throwing himself repeatedly against it in a futile effort to burst it open.

'The window, man!' Finch yelled.

He saw Lovell's face turned towards him, twisted with pain and that unseeing, unhearing desperation of a man who is acting out of blind impulse.

It was Boyce who, coming up behind Lovell, smashed the glass with his forearm and reached in to open the latch. Finch scrambled through, aware as he did so that the other men were running into the yard.

As he ran towards the door, he found himself straining for any sounds from the room upstairs. The sound of flames crackling, with a leisurely crunching noise like wheels moving slowly across gravel, was clearly audible and he thought he heard someone moaning quietly as well but he couldn't be sure for, as he slid the bolts open, the door was thrown back and Lovell had flung violently past him and was making for the staircase door, his feet clattering and skidding on the polished boards.

Finch followed only a few steps behind him, Boyce on his heels, with the two marksmen and four other plain-clothes men whom Finch had ordered to accompany them crowding up the narrow staircase in their rear.

'I've sent five men to cover the back of the house,' Boyce announced, already out of breath.

Finch merely nodded. There was no time to reply. They had reached the tiny landing where Lovell was in the act of bursting open the bedroom door. There was not even time to shout a warning to him that Ron might still be armed and could fire on him at close range for, without hesitating, Lovell had plunged into the smoke that was pouring out of the open doorway.

In the event, no warning was needed for Finch, already on the threshold, could see what lay beyond inside the room.

The body of Ron Lovell was lying just inside the door, sprawled face downwards on the bedside rug, the end of which was buckled under, the gun caught under him with its barrel close to his head. Used as he was to violent death, even Finch averted his eyes from what was left of the side of Ronnie's face.

A little distance away, Charlie lay huddled, curled up on his side as if asleep, except it was a sleep from which he would not awake. From the doorway, Finch could see the wound in his chest from which the blood was still trickling to gather in a dark pool on the floor.

The only moving figure was Betty Lovell's crawling towards them, her face raised, out of the heart, it seemed, of the smoke and flame of the fire that was burning behind her under the window.

Lovell gave a great cry that sounded as if it had been torn out of him and, gathering her up in his arms as a father might a child, his dark face brilliant with an expression of such fierce love that it was transfigured, shouldered his way roughly through the group of men that was now crowding into the room and carried her down the stairs.

Finch let him go without comment and, turning away, began rapping out orders for the fire to be extinguished. It was not a large conflagration, consisting mostly of bedding that had been piled up in a heap under the window, with a few smaller articles of furniture placed on top of it, but it was well alight and, as he and Boyce crossed the room towards it, they saw the flames touch the edge of the curtains and run quickly up them, transforming them in seconds into fiery pennants.

As they tore them down and stamped on the flames, some of the men were already returning with buckets and bowls of water with which to douse the fire and, in a few minutes, nothing remained except the smouldering debris of wood and fabric which they flung through the open window into the yard below, and a patch of charred floorboards from which faint wisps of smoke were still rising.

Finch left them to it and crossed the landing to Charlie's room, where he stripped the bed of sheets, returning to lay them over the two bodies. Curiosity sent him back, when this was done, to examine the further bedroom where Ronnie had lain in hiding, listening to what was said in the kitchen below, and where Geoff Lovell had slept alone.

It was a sparse, bleak room, simply furnished, like Charlie's, with a single bed and a deal chest-of-drawers. A few books were lined up on the windowsill; mostly farming magazines and manuals. The only novel among them was *Lorna Doone*. Intrigued by the title, Finch opened it and saw pasted on the inside cover a plate announcing that it was a school prize awarded to Geoffrey Kenneth Lovell for good attendance. Why had he kept it? Had it been his only success? Or had he been drawn to its theme of violence and forbidden love?

It was a matter of pure speculation that had no relevance to the present investigation and yet, as Finch replaced it on the windowsill, he felt inexplicably close to Lovell and to the lonely and taciturn child that he felt he recognised in the man.

His attention was caught next by a ladder, screwed to the wall, that led upwards to an opening in the ceiling, the wooden cover of which had been removed. Climbing up, Finch stuck his head above the opening. A large attic, with a boarded floor, ran the length of the roofspace, much of which was taken up with the miscellaneous objects that most attics accumulate: trunks and boxes, discarded furniture, old belongings no longer used but which their owners can never quite bring themselves to throw away. There was a smell, too, of dust and hot, close air, trapped beneath the tiles, and the sweet, decaying scent of stored apples.

In the centre, an up-ended crate stood beneath the open skylight, through which an oblong patch of sky, purpling into dusk, was visible. Finch scrambled up into the loft and, mounting the crate, looked down, as Geoff Lovell had done, at the roof sloping steeply away to the darkening garden. It was, he decided, a very brave and desperate man who had made his escape by that route.

As he stood there, he heard in the distance the double warning bells of an ambulance and fire-engine approaching at speed from the main road and, closing the skylight, he went down the stairs to meet them.

The next few hours passed rapidly. Betty Lovell, unconscious but suffering only from shock, was taken away in the ambulance, Geoff Lovell accompanying her. The firemen tore up the square of smouldering floorboards and extinguished the last remnants of the fire. In the ravaged bedroom, stinking of smoke and wet, charred wood, Pardoe examined the bodies, McCullum photographed them, Boyce and Kyle marked their positions on the floor and, finally, the last mortal remains of Ron and Charlie Lovell were carried awkwardly down the narrow stairs and taken away.

In the middle of it all, some enterprising constable made tea which they drank standing up in the kitchen. Finch, holding the cup between two hands, had a free moment at last to look about him. It was dark outside now and, through the uncurtained window, he could see the headlamps of the parked cars shining on the façades of the outbuildings, giving them the unreal, theatrical intensity of brilliant highlights and dense shadows. It seemed a fitting backdrop to the night's activities.

Inside, the kitchen still managed to preserve, at least for him, some of Betty's ordered influence, despite the crowd of men who stood about talking and drinking tea. The blue and white mixing bowl stood on a shelf near the saucepans, which had been his first glimpse of her world. Some newly-washed shirts, neatly folded down and waiting to be ironed, lay in the red plastic laundry basket in one corner.

He had seen her briefly, lying on the sofa in the living-room, Geoff Lovell squatting on his heels beside her, holding her hand; on guard, it seemed to Finch, for he had allowed no one near her except Pardoe and the ambulance men. Not that Finch hoped to get a statement from her; she was in too deep a state of shock.

A little later, they carried her out to the waiting ambulance, Lovell still holding her hand as he walked beside the stretcher, his head bent, his feet slurring on the ground. Watching him leave, Finch realised how close he was to exhaustion.

The night wore on. Most of the men, their tasks completed, went away. McCullum departed, as did Pardoe. Soon there were only Finch, Boyce and a few plain-clothes men left who were making a search of the house.

It was dawn before they finally finished. Finch, standing at the window on the planks that had been laid across the charred hole in the floor, saw the first streaks of light lifting the darkness beyond the trees in the direction, he realised, of Hollowfield. There was, he felt, something symbolic about this, although what exactly his tired mind could not define.

'We're through with the search,' Boyce announced, coming up behind him, his face streaked with dirt and rough with a night's growth of stubble. 'Are you ready to leave?'

'No, not yet,' Finch replied. 'I'll make my own way back. You go on ahead, Tom.'

'If you want me to stay . . . ,' Boyce began but Finch shook his head.

He had a desire to linger, as he had done in the field after the body of the man he now knew was Maguire had been taken away. Was it morbidity? he wondered. Or sentimentality? Or a desire to try to come nearer to an understanding of what had happened?

After all, there was nothing much left to see. In Maguire's case, there had been a heap of earth and a tarpaulin-covered hole. Of Ron and Charlie even less remained: just two shapes on the floorboards, outlined in white tape.

Boyce and the other men tramped off down the stairs. He heard the front door close behind them and then their voices and footsteps as they crossed the yard and made their way up the slope towards the gate in the faint morning light.

After their departure, the house seemed to settle back into silence, to contract and close in on itself once more, as if thankfully resuming its old secretive habits.

Finch remained standing at the window, his back to the room and the taped outlines on the floor, watching the light spread across the sky, confirming the outlines of barn and treetops, restoring colour to the leaves and grass. A few birds stirred and called, anxiously at first and then with growing confidence as the day widened, until their song rose up in a paeon of triumph across the waking fields.

The sight of Geoff Lovell's figure trudging slowly down the track towards the yard did not surprise him. It was as if he had been expecting him and it seemed perfectly natural to Finch to walk down the stairs and open the door to welcome him in. Nor did Lovell appear startled by the Inspector's presence in an otherwise empty house. He nodded briefly before stepping inside and the two men went, by common, unspoken consent, into the kitchen where Lovell filled the kettle and put it on the stove to boil.

'I got a lift back from the hospital,' he explained briefly. 'I started walking and then this lorry stopped.'

His injured arm was in a sling and he was wearing a jacket that someone must have lent him. It was slightly too small for him and was strained across his broad shoulders. His face was heavy with exhaustion, the features blurred as if lack of sleep had robbed them of their outlines.

'I spoke to Betty for a little while,' he went on, setting out cups one-handed. 'She came round and the doctor let me in to see her.'

He was silent for a moment, frowning down at the table and the arrangement of china as if he felt there was something amiss with it. 'She told me what happened.'

Finch, seated at the table, looked up but did not speak. He was himself in that state of tiredness when action of any kind is an effort and it is easier to remain silent and passive. Later, he would pick up the threads of the inquiry again, visit the hospital, take an official statement from Betty Lovell. But, for the time being, he was content to sit and listen while Lovell told it in his own way.

'She said, after I went, Ron tried coming after me,' Lovell continued in a voice that had very little expression. 'But he must have realised it was a waste of time because he was back in a few seconds, bringing with him the little paraffin heater from my room that we put up in the loft in the winter to keep the pipes from freezing. He was furious, she said, and started pulling the clothes off the bed and piling them up on the floor under the window, with some of the furniture. Then he poured the paraffin out of the stove on top of it and told them, "If anyone tries to rush the house, I'll set light to the bloody lot." Charlie was frightened and kept crying and this made Ron even more angry. He was shouting to Charlie to shut up and waving the gun about. Betty said she thought he was frightened, too. He was as white as a ghost and shaking and he kept looking towards the door as if he was thinking of making a run for it.'

The kettle boiled and Lovell broke off to make the tea. The smell of it, fresh and aromatic, was very strong in the clear, morning air.

'If I'd been there, I might have talked him into it,' Lovell went on. His face in profile as he bent over the stove had a haunted, brooding look. 'At least, it might have saved Charlie's life. Then Stebbing arrived, making all that bloody racket.' A paroxysm of rage twisted his mouth. 'God damn that man to hell!'

Finch shifted slightly in his chair but still didn't speak and, after a few seconds, Lovell recovered and took up the account in a calmer voice.

'It was enough to set Ron off again. He was standing at the

window, smoking, when they heard the car and he jumped back and threw the cigarette down on the pile of bedding. The lot went up in a few seconds. There was a sheet of flame as the paraffin caught. It frightened all of them; Ron, as well. He probably didn't realise it would catch fire so quickly.'

It fitted, Finch thought, what he knew of Ron Lovell, and others like him he had had dealings with; men who had never properly grown up, who acted on impulse like children and then were aghast at what they had done. But what must it have been like for Betty Lovell, shut up in a room with two terrified men, neither of whom were capable of rational behaviour?

'Charlie began screaming and ran across the room towards Ron. Betty's not sure what happened next. She doesn't think Ron intended to fire but Charlie was hysterical and going at him with his fists and the next thing she knew the gun had gone off and Charlie fell on the floor.'

He stopped abruptly and Finch spoke for the first time.

'What happened to Ron?'

Lovell pulled himself together with a visible physical effort, straightening his shoulders and then clasping the damaged arm with the other hand as the bruised muscles contracted. But the pain seemed to steady him.

'She's not sure. It was all muddled and confused. There was the noise of the gun going off, and the smoke and flame from the fire and Ron shouting. Anyway, she ran forward to help Charlie and Ron pushed past her as if he was making for the door. The next thing she knew, she heard the gun fire a second time and when she looked round, Ron was lying by the bed. So she doesn't know whether he meant to kill himself or if it was an accident.'

The position of the body, with the gun lying under it, suggested to Finch that it was more probably an accident. In a panic, Ron had been running for the door, had tripped on the edge of the rug and fallen onto the gun. But it was only a theory. They would never positively know what had happened in those last terrifying minutes.

Lovell pushed his chair back violently from the table and left the room, returning in a short time with a bottle of whisky and two glasses which he banged down on the table.

'That's the last of it,' he said. 'I used to keep a couple of bottles in the house for Ron; hidden away so he wouldn't find it and drink it too quickly. He won't need it now.'

Suddenly a spasm crossed his face, twisting and jerking his mouth and, with a muttered exclamation, he put his head in his hands.

'Get this down you,' Finch ordered, splashing whisky into one of the glasses and pushing it across the table towards him. He poured another for himself and drank it quickly, feeling the spirit run like a warm stream through his body. Lovell drank his covertly, turning his head away.

'What'll happen now?' he asked, when he had drained his glass. He still kept his face averted.

'You mean to you?' Finch asked. Lovell nodded. The Inspector, watching his profile closely, decided it was better to tell him the truth.

'A report will have to go to the Director of Public Prosecutions to see if there's a case to answer,' he said quietly.

'It must look bad,' Lovell replied, in a voice as subdued as Finch's. He turned to look directly into the Inspector's face. 'I kept him on here, knowing he'd killed Maguire and after I'd found out he was wanted on an attempted murder charge. I should have handed him over to the police.'

This was true, but Lovell had good reason not to do so, Finch admitted only to himself. It wasn't his place to act as judge and jury but he already knew what would figure in his report: Lovell's escape down the roof, that might have led to death or serious injury, in order to warn him; and the second time he had risked his life by bursting into the bedroom before he knew Ron was dead. It might be enough to persuade a judge, if the case ever came to trial, to give him a suspended sentence or, at most, a short term of imprisonment.

'You knew I burnt Ron's photos?' Lovell was asking, his eyes fixed on Finch's face. He seemed to want to admit to all, confess everything, and Finch understood the reason behind it. Lovell must be accusing himself bitterly of being the cause of their deaths by not staying behind. But, in doing so, he was being unjust to himself. Betty's life had been saved and so possibly had been the lives of some of Finch's own men; for God alone knew how Ronnie might have reacted had they been forced to close in on him. If anyone was directly to blame it was Stebbing.

'I understand why you did it,' Finch replied. Lovell had got rid of them in order to stop the inquiry from going ahead, knowing the state of Ronnie's mind and the danger Finch himself was in every time he called at the farm. As it was, he had only escaped death by Lovell's prompt action in knocking the gun to one side, another fact that he intended mentioning in his report.

'Would you have given him up eventually?' he asked.

'I don't know,' Lovell said slowly. 'We were living from day to day. I hoped, though, that some time Ron would be less on his guard or get so drunk that I could take the guns off him without risking anybody's life.'

Finch nodded but made no reply. He felt Lovell was speaking the truth. The man was too exhausted and too beaten by what had happened to be capable of lying.

'What will you do eventually?' he asked, changing the subject. 'Will you stay on here?'

'No!' Lovell replied positively. 'Not now. Not after this.'

'Stebbing would buy it,' Finch remarked. 'He'd pay a good price, too.'

'I know,' Lovell said bitterly. 'He's been after it ever since he came here.'

'Would you sell?'

'What's it to you?' Lovell demanded, with some of his old, jeering manner.

'Partly nosiness,' Finch admitted. 'Partly real concern. I'd like to feel . . .'

This time it was his turn to look away, embarrassed by Lovell's direct gaze that was fixed on him. There was a silence in which Finch felt there was nothing he could do except mumble some apology and take his leave. Then he heard the chink of glass and the sound of whisky being poured.

'I know what I'd do, given the chance,' Lovell was saying slowly, in the low voice of a man confiding a dream. 'I'd set up somewhere else on a smaller scale. Market gardening mostly.

Early lettuces. Tomatoes under glass. That sort of thing. Perhaps a few chickens as a side-line.'

Finch picked up his glass, resting his elbows comfortably on the table. He was strangely touched by Lovell's confidence.

'It might still be possible,' he said.

'Maybe. I don't know. It's too soon. Anyway, I'll have to see what happens to me first. But I had this idea . . . Just the three of us . . . Charlie helping . . . Betty, as well. She likes plants . . .'

'I know,' Finch said. 'I saw the kitchen garden.'

'And now Charlie's gone. And Betty . . .'

'Give her time,' Finch told him.

Lovell looked at him with a wry smile in which Finch recognised that Lovell understood his own knowledge of their relationship.

'You reckon?' he asked.

'I'm sure,' Finch replied. He didn't add, as he could have done, that there was nothing else she could do except come back to Lovell in the end. She had no one left now, only him. It wasn't much on which to build a marriage, but it was more than a lot of people had. And perhaps the strength of Lovell's affection for her would carry them through.

He liked to think so. He wanted to imagine a happy ending for them, although Christ! he thought, I'm falling into the same sentimental trap that I thought Nancy Fowler had got caught in: the pap world of the happy-ever-after. Maybe, as she had recognised, it wouldn't work that way.

I must go and see her, he added, his thoughts veering off. Tell her what happened. We've found Ron for you with a bloody great hole in his head. Sorry, but he won't be coming back anymore.

He began to put on his jacket and do up his tie.

'You're off?' Lovell asked. He seemed to regret the Inspector's departure.

'I've got things to do,' Finch told him with a briskness he didn't feel.

'And so have I,' Lovell replied, accompanying him to the door. 'The cows have been out all night. I'll have to get them in and milked.'

At the gate, Finch paused for the last time to look back. The sun was fully risen now, although the front of the house was still in shadow. As he watched, he saw Lovell come out of the house and cross the yard, walking into the sunlight, towards the gate that led to the fields beyond.

Unlike Finch, he didn't stop to look back. His dark, square-shouldered figure mounted the slope at a steady pace and presently disappeared from sight behind the trees.